Praise for Harlan Coben

'It is always satisfying to discover a new crime writer – and this is the business . . . this book will keep you up until 2 a.m.' *The Times*

'Harlan Coben. He's smart, he's funny, and he has something to say' Michael Connelly

'An increasingly frightening conspiracy with an unguessable ending . . . hard to put down' *Sunday Telegraph*

'At last a British publisher has given British readers the chance to discover something every US mystery fan already knows – that Harlan Coben is one of the most entertaining and intriguing crime writers around'

Val McDermid, *Manchester Evening Guardian*

'What sets Harlan Coben above the crowd are wit and . . . an entertaining plot' *Los Angeles Times Book Review*

'Fast action, snappy dialogue and plenty of insider hoops material make this a fast, enjoyable read' *Toronto Star*

'Coben . . . scores a hole in one! The characters are deftly etched and the details keenly observed' *Publishers Weekly*

By Harlan Coben

Harlan Coben is one of the most exciting talents in American crime writing. He was the first ever author to win all three major US crime awards, and has established a bestselling series of crime novels starring his powerful creation, Myron Bolitar. Harlan lives in New Jersey with his wife and four children. Visit his website at www.harlancoben.com

Deal Breaker

Drop Shot

HARLAN COBEN

ORION

Deal Breaker
First published in Great Britain by Orion Books Ltd in 2001

Drop Shot
First published in Great Britain by Orion Books Ltd in 2001

This omnibus edition published in 2005
by Orion Books Ltd
Orion House, 5 Upper St Martin's Lane
London WC2H 9EA

Published by arrangement with Dell Publishing,
an imprint of The Bantam Dell Publishing Group,
a division of Random House, Inc

A CIP catalogue record for this book is available from the British
Library.

ISBN 1 89880 088 X

Printed in Great Britain by
Mackays Of Chatham Ltd, Chatham Kent

Deal Breaker

Chapter 1

Otto Burke, the Wizard of Schmooze, raised his game another level.

"Come on, Myron," he urged with neoreligious fervor. "I'm sure we can come to an understanding here. You give a little. We give a little. The Titans are a team. In some larger sense I would like all of us to be a team. You included. Let's be a real team, Myron. What do you say?"

Myron Bolitar steepled his fingers. He had read somewhere that steepled fingers made you look like a thoughtful person. He felt foolish.

"I'd like nothing more, Otto," he said, returning the pointless volley for the umpteenth time. "Really I would. But we've given as much as we can. It's your turn now."

Otto nodded vigorously, as if he had just heard some philosophical whimsy that put Socrates to shame. He tilted his head, angling the painted-on smile toward his team's general manager. "Larry, what do you think?"

Taking his cue, Larry Hanson pounded the conference table with a fist hairy enough to be a gerbil. "Bolitar can go to hell!" he shouted, playing enraged to the hilt. "You hear me, Bolitar? You understand what I'm telling you? Go to hell."

"Go to hell," Myron repeated with a nod. "Got it."

"You being a wiseass with me? Huh? Answer me, dammit! You being a wiseass?"

Myron looked at him. "You have a poppy seed stuck in your teeth."

"Goddamn wiseass."

"And you're beautiful when you're angry. Your whole face lights up."

Larry Hanson's eyes widened. He swung his line of vision toward his boss, then back to Myron. "You're out of your league here, Bolitar. And you fucking know it."

Myron said nothing. The truth of the matter was, Larry Hanson was partially right. Myron was out of his league. He had been in sports representation for only two years now. Most of his clients were borderline cases—guys who were lucky to make the cut and grabbed the league's minimum. And football was far from his specialty. He had only three NFL players, only one of whom was a starter. Now Myron sat across from thirty-one-year-old wunderkind Otto Burke, the youngest owner in the NFL, and Larry Hanson, former-football-legend-turned-exec, negotiating a contract that even in his inexperienced hands would be the biggest rookie contract in NFL history.

Yes, he—Myron Bolitar—had landed Christian "Hot Prop" Steele. Two-time Heisman trophy–winning quarterback. Three straight AP and UPI number-one rankings. All-American four years in a row. If that wasn't enough, the kid was an endorsement wet dream. An A student, good-looking, articulate, polite, and white (hey, it mattered).

Best of all, he was Myron's.

"The offer is on the table, gentlemen," Myron continued. "We think it's more than fair."

Otto Burke shook his head.

"It's a load of crap!" Larry Hanson shouted. "You're a goddamn idiot, Bolitar. You're going to flush this kid's career down the toilet."

Myron spread his arms. "How about a group hug?"

Larry was about to offer up another expletive, but Otto stopped him with a raised hand. In Larry's playing days Dick Butkus and Ray Nitzchke couldn't stop him with body blows. Now this one-hundred-fifty-pound Harvard grad could silence him with but a wave.

Otto Burke leaned forward. He hadn't stopped smiling, hadn't stopped the hand gestures, hadn't stopped the eye contact—like an Anthony Robbins Personal Power infomercial come to life. Disconcerting as all hell. Otto was a small, fragile-looking man with the tiniest fingers Myron had ever seen. His hair was dark and heavy-metal long, flowing to his shoulders. He was baby-faced with a silly goatee that looked as if it'd been sketched on in pencil. He smoked a very long cigarette, or maybe it just appeared long against his tiny fingers.

"Now, Myron," Otto said, "let's speak rationally here, okay?"

"Rationally. Let's."

"Great, Myron, that'll be helpful. The truth is, Christian Steele is an unknown, untested quantity. He hasn't even put on a pro uniform yet. He may be the bust of the century."

Larry snorted. "You should know something about that, Bolitar—about players who amount to nothing. Who crap out."

Myron ignored him. He had heard the insult before. It no longer bothered him. Sticks and stones and all that. "We are talking about perhaps the greatest quarterback prospect in history," he replied steadily. "You made three trades and gave up six players to get his rights. You didn't do all that if you didn't believe he has what it takes."

"But this proposal"—Otto stopped, looked up as

though searching the ceiling tiles for the right word—
"it's not sound."

"Crap is more like it," Larry added.

"It's final," Myron said.

Otto shook his head, the smile unfazed. "Let's talk this through, okay? Let's look at it from every conceivable angle. You're new at this, Myron—an ex-jock reaching for the executive brass ring. I respect that. You're a young guy trying to give it a go. Heck, I admire that. Really."

Myron bit down. He could have pointed out that he and Otto were the same age, but he so loved being patronized. Didn't everybody?

"If you make a mistake on this," Otto continued, "it could be the sort of thing that destroys your career. Do you know what I mean? Plenty of people already feel that you're not up to this—to handling such a high-profile client. Not me, of course. I think you're a very bright guy. Shrewd. But the way you're acting . . ." He shook his head like a teacher disenchanted with a favorite pupil.

Larry stood, glowering down at Myron. "Why don't you give the kid some good advice?" he said. "Tell him to get a real agent."

Myron had expected this whole good-cop, bad-cop routine. He had, in fact, expected worse; Larry Hanson had not yet attacked the sexual appetites of anyone's mother. Still, Myron preferred the bad cop to the good cop. Larry Hanson was a frontal assault, easily spotted and handled. Otto Burke was the snake-infested high grass with buried land mines.

"Then I guess we have nothing more to discuss," Myron said.

"I believe a holdout would be unwise, Myron," Otto said. "It might soil Christian's squeaky-clean image.

Hurt his endorsements. Cost you both a great deal of money. You don't want to lose money, Myron.''

Myron looked at him. "I don't?"

"No, you don't."

"Can I jot that down?" He picked up a pencil and began scribbling. "Don't . . . want . . . to . . . lose . . . money." He grinned at both men. "Am I picking up pointers today or what?"

Larry mumbled, "Goddamn wiseass."

Otto's smile remained locked on autopilot. "If I may be so bold," he continued, "I would think Christian would want to collect quickly."

"Oh?"

"There are those who have serious reservations about Christian Steele's future. There are those"—Otto drew deeply on his cigarette—"who believe he may have had something to do with that girl's disappearance."

"Ah," Myron said, "that's more like it."

"More like what?"

"You're starting to fling mud. For a second there I thought I wasn't asking for enough."

Larry Hanson stuck a thumb in Myron's direction. "Do you believe this fucking sliver of pond film we're sitting with? You raise a legitimate issue about Christian's ex-bimbo, one that goes to the heart of his value as a public relations commodity—"

"Pitiful rumors," Myron interrupted. "No one believed them. If anything, they made the public more sympathetic to Christian's tragedy. And don't call Kathy Culver a bimbo."

Larry raised an eyebrow. "Well, well, aren't we touchy," he said, "for a low-life pissant."

Myron's expression did not change. He had met Kathy Culver five years ago when she was a sophomore in high school, already a budding beauty. Like her sister

Jessica. Eighteen months ago Kathy had mysteriously vanished from the campus of Reston University. To this day no one knew where she was or what had happened to her. The story had all the media's favorite tasty morsels —a gorgeous co-ed, the fiancée of football star Christian Steele, the sister of novelist Jessica Culver, a strong hint of sexual assault for extra seasoning. The press could not help themselves. They attacked like ravenous relatives around a buffet table.

But just recently a second tragedy had befallen the Culver family. Adam Culver, Kathy's father, had been murdered three nights earlier in what police were calling a "botched robbery." Myron wanted very much to contact the family, to do more than merely offer simple condolences, but he had decided to stay away, not knowing if he was welcome, fairly certain he wasn't.

"Now if—"

There was a knock on the door. It opened a crack, and Esperanza stuck her head in. "Call for you, Myron," she said.

"Take a message."

"I think you'll want to take it."

Esperanza stayed in the doorway. Her dark eyes gave away nothing, but he understood.

"I'll be right there," he said.

She slipped back through the door.

Larry Hanson gave an appreciative whistle. "She's a babe, Bolitar."

"Gee, thanks, Larry. That means a lot coming from you." He rose. "I'll be right back."

"We don't have all goddamn day to jerk off here."

"I'm sure you don't."

He left the conference room and met up with Esperanza at her desk.

"The Meal Ticket," she told him. "He said it was urgent."

Christian Steele.

From her petite frame most would not guess that Esperanza used to be a professional wrestler. For three years she had been known on the circuit as Little Pocahontas. The fact that Esperanza Diaz was Latina, without a trace of American Indian blood, did not seem to bother the FLOW (Fabulous Ladies of Wrestling) organization. A minor detail, they said. Latino, Indian, what's the difference?

At the height of her pro wrestling career, the same script was played out every week in arenas all over the U.S. of A. Esperanza ("Pocahontas") would enter the ring wearing moccasins, a suede-fringed dress, and a headband that lassoed her long black hair away from her dark face. The suede dress came off before the fight, leaving a somewhat flimsier and less traditional Native American garb in its stead.

Professional wrestling has a pretty simple plot with painfully few variations. Some wrestlers are bad. Some are good. Pocahontas was good, a crowd favorite. She was cute and small and quick and had a tight little body. Everyone loved her. She would always be winning the fight on skill when her opponent would do something illegal—throw sand in her eyes, use a dreaded foreign object that everyone in the free world except the referee could see—to turn the tide. Then the bad wrestler would bring in a couple of extra cronies, ganging up three against one on poor Pocahontas, pounding mercilessly on the brave beauty to the unequivocal shock and chagrin of the announcers, who had seen the same thing happen last week and the week before.

Just when it seemed there was no hope, Big Chief Mama, a mammoth creature, charged out of the locker room and threw the beasts off the defenseless Pocahontas. Then together Big Chief Mama and Little Pocahontas would defeat the forces of evil.

Massively entertaining.

"I'll take it in my office," Myron said.

As he entered he saw the nameplate on his desk, a gift from his parents.

MYRON BOLITAR
SPORTS AGENT

He shook his head. Myron Bolitar. He still couldn't believe someone would name a kid Myron. When his family first moved to New Jersey, he had told everyone in his new high school that his name was Mike. Nope, no dice. Then he tried to nickname himself Mickey. Unh-unh. Everyone reverted to Myron; the name was like a horror-movie monster that would not die.

To answer the obvious question: No, he never forgave his parents.

He picked up the phone. "Christian?"

"Mr. Bolitar? Is that you?"

"Yes. And please call me . . . Myron." Acceptance of the inevitable, a sign of a wise man.

"I'm sorry to interrupt you. I know how busy you are."

"I'm busy negotiating your contract. I have Otto Burke and Larry Hanson in the next room."

"I appreciate that, Mr. Bolitar, but this is very important." His voice was trembling. "I have to see you right away."

He switched hands. "Something wrong, Christian?" Mr. Perceptive.

"I—I'd rather not discuss it over the phone. Would you be able to meet me at my room on campus?"

"Sure, no problem. What time?"

"Now, please. I—I don't know what to make of this. I want you to see it."

Myron took a deep breath. "No problem. I'll throw Otto and Larry out. It'll be good for the negotiations. I'll be there in an hour."

It took a lot longer.

Myron entered the Kinney garage on Forty-sixth Street, not too far from his Park Avenue office. He nodded to Mario, the garage attendant, walked past the pricing sheet, which had a small disclaimer on the bottom that read "not including 97% tax," and headed to his car on the lower level. A Ford Taurus. Your basic Babe Magnet.

He was about to unlock the door when he heard a hissing sound. Like a snake. Or more likely, air escaping from a tire. The sound emanated from his back right tire. A quick examination told Myron that it had been slashed.

"Hi, Myron."

He spun around. Two men grinned at him. One was the size of a small Third World nation. Myron was big— nearly six-four and two hundred twenty pounds—but he guessed that this guy must have been six-six and closing in on three hundred. A heavy-duty weight lifter, his whole body was puffed up as if he were wearing inflatable life vests under his clothes. The second man was of average build. He wore a fedora.

The big man lumbered toward Myron's car. His arms swung stiffly at his sides. He kept tilting his head, cracking the part of the anatomy that on a normal human being might be called a neck.

"Having some car trouble?" he asked with a chuckle.

"Flat tire," Myron said. "There's a spare in the trunk. Change it."

"I don't think so, Bolitar. This was just a little warning."

"Oh?"

The human edifice grabbed the lapels of Myron's jacket. "Stay away from Chaz Landreaux. He's already signed."

"First change my tire."

The grin increased. It was a stupid, cruel grin. "Next time I won't be so nice." He grabbed a little tighter, bunching up the suit and tie. "Understand?"

"You are aware, of course, that steroids make your balls shrink."

The man's face reddened. "Oh, yeah? Maybe I oughta smash your face in, huh? Maybe I oughta pulverize you into oatmeal."

"Oatmeal?"

"Yeah."

"Nice image, really."

"Fuck you."

Myron sighed. Then his whole body seemed to snap into motion at the same time. He started with a head-butt that landed square on the big man's nose. There was a squelching noise like beetles being stepped on. Blood gushed from the nose.

"Son of a—"

Myron cradled the back of the big man's head for leverage and smashed his elbow into the sweet of the Adam's apple, nearly caving the windpipe all the way in. There was a painful, gurgling choke. Then silence. Myron followed up with a knife-hand strike to the back of the neck below the skull.

The big man slid to the ground like wet sand.

"Okay, that's enough!"

The man with the fedora stepped closer, a gun drawn and pointed at Myron's chest.

"Back away from him. Now!"

Myron squinted at him. "Is that really a fedora?"

"I said, back off!"

"Okay, okay, I'm backing."

"You didn't have to do that," the smaller man said with almost childlike hurt. "He was just doing his job."

"A misunderstood youth," Myron added. "Now I feel terrible."

"Just stay away from Chaz Landreaux, okay?"

"Not okay. Tell Roy O'Connor I said it's not okay."

"Hey, I ain't hired to get no answer. I'm just delivering."

Without another word the man with the fedora helped his fallen colleague to his feet. The big man stumbled to their car, one hand on his nose, the other massaging his windpipe. His nose was busted, but his throat would hurt even worse, especially when he swallowed.

They got in and quickly drove away. They did not stop to change Myron's tire.

Chapter 2

Myron dialed Chaz Landreaux's number on his car phone.

Not being what one would call mechanically inclined, it had taken Myron half an hour to change the tire. He rode slowly for the first few miles, fearing his handiwork would encourage the tire to slip off and flee. When he felt more confident, he accelerated and started back on the road to Christian's.

When Chaz answered, Myron quickly explained what happened.

"They was already here," Chaz told him. Lots of noise in the background. An infant cried. Something fell and broke. Children laughed. Chaz shouted for quiet.

"When?" Myron asked.

"Hour ago. Three men."

"Did they hurt you?"

"Nah. Just held me down and made threats. Said they was going to break my legs if I didn't honor my contract."

Breaking legs, Myron thought. How original.

Chaz Landreaux was a senior basketball player at Georgia State and a probable first-round NBA pick. He was a poor kid from the streets of Philadelphia. He had six brothers, two sisters, no father. The ten of them lived in an area that—if daringly improved—might one day be charitably dubbed "poor ghetto."

During his freshman year, an underling of a big-time agent named Roy O'Connor had approached Chaz—four years before Chaz was eligible to talk to an agent. The man offered Chaz a five-thousand-dollar "retainer" up front, with monthly payments of $250, if he signed a contract making O'Connor his agent when he turned pro.

Chaz was confused. He knew that NCAA rules forbade him from signing a contract while he still had eligibility. The contract would be declared null and void. But Roy's man assured him this would be no problem. They would simply postdate the contract to make it appear Chaz had signed on after his final year of eligibility.

They'd keep the contract in a safety deposit box until the proper time arrived. No one would be the wiser.

Chaz was not sure. He knew it was illegal, but he also knew what that kind of money would mean to his mom and eight siblings living in a two-room hellhole. Roy O'Connor then entered the picture and pitched the final inducement: If Chaz changed his mind at some future date, he could repay the money and tear up the contract.

Four years later Chaz changed his mind. He promised to pay back every cent. No way, said Roy O'Connor. You have a contract with us. You'll stick with it.

This was not an uncommon setup. Dozens of agents did it. Norby Walters and Lloyd Bloom, two of the country's biggest agents, had been arrested for it. Threats too were not uncommon. But that was where it usually ended: with threats. No agent wanted to risk being exposed. If a kid stood firm, the agent backed off.

But not Roy O'Connor. Roy O'Connor was using muscle. Myron was surprised.

"I want you out of town for a little while," Myron continued. "You got someplace to lay low?"

"Yeah, I'll crash with a friend in Washington. But what we going to do?"

"I'll take care of it. Just stay out of sight."

"Okay, yeah, I hear ya." Then: "Oh, Myron, one other thing."

"What?"

"One of the dudes who held me down said he knew you. A monster, man. I mean, huge. Slick-looking motherfucker."

"Did he say his name?"

"Aaron. He said to tell you Aaron said hi."

Myron's shoulders slumped. Aaron. A name from his past. Not a good name either. Roy O'Connor not only had muscle behind him—he had serious muscle.

* * *

Three hours after leaving his office, Myron shook off all thoughts about the garage incident and knocked on Christian's door. Despite the fact that he'd graduated two months earlier, Christian still lived in the same campus dorm he had occupied throughout his senior year, working as a counselor at Reston U's football summer camp. The Titans minicamp, however, started in two days, and Christian would be there. Myron had no intention of having Christian hold out.

Christian opened the door immediately. Before Myron had a chance to explain his tardiness, Christian said, "Thanks for getting here so fast."

"Uh, sure. No problem."

Christian's face was completely devoid of its usual healthy color. Gone were the rosy cheeks that dimpled when Christian smiled. Gone was the wide-open, aw-shucks smile that made the co-eds swoon. Even the famed steady hands were noticeably quaking.

"Come on in," he said.

"Thanks."

Christian's room looked more like a 1950s sitcom set than a modern-day campus dorm room. For one thing, the place was neat. The bed was made, the shoes in a row beneath it. There were no socks on the floor, no underwear, no jock straps. On the walls were pennants. Actual pennants. Myron couldn't believe it. No posters, no calendars with Claudia Schiffer or Cindy Crawford or the Barbi twins. Just old-fashioned pennants. Myron felt as if he'd just stepped into Wally Cleaver's dormitory.

Christian didn't say anything at first. They both stood there uncomfortably, like two strangers stuck together at some cocktail party with no drinks in their hands. Christian kept his eyes lowered to the floor like a scolded child. He hadn't commented on the blood on Myron's suit. He probably hadn't noticed it.

Myron decided to try one of his patented silver-tongued ice-breakers. "What's up?"

Christian began to pace—no easy accomplishment in a room slightly larger than the average armoire. Myron could see that Christian's eyes were red. He'd been crying, his cheeks still showing small traces of the tear tracks.

"Did Mr. Burke get mad about canceling the meeting?" Christian asked.

Myron shrugged. "He had a major conniption, but he'll survive. Means nothing, don't worry about it."

"Minicamp starts Thursday?"

Myron nodded. "Are you nervous?"

"A little, maybe."

"Is that why you wanted to see me?"

Christian shook his head. He hesitated and then said, "I—I don't understand it, Mr. Bolitar."

Every time he called him mister, Myron looked for his father.

"Don't understand what, Christian? What's this all about?"

He hesitated again. "It's . . ." He stopped, took a deep breath, started again. "It's about Kathy."

Myron thought he'd heard wrong. "Kathy Culver?"

"You knew her," Christian said. Myron couldn't tell if it was a statement or a question.

"A long time ago," Myron replied.

"When you were with Jessica."

"Yes."

"Then maybe you'll understand. I miss Kathy. More than anyone can ever know. She was very special."

Myron nodded, encouraging. Very Phil Donahue.

Christian took a step back, nearly banging his head

into a bookshelf. "Everybody sensationalized what happened to her," he began. "They put it in tabloids, had stories about the disappearance on *A Current Affair*. It was like a game to everyone. A TV show. They kept calling us 'idyllic,' the 'idyllic couple.' " He made quote marks in the air with his fingers. "As if *idyllic* meant unreal. Unfeeling. Everyone kept saying I was young, I'd get over it quickly. Kathy was just a pretty blonde, millions more like her for a guy like me. I was expected to get on with my life. She was gone. It was over and done with."

Christian's boyish quality—something that Myron thought would help make him the future endorsement king—had suddenly taken on a new dimension. Instead of the shy, gee-whiz, modest little Kansas boy, Myron saw reality: a scared child huddled in a corner, a child whose parents were dead, who had no real family, probably no real friends, just hero-worshipers and those who wanted a piece of him (like Myron himself?).

Myron shook his head. No way. Other agents, yes, but not him. Myron wasn't like that. But still something akin to guilt stayed there, poking a sharp finger into his ribs.

"I never really believed Kathy was dead," Christian continued. "That was part of the problem, I guess. The not-knowing gets to you after a while. Part of me—part of me almost hoped they'd find her body already, anything to end it. Is that an awful thing to say, Mr. Bolitar?"

"I don't think so, no."

Christian looked at him solemnly. "I kept thinking about the panties. You know about that?"

Myron nodded. The lone clue in the mystery was Kathy's ripped panties, found on top of a campus Dumpster. Rumor had it that they were covered with semen and blood. To the world at large, the panties had confirmed what had long been suspected: Kathy Culver was dead. It was a sad though not uncommon story. She had been raped and murdered by a random psychopath. Her body would probably never be found—or maybe some hunters would stumble across the skeletal remains in the woods one day, giving the press a great eleven o'clock commercial teaser, bringing the cameras back into the story with undying hopes of catching a grief-stricken relative on film.

"They made it seem like it was a dirty thing," Christian continued. " 'Pink,' they said. 'Silk,' they said. They never called them underwear or undergarments or even just plain panties. It was always pink silk panties. Like that was important. One TV station even interviewed a Victoria's Secret model for her comment on them. Pink silk panties. Like that meant she was asking for it. Trashing Kathy like that . . ."

His voice sort of faded away then. Myron said nothing. Christian was working up to something. Myron only hoped it wasn't a breakdown.

"I guess I should get to the point," Christian finally said.

"Take your time. I'm not going anywhere."

"I saw something today. I—" Christian stopped and swung his eyes toward Myron's. They looked at him, pleading. "Kathy may still be alive."

His words hit Myron like a wet slap. Whatever Myron had been preparing himself for, whatever he imagined Christian was leading up to, hearing Kathy Culver might still be alive was not a part of the equation.

"What?"

Christian reached behind him and opened his desk drawer. The desk too was something out of *Leave It to Beaver*. Completely uncluttered. Two cans, one with Bic pens, the other with sharpened number-two pencils.

Gooseneck lamp. Desk blotter with calendar. Dictionary, thesaurus, and *The Elements of Style* all in a row between two globe bookends.

"This came in the mail today."

He handed Myron a magazine. On the cover was a naked woman. Calling her well-endowed would be tantamount to calling World War II a skirmish. Most men are somewhat mammary obsessed, and Myron was not above having similar sentiments, but this was positively freakish. The woman's face was far from pretty, kind of harsh looking. She was giving the camera a look that was supposed to be come-hither but looked more like constipation. Her tongue was licking her lips, her legs spread, her finger beckoning the reader to come closer.

Very subtle effect, Myron thought.

The magazine was called *Nips*. The lead story, according to the words emblazoned across her right breast: "How to Get Her to Shave Dat Thang."

Myron looked up sharply. "What's this all about?"

"The paper clip."

"What?"

But Christian seemed too weak to repeat it. He just pointed. On the top of the magazine Myron spotted a glint of silver. A paper clip was being used as a bookmark.

"It came with that on there," Christian said by way of explanation.

Myron fingered through the pages, catching quick glimpses of flesh, until he arrived at the page marked off by the paper clip. His eyes squinted in confusion. It was an ad page, though it had as many erotic photos as any other. The top of the page read:

Live Fantasy Phone—Pick Your Girl!

There were three rows, four girls in each row, all the way down the page. Myron's eyes scanned down. He could not believe what he was seeing. "Oriental Girls Are Waiting!" "Wet and Juicy Lesbos!" "Spank Me, Please!" "Bitches in Heat!" "Tiny Titties!" (for those who didn't like the cover shot, no doubt) "I Want You to Ride Me!" "Pick My Cherry!" "Make Me Beg for More!" "Wanted: Robocock." "Mistress Savannah Demands You Call Now!" "Horny Housewife!" "Overweight Men Wanted." Each with matching photo—provocative poses involving telephones.

There were some that were far more raunchy. Crossdressers. Women with men's equipment. There were some Myron could not even understand. Like unfathomable science experiments. The telephone numbers were what you'd expect. 1-800-888-SLUT. 1-900-46-TRAMP. 1-800-REAM-MEE. 1-900-BAD-GIRL.

Myron made a face. He wanted to wash his hands.

Then he saw it.

It was in the bottom row, second from the right. It read, "I'll Do Anything!" The phone number was 1-900-344-LUST. $3.99 per minute. Discreetly billed to your telephone or charge card. Visa/MC accepted.

The woman in the picture was Kathy Culver.

Myron felt a coldness seep into him. He turned back to the cover and checked the date. It was the current issue.

"When did you get this?"

"It came in today's mail," Christian said, picking up an envelope. "In this."

Myron's head began to swim. He tried to fight the dizziness and get some kind of footing, but the picture of Kathy kept tipping him back over. The envelope was plain manila. There was no return address—that would have been too easy. It was not postmarked and had no stamps, merely reading:

CHRISTIAN STEELE
BOX 488

No city, no state. That meant it'd been mailed on campus. The address had been handwritten.

"You get lots of fan mail, right?" Myron asked.

Christian nodded. "But they go somewhere else. This was in my private box. The number is unlisted."

Myron handled the envelope carefully, trying not to smudge any potential fingerprints. "It could be trick photography," Myron added. "Someone might have superimposed her head on—"

Christian stopped him with a shake of his head. His eyes were back on the floor. "It's not just her face, Mr. Bolitar," he said, embarrassed.

"Oh," Myron said, ever swift on the uptake. "I see."

"Do you think we should give this to the police?" Christian asked.

"Perhaps."

"I want to do the right thing," Christian said, his hands balling into fists. "But I won't let them drag Kathy through the mud again. You saw what they did when she was the victim. What will they do when they see this?"

"They'll go animal," he agreed.

Christian nodded.

"But it's probably just a prank," Myron continued. "I'll check it out before we do anything else."

"How?"

"Let me worry about that."

"There's one other thing," Christian said. "The handwriting on the envelope."

Myron glanced at it again. "What about it?"

"I can't say for sure, but it looks a lot like Kathy's."

Chapter 3

Myron stopped short when he saw her.

He had just stumbled into the bar in something of a daydream, his mind like a movie camera that couldn't stay in focus. He tried to sift through what he had just seen and learned from Christian, tried to compute the facts and form a solid, well-conceived conclusion.

He came up with nothing.

The magazine was jammed into the right pocket of his trench coat. Porn mag and trench coat, Myron thought. Jesus. The same questions echoed ad nauseam in his head: Could Kathy Culver still be alive? And if she was, what had happened to her? What could have led Kathy from the innocence of her dorm room to the back pages of *Nips* magazine?

That was when he spotted the most beautiful woman he had ever seen.

She was sitting on a stool, her long legs crossed, sipping gently at her drink. She wore a white blouse opened at the throat, a short gray skirt, and black stockings. Everything clung just right. For a fleeting moment Myron thought she was just a by-product of his daydream, a dazzling vision to tantalize the senses. But the knot in his stomach made him quickly dismiss that notion. His throat went dry. Deep, dormant emotions crashed down upon him like a surprise wave at the beach.

He managed to swallow and commanded his legs to move forward. She was, quite simply, breathtaking. Everything else in the bar faded into the background, as though they were only stage props set for her.

Myron approached. "Come here often?" he asked.

She looked at him like he was an old man jogging in a Speedo. "Original line," she said. "Very creative."

"Maybe not," he said. "But what a delivery." He smiled. Winningly, he thought.

"Glad you think so." She turned back to her drink. "Please leave."

"Playing hard to get?"

"Get lost."

Myron grinned. "Stop it already. You're embarrassing yourself."

"Pardon me."

"It's obvious to everyone in this bar."

"Oh?" she remarked. "Do enlighten."

"You want me. Bad."

She almost smiled. "That obvious, huh?"

"Don't blame yourself. I'm irresistible."

"Uh-huh. Catch me if I swoon."

"I'm right here, sweetcakes."

She sighed deeply. She was as beautiful as ever, as beautiful as the day she had walked out on him. He hadn't seen her in four years, but it still hurt to think about her. It hurt even more to look at her. Their weekend at Win's house on Martha's Vineyard came to him. He could still remember the way the ocean breeze blew her hair, the way she tilted her head when he spoke, the way she looked and felt in his old sweatshirt. Simple fragile bliss. The knot in his stomach tightened.

"Hello, Myron," she said.

"Hello, Jessica. You're looking well."

"What are you doing here?" she asked.

"My office is upstairs. I practically live here."

She smiled. "Oh, that's right. You represent athletes now, don't you?"

"Yes."

"Better than working all that undercover stuff?"

Myron did not bother answering. She glanced at him but did not hold the gaze.

"I'm waiting for someone," Jessica said suddenly.

"A male someone?"

"Myron . . ."

"Sorry. Old reflex." He looked at her left hand. His heart back-flipped when he saw no rings. "You never married what's-his-name?" he asked.

"Doug."

"That's right. Doug. Or was it Dougie?"

"You're making fun of someone's name?"

Myron shrugged. She had a point. "So what happened to him?"

Her eyes studied a beer ring on the bar. "It wasn't about him," she said. "You know that."

He opened his mouth and then closed it. Rehashing the bitter past was not going to do any good. "So what brings you back to the city?"

"I'm going to be teaching a semester at NYU."

His heart sped up again. "You moved back to Manhattan?"

"Last month."

"I'm really sorry about your father's—"

"We got your flowers," she interrupted.

"I wanted to do more."

"Better you didn't." She finished her drink. "I have to go. It was nice seeing you."

"I thought you were meeting someone."

"My mistake, then."

"I still love you, you know."

She stood, nodded.

"Let's try again," he said.

"No."

She walked away.

"Jess?"

"What?"

He considered telling her about her sister's picture in the magazine. "Can we have lunch sometime?" he asked. "Just talk, okay?"

"No."

Jessica turned and left him. Again.

Windsor Horne Lockwood III listened to Myron's story with his fingers steepled. Steepling looked good on Win, a lot better than on Myron. When Myron finished, Win said nothing for a few moments, doing more of that steepled-hands-concentration thing. Finally he rested his hands on the desk.

"My, my, haven't we had a special day?"

Myron rented his space from his old college roommate, Windsor Horne Lockwood III. People often said that Myron looked nothing like his name—an observation Myron took as high praise; Windsor Horne Lockwood III, however, looked exactly like his name. Blond hair, perfect length, parted on the right side. His features were classical patrician, almost too handsome, like something crafted in porcelain.

His attire was always thoroughbred prep—pink shirts, polo shirts, monogrammed shirts, khaki pants, golf (read, ugly) pants, white bucks (Memorial Day to Labor

Day) or wing tips (Labor Day to Memorial Day) on his feet. Win even had that creepy accent, the one that did not originate from any particular geographical location as much as from certain prep schools like Andover and Exeter. (Win had gone to Exeter.) He played a mean game of golf. He had a three handicap and was the fifth-generation member of stuffy Merion Golf Club in Philadelphia and third-generation at equally stuffy Pine Valley in southern New Jersey. He had a perennial golf tan, one of those where the color could be found only on the arms (short-sleeve shirts) and a V-shape in the neck (open alligator shirt), though Win's lily-white skin never tanned. It burned.

Win was full-fledged whitebread. He made star quarterback Christian Steele look like a Mediterranean houseboy.

Myron had hated Windsor on sight. Most people did. Win was used to it. People liked to form and keep an immediate impression. In Win's case that impression was old money, elitist, arrogant—in a phrase, a flaming asshole. There was nothing Win could do about it. People who relied solely on first impressions meant little to him.

Win gestured to the magazine on his desk. "You chose not to tell Jessica about this?"

Myron stood, paced, and then sat back down. "What was I going to say? 'Hi, I love you, come back to me, here's a photo of your supposedly dead sister advertising a sex phone in a porno mag?' "

Win thought a moment. "I'd refine the wording a bit," he said.

He flipped through the porno rag, his eyebrow arched as if to say Hmmm. Myron watched. He had decided not to tell Win about Chaz Landreaux or the incident in the garage. Not yet anyway. Win had a funny way of reacting when someone tried to hurt Myron. It wasn't always pretty. Better to save it for later, when Myron would know exactly how he wanted to handle Roy O'Connor. And Aaron.

Win dropped the magazine on his desk. "Shall we begin?"

"Begin what?"

"Investigating. That is what you planned for us, correct?"

"You want to help?"

Win smiled. "But of course." He turned his phone around so that it faced Myron. "Dial."

"The number in the magazine?"

"Well, golly, Myron, I thought we'd call the White House," Win said dryly. "See if we can get Hillary to talk dirty."

Myron took hold of the phone. "You ever call one of these lines?"

"I?" Win feigned shock. "The Debutantes' Darling? The Society Stud? Surely you jest."

"Neither have I."

"Perhaps you'd like to be alone, then," Win said. "Loosen your belt, pull down your trousers, that kind of thing."

"Very funny."

Myron dialed the 900 number under Kathy's photograph. He had made thousands of investigative calls, both during his years in the FBI and in his private work for team owners and commissioners. But this was the first time he'd felt self-conscious.

An awful beeping noise blasted his ear, followed by an operator: "We're sorry. Your call is being blocked."

Myron looked up. "The call won't go through."

Win nodded. "I forgot. We have a block on all 900 calls. Employees were calling them all the time and ringing up quite a bill—not just the sex phones but astrologers, sports lines, psychics, recipes, even dial-a-prayers." He reached behind him and pulled out another phone. "Use this one. It's my private line. No blocks."

Myron redialed. The phone rang twice before being picked up. A woman's voice on tape husked, "Hello, there. You've reached the fantasy phone line. If you're under eighteen or do not wish to pay for this call, please hang up now." Less than a second passed before she continued. "Welcome to the fantasy phone line, where you can talk to the sexiest, most willing, most beautiful, most desirous women in the world."

Myron noticed that the taped voice was speaking far more slowly now, as if she were reading to a kindergarten class. Each word was its own sentence.

"Welcome. To. The. Fantasy . . ."

"In a moment you will talk directly to one of our wondrous, gorgeous, voluptuous, hot girls who are here to heighten your pleasure to new boundaries of ecstasy. One-on-one private conversation. Discreetly billed to your phone. You will talk live with your personal fantasy girl." The voice droned on with its own form of iambic pentameter. Finally the tape gave instructions: "If you have a touch-tone phone, press one if you'd like to talk about the secret confessions of a naughty schoolteacher. Press two if . . ."

Myron looked up at Win. "How long have I been on?"

"Six minutes."

"Twenty-four dollars already," Myron said. "Does the term 'total scam' mean anything to you?"

Win nodded. "Talk about jerking off."

Myron pressed a button, anything to get off this revolving tape. The phone rang ten times—Christ, they knew how to stretch the time—before he heard another female voice say, "Hi, there. How are you today?"

Her voice was exactly what Myron had expected. Low and husky.

"Uh, hi," Myron fumbled. "Look, I'd like—"

"What's your name, honey?" she asked.

"Myron." He slapped his forehead and held back a profanity. Had he really been stupid enough to use his real name?

"Mmmmm, Myron," she said as if testing it out. "I like that name. It's so sexy."

"Yeah, well, thanks—"

"My name is Tawny."

Tawny. Sure.

"How did you get my number, Myron?"

"I saw it in a magazine."

"What magazine, Myron?"

The constant use of his name was beginning to unnerve him. *"Nips."*

"Oooo. I like that magazine. It makes me so, you know."

A way with words. "Listen, uh, Tawny, I'd like to ask you about your ad."

"Myron?"

"Yes."

"I love your voice. You sound really hot. Do you want to know what I look like?"

"No, not real—"

"I have brown eyes. I have long brown hair, kinda wavy. I'm five-six. And I'm a 36-24-36. C cup. Sometimes a D."

"You must be very proud but—"

"What do you like to do, Myron?"

"Do?"

"For fun."

"Look, Tawny, you seem very nice, really, but can I talk to the girl in the ad?"

"I am the girl in the ad," she said.

"No, I mean, the girl whose picture is in the magazine on top of this phone number."

"That's me, Myron. I'm that girl."

"The girl in the photo is a blonde with blue eyes," Myron said. "You said you had brown eyes and brown hair."

Win gave him a thumbs-up, scoring one for the detailed eye of Myron Bolitar, ace investigator.

"Did I say that?" Tawny asked. "I meant blonde with blue eyes."

"I need to talk to the girl in the ad. It's very important."

Her voice went down another octave. "I'm better, Myron. I'm the best."

"I don't doubt that, Tawny. You sound very professional. But right now I need to talk to the girl in the ad."

"She's not here, Myron."

"When will she be back?"

"I'm not sure, Myron. But just sit back and relax. We're going to have fun—"

"I don't want to be rude, but I'm really not interested. Can I talk to your boss?"

"My boss?"

"Yes."

Her tone was different now. More matter-of-fact. "You're kidding, right?"

"No. I'm serious. Please put your boss on."

"Okay, then," she said. "Hold on a second."

A minute passed. Then two. Win said, "She's not coming back. She's just going to see how long the chump will stay on the line and pour dollars down her pants."

"I don't think so," Myron said. "She liked my voice, said I sounded hot."

"Oh, I didn't realize. Probably the first time she's ever said that."

"My thinking exactly." A few minutes later Myron put the receiver back in its cradle. "How long was I on for?"

Win looked at his watch. "Twenty-three minutes." He grabbed a calculator. "Twenty-three minutes times three ninety-nine per minute." He punched in the numbers. "That call cost you ninety-one dollars and seventy-seven cents."

"A rare bargain," Myron said. "You want to hear something weird? She never said anything dirty."

"What?"

"The girl on the phone. She never said anything dirty."

"And you're disappointed."

"Don't you find that a bit strange?"

Win shrugged, skimming through the magazine. "Have you looked through this at all?"

"No."

"Half the pages are advertisements for sex phones. This is clearly big business."

"Safe sex," Myron said. "The safest."

There was a knock on the door.

"Enter," Win called out.

Esperanza opened the door. "Call for you. Otto Burke."

"Tell him I'll be right there."

She nodded and left.

"I have some time on my hands," Win said. "I'll try to find out who placed the ad. We'll also need a sample of Kathy Culver's handwriting for comparison."

"I'll see what I can come up with."

Win resteepled his hands, bouncing the fingertips gently against one another. "You do realize," he began, "that this photograph probably means nothing. Chances are there is a very simple explanation for all this."

"Maybe," Myron agreed, rising from his chair. He had been telling himself the same thing for the past two hours. He no longer believed it.

"Myron?"

"What?"

"You don't think it was a coincidence—Jessica being in the bar downstairs, I mean."

"No," Myron said. "I guess I don't."

Win nodded. "Be careful," he said. "A word to the wise."

Chapter 4

Damn him.

Jessica Culver sat in her family's kitchen, in the very seat she had sat in innumerable times as a child.

She should have known better. She should have thought it through, should have come prepared for any occurrence. But what had she done instead? She had gotten nervous. She had hesitated. She had stopped for a drink in the bar below his office.

Stupid, stupid.

But that wasn't all. He had surprised her, and she had panicked.

Why?

She should have told Myron the truth. She should have told him in a plain unemotional voice the real reason she was there. But she hadn't. She had been drinking unaware, and suddenly he had appeared, looking so handsome and yet so hurt and—

Oh shit, Jessie, you are one fucked-up chick. . . .

She nodded to herself. Yup. Fucked-up. Self-destructive. And a few other hyphenated words she couldn't come up with right now. Her publisher and agent did not see it that way, of course. They loved her "foibles" (their term—Jessie preferred "fuck-ups"), even encouraged them. They were what made Jessica Culver such an exceptional writer. They were what gave Jessica Culver's writing that certain "edge" (again, their term).

Perhaps that was so. Jessie really couldn't say. But one thing was certain: These foibling fuck-ups had turned her life to shit.

Oh, pity the suffering artist! Thy heart bleeds for such torment!

She dismissed the mocking tone with a shake of her head. She was unusually introspective today, but that was understandable. She had seen Myron, and that had led to a lot of "what if-ing"—a verifiable avalanche of useless "what if-ing" from every conceivable height and angle.

What if. She pondered it yet again.

In her typically self-centered way, she had seen the "what if-ing" only in terms of herself, not Myron. Now she wondered about him, about what his life had really been like since the world crumbled down upon him—not all at once—but in small, decaying bits. Four years. She had not seen him in four years. She had shoved Myron into some back closet in her mind and locked the door. She'd thought (hoped?) that would be the end of it, that

the door could stand up to a little pressure without opening. But seeing him today, seeing the kind, handsome
face high above those broad shoulders, seeing the still
why-me stare in his eyes—the door had blown off its
hinges like something in a gas explosion.

Jessica had been overwhelmed by her feelings. She
wanted to be with him so badly that she knew she had to
get out right away.

Makes sense, she thought, *if you're a total fuck-up.*

Jessica glanced out the window. She was waiting for
Paul's arrival. Bergen County police Lieutenant Paul
Duncan—Uncle Paul to her, since infancy—was two
years away from retirement. He had been her father's
closest friend, the executor of Adam Culver's will. They
had both worked in law enforcement—Paul as a cop,
Adam as the county medical examiner—for more than
twenty-five years.

Paul was coming to finalize the details for her father's
memorial service. No funeral for Adam Culver. He
wouldn't hear of it. But Jessica wanted to talk to Paul
about another matter. Alone. She did not like what was
going on.

"Hi, honey."

She turned to the voice. "Hi, Mom."

Her mother came up through the basement. She was
wearing an apron, her fingers fiddling with the large
wooden cross around her neck. "I put his chair in storage," she explained in a forced matter-of-fact tone.
"Just cluttering space up here."

For the first time Jessica realized that her father's
chair—the one her mother must have been referring to—
was gone from the kitchen table. The simple unpadded
four-legged chair her father had sat in for as long as
Jessica could remember, the one closest to the refrigerator, so close that her father could turn around, open the

door, and stretch for the milk on the top shelf without getting up, had been taken away, stored in some cobwebbed corner of the basement.

But not so Kathy's.

Jessie's gaze touched down on the chair to her immediate right. Kathy's chair. It was still here. Her mother had not touched it. Her father, well, he was dead. But Kathy—who knew? Kathy could, in theory, walk through the back door right this very minute, banging it against the wall as she always did, smile brightly, and join them for dinner. The dead were dead. When you lived with a medical examiner, you understood just how useless the dead were. Dead and buried. The soul, well, that was another matter. Jessie's mom was a devout Catholic, attending mass every morning, and during crises like these her religious tenacity paid off—like someone who spent time in a gym finally finding a use for their new muscles. She could believe without question in a divine and joyous afterlife. Such a comfort. Jessica wished she could do the same, but over the years her religious fervor had become a strict couch potato.

Except, of course, Kathy might not be dead. Ergo the chair—Mom's lantern kept lit to guide her youngest back home.

Jessica awoke most mornings bolting upright in her bed, thinking about—no, inventing new possibilities for —her younger sister. Was Kathy lying dead in a pit somewhere? Buried under brush in the woods? A skeleton gnawed on by animals and inhabited by maggots? Was Kathy's corpse stuck in some cement foundation? Was it weighed down in the bottom of some river like the little undersea man in the living-room aquarium? Had she died painlessly? Had she been tortured? Had her body been chopped into small bits, burned, broken down with acid . . .

Or was she still alive?

That eternal spring.

Had Kathy possibly been kidnapped? Was she living in white slavery under the thumb of some Middle East sheikh? Or was she living chained to a radiator on a farm in Wisconsin like something on *Geraldo*? Could she have banged her head, forgotten who she was, and was now living as a street person with amnesia? Or had she simply run away to a different world?

The possibilities were endless. Even those lacking creativity can come up with a million different horrors when their loved one suddenly vanishes—or more painfully, a million different hopes.

Jessica's thoughts were chased away by the tired chugging of a car engine. A familiar Chevy Caprice blanketed with tiny dents pulled up. It looked like a retrieval car at a driving range. She stood and hurried out the front door.

Paul Duncan was a stocky man, compact, with salt-and-pepper hair now turning defiantly toward salt. He walked purposely, the way cops do. He greeted her on the front stoop with a big smile and kiss on the cheek. "Hey, beautiful! How are you?"

She hugged him. "I'm okay, Uncle Paul," she said.

"You look great."

"Thanks."

Paul shaded his eyes from the sun. "Come on, let's go inside. It's hot as hell out here."

"In a minute," she said, putting a hand on his forearm. "I want to talk to you first."

"What about?"

"My father's case."

"I'm not handling that, honey. I don't do homicides anymore, you know that. Besides, it would be a conflict of interest—me being Adam's friend and all."

"But you have to know what's going on."

Paul Duncan nodded slowly. "I do."

"Mom said the police think he was killed in a robbery attempt."

"That's right."

"You don't believe that, do you?"

"Your father was robbed," he said. "His wallet was gone. His watch. Even his rings. The guy stripped him clean."

"To make it look like a robbery."

Paul smiled then, gently—the way, she remembered, he had at her confirmation and Sweet Sixteen party and high school graduation. "What are you getting at, Jess?"

"You don't find this whole thing odd?" she asked. "You don't see a connection between this and Kathy?"

He stumbled a step back, as if her words had given him a gentle push. "What connection? Your sister vanished from her college campus. Your father was murdered by a robber a year and a half later. Where do you see a connection?"

"Do you really believe that they have nothing to do with each other?" she asked. "Do you honestly believe that lightning struck twice in the same place?"

He put his hands in his pockets. "If you mean do I think your family has been the victim of two separate awful tragedies, the answer is yes. It happens all the time, Jess. Life is rarely fair. God doesn't go around divvying out the bad in equal doses. Some families go through life with nary a scratch. Some get too much. Like yours."

"So it's fate," she said. "That's your answer. Fate."

He threw his hands up. "Fate, lightning striking twice—these are your phrases. You're the writer here, not me. I just call it a tragedy. I just call it a tragic, somewhat bizarre coincidence. I've seen a lot stranger. So had your dad.''

The front door opened. Mom stood in the doorway. ''What's going on?''

''It's nothing, Carol. We were just talking.''

Carol looked at her daughter. ''Jessica?''

Her eyes stayed on Paul's, probing. ''Just talking, Mom.''

Jessica turned away and stepped back inside. Paul Duncan watched her, letting loose a silent breath. He had suspected she would be a problem—Jessica never accepted easy solutions to anything in life, even when the answer was simple. Yep, he had hoped it wouldn't happen, but he had definitely foreseen this possibility.

He just wasn't sure what he should do about it.

Midnight.

At ten P.M. Christian Steele had crawled under the blanket, read for ten minutes, and then switched off the light. Since then he had lain on his back in the dark, staring at the ceiling, not moving, not fooling himself into even hoping that sleep was imminent.

''Kathy,'' he said out loud.

His mind floated about aimlessly, settling like a butterfly for only brief moments before moving on. Darkness surrounded him, but not silence. There was no such thing as silence at football camp. Christian heard kegs being thrown, loud music, laughter, singing, swearing. He could distinctly hear Charles and Eddie, his offensive tackles, in the next room. They were permanently set on loud, like a radio turned up before the knob was ripped out. Christian was not above partying too, having fun by consuming alcohol until he hugged the porcelain god and puked up his offering. But not tonight.

God, not tonight.

"Kathy," he said again.

Was it possible? After all this time . . .

So many things were happening at once. School was over. The Titans' minicamp began the day after tomorrow. The scrutiny of the press had grown more intense than ever. He liked the attention, liked being on the cover of *Sports Illustrated,* liked the awe in people's faces when they spoke to him. Nice kid, they always said. Real nice. As though they expected him to be rude just because he could throw a pigskin with precision. As though he should somehow feel as though he belonged to a higher species, far above them, because he happened to be a good athlete.

Christian was excited. He was scared. He knew he had to think about the future. Myron had told him of the dangers and of how short-lived fame could be. Myron was, after all, a classic example. He had told Christian about the importance of cashing in now, that his career would at best last ten years. So much was at stake. So much. He was famous now, but there was a big difference between college famous and pro famous. Soon he'd have it all. Competition. Fame. Real money—not just the alumni secret handouts. . . .

But so what?

"Kathy . . ."

His phone rang.

Christian shot up, his heart beating like a rabbit's. Fast reflexes. Sometimes they played against you. It was only the phone. Probably Charles or Eddie telling him, hey, it's party time! They'd both gotten drafted too. Charles had gone in the second round to Dallas. Eddie in the fifth to the Rams.

He picked up the phone. "Hello?"

No response.

"Hello?" he said again.

Nothing. But the phone had not been hung up. Someone was there, silently holding the receiver to their ear.

"Who is this?"

Nothing.

Christian hung up. He began to lie back down when
the phone rang again. He picked up the receiver.

"Hello?"

Silence again. Christian tried to listen more closely.
Nothing. Or—or was that breathing? Panic seized him.
He couldn't say why. It was just a prankster calling on
his unlisted phone. It might even be Charles or Eddie
playing some kind of joke. Nothing to get upset about.

Except he was upset.

He cleared his throat. "What do you want?"

Still nothing.

"If you call back again, I'll call the cops."

He slammed the phone down. His hand shook. He
was just about to try to settle back down when he remembered something.

Star. Six. Nine.

The phone company had sent something in the mail
today. There had been advertisements on the TV—a
pregnant woman trying to get to the ringing phone,
trudging across the room toward the phone, but when
she arrived the caller had already hung up. Then what?
She picked up the phone and the voice-over—Cliff Rob-
ertson's or someone like that—said something like "You
just missed the call. Was it important? Was it someone
you wanted to talk to? There is only one way to find out.
Press the star and then six and nine." They demon-
strated it on the screen now, in case anyone wasn't sure
how to use a phone. Then the voice-over continued.
"You'll be connected to your previous caller, even if the
number is busy. We'll keep dialing for you, leaving your
phone line free to make or receive other calls."

The pregnant woman listened to a phone ring and then spoke to her relieved husband, who was working on some drafting board at work.

Christian picked up the phone. Then he hit the star, the six, and the nine.

The phone rang.

He rubbed his chin. A moment later a robotic operator came on. "The number is currently busy. We will ring you back when the line is free. Thank you."

Christian replaced the receiver. He sat up and waited. The partying was still going on. He could hear three or four distinct partying areas. Someone shouted, "Yahooo!" A window crashed. People cheered. His larger teammates were playing keg toss, a sort of discus throw involving beer kegs.

The phone rang.

He snatched the receiver as if it were a loose ball on the turf. The phone was ringing back the number—just like the pregnant lady's on the television. After the fourth ring the phone was picked up.

An answering machine.

A voice said, "Hi. We're not in right now. Please leave a message at the beep, and we'll be sure to call you back. Thanks."

The phone slipped from Christian's grip. A chilly hand caressed the back of his neck. A sound—some kind of choking noise—escaped his lips. Christian tried to form words but he couldn't.

The answering machine. The voice.

It was Kathy.

Chapter 5

Myron staggered into his office, punch-drunk from lack of sleep. He had not even bothered climbing into bed the night before. He tried to read, but the words swam in front of his eyes in meaningless waves. He put on the television. Nick at Nite, the cultural equivalent of aerosol cheese. Back-to-back episodes of *F Troop* for three hours. Larry Storch's portrayal of Agarn was, in a phrase, pure thespian genius. Who knew that hitting someone repeatedly with a big hat could be so funny?

But not even such highbrow entertainment could stop his mind from going back to one thought: Jess was back. And like Win had said, it was no coincidence.

At midnight his mother had come down in her robe.

"Hon, you all right?"

"I'm fine, Mom."

"You seemed distracted all night."

"It's nothing. Just have a lot of work."

She looked at him with her a-mother-is-psychic-and-knows look of disbelief. "Whatever you say."

At the age of thirty-one Myron still lived at home. True, he had his own space, his own bedroom and bathroom in the basement. But there was no denying it. Myron still lived with Mommy and Daddy.

Five minutes after his mother had gone back to bed, Christian Steele called Myron on his private line, the one that rang softly in the basement so as not to wake up his parents, both of whom slept so lightly, Myron was sure they'd been some kind of ghetto lookouts in a previous life. He filled Myron in on the weird phone calls.

Myron was familiar with the star-six-nine, known as Return Call. The phone company charged on a "pay-per-use" basis—around seventy-five cents per use. The problem was, Return Call did not trace the number. It automatically redialed the number of the last incoming call received, not letting you know the number. Star-five-seven—Call Trace—would have done the job, though the number is merely reported to the local phone company, which gives it only to the proper authorities.

Still, Myron would call some of his old sources at the phone company, see what he could find out. He knew that star-six-nine worked only for certain local areas. That meant the call was not long distance. A start. Better than nothing. He would also put Caller ID or a trace on Christian's phone. Taps were no longer like you saw on television, the hero anxiously trying to get the caller to stay on the line until it was completed. They were automatic. Caller ID actually showed you the incoming number before you picked up the phone.

But of course, none of that answered the larger questions:

Was it really Kathy's voice Christian had heard? And if so, what did that mean?

Lots of *preguntas*. Not too many answers.

He approached Esperanza's desk. "How's it going?"

She pierced him with a glare, shook her head in disgust, and looked back down at her desk.

"Back on decaf?" he asked.

Another glare. Myron shrugged. "Any messages?"

A head shake. Esperanza muttered something. Myron thought he picked up the Spanish equivalent of "ass-wipe."

"You want to tell me why you're so upset?"

"Right," she said bitingly. "Like you don't know."

"I don't."

The glare was back. Women had a talent for glares. Esperanza had a divine gift.

"Forget it," he said. "Just get me Otto Burke on the phone."

"Now?" Esperanza said, her voice dripping with sarcasm. "Won't you be busy?"

"Just do it, please, okay? You're starting to piss me off."

"Oooo. I'm quaking."

Myron shook his head. He had no time for her moods right now. He crossed the room and opened his office door. He stopped short.

"Hi."

He cleared his throat and closed the door behind him. "Hello, Jessica."

For most athletes, Jessica thought, the spotlight fades slowly. But for a tragic few, it vanishes as though from a sudden power failure, bathing the athlete in dazzling darkness.

Such was the case with Myron.

For most athletes the expectation game helps dim the light gradually. A high school star becomes a college bench warmer. The light dims. A college starter realizes he will not be the team's high scorer. The light dims. The college superstar realizes he will never make it to the pros. The light dims. And then there are those very few, those who are one in a million, those with almost Wolfean "right stuff," who become professional athletes.

For those, the light is blinding, forever damaging the vision of the ones who stare directly into it. That was what made the dimming so important. An athlete could get used to losing the light slowly. His career would peak before tapering off just slightly. He would brighten from the inexperienced rookie to the player in his prime, and then the light would begin to fade as he moved past seasoned vet.

For Myron that had not happened.

He had been one of those select few who basked in the most potent wattage imaginable, as if the spotlight shone on him and from inside of him. His basketball talent had first became apparent in the sixth grade. He had gone on to break every scoring and rebounding record in Essex County, New Jersey, a perennial basketball stronghold. Myron was short for a forward, a program six-six (really only six-four), but he was a physical brute, a bull, and a hell of a leaper for a white man. He was highly recruited, chose Duke, and won two NCAA titles in four years.

The Boston Celtics had drafted him in the first round, the eighth pick overall. Myron's spotlight grew impossibly bright.

And then the fuse blew.

A freak injury, they called it. It was a preseason game against the Washington Bullets. Two players weighing a combined six hundred pounds sandwiched the rookie Myron Bolitar. The doctors threw all kind of terms at the man-child who had never been injured before, not even a twisted ankle. Multiple fractures, they said. Shattered kneecap. Casts. Wheelchair. Crutches. Cane.

Years.

Sixteen months later Myron could walk, though the limp lasted another two years. He never came back. His career was over. The only life he had ever known had been stripped from him. The press had done a story or two, but Myron was quickly forgotten.

Complete blackout.

Jessica frowned. Spotlight. Bad metaphor. Too cliché and inaccurate. She shook her head and looked up at him.

"That explains it," Myron said.

"Explains what?"

"Esperanza's mood."

"Oh." She smiled at him. "I told her we had an appointment. She didn't seem pleased to see me."

"No kidding."

"She'd still kill me for a nickel, huh?"

"Or half that much," he replied. "Want some coffee?"

"Sure."

He picked up his phone. "Can you get me a black coffee? Thanks." He put the receiver back in its cradle and looked up at her.

"How's Win?" she asked.

"Good."

"His family owns the building?"

"Yes."

"I understand Win's become quite a financial whiz—despite himself."

Myron nodded, waited.

"So you're still hanging around with Win," she continued. "You still have Esperanza. Not a lot changes."

"Plenty changes," he said.

Esperanza appeared at the door, the scowl still on her face. "Otto Burke was in a meeting."

"Try Larry Hanson."

She handed the coffee to Jessica, smiled eerily, and left. Jessica studied the cup. "Think she spat in it?"

"Probably," Myron replied.

She put it down. "I need to cut back anyway."

Myron moved around his desk and sat down. The wall

behind him was covered with theater posters. All musicals. His fingers drummed the desk.

"I'm sorry about yesterday," she said. "I wanted to surprise you, catch you off guard. Not the other way around."

"Still seeking the upper hand?"

"I guess so, yeah. Old habit."

He shrugged but said nothing.

"I need your help," she said.

He waited.

She took a breath and plunged. "The police say my father was killed in a robbery attempt. I don't believe it."

"What do you believe?" he asked.

"I think his murder has something to do with Kathy."

Myron was not surprised. He leaned forward, his eyes never staying on hers for very long. "What makes you say that?"

"The police dismiss it as a coincidence," she said simply. "I'm not big on coincidences."

"What about your dad's friend on the force, what's-his-name?"

"Paul Duncan."

"Right, him. Have you spoken to him?"

"Yes."

"And?"

She began tapping her foot, an old, subconscious, annoying habit. She made herself stop. "Paul says it was a robbery too. He spews out all the facts about the crime scene, the missing wallet, the missing jewelry, that kind of thing. He is perfectly logical and objective, which is not his way."

"What do you mean?"

"Paul Duncan is a passionate man. A hothead. Here

his best friend has been murdered, and he seems almost blasé about it. It's not like him.'' She stopped, shifted in her chair. ''Something isn't right here, I don't know how else to explain it.''

Myron rubbed his chin but kept quiet.

''Look, you know I was never very close to my father,'' she continued. ''He wasn't an easy man to love. He was far better with his corpses than with breathing entities. He liked the ideal of family, the concept—it was the actual execution he found wearisome. But I still have to find out the truth. For Kathy.''

''How did your father and Kathy get along?'' Myron asked.

She thought about it a moment. ''Better lately. When we were kids, they weren't very close. Kathy was a mama's girl, always hanging around my mom, wanting to be like her, the whole bit. But when she vanished, I'd venture to guess she was closer to my dad than my mom. He was crushed when she disappeared. He became obsessed. No, 'obsessed' isn't strong enough. All of us were obsessed, of course. But not like my father. It consumed him entirely. Everything about him changed. He had always been the quiet county medical examiner, the man who made no waves. Now he was using his position to keep the pressure on twenty-four hours a day. He became paranoid, convinced the police weren't doing all they could do to find her. He even started his own investigation.''

''Did he find anything?''

''No. Not that I know of.''

Myron looked away. At the far wall. A movie still of the Marx Brothers. *A Night at the Opera.* Groucho looked back but offered no answers.

''What is it?'' she asked.

''Nothing. Go on.''

"There isn't much else. I can only tell you that my father was acting very strangely the past few weeks. He started calling me all the time when previously we'd only talked maybe three times a year, sounding a little teary. It was like he was play-acting the part of perfect Daddy with renewed vigor. I couldn't tell if it was a serious change or just a phase."

Myron nodded, looking off again. He said nothing. Jessica almost thought he'd completely drifted off when he finally spoke, his voice almost inaudibly soft. "What do you think happened to Kathy?" he asked.

"I don't know."

"Do you think she's dead?"

"I—" She stopped. "I miss her. It's . . . I don't want to think she's dead."

He nodded again. "So what do you want me to do?"

"Look into it. Find out what's going on."

"Assuming something is going on."

"Right."

"Why me?"

She thought about it a moment. "I'm not sure," she said. "I thought you'd believe me. I thought you'd help."

"I'll help," he said. "But understand one thing: I have an important business interest in settling this whole thing."

"Christian?"

"I'm his agent," he continued. "I'm responsible for his well-being."

"He still misses my sister," she said.

"Yes."

"Is he okay?"

Myron's face remained set. "He's fine."

"He's a good kid. I like him."

Myron nodded.

Jessica rose and stepped toward the window. Myron averted his eyes. He did not like to look at her for too long at one time. She understood. It hurt her too. She looked down at Park Avenue, twelve stories below. A taxi driver with a turban was shaking his fist at an old woman with a cane. The old woman whacked him and ran. The driver fell. The turban did not even shift.

"Hiding your feelings from me has never been your forte," she said, still staring out the window. "What don't you want to tell me?"

He did not reply.

"Myron . . ."

Esperanza saved him, bursting through the door without knocking. "Larry Hanson is out of the office," she said.

Win came in behind her. "I got something for us on that magazine. . . ." His voice died out when he saw Jessica.

"Hi, Win," she said.

"Hello, Jessica Culver." They embraced. "My goodness, you look utterly fantastic. I read an article on you the other day, calling you the Literary Sex Symbol."

"You shouldn't read such trash."

"It was in my dentist's waiting room. Honest."

An uncomfortable pause followed. Esperanza broke it by pointing at Jessica, making a gagging motion by sticking her finger in her mouth, and then storming out.

"Ever the enchantress," Jessica muttered.

Myron stood. "Where are you staying?"

"At my mom's."

"Same number?"

"Yes."

"I'll call you later. Right now I've got to go with Win."

Jessica looked toward Win. He grinned at her. His

face, as always, gave away nothing. "I have a meeting with my editor this afternoon," she said. "But I'll be home all night."

"Fine. I'll call you then."

An awkward impasse. No one knew exactly how to say good-bye. A wave? A handshake? A kiss?

"We've got to go," Myron said. He sprinted past her, never getting too close. Win shrugged at her in a what-can-you-do fashion and followed. She watched them disappear around the corner. Batman and Robin heading to the Bat-poles.

She left then. She had seen Myron twice now, and they had not yet touched—not even brushed up against one another.

It was an odd thing to wonder about.

Chapter 6

"What did you find out?" Myron asked.

Win whipped the wheel to the right. The Jag XJR responded with nary a squeal. They had been driving without speaking for the past ten minutes, Win's CD player the only sound. Win favored show tunes. *Man of La Mancha* was on now. Don Quixote serenaded his beloved Dulcinea.

"*Nips* magazine is published by HDP," Win answered.

"HDP?"

"Hot Desire Press." Another Bat-turn. The Jag accelerated past eighty.

"Speed limits," Myron said. "Heard of them?"

Win ignored him. "Their editorial office is located in Fort Lee, New Jersey."

"Editorial office?"

"Whatever. We have an appointment with Mr. Fred Nickler, managing editor."

"His mother must be proud."

"Moralizing," Win mused. "Nice."

"What did you tell Mr. Nickler?" Myron asked.

"Nothing. I called and asked if we could see him. He said yes. Seemed like a very pleasant fellow."

"I'm sure he's a prince." Myron looked out the window. Buildings blurred. They fell back into silence. "You're probably wondering what Jessica was doing in my office."

Win gave a halfhearted shrug. It was not his way to pry.

"It's her father's murder. The police say it was a robbery. She thinks otherwise."

"How does she see it?"

"She thinks there's a connection between his murder and Kathy."

"So the plot thickens. Are we going to help her?"

"Yes."

"Goodie. So do we think there is a connection?"

"Yes."

"Yes," Win agreed.

They pulled into the driveway of a building that could have been either a nice warehouse or low-rent office space. No elevator, but then again, only three levels. HDP, Inc., was on the second floor. When they entered the outer office, Myron was a bit surprised. He was not sure what he'd expected, but he had thought the dwell-

ings of a sleaze merchant would not be so . . . nonde-
script. The walls were white with inexpensive but taste-
fully framed art posters—McKnight, Fanch, Behrens.
Mostly scenery shots of beaches and sunset. Nothing
with naked breasts. Surprise number one. Surprise number two was the unremarkable receptionist. She was
strictly standard issue, not an overaged, bleach-blond,
flabby ex-bunny/sexpot/porno starlet with a breathy gig-
gle and seductive wink.

Myron was almost disappointed.

"May I help you?" the receptionist asked.

Win said, "We're here to see Mr. Nickler."

"Your names, please?"

"Windsor Lockwood and Myron Bolitar."

She picked up the phone, buzzed in, and a moment
later said, "Right through that door."

Nickler greeted them with a firm handshake. He was
dressed in a blue suit, red tie, white shirt—conservative
as a Republican senatorial candidate. Surprise number
three. Myron had expected gold chains or a Joey But-
tafuoco earring or at the very least a pinkie ring. But
Fred Nickler wore no jewelry, except for a plain wedding
band. His hair was gray, his complexion a bit washed
out.

Win whispered, "He looks like your uncle Sid."

It was true. The publisher of *Nips* magazine looked
like Sidney Griffin, popular suburban orthodontist.

"Please have a seat," Nickler said, moving back behind his desk. He smiled at Myron. "I was at the Final
Fours when you guys beat Kansas. Twenty-seven points
including the game winner. Hell of a performance. Incredible."

"Thank you," Myron said.

"Never seen anything like it. The way that final shot
kissed the backboard."

"Thank you."

"Just incredible." Nickler renewed his smile, shaking his head in awe at the memory. Then he sat back. "So, what can I do for you gentlemen?"

Myron said, "We have a couple of questions about an ad in one of your, uh, publications."

"Which one?"

"*Nips.*" Saying the word felt grungy. Myron tried not to make a face.

"Interesting," Nickler replied.

"What makes you say that?"

"*Nips* is a relatively new publication, and it's doing poorly—far and away the worst of HDP's monthlies. I'm going to give it another month or two, and then it'll probably fold."

"How many magazines do you publish?"

"Six."

"Are they all like *Nips*?"

Nickler chuckled lightly. "They are all pornographic magazines, yes. And they are all completely legal."

Myron handed him the magazine Christian had given him. "When was this printed?"

Fred Nickler barely glanced at it. "Four days ago."

"That's all?"

"It's our most recent issue—they've barely hit the stands. I'm surprised you found one."

Myron opened to the proper page. "We'd like to know who paid for this advertisement."

Nickler put on a pair of half-moon glasses. "Which one?"

"Bottom row. The Lust Line."

"Oh," he said. "A sex phone."

"Is there a problem?"

"No. But this ad wasn't paid for."

"What do you mean?"

"It's the nature of the business," Nickler explained. "Someone calls me up to place an ad for a dial-a-porn line. I tell him it costs X amount. He says, wow, I'm just starting out, I can't afford it. So if it looks like a good idea, I go in fifty-fifty with him. In other words, I take care of the marketing, if you will, while my partner takes care of the technical side—phones, cables, girls to work the phones, whatever else. Then we split it down the middle. It limits both of our risks."

"Do you do this a lot?"

He nodded. "Ninety percent of my advertising comes for fantasy lines. I'd say I have a piece of the action in three-quarters of them."

"Can you give us the name of your partner on this particular venture?"

Nickler studied the picture in the magazine. "You're not with the police, are you?"

"No."

"Private investigators?"

"No."

He took off his glasses. "I'm fairly small-time," he said. "I have my own little niche. It's the way I like it. No one bothers me, and I don't bother anybody else. I have no interest in a lot of publicity."

Myron shot a glance at Win. Nickler had a family, probably a nice house in Tenafly, told the neighbors he was in publishing. Pressure could be applied. "I'll be frank with you," Myron said. "If you don't help us out, it may blow up into something major. Newspapers, TV, the works."

"Is that a threat?"

"Absolutely not." Myron reached into his wallet and took out a fifty-dollar bill. He placed it on the desk. "We just want to know who put this ad in."

Nickler pushed the bill back toward Myron, his expression suddenly irritated. "What is this, a movie? I don't need a payoff. If the guy has done something wrong, I want no part of him. This business has enough problems as it is. I run a straight operation. No underage girls, nothing illegal in any way, shape, or form."

Myron looked at Win. "Told you he was a prince."

"Think what you want," Nickler said in a voice that said he'd been down this road many times before. "This is a business like any other. I'm just an honest guy trying to make an honest buck."

"Real American of you."

He shrugged. "Look, I don't defend everything about this business. But there are plenty of worse. IBM, Exxon, Union Carbide—these are the real monsters, the real exploiters. I don't steal. I don't lie. I satisfy a societal need."

Myron had a quick comeback, but Win stopped him with a shake of his head. He was right. What was the point in antagonizing the guy?

"Could we have the name and address, please?" Myron asked.

Nickler opened a drawer behind him and pulled out a file. "Is he in some sort of trouble?"

"We just need to talk to him."

"Can you tell me why?"

Win spoke to Nickler for the first time. "You don't want to know."

Fred Nickler hesitated, saw Win's steady gaze, then nodded. "The company is called ABC. They have a p.o. box in Hoboken, number 785. The guy's name is Jerry. I don't know anything else about him."

"Thanks," Myron said, standing. "One more question if you don't mind: Have you ever seen the girl in the ad?"

"No."

"You're sure?"

"Positive."

"If you do or if you think of anything else, will you give me a call?" Myron handed him a card.

Nickler looked as if he wanted to ask a question, his gaze continually drifting back to Kathy's photograph, but he settled for saying "Sure."

Once outside, Win asked, "What do you think?"

"He's lying," Myron said.

Back in the car Myron asked, "Can I use the phone?"

Win nodded, his foot not slackening on the pedal. The speedometer was hovering at seventy-five. Myron watched it as if it were a taxi meter on a long ride, keeping his gaze averted from the blur of a street.

Myron dialed the office. Esperanza answered the phone after one ring.

"MB SportReps."

MB SportReps. The M stood for Myron, the B for Bolitar. Myron had thought of the name himself, though he rarely bragged about it. "Did Otto Burke or Larry Hanson call?"

"No. But you have lots of messages."

"Nothing from Burke or Hanson?"

"You deaf?"

"I'll be back in a little while."

Myron hung up. Otto and Larry should have called by now. They were avoiding him. The question was, why?

"Trouble?" Win asked.

"Maybe."

"I believe we need a rejuvenation."

Myron looked up. He recognized the street immediately. "Not now, Win."

"Now."

"I have to get back to the office."

"It'll keep. You need inner energy. You need focus. You need balance."

"I hate it when you talk like that."

Win smiled, pulling into the parking lot. "Come along now. I'd hate to kick your ass right here in the car."

The sign read MASTER KWAN'S TAE KWON DO SCHOOL. Kwan was nearing seventy now and rarely conducted classes any longer, choosing instead to hire well-tutored underlings to handle that work. Master Kwan stayed in his high-tech office, surrounded by four television screens so he could monitor the classes. Occasionally he leaned forward and barked something into a microphone, scaring some poor student into attention. Like something out of *The Wizard of Oz*.

If Master Kwan's English improved a bit, it might reach the level of pidgin. Win had brought him over from Korea fourteen years ago, when Win was only seventeen. It seemed to Myron that Master Kwan had spoken better English back then.

Win and Myron changed into their white uniforms called *dobok*. Both men wrapped black belts around their stomachs. Win was a sixth-degree black belt, about as high a ranking as anybody in the United States. He had been studying tae kwon do since the age of seven. Myron had picked it up in college, giving him a dozen years of studying and a third-degree black belt.

They approached Master Kwan's door, paused in the doorway until he acknowledged their presence, then bowed at the waist. "Good afternoon, Master Kwan," they said in unison.

Kwan smiled toothlessly. "You here early."

"Yes, sir," Win replied.

"Need help?"

"No, sir."

Kwan dismissed them by spinning back to his television screens. Myron and Win bowed once more and moved into the private *dojang* for the upper-ranked black belts. They began with meditation, something Myron had never quite gotten the full grasp of. Win loved it. He did it for at least an hour a day. Win folded himself into a lotus position. Myron settled for sitting Indian style. Both men closed their eyes, placed their thumbs on the palm directly below the pinkie, and tilted their palms toward the ceiling. They rested their hands on their knees. Instructions echoed through Myron's mind like a mantra. Back straight. Bottom of tongue curled up against the back of the upper teeth. He breathed in through his nose for six seconds, concentrating on pushing the air down into the pit of his gut, making sure that his chest did not move, that only his abdomen expanded. Then he held the air down deep, counting to himself to prevent his mind from wandering. After seven seconds he slowly released the air through the mouth for a ten count, making sure to empty completely his contracting gut. Then he waited four seconds before breathing in again.

Win did this painlessly. He did not count. His mind went blank. Myron always counted, needing it to keep his mind from wandering back to the problems of the day—especially on a day like today. But in spite of himself he began to relax, to feel the tension leave his body with every long exhalation. It almost tingled.

They meditated for ten minutes before Win opened his eyes and said, *"Barro."* Korean for stop.

They performed deep stretching exercises for the next twenty minutes. Win had the flexibility of a ballet dancer, performing full splits effortlessly. Myron had gained a lot of flexibility since taking up tae kwon do.

He believed it had helped him gain six inches on his vertical leap in college. He could almost do a full split, but he couldn't hold it long.

In short Myron was flexible; Win was Gumby.

They went through their forms or *poomse* next, a complicated set of moves not unlike a violent dance step. What many exercised-crazed junkies never realized is that the martial arts are the ultimate aerobic workout. You are in constant motion—jumping, turning, spinning —propelling both arms and both legs nonstop for a half hour at a time. Low block and front kick, high block and punch, middle block and roundhouse kick. Inside blocks, outside blocks, knife-hand, fists, palm strikes, knees and elbows. It was an exhausting and exhilarating workout.

Win moved through his routine flawlessly—ever the contradiction and deception. See Win on the street, and people said arrogant Waspy wimp who couldn't bruise a peach with his best punch. See him in a *dojang,* and he struck fear and awe. Tae kwon do is considered a martial art. Art. The word was not used by accident. Win was an artist, the best Myron had ever seen.

Myron remembered the first time he'd seen Win demonstrate his talent. They were freshmen in college. A group of large football players decided to shave Win's blond locks because they didn't like the way he looked. Five of them sneaked into Win's room late at night— four to hold down his arms and legs and one to carry the razor and shaving cream.

Simply put, the football team had a poor season that year. Too many guys on the injured list.

Myron and Win finished up with light free sparring. Then they dropped to the mat and performed one hundred push-ups on their fists—Win counting out loud in Korean. That done, they sat again for meditation, this time lasting fifteen minutes.

"Barro," Win said.

Both men opened their eyes.

"Feeling more focused?" Win asked. "Feeling the flow of energy? The balance?"

"Yes, Grasshopper. You want me to snatch the pebble from your hand now?"

Win moved from his lotus position into a full stance in one graceful, effortless move. "So," he said, "have you reached any decisions?"

"Yes." Myron struggled to stand in one motion, tipping from side to side as he ascended. "I'm going to tell Jessica everything."

Chapter 7

Yellow stick-on phone messages swarmed Myron's phone like locusts on a carcass. Myron peeled them away and shuffled through them. Nothing from Otto Burke or Larry Hanson or anyone in the Titans organization.

Not good.

He strapped on his headset telephone. He had resisted using one for a long time, figuring they were more suited for air traffic controllers than agents, but he quickly learned that an agent is but a fetus, his office a womb, his telephone an umbilical cord. It was easier with the headset. He could walk around; he could keep his hands free; he could forgo neck cramps from cradling a phone against his shoulder.

His first call was to the advertising director for BurgerCity, a new fast-food chain. They wanted to sign up Christian and were offering pretty good money, but Myron wasn't sure about it. BurgerCity was only regional. A national chain might come up with a better offer. Sometimes the hardest part of the job was saying no. He'd discuss the pros and cons with Christian, let him make the final decision. In the end it was his name. His money.

Myron had already signed Christian to several very lucrative endorsement deals. Wheaties would have Christian's likeness on cereal boxes starting in October. Diet Pepsi was coming up with some promotion involving Christian throwing a two-liter bottle on a perfect spiral to nubile women. Nike was developing a sweatsuit line and cleats known as the Steele Trap.

Christian stood to earn millions from endorsements, far more than he would make playing for the Titans, no matter how reasonable Otto Burke wanted to be. It was strange in a way. Fans grew agitated at the idea of a player trying to get the most out of his playing contract. They called him boorish, selfish, and egomaniacal when he demanded a great deal of money from a wealthy team owner—but they had no problem when he grabbed vault-loads from Pepsi or Nike or Wheaties for promoting products he'd probably never used or even liked. It made no sense. Christian would make more money for spending three days shooting a thirty-second hypocritical spot than he would for spending the season getting blindsided by drooling men with overactive pituitary glands—and that was how the fans wanted it.

No agent minded that setup. Most agents got between three and five percent of their players' total negotiated salary (Myron took four percent), compared with twenty or twenty-five percent for all endorsement money. (Myron took fifteen percent—hey, he was new.) In other words, sign a million-dollar deal with a team, and the agent gets around forty grand. Sign him for a million-dollar commercial, and the agent can nab as much as a quarter mil.

Myron's second call was to Ricky Lane, a running back for the New York Jets and a former college teammate of Christian's. Ricky was one of his most important clients, and Myron was fairly certain it had been Ricky who'd convinced Christian to hire him in the first place.

"I have a kids' camp appearance for you," Myron began. "They're paying five grand."

"Sounds good," Ricky said. "How long do I have to be there?"

"Couple hours. Do a little talk, sign a few autographs, that kind of thing."

"When?"

"A week from Saturday."

"What about that mall appearance?"

"That's Sunday," Myron said. "Livingston Mall. Morley's Sporting Goods." Ricky would get paid another five thousand dollars for sitting at a table for two hours and signing autographs.

"Cool."

"You want me to send a limo to pick you up?"

"No, I'll drive. You hear anything about next year's contract yet?"

"We're getting there, Ricky. Another week at the most. Listen, I want you to come in and see Win soon, okay?"

"Yeah, sure."

"You in shape?"

"The best of my life," Ricky said. "I want that starting job."

"Keep working. And don't forget to make that appointment with Win."

"Will do. Later, Myron."

"Yeah, later."

The calls continued, one blurring into another. He returned calls from the press. They all wanted to know about a pending deal between the Titans and Christian. Myron politely no-commented. Occasionally it was good to use the media as leverage in negotiating, but not with Otto Burke. Matters were proceeding, he told them. An agreement could be expected at any time.

He then called Joe Norris, an old-time Yankee who appeared almost every weekend at a baseball card show. Joe made more in a month now than he had in an entire season in his heyday.

Next up was Linda Regal, a tennis pro who had just cracked the top ten. Linda was worried about aging, offended because a broadcaster had referred to her as a "familiar veteran." Linda was almost twenty.

Eric Kramer, a UCLA senior and probable second round NFL draft pick, was in town. Myron managed to arrange a dinner with him. That meant Myron was a finalist—he and a zillion other agents. The competition was incredible. Example: There are twelve hundred NFL-authorized agents who court the two hundred college players who will be drafted in April. Something has to give. It's usually ethics.

Myron called the New York Jets general manager, Sam Logan, to discuss Ricky Lane's contract.

"The kid is in the best shape of his career," Myron raved. He stood and paced. Myron had a large, fairly gorgeous office on Park Avenue between Forty-sixth and Forty-seventh streets. It impressed people, and appear-

ance was important in a business dominated by
sleazeballs. "I've never seen anything like it. I'm telling
you, Sam, the kid is Gayle Sayers all over again. It's
amazing, really."

"He's too small," Logan said.

"What are you talking about? Is Barry Sanders too
small? Is Emmitt Smith too small? Ricky's bigger than
both of them. And he's been lifting. I'm telling you, he's
going to be a great one."

"Uh-huh. Look, Myron, he's a nice kid. He works
hard. But I can't go any higher than . . ."

The number was still too low. But it was better.

The calls continued without a break. Sometime during the day Esperanza brought him a sandwich, which he
inhaled.

At eight o'clock Myron placed his final office call of
the day.

Jessica answered. "Hello?"

"I'll be at your house in an hour," Myron said. "We
need to talk."

Myron watched Jessica's face for a reaction. She kept
looking at the magazine as if it were just another issue of
Newsweek, her expression frighteningly passive. Every
once in a while she nodded, looked over the rest of the
page, and glanced at the front and back covers of the
magazine, always returning to the picture of Kathy. She
was so nonchalant, Myron almost expected her to whistle.

Only her knuckles gave her away. They were blood-
less white, the pages crinkling in her death grip.

"Are you okay?" he asked.

"I'm fine," she said, her voice calm, almost soothing.
"You said Christian got this in the mail?"

"Yes."

"And you and Win spoke to the man who publishes this"—she hesitated, her face finally showing some signs of disgust—"this thing?"

"Yes."

She nodded. "Did he give you the address of whoever put this ad in?"

"Just a p.o. box. I'm going to scout it out tomorrow, see who picks up the mail."

She looked up for the first time. "I'll go with you."

He almost protested but stopped himself. He didn't stand a chance. "Okay."

"When did Christian give this to you?"

"Yesterday."

That got her attention. "You knew about this yesterday?"

He nodded.

"And you didn't tell me?" she snapped. "I was pouring my heart out to you, feeling like some paranoid schizophrenic, and you knew about this the whole time?"

"I wasn't sure how to tell you."

"Anything else you haven't told me?"

"Christian got a phone call last night. He thinks it was from Kathy."

"What?"

He quickly told her about it. When he reached the part about Christian hearing Kathy's voice, her face drained of all color.

"Has your friend at the phone company learned anything?" she asked.

"No. But we know Return Call only works for specific towns within the 201 area codes."

"How many towns?"

"About three-quarters of them."

"So you're talking about three-quarters of the northern part of New Jersey, the most densely populated state in the U.S.? That limits it down to what, two, three million people?''

''It's not a big help,'' he admitted, ''but it's something.''

Her eyes settled back on the magazine. ''I didn't mean to jump all over you. It's just—''

''Forget it.''

''You're the best person I've ever known,'' she said. ''I mean that.''

''And you're the biggest pain in the ass.''

''Tough to argue that one,'' she said, but there was a hint of a smile.

''Do you want to tell the police about this?'' he asked. ''Or Paul Duncan?''

She thought a moment. ''I'm not sure.''

''The press will eat it up,'' he said. ''They'll drag Kathy through the mud.''

''I don't give a rat's ass what the press does.''

''I'm just telling you,'' Myron said.

''They can call her a slut a million different ways. I don't care.''

''What about your mom?''

''I don't give a rat's ass what she wants either. I just want Kathy found.''

''So you want to tell them,'' Myron said.

''No.''

He looked at her, confused. ''Care to elaborate?''

Her words came slow, measured, the ideas coming to her even as she spoke. ''Kathy has been gone for more than a year now,'' she began. ''In all that time the cops and the press have come up with zip. Not one thing. She's just vanished without a trace.''

''So?''

''But now we get this magazine. Someone sent it to

Christian, which means someone—maybe Kathy, maybe not—is trying to make contact. Think about it. For the first time in over a year there is some form of communication. I don't want that taken away. I don't want a lot of attention scaring away whoever is out there. Kathy might disappear again. This''—she held up the magazine— ''this thing is disgusting, but it's also encouraging. It's something. Don't get me wrong. I'm shocked by this. But it's a solid thread—a thread as confusing as all hell, but nonetheless a thread of hope. If the cops and the press are called in, whoever did this might get scared and vanish again. Permanently this time. I can't risk that. We have to keep this to ourselves.''

Myron nodded. ''Makes sense.''

''So what's next?'' she asked.

''We go to the post office in Hoboken. I'll pick you up early. Say six.''

Chapter 8

Jessica smelled great.

They were at Uptown Station in Hoboken. She stood very close to him. Her hair had that freshly washed smell he had tried for four years to forget. Inhaling made him feel light-headed.

''So this is playing detective,'' she said.

''Exciting, isn't it?''

They had been trying to look inconspicuous—no easy

task when a man is six-four and a woman is a total knee-knocker—for the better part of an hour, having arrived at the post office at six-thirty in the morning. No one had touched Box 785 yet.

Boredom set in quickly. Jessica looked over the prices of different mailing containers. Not very interesting. She read the wanted ads, all of them, found them a bit more interesting. Wanted posters in a post office. Like they wanted you to write the guy a letter.

"You sure know how to show a girl a good time," she said.

"That's why they call me Captain Fun."

She laughed. The melodic sound twisted his stomach.

"Do you like being an agent, Captain Fun?"

"Very much."

"I always thought of agents as a bunch of sleazeballs."

"Thank you."

"You know what I mean. Leeches. Vipers. Greedy, money-hungry, bloodsucking parasites, swindling naïve jocks, doing lunch at Le Cirque, destroying everything that's good about sports—"

"The problems in the Middle East," he interrupted. "That's our fault too. And the budget deficit."

"Right. But you're not any of those things."

"Not a leech, viper, or parasite. That's quite a rave."

"You know what I mean."

He shrugged. "There are plenty of sleazy agents. There are also plenty of sleazy doctors, lawyers—" He stopped, the words sounding familiar. Hadn't Fred Nickler used the same argument in justifying his magazines? "Agents are a necessary evil," he continued. "Without them, athletes get taken advantage of."

"By whom?"

"Owners, management. Agents have done some good

for the athletes. They've helped raise their salaries, assure free agency, get them endorsement money.''

''So what's the problem?''

Myron thought a moment. ''Two things,'' he said. ''First of all, some agents are crooks. Plain and simple. They see a young, rich kid, and they take advantage. But as the athletes get more sophisticated, as more stories like what happened to Kareem Abdul-Jabar become known, most of the crooks will be weeded out.''

''And second?''

''Agents have to wear too many hats,'' he said. ''We're negotiators, accountants, financial planners, hand-holders, travel agents, family counselors, marriage counselors, errand boys, lackeys—whatever it takes to get the business.''

''So how do you do it all?''

''I give two of the biggest hats to Win—accountant and financial planner. I'm the lawyer. He's the MBA. Plus we have Esperanza, who can do almost anything. It works well. We all check and balance one another.''

''Just like the branches of the federal government.''

He nodded. ''Jefferson and Madison would be proud.''

A hand reached out and opened Box 785.

''Show time,'' Myron said.

Jessica snapped her head around to look. The man was slim. Everything about him was too long, eerily elongated, as if he had spent time on a medieval rack. Even his face seemed stretched like a cartoon imprint on Silly Putty.

''Recognize him?'' Myron asked.

She hesitated. ''Something about him . . . but I don't think so.''

''Come on, let's get out of here.''

They hurried down the steps and got in the car. Myron had parked illegally in front of the building, putting a police emergency sign in his front windshield. A gift from a friend on the force. The emergency sign came in handy—especially during sale days at the mall.

The slim man came out two minutes later. He got into a yellow Oldsmobile. New Jersey plates. Myron shifted into drive and followed. Slim took Route 3 to the Garden State Parkway north.

"We've been driving almost twenty minutes," Jessica said. "Why would he go to a mailbox so far from his home?"

"Could be that he's not going to his house. Maybe he's going to work."

"The dial-a-porn office?"

"Maybe," Myron said. "Or it could be that he travels a long way so no one will see him."

He got off at Exit 160, jumped on Route 208 heading north, and pulled off at Lincoln Avenue, Ridgewood.

Jessica sat up. "This is my exit," she said.

"I know."

"What the hell is going on here?"

The yellow Oldsmobile turned left at the end of the ramp. They were now within three miles of Jessica's house. If he took Lincoln Avenue all the way to Godwin Road, they'd be . . .

Nope.

Mr. Slim turned on Kenmore Road, a half-mile before the Ridgewood border. They were still in the heart of suburbia—the suburb in question being Glen Rock, New Jersey. Glen Rock was so named because of a giant rock that sat on Rock Road. The key word here is *rock*.

The yellow Olds pulled into a driveway. 78 Kenmore Drive.

"Look casual," he said. "Don't stare."

"What?"

He didn't answer. He drove past the house without pausing, turned at the next street, and stopped the car behind some shrubs. He picked up the car phone and dialed the office. It was picked up midway through the first ring.

"MB SportReps," Esperanza said.

"Get me all you can on 78 Kenmore Street, Glen Rock, New Jersey. Owner's name, credit check, the works."

"Got it." Click.

He dialed another number. "My friend at the phone company," he explained to Jessica. Then: "Lisa? It's Myron. Look, I need a favor. Seventy-eight Kenmore Road, Glen Rock, New Jersey. I don't know how many lines the guy has, but I need you to check them all. I want to know every number he calls for the next two hours. Right. Hey, what did you find out about that 900 number? What? Oh, okay, I understand. Thanks."

He hung up.

"What did she say?"

"The 900 number isn't operated by the phone company. Some small outfit out of South Carolina takes care of it. She can't get anything on it."

"So what do we do now?" she asked. "Just watch his house?"

"No. I go inside. You wait here."

She arched an eyebrow. "Excuse me?"

"You were the one who didn't want to scare anyone away," he continued. "If this guy has something to do with your sister, how do you think he'll react to seeing you?"

She folded her arms across her chest and fumed. She knew he was right, but that didn't mean she had to be happy about it. "Go," she said.

He got out of the car. It was one of those no-variety

neighborhoods, each house cookie-cut from the same mold—split-levels on three-quarters of an acre. Sometimes the house was backward, the kitchen on the right instead of the left. Most had aluminum siding. The street reeked of middle class.

Myron knocked. The thin man opened the door.

"Jerry?"

Slim's face registered confusion. Up close he was better looking, his face more brooding than freakish. Give him a cigarette and a black turtleneck, and he could be reading poetry in a village café. "May I help you?"

"Jerry, I'm—"

"You must have the wrong house. My name isn't Jerry."

"You look like Jerry."

Something dark crossed his face. "I'm sorry," he said, closing the door. "I really don't have time right now."

"Sure about that, Jer?"

"I already told you—"

"Do you know Kathy Culver?"

It was a sneak attack. And it drew blood. "Wha—what's this all about?" he snapped.

"I think you know."

"Who are you?"

"My name is Myron Bolitar."

"Am I supposed to know you?"

"Well, if you're a big basketball fan . . . actually, no. But I'd like to ask you a few questions."

"I have nothing to say."

Ace of spades time. Myron pulled out the magazine. "Sure about that, Jerry?"

The whites of Slim's eyes grew tenfold, looking like Wedgwood china on the elongated face. "You have me mixed up with someone else. Good-bye."

He slammed the door.

Myron shrugged, headed back to the car.

"Well?" Jessica asked.

"We shook him," Myron said. "Let's see what falls out."

The neighborhood newsstand.

Win remembered a time when the phrase conjured up nostalgia and Rockwellian images of real America. No more. Any street, any corner, any hickville town was the same. Candy, newspapers, greeting cards—and porno mags. Kids could pick up a Snickers bar and get an eyeful, all in one. Porno had become a staple of American life. Hardcore porn. The kind of porn that made *Penthouse* look like *Highlights* magazine.

Win approached the man behind the lottery ticket dispenser. "Pardon me," Win said.

"Yeah?"

"Would you be able to tell me if you have the most recent issues of *Climaxx, Jiz, Orgasm Today, Licks, Quim,* and *Nips*?"

An elderly woman gasped and gave him an icy stare. Win smiled at her. "Let me guess," he said. "Playmate of the Month, June 1926?"

She made a harumph noise and turned away.

"Check over there," the man said. "Between the comic books and Disney videos."

"Thank you."

Win found three of them—*Climaxx, Orgasm Today,* and *Quim.* He tried three other newsstands and was able to pick up *Lick,* but there was no sign of *Jiz* or *Nips.* He finally found copies of them at a hardcore shop on Forty-second Street called King David's Smut Palace. They had a big sign out front that said OPEN 24 HOURS. How very convenient. Win considered himself fairly worldly, but the items and photographs in the "palace" proved that both his life experiences and his imagination had at best been limited.

It was almost noon when he exited the palace. A productive and quasi-educational morning.

With a total of eight magazines lodged under his arm, Win caught a taxi to midtown. He skimmed through a few in the backseat.

"So far so good," he said out loud.

The driver glanced at him in the rearview mirror, shrugged, looked back to the road.

When Win arrived at his office, he spread the magazines across the vast breadth of his desk. He studied them closely, comparing them. Incredible. His suspicion had been sound. It was just as he thought.

Five minutes later, Win put the magazines in his desk drawer. Then he buzzed Esperanza.

"Kindly send Myron to my office as soon as he comes in."

Chapter 9

"I have a confession," Jessica said.

They were coming out of the Kinney garage on Fifty-second Street, the smell of fumes and urine dissipating as they hit the relatively fresh air on the sidewalk. They turned down Fifth Avenue. The line for passports stretched past the statue of Atlas. A black man with long dreadlocks sneezed repeatedly, his hair flapping about like dozens of snakes. A woman behind him tsk-tsked a complaint. Many of the people waiting faced St. Patrick's across the street as though pleading for divine intervention, their faces lined with anguish. Japanese tourists took pictures of both the statue and the line.

"I'm listening," Myron replied.

They kept walking. Jessica did not face him, her gaze fixed on nothing straight ahead. "We weren't close anymore. In fact, Kathy and I barely spoke."

Myron was surprised. "Since when?"

"The last three years or so."

"What happened?"

She shook her head, but she still did not look at him. "I don't know exactly. She changed. Or maybe she just grew up and I couldn't handle it. We just drifted apart. When we saw each other, it was as if she couldn't stand to be in the same room with me."

"I'm sorry to hear that."

"Yeah, well, it's no big thing. Except Kathy called me the night she disappeared. First time in I don't know how long."

"What did she want?"

"I don't know. I was on my way out the door. I rushed her off."

They fell into silence the rest of the way to Myron's office.

When they got off the elevator, Esperanza handed him a sheet of paper and said, "Win wants to see you right away." She glared at Jessica the way a linebacker might glare at a limping quarterback on a blindside blitz.

"Otto Burke or Larry Hanson call?" Myron asked.

She swerved her glare toward Myron. "No. Win wants to see you right away."

"I heard you the first time. Tell him I'll be up in five minutes."

They moved into Myron's office. He closed the door and skimmed over the sheet. Jessica sat in front of him. She crossed her legs the way few women could, turning an ordinary event into a moment of sexual intrigue. Myron tried not to stare. He also tried not to remember the luscious feel of those legs in bed. He was unsuccessful in both endeavors.

"What's it say?" she asked.

He snapped to. "Our slim friend on Kenmore Street in Glen Rock is named Gary Grady."

Jessica squinted. "The name sounds familiar." She shook her head. "But I can't place it."

"He's been married seven years, wife Allison. No kids. Has a $110,000 mortgage on that house, pays it on time. Nothing else yet. We should know more in a little while." He put the paper on his desk. "I think we have to start attacking this on a few different fronts."

"How?"

"We have to go back to the night your sister disappeared. Start with that, and move forward. The whole case needs to be reinvestigated. The same with your father's murder. I'm not saying the cops weren't thorough. They probably were. But we now know some things they don't."

"The magazine," she said.

"Exactly."

"How can I help?" she asked.

"Start finding out all you can about what she was up to when she disappeared. Talk to her friends, roommates, sorority sisters, fellow cheerleaders—anyone."

"Okay."

"Also get her school records. Let's see if there's anything there. I want to see what courses she was taking, what activities she was involved with, anything.''

Esperanza threw open the door. ''Meal Ticket. Line two.''

Myron checked his watch. Christian should be in the middle of practice by now. He picked up the phone. ''Christian?''

''Mr. Bolitar, I don't understand what's going on.''

Myron could barely hear him. It sounded as if he were standing in a wind tunnel. ''Where are you?''

''A pay phone outside Titans Stadium.''

''What's the matter?''

''They won't let me in.''

Jessica stayed in the office to make a few calls. Myron rushed out. Fifty-seventh Street to the West Side Highway was unusually clear. He called Otto Burke and Larry Hanson from the car. Neither one was in. Myron was not astounded.

Then he dialed an unlisted phone in Washington. Few people had this particular number.

''Hello?'' the voice answered politely.

''Hi, P.T.''

''Ah shit, Myron, what the fuck do you want?''

''I need a favor.''

''Perfect. I was just telling someone, gee, I wish Bolitar would call so I could do him a favor. Few things bring me such joy.''

P.T. worked for the FBI. FBI chiefs come and go. P.T. was a constant. The press didn't know about him, but every president since Nixon had had his number on their speed dial.

''The Kathy Culver case,'' Myron said. ''Who's the best guy to talk to about it?''

''The local cop,'' P.T. answered without hesitation.

"He's an elected sheriff or something. Great guy, good friend of mine. I forget his name."

"Can you get me an appointment?" Myron asked.

"Why not? Serving your needs gives my life a sense of purpose."

"I owe you."

"You already owe me. More than you can pay. I'll call you when I have something."

Myron hung up. The traffic was still clear. Amazing. He crossed the Washington Bridge and arrived at the Meadowlands in record time.

The Meadowlands Sports Authority was built on useless swampland off the New Jersey Turnpike in a place called East Rutherford. From west to east stood the Meadowlands Race Track, Titans Stadium, and the Brendan Byrne Arena, named for the former governor who was about as well liked as a whitehead on prom night. Angry protests equal to the French Revolution had erupted over the name, but to no avail. Mere revolutions are hardly worthy adversaries for a politician's ego.

"Oh, Christ."

Christian's car—or he assumed it was Christian's— was barely visible under the blanket of reporters. Myron had expected this. He had told Christian to lock himself in his car and not say a word. Driving away would have been useless. The press would have just followed, and Myron was not up for a car chase.

He parked nearby. The reporters turned toward him like lions smelling a wounded lamb.

"What's going on, Myron?"

"Why isn't Christian at practice?"

"You pulling a holdout or what?"

"What's happening with his contract?"

Myron no-commented them, swimming through the sea of microphones, cameras, and flesh, squeezing his way into the car without allowing any of the slime to ooze in with him.

"Drive off," Myron said.

Christian started the car and pulled out. The reporters parted grudgingly. "I'm sorry, Mr. Bolitar."

"What happened?"

"The guard wouldn't let me in. He said he had orders to keep me out."

"Son of a bitch," Myron muttered. Otto Burke and his damn tactics. Little weasel. Myron should have been looking for something like this. But a lockout? That seemed a tad extreme, even by Otto Burke's standards. Despite the posturing, they had been fairly close to signing. Burke had expressed strong interest in getting Christian to minicamp as soon as possible, to get him ready for the season.

So why would he lock Christian out?

Myron didn't like it.

"Do you have a car phone?" he asked.

"No, sir."

It didn't matter. "Turn back around," Myron said. "Park by Gate C."

"What are you going to do?"

"Just come with me."

The guard tried to stop them, but Myron pushed Christian past him. "Hey, you're not allowed in there!" he called after them. "Hey, stop!"

"Shoot us," Myron said without stopping.

They strode onto the field. Players were hitting the tackle dummies hard. Very hard. No one was holding back. These were tryouts. Most of these guys were fighting for a spot on the team. Most had been high school and college superstars, accustomed to unadulterated greatness on the field. Most would get cut. Most would not allow the dream to end there, scrounging other teams' rosters for a possible opening, holding on, slipping endlessly, dying slowly all the while.

A glamour profession.

The coaches blew whistles. The running backs practiced wind sprints. Kickers were knocking down field goals at the far goal post. Punters boomed slow lazy arcs high into the air. Several players turned and spotted Christian. A buzz developed. Myron ignored it. He had spotted his target, sitting in the first row on the fifty-yard line.

Otto Burke sat like Caesar at the Colosseum, that damn smile still plastered to his face, his arms spread over the seats on either side of him. Behind him sat Larry Hanson and a few other executives. Caesar's senate. Occasionally Otto would lean back and award his entourage a comment that brought on aneurysm-like fits of laughter.

"Myron!" Otto called out pleasantly, waving one of those tiny hands. "Come on over. Have a seat."

"Wait here," Myron told Christian. He climbed the steps. The entourage, led by Larry Hanson, stood in unison and marched away.

Myron snapped a salute at them. "Hut two, three, four. Right face." No one laughed. Big surprise.

"Sit down, Myron," Otto said, beaming. "Let's have a chat."

"You haven't been returning my calls," Myron said.

"Did you call?" He shook his head. "I'll have to get on my secretary about that."

Myron let out a deep breath and sat. "Why was Christian locked out?"

"Well, Myron, it's pretty simple, actually. Christian hasn't signed his contract yet. The Titans don't have time to invest in someone who may not be part of our future." He nodded toward the field. "Do you see who's here for a tryout? Neil Decker from Cincinnati. Fine quarterback.''

''Yeah, he's great. He can almost throw a spiral.''

Otto chuckled. ''That's funny, Myron. You're a very amusing man.''

''I'm so glad you think so. Mind telling me what's going on?''

Otto Burke nodded. ''That's fair, Myron. So let's talk frankly, shall we?''

''Rationally, frankly, whatever you want.''

''Great. We'd like to renegotiate your client's contract,'' he said. ''Downward.''

''I see.''

''We feel your client's value has depreciated.''

''Uh-huh.''

Burke studied him. ''You don't seem surprised, Myron.''

''So what is it this time?'' Myron asked.

''What is what this time?''

''Well, let's start with Benny Keleher. You invited him to your house, plied him with booze, then had a cop arrest him on his ride home for drunk driving.''

Otto looked properly shocked. ''I had nothing to do with that.''

''Amazing how he signed the next day. And then there's Eddie Smith. You had compromising photographs of him taken by a private eye and threatened to send them to his wife.''

''Another lie.''

''Fine, a lie. So let's cut to the chase, then. What has caused this sudden devaluation?''

Otto sat back. He withdrew a cigarette from a gold case with a Titans emblem on the cover. ''It's something I saw in a rather lewd magazine,'' he said. ''Something that truly disheartened me.'' He didn't look disheartened. He looked rather pleased.

"A new low," Myron said. "You should be proud."

"Pardon me?"

"You set it up. The magazine."

Otto smiled. "Ah, so you knew about it."

"How did you get that picture?"

"What picture?"

"The one in the ad."

"I had nothing to do with it."

"Sure," Myron said. "I guess you're just a charter subscriber to *Nips*."

"I had nothing to do with that ad, Myron. Honestly."

"Then how did you get a hold of the magazine?"

"Someone pointed it out to me."

"Who?"

"I am not at liberty to discuss it."

"Very convenient."

"I'm not sure I like your tone, Myron. And let me tell you something else: You're the one who has done wrong in the case. If you knew about the magazine, you had an ethical responsibility to tell me."

Myron looked up at the sky. "You used the word *ethical*. Lightning did not strike. There is no God."

The smile flickered but stayed on. "Much as we'd like to, Myron, we can't just wish this away. The magazine exists, and it must be dealt with. So let me tell you what I've come up with."

"I'm all ears."

"You're going to take our current offer and knock it down by a third. If not, the picture of Ms. Culver goes public. Think about it. You have three days to decide." Otto watched Neil Decker throw a pass. It looked like a duck with a broken wing, crashing well short of the receiver. He frowned, stroked his goatee. "Make that two days."

Chapter 10

Dean of Students Harrison Gordon made sure the door to his office was locked. Double-locked, in fact. He was taking no chances. Not with this.

He sat back down and stared out his office window. Esteemed Reston University in all its glory. The view was a mesh of green grass and brick buildings. No ivy adorned these towers of learning, but it should have. The students were gone for summer break, but the commons still had a sprinkling of people on it—campers from the football and tennis camps, local people who used the campus as a park, the old throwback hippies who pilgrimage to liberal arts institutions like Moslems to Mecca. Lots of red bandannas and ponchos and granola-types. A bearded man tossed a Frisbee. A small boy caught it.

Harrison Gordon saw none of it. He had not spun his chair around to enjoy the view. He had done so to avert his gaze from the . . . thing on his desk. He wanted simply to destroy the damn thing and forget about it. But he couldn't. Something held him back. And something kept drawing him toward it, toward that page near the back. . . .

Destroy it, you fool. If somebody finds it . . .

What?

He did not know. He spun his chair back around, keeping his eyes away from the magazine. The student file marked CULVER, KATHERINE lay to the right. He swallowed. With a shaking hand he sifted through the stacks of transcripts and recommendation letters. It was an impressive file, but Harrison had no time for that now.

The buzz of his intercom—a horrid noise—startled him upright.

"Dean Gordon?"

"Yes," he said, nearly shouting. His heart was beating like a rabbit's.

"I have someone here to see you. She doesn't have an appointment, but I thought you might want to see her."

Edith's voice was hushed, a church-whisper.

"Who is it?" he asked.

"It's Jessica Culver. She's Kathy's sister."

Panic punctured his heart like an icicle.

"Dean Gordon?"

He clamped his hand over his mouth, afraid he might scream.

"Dean Gordon? Are you there?"

There were no true options. He would have to see her and find out what she wanted. To act in any other manner would raise suspicion.

He opened his bottom drawer and scooped the contents of his desk into it. He shut it, took out his key ring, and locked his desk. Better safe than sorry. Last, he unbolted his door.

"Send Ms. Culver in," he said.

Jessica was at least as beautiful as her sister, which was saying something quite extraordinary. He debated on how to greet her and settled for funeral director mode —detached sympathy, warm professionalism.

He shook her hand with gentle firmness. "Miss Culver, I'm so sorry we have to meet under such circumstances. Our prayers are with your family during this difficult time."

"Thank you for seeing me without an appointment."

He waved his hand as if to scoff, It's nothing. "Please have a seat. Can I get you something to drink? Coffee, soda?"

"No, thank you."

He moved back to his chair. He sat and folded his hands on the desk. "Is there something I can do for you?"

"I need my sister's file," Jessica replied.

Harrison felt his fingers bunch, but he kept his face steady. "Your sister's school file?"

"Yes."

"May I inquire as to why?"

"It involves her disappearance."

"I see," he said slowly. His voice, he was surprised to hear, remained calm. "I believe the police were very thorough with the file. They made copies of everything in it—"

"I understand that. I'd like to see the file for myself."

"I see," he said again.

Several seconds passed. Jessica shifted in her chair. "Is there a problem?" she asked.

"No, no. Well, perhaps. I'm afraid it may not be possible to give you the file."

"What?"

"What I mean to say is, I'm not sure you have any legal right to it. Parents certainly do. But I'm not sure about siblings. I'll need to check this with a university attorney."

"I'll wait," Jessica said.

"Uh, fine. Would you mind waiting in the other room, please?"

She stood, turned, stopped. She looked back over her shoulder at him. "You knew my sister, didn't you, Dean Gordon?"

He managed a smile. "Yes, I did. Wonderful young lady."

"Kathy worked for you."

"Filing, answering the phone, that sort of thing," he said quickly. "She was a terrific worker. We all miss her very much."

"Did she seem okay to you?"

"Okay?"

"Before she disappeared," Jessica continued, her eyes boring into his. "Was she acting strangely?"

Beads of sweat popped onto his forehead, but he dared not wipe them away. "No, not that I could see. She seemed perfectly fine. Why do you ask?"

"Just checking. I'll wait out front."

"Thank you."

She closed the door.

Harrison let loose a long breath. What now? He would have to give her the file; to do otherwise would do far more than merely raise suspicion. But he could not, of course, just pull the file out of his bottom drawer and hand it to Jessica. No, he would wait a few minutes, walk down to the filing room to handle her case "personally," then return with the file.

Why, he wondered, did Jessica Culver need the file? Was there something he had missed?

No. He was sure of that.

Harrison had spent the last year hoping, praying, that it was over. But he should have known better. Matters like this never truly die. They hide, take root, grow stronger, prepare for a fresh onslaught.

Kathy Culver was not dead and buried. Like some gothic ghost, she had arisen, haunting him, crying out from some great beyond.

For vengeance.

Myron returned to the office.

"Win buzzed down twice," Esperanza said. "He wants to see you. Now."

"On my way."

"Myron?"

"What?"

Esperanza's lovely dark eyes were solemn. "Is she back? Jessica, I mean."

"No. She's just visiting."

Her face registered doubt. Myron did not press it. He no longer knew what to think himself.

He ran up the stairs two at a time. Win was two floors above him, but he might as well have been in another dimension. As soon as he opened the big steel door, the tireless clamor swarmed in, attacking. The large open space was in perpetual motion. Two, maybe three hundred desks covered the huge floor like throw rugs. Every desk had at least two computer terminals on it. There were no partitions. Hundreds of men sat and stood at every angle, each wearing a white button-down shirt with tie and suspenders, suit jackets draped from the back of their chairs. There were painfully few women. The men were all on the phone, most covering the mouthpiece to scream at someone else. They all looked alike. They all sounded alike. They were all pretty much the same person.

Welcome to Lock-Horne Investments & Securities.

All six floors were exactly the same. In fact, Myron often suspected that Lock-Horne had only one floor and that the elevator was set to stop on the same floor no matter which number you hit from floor fourteen to floor nineteen, giving the illusion of a bigger company.

Office after office made up the compound's perimeter. These were saved for the head honchos, the top dogs, the numero unos, or in securities talk, the Big Producers. The BPs all had windows and sunshine, unlike the peons on the inside, who sickened and paled from the unnatural light.

Win had a corner office with a view of both Forty-seventh Street and Park Avenue—a view that screamed major dinero. His office was decorated in Early American Wasp. Dark-paneled walls. Forest green carpet. Wing-back chairs. Paintings of a fox hunt on the wall. Like Win had ever seen a fox.

Win looked up from his massive oak desk when Myron entered. The desk weighed slightly less than a cement mixer. He'd been studying a computer print-out, one of those never-ending reams with green and white stripes. The desk was blanketed with them. They sort of matched the carpet.

"How did your morning rendezvous go with our friend Jerry the Phone-icator?" Win asked.

"Phone-icator?"

Win smiled. "I spent the whole morning working that one."

"It was worth it," Myron said.

He filled Win in on his encounter with Gary "Jerry" Grady. Win sat back and steepled. Myron then filled him in on his encounter with Otto Burke. Win leaned forward and unsteepled.

"Otto Burke," Win said, his voice measured, "is a scoundrel. Perhaps I should pay him a private visit." He looked up at Myron hopefully.

"No. Not yet. Please."

"Are you quite positive?"

"Yes. Promise me, Win. No visits."

He was clearly disappointed. "Fine," Win said, grudgingly.

"So what did you want to see me about?"

"Ah." Win's face lit up again. "Take a look at this."

He lifted the reams of computer print-outs and unceremoniously dumped them on the floor. Underneath were a pile of magazines. The top one was called *Climaxx*. The subheadline read, "Double Xs for Double the Pleasure." Nifty sales technique. Win fanned them out as if he were doing a card trick.

"Six magazines," he said.

Myron read the titles. *Climaxx, Licks, Jiz, Quim, Orgasm Today,* and of course, *Nips*. "Nickler's publications?"

"God, you are good," Win said.

"Years of training. So what about them?"

"Take a look at the pages I have marked off."

Myron started with *Climaxx*. The cover featured another freakishly endowed woman, this time licking her own nipple. Handy. Win had used leather bookmarks to mark the page. Leather bookmarks in porno magazines. Like cigarettes in an aerobics class.

The page marked off was already too familiar. Myron felt his stomach churn all over again.

Live Fantasy Phone—Pick Your Girl

There were still three rows, still four in each row. His eyes immediately moved down to the bottom row, second from the right. It still read, "I'll Do Anything!" The phone number was still 1-900-344-LUST. Still $3.99 per minute. Still discreetly billed to your telephone or charge card, Visa and MasterCard accepted.

But the woman in the picture was not Kathy Culver.

He quickly scanned the rest of the page. Nothing else was different. The same Oriental girl was still waiting. The same buttock still craved a spanking. "Tiny Titties" had not pubesced.

"This same advertising page is in all six magazines," Win explained. "But only *Nips* has Kathy Culver's picture."

"Interesting." Myron thought a moment. "Nickler probably sells package deals to advertisers—buy space in six for the price of three, that kind of thing."

"Precisely. I would venture to say that all six magazines have the exact same ads."

"But someone stuck Kathy's picture in *Nips*." Myron was getting used to saying the name of the magazine. It no longer felt grimy on his lips, which in itself made him feel grimier.

Win said, "Do you remember Nickler telling us that *Nips* was doing poorly?"

Myron nodded.

"Well, I had a devil of a time locating it. Most of the other rags were fairly easy to find on corner newsstands. But I had to go to a hardcore porno palace on Forty-second Street to come up with *Nips*."

"Yet," Myron added, "Otto Burke was able to get a copy."

"Precisely. I am sure you've considered the possibility that Mr. Burke is behind it."

"The idea has crossed my mind."

There was a knock on the door. Esperanza entered.

"Your handwriting expert is on the phone," she said. "I put it on Win's line."

Win picked up the receiver and handed it to Myron. "Hello."

"Hey, Myron, it's Swindler. I just went over the two samples you gave me."

Myron had given Swindler the envelope *Nips* had come in as well as a letter in Kathy's handwriting.

"Well?"

"They match. It's her or a very professional forgery."

Myron felt his stomach dive. "You're sure?"

"Positive."

"Thanks for calling."

"Yeah, no problem."

Myron handed the receiver back to Win.

"A match?" Win asked.

"Yep."

Win tilted back in his chair and smiled. "Yowzer."

Chapter 11

Myron ran into Ricky Lane in the corridor. He hadn't seen him in three months. Ricky looked a lot bigger. The Jets would be pleased.

"What are you doing here?" Myron asked.

"I made an appointment with Win," Ricky said with a big grin. "Just like my agent advised."

"Good to see you listen to your agent."

"Always. The man is brilliant."

"And he never argues with a client."

Ricky laughed. "Say, I heard Christian got locked out of camp."

News traveled fast. "Where did you hear that?"

"The FAN."

WFAN was New York's all-sports radio station. "Have you spoken to him lately?"

Ricky made a face. "Christian?"

"Yeah."

"Not since my last college football game, what, year and a half ago."

"I thought you were friends." Myron had, in fact, assumed that Ricky had recommended his services to Christian.

"We were teammates," Ricky replied steadily. "We were never friends."

"You don't like him?"

Ricky shrugged. "Not really. None of us did."

"Who is 'us'?"

"Guys on the team."

"What's wrong with him?"

"Long story, man. Not worth telling."

"I'd be interested."

"Put it like this," Ricky said. "Christian was a little too perfect for most of us, okay?"

"An egomaniac?"

Ricky paused, considering. "Not really. I mean, to be straight, I guess a lot of it was jealousy. Christian wasn't just good. Shit, he wasn't even just great. He was incredible. Best I ever seen."

"So?"

"So he expected the same from everyone else."

"He got on people's case when they made mistakes?"

Ricky paused again, shook his head. "No, that ain't it either."

"You're being a tad obtuse, Ricky."

Ricky Lane looked up, looked down, looked left, looked right, looked very uneasy. "I can't explain it," he said. "It's going to sound like a lot of griping, but guys weren't crazy about all the attention he was getting. I mean, we won two national championships, and the only guy they ever talked to was Christian."

"I heard those interviews. He always gave his team-mates all the credit."

"Yeah, a real gentleman," Ricky replied with more than a hint of sarcasm. "All that 'it's a team effort' bullshit just made the press love him even more. Guys on the team thought he was a promo-hog, you know? His own best PR firm. They blamed him for being too popular."

"Did you?"

"I don't know. Maybe. Truth was, I just didn't really like him. We had nothing in common except football. He's a pure Midwest white-boy. I'm a city-slicking black man. It ain't a winning combination."

"That's all it was?"

He gave a half-shrug. "I guess so. But man, this is all ancient history. I don't know why I brought it up. It don't matter no more. Christian just didn't fit in, okay. He was a nice guy, I guess. He was always polite. But that don't play so well in a locker room, you know?"

Myron knew. Juvenile, sexist, homophobic bantering —that was the stuff of locker-room popularity.

"I gotta go, man. Win will be wondering where I am."

"Okay. I'll see you around."

Ricky had almost turned away when Myron thought of something else. "What can you tell me about Kathy Culver?"

Ricky's face blanched. "What about her?"

"Did you know her?"

"A little, I guess. I mean, she was a cheerleader and dated the quarterback. But we never hung out or anything." He looked very unhappy now. "Why you asking?"

"Was she popular? Or was she hated too?"

Ricky's eyes darted about like birds trying to find a safe place to land. "Look, Myron, you always been straight with me, I always been straight with you, right?"

"Right."

"I don't want to say nothing else. She's dead. Might as well let her be."

"What does that mean?"

"Nothing. I just don't like talking about her, okay. It's kinda creepy. I'll see you later."

Ricky hurried down the corridor as if Reggie White were chasing him. Myron watched him. He debated following him but decided against it. Ricky would say no more today.

Chapter 12

Esperanza stuck her head in the door. "Someone—or something—is here to see you."

Myron held up a silencing hand. The headset had been on since his return to his office. "Look, I have to go," he said. "See if you can get him upgraded to first class. He's a big guy. Thanks." He took off the headset. "Who is it?"

She made a face. "Aaron. He didn't give a last name."

He didn't have to. "Send him in."

Seeing Aaron was like falling into a time warp. He was as big as Myron remembered, as big as the lummox in the garage. He was dressed in a freshly pressed white suit, but he wore no shirt with it, displaying plenty of tan pectoral cleavage. He wasn't wearing socks either. Nifty haircut, the swept-back look à la Pat Riley. A saunter for a walk. Designer sunglasses. Designer cologne that smelled suspiciously like insect repellent. Aaron was the pure definition of "supersmooth"—just ask him, he'd tell you.

He smiled widely. "Nice to see you, Myron."

They shook hands. Myron did not squeeze. He was far too mature. That, and Aaron could probably squeeze harder. "Have a seat."

"Wonderful." Aaron made a production of it, spreading out his arms as if he were wearing a cloak. He removed his sunglasses with an audible snap. "I like your office. It's really great."

"Thank you."

"Great address. Great view."

The password is *great*. "You looking to rent space?"

Aaron laughed as if that were the gem of gems. "No," he said. "I don't like being cooped in an office. It's not my style. I like my freedom. I like being out on my own, on the road. I wouldn't do well chained to a desk."

"Wow, that's fascinating, Aaron. Really."

He laughed again. "Ah, Myron, you haven't changed a bit. I'm glad to see it."

They hadn't seen each other since high school. Myron had gone to Livingston High School in New Jersey. Aaron had gone to his archenemy, West Orange High.

The teams played each other twice a year, and it was rarely a pleasant encounter.

In those days Myron's best friend was a huge ox named Todd Midron. Todd was a big, softhearted, simple kid with a lisp. He played Lenny to Myron's George. He was also the toughest kid Myron had ever met.

Todd never lost a fight. Never. No one ever came close to him. He was just too powerful. During a game their senior year, Aaron undercut and nearly injured Myron. Todd took exception. He went after Aaron. Aaron destroyed him. Myron tried to help his friend, but Aaron shrugged Myron off like a dandruff flake. He continued to pulverize Todd, steadily, methodically, glaring at Myron the whole time, not even glancing at his limp victim. The beating was ferocious. By the time it ended, Todd's face was an unrecognizable pulpy mess. Todd spent four months in a hospital. His jaw was wired shut for nearly a year.

"Hey," Aaron said. He pointed to a movie still on the wall. "That's Woody Allen and what's-her-name."

"Diane Keaton."

"Right, Diane Keaton."

"Is there something I can do for you?" Myron asked.

Aaron turned his whole body toward Myron. The glare from his shaved chest was nearly blinding. "I think there is, Myron. In fact, I think there's something we can do for each other."

"Oh?"

"I represent a competitor of yours. A certain dispute has arisen between the two of you. My client wishes to settle it peacefully."

"Are you an attorney now, Aaron?"

He smiled. "Not likely."

"Oh."

"I am referring to a young man named Chaz Landreaux. He recently signed a contract with your company, MB SportReps.''

"I thought of the name myself."

"Pardon me."

"MB SportReps. I came up with the name by myself."

Aaron renewed his smile. It was a good smile. Lots of teeth. "There is a problem with the contract."

"Do tell."

"You see, Mr. Landreaux has also signed a contract with Roy O'Connor at TruPro Enterprises, Incorporated. The contract predates yours. So you see the problem: Your contract is invalid."

"Why don't we let a court of law decide that?"

He sighed deeply. "My client feels it is in everyone's best interest to avoid litigation."

"Gee, what a surprise. So what does your client suggest?"

"Mr. O'Connor would be willing to pay you for your time."

"Very generous of him."

"Yes."

"And if I say no?"

"We hope it won't come to that."

"But if it does?"

Aaron sighed, stood, leaned on Myron's desk. "I'll be forced to make you disappear."

"Like in a magic trick?"

"Like in dead."

Myron put his hand to his chest. "Gasp. Oh. Gasp."

Aaron laughed again, this time without humor. "I know all about your tae kwon do display in the garage. But that guy was a stupid musclehead. I am not. I boxed professionally. I'm a black belt in jujitsu and a grand master in aikido. I've killed people."

"I bet that looks good on a résumé," Myron said.

"Let me put this in very simple terms for you, Myron: You fuck with us, I'll kill you."

"Shiver. Tremble." Myron was not quite as confident as his sarcasm, but he knew better than to show fear. Guys like Aaron are like dogs. They smell fear, they pounce.

Aaron laughed again. He was laughing a lot today. He was either very amused or had been sniffing gas. He turned his back and walked to the door. "This is your final warning," he said. "Landreaux honors his contract with Mr. O'Connor, or both of you end up worm food."

Worm food. First oatmeal. Now worm food.

"I like you, Myron. I'd really hate to see something bad happen. But you understand."

"Business is business."

"Exactly."

Esperanza appeared at the door.

Aaron gave her a sharklike smile. "Well, well," he said. Then he followed up with his best big-guy wink. Esperanza managed to keep her clothes on. Amazing restraint.

"Pick up line two," she said.

"Listen to this call closely, Myron," Aaron added with a final grin. "Appreciate the gravity of the situation. And remember. Worm food."

"Worm food. I'll keep it in mind."

Aaron winked at Esperanza again, blew her a kiss, and left.

"Charming," she said.

"Who's on the phone?"

"Chaz Landreaux."

Myron picked up the headset. "Hello."

"Motherfuckers were at my mom's!" Chaz shouted. "They told her they were going to cut off my nuts and send them to her in a box! My mother, man! They said this to my mother!''

Myron felt his fingers tighten into fists. ''I'll take care of it,'' he said slowly. ''They won't bother her again.''

Enough game playing. It was time to act.

It was time to tell Win about Roy O'Connor.

Win smiled like a kid on a snow day listening to the radio for a school closing. ''Roy O'Connor,'' he said.

''I don't want him hurt. Promise me.''

Win's eyes drifted dreamily. He might have nodded a yes, but Myron couldn't say for sure.

Chapter 13

Baumgart's on Palisades Avenue. Their old stomping grounds.

Peter Chin greeted them at the door, his eyes widening in delight and surprise when he spotted Jessica. ''Miss Culver! How wonderful to see you again.''

''Nice to see you, Peter.''

''You look as lovely as ever. You beautify my restaurant.''

Myron said, ''Hi, Peter.''

''Yeah, whatever.'' He dismissed Myron with a hand wave. His full attention was on Jessica; a crocodile gnawing on his foot wouldn't have changed that. ''You look a little too thin, Miss Culver.''

"The food's not as good in Washington."

"Funny," Myron said. "I was thinking she looked a little chunky."

Jessica eyed him. "Dead man."

Baumgart's was an institution in Englewood, New Jersey. For fifty years it was an old Jewish deli and soda fountain, noted for its superb ice cream and desserts. When Peter Chin bought it eight years ago, he kept all of the tradition but added the best nouvelle Chinese cuisine in the state. The combination was a smash. The normal order might consist of Peking duck, sesame noodles, chocolate milk shake, french fries and a death-by-chocolate sundae for dessert. When Myron and Jessica had lived together, they ate at Baumgart's at least once a week.

Myron still came once a week. Usually with Win or Esperanza. Sometimes alone. He never brought a date here.

Peter walked them past the soda fountain and put them in a booth under a huge painting. Modern art. It was a portrait of either Cher or Barbara Bush. Maybe both. Very esoteric.

Myron and Jessica sat across the table from each other, silently. The moment seemed weighed down, overwhelming. Being here together again—they had expected it to generate some light nostalgia. But the effect was more like a body blow.

"I've missed this place," she said.

"Yes."

She reached her hand across the table and took his. "I've missed you."

Her face was aglow, the way it used to be when she looked at him as though he were the only person in the entire world. Myron felt something squeeze his heart, making it nearly impossible to breathe. The rest of the world broke apart, diffused. There were only the two of them.

"I'm not sure what to say."

She smiled. "What? Myron Bolitar at a loss for words?"

"Ripley's, huh?"

Peter came by. Without preamble, he said, "You'll start with the crispy duck appetizer and squab package with pine nuts. For your main course you'll have soft-shell crab in special sauce and the Baumgart lobster and shrimp."

"Can we choose dessert?" Myron asked.

"No. Myron, you'll have the pecan pie à la mode. And for Miss Culver." He stopped, building suspense like a game-show host.

She smiled expectantly. "You don't mean . . ."

Peter nodded. "Banana pudding cake with vanilla wafers. There's only one piece left, but I put it away for you."

"Bless you, Peter."

"Each man does what he can. You didn't bring wine?" Baumgart's was BYO.

"We forgot," Jessica said. She was dazzling Peter with her smile. Not fair. Jessica's looks were like a *Star Trek* laser set on stun. Her smile, kill.

"I'll send someone across the street to get a bottle. Kendall-Jackson Chardonnay?"

"You have a good memory," she said.

"No. I just remember what is important." Myron rolled his eyes. Peter bowed slightly and left.

She turned the smile back to Myron. He felt frightened and helpless and deliriously happy.

"I'm sorry," she said.

He shook his head. He was afraid to open his mouth.

"I never meant—" She was unsure how to continue.

"I made a lot of mistakes in my life," she said. "I am dumb. I am self-destructive."

"No," Myron said. "You're perfect."

Her voice grew dramatic, her hand against her chest. " 'Take the blinders from your eyes and see me as I really am.' "

He thought a moment. "Dulcinea to Don Quixote in *Man of La Mancha*. And it's 'take the clouds,' not blinders."

"Very impressive."

"Win was playing it in the car." This was an old game of theirs. Guess the Quote.

She fiddled with her water glass, making little water circles and then inspecting them for clarity and definition. Eventually she created an aquatic Olympics logo. "I'm not sure what I'm trying to say to you," she said at last. "I'm not sure what I want to happen here." She looked up. "One last confession, okay?"

He nodded.

"I came to you because I thought you would help. That was true. But that wasn't the only reason."

"I know," he said. "I try not to think about it too much. It terrifies me."

"So what do we do now?"

His chance. He hoped there would be others. "Did you get your sister's file?"

"Yes."

"Have you gone through it yet?"

"No. I just picked it up."

"Then why don't we open it now?"

She nodded. The crispy duck and squab package with pine nuts appeared. Jessica took out a manila envelope and slit the seal. "Why don't you look at it first?"

"Okay," he said. "But save me some food."

"Chance."

He started sifting through the papers. The top page was Kathy's high school transcript. After her junior year her ranking had been twelfth in a class of three hundred. Not bad. But by the end of senior year her ranking had slipped considerably—to fifty-eighth.

"Her grades dropped senior year of high school," Myron said.

"Whose didn't drop senior year?" Jess countered. "She was probably just goofing off."

"Probably." But usually that meant A students got B's or C's. Kathy had gotten one A, three D's and an F in her final semester. Her clean record was also muddied with several detentions—all in her senior year. Strange. But probably meaningless.

"Do you want to fill me in on what happened today?" Jessica asked between bites.

She was even beautiful when pigging out. Amazing. He started by telling her about Win's discovery in the six magazines.

"So what does it mean," she asked, "her picture being only in that one rag?"

"I'm not sure."

"But you have an idea?"

He did. But it was too early to say anything. "Not yet."

"Did you hear from your friend at the phone company?"

He nodded. "Gary Grady placed two calls after we left. One was to Fred Nickler's office at Hot Desire Press. The other was someplace in the city. There was no answer when we called it. We got the information kind of late in the day."

"And the handwriting analyst?"

Best to dive right in. "The handwriting matches. It's either Kathy's or a very good forger."

That slowed her chopsticks. "My God."

"Yes."

"Then she's alive?"

"It's still just a possibility. Nothing more. That envelope could have been written before she died. Or like I said, it could be a clever forgery."

"You're reaching."

"I'm not so sure," he said. "If she's alive, where is she? Why is she doing all this?"

"Maybe she's been kidnapped. Maybe she's being forced to."

"Forced to address envelopes? Now who's reaching?"

"Do you have a better explanation?" she asked.

"Not yet. But I'm working on it." He started looking through the file again. "You ever hear of a guy named Otto Burke?"

"The big record company magnate who owns the Titans?"

"Right. He also knew about the magazine." Myron quickly summarized his visit to Titans Stadium.

"So you think Otto Burke might be behind it?" she asked.

"Otto has a motive: knocking down Christian's asking price. He certainly has the resources: lots of money. And it would also explain why Christian got a copy in the mail."

"He was sending Christian a message," she added.

"Right."

"But how would Burke forge my sister's handwriting?"

"He could have hired an expert."

"Where did he get a writing sample?"

"Who knows? It can't be that difficult."

Her eyes glazed over. "So this was all a hoax? This was all some plot to gain leverage in a negotiation?"

"It's possible. But I don't think so."

"Why not?"

"Something just doesn't mesh. Why would Burke go through all that trouble? He could have blackmailed us with just the photo. He didn't have to put it in a magazine. The photo was enough."

She grasped on to his hope as if it were a life preserver. "Good point," she said.

"The question then becomes," he continued, "how did Otto get a copy of the magazine?"

"Maybe someone in his organization picked up a copy at a newsstand."

"Very unlikely. *Nips*"—the word felt grungy again, good—"has a very low circulation rate. The chances that someone in the Titans organization bought that particular magazine, had time to read it carefully, somehow spotted Kathy's picture in the bottom row on a page of ads in the back—it's fairly remote at best."

Jessica snapped her fingers. "Someone mailed it to him too."

He nodded. "Why should Christian have been the only one? For all we know, dozens of people were sent that magazine."

"How do we find out?"

"I'm working on it."

He managed to salvage a sliver of crispy duck before it was sucked into the black hole. It was delicious. He turned his attention back to Kathy's files. Her bad grades continued during her first semester at Reston. By second semester, her grades had picked up considerably. He asked Jessica about this.

"She settled into college life, I guess," she said. "She joined the drama group, became a cheerleader, started dating Christian. She went through culture shock in her first semester. It's not uncommon.''

"No. I guess not.''

"You don't sound convinced.''

He shrugged. Myron Bolitar, Señor Skepticalo.

Kathy's recommendation letters were next. Three of them. Her high school guidance counselor called her "unusually gifted.'' Her tenth-grade history teacher said, "Her enthusiasm for life is contagious.'' Her twelfth-grade English teacher said, "Kathy Culver is bright, witty, and fun-spirited. She will be a welcome addition to any institution of learning.'' Nice comments. He scanned down to the bottom of the page.

"Uh-oh,'' he said.

"What is it?''

He handed her the glowing recommendation letter from Kathy's twelfth-grade English teacher at Ridgewood High School. A Mr. Grady.

A Mr. Gary, aka "Jerry'' Grady.

Chapter 14

Myron was startled awake by the telephone. He'd been dreaming about Jessica. He tried to remember specifics, but the details disintegrated into small pieces and blew away, leaving behind only a few frustrating snippets. The clock on his nightstand read seven o'clock. Someone was calling him at home at seven o'clock in the morning. Myron had a pretty good idea who it was.

"Hello?"

"Good morning, Myron. I hope I didn't wake you."

Myron recognized the voice. He smiled and asked, "Who is this?"

"It's Roy O'Connor."

"*The* Roy O'Connor?"

"Uh, yes, I guess so. Roy O'Connor, the agent."

"The superagent," Myron corrected. "To what do I owe this honor, Roy?"

"Would it be possible for us to meet this morning?" The voice had a discernible quake to it.

"Sure thing, Roy. My office, okay?"

"Uh, no."

"Your office, Roy?"

"Uh, no."

Myron sat up. "Should I keep guessing places and you can say hotter or colder?"

"You know Reilly's Pub on Fourteenth Street?"

"Yes."

"I'll be in the booth in the back right-hand corner. One o'clock. We'll have lunch. If that's okay with you."

"Peachy, Roy. Want me to wear anything special?"

"Uh, no."

Myron hung up, smiled. A night visit from Win, usually while sleeping soundly in your bedroom, your innermost sanctuary. Worked every time.

He got out of bed. He heard his mother in the kitchen above him, his father in the den watching television. Early morning at the Bolitar house. The basement door opened.

"Are you awake, Myron?" his mother shouted.

Myron. What a goddamn awful name. He hated it with a passion. The way he looked at it, he'd been born with all his fingers and toes, he didn't have a harelip or a cauliflower ear or a limp of any kind—so to compensate for his lack of ill fortune, his parents had christened him Myron.

"I'm awake," he answered.

"Daddy bought some fresh bagels. They're on the table."

"Thanks."

He got out of bed and climbed the steps. With one hand he felt the rough beard he'd have to shave; with the other he picked the yellow sleep-buggers out of the corner of his eyes. His father was sprawled on the den couch like a wet sock, wearing an Adidas sweatsuit and eating a bagel oozing with whitefish spread. As he did every morning, Myron's father was watching a videocassette of people exercising. Getting in shape through osmosis.

"Good morning, Myron. There're some bagels on the table."

"Uh, thanks." It was like one parent never heard the other.

He entered the kitchen. His mom was nearly sixty, but she looked much younger. Say, forty-five. She acted much younger too. Say, sixteen.

"You came in late last night," she said.

Myron made a grunting noise.

"What time did you finally get home?"

"Really late. It was almost ten." Myron Bolitar, the late-night scream machine.

"So," Mom began, struggling to look and sound casual, "who were you out with?" Mistress of the Subtle.

"Nobody," he said.

"Nobody? You were out all night with nobody?"

Myron looked left and right. "When are you going to bring in the hot lights and jumper cables?"

"Fine, Myron. If you don't want to tell me—"

"I don't want to tell you."

"Fine. Was it a girl?"

"Mom . . ."

"Okay, forget I asked."

Myron reached for the phone and dialed Win's number. After the eighth ring he began to hang up when a weak, distant voice coughed. "Hello?"

"Win?"

"Yeah."

"You okay?"

"Hello?"

"Win?"

"Yeah."

"What took you so long to answer the phone?"

"Hello?"

"Win?"

"Who is this?"

"Myron."

"Myron Bolitar?"

"How many Myrons do you know?"

"Myron Bolitar?"

"No, Myron Rockefeller."

"Something's wrong," Win said.

"What?"

"Terribly wrong."

"What are you talking about?"

"Some asshole is calling me at seven in the morning pretending to be my best friend."

"Sorry, I forgot the time." Win was not what one would call a morning person. During their years at Duke, Win was never out of bed before noon—even on the days he had a morning class. He was, in fact, the heaviest sleeper Myron had ever known or imagined. Myron's parents, on the other hand, woke up when somebody in

the Western hemisphere farted. Before Myron moved
into the basement, the same scenario was played out
nightly:

Around three in the morning, Myron would get out of
bed to go to the bathroom. As he tiptoed past his parents' bedroom, his father would stir ever so slowly, as
though someone had dropped a Popsicle on his crotch.

"Who's that?" his father would shout.

"Just me, Dad."

"Is that you, Myron?"

"Yes, Dad."

"Are you okay, son?"

"Fine, Dad."

"What are you doing up? You sick or something?"

"I'm just going to the bathroom, Dad. I've been going to the bathroom by myself since I was fourteen."

During their sophomore year at Duke, Myron and
Win lived in the smallest double on campus with a bunk
bed that Win said "creaks slightly" and Myron said
"sounds like a duck being run over by a back hoe." One
morning, when the bed was quiet and he and Win were
asleep, a baseball crashed through their window. The
noise was so deafening that their entire dorm jumped out
of bed and rushed to see if Myron and Win had survived
the wrath of whatever gigantic meteorite had fallen
through the roof. Myron rushed to the window to yell
obscenities. Dorm members stamped across the under-
wear-carpeted floor to join in the tirade. The ensuing
reverberations were loud enough to disturb a diner waitress on her coffee break.

Win just lay asleep, a blanket of broken glass strewn
over his blanket.

The next night, Myron called through the darkness of
his bottom bunk. "Win?"

"Yes."

"How do you sleep so soundly?" But Win didn't answer because he'd fallen asleep.

On the phone Win asked, "What do you want?"

"Did all go well last night?"

"Mr. O'Connor hasn't called you yet?"

"He has." End of subject. Myron didn't want details.

"I know," Win continued, "that you did not awaken me to question my effectiveness."

"Kathy Culver got only one A in her senior year at Ridgewood High. Guess who her teacher was."

"Who?"

"Gary Grady."

"Hmm. Dial-a-porn and high school English. Interesting vocational mix."

"I was thinking we could go see Mr. Grady this morning."

"At the school?"

"Sure. The two of us can pretend we're concerned parents."

"For the same kid?"

"Putting the rainbow curriculum to the test."

Win laughed. "This is going to be fun."

Chapter 15

"How do we find him?" Win asked.

They arrived at Ridgewood High School at nine-thirty. It was a warm June day, the kind of day where you stared at the window and daydreamed about the end of school. Not much movement around the building—as though the entire school, even the edifice, were coasting toward summer vacation.

Myron remembered how miserable such days were. It gave him an idea.

"Let's pull the fire alarm," he said.

"I beg your pardon."

"We'll get everyone outside. It'll be easier to spot him."

"Idiotically ingenious," Win said.

"Besides, I always wanted to pull a fire alarm."

"Walk on the wild side."

No one noticed them when they entered the school. There were no guards, no locks on the door, no hall monitors of any kind. This was not an urban high school. Myron found a fire alarm not too far from the entrance.

"Kids, don't try this at home," Myron said. He pulled. Bells went off. Then cheers from the kids. Myron felt good about his deed. He thought about pulling alarms more often but decided some might construe the act as immature.

Win held the door open and pretended to be a fire marshal. "Single file," he told the students. "And remember: Only you can prevent fires."

Myron spotted Grady. "Bingo."

"Where?"

"Turning the corner. On the left. Mr. Fashion."

Gary Grady was wearing a yellow Century 21–like blazer with Keith Partridge orange-striped pants. Win looked visibly pained at the sight. They made their approach.

"Hi, Jerry."

Grady's head shot around. "That's not my name."

"Yeah, you told me. It's your alias, right? When you

do business with Fred Nickler. Your real name is Gary Grady.''

Nearby students stopped walking.

"Keep moving!" Gary snapped.

The students restarted their grudging trudge.

"Impatient teachers," Myron said.

"Sad," Win agreed.

Gary's thin face seemed to stretch even further. He stepped closer so that no one could overhear.

"Perhaps we can continue this conversation later," he whispered.

"I don't think so, Gary."

"I'm in the middle of a class."

"Tough tittie," Myron said.

Win arched an eyebrow. "Tough tittie?"

"Something about being back in high school," Myron said. "Besides, I thought it appropriate considering the situation."

Win considered for a moment. "Okay, I can accept that."

Myron turned back to Gary. "The fire drill will last a little while. Then it will take a little while for the kids to file back in. Then they'll want to goof around in the halls for a while. By then we'll be all done."

Gary crossed his arms over his chest. "No."

"Option two, then." Myron took out a copy of *Nips*. "We can play Show and Tell with the principal."

Grady coughed into his fist. A loud fire whistle sounded. Sirens came closer. "I don't know what you're talking about," he said, taking a few more steps away from the kids.

"I followed you."

"What?"

Myron sighed, gave him exasperation. "You were in Hoboken yesterday morning. You picked up the mail at an address used for advertising sex lines in porno rags. Then you went home to Glen Rock, saw me, panicked, and called Fred Nickler, the managing editor of said rags.''

''Amateur,'' Win added with disgust.

''Now, we can discuss this with you or with the school board. Up to you.''

Gary glanced at his watch. ''You have two minutes.''

''Fine.'' Myron gestured to the right. ''Why don't we step into the teachers' lavatory? I assume you have a key.''

''Yes.''

He opened the door. Myron had always wanted to see a teachers' bathroom, see how the other half lives. It was unremarkable in every way.

''Okay, you have me here,'' Gary said. ''What do you want?''

''Tell me about this ad.''

Gary swallowed. His enlarged Adam's apple bobbed up and down like a boxer's head avoiding jabs. ''I don't know anything about it.''

Myron and Win exchanged a glance.

''Can I stick his head in a toilet?'' Win asked.

Gary straightened his back. ''If you are trying to frighten me, it won't work.''

Win's voice was semipleading. ''One quick dunk?''

''Not yet.'' Myron turned his attention back to Gary. ''I have no interest in busting you, Gary. You're a perv, that's your business. I want to know about your connection with Kathy Culver.''

Sweat appeared above Gary's upper lip. ''She was a student of mine.''

''I know. Why is her picture in *Nips*? In your ad?''

''I have no idea. I saw it for the first time yesterday.''

''But that's your ad, right?''

He hesitated, giving silent half-shrugs to no one in particular. "Okay," he said, "I admit it. I advertise in Mr. Nickler's publications. No law against that. But I did not put that picture of Kathy in the ad."

"Who did?"

"I don't know."

"But you admit operating sex lines?"

"Yes. It's harmless. I do it to make extra money. Nobody gets hurt."

"Another prince," Myron said. "How much extra money?"

"In the business's heyday I was making twenty thousand dollars a month."

Myron wasn't sure he heard right. "Twenty thousand dollars a month from phone sex?"

"In the mid-eighties, yes. Before the government got involved and began to crack down on 900 lines. Now I'm lucky to clear eight grand a month."

"Damn bureaucrats," Myron said. "So how does Kathy Culver fit into all this?"

"What do you mean?"

"Gee, Gary, a naked picture of her is in your ad this month. Maybe that's what I mean."

"I already told you. I had nothing to do with that."

"Then I guess it's a coincidence, her being a student of yours and all."

"Yes."

"I won't hold him under long," Win promised. "Please."

Myron shook his head. "You wrote her a glowing recommendation letter for college, correct?"

"Kathy was a wonderful student," Gary replied.

"And what else?"

"If you are suggesting that my relationship with Kathy was something other than student-teacher—"

"That's exactly what I'm suggesting."

Once again he crossed his arms over his chest. "I will not dignify that with a response. And I am now terminating this conversation."

Gary was addressing them in that way teachers do. Sometimes teachers forget that life is not a classroom.

"Dunk him," Myron said.

"With pleasure."

Gary probably had two inches on Win. He leaned up on his toes and gave Win his most withering glare.

"I'm not afraid of you," Gary said.

"Mistake number one."

Win moved with a speed that videocameras would not catch. He took hold of Gary's hand, twisted it, and pulled down. Hapkido move. Gary dropped to the tile floor. Win pressed his knee against the point of Gary's elbow. Gently. Not too much pain. Just enough to let him know who was in control.

"Damn," Win said.

"What?"

"All the toilets are clean. I hate when that happens."

"Anything to add before the dunk?" Myron asked.

Gary's face was white. "Promise me you won't tell anyone," he managed.

"You'll tell us the truth?"

"Yes. But you have to swear you won't tell anyone. Not the principal, no one."

"Okay." Myron nodded to Win. Win let go. Gary took back his hand and caressed it as though it were an abused puppy.

"Kathy and I had an affair," he said.

"When?"

"Her senior year. It lasted a few months, that's all. I haven't seen her since, I swear."

"And that's everything?"

He nodded. "I don't know anything else. Somebody else put that picture in the ad."

"If you're lying, Gary—"

"I'm not. Hand to God."

"Okay," Myron said. "You can go."

Gary rushed out. He had not even paused to check his hair in the mirror.

"Scum," Myron said. "The man is pure unadulterated scum. Seduces his students, operates a dial-a-porn line."

"But a snappy dresser," Win said. "So what next?"

"We finish the investigation. Then we go to the school board. We tell them all about Mr. Grady's extracurricular activities."

"Didn't you just promise him you weren't going to tell?"

Myron shrugged. "I lied."

Chapter 16

In something of a trance, Jessica thanked Myron and hung up the phone. She half-stumbled into the kitchen and sat down. Her mother and her younger brother Edward looked up.

"Honey," Carol Culver began, "are you okay?"

"Fine," she managed.

"Who was on the phone?"

"Myron."

Silence.

"We were talking about Kathy," she continued.

"What about her?" Edward asked.

Her brother had always been Edward, not Ed or Eddie or Ted. He was only a year out of college and already he owned a successful computer business, IMCS (Interactive Management Computer Systems), which developed software systems for several prestigious corporations. Edward wore only jeans, even in the office, and obnoxious T-shirts, the kind with chintzy iron-on decals that say stuff like "Keep on Truckin'." He didn't own a tie. He had a wide, almost-feminine face with delicate porcelain features. Women would kill for his eyelashes. Only the buzz-cut hair—and the pithy phrase on his T-shirt—hinted at what Edward was proud to be: COMPUTER WEENIES HAVE THE BEST HARDWARE.

Jessica took a deep breath. She could not be concerned with delicacies or feelings anymore. She opened her purse and pulled out a copy of *Nips*. "This magazine hit the stands a few days ago," she said.

She tossed it on the table, cover up. A cross between puzzlement and disgust blanketed her mother's face.

Edward remained stoic. "What the hell is this?" he asked.

Jessica flipped to the page in the back. "There," she said simply, pointing to the picture of Kathy in the bottom row.

It took a few moments for them to comprehend what they were seeing, as though the information had been waylaid somewhere between the eye and brain. Then Carol Culver let out a groan. Her hand flew to her mouth, smothering a scream. Edward's eyes narrowed into thin slits.

Jessica did not give her time to recover. "There's more," she said.

Her mother looked up at her with hollow, haunted eyes. There was no life behind them anymore, as though a final cold gust had put out a flickering flame.

"A handwriting expert checked the envelope it came in. The writing matches Kathy's."

Edward inhaled sharply. Carol's legs finally gave out, folding at the knees. She landed hard in her chair and crossed herself. Tears came to her eyes.

"She's alive?" Carol managed.

"I don't know."

"But there's a chance?" Edward followed up.

Jessica nodded. "There's always been a chance."

Stunned silence.

"But I need some information," Jessica continued. "I need to know what happened to Kathy. What made her change."

Edward's eyes narrowed again. "What do you mean?"

"Kathy had an affair with her high school English teacher. Senior year."

More silence. Jessica was not so sure it was stunned.

"The teacher, a maggot named Gary Grady, has admitted it."

"No," her mother said weakly. She lowered her head, her crucifix dangling like a pendulum. She began to weep. "Sweet Jesus, not my baby . . ."

Edward stood. "That's enough, Jess."

"It's not enough."

Edward grabbed his jacket. "I'm out of here."

"Wait. Where are you going?"

"Good-bye."

"We need to talk this out."

"The hell we do."

"Edward—"

He ran out the back door, slamming it behind him.

Jessica turned back to her mother. Her sobs were gut-wrenching. Jessica watched for a minute or two. Then she turned and left the kitchen.

Roy O'Connor was already in the back booth when Myron arrived. His glass was empty, and he was sucking on an ice cube. He sounded like an aardvark near an anthill.

"Hey, Roy."

O'Connor nodded to the seat across the table, not bothering to stand. He wore gold rings that disappeared under the folds of flesh in his chubby unstained hands. His fingernails were manicured. He was somewhere between forty-five and fifty-five years old, but it was impossible to tell where. He was balding, wearing the ever-desirable swept-over look, parting his hair just below the armpit.

"Nice place, Roy," Myron said. "A table in the back, low lights, soft romantic music. If I didn't know better—"

O'Connor shook his head. "Look, Bolitar, I know you think you're a regular Buddy Hackett, but give it a rest, okay?"

"I guess flowers are out, then." Pause. Then: "Buddy Hackett?"

"We need to talk."

"I'm all ears."

A waitress came over. "Can I get you gentlemen something to drink?"

"Another," Roy said, pointing to his glass.

"And for you?"

"Do you have Yoo-Hoo?" Myron asked.

"I think so."

"Great. I'll have one."

She left. Roy shook his head. "A fucking Yoo-Hoo," he mumbled.

"Did you say something?"

"Your goon visited me last night."

"Your goons visited me first," Myron said.

"I had nothing to do with that."

Myron gave him his best "come off it" look of pure skepticism. The waitress put down the drinks. Roy scooped up his martini as if it held a life-saving antidote. Myron, by contrast, sipped his Yoo-Hoo daintily. Ever the gentleman.

"Look, Myron," O'Connor continued, "it's like this. I signed Landreaux. I gave him money up front. I gave him money every month. I kept my part of the bargain."

"You signed him illegally."

"I'm not the first guy to do it," he said.

"Nor the last. What's your point, Roy?"

"Look, you know me. You know how I operate."

Myron nodded. "You're a chicken-shitted crook."

"I might have threatened the kid. Fine. I've done that before. But that's it. I'd never really hurt anybody."

"Uh-huh."

"Word would get out to the athletes. I'd be ruined."

"Damn shame that would be."

"Bolitar, you're not making this any easier."

"I'm not trying to."

O'Connor grabbed the drink again. He finished it and signaled to the waitress for another. "I've gotten involved with the wrong people," he said.

"What do you mean?"

"I worked up some big-time gambling debts. Debts I couldn't pay off."

"So they took a piece of your business."

Roy nodded. "They control me now. Your—your friend from last night." A Geiger counter could have

registered the quake in his voice when he mentioned
Win. "I want to do just what he said, but I don't have the
power anymore."

Myron took another sip of his Yoo-Hoo, hoping he
wasn't getting one of those chocolate mustaches. "My
friend won't be pleased to hear that."

"You have to tell him it's not me."

"Then who is it?"

Roy sat back, shaking his head. "I can't say. But I
can tell you they play for keeps. And they don't understand a thing about this business. They think they can
just scare everyone into compliance. They want to make
an example out of someone."

"And Landreaux is the example?"

"Landreaux. And you. They want to hurt Landreaux.
They want to kill you. They're putting out a contract on
your head."

Another cool sip. Myron said nothing.

"You don't seem very worried," Roy said.

"I laugh in the face of death," Myron replied. "Well,
maybe not laugh. More like a snicker. A quiet snicker."

"Jesus, you're a lunatic."

"And I wouldn't do it directly in death's face. So it's
more like a quiet snicker behind his back."

"Bolitar, this isn't funny."

"No," Myron agreed. "It's not. I strongly suggest
you call them off."

"Haven't you heard a word I've said? I got no control
here."

"If something happens to me, my friend will be very
upset. He'll take it out on you."

Roy swallowed. "But I'm powerless. You have to believe that."

"Then tell me who's calling the shots."

"I can't."

Myron shrugged. "Maybe we can be buried next to one another. One of those romantic tragedy things."

"They'll kill me if I say anything."

"What do you think my friend will do to you?"

Roy shuddered. He sucked on the ice again, trying to salvage the last remnants of the whiskey. "Where is that damn bimbo with my drink?"

"Who's calling the shots, Roy?"

"You didn't hear it from me, right?"

"Right."

"You won't tell them?"

"Mum's the word."

One more ice suck. Then Roy said, "Ache."

"Herman Ache?" Myron asked, surprised. "Herman Ache is behind this?"

Roy shook his head. "His younger brother. Frank. He's out of control. I don't know what the psycho will do next."

Frank Ache. It made sense. Herman Ache was one of New York's leading mobsters, responsible for countless misery. But next to his younger brother Frank, Herman was an Alan Alda clone. Aaron would enjoy working for someone like Frank.

This was not good news. Myron toyed with the idea of dropping the snicker altogether. "Anything else you can tell me?"

"No. I just don't want anyone hurt."

"You're some guy, Roy. So selfless."

O'Connor stood. "I got nothing more to say."

"I thought we were going to have lunch."

"Have it by yourself," O'Connor said. "It's on my tab."

"Won't be the same without your company."

"Yet somehow you'll muddle through."

Myron picked up the menu. "I'll try."

Chapter 17

Who else to call?

The answer, Jessica realized, was obvious.

Nancy Serat. Kathy's roommate and closest friend.

Jessica sat at her father's desk. The lights were turned off, the shades were pulled down, but the sunlight was still strong enough to sneak through and cast shadows.

Adam Culver had done everything he could to make his home office radically different from the cement, institutional, macabre feel of the county morgue. The results were mixed. The converted bedroom had bright yellow walls, plenty of windows, silk flowers, white Formica desk. Teddy bears encircled the room. William Shakesbear. Rhett Beartler with Scarlett O'Beara. Bear Ruth. Bearlock Holmes. Humphrey Beargart with Lauren Bearcall. The whole atmosphere was cheerful, albeit a forced cheerful, like a clown you laugh at but find a little scary.

She took her phone book from her purse. Nancy had sent the family a card a few weeks ago. She had won some fellowship and was staying on campus to work in admissions. Jessica looked up her number and dialed.

On the third ring the answering machine picked up. Jessica left a message and hung up. She was about to start going through the drawers when a voice stopped her.

"Jessica."

She looked up. Her mother stood in the doorway. Her

eyes were sunken, her face a skeletal death mask. Her body swayed as though she were about to topple over.

"What are you doing in here?" Carol asked.

"Just looking around," she said.

Carol nodded, her head bobbing on the string that was her neck. "Find anything?"

"Not yet."

Carol sat down. She stared straight ahead, her eyes unfocused. "She was always such a happy child," she said slowly. Her fingers fiddled with prayer beads, her gaze still far off. "Kathy never stopped smiling. She had such a wonderful, happy smile. It lit up any room she entered. You and Edward, well, you were both more brooding. But Kathy—she had a smile for everyone and everything. Do you remember?"

"Yes," Jessica said. "I remember."

"Your father used to joke that she had the personality of a born-again cheerleader," Carol added, chuckling at the memory. "Nothing ever brought her down." She stopped, the chuckle fading away. "Except, I guess, me."

"Kathy loved you, Mom."

She sighed deeply, her chest heaving as though even a sigh took great effort. "I was a strict mother with you girls. Too strict, I guess. I was old-fashioned."

Jessica did not reply.

"I just didn't want you or your sister to . . ." She lowered her head.

"To what?"

She shook her head. Her fingers moved across the beads at a more fervid pace. For a long time neither of them spoke. Then Carol said, "You were right before, Jessica. Kathy changed."

"When?"

"Her senior year."

"What happened?"

Tears sprang to Carol's eyes. Her mouth tried to form words, her hands moving in gestures of helplessness. "The smile," she replied with something like a shrug. "One day it was gone."

"Why?"

Her mother wiped her eyes. Her lower lip quivered. Jessica's heart reached out to her, but for some reason the rest of her couldn't. She sat and watched her suffering, strangely uninvolved, as if she were watching a late-night tearjerker on cable.

"I'm not trying to hurt you," Jessica said. "I just want to find Kathy."

"I know, sweetheart."

"I think," Jessica continued, "that whatever changed Kathy is connected to her disappearance."

Her mother's shoulders sagged. "Merciful God."

"I know it hurts," Jessica said. "But if we can find Kathy, if we can find who killed Dad—"

Carol's head shot up. "Your father was killed in a robbery."

"I don't think so. I think it's all connected. Kathy's disappearance, Dad's murder, everything."

"But—how?"

"I don't know yet. Myron is helping me find out."

The doorbell rang.

"That'll be Uncle Paul," her mother said, heading for the door.

"Mom?"

Carol stopped but did not turn around.

"What's going on? What are you afraid to tell me?"

The doorbell rang again.

"I better get that," Carol said. She hurried down the stairs.

* * *

"So," Win began, "Frank Ache wants to kill you."

Myron nodded. "Seems so."

"A shame."

"If he'd only get to know me. The real me."

They sat in the front row at Titans Stadium. Out of the goodness of his heart, Otto had agreed to let Christian practice. That, and the fact that veteran quarterback Neil Decker was beyond horrendous.

The morning session had been a lot of wind sprints and walking through plays. The afternoon session, however, was a bit of a surprise. The players were in full gear, almost unheard of this early on in the year.

"Frank Ache is not a kind fellow," Win said.

"He likes torturing animals."

"Excuse me?"

"A friend of mine knew him growing up," Myron explained. "Frank Ache's favorite hobby was to chase down cats and dogs and bash in their heads with a baseball bat."

"I bet that impressed the girls," Win said.

Myron nodded.

"I assume, then, that you will be in need of my unique services."

"For a few days, anyway," Myron replied.

"Goodie. May I also assume that you have a plan?"

"I'm working on it. Feverishly."

Christian jogged out on the field. He moved in that effortless way great athletes do. He got into the huddle, broke it, and approached the line of scrimmage.

"Full contact!" a coach yelled out.

Myron looked at Win. "I don't like this."

"What?"

"Full contact on the first day."

Christian started calling out numbers. Then he gave a

few hut-huts before the ball was snapped to him. He faded back to pass.

"Oh, shit," Myron said.

Tommy Lawrence, the Titans' All-Pro linebacker, charged forward unblocked. Christian saw him too late. Tommy placed his helmet into Christian's sternum and slammed him to the ground—the kind of tackle that hurts like hell but doesn't do any permanent damage. Two other defenders piled on.

Christian got up, wincing and holding his chest. Nobody helped him.

Myron stood.

Win stopped him with a shake of his head. "Sit down, Myron."

Otto Burke came down the stairs, entourage in tow.

Myron glared at him. Otto smiled brightly. He made a tsk-tsk noise. "I traded a lot of popular veterans to get him," he said. "It looks like some of the guys aren't too thrilled."

"Sit down, Myron," Win repeated.

Myron hesitated, then complied.

Christian limped back to the huddle. He called the next play and again approached the line of scrimmage. He surveyed the defense, yelled out numbers and hut-huts, then took the snap from the center. He stepped back. Tommy Lawrence blitzed again over left guard, completely untouched. Christian froze. Tommy bore down on him. He leaped like a panther, his arms stretched out for a bone-crushing tackle. Christian moved at the very last moment. Not a big move. Just a slight shift, actually. Tommy flew by him and landed on the ground. Christian pumped and threw a bomb.

Complete pass.

Myron turned around, grinning. "Hey, Otto?"

"What?"

"Kiss my grits."

Otto's smile did not falter. Myron wondered how he did that, if his mouth was frozen that way, like the threat a little kid hears from his mom when he's making faces. Otto nodded and walked away. His entourage followed in a row, like a family of mallard ducks.

Win looked at Myron. "Kiss my grits?"

Shrug. "Paying homage to Flo on *Alice*."

"You watch too much television."

"Listen, I've been thinking."

"Oh?"

"About Gary Grady," Myron said.

"What about him?"

"He has an affair with a student. She vanishes a year or so later. Time passes and her picture ends up in a porno ad he runs."

"Your point being?"

"It's crazy."

"So is everything about this case."

Myron shook his head. "Think about it. Grady admits having an affair with Kathy, right? So what would be the last thing he'd want to do?"

"Publicize it."

"Yet her picture ends up in his ad."

"Ah." Win nodded. "You believe someone is setting him up."

"Exactly."

"Who?"

"Fred Nickler would be my bet," Myron said.

"Hmm. He did hand over Grady's p.o. box without much debate."

"And he has the power to switch photos in his own magazine."

"So what do you suggest?" Win asked.

"I'd like you to check out Mr. Fred Nickler very

thoroughly. Maybe talk to him again. *Talk*," Myron repeated. "Not visit."

On the field Christian was fading back again. For the third straight time Tommy Lawrence blitzed over left guard untouched. In fact, the left guard stood with his hands on his hips and watched.

"Christian's own lineman is setting him up," Myron said.

Christian side-stepped Tommy Lawrence, cocked his arms, and whipped the ball with unearthly velocity directly into his left guard's groin. There was a short *oomph* sound. The left guard collapsed like a folding chair.

"Ouch," Win said.

Myron almost clapped. "*The Longest Yard* revisited."

The left guard was, of course, wearing a cup. But a cup was far from full protection against a speeding missile. He rolled on the ground, back curved fetal-like, eyes wide. Every man in the general vicinity gave a collective, sympathetic "Ooo."

Christian walked over to his left guard—a man weighing in excess of 275 pounds—and offered him a hand. The left guard took it. He limped back to the huddle.

"Christian has balls," Myron said.

Win nodded. "But can the same be said of the left guard?"

Chapter 18

As soon as Myron entered the Reston University campus, his car phone rang.

"Listen, putz, I got what you want," P.T. said. "My friend's name is Jake Courter. He's the town sheriff."

"Sheriff Jake," Myron said. "You're kidding, right?"

"Hey, don't let the title fool you. Jake used to work homicide in Philly, Boston, and New York. Good man. He said he'd meet with you today at three."

Myron checked his watch. It was one o'clock now. The station was five minutes away. "Thanks, P.T."

"Can I ask you something, Myron?"

"Shoot."

"Why you looking into this?"

"It's a long story, P.T."

"This have to do with her sister? That great piece of tail you used to nail?" He cackled.

"You're all class, P.T."

"Hey, Myron, I want to hear about it sometime. The whole story."

"It's a promise."

Myron parked the car and headed into the old athletic center. The corridor was a bit more beaten up than Myron had expected. Three rows of framed photographs of past athletic teams—some from as far back as a hundred years ago—lined the walls. Myron approached a beaded-glass door that looked like something out of an old Sam

Spade film. The word FOOTBALL was stenciled in black.
He knocked.

The voice was like an old tire on an unpaved road.
"What?"

Myron stuck his head. "Busy, Coach?"

Reston University football coach Danny Clarke
looked up from his computer. "Who the hell are you?"
he rasped.

"Fine, thanks. But let's dispense with the pleasantries."

"That supposed to be funny?"

Myron tilted his head. "You didn't think so?"

"I'll ask one more time: Who the hell are you?"

"Myron Bolitar."

The coach's scowl did not change. "Am I supposed
to know you?"

It was a hot summer day, the campus was practically
empty, and here sat the school's legendary football
coach wearing a suit and tie, watching videotapes of
high school prospects. A suit and tie and no air conditioning. If the heat bothered Danny Clarke, it didn't
show. Everything about him was well groomed and tidy.
He was shelling and eating peanuts, but no mess was
visible. His jaw muscles bunched as he chewed, making
little knobs appear and disappear near his ears. He had a
prominent vein in his forehead.

"I'm a sports agent."

He flicked his eyes away like a ruler dismissing an
underling. "Get out of here. I'm busy."

"We need to talk."

"Out of here, asshole. Now."

"I just—"

"Listen up, shithead." He pointed a coach finger at
Myron. "I don't talk to bottom-feeders. Ever. I run a
clean program with clean players. I don't take payoffs

from so-called agents or any of that bullshit. So if you got an envelope stuffed with green, you can go shove it up your ass."

Myron clapped. "Beautiful. I laughed, I cried, it became a part of me."

Danny Clarke looked up sharply. He wasn't used to having his orders questioned, but part of him seemed almost amused by it. "Get the hell out of here," he growled, but more gently now. He turned back to the television. On the screen a young quarterback threw a long, tight spiral. Caught. Touchdown.

Myron decided to disarm him with tact. "The kid looks pretty good," he said.

"Yeah, well, it's a good thing you're a scum-sucking leech and not a scout. The kid can't play a lick. Now take a hike."

"I want to talk to you about Christian Steele."

That got his attention. "What about him?"

"I'm his agent."

"Oh," Danny Clarke said. "Now I remember. You're the old basketball player. The one who hurt his knee."

"At your service," Myron said.

"Is Christian okay?"

Myron tried to look noncommittal. "I understand he didn't get along with his teammates."

"So? You his social coordinator?"

"What was the problem?"

"I can't see how it matters now," he said.

"Then humor me."

It took the coach some time to relax his glare. "It was a lot of things," he said. "But I guess Horty was the main problem."

"Horty?" Clever interrogation techniques. Pay attention.

"Junior Horton," he explained. "A defensive lineman. Good speed, good size, good talent. The brains of a citrus beverage.''

"So what does this Horty have to do with Christian?''

"They didn't see eye to eye.''

"How come?''

Danny Clarke thought a moment. "I don't know. Something to do with that girl who disappeared.''

"Kathy Culver?''

"Right. Her.''

"What about her?''

He turned back to the VCR and changed tapes. Then he typed something on his computer. "I think maybe she dated Horty before Christian. Something like that.''

"So what happened?''

"Horty was a bad apple from the get-go. In his senior year I found out he was pushing drugs to my players: cocaine, dope, Lord knows what else. So I bounced him. Later, I heard he'd been supplying the guys with steroids for three years.''

Later my ass, Myron thought. But for once he kept the thought to himself. "So what does this have to do with Christian?''

"Rumors started circulating that Christian had gotten Horty thrown off the team. Horty fueled them, you know, telling the guys that Christian was turning them all in for using steroids, stuff like that.''

"Was that true?''

"Nope. Two of my best players showed up game day so stoned, they could barely see. That's when I took action. Christian had nothing to do with it. But you know how it is. They all figured Christian was the star. If he wanted his ass wiped, the coaches asked Charmin or Downy.''

"Did you tell your guys Christian had nothing to do with it?''

He made a face. "You think that would have helped? They would have thought I was covering for him, protecting him. They would have hated him even more. As long as it didn't affect their play—and it didn't—it was not my concern. I just let it be."

"You're a real character developer, Coach."

He gave Myron his best intimidate-the-freshman glare. The forehead vein started pulsing. "You're out of line, Bolitar."

"Wouldn't be the first time."

"I care about my boys."

"Yeah, I can tell. You let Horty stay as long as he pumped your boys with dangerous albeit play-enhancing drugs. When he graduated to the big leagues—to the stuff that had a negative on-the-field impact—all of a sudden you became a righteous drug czar."

"I don't have to listen to this bullshit," Danny Clarke ranted. "Especially from a no-good, bloodsucking vampire. Get the hell out of my office. Now."

Myron said, "You want to catch a movie together sometime? Maybe a Broadway show?"

"Out!"

Myron left. Another day, another friend. Charm was the key.

He had plenty of time to kill before he visited Sheriff Jake, so he decided to take a stroll. The campus was like a ghost town, except no tumbleweeds were skittering along the ground. The students were gone for summer break. The buildings stood lifeless and sad. In the distance a stereo was playing Elvis Costello. Two girls appeared. Co-ed types wearing crotch-riding shorts and halter tops. They were walking a hairy, little dog—a Shih Tzu. It looked like Cousin It after one too many spins in the dryer. Myron smiled and nodded as the girls passed him. Neither one fainted or disrobed. Astonishing. The little dog, however, snarled at him. Cujo.

He was nearly at his car when he spotted the sign:

CAMPUS POST OFFICE

He stopped, looked around the grounds, saw nobody. Hmm. It was worth a try.

The inside of the post office was painted institutional green, the same color as the school bathroom. A long V-shaped corridor was wallpapered with p.o. boxes. He heard the distant sound of a radio. He couldn't make out the song, just a strong, monotonous bass beat.

Myron approached the mail window. A kid sat with his feet up. The music was coming from the kid's ears. He was listening to one of those Walkman clones with the minispeakers that bypass the ears and plug directly into the cerebrum. His black high-tops rested on a desk, his baseball hat tipped down like a sombrero at siesta time. There was a book on his lap. Philip Roth's *Operation Shylock*.

"Good book," Myron said.

The kid did not look up.

"Good book," Myron said again, this time yelling.

The kid pulled the speakers out of his ears with a sucking pop. He was pale and red-haired. When he took off his hat, his hair was Afro-wild. Bernie from *Room 222*.

"What?"

"I said, good book."

"You read it?"

Myron nodded. "Without moving my lips."

The kid stood. He was tall and lanky.

"You play basketball?" Myron asked.

"Yeah," the kid said. "Just finished my freshman year. Didn't play much."

"I'm Myron Bolitar."

The kid looked at him blankly.

"I played ball for Duke."

Blink, blink.

"No autographs, please."

"How long ago did you play?" the kid asked.

"Graduated ten years ago."

"Oh," the kid replied, as though that explained everything. Myron did some quick math in his head. The kid had been seven or eight when Myron won the national title. He suddenly felt very old.

"We used peach baskets back then."

"What?"

"Never mind. Can I ask you a few questions?"

The kid shrugged. "Go ahead."

"How often are you on duty in the post office?"

"Five days a week in the summer, nine to five."

"Is it always this quiet?"

"This time of year, yeah. No students, so there's almost no mail."

"Do you do the mail sorting?"

"Sure."

"Do you do pick-ups?"

"Pick-ups?"

"Campus mail."

"Yeah, but there's only that slot by the front door."

"That's the only campus mailbox?"

"Um-hmm."

"Been getting a lot of campus mail lately?"

"Next to none. Three, four letters a day."

"Do you know Christian Steele?"

"Heard of him," the kid said. "Who hasn't?"

"He got a big manila envelope in his box a few days

ago. There was no postmark, so it had to be mailed from campus.''

"Yeah, I remember. What about it?''

"Did you see who mailed it?'' Myron asked.

"No,'' the kid said. "But they were the only pieces of mail I got that whole day.''

Myron cocked his head. "They?''

"What?''

"You said 'they. They were the only pieces.' ''

"Right. Two big envelopes. Exact same except for the address.''

"Do you remember who the other one was addressed to?''

"Sure,'' the kid said. "Harrison Gordon. He's the dean of students.''

Chapter 19

Nancy Serat dropped her suitcase on the floor and re-wound the answering machine. The tape raced back, shrieking all the way. She had spent the weekend in Cancún, a final vacation before starting her fellowship at Reston University, her alma mater.

The first message was from her mother.

"I don't want to disturb you on vacation, dear. But I thought you'd want to know that Kathy Culver's father died yesterday. He was stabbed by a mugger. Awful. Anyway, I thought you'd want to know. Give us a call

when you get back in. Your father and I want to take you
out to dinner for your birthday."

Nancy's legs felt weak. She collapsed into the chair,
barely hearing the next two messages—one from her
dentist's office reminding her of a teeth cleaning on Friday, the other from a friend planning a party.

Adam Culver was dead. She couldn't believe it. Her
mother had said it was a mugger. Nancy wondered. Was
it really random? Or did it have something to do with his
visit on . . . ?

She calculated the days.

Kathy's father had visited on the day he died.

A voice on the machine jarred her back to the present.

"Hello, Nancy. This is Jessica Culver, Kathy's sister.
When you get in, please give me a call. I need to talk to
you as soon as possible. I'm staying with my mom. The
number here is 555-1477. It's kind of important. Thank
you."

Nancy suddenly felt very cold. She listened to the rest
of the messages. Then she sat without moving for several
minutes, debating her options. Kathy was dead—or so
everyone believed. And now her father, hours after talking to Nancy, was dead too.

What did it mean?

She remained very still, the only sound her own
breaths coming in short, hitching gasps. Then she picked
up the phone and dialed Jessica's number.

The dean's office was closed, so Myron proceeded
straight to his house. It was an old Victorian with cedar
shingles on the west end of the campus. He rang the
doorbell. A very attractive woman opened the door. She
smiled solicitously.

"May I help you?"

She wore a tailored cream suit. She was not young,

but she had a grace and beauty and sex appeal that made Myron's mouth a little dry. In front of such a lady Myron wanted to remove his hat, except he wasn't wearing one.

"Good afternoon," he said. "I'm looking for Dean Gordon. My name is Myron Bolitar, and—"

"The basketball player?" she interrupted. "Of course. I should have recognized you right away."

To grace, beauty, and sex appeal, add knowledge of basketball.

"I remember watching you in the NCAAs," she continued. "I cheered you all the way."

"Thank you—"

"When you got hurt—" She stopped, shook the head attached to the Audrey Hepburn neck. "I cried. I felt like a part of me was hurt too."

Grace, beauty, sex appeal, basketball knowledge, and alas, sensitivity. She was also long-legged and curvy. All in all, a nice package.

"That's very kind of you, thank you."

"It's a pleasure to meet you, Myron."

Even his first name sounded good coming from those lips. "And you must be Dean Gordon's wife. The lovely dean-nessa."

She laughed at the Woody Allen rip-off. "Yes, I'm Madelaine Gordon. And no, my husband is not home at the moment."

"Are you expecting him soon?"

She smiled as though the question were a double entendre. Then she gave him a look that flushed his cheeks. "No," she said slowly. "He won't be home for hours."

Heavy accent on the word *hours*.

"Well then, I won't bother you anymore."

"It's no bother."

"I'll come by another time," he said.

Madelaine (he liked that name) nodded demurely. "I'll look forward to it."

"Nice meeting you." With Myron, every line was a lady-slayer.

"Nice meeting you too," she singsonged. "Good-bye, Myron."

The door closed slowly, teasingly. He stood there for another moment, took a few deep breaths, and hurried back to his car. Whew.

He checked his watch. Time to meet Sheriff Jake.

Jake Courter was alone in the station, which looked like something out of Mayberry RFD. Except Jake was black. There were never any blacks in Mayberry. Or Green Acres. Or any of those places. No Jews, Latinos, Asians, ethnics of any kind. Would have been a nice touch. Maybe have a Greek diner or a guy named Abdul working for Sam Drucker at the grocery store.

Myron estimated Jake to be in his mid-fifties. He was in plainclothes, his jacket off, his tie loosened. A big gut spilled forward like something that belonged to someone else. Manila files were scattered across Jake's desk, along with the remnants of what might be a sandwich and an apple core. Jake gave a tired shrug and wiped his nose with what looked like a dishrag.

"Got a call," he said by way of introduction. "I'm supposed to help you out."

"I'd appreciate it," Myron said.

Jake leaned back and put his feet on the desk. "You played ball against my son. Gerard. Michigan State."

"Sure," Myron said, "I remember him. Tough kid. Monster on the boards. Defensive specialist."

Jake nodded proudly. "That's him. Couldn't shoot worth a lick, but you always knew he was there."

"An enforcer," Myron added.

"Yep. He's a cop now. In New York. Made detective second grade already. Good cop."

"Like his old man."

Jake smiled. "Yeah."

"Give him my regards," Myron said. "Better yet, give him an elbow to the rib cage. I still owe him a few."

Jake threw back his head and laughed. "That's Gerard. Finesse was never his forte." He blew his nose into the dishrag. "But I'm sure you didn't come all this way to talk basketball."

"No, I guess not."

"So why don't you tell me what this is all about, Myron?"

"The Kathy Culver case," he said. "I'm looking into it. Very surreptitiously."

"Surreptitiously," Jake repeated with a raised eyebrow. "Awfully big word, Myron."

"I've been listening to self-improvement tapes in the car."

"That right?" Jake blew his nose again. Sounded like a ewe's mating call. "So what's your interest in this—aside from the fact that you represent Christian Steele and you used to have a thing for Kathy's sister."

Myron said, "You're thorough."

He took a bite out of the half-eaten sandwich on his desk, smiled. "Man does love to be flattered."

"It's like you said. Christian Steele. He's a client. I'm trying to help him out."

Jake studied him, waiting again. It was an old trick. Stay silent long enough, and the witness would start talking again, elaborating. Myron did not bite.

After a full minute had passed Jake said, "So let me get this straight. Christian Steele signs on with you. One day you start chatting. He says, 'You know, Myron, the way you been licking my lily-white ass and all, I'd like you to go play Dick Fuckin' Tracy and find my old squeeze who's been missing for the last year and a half and the cops and feds can't find.' That how it went, Myron?''

"Christian doesn't curse," Myron said.

"Okay, fine, you want to skip the dance? Let's skip it. You want me to give, you have to give back.''

"That's fair enough," Myron said. "But I can't. Not yet, anyhow.''

"Why not?''

"It could hurt a lot of people," Myron said. "And it's probably nothing.''

He made a face. "What do you mean, hurt?''

"I can't elaborate.''

"Fuck you can't.''

"I'm telling you, Jake. I can't say anything.''

Jake studied him again. "Let me tell you something, Bolitar. I'm no glory hound. I'm like my son was on the court. Not flashy but a workhorse. I don't look for clippings so I can climb up the ladder. I'm fifty-three years old. My ladder don't go no higher. Now this may seem a bit old-fashioned to you, but I believe in justice. I like to see truth prevail. I've lived with Kathy Culver's disappearance for eighteen months. I know her inside and out. And I have no idea what happened that night.''

"What do you think happened?" Myron asked.

Jake picked up a pencil and tapped it on the desk. "Best guess based on the evidence?''

Myron nodded.

"She's a runaway.''

Myron was surprised. "What makes you say that?''

A slow smile spread across Jake's face. "That's for me to know and you to find out.''

"P.T. said you would help.''

Jake shrugged and took another bite from yet another

sandwich scrap. "What about Kathy's sister? I understand you two were pretty heavy."

"We're friends now."

Jake gave a low whistle. "I've seen her on TV," he
said. "Hard to be friends with a woman who looks like
that."

"You're a real nineties guy, Jake."

"Yeah, well, I forgot to renew my subscription to
Cosmo."

They stared at each other for a while. Jake settled
back in his chair and examined his fingernails. "What
do you want to know?"

"Everything," Myron said. "From the beginning."

Jake folded his arms across his chest. He took a deep
breath and let it loose slowly. "Campus security got a
call from Kathy Culver's roommate, Nancy Serat. Kathy
and Nancy lived in the Psi Omega sorority house. Nice
house. All pretty white girls with blond hair and white
teeth. Kind that all look alike and sound alike. You get
the picture."

Myron nodded. He noticed that Jake was not reading
or even consulting a file. This was coming from memory.

"Nancy Serat told the rent-a-cop that Kathy Culver
hadn't returned to her room for three days."

"Why did Nancy wait so long to call?" Myron asked.

"Seems Kathy wasn't spending too many nights in
the sorority house anyhow. She slept in your client's
room most of the time. You know, the one who doesn't
like to curse." Brief smile. "Anyhow, your boy and
Nancy got to talking one day, both figuring Kathy had
been spending all her time with the other. That's when
they realized she was missing and called campus security.

"Campus security told us about it, but no one got

very excited at first. A co-ed missing for a few days is hardly an earth-shattering event. But then one of the rent-a-cops found the panties on top of a waste bin, and well, you know what happened then. The story spread like a grease stain on Elvis's pillow.''

"I read there was blood on the panties," Myron said.

"A media exaggeration. There was a bloodstain, dry, probably from a menstrual cycle. We typed it. B negative. Same type as Kathy Culver's. But there was also semen. Enough antibodies for a DNA and blood test."

"Did you have any suspects?"

"Only one," Jake said. "Your boy, Christian Steele."

"Why him?"

"Usual reasons. He was the boyfriend. She was on her way to see him when she vanished. Nothing very specific or damaging. But the DNA test on the semen cleared him." He opened a small refrigerator behind him. "Want a Coke?"

"No, thanks."

Jake grabbed a can and snapped it open. "Here's what you probably read in the papers," he continued. "Kathy is at a sorority cocktail party. She has a drink or two, nothing serious, leaves at ten P.M. to meet Christian, and disappears. End of story. But now let me fill it in a little."

Myron leaned forward. Jake took a swig of Coke and wiped his mouth with a forearm the size of an oak trunk.

"According to several of her sorority sisters," he said, "Kathy was distracted. Not herself. We also know she got a phone call a few minutes before she left the house. She told Nancy Serat the call was from Christian and she was going to meet him. Christian denies making the call. These were all intracampus calls, so there is no way for us to tell. But the roommate says Kathy sounded strained on the phone, not like she was talking to her true love, Mr. Clean-Mouth.

"Kathy hung up the phone and went back downstairs with Nancy. Then she posed for the now-famous last photograph before leaving for good."

He opened his desk drawer and handed Myron the photograph. Myron had, of course, seen it countless times before. Every media outlet in the country had run the photograph with morbid fascination. A picture of twelve sorority sisters. Kathy stood second from the left. She wore a blue sweater and skirt. Pearls adorned her neck. Very preppy. According to Kathy's sorority sisters, Kathy left the house alone immediately after the picture was taken. She never returned.

"Okay," Jake said, "so she leaves the cocktail party. Only one person saw her for sure after that."

"Who?" Myron asked.

"Team trainer. Guy named Tony Gardola. He saw her, strangely enough, entering the team's locker room around quarter after ten. The locker room was supposed to be empty at that hour. Only reason Tony was there was that he forgot something. He asked her what she was doing there, and she said she was meeting Christian. Tony figured what the hell, kids today. Might be having a kinky locker-room encounter. Tony decided it was in his best interest not to ask too many questions.

"That's our last *firm* report on her whereabouts. We have a possible sighting of her on the western edge of campus at around eleven P.M. Someone saw a blond woman wearing a blue sweater and skirt. It was too dark to make a positive ID. The witness said he wouldn't have even noticed, except she seemed in a rush. Not running but doing one of those quick-walks."

"Where on the western edge of campus?" Myron asked.

Jake opened a file and took out a map, still studying Myron's face as though it held a clue. He spread the map out and pointed. "Here," he said. "In front of Miliken Hall."

"What's Miliken Hall?" Myron asked.

"Math building. Locked tight by nine o'clock. But the witness said she was moving west."

Myron's eyes traced a path to the west. There were four other buildings labeled FACULTY HOUSING. Myron remembered the spot.

It was where Dean Gordon lived.

"What is it?" Jake asked.

"Nothing."

"Bullshit, Bolitar. You see something."

"It's nothing."

Jake's eyebrows furrowed. "Fine. You want to play it that way? Then get the fuck out. I still got my ace in the hole, and I ain't showing it."

Myron had planned for this. Jake Courter would have to be given something. That was fine, as long as Myron could turn it to his advantage.

"It seems to me," Myron said slowly, "that Kathy was walking in the general direction of the dean's house."

"So?"

Myron said nothing.

"She worked for him," Jake said.

Myron nodded.

"What's the connection?"

"Oh, I'm sure it's completely innocent," Myron said. "But you might want to ask him about it. You being so thorough and all."

"Are you saying—"

"I'm not saying anything. I am merely making an observation."

Again Jake studied him. Myron looked back coolly. A visit from Jake Courter would probably not crack Dean Gordon, but it should soften him a bit. "Now about that ace in the hole . . . ?"

Jake hesitated. "Kathy Culver inherited money from her grandmother," he said.

"Twenty-five grand," Myron added. "All three kids got the same. They're sitting in a trust account."

"Not exactly," Jake said. He stood, hitched his pants up. "You want to know why I said the evidence pointed to Kathy being a runaway?"

Myron nodded.

"The day Kathy Culver vanished, she visited the bank," Jake continued. "She cleared out her inheritance. Every penny."

Chapter 20

Myron started back toward New York. He flipped on the radio. Wham's classic hit "Careless Whisper" was playing. George Michael was bemoaning the fact that he would never dance again because "guilty feet have got no rhythm." Deep, Myron thought. Very deep.

He picked up the car phone and dialed Esperanza.

"What's up?" he asked.

"You coming back to the office?"

"I'm on my way there now."

"I wouldn't make any stops," she said.

"Why?"

"You have a surprise client waiting for you."

"Who?"

"Chaz Landreaux."

"He's supposed to be hiding in Washington."

"Well, he's here. And he looks like shit."

"Tell him to sit tight. I'm on my way."

"It's like this," Chaz began. "I want to cancel our contract."

He paced the office like an expectant father, and he did indeed look like shit. The cocky grin was nowhere to be seen. The swagger was more like a hunch. He kept licking his lips, darting his eyes, bunching and unbunching his fingers.

"Why don't you start at the beginning?" Myron tried.

"Ain't no beginning," Chaz snapped. "I want out. You gonna fight me on it?"

"What happened?"

"Nothing happened. I changed my mind, is all. I want to go with Roy O'Connor at TruPro now. They're big-time. You're a nice guy, Myron, but you don't have their connections."

"Uh-huh."

Silence. More pacing.

"Can I have the contract or what?"

"How did they get to you, Chaz?"

"I don't know what the fuck you're talking about. How many times do I have to say it? I don't want you, okay?" Chaz was on the edge and teetering. "I want TruPro."

"It's not that easy," Myron said.

"You gonna fight me on this?" he asked again.

"They won't stop with this, Chaz. You're in over your head. You have to let me help you."

He stopped. "Help me? You wanna help me? Then give me back my contract. And don't pretend you give a shit about me. You just want your piece."

"Do you really believe that?" Myron asked.

He shook his head. "You don't get it, man. I don't want you. I want to go with TruPro."

"I get it. And like I said before, it's not that easy. These guys got you by the balls. You think you can make them let go by doing what they say. But you can't. Not for good anyway. Whenever they want something, they'll just reach back into your pants and give another squeeze. They won't stop, Chaz. Not until they've squeezed you for everything they can."

"Man, you don't know shit. I don't have to explain nothing to you." He approached the desk, but his eyes looked away. "I want that goddamn contract. I want it now."

Myron picked up his phone. "Esperanza, bring me Chaz's contract. The original." He hung up. "It'll just be a moment."

Chaz said nothing.

"You don't know what you're mixed up in," Myron continued.

"Fuck off, man. I know exactly what I'm mixed up in."

"Let me help, Chaz."

He snorted. "What can you do?"

"I can stop them."

"Oh yeah, I can tell. You done a great job so far."

"What happened?"

But he just shook his head.

Esperanza came in and handed Myron the contract.

Myron in turn handed it to Chaz. He grabbed it and hurried to the door.

"Sorry, Myron. But this is business."

"You can't beat them, Chaz. Not on your own. They'll suck you dry."

"Don't worry about me. I can take care of myself."

"I don't think you can."

"Just stay the fuck out. It ain't your business no more."

He took off without a backward glance. When he was gone, Win opened the door between the conference room and Myron's office. "Interesting conversation," Win said.

Myron nodded, thinking.

"We've lost a client," Win said. "Too bad."

"It's not that simple, Win."

"That's where you're mistaken," Win replied steadily. "It's just that simple. He dumped you for another agency. As he so eloquently put it, 'It ain't your business no more.' "

"Chaz is being pressured."

"And you offered to help him. He refused."

"He's a scared kid."

"He's an adult who makes his own decisions. One of which was to tell you to fuck off."

Myron looked up. "You know what they'll do to him."

"It's a world of free will, Myron. Landreaux chose to take the money in college. And he chose to go back to them now."

"Will you follow him?"

"Pardon?"

"Follow Chaz. See where he takes those contracts."

"You complicate the simple, Myron. Just let it be."

"I can't. You know I can't."

Win nodded. "I guess I do." He thought a moment. "I'll do it for the sake of our business," he said. "For the added revenue. If we get Landreaux back in our stable, it will be very profitable. You may enjoy playing superhero, but as far as I'm concerned, this is no moral crusade. I am doing this for the money. That is the only reason. The money."

Myron nodded. "I wouldn't want it any other way."

"Fine. As long as we are clear on that point. And I want you to take this."

Win handed him a Smith & Wesson .38 and a shoulder holster. Myron put it on. Carrying a gun was incredibly uncomfortable, yet the weight felt good, like a reminder of some kind of protective bubble. Sometimes the sensation made you feel heady, invincible even.

That was usually when you got popped.

"Be extra careful," Win said. "The word has hit the streets."

"What word?"

"A price has officially been put on your head," Win said, as if it were amusing cocktail conversation. "Thirty thousand dollars to the man who takes you out."

Myron made a face. "Thirty thousand? Hell, I used to be a fed. I should be worth sixty, seventy grand minimum."

"Bad economy. Times are tough."

"I'm being discounted?"

"Appears so, yes."

Myron opened the revolver and checked the bullets. Just as he suspected. Win had loaded the gun with dumdums—bullets with cross-hatched tips to expose the lead. Wasn't enough to be using hollow-point Winchester Silvertip bullets. Win had to doctor them for that extra little crunch. "These are illegal."

Win put his hand against his chest. "My. Oh. My. How. Awful."

"And unnecessary."

"If you say so."

"I say so."

"They are effective."

"I don't want them," Myron said.

"Fine." He handed Myron uncut bullets. "Be a wimp."

Chapter 21

Jessica listened to the message on the answering machine.

"Hi, Jessica. It's Nancy Serat. I'm so sorry to hear about your father. He was such a nice man. I can't believe it. He was here the morning he died. So weird. He was so nostalgic that day. He told me all about that favorite yellow sweater he gave Kathy. Such a sweet story. I wish I could have been more helpful. I just can't believe—well, I'm rambling, sorry. I do that when I'm nervous. Anyway I'll be out until ten o'clock tonight. You can come by then or give me a call. Bye."

Jessica rewound the message and played it back. Then a third time. Nancy Serat had seen her father on the morning of his murder.

Another coincidence?

She thought not.

* * *

Myron called his mother. "I won't be home for a few days."

"What?"

"I'm going to stay with Win."

"In the city?"

"Yes."

"New York City?"

"No, Mom. Kuwait City."

"Don't be such a wise guy with your mother, save it for your friends," she said. "So why are you staying in the city?"

Hmm. Should he tell her the truth? *Because, Mom, a mobster has a contract out on my head and I don't want to put you and Dad in danger.* Nah. Might make her worry. "I'm going to be working late the next few nights."

"You sure about this?"

"Yes."

"Be careful, Myron. Don't walk around alone at night."

Esperanza opened the door. "Urgent call on line three," she said, loud enough for Myron's mother to hear.

"Mom, I gotta go. Urgent call."

"Call us."

"I will." He hung up and looked up at Esperanza. "Thanks."

"Don't mention it."

"Is there anyone on the phone?"

She nodded. "Timmy Simpson again. I tried to handle it, but he says his problem needs your particular expertise."

Timmy Simpson was a rookie shortstop for the Red Sox. A major-league pain in the ass.

"Hi, Timmy."

"Hey, Myron, I've been waiting here two goddamn hours for your call."

"I was out. What's the problem?"

"I'm here in Toronto, okay, at the Hilton. And this hotel's got no hot water."

Myron waited. Then he said, "Did I hear you correctly, Timmy? Did you say—"

"Unfuckinbelievable, ain't it?" Timmy shouted. "I go in the shower, right, wait five minutes, then ten minutes. The water's fucking freezing, Myron. Ice cold. So finally I call down to the front desk, right? Some pissant manager tells me they're having some kind of plumbing problem. Plumbing problem, Myron, like I'm staying in a fuckin' trailer park or something. So I say, when's it going to be fixed? He gives me this whole long spiel how he don't know. Can you believe this shit?"

No, Myron thought. "Timmy, why exactly are you calling me?"

"Jesus Christ, Myron, I'm a pro, right? And I'm stuck in this hellhole with no hot water. I mean, isn't there something in my contract about that?"

"A hot water clause, perhaps?" Myron tried.

"Or something. I mean, come on. Where do they get off? I need a shower before a game. A *hot* shower. Is that too much to expect? I mean, what am I going to do?"

Stick your head in the toilet and flush, Myron thought, massaging his temples with his fingertips. "I'll see what I can do, Timmy."

"Talk to the hotel manager, Myron. Make him understand the importance."

"As far as I'm concerned," Myron said, "those orphans in Eastern Europe are a minor annoyance in comparison to this. But if the hot water doesn't come back

on soon, check into another hotel. We'll send the bill to
the Red Sox.''

"Good idea. Thanks, Myron.''

Click.

Myron stared at the phone. Unbelievable. He leaned
back and wondered how to handle his three big problems: Chaz Landreaux's sudden departure, Kathy Culver's possible re-emergence, and the Toronto Hilton's
plumbing. He decided to forgo the last. Only so much
one man can do.

Problem 1: Chaz Landreaux was climbing into bed
with Frank Ache. There was only one way out of that.
Big brother Herman.

Myron picked up the phone and dialed. He still knew
the number by heart. It was picked up on the first ring.
"Clancy's Tavern.''

"It's Myron Bolitar. I'd like to see Herman.''

"Hold on.'' Five minutes passed before the voice
came back on. "Tomorrow. Two o'clock.''

Click. No need to wait for an answer. Whatever time
Herman Ache agreed to see you, you were free.

Problem 2: Kathy Culver. *Nips* magazine had been
mailed from a campus box. It had been mailed not only
to Christian Steele but also to Dean Harrison Gordon.
Why? Myron knew that Kathy had worked for the dean.
Was there more to her job than just filing? An affair,
perhaps? And what about the dean's lovely wife? Did
she wear underwear?

But Myron was digressing.

The catalyst of this whole thing was the ad in *Nips*.
Gary Grady claimed he had nothing to do with it.
Maybe. Maybe not. But either way the picture had to go
through Fred Nickler. Good ol' Freddy was at the center
of this.

Myron looked up the number and dialed.

"HDP. May I help you?"

"I'd like to speak to Fred Nickler."

"Whom shall I say is calling?"

"Myron Bolitar."

"Please hold."

A minute passed. Then Fred Nickler came on. "Hello?"

"Mr. Nickler, this is Myron Bolitar."

"Yes, Myron. What can I do for you?"

"I'd like to come by and ask you a few more questions about the ad."

"I'm afraid I'm quite busy right now, Myron. Why don't you give me a call tomorrow? Maybe we can set something up."

Silence.

"Myron? You there?"

"Do you know who took that picture, Mr. Nickler?"

"Of course not."

"Your friend Jerry denies any knowledge of it."

"Myron, please. You're a man of the world. What did you expect him to say?"

"He says he had nothing to do with putting that picture in the ad."

"Well, that's quite impossible. He was the advertiser. He submitted the photograph."

"Then you have a copy of the photo?"

Pause. "It has to be in the file somewhere."

"Maybe you can pull it out, and I'll come pick it up."

"Listen, Myron, I hate to be rude, but I'm really busy right now. It will just be the same photograph you already saw."

"Kathy's picture was only in *Nips,*" Myron said.

"Pardon me?"

"Her picture. It wasn't in any of your other magazines. Only *Nips.*"

Pause. "So?" But his voice was suddenly tottery.

"So the same ad was in all six magazines. The same exact page with the same exact pictures. Except for one small change in *Nips*. Someone had changed just one photograph in the bottom row. Someone had switched pictures for just that one magazine and not the others. Why?"

Fred Nickler coughed. "I really don't know, Myron. Tell you what: I'll check on it and let you know. Gotta zillion calls waiting. Gotta run. Bye."

Another click.

Myron sat back. Fred Nickler was starting to panic.

With a shaking hand Fred Nickler dialed the number. After three rings the phone was picked up.

"County police."

Fred cleared his throat. "Paul Duncan, please."

Chapter 22

Nine P.M.

Myron called Jessica. He filled her in on his dean discovery.

"Do you really think Kathy was having an affair with the dean?" Jessica asked.

"I don't know. But after seeing his wife, I'd tend to doubt it."

"Good-looking?"

"Very," Myron said. "And she knows her basketball. She even cried when I got hurt."

Jessica made a noise. "The perfect woman."

"Do I detect a note of jealousy?"

"Dream on," Jessica said. "The fact that a man is married to a beautiful woman does not preclude him from having affairs with pretty co-eds."

"True enough. So the question is: How did Dean Gordon get his name on this infamous mailing list?"

"I haven't got a clue," she said. "But I too found out something interesting today. My father visited Nancy Serat, Kathy's roommate, the morning he died."

"Why?"

"I don't know yet. Nancy just left a message on my machine. I'm meeting her in an hour."

"Good. Call me if you hear anything else."

"Where are you going to be?" she asked.

"I work nights at Chippendale's," Myron said. "Stage name Zorro."

"Should be Tiny."

"Ouch."

An uncomfortable silence engulfed them. Jessica finally broke it. "Why don't you come by the house tonight?" she asked, struggling to keep her tone level.

Myron's heart pounded. "It'll be late."

"That's okay. I'm not sleeping much. Just knock on my bedroom window. Zorro."

She hung up. For the next five minutes Myron sat perfectly still and thought about Jessica. They had first started dating a month before his career ended. She stayed with him. She nursed him. She loved him. He pushed her away under some macho disguise of protecting her. But she wouldn't leave. Not then, anyway.

Esperanza opened the door without knocking. She looked at him and snapped, "Stop it."

"What?"

"You're making that face again."

"What face?"

She imitated him. "That repulsive lovesick-puppy face."

"I wasn't making any face."

"Right. You disgust me, Myron."

"Thank you."

"You know what I think? I think you're more interested in getting back in Jessica's pants than you are in finding her sister."

"Jesus, what the hell is with you?"

"I was there, remember? When she left."

"Hey, I'm a big boy. I can take care of myself."

Esperanza shook her head. "Déjà vu all over again."

"What?"

"Take care of yourself. Bullshit. You sound just like Chaz Landreaux. Both of you have your head up your ass."

Esperanza's dark face reminded him of Spanish nights, golden sand, full moons against starless skies. There had been moments of temptation between them, but one or the other had always realized what it would mean and stopped it. Such temptations no longer came their way anymore. Aside from Win, Esperanza was his closest friend. Her concern, Myron knew, was genuine.

He changed subjects. "Was there a reason for your unannounced entrance?"

"I found something."

"What?"

She read from a steno pad. Why she had a steno pad he could not say. She could not take dictation or type a lick. "I finally tracked down the other number Gary Grady called after your visit. It belongs to a photography studio called—get this—Global Globes Photos. Located off Tenth Avenue, near the tunnel.''

"Sleazy area.''

"The sleaziest," she said. "I think the studio specializes in pornography.''

"Nice to have a specialty." Myron checked his watch. "Any word from Win?''

"Not yet.''

"Leave the photographer's address on his voice mail. Maybe he'll finish in time to meet me.''

"You going tonight?" she asked.

"Yes.''

Esperanza closed the pad with a snap. "Mind if I tag along?''

"To the photography studio?''

"Yes.''

"Don't you have class tonight?" Esperanza was getting her law degree from NYU at night.

"No. And I've done all my homework, Daddy. Really I have.''

"Shut up and come on.''

Chapter 23

Hookerville.

There were all kinds. White, Black, Asian, Latino—a verifiable United Nations of prostitutes. Most were young, very young, stumbling on too-high heels, like children playing dress-up, which in a real sense they were. Most were thin, dried-up, needle tracks covering their arms like dozens of tiny insects, their skin pulled tightly around cheekbones, giving their faces a haunted skull look. Their eyes were hollow and set deep, their hair lifeless and strawlike.

Myron muttered, " 'Don't they know they're making love to what's already dead?' "

Esperanza paused, thinking. "Don't know that one."

"Fontine in *Les Misérables*. The musical."

"I can't afford Broadway musicals. My boss is cheap."

"But cute."

He watched a blond girl in sixties hot-pants negotiate with a sleazeball in a Ford station wagon. He knew her story. He had seen girls (boys sometimes) just like her get off the bus at the Port Authority, a Greyhound bus that had originated in West Virginia or western Pennsylvania or that great, barren mono-expanse New Yorkers simply referred to as the Midwest. She had run away from home—maybe to avoid abuse, but more likely because she was bored and "belonged" in a big city. She had high-stepped off the bus with a wide smile, mesmerized, without a penny. Pimps would eye her and wait with the patience of a vulture. When the time was right, they would sweep down and claim their carcass. They'd introduce her to the Big Apple, get her a place to stay, some food, a hot shower, maybe a room with a Jacuzzi and dazzling lights and a cool CD player and cable TV with a remote. They'd promise to set her up with a photographer, get her a few modeling gigs. Then they'd teach her how to party, *really* party, not that candy-ass shit she'd done in Hicks Falls with some beer and a zit-infested senior pawing at her in the backseat of a pickup.

They'd show her how to have a good time with the prime stuff, the numero-uno white powder.

But things would change. Someone would have to pay for all these good times. The modeling job would fall through, and she couldn't just be a freeloader. Besides, the partying was more a need now than a luxury. Like food or breathing. She could no longer exist without a snort or a pinch from her favorite needle.

It didn't take long to plummet and hit bottom. And once there she didn't have the strength—not even the desire, really—to get up.

She ended up here.

Myron parked. He and Esperanza got out of the car silently. Myron felt his stomach churn. It was night, of course. Places like this existed only at night. They fled with the onslaught of sunlight.

Myron had never been with a whore, but he knew Win had engaged their services on plenty of occasions. Win liked the convenience. His favorite spot was an Asian whorehouse on Eighth Street called Noble House. Back in the mid-eighties, Win and a few friends would have what they called "Chinese night" in Win's apartment—Hunan Garden would deliver food, Noble House women. The truth was, Win had no feelings for women. He didn't trust them. Whores were what he wanted. It wasn't just the lack of attachment. Win never let women attach. But prostitutes were throwaways. Disposable.

Myron didn't think Win still partook in such events—not in this disease-ridden era—but he didn't know for sure. They never talked about it.

"Pretty spot," Myron said. "Scenic."

Esperanza nodded.

They passed a nightclub of some sort. The music was loud enough to crack the sidewalk. A teen—Myron couldn't say if it was male or female—with green spiked

hair bumped into him. Looked like the Statue of Liberty.
There were lots of motorcycles, ear and nipple rings,
tattoos, chain jewelry. A constant whore chorus of
''Hey, baby'' pelted him from every conceivable angle,
their faces blurring into one mass of human debris. The
place was like a carnival freak show.

The sign above the door read CLUB F.U. The logo was a
raised middle finger. Subtle. A chalkboard read the following:

HEAVY ''MEDICAL'' NIGHT!
LIVE BANDS!
Featuring the only local appearances by:
PAP SMEAR
and RECTAL THERMOMETER

Myron could see through the open door. People
weren't dancing. They were jumping up and down, heads
lolling lifelessly as if their necks were rubber bands,
their arms tucked against their sides. Myron focused in
on one kid, maybe fifteen years old, lost in the violet
bliss, sweat matting his long hair to his face. He wondered if the group onstage was Pap Smear or Rectal
Thermometer. Didn't matter. Sounded like someone had
jammed a rutting pig into a Cuisinart.

The whole scene was like Dickens meets *Blade Run-
ner.*

''The studio is next door,'' Esperanza said.

The building was either a disastrous brownstone or a
small warehouse. Whores hung out the windows like
shreds of leftover Christmas decorations.

''This is it?'' Myron asked.

''Third floor,'' Esperanza answered. She did not seem
intimidated by the surroundings in the least, but she had
come from streets not much better than this. Her face

remained a placid pool. Esperanza never showed weakness. Her temper flared often, but for all their times together, Myron had never seen her cry. She could not say the same of him.

Myron approached the stoop. An overweight whore stuffed into a bodysuit that doubled as sausage casing licked her lips and stepped in front of him.

"Hey, yo, want a blow job? Fifty bucks."

Myron tried not to close his eyes. "No," he said softly, lowering his head. He wanted to offer words of wisdom, words that could transform her, change her circumstances. But he just said, "I'm sorry," and hurried past. The fat girl shrugged and moved on.

It was a walk-up. No surprise there. The stairwells were littered with people, most unconscious or maybe dead. Myron and Esperanza carefully climbed over them. A cacophony of music—everything from Neil Diamond to what might have been Pap Smear bellowed through the corridor. There were other sounds too. Broken bottles, shouts, curses, crashing, a baby crying. An orchestra from hell.

When they reached the third floor, they saw a glassed-in office. No one was inside, but the pictures on the wall —not to mention the bullwhip and handcuffs—left little doubt that they had arrived at the right place. Myron tried the knob. It turned.

"You stay out here," he said.

"Okay."

He moved in. "Hello?"

No one answered him, but music was coming from the other room. Sounded like calypso music. He called out again and stepped into the studio.

Myron was struck by how professional the setup was. It was clean, brightly lit, with one of those big white umbrella things you always see in photo studios. There were half a dozen cameras set up on tripods, and over-head was a variety of different-colored lights.

Of course, the setting was not the first thing that struck him. Other things caught his eye first. The naked woman sitting on a motorbike, for example. To be accurate, she wasn't fully naked—she had on a pair of black boots. Nothing else. Not a look every woman could pull off, but it seemed to work for her. She had not seen him yet, intensely studying the magazine in her hand. *The National Sun.* Headline: Boy 16 Becomes Grandmother. Hmm. He stepped closer. She was big-breasted, very Russ Meyer, but Myron could see scars under the large swellings. Implants, the fashion accessory of the eighties.

She looked up, startled.

Myron smiled warmly. "Hi."

She screamed. Piercingly. "Get the fuck out of here!" she shrieked, covering her chest. Modesty. So rare nowadays. It was nice to see.

Myron said, "My name—"

Another piercing scream. Myron heard a noise behind him and spun. A skinny kid wearing no shirt stood smiling. He popped open a switchblade, a maniacal grin plastered across his face. His Bruce Lee–like build shimmered in the light. He crouched low and beckoned Myron forward. Very *West Side Story*. If only the kid would snap his fingers.

Another door opened, and red light leaked out. A woman stepped into view. She had what looked like curly red hair, but Myron couldn't be sure if that was her color or if it just appeared red because of the light from the darkroom.

"You're trespassing," she said to Myron. "Hector has the right to kill you where you stand."

"I don't know where you got your law degree," Myron said, "but if Hector isn't careful, I'm going to take away his toy and shove it where the sun don't shine."

Hector giggled. He began to toss the knife back and forth between his hands.

"Wow," Myron said.

The topless model fled to the dressing room, which was cleverly marked UNDRESSING ROOM. The woman from the darkroom stepped fully into the studio and closed the darkroom door. Her hair was indeed red, more like burnt auburn actually. Her skin was what some might call peaches and cream. She was maybe thirty and looked, strange as it might sound, perky. The Katie Couric of the porno world.

"Are you the owner?" Myron asked.

"Hector is very good with a blade," she replied coolly. "He could slice out a man's heart and show it to him before he died."

"That must liven a party."

Hector stepped closer. Myron did not move.

"I could demonstrate my skills in the martial arts," Myron began. He quickly withdrew his gun and aimed it at Hector's chest. "But I just showered."

Hector's eyes widened in surprise.

"Let this be a lesson to you, Blade Boy," Myron continued. "Half the people in this building probably carry guns. You go around waving that toy, and someone without my tender heart will ace you."

The redhead did not seem taken aback by the gun. "Get out of here," she said to Myron. "Now."

"Are you the owner?" Myron tried again.

"You got a warrant?"

"I'm not a cop."

"Then get your ass out of here." She undulated a lot when she talked. Her hips and legs in constant motion.

She signaled to Hector, who closed up the switchblade. "You can go, Hector."

"Not so fast, Hector," Myron said. "Get in the dark-room. I don't want you getting any ideas about coming back with a gun."

Hector looked toward the redhead. She nodded, and he went.

"Close the door," Myron said.

He closed it. Myron walked over and pulled the dead bolt.

The redhead put her hands on her hips. "Happy now?"

"Nearly ecstatic."

"Now get out."

"Listen," Myron said with his melt-'em, warm smile, "I don't want any trouble. I'm just here to buy some photographs. My name is Bernie Worley. I work for a new porno magazine."

She made a face. "Do I really look that stupid? Bernie Worley, here to buy some photographs. Give me a fuckin' break."

There was a sudden noise. People. Lots of them. A commotion, even by this place's standard. In the corridor. Right where he had left Esperanza. Alone.

Myron turned and ran, feeling his heart leap to his throat. If something had happened to her—

He threw open the door. Dozens of people surrounded Esperanza, most kneeling. She stood in the middle, smiling and—he couldn't believe it—signing autographs.

"It's Pocahontas!" someone shouted.

"Make mine out 'With love to Manuel.' "

"You're still my favorite!"

"I remember when you beat Queen Carimba. What a fight!"

"That Highway Hannah. Such a dirty fighter. When she threw salt in your eyes, I could have killed her."

Esperanza caught Myron's eye, shrugged, went back to signing old matchbooks and scraps of paper. The red-head followed him out the door. When she saw Esperanza, her entire being lit up. "Poca?"

Esperanza looked back up. "Lucy?"

They hugged. They stepped back into the studio, Myron following.

"Where you been, girl?" Lucy asked.

"Here, there."

The two women kissed. On the lips. A little too long. Esperanza turned around. "Myron?"

"Huh?"

"Your eyes are bulging."

"They are?"

"I don't tell you everything."

"Apparently not," he said. "But at least I know why my startling good looks didn't faze your friend."

Both women found that laughable. "Lucy, this is Myron Bolitar."

Lucy looked him up and down. "He your boy-friend?"

"No. Just a good friend. And my boss."

"He looks like a guy I know, worked a kinky show at a club down the street. He had this act where he peed on different women."

"It wasn't me," Myron assured her. "I have enough trouble peeing in a public urinal."

Lucy turned her attention to Esperanza. "You look good, Poca."

"Thanks."

"Out of the wrestling game, huh?"

"Completely."

"But you're still working out?"

"As often as I can."

"Nautilus?"

"Um-hmm."

"It shows," Lucy said with a wicked smile. "You really look hot."

Myron cleared his throat. "Hey, how about those Knicks?"

The women ignored him. "You still taking pictures of the wrestlers?" Esperanza asked.

"Not much anymore. I'm mostly into this shit."

Esperanza looked back at Myron. "Lucy—that isn't her real name, we just call her that because of her hair—she used to do the promo photos of all the wrestlers."

"So I gathered," Myron said. "Do you think she can help us out?"

"What do you want to know?" Lucy asked.

Myron handed her the copy of *Nips*. He pointed to Kathy's picture. "I want to know about this," he said.

Lucy studied the photograph for a second. "He a cop?" she asked Esperanza.

"A sports agent."

"Oh." She did not ask for further elaboration. "Because this could get us in trouble."

"How so?" Myron asked.

"The photograph. The girl is topless."

"So?"

"So it's illegal. Topless girls aren't allowed in 900 ads. We're going to get screwed if the government sees this."

"We?" Myron repeated. Again the clever interrogation techniques.

"I'm one of the owners of these dial-a-porn companies. A lot of the lines work out of this building."

"I'm not sure I understand," Myron said. "What do

you mean, topless girls are illegal? Almost every girl in
that magazine is naked.''

"Not in the ads for 900 lines," Lucy corrected.
"Couple years back a law was passed. Nine hundred
lines had to go clean. Look here." She turned a page and
pointed at another ad. "The girl might look suggestive,
but she can't be naked. And look at the name of the
lines. Stuff like 'Secret Confessions' or 'Talk to Girls.'
Now look at the ones for the 800 lines. Hard core. 'Cum
Between My Tits,' stuff like that."

Myron remembered his conversation with Tawny on
the 900 line. He had been struck by the fact that she said
nothing dirty. "So you can only have phone sex on the
other lines?"

"Right. You see, you need real permission for those.
That's how the government sees it. Any asshole can call
a 900 line. The charges are automatic. They start almost
immediately after your call is answered. But not with an
800 line or one of the other numbers. You have to use
either your credit card or a callback. That's the way you
get billed."

"So all that talk about 900 lines being dirty—"

"Is bullshit," Lucy finished. "They're cons. We can't
say one dirty thing on those lines. We use them as lures
mostly, because they're so easy to use. A guy just has to
dial. No credit card. No callbacks. Most of the time we
talk about skinny-dipping or massages—suggestive but
not sexual. Get him excited, you know what I mean?"

"I think so, yes."

"These guys call horny anyway. I mean, most are so
hard up, they'll stick it in a knothole to get relief. What
we try to do is get him to say the first dirty word, which
usually isn't too difficult. Once he does, we say, 'Oh,
baby, I can't talk dirty on this line, but you should call

me back at X number with a credit card.' The guys calls it and gets charged all over again.''

"Aren't they afraid of how it'll look on their credit card bill?'' Myron asked.

Lucy shook her head. She was still undulating. It was a combination of irritating and erotic. "The company names are usually pretty discreet,'' she explained. "We bill under names like Norwood Incorporate or Telemark —not Hot Lesbos or Sucking Starlet. You want to see it?''

"See what?''

"The operation upstairs. Where we answer some of the calls. Lots of people work out of their homes, but I got a crew of six or seven working the lines now.''

Myron shrugged. "Yeah, sure.''

Lucy took them up one level. Some sort of sickening stench engulfed the stairwell. When they reached the landing, Lucy opened a door. They stepped through and quickly closed it behind them.

"This is Fantasies Forever Lines,'' Lucy said. "Not to mention Dick-a-Lick, Hootersline, Telefun, and a dozen others.''

Myron could not believe what he was seeing. His mouth dropped open. He had expected ugly women or fat women or old women. But he had not expected this.

They were men. All but one of the workers were male.

"Gay lines?'' Myron asked.

Lucy shook her head, smiling. "Very few gay calls come in. Maybe one in a hundred.''

"But . . . these are men.''

Myron Bolitar, the essence of keen observation.

He heard a man in a gruff, truck-driver voice say, "Yeah, big man, slide it all the way in. That's it. Oh, yeah, that feels good.''

Lucy smiled at the man. The man rolled his eyes and continued, "Don't stop, Stallion. Ride me."

Esperanza, Myron was glad to see, looked equally confused. "What's going on, Lucy?" she asked.

"It's the times," Lucy said. "In this economy men are a cheaper source of labor. Most of the girls are on the streets. These are brothers, cousins, street kids."

"But their voices—"

"They use a voice changer. Sharper Image sells them, but I get them cheaper in the Village. You can make little girls sound like Barry White, or vice versa. These guys can become a husky woman, a teenage virgin, a little girl — whatever the line calls for."

Myron was stunned. "Do the customers know this?"

"Of course not." She turned to Esperanza. "Dumb. But he is kinda cute."

Myron Bolitar, Lesbian Fantasy Man.

The room looked like any telemarketing office. The phones were high-tech. Dozens of lines lit up, each marked for what role was to be played. Horny Housewife. Dominatrix. Cross-dressers. Busty Babes. Even Foot Fetish. Each employee also had another phone for Visa and MasterCard verification.

"The lines with a C next to them got to be kept clean," Lucy explained. "We also have another hundred or so people working phones from their homes. Most of those are women."

"Horny housewives?"

"Some of them. Most are just plain housewives. Anyway, that's why I found the ad strange. A 900 line shouldn't have a topless girl."

They left the room and walked back down to the studio. Myron almost tripped over a wino who chose the moment Myron was stepping over him to stand up.

"Is ABC one of the companies upstairs?" Myron asked.

"Yeah."

"And we know Gary Grady called you yesterday. Can you tell us why?"

"Who?"

"Gary Grady."

Lucy shook her head. "Don't know him."

"How about Jerry?"

"Oh yeah, him." She gave a small laugh. "I figured that wasn't his real name. He was always real secretive."

"So what did he want?"

She nodded as though something had just occurred to her. "I get it now."

"Get what?"

"He was asking me about a photograph I'd taken a couple years back."

"This one?" Myron asked, pointing to Kathy's picture again.

"Yeah. One of his girls."

Myron and Esperanza exchanged a glance. "You mean there were others?"

"Few. Half dozen, maybe more."

Myron felt the rage consume again. "Underage girls?"

"How the fuck am I supposed to know?"

"You didn't ask?" Myron asked.

"Do I look like a cop? Look, man, if you're here to hassle me—"

"He's not," Esperanza said. "You can trust him."

"The fuck I can, Poca. He comes busting in here with a fucking gun, scares the piss out of my model."

"We need your help," Esperanza said. "*I* need your help."

"I don't want to hurt you, Lucy," Myron said. "I'm just interested in the girl in the picture."

Lucy hesitated. "All right," she said at last. "But back off."

Myron gave a quick nod of agreement. "Jerry brought this girl to you?"

"Yeah, when I had my other studio a couple blocks away. Like I said, he brought in a few girls over the years. He wanted their photos for all kinds of stuff. Porno mags, smut film stills, that kind of thing. Most were a cut or two above the average hosebag who comes through the door. But he usually keeps the photos under wraps until they're a little older. Legal age, I guess."

The rage again. Myron's hands tightened into fists. "So Jerry asked you about this picture yesterday?"

"Yeah."

"What did he want to know?"

"If I sold any copies recently."

"Have you?"

Pause. "Yeah. Couple months ago."

"Who bought them?"

"You think I keep records?"

"A he or a she?"

"A he."

"Do you remember what he looks like?"

She took out a cigarette, lit it, took a deep puff. "I'm not real good with faces."

"Anything, Lucy," Esperanza added. "Young, old, anything you can remember."

Another puff. Then: "Old. Not ancient, but not a young guy. Might have been my father's age. And he knew what he was doing." She looked at Myron. "Not like you. Bernie Worley. Jesus."

Myron pressed on. "What do you mean, he knew what he was doing?"

"The man paid me top dollar under one condition: I hand over every photo and negative in front of him right now. Smart. He wanted to make sure I didn't have time to make any extra copies or an extra set of negatives."

"How much did he pay you?"

"Sixty-five hundred altogether. In cash. Five grand for the photos and negatives. Plus another grand for Jerry's phone number. Said he wanted to get in touch with the girl personally. Then he gave me another five hundred if I didn't say anything to Jerry."

In the background there was yet another blood-curdling scream. It went ignored. "Would you know the man if you saw him again?" Myron asked.

"I don't know," she said. "I can't picture him now, but if we met up face to face . . . who knows?" There was a pounding noise from the darkroom. "Mind if I let Hector out now?"

"We were just leaving," Myron said. He handed her a card. "If you remember anything else—"

"Yeah, I'll call." She looked over to Esperanza. "Don't be a stranger, Poca."

Esperanza nodded but said nothing. They were quiet the entire way down. When they stepped into the hot air, surrounded by the night street, she said, "Didn't mean to shock you in there."

"Not my business," he said. "I was a little surprised, that's all."

"Lucy is a lesbian. I experimented with it a little. Long time ago."

"You don't have to explain," he said. But he was glad she told him. Myron had no secrets from Esperanza. He didn't like thinking she had some from him.

They were about to head back to the car when Myron felt the muzzle of a gun against his ribs.

A voice said, "Stay cool, Myron."

It was the man with the fedora hat from the garage. He reached into Myron's jacket and took out the .38. A second man, this one with a Gene Shalit–like mustache, grabbed Esperanza and pressed his gun against her temple.

"If Myron moves," Fedora said to the other man, "blow the bitch's brains all over the sidewalk."

The man nodded, half-smiling.

"Come on," Fedora said, nudging Myron forward with the gun. "Let's take a little walk."

Chapter 24

Jessica parked in front of the house Nancy Serat was renting for the semester. It was more a cottage really, located at the end of a dark street about a mile from the campus of Reston University. Even at night Jessica could see the house's salmon-pink hue, which seemed to clash with the planet earth. The landscape looked like the trees had vomited—the front yard of *The Munsters*. A faded 118 ACRE STREET was stenciled on the weatherbeaten sign. A blue Honda Accord with a Reston University bumper sticker sat in the driveway.

Jessica headed down the broken remnants of what must have once been a cement path. She rang the bell and immediately heard a scurrying sound. Several seconds passed. No one approached the door. She tried again. No scurrying sound this time. No sound at all.

"Nancy?" she called out. "It's Jessica Culver."

She hit the bell a few more times, though in a house this small there was not much chance she hadn't been heard. Unless Nancy was in the shower. A possibility. The lights, she could see through the window shades, were on. The car was in the driveway. Jessica had heard movement.

Nancy had to be home.

Jessica reached out for the knob. Under normal conditions some filter in her mind would probably have stopped her from simply trying to open the door of a virtual stranger (she had only met Nancy once). But these conditions were hardly normal. She took hold of the knob and turned.

Locked.

Now what?

She stood at the door five more minutes ringing the bell. Still nothing. Jessica circled the house, using a distant streetlight and the house's glow-in-the-dark properties to guide her. She stumbled over a tricycle that looked like something recovered from an archaeological dig. Her feet got tangled in the high grass, the prickly ends tickling her calves. As she circled, Jessica peeked through the small openings in the window shades. She could make out rooms and spotted an occasional piece of furniture or wall hanging, but no people.

In the backyard she saw the shades were not pulled down in the kitchen. The lights were off too. It was pitch black here, the pink not getting the illumination of the streetlight to cast its glow. She peered through the kitchen window, cupping her hands around her face to cut off the reflection. A sliver of light from the front room slashed across the room. On the table sat a purse. And a set of keys.

Someone was home.

A sound behind her made her jump. Jessica spun, but it was too dark to make out what it was. Her heart beat wildly in her chest. Crickets singsonged unceasingly. She pounded on the door with both fists.

"Nancy! Nancy!"

She heard the panic in her voice and scolded herself for it. *Get a grip. You're spooking yourself.*

She stopped, took a few deep breaths, felt herself relax. She took another look through the window, pressing her face right up against the glass. She was watching the sliver of light when it happened.

Someone walked by.

Jessica jumped back. She hadn't seen the person, hadn't seen anything, except the sliver of light disappear for the briefest of seconds. She looked again. Nothing. But someone had gone past and blocked off the light. She put her hand on the kitchen doorknob.

This time the door was not locked. The knob turned easily.

Don't just go in, dodo! Call the cops!

And say what? I knocked on a door and no one answered? That I then started peeking through windows and saw someone moving around?

That doesn't sound so bad.

Sounds bad enough to me. Besides, I'd have to find a phone. By the time I do that, whatever is going on may be over. I may have lost my one opportunity. . . .

Opportunity for what?

She pushed the voice away. Then she opened the door. She waited for the door to squeak madly, but it slid open with remarkable silence. She stepped into the kitchen and left the door open. Better for the quick getaway.

"Nancy?

"*Kathy?*"

She clasped her hand over her mouth. She hadn't meant that. Kathy wasn't here. Jessica wished like hell she were, but that would be too easy. Kathy wasn't here. And if she were, she certainly would not be afraid to open the door for her sister. Her baby sister. The sister with the bright smile. The sister whom she loved. . . .

The sister you let slip away. The sister you impatiently rushed off the line the night she vanished.

For several minutes Jessica just stayed in the kitchen. There were no sounds, except those maddening crickets. No running water. No shower. No scurrying. No footsteps. She opened the purse and extracted the wallet. Driver's license and assorted credit cards—all in the name of Nancy Serat. She flipped to the back and stopped suddenly at a wallet-size photograph.

The picture. The sorority sisters picture. The last picture of Kathy.

She dropped the wallet as though it were something scaly and alive. Enough, Jessica said to herself. She moved toward the light. One foot slid out, the other followed. In a matter of seconds Jessica was at the door. It was open a crack, allowing the light to cast its sliver now unimpeded. She pushed through, crouching like a cop with a gun, preparing for the worst.

And the worst was what she got.

Jessica stumbled back. "Jesus Christ—"

Nancy lay flat on her back, her hands at her sides. Her eyes stuck out like two golf balls, staring at Jessica. Her face was a deep purplish-blue, like a giant bruise. Her mouth was wide and twisted in pure agony. The tongue lolled out like a dead fish. Nancy Serat's entire expression was still frozen in a look that begged and screamed with its every cell for oxygen. A thin line of still-wet saliva clung to her chin.

A cord of some kind—no, a wire—was wrapped

around Nancy's neck, barely visible. Most of it had sliced clean through the skin and was embedded deep in the flesh. A circling lash of blood marked the spot where the wire had entered.

Jessica stared, lost. The world vanished for several moments, leaving behind only the horror. She forgot about the scurrying when she first rang the bell. She forgot the shadow that had cut off the sliver of light.

Jessica did not hear the approaching footsteps. Still staring at Nancy's face, unable to tear her eyes away, she felt a sudden, sharp pain in her head. She saw white flashes. Her body folded at the waist and pitched forward. A tingling numbness followed.

Then nothing.

Chapter 25

Fedora Hat knew what he was doing.

"Stay a few steps behind me," he barked at his new partner.

In the garage Fedora and Musclehead (who, Myron was happy to see, seemed to be out of commission) had underestimated Myron. Fedora would not make the same mistake twice. Not only had he always kept eyes and gun on Myron but he was making sure that his new partner (the Mustache) kept both himself and Esperanza a safe distance away.

Smart.

Myron had been tempted to make a move, but even
his best move was useless in this circumstance. If he
managed to get the gun away from Fedora, there was no
way he'd be able to turn it on the Mustache before he'd
shoot either him or Esperanza.

He would have to wait and watch. He knew what Fedora and Mustache intended to do. They hadn't been
hired to buy him ice cream or teach line dancing or even
beat him up. Not this time.

"Let her go," Myron said. "She has nothing to do
with this."

"Keep moving," Fedora replied.

"You don't need her."

"Move."

Mustache spoke for the first time. "I might want a
little company later," he sneered. Then he stopped and
pressed the gun against Esperanza's right cheek while he
licked—actually licked—her left cheek with a wet cow-
like tongue. Esperanza stiffened. Mustache looked at
Myron. "You got a problem with that, pal?"

Myron knew words would be either superfluous or
harmful at this stage. He kept his mouth shut.

They turned a corner. The stench of garbage was
overwhelming. It was piled at least six feet high on both
sides of the narrow alley. Fedora quickly scanned the
area. It appeared to be abandoned.

"Go," he said, giving Myron another poke with the
gun. "End of the alley."

Myron felt as if he were walking a plank. He tried to
take it as slowly as possible.

"What are we going to do with the piece of ass?"
Mustache asked.

Fedora's eyes never left Myron. "She's seen us," he
said. "She's a witness."

"But we weren't hired to ace her," Mustache whined.

"So?"

"So let's not just waste a piece like this"—he smiled—"especially when we can fuck it first."

Mustache laughed at his suggestion. Fedora did not. He stepped back, aiming the gun at Myron's back. Myron turned to face him. They were separated by about six feet. Myron was against the back wall. There was no avenue of escape. The nearest window was at least twelve feet off the ground. No room to move at all.

Fedora raised the gun so that it stared Myron right in the face. Myron did not blink. He looked into Fedora's eyes.

And then they were gone. Fedora's eyes were gone. Along with half his head.

The bullet had ripped off the skull at the midway point, splitting Fedora's head open like a coconut. He slid to the ground, the fedora floating down after him.

A dum-dum bullet.

Mustache cried out and dropped the gun. He held his hands up. "I surrender!"

Myron ran forward. "Don't! He's surren—"

But the gun exploded again. Mustache's face disappeared in a spray of red mist. Myron stopped, closed his eyes. Mustache joined Fedora on the filthy cement. Esperanza came over and wrapped her arms around Myron. They both turned toward the alley's entrance.

Win stepped into view, studying his handiwork as though it were a statue he wasn't sure he liked. He was dressed in a gray suit, his red tie still in a perfect Windsor knot. His blond hair was neat, conservative, parted as always on the left. The .44 was in his right hand. His cheeks were rosy, and there was just a hint of a smile on his face.

"Good evening," Win said.

"How long have you been here?" Myron asked. He

hadn't spotted Win when they exited the photography studio. But he had known he was there. With Win you just knew. One of life's constants.

"I arrived as you entered the dwelling of ill repute," Win answered. He smiled. "But I wanted my appearance to have that flair of drama."

Myron let go of Esperanza.

"We better get moving," Win said. "Before the authorities arrive."

They walked away from the corpses in silence. Esperanza was shaking. Myron did not feel so hot either. Only Win seemed completely unaffected by what had transpired. As they approached the car, the same fat young prostitute clad in sausage casing approached Win.

"Hey, yo, want a blow job? Fifty bucks."

Win looked at her. "I would rather have my semen sucked out with a catheter."

"Okay," the girl said. "Forty bucks."

Win laughed and walked away.

Chapter 26

"All units. One-eighteen Acre Street. All units. One-eighteen Acre Street."

Paul Duncan heard the call on his police scanner. He was only a few blocks from the scene, but this was not his district. Far from it. He could certainly not answer the call. That would only draw attention and questions. Questions like what was he doing here.

Pieces were starting to come together. Fred Nickler, the publisher of those sleazy rags, had called him earlier in the day. What he had told Paul explained a lot. Not everything. Not by a long shot. But he now understood Jessica's behavior the other night. She had learned about Kathy's picture. Myron Bolitar must have told her.

But how had Myron gotten a copy of it?

Not important. Not really. What was important was that Myron Bolitar was involved. He could not be underestimated. Jessica was a big enough pain in the ass on her own. But now she had Myron on her side and probably that Win Lockwood, Myron's psychotic Tonto. Paul knew something about their past work for the feds. Not a lot. Myron and Win had answered only to top government officials. Their work was almost always classified. But Paul knew their reputations. That was enough.

A police car sped past Paul, sirens screaming. They were probably on their way to 118 Acre Street. Paul turned up his scanner. He wanted to hear every word that was said.

He debated calling Carol, but what could he tell her? She hadn't been specific on the phone, just telling him about the phone message from Nancy to Jessica. So what did Jessica know? How had she found out?

And what would Carol ultimately be pressured into saying?

Two ambulances flew by him. They too had their sirens on full blast. Paul swallowed. He wanted to pull over, but he wanted more to drive as far away as possible.

Once again Paul Duncan thought of his friend Adam Culver. Dead. Murdered. With everything that had happened, there had been no time for Paul to mourn.

Yes, mourn.

That might sound strange—Paul Duncan mourning
Adam Culver. Especially if anyone knew how Adam had
spent the last precious hours of his life.

Win and Myron dropped Esperanza off at the apartment she shared with her sister and cousin in the east
part of Greenwich Village. Myron escorted her to the
door.

"You okay?"

She nodded. Her face was deathly pale. She had not
spoken a word since the shooting. "Win—" She
stopped, shook her head. It took her a full minute to pull
herself together. "He saved us. I guess that's what
counts."

"Yes."

"I'll see you in the morning."

Myron returned to the car. He called Jessica. She
wasn't home yet, but Myron did manage to wake her
mother. They drove to a twenty-four-hour diner on Sixth
Avenue—one of those Greek diners with a menu the
approximate length of a Tolstoy novel. Win was a vegetarian. He ordered a salad and french fries. Myron ordered a Diet Coke. He couldn't eat.

After they were settled in, Myron asked, "What happened with Chaz?"

Win was picking at a basket of stale bread. His face
registered displeasure, but he settled on a small packet of
Saltines. "Mr. Landreaux hurried straight from our esteemed offices to a building at 466 Fifth Avenue," he
began. "He took the elevator to the eighth floor, which is
rented by Roy O'Connor and TruPro Enterprises. When
Landreaux entered the elevator, he had your contract
tightly clutched in his paw. When he exited, the contract
was no longer visible. He had no pockets that could hold

such a document. Conclusion: Mr. Landreaux gave the
contract to someone at TruPro Enterprises.''

"Your powers of deduction," Myron said. "In a
word: uncanny.''

Win smiled. "I assume you are feeling better.''

Myron shrugged.

"We are not the same, you and I," Win added. "You
call it execution, what I did to that vermin. I call it extermination.''

"You didn't have to kill him.''

"I *wanted* to kill him," Win said with flat inflection.
"And I doubt any of us will mourn his death for very
long.''

True enough, but the argument did not ease Myron's
mind. He wanted to drop the subject. "Where did Chaz
go after he left TruPro?''

Win took a dainty bite out of the corner of the Saltine.
"Before I get into that, I should point out that Mr. Landreaux was escorted from the building by a large man
who fit the description of your friend Aaron. Large. Confident. Athletic. Suit with no shirt. Sunglasses, though
the sun had already set.''

"Sounds like Aaron.''

"They split up on the street. Aaron got into a stretch
limousine. Chaz Landreaux walked to the Omni Hotel.''

"Which Omni?" Myron asked. Manhattan had several.

"The one near Carnegie Hall. Landreaux met up with
his mother in the lobby. Their reunion was rather moving. Mother and son embraced. Both were crying.''

"Hmm," Myron said.

The waitress arrived with the food and drinks. She put
them down, scratched her butt with a pencil, and returned to the kitchen.

"So where did they go after that?''

"Upstairs. They ordered room service."

Myron thought a moment. "What is Chaz's mother doing up from Philadelphia?"

"I would assume," Win said, pulling a napkin out of the dispenser and spreading it on his lap, "based on their mutual anguish, that Frank Ache reached Chaz Landreaux through a family member."

"A kidnapping?"

Win shrugged. "A possibility. Frank just sent two men to try to kill you. I highly doubt he is going to become squeamish over a ghetto abduction."

Silence.

"We're wading in some deep doo-doo," Myron said.

"Indeed. Too deep."

Chaz had a big family. If Frank really wanted to hit him where he lived, he'd take one of his siblings. "We'll settle it tomorrow," Myron said. "I scheduled a meeting with Herman Ache. Two o'clock. Usual place."

"Should I attend?"

"Most definitely."

Win ate his salad. "You do know that this won't be easy."

Myron nodded.

"Herman Ache does not like to intervene in his brother's business."

"I know."

Win put down his fork. "If I may be so bold as to offer a suggestion."

"I'm listening."

"Frank Ache sent two professionals after you. Their untimely deaths will not dissuade him from trying again."

"Uh-huh. So what's your suggestion?"

"Cut your losses now. Make an exchange. You let

them keep Landreaux. They call off the contract on your head.''

"I can't do that."

"You can. You choose not to."

"Semantics."

"You don't have to help him."

"I *want* to help him," Myron answered.

Win sighed. "A man must try to illuminate even those who prefer to sit in the darkness. Do you have a plan yet?"

"I'm still working on it."

"Feverishly?"

Myron nodded.

"In the meantime," Win said, "what did you learn from the photographer?"

Myron filled him in on the meeting with Lucy.

"So who bought the nude pictures?" Win asked.

"A name springs to mind," Myron said.

"Who?"

"Adam Culver."

"Kathy's father?"

Myron nodded. "Think about it. The buyer was in his fifties. He wanted all copies and all negatives on the spot. He left nothing to chance."

"The father protecting the daughter?"

"It makes sense," Myron said.

"But Kathy was missing for over a year. How did Adam Culver suddenly learn about the photographs?"

"Maybe he knew about them all along."

"Then why did he wait so long to buy them?"

Myron shrugged. "We'll know more tomorrow. I'm going to send Esperanza over to the studio with a picture of Adam, see if Lucy recognizes him."

Win took another bite of his salad. "It's a rather strange development."

"Yes."

"But"—Win stopped to finish chewing—"here is something else you may not have considered: If Adam Culver purchased all the pictures and negatives in order to protect his daughter, how did her photograph end up in the magazine?"

Myron had considered that. He just didn't have an answer.

The waitress put down the check. Myron picked up the tab for both of them. The total was $8.50. Mr. Magnanimous. They drove uptown. Win lived in the San Remo building overlooking Central Park West. Very fancy address. They were on Seventy-second Street when the car phone rang.

Myron looked at his multicolored Swatch. A gift from Esperanza.

Past midnight.

"Rather late for a call to your car," Win noted.

Myron picked up the phone. "Hello?"

The voice came fast. "Bolitar, it's Jake Courter. Get your ass down to St. Barnabas Hospital in Livingston right away."

"What happened?"

"Just get down here. Now."

Chapter 27

"We got the call around eleven-thirty," Jake said, ushering Myron through the lobby of St. Barnabas. Jake's face was set, his eyes red and puffy. They hurried past the circular visitors' desk and waited for an elevator.

"Is Jessica okay?" Myron asked.

"She is going to be fine," he said. Then he added, "Wish I could say the same about Nancy Serat."

"What happened?"

"She was garroted with a wire." The elevator arrived. Jake pressed the button for the fifth floor. "When no one answered the door, Jessica let herself in through the back. The killer must have still been there. He knocked her over the head and ran. When she came to, she called us. I'd say she's pretty lucky the perp didn't waste her."

The elevator opened with a *ding*. "What room is she in?" Myron asked.

"Five fifteen."

Myron sprinted down the corridor. He turned the corner. Jessica was in the bed, her face ashen. A doctor stood next to her, preparing a needle. Jake came up behind Myron but stayed in the doorway.

Her voice was wobbly. "Myron?"

"I'm here," he said, taking her hand. She looked small and frail and alone. "I won't leave."

The doctor pricked her with the needle. "You need your rest," he said.

"I'm fine," Jessica insisted weakly. "I want to get out of here."

"We think it's best if you stay overnight for observation."

"But—"

"Listen to him, Jess," Myron interrupted. "There's nothing we can do tonight."

The drug began to take effect. Her eyes fluttered back. "Nancy . . ."

"It's okay," Myron soothed.

"Her face was blue. . . ."

"Shhh."

Jessica slipped into unconsciousness. Myron looked up at the doctor. "Is she going to be okay?"

"She'll be fine. I think the shock of what she saw was worse than the blow to her head."

Jake put his hand on Myron's shoulder. "Come on, I'll buy you a cup of coffee."

"I want to stay."

"You can come back later. Right now we need to talk."

Myron gazed down at Jessica. She was deep in sleep.

"She'll be out for a while," the doctor assured him.

They walked down the corridor silently and took the elevator back to the lobby. The place had that hospital smell—that unique combo of something antiseptic and the hospital food. Win had parked the car and was now sitting in the waiting area. He stood when he saw them.

"That your friend Win?" Jake asked, motioning with his chin. "The one P.T. told me about?"

"Yes."

"Tell him to stay here. I want to talk to you alone."

Myron signaled to Win. Win nodded, sat back down, picked up a newspaper, crossed his legs. Jake looked him over for a minute. "He as crazy as P.T. says?"

"Pretty much."

"Come on."

They grabbed coffee and found a table in the corner. "The crime scene unit is going over Nancy's house now. They'll beep me if they find anything."

"So what do you know so far?" Myron asked.

"Not much. Nancy spent the last few days in Cancún —a graduation present from her parents."

"Have they been told?"

He shook his head. "I'm going over there right after we talk."

Silence. Jake broke it. "So how did Jessica get involved in this?"

"She wanted me to look into her father's murder. She didn't buy the fact that he was killed in a botched robbery."

Jake nodded. "She thought her old man's murder had something to do with her sister."

"Yes."

"I figured as much. I got the file in the car."

Myron sat up. "Adam Culver's homicide file?"

"Hey, I ain't an idiot, Bolitar. You start investigating after eighteen months. Why? Had to be the father's murder. You saw a connection. But I gotta be honest. I don't see it. No connections in that file at all. A few inconsistencies maybe. But no connection."

"What sort of inconsistencies?" Myron asked.

"Adam Culver was supposed to be in Denver when he was killed. At a medical examiners' conference at the Hyatt Regency. But he never showed, missed his morning flight."

"Does the file say why?"

"Adam didn't feel well. A reasonable explanation."

"Who told them that?"

"His wife."

Pause. "What else?"

"Nothing else. The crime scene—a quiet street—was unremarkable. He was stabbed through the heart."

"What was he doing out?"

"The wife said he went out to buy some groceries."

Myron chewed that one over for a moment. "Odd thing to do," he said, "when you're not feeling well."

"Yeah, that's easy for us to say, sitting here like this. But the cops were concentrating on finding a mugger. No one really gave a shit about a missed flight or what it might mean."

"Any witnesses to the murder?"

"None. The file is pretty bare-bone." Jake leaned forward and tried to stare Myron down. Myron did not look away. "Now," Jake said slowly, "you start talking to me. And don't give me no 'I don't want no one hurt' crap. Too late for that now. Why are you really involved in all this?"

"I told you. Jessica."

Jake leaned farther forward until their faces were only inches apart. "Stop jerking me around," he spat out. "I ain't blind. I can see Jessica Culver is great tail. But don't start giving me this bullshit that you just decided to drop everything and help on a whim. You ain't that hard up."

"There was also Christian to consider," Myron said.

"What about him?"

"He's my top client. He was still upset about his fiancée's disappearance."

Jake made a snorting nose. "Yeah, I bet."

"What's that supposed to mean?"

"It means," Jake said, "that I'm not convinced Christian is completely innocent in all this."

"But you said the DNA test on the semen—"

"I'm not saying he raped her."

"Then what are you saying?"

"That he might be involved," Jake replied. "Your client had no solid alibi for the time of the disappearance. He claims he was in bed at eleven o'clock, but no one can confirm it."

"He has a single room," Myron said. "Who's going to confirm he was in bed when he lived alone?"

"It's suspicious," Jake replied.

"How? Kathy Culver was seen entering the team locker room after ten, right?"

Jake nodded.

"And you know Christian was meeting with the offensive coordinator until ten-thirty," Myron continued. "That's confirmed."

"But that's where his alibi ends."

"He went to bed after that. Kathy was seen wandering around on the other side of the campus at eleven o'clock. I don't see the connection."

"Maybe there is none," Jake said simply. "But he's the boyfriend. The boyfriend is always a prime suspect. And there was something else."

"What?"

"His teammates."

"What about them?"

Jake finished his coffee. He tapped the cup to get the last few drops. "They were cooperative, I guess, but some of them seemed awfully vague. Nothing I could pin down, but some of them looked more nervous than they should. Like they were covering something up. Like maybe, just maybe, they were protecting their star quarterback before the big game."

Except, Myron thought, nobody on the team liked Christian. His teammates would not have gone out of their way to protect him. Just the opposite, in fact.

So why were they nervous?

Jake settled back and smiled, marking a change in tactics. "Now, Myron, I've been awfully sweet, haven't I? I've told you all I know, and you're still holding back on me. That ain't nice. Something else—something you haven't shared with me yet—put a real hairy bug in your ass. Now I visited our friend Dean Gordon a few hours ago, just like you suggested. The man was cordial, friendly, not at all a pompous ass. Which ain't like him. In fact, I think he was scared shitless. Now why's that?"

"Did he tell you anything?"

"Oh, he was real helpful. Kathy was a wonderful girl, an honor student, a hard worker, blah, blah, blah. Oh, yeah. He also told me your ex upstairs paid him a visit. Seems Jessica wanted her sister's file. Imagine that."

"We were trying to gather as much info as possible."

"Information on what?"

Myron eyed his coffee. It looked like sewer sludge. "On the morning Adam Culver was murdered, he visited Nancy Serat."

Jake's eyes widened a bit. "How do you know that?"

"Nancy left a message on Jessica's phone to meet her at ten o'clock tonight. She also said that she'd seen Adam Culver on the morning of the murder."

"Jesus Christ." Jake crossed his arms, resting them on his belly. "So Adam Culver visits Nancy Serat in the morning. He finds something out. Something big. Something so big he cancels his trip."

"Something so big," Myron added, "it gets him killed."

Jake nodded, thinking. "Then the killer has to get rid of the source."

"Nancy Serat."

"Right." Jake stopped. "But I questioned that girl for hours. I asked her everything. . . ." His voice faded off, and a shadow crossed his face. Myron knew what he was wondering. Any cop worth a damn would be asking the same questions. Did I fuck up? Did I miss something? Is a young girl dead because of me?

"If Nancy knew something that important," Myron said, "the killer wouldn't have waited eighteen months to silence her. I think it's a little more complicated than our scenario. I think Adam Culver had already put most of it together. Nancy had the final piece, a piece that by itself meant nothing to anyone—except Adam Culver."

"You trying to make me feel better?"

"No. It's how I see it. If I thought you fucked up, I'd say so."

"You didn't see her body," Jake said quietly. "Strangulation ain't pretty. The damn wire nearly sliced her head off. Not a nice way to go, Myron." He stopped, shook his head. "After seeing that, I know what Jessica is asking herself, because I keep asking myself the same thing."

"What's that?"

"Did Kathy meet a similar fate?"

Silence. They drank some coffee. Myron's was already cold, but he didn't complain. Cold, sludgelike coffee seemed to fit the occasion.

"P.T. told me all about you," Jake said after a massive slurp. "Said you were smart, that I could trust you. He don't say that about too many folks. Said you and that Win fella were as good as they come. A little too maverick, but right now I could use that. I'm a cop. I have to follow rules. You don't. More power to you. But this is my territory, and I ain't gonna sit around like some fucking movie extra." He put his hands on the table. They were big and callused and had no rings. "So now I want you to tell me everything, Myron. Right now. Just you and me. It won't get out, you have my word. Don't hold anything back. You understand?"

Myron nodded.

"So start talking, boy. I'm all ears."

Myron took out the magazine and handed it to Jake. "It all started with this."

Chapter 28

The morning papers had no mention of Nancy Serat's murder, but the radio was beginning to pick up early reports of a murdered woman. Just a question of time. Myron took Route 280 east to the New Jersey Turnpike north. Scenic road. Like driving through west Beirut on a good day. Problem was, people unfairly judged New Jersey by this road. It was like judging a woman's beauty by the size of her feet.

Billy Joel was on the radio, singing, "I love you just the way you are." Big talk, Myron mused, when you've been married to Christie Brinkley.

Exit 16W led him directly into the Meadowlands parking lot. Murder and intrigue were all well and good, but agenting paid the bills. He had a meeting with Otto Burke. Otto was expecting a response to his demand vis-à-vis Christian's contract. Myron had prepared one for him.

He had spent the night in Jessica's hospital room, trying to get comfortable in a chair that doubled as a medieval torture device. But he had not minded. He liked watching her sleep. It brought back memories.

He'd always hoped they'd one day sleep together again, though last night was not precisely what he had had in mind.

Jess had woken up two hours ago. Belligerent. Testy. Demanding. In a word: herself. Before her brother Edward took her home, Myron had told her all he knew—especially about his visit to Lucy's photo studio. She had given him a photograph of her father to show Lucy. Myron was surprised to see Jessica carried one in her wallet. But he was far more surprised to catch a fleeting glimpse of a picture from four summers ago—a picture she tried to skip past without his seeing. But he had seen it, and he remembered the precise moment it had been taken. Their last weekend in Martha's Vineyard. Just the two of them. Tan, happy, relaxed. A barbecue at Win's summer house. The pinnacle before the inevitable slide.

Myron had not had a chance to change clothes. He looked as if he'd spent the evening in the bottom of a laundry hamper.

Otto was waiting for him in the owner's box on Titans Stadium mezzanine level. Larry Hanson was with him. Otto greeted Myron with a bony handshake and a wide smile. Mr. Sunshine. Larry offered a quick wave. He did not meet Myron's eye. It was no wonder. Larry Hanson was a tough guy, a loud brute even, but he tried to play fair. He didn't like to cheat, and he did not like what Otto was doing now. He looked, in fact, as if he wanted to blend into the wall.

"Please, Myron," Otto said, spreading his arms like Carol Merrill on *Let's Make a Deal*, "sit wherever you like."

"Always the perfect host, Otto."

"I do try, Myron. Thank you for noticing."

"Sarcasm, Otto. It's called sarcasm."

Otto kept the smile aglow. His goatee was exactly the

same as always, never heavier or lighter. Must trim it
every day, Myron thought. They sat in two seats facing
the field. Fifty yard line. Fans would kill for these seats.
Down below, players were scattered across the field. Myron spotted Christian walking toward the sideline. His
helmet was off, his head held high. Christian didn't
know about Nancy Serat's murder—her name had not
yet been released—but the press would be all over him
soon enough. Myron could protect him only so much,
though he did entertain hopes that the news of Christian's signing would deflect some attention away from
the murder.

"So," Otto said with a clap of his hands, "are you
ready to sign?"

Down on the field Christian was being introduced to a
bunch of long-haired men. Myron recognized the men
from a video on MTV. They were Otto Records' latest
find. A group called StillLife. Good sound, but did they
have the raw talent, of, say, Pap Smear?

"Sure," Myron said. "We would like nothing more."

"Great. I have a pen."

"How handy. I have a contract." He handed it to
Otto. Otto read it quickly. His mouth was smiling, but
his eyes frowned. He passed it to Larry Hanson.

"I'm confused, Myron. This looks like your last
offer."

"Very perceptive, Otto."

"I thought we had an agreement," he said.

"We do. There it is."

"I think you're forgetting"—he paused, searching for
the right word—"Christian's sudden devaluation."

"You make him sound like a foreign currency."

Otto laughed. He looked over to Larry as if to say,
laugh too. Larry could only muster a smile. "Okay, Myron, I'll accept that. We are all, to some extent, commod-

ities. Your client, however, is now trading at a lower rate against the U.S. dollar.''

''Thanks for keeping within the metaphor, Otto, but I don't see it that way.'' Myron looked at Larry Hanson. ''How's his play been, Larry?''

''Well, it's very early,'' Larry said, clearing his throat. ''You really can't tell too much after such a short time period.''

''But if you had to grade him so far?''

Another throat clear. ''Let's just say,'' he replied, ''that Christian's play has not been a disappointment.''

''There you go,'' Myron said, matching Otto's smile. ''His value has, if anything, increased with his recent on-the-field display. You have now had a tasty morsel of his potential. I don't see how you could expect us to drop our asking price.''

Otto rose, nodding his head. He clasped his hands behind his back and walked to the bar. ''Care for a drink, Myron?''

''Do you have any Yoo-Hoo?''

''No, I don't.''

''Nothing, then.''

Otto poured himself a 7-Up. He did not ask Larry Hanson if he wanted anything. ''I will admit,'' Otto said, ''that Christian's play so far has been impressive, though I must caution you, Myron—and you too, Larry—that there is a big difference between practice and games. Between how an athlete performs in a scrimmage and how he performs in a pressure situation.''

Myron and Larry exchanged a glance. The glance said, Pretentious asshole.

''But let me also add,'' Otto continued, ''that our product is dependent on more than just performance. If, for example, our team were to win the Super Bowl but were also involved in a major drug or sex scandal, the overall value of the product may decline.''

"Can you demonstrate that with a graph?'' Myron asked. "I'm not sure I understand.''

"It means,'' Otto said, "that the photograph in that sleazy publication makes Christian worth less money to us.''

"But it's not a picture of him.''

"It's a picture of his fiancée.''

"Ex-fiancée.''

"His fiancée who vanished under mysterious circumstances.''

"Christian and I are willing to take the chance,'' Myron said. "It was in a small publication. It hasn't gotten out so far. We don't think it will.''

Otto sipped his 7-Up. He seemed to enjoy it, even adding an "aaah'' like he was taping a commercial. "But the press might find out.''

"I don't think so,'' Myron said. "I've discussed it with Christian. We both feel the same.''

"Then you are both fools.''

The facade had dropped open a crack.

"Now, Otto, that wasn't very nice.''

The facade slid back up, smooth as an electric car window. "Let me remind you of our previous discussion on this very subject, Myron. See if you can follow this. You were to take our agreement and knock it down by a third. If not, the picture of the au naturel Ms. Culver goes public, thereby ruining your player's endorsement career.''

"But he didn't do anything, Otto. It's only a picture of Kathy Culver.''

"It doesn't matter. Advertisers do not like the smallest whiff of controversy. Remember this, Myron: In business, appearance is far more important than reality.''

"Appearance versus reality," Myron said. "That I have to write down."

Otto took out a contract of his own. "Sign it," he said. "Now."

Myron just smiled at him.

"Sign it, Myron. Or I'll ruin you."

"I don't think so, Otto."

Myron began to unbutton his shirt.

"What do you think you're doing?"

"Don't get excited, Otto. I'm stopping after the third button. Just enough to show you this." He pointed to the small microphone on his chest.

"What the hell—?"

"It's a wire, Otto. It leads to a tape recorder stuck in my belt. You can make the picture public, that's up to you. It may damage Christian, it may not. I, in turn, will make this tape public. I will also sue your sorry ass for any damages Christian may have suffered because of your actions, and I will also see to it that you are arrested for extortion and blackmail." Myron smiled. "I always wanted to own a record company. Chicks dig that, don't they, Otto?"

Otto looked at him coolly. "Larry?"

"Yes, Mr. Burke."

"Take the tape away from him. Forcibly, if necessary."

Myron looked at Hanson. "You're a big guy, Larry," Myron said. "And I know you were one of the toughest fullbacks ever to play this game. But if you get out of that chair, I'll put you in a body cast."

Larry Hanson merely nodded. Not afraid, but not moving either.

"There are two of us," Otto urged. "I can call in security guards to help."

"I don't think so, Mr. Burke." Larry was almost

smiling. "And I don't think a few security guards are going to scare him very much. Are they, Myron?"

"Not likely."

"I think we should sign his contract, Mr. Burke. I think it's best for all."

"I've even drawn up a press release," Myron said. "Says how happy Christian is to be playing for such an outstanding and reputable organization as the Titans."

Otto thought a moment. "If I sign," he said, "you'll hand over the tape?"

"Not likely."

"Why not?"

"You keep the magazine and I keep the tape. Think of it as our own little balance of terror. A throwback to the cold war."

"But you have my word—"

"Please, Otto, it hurts when I laugh."

Otto thought a moment. He was shaken but calm. A guy his age doesn't reach this level without learning to take a few knocks.

"Myron?"

"Yes."

"I can't tell you how thrilled the Titans are to have Christian Steele, the quarterback of the future, with us."

"Just sign right here, Otto."

"My pleasure, Myron."

"No, Otto. Mine."

Otto signed. Myron and Otto shook hands. The deal was done.

"Shall we meet the press jointly, Myron?"

"Sounds wondrous, Otto."

"There's a shower downstairs. I'll make sure you're provided with shaving equipment, if you like."

"Very kind of you."

Otto's smile was back. The man was never down

long. He picked up the phone. "Christian Steele has been signed," Otto said. Then, looking back and winking at Myron, he added, "At the highest salary ever given to a rookie."

Myron winked back and gave him the thumbs up. Lifelong chums. He checked his watch. There would be just enough time to shower and do the press conference before he would have to head back into the city for his meeting with Herman Ache.

He had no idea how he was going to handle the evil Ache brothers. But he was still working on it. Feverishly.

Chapter 29

Jessica arrived at the house in Ridgewood at ten o'clock. The doctor had wanted to run some more tests in the morning. Jessica refused. They finally reached a compromise whereby Jessica promised to visit him in his office sometime during the week. Edward had driven her home in silence.

When they arrived, Jessica noted that her mother's car was not in the driveway. Good. Not in much of a mood to handle a hysterical mother on top of everything else, Jessica had insisted that no one tell her mother about last night's incident. Mom had enough on her mind. No reason to get her unnecessarily upset.

Jessica headed straight for the study. Her father had been up to something, that much was clear. There were too many weird happenings for it to have been any other way. He had visited Nancy Serat on the morning of his death. He had skipped out on a medical examiners' convention in Denver because he hadn't felt well—something he would never do. He had possibly even purchased nude photographs of Kathy.

You didn't have to be Sherlock Holmes to realize something was amiss.

She flicked on the track lights, illuminating the room a bit too harshly for her taste. She used the dimmer. Downstairs, Edward was in the kitchen opening the refrigerator.

She began to rifle through her father's drawers. She had no idea what she was looking for. Perhaps a small box with the words BIG CLUE scrawled across the top. That would be nice. She tried not to think about Nancy Serat, about her blue face frozen in terror, but the thought stayed anchored front and center. She thought of more pleasant things, like waking to see Myron folded up in that hospital chair like a contortionist from Le Cirque du Soleil. The image made her smile.

In the file drawer she found a folder marked CMA. Her father's Merrill Lynch Cash Management Account. She pulled it out. The CMA statement is a financial instrument of great beauty. Everything in one statement—your stocks, bonds, other holdings, checks, Visa card transactions. Jessica had one of her own.

She checked the charges and checks cleared on the most recent statement. Nothing unusual. Problem was, the statement ended three weeks ago. She needed something more recent.

She flipped to the last page. On the bottom in small print it read "You have an alphabetic character in your Merrill Lynch account number. Please use nine-eight-two-three-three-four as your account access number for CMA-DATA.''

CMA-DATA. The 800 line. She had used it before with her own account, whenever she found a discrepancy. She dialed the number and immediately heard a taped voice say, "Welcome to the Merrill Lynch Financial Service Center. Enter your Merrill Lynch account number or your account access number.''

Jessica entered the number.

"Enter your selection. You may interrupt the dialogue at any time. For your current balance and purchasing power, enter one. For check clearing information, enter two. For most recent funds received, enter three. For most recent Visa transactions, enter six.''

She decided to start with the charges and then look at the checks. She pressed six.

The voice said, "Visa draft for $28.50 is on delay debit as of May twenty-eighth. Visa draft for $14.75 is on delay debit as of May twenty-eighth.''

The machine was not telling her where the charges were coming from. The same would be true for the checks. Knowing just the amounts would do her no good.

"Visa draft for $3,478.44 is on delay debit as of May twenty-seventh.''

She froze. Three thousand dollars? For what? She hung up, hit the redial button, and put in the account access number.

"Enter your selection.''

This time she pressed zero for a customer service representative.

"Good morning,'' a pleasant-voiced woman sing-songed. "May I help you?''

"Yes, there's a Visa charge on my account for over

three thousand dollars. I'd like to know where the charge came from.''

''Your account number, please?''

''Nine-eight-two-three-three-four.''

There was some keyboard clacking in the background. ''And you are?'' the rep asked.

Jessica checked the statement. A joint account, thank God. ''Carol Culver,'' she said.

''Hold one moment, Mrs. Culver.''

More clacking. ''Yes, I have it here. $3,478.44. Eye-Spy Shop in Manhattan.''

Eye-Spy? What the hell was that all about?

''Thank you,'' Jessica said.

''Anything else today, Mrs. Culver?''

''Yes. My husband and I have all our records on a personal computer, and I'm afraid the computer has had a disk failure. Can I ask you to give me the most recent checks that have been written against the account?''

''Certainly.''

More clacking. ''Check one-nineteen for $295 to Volvo Finance, written on May twenty-fifth.''

Car payment.

''Check one-eighteen for $649 to Getaway Realty, also written on May twenty-fifth.''

Hold the phone. ''Did you say Getaway Realty?''

''Yes, that's correct.''

''Does it say where they're located?''

''I'm afraid I don't have that information.''

They went through the rest of the month's checks. Nothing unusual. Jessica thanked the woman and hung up.

$649 to Getaway Realty? $3,478.44 to Eye-Spy? More and more amiss.

Edward knocked on the door. ''Hi,'' he said.

''Hi.''

He stepped into their father's study, head lowered.

"I'm sorry about the other day," Edward said. He blinked several times, his to-die-for eyelashes waving up and down. "About running out like that."

"It's okay."

"You hit a raw nerve," he said. "Asking all those questions and everything."

"They need to be asked," she replied. "I think everything is connected. What happened to Kathy. What happened to Dad. What made Kathy change."

Edward flinched at the word *change*. Then he shook his head. His T-shirt of the day featured Beavis and Butt-head. "You're wrong," he said. "It doesn't have anything to do with what happened to her."

"Maybe," she said. "Only way to find out is if you tell me."

"I don't feel comfortable about it. It's painful."

"I'm your sister. You can trust me."

"We were never very close," he said bluntly. "Not like you and Kathy."

"Or you and Kathy," Jessica said. "But I still love you."

She waited.

"I don't know where to begin exactly," he said. "It started her senior year of high school. You had just moved to Washington. I was at Columbia. I was living off campus with my friend Matt. Remember him?"

"Of course. Kathy dated him for two years."

"Almost three," Edward corrected. "Matt and Kathy were like something out of another century. They were together three years, and he never got, well, below the neck. I mean, never. And it wasn't just from a lack of trying. Matt was as straightlaced as any guy I knew, but that didn't mean he didn't push it now and again. But Kathy held him off."

Jessica nodded, remembering. Kathy had still been confiding in her at that stage.

"Mom loved Matt," Edward continued. "She thought he was the greatest. She used to invite him over for tea like something out of *The Glass Menagerie*. A gentleman caller sitting on the porch with the youngest daughter. Dad liked him too. Everything seemed to be going well. They planned on getting engaged in another year, married after he graduated, the whole Chevy-and-apple-pie love story. Then one day Kathy called him on the phone and just dumped him. No explanation.

"Matt was shocked. He tried to talk to her, but Kathy wouldn't see him. I tried to talk to her too, but she just blew me off. Then I started hearing rumors."

Jessica shifted in her chair. "What kind of rumors?" she asked.

"The kind," Edward said slowly, "a brother doesn't like to hear about his sister."

"Oh."

"Worse than oh. Guys were trashing her nonstop. Someone had finally found the key to Miss Prude's chastity belt, they said, and now they couldn't get it back closed. I even got into a fight. Got the shit beaten out of me protecting Kathy's honor." He spat out the word *honor* as though it had an offensive taste.

"She changed at home too. She never went to mass anymore. I thought Mom would have a stroke—you know how she gets about stuff like that."

Jessica nodded. She knew only too well.

"But she never said a word. Kathy started staying out late. She went to college parties. Some nights she wouldn't even come home."

"Didn't Mom stop her?" Jessica asked.

"She couldn't, Jess. It was unbelievable. Kathy had spent her entire life in fear of the woman. Now it was like Kathy had found Kryptonite. Mom couldn't touch her.''

''What about Dad?''

''He was never as strict as Mom, you know that. He wanted to be everyone's buddy, not the bad guy. But strangely enough, Kathy grew closer to Dad during all this. He was thrilled by the sudden attention. I think he was afraid if he laid down the law, he'd push her away from him.''

Sounded like her father. ''What did you do?'' she asked.

''I confronted her.''

''What did she say?''

''Nothing really. She wouldn't deny it or admit it. She would just stand there and smile eerily. She said I didn't understand, that I was 'naïve.' Naïve. Can you believe Kathy could call someone else naïve?''

Jessica thought a minute. ''But none of that explains what started it, what made her change in the first place.''

Edward opened his mouth, stopped. He spread his hands, then dropped them back to his sides as though they were too heavy to hold up. His voice was barely audible. ''Something with Mom,'' he said.

''What with Mom?''

''I don't know. I think maybe Mom does. Kathy became withdrawn from you and me. But she still loved us. It was Mom got the brunt of it.''

Jessica leaned back in her father's chair, considering his last comment. ''I knew Kathy had changed the last couple of years, but I had no idea . . .'' Her voice sort of faded away.

''But it ended, Jess. You have to remember that.''

''What ended?'' she asked.

''This stage Kathy went through. That's why I don't

think it's related to her disappearance. By the time she disappeared, it was all in the past.''

"What do you mean, in the past?''

"She changed back. Oh, I don't mean she started going to mass every Sunday or became buddies with Mom. But whatever had twisted her out of shape had finally let go. She was regaining her old self. I think Christian had a lot to do with that. I think he helped bring her back from the edge. The slutty behavior certainly stopped. So did the drugs, the drinking, the partying. Other things too. The smile even came back a little.''

Jessica remembered Kathy's school transcript. The terrible grades in her senior year and the beginning of college. Then the sudden turnabout back toward excellence that had started her second semester freshman year —when she met Christian. It added up with what Edward was saying.

So was the past irrelevant? Was this period of her life, as Edward had insisted, all behind her? Perhaps. But Jessica doubted it. If it were truly dead and buried, why was her picture now appearing in a pornographic magazine? And that of course led to the central question in all this:

What had made Kathy change in the first place?

Jessica still did not know. But she now had a pretty good idea who might.

Chapter 30

There were several things Myron enjoyed more than visiting Herman Ache. Having his eyeball removed with a grapefruit spoon, for example.

"I heard your press conference on the radio," Win said. The top was down on Win's racing-green Jaguar XJR. Myron was not big on having the top down. It was just a question of time before a bug got stuck in his teeth. "I trust that Christian was pleased with the deal."

"Very."

"The press still hasn't picked up on Nancy Serat."

"Jake hasn't released her name yet. Once they do—"

"Party time."

"Exactly."

"Does Christian know?" Win asked.

"Not yet. He was so damn happy. I just wanted to let him enjoy it a little longer."

"You should warn him."

"I will. Jake promised to let me know the second it got out."

"You seem to like this Jake fellow," Win noted.

"He's a good man. We can trust him."

Win wiggled his fingers, regripped the wheel, accelerated. "I don't trust officers of the law," Win said. "It's safer that way."

The car was going very fast. The West Side Highway was not built for such speed—a four-lane highway with traffic lights every twenty yards. Plus the "ongoing"

construction didn't help. The construction had been going on for as long as anyone could remember. History
books stated that Peter Minuit, the Dutchman who purchased Manhattan from the Indians in 1626, often com-
plained about the delays around Fifty-seventh Street.

But none of that deterred Win's hefty accelerator
foot. The Javits Center was a blur. So was the Hudson
River, for that matter.

Myron said, "Could you slow down a tad?"

"No need to worry. The car has a driver-side air
bag."

"Wonderful."

They were getting closer to Ache's office. Myron's
stomach knotted—not helped by the smog blasting into
his face because the top was down. His nerves were as
taut as a freshly strung tennis racket. Win, on the other
hand, looked relaxed. Then again, Frank Ache didn't
have a contract out on his head.

Win's car phone rang. He picked it up. "Hello?" He
handed the phone to Myron. "It's P.T."

Myron took the receiver. "What's up?"

"Hey, Myron, how you feeling today?"

"Can't complain."

"Glad to hear it. Say, you'll never guess what happened last night."

"What?"

"Two of New York's finest hit men were found dead
in an alley. Sad, ain't it?"

"Tragic," Myron agreed.

"They worked for Frank Ache."

"That a fact?"

"Forty-four Magnum with dum-dum bullets were
used. Blew their heads clean off."

"Such a loss."

"Yeah, I'm losing sleep over it too. Anyway, word out

on the street is, this ain't over. Corpses don't exactly waylay the wants of a guy like Frank Ache. The contract is still out on whatever ugly slob pissed Frank off.''

Myron said, ''Ugly?''

''Well, it's been nice talking to you, Myron. Take care.''

''You too, P.T.''

Myron hung up.

''The contract is still in place?'' Win asked.

''Yep.''

''They won't hit you in Herman's office,'' Win said. ''He would never allow it.''

Myron knew that was true. There was a certain code, even among men who have probably ordered the deaths of hundreds of people. Some idiots believed that these codes were based on some sort of ethics. Not even close. The codes were two things to mobsters: (1) a device to make them appear almost human, and (2) a way of protecting themselves and their position. Ethics are to a mobster what honesty is to a politician.

A construction site slowed them near Twelfth Street, but they still made it with time to spare. The air smelled of pizza—probably because they parked in front of a pizzeria called The First Original Ray's Pizza of New York, Really, We're Not Kidding, Honest, We're It. A tall woman in a blue business suit and fancy sunglasses strolled purposefully down the sidewalk. Myron smiled at her, and she returned it. He would have preferred a faint or even a small swoon, but you can't have everything.

At two in the afternoon Clancy's Tavern was already in full swing. Myron stopped right outside the door, fixed his hair, turned left, smiled, turned right, smiled, looked up, smiled.

Win looked a question at him.

"The feds take pictures of everyone who comes in here," Myron said. "I just wanted to look my best."

"Now you tell me. I look like hell."

Clancy's patrons were all men. Not exactly a swinging pick-up joint. A jukebox played Bob Seger. The decor was Early American Beer. Lots of those neon signs, the ones that spell out company names. Budweiser, Bud Light, Miller, Miller Lite, Schlitz. A clock courtesy of Michelob. A mirror from Coors. Coasters from Pabst. The mugs had Rolling Rock logos emblazoned across them.

Myron knew that there were probably a million FBI bugging devices in here. Herman Ache didn't care. Anybody who said something truly damaging in the tavern itself was beyond stupid and deserved to get nailed. The real talk went on in the back rooms. Ache made sure they were swept for bugs every day.

Win drew a few curious glances when they entered. Prep was not exactly the "in" style of Clancy's clientele. But no one stared too long. This was a bar where no one stared at anyone too long.

"Is that your friend Aaron?" Win asked.

Aaron was at the back of the bar wearing his customary white suit. This time he wore a shirt, albeit one of those pectoral-displaying sleeveless muscle T's. It was as if Aaron's wardrobe had entered some molecular transformer with issues of *GQ* and *Pumping Iron*. Aaron waved them to come forward with a hand the size of a manhole cover.

"Hello, Myron," Aaron said. "A genuine pleasure to see you again."

Myron Bolitar, Mr. Popularity. "Aaron, I'd like you to meet Win Lockwood."

Aaron angled the smile at Win. "Pleasure, Win."

They shook hands with death stares, each sizing the other man up. Neither flinched.

"They're waiting in the back," Aaron said. "Come on."

Aaron led them to a locked door with a one-way mirror. The door opened immediately. They entered. Two hoods stood stonefaced. In front of them was a long corridor. There was—and this was new—a metal detector, like at the airport.

Aaron shrugged, as if to say, A sign of the times. "Hand over your weapons, if you'd be so kind. Then step through."

Myron took out his thirty-eight, Win a brand-new forty-four. Last night's forty-four had no doubt been destroyed. They stepped through. The metal detector did not ding, but the two hoods still searched with one of those gizmos that looked suspiciously like vibrators. Then they searched again, this time by hand.

"Very thorough," Win said.

"Almost enjoyable," Myron added. "I thought he was going to ask me to turn my head and cough."

"Hey, funny man," one of the hoods groused, "this way."

The two hoods took over, escorting them down the corridor. Aaron stayed back and watched. Myron did not like that. The walls were white, the carpet office-orange. Lithographs of the French Riviera lined the walls. The front of Clancy's Tavern looked like a dive; the back like a dentist's office.

Two other men appeared at the other end of the corridor. They were both carrying guns.

Myron leaned toward Win's ear. "Uh-oh."

Win nodded.

The two men pointed their guns at Myron and Win. One barked, "Hey, you, Goldilocks. Get over here."

Win looked at Myron. "Goldilocks?"

"I think he means you."

"Oh. The blond hair. I get it now."

"Yeah, Goldie, get your butt down here."

"Later," Win said. He moved down the corridor. The two hoods from the metal detector took out their guns. Four men, four guns. Lots of firepower. Not taking any chances after last night.

"Hands on your head. Let's go."

Win and Myron, separated by approximately ten feet, did as they were told. One of the hoods from the metal detector approached Myron. Without warning, he punched the butt of his gun against Myron's kidney.

Myron dropped to his knees. Nausea swam through him. The man followed up with a kick to the ribs. Then another. Myron slid to the ground. The other man joined in. He stomped on Myron's upper legs like they were small brushfires. One stomp landed on the already-sore kidney. Myron thought he was going to vomit.

In something of a haze Myron spotted Win. He had not moved, his face displaying something akin to noninterest. Win had sized up the situation and made a quick determination: There was nothing he could do to help. Worrying and fretting were worthless. Win was spending his time calmly studying the men. He didn't like to forget a face.

The kicks came in a nonstop flurry. Myron curled into a fetal position and tried to ride it out. The kicks hurt like hell, but they were too rushed to do serious damage. One landed near his eye. He'd have a shiner for sure.

Then a voice shouted, "What the hell— Stop this moment!"

The kicks halted immediately.

"Get away from him!"

The men backed off. "Sorry, Mr. Ache."

Myron rolled onto his back. With some effort he managed to sit up. Herman Ache stood by an open door. "Are you okay, Myron?"

Myron winced. "Never better, Herman."

"I can't tell you how sorry I am," Herman Ache said. Then glaring at his men. "But some people will be even sorrier."

The men cowered away from the older man. Myron almost rolled his eyes. This was all an act. Herman Ache's men did not beat up men in Herman's corridor without permission. This had been a setup. Now Myron supposedly owed Herman, even before the negotiating started. Not to mention the fact that pain is a great fear-inducer, the perfect prenegotiation cocktail.

Aaron came down the hall. He helped Myron to his feet and sort of half-shrugged as if to say *Cheap move, but what can you do?*

"Come," Herman beckoned. "Let's talk in my office."

Myron moved tentatively into the office. He had not been here in several years, but not much had changed. Golf was still the theme. LeRoy Neiman painting of some golf course on the main wall. Lots of those stupid cartoon/artworks of old-fashioned golfers. Aerial photographs of golf courses. In one corner of the office was a movie screen showing a shot of a fairway. In front of the screen was a golf tee. The player hits the ball against the screen. A computer then calculates where it would have landed and changes the image on the screen to match that. Then the player takes his second shot. Fun city.

"Nice office," Win said.

Figures.

"Thank you, son." Herman Ache smiled. Capped teeth. He was in his early sixties, tan, fit, wearing white pants and a yellow golf shirt with a Nicklaus golden bear where an alligator normally went—as if he were on his way to a gin tournament in Miami Beach. Herman Ache had gray hair. Not his own. A toupee or one of those Hair Club systems, a good one, one most people would probably not spot. He had liver spots on his hands. His face was wrinkle free, probably from collagen shots or a face-lift. The neck gave him away. The flesh was baggy and Reaganesque. Looked like a big scrotum.

"Please, gentlemen, have a seat."

They did so. The door was closed behind them. Aaron, two new hoods, and Herman Ache. Nausea's grip on Myron's stomach began to slacken.

Herman picked up a golf club and sat on the edge of his desk. "I understand," he said, "that you and Frank are having a misunderstanding, Myron."

"That's what I wanted to talk to you about."

Herman nodded. "Frank?"

The door opened. Frank entered. You could tell that they were brothers, both having almost identical facial features, but that was where the similarities ended. Frank had at least twenty pounds on his older brother. He was pear-shaped with small Paul Schaefer shoulders and a rubber tire that would be the envy of the Michelin Man. Frank was completely bald, forgoing the hair weave. His teeth were black with spaces between them. His face was permanently set on angry scowl.

Both brothers had grown up on the streets. Both had started out as small-time hoods and worked their way up. Both had seen their own children gunned down over the years. Both had gunned down plenty of other people's children. Herman liked to pretend that he dwelled on a loftier plane than his coarse younger brother—a plane of fine books, the arts, golf. But the escape was not that easy. Two sides of the same coin. Frank gratingly reminded Herman of his origins and perhaps true nature.

But Frank was comfortable and accepted in his world. Herman was not.

Frank was dressed in a powder blue sweat suit with neon yellow trim. The jacket was unzipped and—taking a fashion tip from Yves St. Aaron—he wore no shirt. His chest hairs were matted with either some type of oil or sweat. Quite a turn-on. The form-fitting pants were a few sizes too small, outlining a bulge in his crotch. Myron started feeling nauseous again.

Frank did not speak. He sat at his brother's desk and waited.

"Now, Myron," Herman continued, "I understand this is all about some black boy who plays basketball."

"Chaz Landreaux," Myron said. "And I'm not sure he'd be crazy about being called 'boy.' "

"Pardon an old man who is not up on all the politically correct terms. I meant no disrespect."

Win sat quietly, studying his surroundings.

"Let me tell you how I see it," Herman continued. "And I'm trying to be objective here. Your Mr. Landreaux made a deal. He took the money. For four years he helped his family with that money. Then when it was time to pay up, he reneged."

"That's objective? Chaz Landreaux is just a kid—"

"Spare me the lecture," Herman interrupted gently. "We're not social workers here. You know that. We are businessmen. We made an investment in this young man. We risked several thousand dollars on him. The investment was finally about to pay dividends when you interfered."

"I didn't interfere. He came to me. He's a scared kid. O'Connor got his hooks in him when he was eighteen. There are rules against approaching kids that young for a reason. Now the kid's trying to get out before he slides in too deep."

Herman looked skeptical. "Oh, come on now, Myron. Kids grow up fast nowadays. He knew exactly what he was doing. So it was against the rules—big deal. The kid knew the rules. He wanted the money anyway."

"He'll pay it back."

Frank Ache spoke for the first time. "Fuck he will."

Myron waved. "Hi, Frank. Boss threads."

"And fuck you too, bug shit. Deal's a deal."

Myron turned to Win. "Bug shit?"

Win shrugged.

"The deal," Myron continued, "was that Chaz could back out at any time and pay back the money. Roy O'Connor told him that."

"I don't give a fuck what O'Connor said."

Herman said, "Please, Frank, we don't need to get hostile."

"Ah, fuck him, Herman. This asshole wants to fuck me over. He wants to steal food off my fucking table. Not just this Landreaux nigger. That's just the start. We got dozens of prospects signed like this. We lose one, we lose them all. I say we let the other agents know we ain't to be messed with. I say we waste Bolitar right now."

Myron said, "I don't like that idea."

"Who the fuck asked you?"

"Just giving my opinion."

"Please, Frank, this isn't helping. You promised to let me handle this."

"Handle what? Kill the son of a bitch. End of story."

"Wait in the other room. I'll take care of it, I promise."

Frank glared at Myron. Myron did not bother glaring back. He knew this was part of the act. He knew that they were trying to intimidate him in much the same way Otto Burke and Larry Hanson had. But for some odd reason, the air of death gave the Mutt and Jeff routine a whole new dynamic.

Win, however, remained pensive.

"Come on, Aaron," Frank growled. "Let's get the fuck out of here." He stood. "But the contract is still on."

"Fine," Herman said. "If you want to kill him, I won't get in the way."

"He's as good as dead."

Frank and Aaron left. Frank slammed the door. Overacting, Myron thought, but an effective cameo appearance.

Myron said, "He's fun."

Herman moved to the corner of the room. He took a slow practice swing with the club. "I wouldn't mess with him, Myron. Frank is really angry. Me, I've always liked you. From the early days. But I'm not sure I can help you on this one."

The "early days" had begun Myron's sophomore year at Duke. It was not something he liked to remember. His father had been gambling. And losing. On the day before a game against Georgia State, Myron returned to his dorm to find his father and two of Herman Ache's hoods. The two hoods told Myron that if Georgia State did not cover the twelve-point spread, his father would lose a finger. His father was crying, the first time Myron had ever seen his father cry. Myron made three turnovers in the last forty seconds to make sure Duke won by only ten.

Father and son never talked about it.

"Why is this kid, this Chaz Landreaux, so important to you, Myron?"

"I think he's worth saving."

"Saving from what?"

"He's just a kid, Herman. Frank is putting the screws to him. I want it to stop."

Herman smiled, changed clubs, took a few more swings. Then he picked up his putter. "Still a crusader, eh, Myron?"

"Hardly. I'm just trying to help the kid."

"And yourself."

"Fine. And myself."

Myron realized that Herman Ache was wearing golf cleats. Jesus. To most people golf is an idiotic excuse for a sport. For others it's a life-consuming obsession. There is no in between.

"I don't think," Herman said, reading the break in his carpet, "I can stop Frank. He's very determined."

"You run the show," Myron said. "Everyone knows that."

"But Frank is my brother. I don't step on his toes unless it's absolutely necessary. I don't think that's the case here."

"What did Frank do to him?"

"Pardon?"

"How did he scare the kid?"

"Oh," Herman said. Another club changed. This time he exchanged the putter for a wood. "He kidnapped his sister. Twin sister, I think."

Myron felt his stomach dive anew. They'd been right. Not much satisfaction in that. "Is she okay?"

"Oh, I wouldn't worry," Herman said, as if that were a truly foolish question. "They won't hurt her. Long as Landreaux continues to cooperate."

"When are they going to let her go?"

"Two more days. Something about making sure the contract is official and Landreaux doesn't have second thoughts."

"What do you want, Herman? What's it going to cost to get Frank off?"

He put on a golf glove and took a very deliberate swing, watching his hands. "I'm an old man, Myron. A *rich* old man. What could you possibly give me?"

Win sat forward, moving for the first time. "Your club is too far open on your swing, Mr. Ache. Try turning your wrists a little more. Shift your grip to the right a little."

The sudden change in subject caught everyone by surprise. Herman looked at Win. "I'm sorry. I never caught the name."

"Windsor Horne Lockwood III."

"Ah, so you are the immortal Win. Not exactly what I expected." He tested the new grip. "Feels odd."

"Give it a few weeks," Win said. "Do you play often?"

"As often as I can. It's more than just a game to me. It's . . ."

"Sacred," Win finished for him.

His eyes livened. "Exactly. You play, Mr. Lockwood?"

"Yes."

"Nothing like it, is there?"

"Nothing," Win agreed. "Where do you play?"

"Not easy for my kind to find good courses. I joined a club in Westchester. St. Anthony's. You know it?"

"No."

"It's not much of a course. Eighteen holes, of course. Very rocky. You have to be half mountain goat."

Golf stories. Myron loved them. Didn't everyone?

"I don't understand something," Myron said, playing along. "With all your, uh, influence, why don't you play anywhere you want?"

Herman and Win looked at him as though he were a

naked infidel praying in the Vatican. "Excuse him," Win said. "Myron does not understand golf. He thinks a nine iron is a vitamin supplement."

Herman laughed. The hoods joined suit. Myron didn't get it.

"I understand fine," Myron said. "Golf is a bunch of silly-dressed men using massive tracts of real estate to play with a ball and stick."

Myron laughed. No one joined suit. Golfers are not known for their sense of humor.

Herman put the club back in the bag. "A man does not force or buy or bully his way onto a golf course," he explained. "I have too much respect for the game, for the traditions, to do anything so crass. It would be like putting a gun against a priest's head to get the front pew."

"Sacrilege," Win said.

"Exactly. No *real* golfer would do it."

"He has to be invited," Win added.

"Right. And you don't merely play a great course. You pay homage to it. I'd love to be invited to one of the world's great courses. It would be my dream. But it is not meant to be."

"How about being invited to two of them?" Win asked.

"Two—" Herman stopped. His eyes widened for a millisecond, then quickly dimmed as though afraid he was being teased. "What do you mean?"

Win pointed to a picture on the left wall. "Merion Golf Club," he said. Then he pointed to a picture on the far wall. "And Pine Valley."

"What about them?"

"I assume you've heard of them?"

"Heard of them?" Herman repeated. "They're the

top two courses on the East Coast, two of the best in the world. Name a hole. Go ahead, any hole, either course.''

"Sixth hole at Merion."

Herman's face glowed like a little kid's on Christmas morning. "One of the most underrated holes anywhere. It sets up with a semiblind tee-shot to a fairway that favors a soft fade. Start your tee-shot at middle bunker, then cut back to the center, keeping clear of the boundary, which comes in on the right. Long-to-middle iron to the modestly elevated green, careful of the bunkers on the left and right."

Win smiled. "Very impressive."

Snore.

"Don't tell me, Mr. Lockwood, that you've played Merion and Pine Valley." Something well past awe resonated in Herman's voice.

"I'm a member of both."

Herman inhaled sharply. Myron half-expected him to cross himself. "A member," he began incredulously, "of both?"

"I'm a three handicap at Merion," Win continued. "A five handicap at Pine Valley. And I'd like you to be my guest at both for a weekend. We'll try to get in seventy-two holes a day, thirty-six at each course. We'll start at five A.M. Unless that's too early."

Herman shook his head. Myron thought his eyes looked teary. "Not too early," he managed.

"Next weekend okay for you?" Win asked.

Herman picked up the phone. "Let the girl go," he said. "And the contract is off. Anyone touches Myron Bolitar, they're dead."

Chapter 31

Win and Myron went back to the office. Myron felt sore from the beating, but nothing was broken. He would persevere. He was that kind of guy. Terribly brave.

Esperanza said, "You look like shit."

"You're so hung up on appearances."

He tossed her the photograph of Adam Culver. "See if your friend Lucy recognizes him."

She snapped a salute. *"Jawohl, Kommandant."* Of all the old shows, Esperanza's favorite was *Hogan's Heroes.* Myron was not a big fan, though he always wished he could have been there when some young TV hotshot said, "Hey, I got an idea for a sitcom! Set it in a POW camp in Nazi Germany. Laughs galore."

"How many calls?" he asked.

"About a million. Mostly the press wanting your comments on Christian's signing." She smiled. "Nice job on that one."

"Thank you."

"That Otto Burke," she said, a pencil near her mouth. "Is he single?"

Myron looked at her, horrified. "Why would you want to know?"

"He's kinda cute."

The nausea was back. "You're hitting me up for a raise, aren't you? Please say yes."

Esperanza smiled coyly but said nothing. He started for his office.

"Hold it," she said. "A strange message just came in for you a few minutes ago."

"From?"

"A woman named Madelaine. Wouldn't give her last name. Sounded sultry."

The dean-nessa. Hmm.

"She leave a number?"

Esperanza nodded, handed it to him. "Remember: The condom is your friend."

"Thanks, Mom."

"Speaking of which, your mother called twice, your father once. I think they're worried about you."

He entered his office. His little private sanctuary. He liked it in here. Myron held most of his negotiations and important meetings in the traditionally decorated conference room, freeing him up to make his office whatever he wanted it to be. He had, of course, his view of the Manhattan skyline to his left. On the wall behind his desk he had framed posters from Broadway musicals: *Fiddler on the Roof, The Pajama Game, How to Succeed in Business Without Really Trying, Man of La Mancha, Les Misérables, La Cage aux Folles, A Chorus Line, West Side Story, Phantom.*

Another wall had movie stills: Humphrey Bogart and Ingrid Bergman in *Casablanca,* Woody Allen and Diane Keaton in *Annie Hall.* Katharine Hepburn and Spencer Tracy in *Adam's Rib.* Groucho, Chico, and Harpo in *A Night at the Opera.* Adam West and Burt Ward in *Batman,* the TV show, the real Batman, the one where Burgess Meredith played the Penguin and Cesar Romero played the Joker. The Golden Age of Television.

The final wall had photographs of Myron's clients. In a few days Christian Steele cloaked in Titans blue would join the group.

He dialed Madelaine Gordon's number. The answering machine picked up. Her silky voice. Hearing it again made his throat dry. He hung up, not leaving a message. He checked the time on the far wall. The clock was shaped like a giant watch with a Boston Celtics insignia in the center.

Three-thirty.

Still time to get to the campus. Madelaine was not important, but Myron very much wanted to see the dean. And he wanted to show up unexpectedly.

At Esperanza's desk he said, "I'm going out for a while. You can reach me in the car."

"Are you limping?" she asked.

"A little. Ache's men roughed me up."

"Oh. See you later."

"Hurts like hell, but I can take it."

"Uh-huh."

"Don't make a scene."

"Inside," she said. "I'm dying."

"Please see if you can reach Chaz Landreaux. Tell him we need to talk."

"Okay."

He left. He picked up his car in the garage. Win was into cars. He loved his racing-green Jag. Myron drove a blue Ford Taurus. He was not what one might call a car man. A car got him from point A to point B, that was all. It was not a status symbol. It was not a second home. It was not his baby.

The drive didn't take long. Myron took the Lincoln Tunnel. He passed the famed York Motel. Long sign:

$11.99 PER HOUR
$95 PER WEEK
MIRRORED ROOMS
NOW FEATURING SHEETS!

He paid the toll on the Parkway. The woman in the booth was very friendly. She almost looked at him when she tossed him the change.

He called his mother on the car phone and reassured her he was okay. She told him to call his father, he was the worried one. Myron called his father and reassured him he was okay. He told him to call his mother, she was the worried one. Great communication. The secret to a happy marriage.

He thought about Kathy Culver. He thought about Adam Culver. He thought about Nancy Serat. He tried to draw little lines, connecting them. The lines were tenuous at best. He was sure Fred Nickler, Sir Sleaze Rag, was one line. That picture hadn't sneaked into *Nips* by itself. Fred seemed to run a tight operation. He had to know more than he was saying. Win was digging into his background, seeing what he could unearth.

Half an hour later, Myron arrived at the campus. Extra-deserted today. No one on the commons. Very few cars. He parked near the dean's house and knocked on the door. Madelaine (he still liked the name) answered. She smiled when she saw him, clearly pleased, tilting her head a little. "Well, hello, Myron."

"Hi." The Return of Mr. Smooth.

Madelaine Gordon was dressed for tennis. Short white skirt. Great legs. White shirt. He noticed that the shirt was see-through. Keen observation, the signs of a master investigator. Madelaine noticed him noticing. She did not seem particularly offended.

"I'm sorry to intrude," Myron said.

"No intrusion," she said. "I was just about to take a shower."

Hmm. "Your husband's not in, is he?"

She crossed her hands under her breasts. "Not for hours yet," she said. "You got my message?"

He nodded.

"Would you care to come inside?"

Myron said, " 'Mrs. Robinson, you're trying to seduce me, aren't you?' "

"Pardon me?"

"The Graduate."

"Oh." Madelaine wet her lips. She had a very sexy mouth. People overlook the mouth. They talk about the nose, the chin, the eyes, the cheekbones. Myron was a mouth man. "I guess I should be offended," she continued. "I mean, I'm not that much older than you, Myron."

"Good point. Quote withdrawn."

"So," she said. "I'll ask again. Would you like to come inside?"

Myron said, "Sure." Bowling her over with quick wit. What chance did she have against such sparkling repartee?

She disappeared back into the house, creating an air vacuum that sucked Myron—against his will, of course —in after her. The inside was nice, the kind of house that obviously saw plenty of company. Big open room on the left. Tiffany lamps. Persian rugs. Busts of French guys with long, curly hair. Grandfather clock. Painted portraits of stern-faced men.

"Care to sit down?" she said.

"Thank you."

Sultry. That had been the word Esperanza used. It fit. Not just Madelaine's voice but her mannerisms, her walk, her eyes, her persona.

"How about a drink?" she asked.

He noticed she already had one made for herself. "Sure, whatever you're having."

"A vodka tonic."

"Sounds good." Myron hated vodka.

She mixed the drink. He sipped it, trying not to make a face. He wasn't sure if he was successful. She sat down next to him. "I've never been this forward before," she said.

"That a fact?"

"But I'm very attracted to you. It's one of the reasons I loved watching you play. You're really very handsome. I'm sure you're sick of hearing that."

"Well, I don't know if *sick* is the right word."

Madelaine crossed her legs. It wasn't Jessica's leg cross, but it was still worth watching. "When you came to the door yesterday, I didn't want to miss out on the opportunity. I decided to throw caution to the wind and just go for it."

Myron could not stop grinning. "I see."

She stood and reached out her hand to him. "Now how about that shower?"

"Uh, can we talk first?"

Puzzlement shadowed her face. "Is there something wrong?"

Myron feigned embarrassment. "Aren't you married?"

"And that bothers you?"

Not really. "Yes. I guess it does."

"Admirable," she said.

"Thank you."

"Stupid too."

"Thank you."

She laughed. "Actually, it's sweet. But Dean Gordon and I have what we call a semi-open marriage."

Hmm. "Could you elaborate a little?"

"Elaborate?"

"Just to make me feel more comfortable about all this."

She sat back down. The white skirt might as well not

have been there. Her legs could best be described as scrumptious. "I've never had to elaborate before," she said.

"I realize that. But I'm interested."

Arched eyebrow. "In?"

"Can we start with your definition of *semi-open*?"

She sighed. "My husband and I have been close friends since childhood. Our parents summered together in Hyannis Port. We were both from the 'right families.' " She made little quote marks in the air when she said "right families." "We thought that would be enough. But it wasn't."

"So why not divorce?"

She looked a question. "Why am I telling you this?"

"My honest blue eyes," he said. "They're hypnotic."

"Maybe they are."

Now Myron gave her aw-shucks modesty. Mr. Adaptable Face.

"My husband is politically connected. He was an ambassador. He's next in line to be university president. If we get divorced—"

"That ends," Myron finished.

"Yes. Even these days, the hint of scandal can destroy a career and a lifestyle. But more than that, Harrison and I are still dear friends. Best friends, really. It's just that we need limited outside stimulation."

"Limited?"

"Once every two months," she said.

Yikes. "How did you come up with that number?" he asked. "Some kind of new algorithm, perhaps?"

She smiled. "Lots of discussions. Negotiations, really. Once a month seemed like too much. Once a semester too little."

Myron nodded at her. *Toto, we're not in Kansas anymore.*

"And we always use a condom," she added. "That's part of the arrangement."

"I see."

"Do you have one?" she asked. "A condom."

"On?"

She smiled. "I have some upstairs."

"Can I ask one more thing?"

"If you must."

"How do you and your husband know that the other has kept to their, er, limit?"

"Easy," she said. "We tell each other. Everything. Helps spice things up a little."

Madelaine was seriously strange, which only made her more attractive to Myron.

"Your husband. Does he ever fool around with coeds?"

She leaned forward and put her hand on his thigh. Upper thigh. Upper, upper thigh. "That kind of thing turn you on?"

"Yeah." He tried a rakish smile. But rakish was not him. He could see in her eyes that she wasn't buying it.

Madelaine took back her hand. "What are you up to, Myron?" she asked.

"Up to?"

"I feel like I'm being used," she said. "But not the way I had in mind."

Man. "Just getting in the mood."

"I don't think so, Myron." She studied him for moment. "Be honest for a second. Are we going to go to bed?"

"No," he said. "We're not."

"I've never been turned down before."

"And I've never turned down a proposition like this

before," Myron said. "Come to think of it, I've never had a proposition like this before."

"Is it because I'm married?"

"No."

"Are you involved with someone else?" she asked.

"Worse. I'm on the cusp of something that means a great deal to me. I don't know which way I'm going to fall. I'm confused."

"That's sweet."

Again he gave her aw-shucks.

"If it doesn't work out . . . ?" she said.

"I'll be back."

She kissed him then. Hard. It was a damn good kiss. He felt it in his toes.

"Just the overture," she said.

He'd be dead before the second scene. "I really do have to talk to your husband. Do you know when he'll be home?"

"Not for a while. But he's at the office across campus. By himself. You'll have to knock loudly for him to hear you."

He rose. "Thanks."

"Myron?"

"Yes?"

"We never use names when we discuss our affairs. I don't know if Harrison fools around with co-eds. I would doubt it highly."

"How about Kathy Culver?"

She visibly jumped. Her face stiffened. "I think you better leave now."

"The honest blue eyes," Myron said. "Watch the honest blue eyes."

"Not this time. And when I watched you play, it wasn't your eyes I looked at."

"Oh?"

"Your ass," she said. "It looked nice in those little shorts."

Myron felt cheap. Or ecstatic. Probably ecstatic. "Were they having an affair?" he asked.

She said nothing.

"I'll shake my ass if I have to."

"They weren't having an affair," she said firmly. "That much I know."

"So why did you get all bent out of shape?"

"You were asking if my husband had an illicit affair with a co-ed who was probably murdered. I was taken aback."

"Did you know Kathy Culver?"

"No."

"Did your husband ever talk about her?"

"Not really. I just know she worked in his office." She looked at the grandfather clock, stood, and led him to the door. "Talk to my husband, Myron. He's a good man. He'll tell you everything you need to know."

"Like?"

She shook her head. "Thanks for visiting."

Madelaine was in shutdown mode. Probably hurt by his interrogation technique. Using his brawny body to get his way. Myron had never done that before. He liked it. Better than pistol-whipping a suspect, anyway.

He turned and left. Madelaine was probably watching his ass. He put a little wiggle in his step and hurried across campus.

Chapter 32

Jessica found Getaway Realty in the Bergen County Yellow Pages. Their office was a converted cottage next to a McDonald's off Route 17 on the New Jersey side of the New York–New Jersey border. The drive was only twenty minutes, but it felt as if she'd arrived in the rural past. She actually saw a feed store.

Only one person was in the office.

"Well, hello there," the man said with a too-wide smile. He was mid-fifties, bald, with a long, scraggly gray beard, like a college professor's. He wore a flannel shirt, black tie, Levi's jeans, and red Chuck Taylor Converse sneakers.

"I'm Tom Corbett, president of Getaway Realty." He handed her a card. "What can I do for you today?"

"I'm Dr. Adam Culver's daughter," she said. "He wrote a check to your office on May twenty-fifth for $649."

"Yeah, so?"

"He passed away recently. I'd like to know what it was for."

Corbett took a step back. "I'm awfully sorry to hear that," he said. "Nice man, your father."

"Thank you. Can you tell me why he came to you?"

He thought a moment, shrugged. "Don't see why not. He rented a cabin."

"Near here?"

"Five, six miles. In the woods."

"For how long?"

"A month. Starting May twenty-fifth. Still has it for a few more weeks, if you'd like to use it."

"What kind of cabin?" she asked.

"What kind? Well, it's pretty small. One bedroom, one bathroom with shower stall, living room, kitchenette."

This made no sense. "Do you think you could give me the directions and a spare key?"

He thought that one over too, chewing on the inside of his mouth. "It's a bit remote," he said. "Kinda hard to find, darling."

Aside from *babe* and *honey-bun,* there were few things Jessica enjoyed being called more than *darling.* But now was not the time to explain her sentiments. She bit her lip and held back.

"The cottage's away from it all," Tom continued. "Way away, if you know what I mean. A little hunting, a little fishing, but mostly just peace and quiet." He picked up a key chain as heavy as a barbell. "I'll drive you."

"Thank you."

He drove a Toyota LandCruiser and chatted the whole way, as though she were a client. "Here's our local grocery store."

It was an enormous A&P Superstore.

She was surprised when he turned onto an unpaved road. They were heading straight into the woods.

"Nice, ain't it? Real pretty."

"Uh-huh."

Green foliage surrounded them. Jessica was not much of the outdoor sort. To her, the great outdoors meant bugs and humidity and dirt and no running water and no bathroom. Man had evolved for millions of years to escape the woods. Why rush back? But more important, her father had felt the same. He hated the woods.

Why would he rent a cabin out here?

Tom pointed to a gully up ahead. "Two years ago, guy got killed by a hunter over there. Accident. The hunter thought he was a deer, shot him in the head."

"Uh-huh."

"Couple of dead bodies been found in the woods. Three in the past two years, I think. Found one girl just a couple months back. Runaway, they guessed. Hard to tell 'cause she was all decayed and stuff."

"You're a hell of a salesman, Tom."

He laughed. "Yeah, well, I can tell when someone ain't a buyer."

Jessica, of course, knew all about the bodies. The police hadn't caught the killer, but the general consensus was that the psychopath had gotten hold of one more young girl, one that had not yet been found:

Kathy Culver.

Could Kathy's fate have been that simple and that horrible? Had she been another victim of a random psychopath, just as everyone thought?

No, Jessica told herself. Too many holes.

"When I was a kid growing up around here," Tom said, "these woods were filled with legends. Guy with a hook hand lived in here, the old-timers said, used to kidnap bad little boys and gut them with his hook."

"Charming."

"Sometimes I wonder if he moved on to young ladies."

Jessica said nothing.

"Used to call him Dr. Hook," he continued.

"What?"

"Dr. Hook. That's what we all called him."

"Isn't that a singer?" she asked.

"A what?"

"Never mind."

They drove another mile away from civilization. "That's the house," Tom said. "Up there behind the trees."

It was a small wooden cabin with a big front porch. "Rustic, ain't it?"

Decrepit would have been a better adjective. Jessica checked the porch, but there were no toothless hillbillies playing dueling banjos.

"Did my father say why he wanted to rent this cabin?"

"Just said he needed someplace to get away from it all in these woods."

It still made no sense. Dad was going to be gone at a medical examiners' conference for a week out of the month, anyway. And Adam Culver was not the get-away-from-it-all type. He dealt with the dead. On vacations he wanted to be in Vegas or Atlantic City or someplace with lots of people and action. Now he was renting the Waltons' cabin.

Tom used the key to unlock the door. He pushed it open and said, "After you."

Jessica stepped into the living room. And stopped short.

Tom came in behind her. His voice was a whisper. "What the hell is this?" he asked.

Chapter 33

Dean Gordon's office was in Compton Hall. The building was only three stories high but wide. Greek columns out front screamed House of Learning. Brick exterior. White double doors. Directly inside was a bulletin board filled with old notices. Meetings of the usual campus groups: the African American Change Committee, the Gay-Lesbian Alliance, the Liberators of Palestine, the Coalition to Stop the Domination of Womyn (never spelled *women,* for the sexism the name implies), the South African Freedom Fighters—all taking the summer off. College fun days.

There was no one inside the huge lobby. The motif was marble. Marble floors, banisters, columns. The walls were covered with huge portraits of men in graduation robes, most of whom would flip if they could read the bulletin board. All the lights were on. Myron's footsteps clacked and reverberated in the still room. He wanted to shout "Echo," but was far too adult.

The dean of students' office suite was at the end of the left corridor. The door was locked. Myron knocked hard. "Dean Gordon?"

Shuffling behind the dark-paneled doors. Several seconds later, the door opened. Dean Gordon was wearing tortoiseshell glasses. He had wispy hair, conservatively cut, a handsome face with clear brown eyes. His features were gentle, as though the facial bones had been rounded

off to soften his appearance. He looked kind, trustworthy. Myron hated that.

"I'm sorry," the dean said. "The office is closed
until tomorrow morning."

"We need to talk."

Confusion crossed his face. "Do I know you?"

"I don't think so."

"You're not a student here."

"Hardly."

"May I ask who you are?"

Myron looked at him steadily. "You know who I am.
And you know what I want to talk about."

"I don't have the slightest idea to what you are referring, but I am really quite busy—"

"Read any good magazines lately?"

Dean Gordon's whole body twitched. "What did you
say?"

"I guess I could come back when the office was
crowded. Maybe bring some reading material for the
school's trustees, though I understand they only read the
articles."

No response.

Myron smiled—knowingly. At least, he hoped that
was how it looked. Myron had no idea what part the
dean played in this little mystery. He had to step tentatively here.

The dean coughed into his fist. Not a real cough or
throat-clear. Just something to stall, give him a chance to
think. Finally he said, "Please come in."

He disappeared back into his office. No sucking vacuum this time, but Myron still followed. They passed a
few chairs in the waiting room, a secretary's desk. The
typewriter was hidden by a khaki-colored dust cover.
Camouflaged in the event of war.

Dean Gordon's office was cookie-cut university executive. Lots of wood. Diplomas. Old sketches of the Reston University chapel. Lucite blocks with clippings or awards on the desk. Bookshelves with all nonfiction titles. The books hadn't been touched. They were props, creating the mood of tradition, professionalism, competence. The prerequisite picture of the family. Madelaine and a girl who looked about twelve or thirteen years old. Myron picked up the photograph.

"Nice family," he said. Nice wife.

"Thank you. Please have a seat."

Myron sat. "Say, where did Kathy work?"

The dean stopped in midseat. "Pardon me?"

"Where was her desk?"

"Whose?"

"Kathy Culver's."

Dean Gordon lowered himself the rest of the way, slowly, as into a hot tub of water. "She shared a desk with another student in the room next door."

Myron said, "Convenient."

Dean Gordon's eyebrows frowned. "I'm sorry. I missed your name."

"Deluise. Dom Deluise."

The dean allowed himself a small brittle smile. He looked tight enough to pop a wine cork with his butt. No doubt being sent the magazine had put the screws in. No doubt Jake's visit yesterday had tightened them a little. "What, Mr. Deluise, can I do for you?"

"I think you know." Again the knowing smile. Combined with the honest blue eyes. If Dean Gordon were female, he'd be naked by now.

"I'm afraid I don't have the slightest idea," the dean said.

Myron continued the knowing smile. He felt like an idiot or a morning network weatherman, if there was a difference. This was an old trick he was trying. Pretend you know more than you do. Get him talking. Play it by ear. Impromptu.

The dean folded his hands and put them on his desk. Trying to look as if he were in control. "This whole conversation is very strange. Perhaps you could explain why you're here."

"I thought we should chat."

"About?"

"Your English department, for starters. Do you still make students read *Beowulf*?"

"Please, whatever your name is, I don't have time for games."

"Neither do I." Myron took out his copy of *Nips* and tossed it on the desk. The magazine was starting to look creased and worn from all the handling, as if it belonged to a hormonal adolescent.

The dean barely glanced at it. "What is this?"

"Now who's playing games?"

Dean Gordon leaned back, his fingers fiddling with his chin. "Who are you?" he asked. "Really."

"It's not important. I am merely a messenger."

"Messenger for who?"

"For *whom*," Myron corrected. "Prepositional phrase. And you a college dean."

"I don't need any smart talk, young man."

Myron looked at him. "Get real."

The dean sucked in air as if he were about to plunge underwater. "What do you want?"

"Isn't the pleasure of your company enough?"

"This is not a joking matter."

"No, it's not."

"So kindly stop playing games. What do you want with me?"

Myron tried the knowing smile again. Dean Gordon

looked puzzled for a brief moment but then returned the smile. It too was knowing.

"Or should I say," the dean added, "how much?"

He seemed more in control now. He had dealt with the blow and was carrying on. A problem had arisen. But there was a solution. There always was in his world.

Money.

He took out a checkbook from his top drawer. "Well?"

"Not that simple," Myron said.

"What do you mean?"

"Don't you think someone should pay?"

He shrugged. "Let's talk figures."

"Don't you think this is worth something more than just money?"

He looked bewildered, as though Myron had just denied the existence of gravity. "I don't understand what you mean."

"What about justice?" Myron asked. "Kathy is owed. Big-time."

"I agree. And I am willing to pay. But what good is revenge going to do her now? You are the messenger, are you not?"

"I am."

"Then go back and tell Kathy to take the money."

Myron's heart collapsed. This man, a man who was clearly involved in what had happened that night, believed Myron was a messenger for a living, breathing Kathy Culver. Tread gently, fair Myron. Ever gently.

But how to play this . . .

"Kathy is not happy with you," he tried.

"I meant her no harm."

Myron put his hand on his chest and lifted his head dramatically. "Be thy intents wicked or charitable, thou com'st in such a questionable shape."

"What's that supposed to mean?"

Myron shrugged. "I like to work Shakespeare into conversations. Makes me sound smart, don't you think?"

The dean made a face. "Can we return to the matter at hand?"

"Sure."

"You say Kathy does not want money."

"Yup."

"What then does she want?"

Good question. "She wants the truth to come out." Noncommittal, vague, open-ended.

"What truth?"

"Stop playing dumb," Myron snapped, feigning annoyance. "You weren't about to write a check to her favorite charity, were you?"

"But I didn't do anything," he half-whined. "Kathy took off that night. I haven't seen her since. How was I supposed to know what to think or do?"

Myron gave him a skeptical look. He did that because he had no idea what else to do. He was now playing Jake's game, the keep-silent-and-hope-he-ties-his-own-noose game. This worked especially well with political types. They're born with a defective chromosome that will not allow for prolonged silence.

"She has to understand," he continued. "I did my best. She disappeared. What was I supposed to do? Go to the police? Was that what she wanted? I didn't know anymore. I was thinking of her. She might have changed her mind. I didn't know. I was trying to consider her interests."

The skeptical look came easier after that last sentence. Myron only wished he knew what the hell the dean was talking about. They sat there staring at one another. Then something happened to Dean Gordon's face. Myron wasn't sure exactly what it was, but his whole demeanor seemed to slump. His eyes grew twisted, pained. He shook his head.

"Enough," he said in a quiet voice.

"What's enough?"

He closed the checkbook. "I won't pay," he said. "Tell Kathy I'll do whatever she wants. I'll stand by her no matter what the cost. This has gone on long enough. I can't live like this. I am not an evil man. She's a sick girl. She needs help. I want to help."

Myron had not expected this. "Do you mean that?"

"Yes. Very much."

"You want to help your former lover?"

His head shot up. "What did you say?"

Myron had been skating blindly on thin ice. His last comment, it seemed, had been something of a blowtorch.

"Did you say 'lover'?"

Uh-oh.

"Kathy didn't send you," he continued. "She has nothing to do with you, does she?"

Myron said nothing.

"Who are you? What is your real name?"

"Myron Bolitar."

"Who?"

"Myron Bolitar."

"Are you a police officer?"

"No."

"Then what exactly are you?"

"A sports agent."

"A what?"

"I represent athletes."

"You— So what do you have to do with this?"

"I'm a friend," Myron said. "I'm trying to find Kathy."

"Is she alive?"

"I don't know. But you seem to think so."

Dean Gordon opened his bottom drawer, took out a cigarette, lit it.

"Bad for you," Myron said.

"I quit smoking five years ago. Or so everyone thinks."

"Another little secret?"

He smiled without humor. "So you were the one who sent me the magazine."

Myron shook his head. "Nope."

"Then who?"

"I don't know. I'm trying to figure that out. But I know about it. And now I also know you're hiding something about Kathy's disappearance."

He inhaled deeply and let loose a long stream of smoke. "I could deny it. I could deny everything we said here today."

"You could," Myron countered. "But of course I have the magazine. I have no reason to lie. And I also have a friend in Sheriff Jake Courter. But you're right. In the end it would be my word against yours."

Dean Gordon took off his glasses and rubbed his eyes. "No," he said slowly, "it won't come down to that. I meant what I said before. I want to help her. I *need* to help her."

Myron was not sure what to think. The man looked in genuine pain, but Myron had seen performances that would put Olivier to shame. Was his guilt real? Was his sudden catharsis the result of having a conscience, or was it self-preservation? Myron didn't know. He didn't much care either, as long as he got to the truth.

"When was the last time you saw Kathy?" Myron asked.

"The night she vanished," he said.

"She came to your house?"

He nodded. "It was late. I guess around eleven, eleven-thirty. I was in my study. My wife was upstairs in bed. The doorbell rang. Not once. Repeatedly, urgently. Interspersed with heavy door-pounding. It was Kathy."

His voice was on autopilot, as if he were reading a fairy tale to a child. "She was crying. Or rather she was sobbing uncontrollably. So much so that she couldn't speak. I brought her into my study. I poured her some brandy and wrapped an afghan around her shoulders. She looked"—he stopped, considered—"very small. Helpless. I sat down across from her and took her hand. She jerked it back. That was when the tears stopped. Not slowly, but all at once, as though a switch had been thrown. She became very still. Her face was completely blank, no emotion whatsoever. Then she started talking."

He reached into the drawer for another cigarette. He put it in his mouth. The match lit on the fourth try.

"She started from the beginning," he continued. "Her voice was remarkably steady. It never cracked or wavered—uncanny, when you consider the fact that she was hysterical just moments earlier. But her words belied her placid tone. She told me stories—" He stopped again, shook his head. "They were surprising, to say the least. I had known Kathy for almost a year. I considered her a thoughtful, sweet, proper young woman. I am not making moral judgments here. But she had always been what I considered old-fashioned. And here she was telling me stories that would make a sailor blush.

"She started by telling me that she used to be everything I always thought she was. The girl next door. Everyone's favorite. But then she changed. She became, in her own words, 'a free-wheeling slut.' She started with some boys in her high school class. But she quickly moved onto bigger things. Adults, teachers, friends of

her parents. Biracial, homosexual, two-on-ones, even or-
gies. She took pictures of her encounters. For posterity,
she said with a sneer.''

"Did she mention any names?'' Myron asked. "Of
the teachers or adults or anyone?''

"No. No names.''

They fell into silence. Dean Gordon looked exhausted.

"What happened next?'' Myron prompted.

He lifted his head slowly, as though it took great effort. "Her story began to change direction,'' he said.
"For the better. She said she realized that what she was
doing was wrong and stupid. She began, she said, to
work through her problems. That was when she met
Christian and fell in love. She wanted to put it all behind
her, but it wasn't easy. The past wouldn't just go away.
She tried and tried, and then . . .'' His voice trailed off.

"And then?'' Myron prompted.

"Then Kathy just looked at me—I'll never forget this
—and she said, 'I was raped tonight.' Just like that. Out
of nowhere. I was stunned, of course. There were six of
them, she said. Or seven, she wasn't sure. A gang-rape in
the locker room. I asked her when. She told me it had
started less than an hour ago. She had gone to the locker
room to meet someone. A blackmailer, she said. A former, uh, suitor, who had threatened to reveal her past.
She was going to pay for his silence.''

The big cash withdrawal from her trust account, Myron thought.

"But when she got to the locker room, the blackmailer wasn't alone. Several of his teammates were with
him, including another past suitor. They didn't hit her,
she said. They didn't beat her. And she didn't fight.
There were too many of them, and they were too

strong." He closed his eyes, his voice a whisper. "They took turns with her."

Silence.

"As I said before, Kathy told me all this in the most dispassionate tone I had ever heard her use. Her eyes were clear, determined. She told me there was only one way to bury her past. Once and for all. She would have to confront it head-on. She'd have to push it out into the bright sunshine where it would wither and die like a medieval vampire. She said she knew what she had to do."

More silence.

"What?" Myron asked.

"Prosecute the boys who raped her. Face up to her past and then put it behind her. Otherwise it would follow her around for the rest of her life."

"What did you say?"

Dean Gordon winced at the question. He stamped out the cigarette. He glanced down at the bottom drawer but didn't reach for another. "I told her to calm down." He laughed at the memory. "Calm down. By now, the girl was so unemotional, so detached, that she could have been reading a telephone directory. And I told her to calm down. Jesus."

"What else?"

"I told her that I thought she was still in shock. I meant that too. I told her that she should consider everything, weigh all her options, not rush into a decision that would undoubtably affect the rest of her life. I told her to think about what it would mean to have her past dragged out—to her family, to her friends, to her fiancé, to herself."

"In other words," Myron said, "you tried to talk her out of pressing charges."

"Perhaps. But I never said what I was really thinking:

A self-described free-wheeling slut who had gotten involved in pornography and wild sex was going to claim she was raped by a group of college boys, two of whom she admitted having past liaisons with. I wanted her to think about all that before she did something rash.''

"Don't be so easy on yourself," Myron said. "You didn't give a damn about her. She came to you for help, and you thought about everything but her. You thought about your precious institution. You thought about the scandal. You thought about the football team on the eve of a national championship. You thought about your own career, how it would come out that she worked for you, how she felt comfortable visiting your house late at night. You'd be tied in. People would investigate you closer, maybe unearth your unusual marital arrangement.''

That prodded him upright. "What about my marital arrangement?''

"Does the phrase 'once every two months' mean anything to you?''

His mouth dropped open. "How . . . ?" He stopped, almost smiled. "You are a very well-informed young man.''

"All-knowing," Myron corrected. "Godlike.''

"I won't comment on my marriage, but I would be less than honest if I did not admit that those selfish considerations crossed my mind. But I was also concerned for Kathy. A mistake like this—''

"A rape, Dean. Not a mistake. Kathy was raped. She didn't make a 'mistake.' She wasn't the victim of an indiscretion. A bunch of football players pinned her down in a locker room and took turns with her against her will.''

"You're simplifying the situation.''

"You're the one who simplified the situation. You just put Kathy last."

"That's not true."

Myron shook his head. No time for this now. "So what happened after you bestowed your stellar counsel upon Kathy?"

He tried to shrug but couldn't pull it off. "She looked at me funny, as though I had betrayed her when all I was trying to do was help. Or maybe she saw in my words the same thing you did. I don't know. She stood up then and said that she would be back tomorrow morning to press charges. Then she left. I never heard from her again until that magazine came in the mail. And the phone call a few nights ago."

"What phone call?"

"A few nights ago, very late, I got a phone call. A female voice—maybe Kathy's, maybe not—said, 'Enjoy the magazine. Come and get me. I survived.' "

" 'Come and get me. I survived'?"

"Something like that, yes."

"What did she mean?"

"I haven't the slightest idea."

"What did you think when you first heard about Kathy's disappearance?"

"That she ran away. Decided it was all too much. I thought she'd come back when she was ready. The police thought that too, until they found her undergarments. Then they suspected violence. But I knew the undergarments were probably from the rape, not the disappearance. So in my mind I still considered her a runaway."

"Didn't the possibility that the rapists wanted to silence her cross your mind?"

"It crossed my mind, yes. But these boys weren't capable of—"

"Rapists," Myron corrected. " 'Boys' who gang-raped a young girl who never did them any harm. You didn't think they had the capability to commit murder?''

"If they wanted her dead, they would never have let her go,'' the dean countered steadily. "That's what I thought.''

"So you kept your mouth shut.''

He nodded. "That was a mistake. I know that now. I was hoping she had just run away for a few days to straighten herself out. When a week passed, I realized it was too late to say anything.''

"You chose to live with the lie.''

"Yes.''

"She was just a student, after all. She came to you for help during the hardest time of her life. And you turned her away.''

"Don't you think I know that?'' he shouted. "Don't you think this has been tearing me apart for the past year and a half?''

"Yeah, you're a real humanitarian.''

"What the hell do you want from me, Bolitar?''

Myron stood. "Resign. Immediately.''

"And if I refuse?''

"Then I'll drag you down, and it'll be uglier than you ever imagined. First thing tomorrow morning. Turn in your letter of resignation.''

He looked up, his fingers supporting his chin. Time passed. His face began to soften as though from a masseur's touch. His eyes closed, and his shoulders slumped. Then he nodded slowly. "All right,'' he said. "Thank you.''

"This isn't penitence. You don't get off that easy.''

"I understand.''

"One last thing: Did Kathy mention any names at all?''

"Names?''

"Of the rapists?"

He hesitated. "No."

"But you have a guess?"

"It's not based on anything concrete."

"Go on."

"A few days after she disappeared, I noticed a certain student was tossing around a lot of money. A trouble-maker. He bought a new BMW convertible that came to my attention because he drove it across the commons. Ripped up a lot of grass."

"Who?"

"An ex–football player. He was kicked off the team for selling drugs. His name was Junior Horton. They call him—"

"Horty."

Myron left without another word, hurrying to get out of the building. It was a beautiful day. Warm but not humid, the sun weakening in the late afternoon but not quite ready to set. The air smelled of freshly cut grass and blooming cherry blossom trees. Myron wanted to spread out a blanket. He wanted to lie down and think about Kathy Culver.

No time.

The phone in his Ford Taurus was ringing when he unlocked the door. It was Esperanza.

"Dead end with Lucy," she said. "Adam Culver wasn't the guy who bought the pictures."

Another theory blown to hell. He was about to start his car when he heard Jake Courter's voice.

"Thought I might find you here."

Myron looked out the open window. "What's up, Jake?"

"We're about to release Nancy Serat's name to the press."

Myron nodded. "Thanks for letting me know."

"That's not why I'm here."

Myron did not like his tone.

"We also have a suspect," Jake continued. "We've brought him in for questioning."

"Who?"

"Your client," Jake said. "Christian Steele."

Chapter 34

"What about Christian?" Myron asked.

"Nancy Serat had just rented that house a week ago," Jake replied, "a day or two before she left for Cancún. She hadn't even unpacked yet."

"So?"

"So how come Christian Steele's fingerprints—clean, fresh prints—are all over the place? On the front doorknob. On a drinking glass. On the fireplace mantel."

Myron tried not to looked stunned. "Come on, Jake. You can't make an arrest on something like that. The press will eat him alive."

"Like I give a flying shit."

"You have nothing."

"We can place him at the scene."

"So what? You can place Jessica at the scene. Gonna arrest her too?"

Jake unbuttoned his jacket, allowing his belly to expand. He was wearing a brown suit, circa 1972. In a word: lapels. No slave to fashion, that Jake. "Okay, smart-boy," he said, "you want to tell me what your client was doing at Nancy Serat's house?"

"We'll ask him. He'll talk to you. Christian's a good kid, Jake. Don't ruin him on speculation."

"Yeah. I'd hate to ruin your commissions."

"Low blow, Jake."

"You're not objective, Bolitar. The kid's your most valuable client, your ticket to the bigs. You don't want him to be guilty."

Myron looked at him but said nothing.

"Leave your car here," Jake said. "I'll drive you to the station."

It was only a mile away. When they pulled into the lot, Jake said, "The new DA is here. Young hotshot named Roland."

Uh-oh. "Cary Roland?" Myron asked. "Curly hair?"

"You know him?"

"Yeah."

"He's a publicity hound," Jake said. "Gets a hard-on watching himself on TV. He practically creamed when he heard Christian's name."

Myron could imagine. Old buddies, he and Cary Roland. This was not a good development. "Has he released Christian's name?"

"Not yet," Jake said. "Cary decided to put it off until eleven. Gets a live feed from all the networks that way."

"And plenty of time to tighten the perm."

"That too."

Christian was sitting in a small room, no bigger than eight by eight. He sat in a chair behind a desk. No hot lights. No one else was in the room.

"Where's Roland?" Myron asked.

"Behind the mirror."

One-way glass, even in a rinky-dink station like this. Myron stepped into the room, looked in the mirror, adjusted his tie, and refrained from giving Roland the finger. Mr. Mature strikes again.

"Mr. Bolitar?"

Myron turned. Christian waved to him as if he'd spotted a familiar face in the stands.

"You okay?" Myron asked.

"I'm fine," Christian said. "I just don't understand what I'm doing here."

A uniformed officer came in with a tape recorder. Myron turned to Jake. "Is he under arrest?"

Jake grinned. "I almost forgot, Bolitar. You're a lawyer too. Nice to be dealing with a professional."

"Is he under arrest?" Myron repeated.

"Not yet. We'd just like to ask him a few questions."

The uniformed officer took care of the preliminaries. Then Jake started.

"My name is Sheriff Jake Courter, Mr. Steele. Do you remember me?"

"Yes, sir. You're handling my fiancée's disappearance."

"That's correct. Now, Mr. Steele, do you know a woman named Nancy Serat?"

"She was Kathy's roommate at Reston."

"Are you aware that Nancy Serat was murdered last night?"

Christian's eyes widened. He turned to Myron. Myron nodded. "My God . . . no."

"Were you friends with Nancy Serat?"

His voice was hollow. "Yes, sir."

"Mr. Steele, can you tell us where you were last night?"

Myron interrupted. "What time last night?"

"From the time he left practice till he went to sleep."

Myron hesitated. This was a trap. He could try to defuse it, or he could let Christian handle it on his own. Under most circumstances Myron would have stepped in and sounded a subtle warning of what the wrong answer might mean. But this time he sat back and watched.

"If you want to know if I was with Nancy Serat last night," Christian said slowly, "the answer is yes."

Myron breathed again. He looked back at the one-way mirror and stuck out his tongue. The demise of Mr. Mature.

"What time was that?" Jake asked.

"Around nine o'clock."

"Where did you see her?"

"At her house."

"The one at 118 Acre Street?"

"Yes, sir."

"What was the purpose of your visit?"

"Nancy returned from a trip that morning. She called and said she needed to talk to me."

"Did she tell you why?"

"She said it had something to do with Kathy. She wouldn't tell me anything else over the phone."

"What happened when you arrived at the house at 118 Acre Street?"

"Nancy practically shoved me out the door. She said I had to leave right away."

"Did she say why?"

"No, sir. I asked Nancy what was going on, but she was insistent. She promised to call me in a day or two and tell me everything, but for now I had to go."

"What did you do?"

"I argued with her for a minute or two. She started getting upset and saying stuff that made no sense. I finally just gave up and left."

"What sort of 'stuff' was she saying?"

"Something about sisters reuniting."

Myron sat up.

Jake asked, "What about sisters reuniting?"

"I don't remember exactly. Something like 'Time for sisters to reunite.' She really wasn't making much sense, sir."

Jake looked at Myron. Myron looked back.

"Do you remember anything else she said?"

"No, sir."

"Did you go straight home after that?"

"Yes, sir."

"What time did you arrive home?"

"Ten-fifteen, I guess. Maybe a little later."

"Is there anybody who can confirm the time?"

"I don't think so. I just moved into a condominium in Englewood. Maybe a neighbor saw me, I don't know."

"Would you mind waiting here for a minute?"

Jake signaled for Myron to follow him. Myron nodded, leaned over to Christian. "Don't say another word until I get back."

Christian nodded.

They stepped into the other room. The other side of the mirror, so to speak. County District Attorney Cary Roland had gone to Harvard Law School with Myron. A bright guy. Law review. Clerk for a Supreme Court justice. Cary Roland had first shown signs of political ambition while exiting his mother's womb.

He looked the same. Gray suit with vest (yes, he'd worn suits to class). Hook nose. Small, dark eyes. Loose curly hair, like a seventies Peter Frampton's, only shorter.

Roland shook his head. Then he made a noise of disgusted belief. "Creative client, Bolitar."

"Not as creative," Myron said, "as your barber."

Jake held back a laugh.

"I say we book him," Roland continued. "We'll announce it at the press conference."

"Now I see it," Myron said.

"See what?"

"The hard-on. When you said 'press.'"

Snickers.

Roland fumed. "Still a comedian, eh, Bolitar? Well, your client is about to go down."

"I don't think so, Cary."

"I don't care what you think."

Myron sighed. "Christian gave you a reasonable explanation for being at Nancy Serat's house. You got nothing else, ergo you got nothing. Besides, imagine the headlines if Christian's innocent. Young DA Makes Major Blunder. Tarnishes Name of Local Hero for Own Gain. Hurts Titans' Chances for Superbowl. Becomes Most Hated Man in State."

Roland swallowed. He hadn't considered that. Blinded by the lights. The TV lights. "Sheriff Courter, what do you think?"

Backpedal time.

"We have no choice," Jake said. "We have to let him go."

"Do you believe his story?"

Jake shrugged. "Who the hell knows? But we don't have enough to keep him."

"Okay," Roland said with a weighty nod. Important man. "He's free to go. But he better not leave town."

Myron looked at Jake. "Not leave town?" He laughed. Hard. "Did he just say not to leave town?"

Jake was trying to hold it in. But his lip was quivering pretty good.

Roland's face turned red. "Infantile," he spat out. "Sheriff, I want daily updates on this case."

"Yes, sir."

Roland gave everyone his most frightening glare. No one fell to their knees. He stormed out.

"Must be nonstop laughs," Myron said, "working with him."

"Gobs of fun."

"Can Christian and I go now?"

Jake shook his head. "Not until I hear all about your visit with Dean Gordon."

Chapter 35

Myron filled Jake in. Then he drove Christian home. On the way he filled Christian in too. On everything. Christian wanted to know. Myron wanted to spare him, but he knew he didn't have the right to keep things from him.

Christian did not interrupt with questions. In fact, he said nothing. On the field he was famous for his composure under any situation. Right now, Christian had on his best game face.

When Myron finished, neither spoke for several minutes. Then Myron said, "Are you okay?"

Christian nodded. His face was pale. "Thank you for being up-front with me," he said.

"Kathy loved you," Myron said. "Very much. Don't forget that."

He nodded again. "We have to find her."

"I'm trying."

Christian shifted in the car seat so he could face Myron. "When I was being wooed by all these big agencies, the whole process felt—I don't know—so impersonal. It was all about money. Still is, I know that. I'm not being naïve here, but you were different. I instinctively knew I could trust you. I guess what I'm trying to say is, you've become more than just an agent to me. I'm glad I chose you."

"Me too," Myron said. "This might not the best time to ask, but how did you hear about me in the first place?"

"Someone gave you a glowing recommendation."

"Who?"

Christian smiled. "You don't know?"

"A client?"

"No."

Myron shook his head. "I have no idea."

Christian settled back in his seat. "Jessica," he said. "She told me your life history. About your playing days, your injury, what you went through, how you worked for the FBI, how you went back to school. She said you were the best person she knew."

"Jessica doesn't get out much."

They fell back into silence. The New Jersey Turnpike had a center-lane closure, slowing them down to a crawl. Should have taken the western spur. Myron was about to change lanes when Christian said something that almost made him slam on the brakes.

"My mother once posed in the nude."

Myron thought he'd heard wrong. "What?"

"When I was a little kid. I don't know if they were ever printed in a magazine or anything. I doubt it. She wasn't very attractive by then. She was twenty-five but looked sixty. She worked as a prostitute in New York. On the streets. I don't know who my father was. She figured he was one of the guys at a bachelor party, but she had no idea which one.''

Myron sneaked a glance at him. Christian stared straight ahead. The game face was still on.

''I thought your mother and father raised you in Kansas,'' Myron said carefully.

Christian shook his head. ''Those were my grandparents. My mom died when I was seven. They legally adopted me. We had the same last name, so I just pretended they were my real parents.''

Myron said, ''I didn't know. I'm sorry.''

''Don't be. They were wonderful parents. I guess they made a lot of mistakes with my mom, the way she ended up and all. But they were kind and loving to me. I miss them a lot.''

The silence was heavier now. They drove past the Meadowlands. Myron paid the toll at the end of the turnpike and followed the signs to the George Washington Bridge. Christian had bought a place two miles before the bridge, six miles from Titans Stadium. A set of three hundred prefab condos loftily labeled Cross Creek Pointe, one of those New Jersey housing developments that looked like something out of *Poltergeist*.

As they cruised to a stop, the car phone rang. Myron picked it up.

''Hello?''

''Where are you?''

It was Jessica.

''In Englewood.''

''Take Route four west to seventeen north,'' she said quickly. ''I'll meet you in the Pathmark parking lot in Ramsey.''

''What's going on?''

''Just meet me there. Now.''

Chapter 36

The moment Myron saw Jessica standing in the dusky glow of the Pathmark fluorescent parking lights, looking achingly beautiful in a pair of hip-hugging blue jeans and a red blouse open at the throat, he knew there was trouble. Big trouble.

"Very bad?" he asked her.

She opened the car door and slid in next to him. "Worse."

He couldn't help it. He couldn't stop thinking of how beautiful she was. She looked a little pale, her eyes a bit too sunken. She did not have crow's-feet quite yet, but new lines had etched their way into her face. Had they been there yesterday or the day she visited his office? He wasn't sure. But he thought she had never looked so devastating. The imperfections, if you wanted to call them that, just made her more real and hence more desirable. Myron had thought Dean-nessa Madelaine was attractive, but she was nary a penlight next to Jessica's blinding beacon.

"Want to tell me about it?"

She shook her head. "I'd rather just show you." She started giving directions. When they reached a road appropriately called Red Dirt Path, she said, "My father rented a cabin out here."

"In these woods?"

"Yes."

"When?"

"Two weeks ago. He had it for the month. According to the realtor, he wanted some peace and quiet. A place to get away from it all."

"Doesn't sound much like your father," Myron said.

"Not like him at all," she agreed.

A few minutes later, they arrived at the cabin. Myron had a hard time believing that Adam Culver, a man he had gotten to know fairly well during his time with Jessica, would want to vacation out here. The man liked to gamble. He liked the ponies, the roulette wheel, the blackjack table. He liked action. His idea of a quiet time was a Tony Bennett concert at the Sands.

Jessica got out of the car. Myron followed. Her posture was arrow-perfect. So was the walk, something Myron had always loved to watch in the past. But there was an unmistakable teeter in her step, as though her legs were not sure they could sustain the lovely torso over the long haul.

Their footsteps creaked on the steps of the wooden porch. Myron spotted plenty of dry rot. Jessica unlocked the front door and pushed it open.

"Take a look," she said.

He did. He said nothing. He could feel her eyes on him.

"I checked his charge card," she said. "He spent over three thousand dollars at a place in the city called Eye-Spy."

Myron knew the store. This was definitely their handiwork. Three videocameras were sprawled across the couch. Panasonic. All with mounting material, so they could be hung up somewhere. There were also three small television monitors. Also Panasonic. The kind you might see at a high-rise's security station. Two VCRs. Toshiba. Lots of cables and wires and stuff like that.

But that stuff wasn't the most bothersome thing he

saw. Alone, those electronic goods could have meant one of several things. But two other items—items that drew Myron's eye and held it like a baby near a shiny coin—changed everything. They were the added catalyst. They completed a mixture that was far too noxious to be ignored.

Propped against the wall was a rifle. And on the floor next to it, a set of handcuffs.

Jessica said, "What the hell was he doing?"

He knew what she was thinking. The dead girls found near here. The television images of their battered, decayed bodies hovered above them like the most haunting of ghosts.

"When did he buy this stuff?" Myron asked.

"Two weeks ago." Her eyes were clear, controlled. "Listen, I've had time to think about this. Even if our worst fears are true, it doesn't explain anything. What about the picture in the magazine? Or Kathy's handwriting on that envelope? Or the phone calls? Or for that matter his murder?"

Myron looked at her. He knew she was seeking an explanation—any explanation but the one that stared them straight in the face. "Are you okay?" he asked.

She crossed her arms under her breasts, a hand on each elbow, as if she were hugging herself. "I feel," she said, "unanchored."

"Can you take more?"

Her hands dropped to her sides. "Why? What is it?" He hesitated.

She exploded. "Goddamn it, don't coddle me!"

"Jess—"

"You know I hate that protect-the-little-lady bullshit of yours! Tell me what the hell is going on!"

"Kathy was gang-raped by some of Christian's teammates on the night she disappeared."

Jessica looked as if she'd just been slapped with an open hand. Myron reached out. "I'm sorry," he said.

"Just tell me what happened. Everything."

He did. Her clear, controlled eyes went blank, lifeless. She remained uncharacteristically silent.

"Bastards," she managed. "The goddamn bastards."

He nodded.

"One of them killed her," she said. "Or all of them. To shut her up."

"It's possible."

She paused, thinking. Then the eyes came back to life. "Suppose," she began slowly, "that my father learned about the rape."

Myron nodded.

"What would he do?" she continued. "How would you react—if it was your daughter?"

"I'd be enraged," Myron replied.

"Would you be able to control yourself?"

"Kathy is not my daughter," he said. "And I'm still not sure I can control myself."

Jessica nodded. "So maybe, just maybe, that explains this whole setup. The electronics, the cuffs, the rifle. Maybe he was using this hideaway, deep in the woods, so he could grab a rapist and exact a little private justice."

"Kathy was gang-raped. There were six of them. This place looks built for one."

"But," she continued with the hint of an eerie smile, "suppose my father was in the exact same position we are in now."

"I don't follow."

"Suppose he knew the name of only one rapist. Maybe this Horton guy. What might he do then? What might *you* do then?"

"I might," Myron said, "kidnap him and make him tell."

"Exactly."

"But it's a hell of a reach. Why would I videotape it? Why would I need cameras and monitors?"

"Tape the confession, make sure no one comes down the road, I don't know. You have a better scenario?"

He did not. "Have you gone through the rest of the house yet?"

"I didn't have a chance. The realtor brought me here. He practically burst a blood vessel when he saw this stuff."

"What did you tell him?"

"That I knew all this was here. That my father was a private investigator working undercover."

Myron made a face.

"Hey, it was the best I could come up with."

"And he bought that?"

"I think so."

Myron shook his head. "I thought you were a writer."

"I'm not good with spur-of-the-moment. I'm a lot better with the written than the oral."

"Based on past experience," he said, "I'd have to disagree."

"Nice time," she said, "for a come-on."

He shrugged. "Just trying to keep things loose."

She almost smiled.

"Let's look around," he said.

There wasn't much to search. The living room had no drawers or closets. Everything was in plain view—the electronic equipment, the handcuffs, the rifle. The kitchenette held no surprises. Same with the bathroom. That left the bedroom.

It was small. The size of a guest bedroom at a beach

house. The double bed took up almost the entire room. There were reading lights on either side of the bed, attached to the wall because there was no room for night tables. No dressers either. The bed was made with flannel sheets. They checked the closet.

Bingo.

Black pants, black T-shirt, black sweatshirt. And worst of all, a black ski mask.

"Ski mask in June?" Myron said.

"He might have needed it to kidnap Horton," she tried. But her tone would not make the leap.

Myron dropped to the floor and looked underneath the bed. He saw a plastic bag. He stretched out his hand, grabbed it, and dragged it along the dust-blanketed floor toward him. The bag was red. The initials BCME were emblazoned across the front.

"Bergen County Medical Examiner," Jessica explained.

It looked like one of those old Lord and Taylor's bags, the kind that snapped closed on the top. Myron pulled it back. The bag opened with a pop. He pulled out a pair of gray no-frills sweat pants with a drawstring. Then he reached back in and withdrew a yellow pullover with the letter T in red. Both were covered with caked-on dirt.

"Recognize these?" he asked.

"Just the yellow sweater," she said. "It's my dad's old varsity sweater from Tarlow High School."

"Funny thing to hide under a bed up here."

Jessica's eyes lit up. "Nancy's message! Jesus Christ, she said my dad told her all about Kathy's yellow sweater."

"Whoa, slow down a second. What did Nancy say exactly?"

"She said—and I quote verbatim—'He told me all

about that favorite yellow sweater he gave Kathy. Such a sweet story.' Those were her exact words. My father never wore it. Kathy did. Like a nightshirt or kick-around-the-house shirt.''

''Did your dad give it to her?''

''Yes.''

''So how did he get it back?''

''I don't know. I imagine it was in her personal belongings at school.''

''Which doesn't explain why he asked Nancy Serat about it. Or why it's hidden under his bed.''

They stood in silence.

''We're missing something here,'' she said.

''Maybe your father saw something in these clothes we can't see yet.''

''What do you mean?''

''I don't know,'' Myron admitted. ''But these clothes were clearly significant to him. Maybe he found them somewhere unusual. Or maybe the police found them.''

''But Kathy was wearing blue the night she left. That's been established.''

Myron remembered the testimony of the sorority sisters and the photograph. But then again . . .

''One way to check on that.''

''How?''

He ran out to the car. Darkness had finally laid claim on the long summer day. He turned on the phone, hoping they weren't too far out of a calling area. Three of those little bars lit up. Enough for the phone to work. He tried Dean Gordon's office. It rang twenty times. No answer. He tried the dean's house. It was picked up on the third ring.

Dean Gordon said, ''Hello?''

''What was Kathy wearing when she came to your house?'' No need for identification or pleasantries.

"Wearing? A blouse and skirt of some kind."

"What color?"

"Blue. I think the blouse was ripped a bit."

Myron hung up.

Jessica said, "Back to square one."

Maybe, Myron thought. But the flash of an image seared across his mind. He couldn't grasp it, couldn't even make out what it was exactly. But it had been there, and it would come back.

"Let's go," she said softly, taking his hand. The car light provided enough illumination to see the look in her eyes. They were beautiful eyes, so light colored they were almost yellow. "I want to get away from here."

He closed the car door, feeling suddenly choked up. The car light went out, basking them in darkness. He couldn't see her face anymore. "Where do you want to go?"

From the darkness he heard her voice. "Someplace," she said, "where we can be alone."

Chapter 37

They found a high-rise Hilton in Mahwah.

Myron checked them in to the best available suite. Jessica stood next to him. The hotel concierge swung his line of vision from Myron to Jessica, eyeing her lustily and Myron jealously. A formal affair was in full swing in the lobby. Men in tuxes, women in long gowns. But every man stared agog at Jessica, who was dressed in jeans and a button-down red blouse.

Myron was used to it. When they were first together, he had taken an almost perverse pleasure in seeing men stare, the familiar you-look-but-I-touch-ha-ha school of macho sneering. But then he started seeing things in the looks that weren't there, and the even more familiar male insecurity burrowed through his rationality.

Jessica was practiced at this. She knew how to ignore the looks without looking cold, bothered, or interested.

Their room was on the sixth floor. They had barely closed the door when they kissed. Jessica's tongue circled and gently darted, making his whole body spasm helplessly. He began to unbutton her blouse. His mouth went dry. He actually gasped when he saw her again. Breathlessness made him heady. He cupped a warm breast, feeling the delicious weight in his hand. She moaned into his mouth.

They moved to the bed.

Their lovemaking had always been intense, all-consuming, but this was somehow more animalistic, needier, and yet more tender.

Later, much later, Jessica sat up, kissed him gently on the cheek. "That," she said, "was awesome."

Myron shrugged. "Not bad."

"Not bad?"

"For me. For you it was awesome."

She swung her legs out of bed and slipped into a hotel robe. "I did enjoy myself," she said.

"Sounded like it."

"I was a tad noisy, huh?"

"The Who in concert is a tad noisy. You were loud."

She stood above the bed, smiling. The robe was tied loosely, showing plenty of cleavage and legs that were so long, they were almost intimidating. "I didn't hear you complain."

"How could you," Myron said, "over all your screaming?"

"What time is it?"

"Midnight." He reached for the phone. "Hungry?"

She gave him a look he felt in his toes. Well, not exactly his toes. "Famished," she said.

"For food, Jess. Food."

"Oh."

"Ever learn about the male's 'time for recovery' in health class?"

"Must have been absent that day."

"The three R's. Replenishment, restoration, recuperation." He looked at the menu. "Damn."

"What?"

"No oysters."

"Myron?"

"Yes."

"There's a hot tub in the bathroom."

"Jess . . ."

She looked at him with who-me innocence. "We can soak until the food comes. Recuperate. One of the three R's."

"Just soak?"

"Just soak."

She had said soak. He was sure of it. Soak. Not soap. But that was how it started. She soaped him back to life. Myron tried to fight it, almost afraid of how good it felt. But he couldn't. Jess toyed with him, pushed him to the edge, let him teeter, then pulled him back. Myron was helpless. Words like *heaven, ecstasy, paradise, ambrosia* floated through his mind.

Total surrender.

With a whispered "Now," she let him go. His nerve

endings surged and sang. The white-hot explosion was so powerful, his ears popped. The bright light hurt his eyes.

"Awesome," he managed.

She lay back, smiling. "Not bad."

There was a knock on the door. Probably room service. Neither one of them moved.

"Why don't you get it," she said.

"My legs," he said. "They can't move. I may never walk again."

Another knock.

"I'm not dressed," she said.

"And what am I, ready for a press conference?"

"Bet you'd get good coverage."

Myron moaned at the joke.

Another knock.

"Come on, Myron. Just throw a towel around your shapely ass and get moving."

The second woman to mention his ass in the same day. Yowzer. He grabbed the bath towel and headed for the door. Another knock.

"One second."

He opened the door. It wasn't their food.

"Maid service," Win said. "May I turn down your bed?"

"Didn't you see the Do Not Disturb sign?"

Win glanced at the doorknob. "Sorry. No speaka da English."

"How the hell did you find us?"

"I traced down your charge card," he said, as though it were the most natural thing in the world. "You checked in here at eight twenty-two P.M." Win leaned his head in the doorway. "Hello, Jessica."

From the bathroom. "Hi, Win." Myron heard her

stepping out of the Jacuzzi. The image of water cascading down her naked body came to him like a deep punch.

"Come on in," he grumbled.

"Thank you." Win handed him a manila folder. "Thought you might want to take a look at this."

Jessica came in from the bathroom. The robe was tied tighter. She was drying her hair with a towel. "What's up?" she asked.

"The police rap sheet of one Fred Nickler, aka Nick Fredericks," Win said.

"Imaginative alias," Myron said.

"For an imaginative fellow."

Jessica sat on the bed. "He's the porno publisher, right?"

Myron nodded. The rap sheet was not very long. He started with the most recent dates. Traffic violations, two DWIs, one arrest for mail fraud.

"Nineteen seventy-eight," Win said.

Myron skipped down. June 30, 1978. Fred Nickler had been arrested for endangering the welfare of a child. Charges dropped.

"So?"

"Mr. Nickler was involved in kiddie porn," Win explained. "He was only a small-time photographer back then. But he was nabbed with his hand, so to speak, in the cookie jar. More precisely, taking photographs of an eight-year-old boy."

Jessica said, "Jesus."

Myron remembered their meeting. " 'Just an honest guy trying to make an honest buck.' "

"Indeed."

Jessica asked, "Why were the charges dropped?"

"Ah," Win said, pointing a finger in the air, "that's where things get interesting. In many ways it's not an uncommon story. Fred Nickler was only the photographer. A little fish. The authorities wanted the bigger fish. The little fish ratted out the big fish in exchange for leniency.''

"And they dropped the charges completely?" Myron said. "Not even a misdemeanor?"

"Not even. It seems that Mr. Nickler also agreed to help out the police from time to time."

"So what's the significance?"

"This entire arrangement was negotiated between Nickler and the officer in charge of the investigation," Win said. He shot a quick glance at Jessica.

"The officer in charge of the investigation was your friend Paul Duncan."

Chapter 38

"That's our man," Win said. "Mr. Junior Horton."

Horty looked like an ex–football player. Big and wide, all veins and bulges. His arms looked like corded wood. He was dressed for a rap video. His button-down St. Louis Cardinals baseball shirt was untucked. His baggy shorts reached down past his knees. No socks. Black Reebok high-tops. A Chicago White Sox baseball cap. Dark sunglasses and lots of jewelry.

It was nine in the morning. One Hundred Thirty-second Street in Manhattan. The street was quiet. Horty was making a drug deal. He had been in and out of jail plenty of times, his one long stint of freedom during his time at

Reston U. Drugs, mostly. Armed robbery, once. Two sexual assault charges. Twenty-four years old and a complete punk. Like most inmates he had spent his prison time lifting weights. Pumping iron. Our penal institutions develop violent men's physical strength, so when they get out, they'll be able to intimidate and maim with far greater skill. Nice system.

Jessica was not with them. She was packing her father's office—that is, the morgue—and checking for any additional bombshells. Myron had managed to talk her out of confronting Paul Duncan until they knew a little more. She listened grudgingly, but that was how Jessica usually listened anyway.

Horty finished the transaction with a kid who looked no older than twelve, slapped him five, headed west. He wasn't wearing a Walkman, but he walked as though he were. Very jittery. His eyes were red. Every few steps he would snort the air and wipe his nose with the back of his hand.

"Boys and girls, can you say 'Cokehead'?"

"Probably has the flu," Win said.

"The Colombian strain."

They ducked out of sight as he approached. When Horty reached the lip of the alley, Myron stepped in front of him.

"Junior Horton?"

Horty gave him a scornful street glare. "Who the fuck wants to know?"

"Snappy comeback," Myron said.

"Get the fuck out of my way or I kick your ass." He spotted Win. "Both your ass."

"Asses," Win corrected. "One ass. Two asses. Plural."

"What the fuck—"

"We want to talk to you," Myron said.

"Hey, fuck you, man."

Myron turned to Win. "He's a real badass."

"Indeed," Win said. "I may wet myself."

Horty stepped toward Win. He had at least six inches and sixty pounds on him. Horty probably thought he was being clever, going after and intimidating the little guy. Myron tried not to smile when Horty spat, "Gonna fuck you up big-time."

"If you curse again," Win said in the tone of pre-school teacher, "I will be forced to silence you."

"You?" Horty laughed heartily. He flexed for a moment and then lowered his nose until it almost touched Win's. Win did not move. "Little piece of upper-crust whitebread gonna shut me up? Fuck—"

Win barely moved. His arm shot up, delivered a palm strike to the solar plexus, and was back at his side in what seemed like a tenth of a second. Horty stumbled back, gasping, unable to get any oxygen into his lungs.

"I asked you not to curse," Win said.

It took Horty nearly half a minute to recover. When he did, the lips started flapping again. "Fucking cheap-shot motherfucker," he said rising. "I gonna tear you a brand-new asshole."

He charged Win, his arms outstretched as though tackling a fullback. Win sidestepped him and delivered a quick roundhouse kick, again hitting the solar plexus. Horty folded and went down. His face was a mixture of fury, pain, surprise, and of course, embarrassment. He looked around to make sure nobody was watching. He was, after all, getting his butt whipped by Mr. Wonder-bread.

"There are two hundred and six bones in the body," Win said evenly. "Next time I break one."

But Horty wasn't listening. His eyes bulged. Rage twisted his face—not to mention his limited ability to reason. Horty stood, stumbling, pretending he was more hurt than he was. The element of surprise. When Horty was close enough, he made his move.

He must have been really coked up, Myron mused. Or really stupid. Probably both.

Win leaned away and snapped a sidekick toward Horty's lower leg. There was a cracking sound, like stepping on a dry twig. Horty screamed and went down. Win raised his leg for an ax kick, but Myron stopped him with a shake of his head.

"Two hundred five," Win said, lowering his foot gently, "and counting."

"You broke my f—" He stopped, holding his leg and rolling back and forth. "You broke my leg!"

"Your right tibia," Win corrected.

"Who the—who are you?"

Myron said, "We're going to ask you a few questions. You're going to answer them."

"My leg, man. I need a doctor."

"When we're finished."

"Look, I just work for Terrell. He gave me this territory. You gotta a problem with that, you speak to him, okay?"

"We don't want to talk to you about that."

"Please, man, I'm begging you. My leg."

"You used to attend Reston University."

A surprised look replaced the pained one. "Yeah, so? You want my résumé?"

"You knew Kathy Culver."

Panic now. "You guys cops?"

"No."

Silence.

"You knew Kathy Culver."

"Kathy who?"

Win said, "Number two-oh-five. The left femur. The femur is the largest bone in the body—"

"Okay, I knew her. So what?"

"How did you meet?" Myron asked.

"At a party. Her first week of school."

"Did you ever date?"

"Date?" Horty laughed at that one. "No. She wasn't the kind you date."

"What kind was she?"

"The kind who sucked off my Johnson first night. Willie's too."

"Who is Willie?"

"My roomie."

"He play football?"

"Yeah." Then he added, "But only special teams," as if that made him a lower species of being.

"Go on."

"Man, why you want to hear this?"

"Go on."

Horty shrugged. The leg was swelling badly, but the coke was numbing the pain enough to keep him going. "You see, we had this party. At Moore House. Where all the brothers lived. Kathy, she was like the only white chick there. So she comes in dressed like a prime-time ho. I mean, she was all that, you know? We start rapping and shit, you know. Did a little nose-candy like a Hoover vac. She liked the stuff. Then we start slow-dancing." The grin returned with the memory. "Grinding, you know. She put her hand on the Black Blade right there on the dance floor. Starts rubbing it and shit. So I take her upstairs, and she sucks me off. But that ain't all. She takes a camera—a fucking camera!—out of her bag and asks me to take pictures. No shit! Close-ups, she wants, of her and the Black Blade."

Myron's stomach began to churn again. Win looked on with his usual noninterest.

Horty continued. "Next night, she come back. Takes on me and Willie at the same time. We take more pictures, have a good old time. 'Cept this time I had my camera too."

"So you took some pictures of your own."

"Shit, yeah."

"Did you and Kathy have any more, uh, encounters?"

"Nope. She moved on to other dudes, though. Prime-looking babe for such a ho. All blond and built and shit."

"You talk to her after that?"

He shrugged. "Little. Not much. But once she started up with Christian, man, it was a whole other story."

"What do you mean?"

"She be all nose up in the air, like her shit don't stink no more. Two of them all lovey-dovey and shit, like they was going steady on a TV show. All of a sudden the slut thinks she's some fucking pure-ass cherry. I mean, the ho been riding the Blade like a fucking bronco, and now she don't even say how-do. That ain't right. That just ain't right."

Mr. Etiquette.

"So you decided to blackmail her," Myron said.

"No way. Unh-unh."

"We know about it, Horty. We know she paid you for the pictures."

Horty made a snorting sound. "Aw, shit, that ain't blackmail. That's a business transaction. I just called her one day and told her I might have to knock her down a few pegs. And then I said a picture was worth a thousand words. She kinda agreed with all that and said she'd be willing to pay for such wonderful pictures. I told her they was real valuable to me. Had a lot of sentimental value and shit. But we finally reached an agreement. A mutually beneficial agreement," he stressed, "not black-mail." He took hold of his leg and winced. "End of story, man."

"You left something out."

"What?"

"The gang-rape in the locker room."

He did not seem surprised. He half-smiled and said, "Rape? Man, you ain't listening. This woman had Horty's Three H's: Hot, Horny, Ho. Shit, she'd jump naked into a rock pile if she thought they'd be a snake in it. She loved it. We all had a good time."

Win looked at Myron. The look said Keep your cool.

"How many of you?" Myron asked.

"Six."

"Why," he said in a low voice, "didn't you just take the money, Horty? Why did you have to rape her?"

"I just told you, man—"

"She didn't come to that locker room for consensual sex with six people. You raped her."

"Can't be, man," he said with a shake of his head, "She a ho through and through. And once a ho, always a ho. That just the way it is. Fucking cunt acting all high and prissy and shit. Quarterback's girl. Miss fucking all-American cheerleader. Who the fuck did she think she was? So yeah, I showed her. I reminded her where she come from, what she really is. Not some fucking prom queen. A slut. A dick-loving ho."

Win now stepped in front of Myron. Preventive mea-sure.

" 'Sides," Horty continued, "I owed her boyfriend. Big-time."

"Christian Steele?"

"Yeah. He did me wrong. I did him wrong. Passed

around his little ho. Just a little payback, my man. To the prick who got me thrown off the team.''

"No," Myron said. "It wasn't Christian."

"What you talking about?''

"I spoke with Coach Clarke. Two guys showed up for a game high. That's why you were thrown off. Christian had nothing to do with it."

"Oh," Horty said with a shrug. "Ain't that something."

"Your remorse," Myron said, "is very touching."

"I gotta get to a doctor, man. My leg is killing me."

"Weren't you worried about getting caught?''

"What?''

"Weren't you afraid she'd report the rape?''

Horty made a face as if Myron had suddenly started speaking Japanese. "You crazy, man? Who she gonna tell? She just gave me major cash to keep it all quiet. She say anything, it all gets out. The whole ugly truth. Everyone would know—Christian, her mammy, her pappy, her teachers. Everyone would know what she just paid all that money to hide. And what if she was dumb enough to tell? There were pictures and witnesses of her doing Willie and me at the party. Who gonna believe she was raped after seeing that?''

Dean Gordon had made the same argument, Myron remembered. Great minds thinking alike.

"Hey, look, man, my leg's killing me."

"Did you ever see Kathy again?" Myron managed.

"Nope."

"Were you the one who threw away the panties?''

"Nope. One of the other guys had them. Thought he'd keep them as a souvenir. When he heard she was missing, he got scared, threw them away."

"Who?''

"I ain't giving names."

"Yes," Win said. "You are." He rested his foot against the broken tibia. That was enough.

"Okay, okay. Like I said, they was six of us. Three brothers, two white dudes, one chink."

Equal opportunity rapists.

"One was the place kicker. Guy named Tommy Wu. Then there was Ed Woods, Bobby Taylor, Willie and me."

"That's five."

Horty hesitated. "Give me a break, man. The other dude was the one who threw away the panties. But he's a friend, man. Still gives me money when I'm down, you know. I can't just give him up. He's big-time."

"What do you mean, big-time?"

"Plays pro ball and shit. I can't give you his name."

Win put the slightest pressure on the leg. Horty bucked.

"Ricky Lane."

Myron froze. "The running back for the Jets?" Dumb question. How many Ricky Lanes who now play pro football went to Reston University?

"Yeah. Now look, man, that's all I know."

Win said to Myron, "Do you have any other questions for him?"

Myron shook his head.

"Then leave," Win said.

Myron did not move.

"I said," Win continued, "leave."

"No."

"You heard what he said. You'll never convict him. He pushes drugs to kids, rapes innocent women, blackmails, steals, whatever, and laughs about it."

Horty sat up. "What the fuck is this?"

"Leave," Win repeated.

Myron hesitated.

"Yo, man, I told you everything I know." There was a tremble in Horty's voice.

Myron did not move.

Horty shouted, "Don't leave me alone with this crazy motherfucker!"

"Leave," Win said.

Myron shook his head. "No. I'll stay."

Win studied Myron. Then he nodded and approached Horty, who was trying to claw away but not getting far.

"Don't kill him," Myron said.

Win nodded. He went to work with the careful precision of a surgeon. His face never changed expression. If he heard Horty's cries, he never showed it.

After a short time Myron told him to stop. Reluctantly Win stepped away.

They left.

Chapter 39

Ricky Lane lived in a New Jersey condo development similar to Christian's. Win waited in the car. As Myron approached the door, he felt rather than heard the bass from Ricky's stereo. It took three rings of the bell and several knocks before Ricky appeared.

"Hey, Myron."

He was wearing a silk shirt that was either very fashionable or a pajama top. Hard to tell. The shirt was unbuttoned, revealing a well-defined physique. His pants were held up by a drawstring. He was also wearing slippers. Maybe they were pajamas. Or lounging clothes. Or he was trying out for a walk-on role on *I Dream of Jeannie*.

"We need to talk," Myron said.

"Come on in."

The music was deafening and awful. Made Pap Smear sound like Brahms. The motif was sleek modern. Lots of Fiberglas. Lots of black and white. Lots of rounded edges. The stereo took up a whole wall. The lights on the equalizer looked like something on *Star Trek*.

Ricky flipped the stereo off. The silence was abrupt. Myron felt his chest stop vibrating.

"So what's up?" Ricky asked.

Myron tossed him a glass jar. Ricky caught it, looked a question.

"Pee in it," Myron said.

"What?"

"I want you to urinate into this jar."

Ricky looked at the jar. Then at Myron. "I don't get it."

"Your new size," Myron said. "You're taking steroids."

"No way, man. Not me."

"Then give me a urine sample. Right now. I'll have it tested at a lab."

Ricky stared at the jar. He said nothing.

"Go ahead, Ricky. I don't have all day."

"You're my agent, Myron. You ain't my mother."

"True enough. Are you taking steroids?"

"It's none of your business."

"I'll take that as a yes."

"Take it any way you'd like."

"Did Horty sell them to you? Or have you gotten a new supplier since college?"

Silence.

Ricky said, "You're fired, Myron."

"I'm devastated. Now tell me about raping Kathy Culver."

More silence. Ricky was struggling to look casual, but his body language was all wrong.

"I know all about it," Myron continued. "Your buddy Horty told all. Nice guy, by the way. A real sweetheart."

Ricky stumbled back. He put the jar down on a shiny cube that Myron guessed was a table. He turned away. His voice was barely audible. "I never touched her."

"Bullshit. You and five other guys jumped her in the locker room. You took turns raping her."

"No. That's not how it happened."

Myron waited. Ricky buttoned his shirt, his back still facing Myron. He took a CD out of the stereo and tucked it back into its case.

"I was there," Ricky began, his voice low. "In the locker room. I was stoned. We all were. Stoned out of our minds. Horty had just gotten in a new supply, and . . ." He sort of shrugged away the rest of the sentence.

"It started as a dare, you know. We knew we'd never go through with it. We figured we'd walk right to the edge but never jump. We kept waiting for someone to call it off." He stopped again.

Myron said, "But no one called it off."

He nodded slowly. "It stopped. But too late. It stopped when it was my turn, and I said no."

"After all the others had gone?"

"Yes. I stood there and watched them. I even cheered."

Silence.

"You kept her panties?"

"Yes."

"When you heard the police were investigating, you tossed them in that garbage bin."

He faced Myron. "No," he said with something close to a hint of a smile. "I wouldn't have been stupid enough to leave them on top of a Dumpster. I'd have burned them."

Myron considered that for a moment. It was, he thought, an excellent point. "Then who threw them away?"

Ricky shrugged. "Kathy, I guess. I gave them to her."

"When?"

"Later."

"What time later?"

"Around midnight, I think. After it happened . . . after she left the locker room, it was like someone had given us the antidote. Or like someone turned on the lights, and we finally saw what we'd done. We all went silent and just drifted away. Except Horty. He was laughing like a goddamn hyena, getting more and more stoned. The rest of us went back to our rooms. None of us said one word. I got into bed, for a little while anyway. Then I got dressed and went back out. I didn't have a plan. Not really. I just wanted to find her. Say something to her. I just wanted to . . . shit, I don't know."

His fingers were playing with his hair, twisting it like a little kid. He looked smaller now. "I finally found her."

"Where?"

"Crossing the campus."

"Where specifically?"

"The middle, I guess. On the commons."

"What direction was she walking in?"

He thought a moment. "South."

"Like maybe she was coming from the faculty housing?"

"Yes."

After she left Dean Gordon's, he thought.

"Go on."

"I approached her. Called out her name. I thought she'd just run away, you know. It was dark and all. But she didn't. She just turned and stared at me. She wasn't scared. She wasn't shaking. She just stood there and stared me down. I said I was sorry. She didn't say anything. I gave her the panties. I told her she could use them as evidence. I even told her I'd testify. I didn't plan on saying that. It just came out. Kathy took the panties and walked away. She never said anything."

"Was that the last time you saw her?"

"Yes."

"What was she wearing?"

"Wearing?"

"When you last saw her?"

He looked up, trying to recall. "Something blue, I think."

"Not yellow?"

"No. Definitely not yellow."

"She hadn't changed clothes since the rape?"

"I don't think so. No, they were the same clothes."

Myron headed for the door. "You're going to need more than a new agent, Ricky. You're also going to need a good lawyer."

Chapter 40

Jake was sitting next to Esperanza in the waiting area. He stood when Myron and Win entered.

"Got a minute?"

Myron nodded. "My office."

Jake said, "Alone."

Without a word Win spun and left.

"Nothing personal," Jake said. "But the guy gives me the creeps."

"Come on in." He stopped at Esperanza's desk. "Did you reach Chaz?"

"Not yet."

He handed her an envelope. "There's a photograph inside. Bring it to Lucy. See if she recognizes him."

Esperanza nodded.

Myron followed Jake into his office. The air conditioning was on full blast. It felt good.

"So what brings you to the Big Apple, Jake?"

"I was over at John Jay," he said, "checking something out."

"The crime lab?"

"Yup."

"Find something?" Myron asked.

Jake did not reply. He examined the pictures on the client wall, leaning forward and squinting. "Heard of some of these guys," he said. "But no superstars up here."

"No, no superstars."

"Nothing like Christian Steele."

Myron sat down. He threw his legs up on the desk. "You still think he killed Nancy Serat?"

Jake did something with his shoulders. Might have been a shrug. "Let's just say Christian is no longer our main suspect."

"Who is?"

Jake moved away from the client wall. He sat down and crossed his legs. "I've been poking into Adam Culver's homicide. Found out something interesting. Seems the cops concentrated solely on the murder scene and surrounding neighborhood. No reason for them to check anything else. They were convinced he was a victim of random street violence. I took a different avenue. I canvassed Culver's neighborhood in Ridgewood. Nice town. Real white. No brothers at all. You been there, I assume?"

Myron nodded.

"Anyway, I talked to a guy who lives two houses down from the Culvers. He says he was walking his dog on the night in question. He wasn't sure of the time, but he guessed it was eight o'clock or so. Seems he heard a big fight going on at the Culvers' house. Major blowup. He said he'd never heard anything like that before. It was so bad he almost called the cops, but he didn't want to pry. They'd been neighbors for twenty years and all. So he just let it slide."

"Did he know what the fight was about?"

Jake shook his head. "Nope. Just loud voices. Adam's and Carol's."

Myron sat quietly, still leaning back in his chair. Adam and Carol Culver had fought hours before Adam's murder. Myron tried to put it together with what he already knew. For the first time things were beginning to fit.

"What else do you got?" Myron asked.

"On Adam Culver's murder? Nothing."

Silence.

"There were," Jake continued, "a few hairs found at Nancy Serat's murder scene. On the body itself. More specifically, clutched in Nancy's hand."

Myron sat up. "Like maybe she tore them off the killer?"

"Maybe," Jake said. "But we checked the hairs at our own facilities and got a confirmation this morning at John Jay. There's no question. The hairs belong to Kathy Culver."

Myron felt his flesh turn to cold stone. He couldn't speak.

"We had some of her hairs on file," Jake continued. "From before. In case we ever found a body or wanted to check a location. Got them from her hairbrush at school. Both labs have done every comparison test conceivable. Neither one has any doubt. They're Kathy's hairs."

Myron shook his head. He felt dizzy. Inside his head the Robot from *Lost in Space* was shouting "That does not compute!" over and over again.

"You have any thoughts on this, Myron?"

"Just the same ones you're having."

Jake nodded. "What Christian said."

" 'Time for sisters to reunite,' " Myron quoted.

"Yup. Kinda takes on a whole new meaning now, don't it."

"But it still doesn't explain anything," Myron said. "Let's assume Kathy Culver is alive. Let's assume that Nancy Serat knows this. Why would Kathy kill her?"

Jake shrugged. "Sounds to me like Kathy may have gone off the deep end. I mean, first she's got this whole weird past. Then she falls in love with a guy. Then she's blackmailed. Then she's gang-raped. Then the dean turns his back on her. She cracks. Has a breakdown. Runs away. Maybe she tells Nancy Serat, maybe she doesn't. But somehow Nancy finds out. Nancy arranges a reunion—probably a surprise reunion—between sisters. Kathy gets there early. She's not happy about Nancy's surprise.''

"So she kills her?''

"Could be,'' Jake said. "Kathy's loony-tunes. She doesn't want to be found. Shit, she probably killed her old man for the same reason. She's nuts. Maybe she wants revenge for some reason. On her father, on her best friend—even on Christian and Dean Gordon and whoever else she sent that nutty magazine to.''

Didn't feel right to Myron. "Then what about the big fight between Adam and Carol Culver? How does that fit in?''

"Hell if I know,'' Jake said. "I'm making this shit up as I go along. Maybe the fight was just a coincidence. Maybe ol' Adam was on edge because he was about to meet with his daughter. Maybe the mother knows more than she's saying.''

Myron thought about it. It was confusing, but the last part made sense. Maybe Carol Culver did know more than she was saying. More than maybe. Myron even had some idea now of what she was hiding.

It was time to pay Carol Culver a visit.

Chapter 41

Myron pulled up in front of the familiar Victorian house on Heights Road in Ridgewood. He hesitated. He should have told Jessica about this, but there are things a woman might be more willing to tell a casual acquaintance than a daughter. This might be one of them.

Carol Culver answered the door. She was wearing an apron and those industrial rubber gloves. She smiled when she saw him, but the smile did not reach her eyes. "Hello, Myron."

"Hello, Mrs. Culver."

"Jessica isn't home right now."

"I know. I wanted to talk to you, if you have a minute."

The smile stayed. But a shadow crossed over the face. "Come on in," she said. "Can I get you something to drink? Maybe a little tea?"

"That would be nice."

He stepped inside. He and Jessica had not visited here often during their time together. A major holiday or two, that was it. Myron never liked the house. Something about it was stifling, as though the air were too heavy for normal breathing.

He sat down on a couch that was hard as a park bench. The decor was solemn. Lots of religious memorabilia. Lots of madonnas and crosses and gold-leaf paintings. Lots of halos and serene faces looking skyward.

Two minutes later Carol reappeared, minus the gloves

and apron, plus some tea and shortbread cookies. She was an attractive woman. She didn't really look like her daughters, but Myron had seen pieces of her in both of them. Jessica's straight posture. Kathy's shy laugh.

"So how have you been?" she asked.

"Fine, thank you."

"It's been a long time since we've seen you, Myron."

"Yes."

"Are you and Jessica . . . ?" She feigned embarrassment. She did that a lot. "I'm sorry. That's none of my business."

She poured the tea. Myron sipped it and nibbled on a cookie. Carol Culver did likewise.

"Tomorrow's the memorial service," she said. "Adam donated his corpse to a medical school, you know. The spirit was all that mattered to him. The body was worthless tissue. I guess that's part of being a pathologist."

Myron nodded, took another sip.

"Well, I just can't believe this weather," she rambled, a distracted smile frozen to her face. "It's so hot out. If we don't have rain soon, the whole front lawn will be brown. And we just paid to have it reseeded last season—"

"The police will be here soon," Myron interrupted. "I thought we should talk first."

She put her hand to her chest. "The police?"

"They'll want to talk to you."

"Me? What about?"

"They know about the fight," he said. "A neighbor was walking a dog. He heard you and Dr. Culver."

She stiffened. Myron waited, but she said nothing.

"Dr. Culver wasn't feeling sick that night, was he?" The color ebbed from her face. She put down her cup of tea and dabbed the corners of her mouth with a cloth napkin.

"He never intended to go to that medical conference in Denver, isn't that right, Mrs. Culver?"

She lowered her head.

"Mrs. Culver?"

No movement.

"I know this isn't easy," Myron said gently. "But I'm trying to find Kathy."

Her eyes remained on the floor. "Do you really think you can, Myron?"

"It's possible. I don't want to give you false hope, but I think it's possible."

"Then you think she might be alive?"

"There's a chance, yes."

She finally raised her head. The eyes were wet. "You do what you have to do to find her, Myron." Her voice was surprisingly steady and strong. "She's my daughter. My baby. She has to come first. No matter what."

Myron waited for Carol Culver to continue, but she fell back into silence. After nearly a full minute, Myron said, "Dr. Culver just pretended he was going to that medical conference."

She took a deep breath and nodded.

"You thought he'd left that morning."

Another androidlike nod.

"Then he surprised you here."

"Yes."

Myron's soft voice seemed to boom in the room. An antique clock ticked maddeningly. "Mrs. Culver, what did he see when he arrived?"

Tears began to flow. She lowered her head again.

"Did he see you," Myron continued, "with another man?"

Nothing.

"Was the man Paul Duncan?"

She lifted her head. Her eyes met his. "Yes," she said. "I was with Paul."

Myron waited again.

"Adam set a trap," she continued, "and we got caught." The words were once again steady and strong. "He had become suspicious. I don't know how. So he did just what you said—pretended to go to a conference in Denver. He even had me arrange his flights, so I would be sure he was gone."

"What happened when your husband saw you?"

Shaking fingers rubbed her cheeks. She stood, turned away. "Exactly what you'd expect to happen when a man finds his wife and best friend in bed. Adam went crazy. He'd been drinking pretty heavily, which didn't help matters. He shouted at me, called me horrible names. I deserved that. I deserved a lot worse. He threatened Paul. We tried to calm him down, but of course that was impossible."

She picked up the tea again. Each word was making her a little stronger, making it a little easier to breathe. "Adam stormed out. I was scared. Paul went after him. But Adam drove off. Paul left after that."

"How long have you and Paul Duncan . . . ?" His voice just sort of mumbled away.

"Six years."

"Did anybody else know?"

Her composure gave way. Not slowly. But as if a small bomb had blown it off her face. She crumbled, weeping freely. A realization came to Myron. He felt his blood freeze.

"Kathy," he whispered. "Kathy knew."

The sobbing grew more intense.

"She found out," he continued, "during her senior year."

Carol tried to stop her tears, but that took time. Myron remembered how Kathy had worshiped her mother, the perfect woman, the woman who balanced old-fashioned values with a sense of the modern. Carol Culver had been a homemaker and a shop owner. She had raised three beautiful children. She had instilled in her children more than just a sense of what is now popularly called "family values." For her values had been a rigid doctrine that she insisted her children follow. Jessica had rebelled. So had Edward. Only Kathy had been successfully locked in, like a lion kept in too small a cage.

And she had finally broken free.

"Kathy . . ." Carol Culver stopped, shut her eyes tightly. "She walked in on us."

"And that was when she changed," Myron finished.

Carol Culver nodded, her eyes still squeezed closed. "I did that to her. Everything that happened was because of me. God forgive me." Then she shook her head. "No. I don't deserve forgiveness. I don't want it. I just want my baby back."

"What did Kathy do when she saw you two?"

"Nothing. At first. She just turned and ran away. But the next day she broke up with her boyfriend Matt. And from there—she made sure I paid for what I'd done. For all the years I'd been a hypocrite. For all the years I lied to her. She wanted to hurt me in the worst way possible."

"She began to sleep around," Myron said.

"Yes. And she made sure I knew all about it."

"By telling you?"

Carol Culver shook her head. "Kathy wouldn't talk to me anymore."

"So how did you find out?"

She hesitated. Her face was drawn, her skin pulled

tight against her cheekbones. "Photographs," she said simply.

Something else clicked into place. Horty and the camera. "She gave you photos of herself with men."

"Yes."

"White men, black men, sometimes more than one."

Her eyes closed again, but she managed to say, "And not just men. It started slowly. A couple of nude pictures of her. Like the one in that magazine."

"You saw that same picture before?"

"Yes. It even had the name of a photographer stamped on the back."

"Global Globes Photos?"

"No. It was something like Forbidden Fruit."

"Do you still have the picture?"

She shook her head.

"You threw them away?"

She shook her head again. "I wanted to destroy them. I wanted to burn them and pretend I'd never seen them. But I couldn't. Kathy was punishing me. Keeping them was a form of penitence. I never told anyone about them, but I couldn't just throw them away. You see that, Myron, don't you?"

He nodded.

"So I hid them in the attic. In an old storage box. I thought they'd be safe there."

Myron saw where this was going. "Your husband found them."

"Yes."

"When?"

"A few months ago. He never told me about it. But of course I knew by the way he was acting. I checked the attic. The pictures were gone. Adam assumed that Kathy had hidden them up there. He had no idea she'd sent them to me. Or maybe he did. Maybe that's how he became suspicious of Paul and me. I don't know."

"Do you know what your husband did with those pictures, Mrs. Culver?"

"No. They were so awful. So painful to look at. I think Adam destroyed them."

Myron doubted it. They both sat in silence for several minutes. Finally Myron said, "Jessica is going to want to know."

Carol Culver nodded. "You tell her, Myron."

She showed him to the door. He stopped at his car and turned back around. He studied the gray Victorian house. Twenty-six years ago a young family had moved in. They'd put up swings in the backyard and a basketball hoop in the driveway. They'd owned a station wagon, carpooled to Little League and choir practice, attended PTA meetings, hosted birthday parties. Myron could almost see it all happening, like a life insurance commercial playing in his head.

He slid into his car and drove away.

Chapter 42

Myron was thinking about threads again.

Threads like Gary Grady. Dean Gordon. Nancy Serat. Carol Culver. Christian Steele. Fred Nickler. Paul Duncan. Ricky Lane. Horty and the thugs. But there was one thread he had overlooked.

Otto Burke.

Suppose Jake was right. Suppose the magazines had been sent out to wreak vengeance or maybe to satisfy some misguided or irrational anger. Either way, it meant that everyone who had received a copy of *Nips* was in some way connected to Kathy Culver.

Except Otto Burke.

How did he fit in? Otto hadn't even known Kathy Culver.

Or had he?

Myron got off Route 4 at the Garden State Plaza Mall and took Route 17 south to Route 3. New Jersey, land of routes. He pulled into the Meadowlands and parked near the Titans' executive offices. He found the general manager's office and asked for Larry Hanson.

He was let in almost immediately. He quickly explained the reason for his visit.

Larry Hanson watched him without expression. His huge hands were folded on his desk. His neck strained the top button. Larry was about fifty, but he hadn't gone to flab. He looked, Myron thought not for the first time, like Sergeant Rock in the old comic strips. Should have been chewing on a big cigar.

The office was adorned with trophies. Larry had been named league MVP twice. He'd been All-Pro twelve times. He had been elected into the Football Hall of Fame on the first ballot. There were plenty of his old football photos, from high school through college and into the pros. Black-and-whites and colors. Same crew cut. Same gritty smile. Different poses, including plenty of knee-up, straight-arm favorites from yesteryear.

When Myron finished, Larry studied his big hands for a minute, as if they were something he'd never noticed before.

"Why ask me?" he said. "Why don't you ask Otto Burke about the magazine?"

"Because he won't tell me."

"And what makes you think I will?"

"Because you're not a complete asshole."

Larry's mouth twitched toward a smile, but he caught himself. "Coming from you," he said, "that really means a lot."

Myron said nothing.

"This is important, huh?"

Myron nodded.

Larry sat back. "Burke didn't get the magazine in the mail. He heard about it from a private detective."

Myron shifted in his chair. "Otto was having Christian investigated?"

Larry's tone was flat. "A man of Otto Burke's unquestionable integrity would never stoop to such a level."

"Under the desk," Myron said, "you're crossing your fingers."

Again the twitch/smile. "This doesn't leave this room, Bolitar. You understand?"

"Cross my heart." Myron motioned such with his hand.

"Burke has a whole security division," Larry explained. "They poke into everyone on the payroll. Including yours truly. They also have a source network all over the place. The credo is pretty simple: If you got dirt on a Titan, Burke will pay top dollar for it. So one of these sources came across the magazine."

"How?"

"I don't know. Maybe he's a steady reader."

"Do you know his name?"

"Brian Sanford. A true sleazeball. He works out of Atlantic City. The casino route. Spies on gamblers, that kind of thing. A Titan puts a quarter in a slot machine, he reports it, especially since that whole Michael Jordan thing started. Burke likes to be kept informed. Gives him the edge in negotiating.''

Myron stood. ''Thanks. I appreciate it.''

''Hey, Bolitar. This don't make us buddies or nothing. We talk again, I still hate your guts. You got it?''

Myron said, ''We're having a warm moment now, aren't we, Larry?''

Hanson leaned his elbows on the desk, pointing a finger at Myron. ''I still think you're a little pissant piece of dog shit. And next time I see you, I'll prove it.''

Myron spread his arms. ''Come on, Larry. How about that hug now?''

''Wiseass.''

''Does that mean no?''

''Do me a favor, Bolitar.''

''Name it, bright eyes.''

''Get the fuck out of my office.''

Chapter 43

Myron called Brian Sanford. Answering machine. Myron said he had a real big case, one that paid ten grand, and he'd stop by his office tonight at seven o'clock. Brian Sanford would be there. For ten grand, a guy like Sanford would let his mother take a bullet in the gut.

Myron dialed his office.

Esperanza said, "MB SportReps."

"Did you show Lucy the photo?"

"Yep."

"And?"

"You found your buyer."

Myron said, "Lucy was sure?"

"Positive."

"Thanks."

He hung up. An hour to kill. Myron headed over to the county medical examiner's office—Dr. Adam Culver's old office. Just a hunch, but worth checking out.

The building was a one-level brick building. Institutional, almost like a small elementary school. The furniture was metal chairs with thin padding, again like a schoolteacher's. The waiting room magazines were pre-Watergate. The tiled floor was worn and yellowed with age, like the "before" shot on a Mr. Clean commercial. There was nothing even remotely decorative.

"Is Dr. Li in?" he asked the receptionist.

"I'll buzz her."

Sally Li was dressed in hospital scrubs, but there was no blood or anything on them. She was Chinese, approaching forty, but she could have passed for much younger. She wore bifocals. A pack of cigarettes was stashed in her front pocket. Cigarettes with a surgeon's gown. Like bowling shoes with a tuxedo.

They had met a couple of times in the past. Sally Li came to many Culver family functions. She had been Adam's right-hand woman for the past decade. Myron greeted her with a kiss on the cheek.

"Jessica told me you were looking into Adam's death," she said without preamble.

He nodded. "Can we talk for a minute?"

"Sure." She led him to her office. Again, institutional. No personal stuff. Lots of pathology textbooks. A

metal desk. Metal chair. A small tape recorder she probably used during autopsies. Her degrees on the wall. She
wasn't married, had no children, so there was no picture
on the desk. Big ashtray, though. Overflowing.

She struck a match, lit up, and said, "How's tricks?"

"An MD smoking," Myron said. "Tsk, tsk."

"My patients never complain."

"Good point."

She took a deep drag. "So what do you want to
know?"

"Did you and Adam ever have an affair?"

"Yes." No hesitation. She looked him right in the
eye. "About four years ago. Lasted a week."

"Did Adam have a lot of affairs?"

"Got me. A few, I guess. Why do you ask?"

"I'm just trying to put a few things together."

"Vis-à-vis his murder?"

"Right."

She took off her glasses. "What does Adam's love
life have to do with it?"

"Probably nothing," Myron admitted. "How had
Adam been acting the last couple months?"

"A bit wacko," she said. Again no hesitation.

"In what way?"

She gave that one some thought. "Businesswise, he
wasn't letting me help him on a lot of big cases. He was
keeping them all to himself."

"And that was unusual?"

"That was unheard of. We always worked on big
cases together."

"These cases," Myron said. "Were they the girls
found in the woods upstate?"

She looked at him. "You want to tell me how you
knew that?"

"Just a guess."

"Hell of a guess, Myron."

"You said big cases. I read the papers. Those are the big cases they keep talking about."

Sally didn't believe him, but she didn't push it either. Myron said, "So what else was there?"

She took another deep drag. "He was very distracted. You'd talk to him, he'd nod, but he wouldn't listen."

"Anything else?"

Sally crushed out the cigarette, though it still had plenty to go. She lit another. "A new way to quit smoking," she said. "I smoke the same amount of cigarettes, but I take less puffs each day. Gradual slowdown until I quit entirely. At this rate it should take no more than twelve years."

"Good luck."

"Thanks."

"So what else was there?"

Another puff. "Adam was ordering a lot of weird tests on the last girl they found in the woods."

"What do you mean, weird tests?"

"Superfluous tests. In my opinion, anyway."

Myron said, "You never got a positive ID on her, right?"

"Right."

"So maybe he was running the tests to see if he could get a handle on her whereabouts."

"Maybe. But he sent them out one at a time. He'd wait for one test to come back before he'd ask for the next one. Anthropological measurements, shape and size of cranium, pelvic bones, ossification of the bones, fusing of sutures on the skull—all one at a time."

"So what do you make of that?"

She shrugged again. "I don't make anything out of that. It's just an example of what I meant by acting strangely. Distracted. The case was a weird one to start off. The girl's skull had been crushed by the perp, but that wasn't what killed her. In other words, she had been buried alive in those woods. She died trying to claw her way out.''

Silence.

"This girl," Myron said, "what was she wearing?"

Sally stiffened a little. Then she leaned forward. "Okay, Myron, what's going on?"

"Nothing. Why?"

"You know why."

Myron stopped. "The girl's clothes are missing."

"Yes."

He felt his heart crash into the pit of his stomach, like a skydiver with a ripped parachute. "Oh, shit."

"What is it?"

"Sally, I need you to run a test for me."

Chapter 44

The address of Brian Sanford, private investigator, was a go-go bar conveniently located one block from Merv Griffin's Resorts. Atlantic City was like that. The big hotels were like beautiful flowers untouched and un-bothered by the unseemly weeds of poverty and sleaze that surrounded them. The big flowers had not beautified the neighborhood as promised by the casino owners. The contrast, if anything, had made the weeds more glaringly hideous.

The go-go bar was called Eager Beaver, and it was exactly what one would expect. Blinking sign with missing letters on the outside. Lots of lowlights around the bar, lots of bright spotlights on the stage. Bored women danced in shifts, most of them unattractive. Lots of flab. Lots of implants. Lots of herpes.

Myron made the key mistake of entering what might loosely be designated a bathroom. The urinals were stuffed with ice cubes—an adequate substitute, Myron supposed, for an actual flushing mechanism. No doors were on the stalls, which did not deter the defecators at all. One man smiled and waved to Myron from a squat.

Myron decided he could wait.

He called over a bartender. "Could you tell me how to get to Brian Sanford's office?"

"Michelob, Bud, Bud Light, Coors."

"I just want to know—"

"Michelob, Bud, Bud Light, Coors."

Myron took out five dollars. The bartender pocketed it.

"Door in the back. Take the stairs up a level."

He didn't wait for Myron to thank him. Capitalism.

A dancer on break approached him. She smiled. Each tooth was angled in a different direction, as if her mouth were the masterwork of a mad orthodontist.

"Hi," she said.

"Hi."

"You're really cute."

"I don't have any money."

She spun and walked away. Ah, romance.

The stairs did not creak. They cracked. Myron kept waiting for them to collapse. On the landing there was only one door. It was open. Myron knocked on the wall and peeked in.

Myron called out, "Hello."

A man he assumed was Brian Sanford came to the door. All smiles. Dressed in a beige suit that had last been pressed during the Bay of Pigs. "You the guy who left the message?"

"Yes."

The office was a minicasino. No desk but a roulette table. A one-armed bandit in the corner. Decks of cards everywhere. Souvenir dice, the kind that have a hole drilled in them, littered the floor. So did racing forms. Keno cards too.

The man put out his hand. "Brian Sanford. But everyone calls me Blackjack. You know who gave me that nickname?"

Myron shook his head.

"Frankie. That's what I call Frank Sinatra. Frankie. Not Frank. Frankie, I call him." He paused, waited.

Myron said, "Good nickname."

"See, Frankie and me were playing at the Sands one night, right, and I was on one of my streaks, you know. And Frankie turns to me and says, 'Yo, check out Blackjack. He can't lose.' Just like that. Frankie says, 'Hey, Blackjack.' Out of nowhere. The name stuck. Now everyone calls me Blackjack. All 'cause of Frankie."

"Great story," Myron said.

"Yeah, well, you know how it is. So what can I do for you, Mr. . . . ?"

"Olson. Merlin Olson."

Blackjack smiled knowingly. "Okay, I can play it that way. Have a seat, Mr. Olson."

Myron sat.

"But before we start, Mr. Olson, I have to tell you one thing right up front."

He was holding dice in his hand, moving them around in his hands the way some people do with those Chinese balls that are supposed to help circulation.

"What's that?"

"I'm a very busy man. Lots of big stuff going on right now. You know how I started in this business?"

Myron shook his head.

"I used to be chief of security for Caesars Palace in Vegas. Head chief. You know how it is. I was in Vegas, right? But Donny—that's what I call Donald Trump, Donny—Donny asked me to head up security for his first hotel on the strip. Then he started nagging me to set up the Taj Mahal's security. I told him, I said, 'Donny, I got too much on my plate, you know?' "

Myron looked up. A small crop plane flew overhead, leaving mucho cow manure in its wake.

"So my problem is this, you see. I got a meeting tomorrow morning with Stevie—Steve Wynn. First thing, seven A.M. sharp. Great guy, Stevie. Morning guy. Up at five every day. You know he's practically blind? Got cataracts or something. He keeps it hidden. Only tells his closest friend. So anyway Stevie wants me to do something for him. Normally I'd tell him no, but it's a personal favor and Stevie's a good friend. Not like Donny. I'm not crazy about Donny. Thinks he's some hot stud now that he's got Marla."

"Mr. Blackjack—"

"Please," he said throwing up his hands, "just call me Blackjack."

"I'd like to ask you a few questions, uh, Blackjack. I need your particular expertise on an important matter."

He nodded. Very understanding. He didn't hitch up his pants importantly, but he should have. "What's this all about?"

"You performed some work for a friend of mine recently," Myron said. "Mr. Otto Burke."

A big smile now. "Sure. Otto. Swell kid. Smart as a whip. He calls me whenever he comes down."

Probably calls him Ottie, Myron thought.

"You gave him a magazine a few days ago. An issue of *Nips*."

Blackjack looked wary now. He rolled the dice on the table. A three. "What about it?"

"We need to know how you located it."

"Who is 'we'?"

"I work with Mr. Burke." Even saying it made Myron feel nauseous.

"So why didn't Ken call? He's the usual contact."

Myron leaned forward. Conspiratorial. "This is bigger than Ken, Blackjack. We don't feel anyone can be trusted with this but you."

He nodded. Again very understanding.

"Frankly, Blackjack—and this has to remain hush-hush."

"Of course."

"You're our first choice to replace Ken. But we know how busy you are."

His eyes gleamed a bit. "I appreciate that, Mr. Olson, but for someone like Otto Burke, I could try to open—"

"Let's talk about this case first, okay? How did you come across the magazine?"

The wary look again. "Don't take this the wrong way," he said, "but how do I know you work with Otto? How do I know you're not some schmo off the street?"

Myron smiled. "I knew it."

"What?"

"I told Otto you were the right guy for the job. You're not sloppy. You're careful. We like that. We need that."

Blackjack shrugged. He picked up the dice, gave another roll. Snake eyes. "I'm a professional," he said.

"Clearly," Myron agreed. "So why don't you call Otto yourself on the private line? He'll confirm everything. I'm sure you know the number."

That slowed him down a bit. He swallowed, trying to disguise it, looked around like a cornered rabbit. Myron could see the wheels churning. "Uh, no reason to bother Otto with this," Blackjack said. "You know how he hates that. I can tell you're an honest Joe. Besides, how would you know about the magazine if Otto hadn't told you?"

Myron shook his head. "You're an amazing man, Blackjack."

He waved a hand of modesty.

"How did you find the magazine?" Myron asked.

"Shouldn't we talk about my fee? On the phone you said something about ten grand."

"Otto said you were a trustworthy guy. He said to bill him through Ken. Whatever you think is fair."

Another nod. He picked up the dice. Rolled again. Another three. Practice, practice. "I didn't find the magazine," Blackjack said. "It found me."

"What do you mean?"

"I was hired to do a job. Part of it was to send out copies of that mag to some people."

"Was Christian Steele one of those people?"

"Yup. That's how I got suspicious. I mean, the envelopes were given to me already addressed and sealed. I didn't recognize any of the names except Christian's. Otto had already put out word he wanted anything, *anything,* on Steele. So I opened it up and took a peek. That's when I saw the picture."

"Who hired you to mail out the magazines?"

Blackjack placed one chip on red, one chip on odd. He spun the roulette wheel. "You wanna put down a couple of chips?"

"No. Who hired you?"

"Well, that's the weird part. I don't know. I got this

big package in the mail with very specific instructions. Plus cash. But no name.''

"Any return address?''

"Nope. Just a postmark.''

"From where?''

"Right here in Atlantic City. I got it about ten, twelve days ago.''

The roulette wheel stopped. Twenty-two. Black.

Blackjack said, "Damn.''

"Do you still have the instructions?''

"Yeah, sure.'' He opened a drawer and handed him a piece of paper. "Here.''

The letter had been typed:

Dear Mr. Sanford,

For the sum of $5,000 (plus expenses) I would like you to perform the following services:

1. Enclosed find seven envelopes. Two of them should be mailed from the campus mail box at Reston University on Friday. The other three should be mailed from a post office box in their respective towns.

2. Please mail out the following New Jersey Bell literature to each person on the list at the same time.

3. Please arrange a phone number in the 201 area code, one that will work on Return Call. This number should be immediately disconnected should anyone call it back or answer it. I would like you to hook up an answering machine with the enclosed tape to that phone. I would then like you to make calls to each of the numbers listed below from that number. On the first two nights—Saturday and Sunday—you will simply call repeatedly, hold the line when they answer, and say nothing until they

*hang up. On Monday, you will call and say the
following: "Enjoy the magazine. Come and get me.
I survived." Please make your voice sound female
and vague. (As you know, there are phones that can
disguise voices and make them sound female.)*

*4. Enclosed is a money order for $3,000. Upon
completion of this exercise I will contact you
personally on or around the ninth of the month and
pay off the remaining $2,000 plus expenses.*

*My name must remain anonymous. Thank you for
understanding.*

Myron looked up. "I assume the New Jersey Bell
literature explained Return Call."

Nod.

"Who were the seven people?"

Blackjack shrugged. The dice were rolled yet again.
Another snake eyes. The guy had the touch. "I don't
remember. Christian was one. Some dean was another. I
mailed another from a town called Glen Rock."

"To a Gary Grady."

"Yeah, that's the name. I also mailed three from New
York."

"One of those to Junior Horton?"

"Uh, yeah, I think so. Junior. That rings a bell."

"And the last one?"

"Some other place in New Jersey. Near Glen Rock."

Myron stopped. "Ridgewood?"

"Yeah. Something-wood anyway. A woman's name. I
remember because all the rest were men."

Myron said, "Carol Culver?"

He thought a moment. "Yeah. That's it. A name with
two C's."

Myron's shoulders slumped.

"Hey, buddy, you all right?"

"Fine," he said softly. "What about the phone calls?"

"The numbers were on another page. I threw them away when I finished. I called Steele and hung up a few times. By the time I called him back to give him the message calls, the line was disconnected. Guess he'd moved."

Myron nodded. Christian had moved from the campus to the condo.

"The guy in New York—Junior—he was never home so I never reached him either. The others all got hang-ups and then the message calls."

"How many of them used Return Call?"

"Just two. Christian and the guy from Glen Rock. It wouldn't have worked for the guys in New York anyhoo. Return Call only works for that area code."

"Have you heard from your client yet?"

"Nope. And yesterday was the ninth. I tell you, he better not stiff Blackjack Sanford." Another mental pants-hitch. "If he knows what's good for him."

"Uh-huh. Anything else you can tell me?"

"About this case? Nope. Hey, you wanna go over to Merv's? They know me over there. I can get us on a good table. Play a little blackjack maybe. Watch the legend in action."

Tempting, Myron thought. Like having electrolysis performed on his testicles. "Maybe some other time."

"Yeah, okay. Say, how much you think I should bill Otto for? Like you said, I want to be fair."

"Oh, I'd bill him for the full amount."

"The whole ten G's?"

"Yes. You've been very helpful, Blackjack. Thank you."

"Yeah, take care. Come by anytime."

"Oh, one more thing."

"What's that?"

Myron said, "Mind if I use your bathroom?"

Chapter 45

It was ten-thirty when Myron arrived at Paul Duncan's house. Lights were still on. Myron had not called to make an appointment. He wanted the element of surprise.

The house was a simple Cape Cod. Nice. Needed a new coat of paint maybe. The front yard had lots of budding flower beds. Myron remembered that Paul liked gardening in his down time. Lot of cops did.

Paul Duncan answered the door holding a newspaper. A pair of reading glasses were low on his nose. His gray hair was neatly combed. He wore navy-blue Hagar slacks and a twist-a-flex Speidel watch. The casual man from Sears. A television played in the background. An audience applauded wildly. Paul was alone, except for a sleeping golden retriever curled in front of the television as if it were a fire on a snowy night.

"We need to talk, Paul."

"Can't this wait until the morning?" His voice was strained. "After Adam's memorial service?"

Myron shook his head and stepped into the den. The television audience applauded again. Myron glanced at the screen. Ed McMahon's *Star Search*. The spokes-models weren't on, so Myron turned away.

Paul closed the door. "What's this all about, Myron?"

A coffee table had *National Geographic* and *TV Guide*. Also two books—the latest Robert Ludlum and the King James Bible. Everything was very neat. A portrait of the golden retriever in its younger days hung on the wall. Lots of little porcelain figurines adorned the room. A couple of Rockwell plates too. Hardly a swinging bachelor pad or den of lust.

"I know about your affair with Carol Culver," Myron said.

Paul Duncan played stiff-lip. "I don't know what you're talking about."

"Then let me try to clarify myself. The affair's been going on for six years. Kathy caught you and Mommy a couple years back. Adam also caught you two on the night he was murdered. Any of this ring a bell?"

His face went ashen. "How . . . ?"

"Carol told me." Myron sat. He picked up the Bible and flipped through it. "Guess you skipped the part about not coveting your neighbor's wife, huh, Paul?"

"It's not what you think."

"What's not what I think?"

"I love Carol. She loves me."

"That sounds swell, Paul."

"Adam treated her awfully. He gambled. He whored. He was cold to his family."

"So why didn't Carol divorce him?"

"She couldn't. We're both devout Catholics. The Church wouldn't allow it."

"The Church prefers marital infidelity?"

"That's not funny."

"No, it's not."

"Who are you to judge us? You think any of this was easy?"

Myron shrugged. "You didn't stop. Not even after Kathy saw you."

"I love Carol."

"So you say."

"Adam Culver was my closest friend. He meant a great deal to me. But when it came to his family, he was a bastard. He provided for them materially, but that's it. Ask Jessica, Myron. She'll tell you. I've always been there. From the time she was a little girl. Who took her to the hospital when she fell off her bike? Me. Who built her swingset? Me. Who drove her down to Duke her freshman year? Me."

"Did you also dress up as the Easter Bunny?" Myron asked.

He shook his head. "You don't understand."

"Correction: I don't give a shit. There's a difference. Now let's go back to the day Kathy caught you two. Tell me what happened."

His face became irritated. "You know what happened. She walked in on us."

"Were you naked?"

"What?"

"Were you and Mrs. Culver in the throes of passion?"

"I won't dignify that with an answer."

Time to rattle his cage a bit. "What position? Missionary, doggie, what? Were either of you wearing handcuffs or a pig's mask?"

He moved so he was standing directly over Myron. Everyone thought this was tremendously intimidating, towering over a seated foe. Fact was, Myron could deliver a palm strike to the groin before an ordinary man could even cock his fist.

"Watch it, son," Paul said.

"How did Kathy react to seeing you two lovebirds?"

"There was no reaction. She ran away."

"Did either of you follow her?"

"No. Frankly, we were both too shocked."

"I bet. Did you ever discuss the matter with Kathy?"

Paul stepped away, circled, sat in the chair next to Myron. "She only mentioned it to me once."

"When?"

"A few months later."

"What happened?"

He looked away, his eyes darting about, searching for a safe place to land. "This isn't easy to say."

Myron nodded, feigned sympathy. "Go on."

"Kathy made a pass at me."

"Did you catch it?"

"What?"

"As in 'catch her pass.' "

He flashed the irritated face again. "Of course not."

"You turned her down?"

"I pretended I didn't know what she was talking about."

"Did she persist?"

"Yes. But I kept ignoring her."

"Bet you were real excited, though. Mother and daughter. Both good-lookers. Your fantasies must have been in overdrive."

Irritation turned to rage. He finally took off his reading glasses. Very dramatically. "Last warning, pal."

"Uh-huh. So now tell me about Fred Nickler."

Piss him off. Quick subject change. Keep him off balance.

"Who?"

"For a cop," Myron said, "you're a lousy liar. Nineteen seventy-eight. You let Nickler plea-bargain a kiddie porn charge. I know all about your connection with him, Paul. What I don't know is how he fits into all this.''

"He helped me out from time to time. With cases.''

"Including the disappearance of Kathy Culver?''

"In a manner of speaking, yes.''

"How?''

"I guess there's no reason not to tell you.'' He coughed into a shaking fist. The golden retriever opened an eye but didn't move. "Adam found photographs of Kathy in his attic. He brought them to me in the strictest confidence. On the back of one was the name of a photography studio called Forbidden Fruit. I couldn't find them anywhere. So Adam and I visited Nickler. Nickler told us that Forbidden Fruit was now called Global Globes. He gave me the address.''

"Then you went and bought all the pictures and negatives of Kathy?'' A throwaway question. Lucy had already identified Paul Duncan from a photograph.

"Yes. We wanted to protect Kathy's name. But we also wanted the name of the animal that'd brought Kathy to the studio.''

"Gary Grady.''

"You know about that?''

"I am,'' Myron said, "well informed.''

"Well, I checked Grady out completely. He was shady, no question about it. A high school teacher with all those sex lines. He advertised in at least fifty pornographic magazines. I tailed him for a couple of weeks, did a lot of it on my own time. I also had his phone tapped for a while. But in the end we came up with nothing.''

"How did Adam react to that?''

"Not well. Adam was always coming to me with some new angle on Kathy's case, mostly out of pure desperation. I don't blame him. She was his youngest daughter. The one child he had a decent relationship with. Adam was willing to do anything to find her. He even wanted to kidnap Grady and torture him until he talked. I told him I'd do anything to help, but that we had to keep within the limits of the law. He didn't like hearing that."

"Tell me about the night Adam died."

Paul took a deep breath. "He set us up beautifully."

"I know all about that. What happened after he caught you and Carol in bed?"

Paul Duncan rubbed his eyes with his palms. "He went berserk. He started calling Carol names. Awful names. We tried to talk to him, but what could we say? After a while he told her he wanted a divorce and ran out."

"What did you do then?"

"I went home."

"Did you stop on the way?"

"No."

"Anybody who can confirm you were home?"

"I live alone."

"Anybody who can confirm you were home?" Myron repeated.

"No, dammit. That's why Carol and I didn't tell anyone. We knew how it would look."

"Not good," Myron agreed.

"I didn't kill him. I wronged him. I was a terrible friend. But I didn't kill him."

Myron gave a small shoulder shrug. "You seem like a pretty good candidate, Paul. You lied about the night of his murder. You were having a long-term affair with his wife, a wife who could marry you only if her husband died. He confronted you two in his bed on the night of the murder. His missing daughter was the only person who knew about your secret liaison. Her photograph appears in a magazine published by your source. No, Paul, I'd say it looks pretty goddamn shitty.''

"I had nothing to do with any of that."

"What did you do with Kathy's pictures?"

"I gave them to Adam, of course."

"Did you keep any for yourself? Maybe as a little souvenir?"

"Of course not!"

"And you never saw any of the pictures again?"

"Never."

"Yet somehow Kathy's picture ended up in a porno mag."

Paul nodded slowly.

"A porno mag published by your buddy Fred Nickler."

Another nod.

"So now comes the big question, Paul: How did Kathy's picture end up in Nickler's magazine?"

Using both arms for leverage Paul Duncan stood. He moved to the television and flicked it off. The junior dancers faded away. The dog did not move. Paul studied the blank screen for a while and then said, "It's going to sound crazy."

"I'm listening."

"Adam arranged it. He put Kathy's picture in that magazine."

Myron waited. His spine began to tingle.

"I don't understand it either," Paul continued. "Nickler called me yesterday. He was all upset, said you were nosing around and realizing something was up. I had no idea what he was talking about. Then he explained it to me. Adam had told Nickler to put that picture in his magazine. You see, Adam had met Nickler when we were trying to find the photographer's studio. So Adam went back to him, pretended he was still working on a case with me. He told Nickler to put Kathy's picture in Gary Grady's ad. He also told him not to say anything if anybody asked about it—except to give out Gary's alias and address.''

''Enough clues,'' Myron said, ''so someone would find Grady.''

''It seems so, yes.''

''Did Nickler tell you why he placed the picture only in *Nips*?''

''No. I can call and ask him, if you'd like.''

Myron shook his head. ''Not necessary.''

''That's all I know. I can't for the life of me figure out what Adam was doing. Maybe he wanted to set up Grady. Or maybe he just snapped. But the truth is, I have no idea why Adam would put his own daughter's picture in that magazine.''

Myron rose. He had a very good idea why.

Chapter 46

Win gazed into the mirror. Despite the fact that the hour was closing in on midnight, his evening was just beginning. He patted his hair, smiled at his reflection, and said, ''God, I am handsome.''

Myron grunted.

''Are you going to call Jessica?'' Win asked.

''I want to go over it again.''

''Now?''

"Now."

"And make my nubile lass wait?"

"She'll survive."

"You don't understand. This girl is very special to me."

"What's her last name?"

Win thought a moment, shrugged. "Okay, what do you wish to review?"

"I've told you everything I know," Myron said. "I want to know how you see it."

Win turned away from the antique mirror. His Central Park West apartment had been a gift from his grandfather. It was huge, worth millions, and decorated like Versailles. Myron was afraid to touch anything. He was sitting in an antique chair with wooden arms digging into his ribs.

"Do you mind if I break the case down into three separate entities?" Win said.

"Whatever you want."

"Fine. Then let us begin. Entity one: Kathy Culver's disappearance. During her senior year of high school, Kathy's personality changed for reasons her mother has now revealed to you. Kathy then sought to hurt said mother with promiscuity. Ergo the lewd photographs, which Kathy mailed to Carol. But Kathy Culver did not see the danger in her actions. She took for granted that she could just end it whenever she so desired. But that was not the case. When she wanted to stop—when she met Christian, it seems—she could not just backslide out."

Myron nodded.

"Enter Mr. Junior Horton. He decided to cash in on the new, unsullied Kathy Culver through blackmail. Kathy agreed to pay him in exchange for silence and photographs. On the night in question Mr. Horton called

Kathy at her sorority house. She agreed to meet him in the locker room. Once there, she was gang-raped by Junior Horton and several cohorts."

Win stopped and moved toward a decanter. "Care for a little cognac?"

"No, thanks."

He poured some into a snifter. "The rape bent her past the breaking point," he continued. "She snapped. She suddenly craved redemption and justice above all else. So she headed immediately to Dean Gordon's office to report the attack. Dean Gordon had been her employer, and she probably considered him a friend. She told him what had happened to her in the locker room. His reaction was either superfluous or detrimental to her resolve. Take your pick."

"Probably detrimental," Myron added.

"Yes, probably detrimental. Either way, Kathy left Dean Gordon's house disheartened. She walked around the campus in a sort of catatonic daze, I imagine. Ricky Lane approached her. He apologized and gave her the panties—that is, evidence of the crime against her. After that—who knows? We slam into a big brick wall. The only thing we know for sure is that the panties were found on top of a waste bin several days later. Are there any questions so far?"

Myron shook his head.

"Then let's move on to Entity two: Adam Culver's involvement. Sometime after Kathy disappears, her father finds the lewd photographs of his little princess in the attic. We know that they were hidden there by Carol Culver. But Adam, I am sure, did not realize that. He would have naturally assumed that Kathy had hidden them there. He would also have naturally assumed that the pictures were connected to his daughter's disappearance."

"Logical," Myron agreed.

"Yes, quite." Win twirled his cognac, studying the color. "Adam Culver then enlists the aid of Paul Duncan in his investigation. They track down the photographs' place of origin with the help of Fred Nickler. They also find out about Gary Grady. They continue their investigation, but nothing new develops. Paul wants to give up. Adam is desperate—so desperate that he tries to draw out the assailant in a most unorthodox manner."

Win paused, considering. "Here," he said, "is where it gets very interesting. We know Adam Culver had the photographs. We know he arranged to have them put in a pornographic magazine. I find it significant that the picture was placed only in *Nips* magazine."

Myron leaned forward. They were on the same wavelength. "The magazine with the smallest—almost non-existent—circulation."

"That fact disturbed you from the beginning," Win said.

Myron nodded. "Someone didn't want that magazine seen by a lot of people."

"Like her father."

"Right."

"And," Win continued, "we know that Adam Culver liked to frequent the casinos of Atlantic City. He might have met your friend Blackjack during one of his visits or at least heard his name. He could have hired someone else to forge his daughter's handwriting. He probably had a tape with her voice from an old answering machine. Ergo, Adam Culver set the whole thing up. He sent out the magazine to everyone who might have been involved in Kathy's disappearance. Her fiancé, for one. People in the picture, like Junior Horton."

"Why did he send one to his wife?" Myron asked.

"I don't know."

"And Dean Gordon?"

"Perhaps the dean was in one of those attic photographs. Or perhaps Adam found out about Kathy's visit to the dean's house that night. Most likely Adam was merely considering every possibility. But it's not really that relevant to the case. What is relevant, however, is the question of why Adam did not once again enlist the help of Paul Duncan."

"Because," Myron said, "Adam found out that Paul was sleeping with his wife."

Win nodded. "Paul was no longer a friend or trustworthy. Adam was now on his own. He sent the package to Sir Blackjack, making sure it would never be traced back to him. Then Adam set up his second little sting operation, the one on his wife and Paul. He walked in on them, ran out, and was killed."

"So who murdered him?" Myron said.

Win put down the snifter on a harpsichord from the seventeenth century. He steepled his fingers, bouncing them gently off one another. "There are two strong possibilities," he said. "First, Paul Duncan. We cannot just dismiss him. He had motive and opportunity. Second, Adam wanted to stir up the killer, that much is clear. But perhaps the magazine stirred up more trouble than he'd anticipated."

"Except for one thing," Myron interjected. "The magazines hadn't been sent out yet. Adam was dead two days before Blackjack mailed them."

"So perhaps someone discovered what Adam was up to before they were mailed."

"Otto Burke?"

Win shrugged.

"But Otto has no connection to Kathy Culver," Myron said.

"None that we are aware of. Which leads us to Entity

three: the unknowns. A major unknown, as I see it, is Nancy Serat. We can assume that she gave Adam Culver valuable information. But we do not know who killed her. Or what she meant when she told Christian it was time for sisters to reunite. And we especially do not know why Kathy Culver's hair was found on her dead body.''

Win rechecked his hair. Perfect. He smiled, winked, did everything but kiss his own reflection. ''We also have no explanation for Adam Culver's cabin in the woods. He could have become desperate enough to grab suspects and do his own interrogations. Or he could have been seeking retribution for all in the wicked photographs. On someone like Gary Grady. Or Junior Horton. But for some reason my mind cannot fully accept either of these rationales.''

Myron nodded. It didn't feel right to him either.

''And so now we've reached the final unknown. The most significant unknown of all: Miss Kathy Culver herself. Is she alive? Is she behind all this? Is she involved in any way at all?''

Win picked the snifter off the harpsichord. He took a sip of cognac, let it roll around his tongue, swallowed. ''The end.''

They both sat in silence. Myron churned the facts though his head yet again. None of them changed. Win studied his face.

''This was all a mental exercise,'' Win said. ''A test drive, as it were.''

Myron said nothing.

''You know what happened. You knew before I said a word.''

Myron handed Win the telephone. ''Cancel your date. We have a lot of work to do.''

Chapter 47

The memorial service.

Myron slipped in late and ducked behind a pillar. He was in desperate need of a shower, a shave, a nap. And he looked it.

He spotted Jessica in the front pew. She sat on one side of her mother, Edward on the other. All three were crying.

The priest delivered the standard death spiel like an actor who knew his lines too well. Nothing new or original was said. There was no coffin, no well-dressed corpse in peaceful repose. The priest seemed bothered by this, by the absence of his customary prop. He kept motioning down on cue, only to draw back when he realized that there was nothing in front of him.

Myron stayed out of sight. The church was crowded. Paul Duncan sat in the second row, directly behind Carol. Every once in a while Paul would put his hand on her shoulder, but he'd never leave it there long. Appearances. Christian was next to him, head lowered in prayer. Otto Burke and Larry Hanson were a few rows back. Good PR move. The press would undoubtedly be made aware of Otto Burke's heartfelt concern for his players' personal plights. Again, appearances.

Win was near the back. To his right sat Sally Li. Her face looked drawn, as if she could use a cigarette. Myron had spoken to her late last night. She had done the test. It had come out as he'd suspected.

Dean Gordon and his wife Madelaine were off to the left. Dean Gordon looked grim. Madelaine Gordon looked good in black. Myron recognized a few other faces in the crowd, but he couldn't put a name or place to any of them. It didn't matter.

The priest made a few last comments about the hereafter, God's will, and reuniting with the beloved in Heaven. Jessica's sob racked her whole body. No one put an arm around her. No one comforted her. She looked small and frail. Myron felt a lump rise in this throat.

Here we go.

When the ceremony ended, Myron did not hesitate. He walked purposively down the aisle. Jessica ran toward him without hesitation. They hugged, both closing their eyes. The mourners turned away and began to head for the exit. Win kept close to Otto Burke, Larry Hanson, and Dean Gordon.

Jessica finally released her grip. "Where were you?" she asked.

Myron swallowed. He nodded to Paul Duncan, shook hands with Edward and Christian, lightly kissed Carol on the cheek.

"I don't know how to say this," Myron said.

"What's the matter?"

He looked her straight in the eye. "I found Kathy. She's alive."

The group went silent.

Jessica opened her mouth, closed it.

"I'm meeting her tonight," Myron said.

Jessica finally found her voice. "I don't understand."

"It's a long story. But she's alive. I'll bring her home to you tonight."

Jessica looked at Carol. Carol looked back. Everyone looked at everyone else.

"I'll go with you," Jessica said.

"You can't."

"Like hell I can't."

"I promised her," Myron said. "Just me. Alone. She's scared."

"Of what?"

"Of the person who tried to kill her."

"Who?"

Myron shook his head. "She wouldn't tell me. Not on the phone." He took hold of Jessica's hand. It was cold and stiff. Like marble. "I'll bring her right to the house. I promise. We'll all talk then. But we can't risk scaring her off."

Jessica shook her head. She looked lost. "Where are you meeting her?"

"It's in the woods."

"What woods?" Jessica pulled back a little. "You're not making any sense."

"I can't tell you, Jess. I promised her. Kathy said it's the spot where she was left for dead. She wants to show me where it happened."

More silence.

Paul Duncan said, "Dear God."

Carol practically fainted into his arms.

"Where has she been?" Jessica asked.

"I only know bits and pieces from my investigation. She spent most of the time recovering from her injuries. She also spent some time in the Caribbean. An island called Curaçao. I picked up her trail from an entry that night in St. Mary Hospital's registry. On the night she vanished, a patient was found unconscious in the middle of a road. She gave her name as Katherine Pierce."

Carol gasped. "Pierce? That's my maiden name."

Myron nodded. "I don't know all the details yet. She was hit over the head. The blow cracked her skull. The assailant thought she was dead. But she wasn't. He buried her in the woods. She woke up and managed to dig herself out. It's a miracle she survived.''

Jessica's eyes filled with tears. ''She's alive?''

''Yes.''

''You're sure?''

''Yes.''

Jessica hugged her mother then. Edward joined in. Christian and Paul watched dumbfounded. Myron turned toward the door. Win was standing there. His nod was almost imperceptible.

Chapter 48

Myron parked his car on the dirt road. He was alone. The car's clock read 8:30 P.M. He grabbed his flashlight and headed toward the meeting spot.

The brush was thick. Several branches whipped across his face. He listened for other sounds. Crickets hummed away. Nothing else. The flashlight sliced through the heavy darkness, carving a path for him to follow. Myron heard his feet crunch on twigs and leaves. His mouth felt bone-dry. It always felt that way at moments like this.

He was getting close now, no more than twenty or thirty yards away.

''Kathy?'' he called out.

No answer.

"It's Myron, Kathy. I'm alone."

No reply. But then Myron heard a shuffling from in front of him. Something came into view. A head. A head of long blond hair.

"It's okay," Myron said gently. "I'm here alone."

She stepped toward him tentatively. Her right hand shaded her eyes from the flashlight's harsh glare. Myron pointed the beam away. "It's all right," he said.

She continued to move toward him, a dim silhouette. Her steps were slow, plodding, like a B-movie monster come to life.

"It's okay," Myron said again. "No one is going to hurt you."

"I wish that were true."

The voice had not come from her. It had come from behind him. Myron closed his eyes. His shoulders slumped. "Hello, Christian."

"Don't move, Mr. Bolitar. Put your hands up."

"Why bother?"

"What?"

"You're going to kill us. Just like you tried to kill Kathy. Just like you killed her father and Nancy."

"I never meant to hurt anybody," he said.

"But you did."

Christian cocked the gun. "Hands up. Now."

Myron raised his hands slowly. "Kathy opened up to you that night. She told you everything—every sordid detail of her past. She wanted to clean the slate."

"She lied to me!" Christian shouted. "All the time we were together—it was all a lie."

"So you tried to kill her."

"Kathy wanted me to still love her, Mr. Bolitar. But don't you see? I never loved her. I loved a lie. She wanted me to stand beside that lie while she told her story to the world. She wanted me to sell out my teammates, toss away a chance at a national championship and Heisman trophy—all for the sake of a lying whore.''

"A lying whore," Myron said, "like your mother."

He nodded. "Mr. Bolitar, tell her. Tell her what that game meant. In terms of money, fame, pride. You understand, Mr. Bolitar. It helped get me that contract."

"So you hit her over the head."

"I didn't mean to. It just happened. I thought she was dead. I couldn't find a pulse."

"So you drove her out here and buried the body. You hoped she'd never be found, but if she were, it'd be blamed on a serial killer."

Christian stepped closer. He raised the gun. "Enough talk," he said. "I'm not going to let you stall around until someone shows up."

"No need. Someone's been here all the time."

Win came out from behind a tree, no more than a yard away from Christian. He pressed the .44 against Christian's ear and said, "Drop it, or your brain becomes squirrel lunch."

Christian dropped the gun.

"It's over," Myron shouted.

From a farther distance two uniformed police arrived. They handcuffed Christian.

Jake Courter stumbled behind them, high-stepping through the long grass. "Too old for this shit," he mumbled. When he reached the clearing he said, "Nice setup, Bolitar."

"Lots of details. The secret to a good scam."

"Gonna tell me what's going on now?"

"Sure. Jess?"

Jessica took off the blond wig and stepped forward. Christian's mouth dropped open. "What the—"

"You killed Kathy," Myron said, "but not from the

blow to the head. She suffocated trying to claw her way out of the dirt.''

Jake looked confused. "Where's the body?"

"In the morgue. Where it's been since the police found it two months ago. Sally Li confirmed the identity last night."

"So why hadn't it been identified before?"

"Because the county medical examiner was Kathy's father. He knew who it was right away, but he pretended otherwise."

"Why?"

"Think about it a second, Jake. From Adam Culver's perspective. Your case had gone nowhere in eighteen months. Adam knew that. He also knew the body provided no new clues. So he figured that the only way to catch Kathy's killer was to draw him out. How? By making the killer think Kathy might still be alive. After all, she'd been alive when he dumped her in the woods. So Adam kept the corpse's identity a secret from everyone —the police, his friends, even his own family. He also figured that the nude photographs were tied into all this. So he used them."

"You mean he put that ad in the magazine?"

Myron nodded. "Adam Culver arranged everything. Even the mysterious phone calls saying 'Come and get me. I survived.' He did everything he could to make it look like Kathy was alive."

Jake nodded. "So what you guys were just doing—"

"Was finishing up Adam Culver's plan. Our performance at the church this morning sowed the final seeds of doubt."

"You were forcing Christian to make a play for you."

"Exactly."

"Incredible. So everyone was in on on this?"

"Jessica was," Myron said. "So were her mother and

brother. It would have been too cruel to lie to them. But Paul Duncan didn't know. Neither did anybody else, and Win made sure that all the suspects—Otto, the dean, even Gary Grady—knew about Kathy's 'survival.' ''

"Then you weren't sure it was Christian?"

"No, I was sure."

"You were trying to play it fair."

Myron nodded. "That's why I didn't tell you anything. I wanted you to see what happened without any preconceived notions."

"Fair enough," Jake said. "Go on."

"Adam Culver understood that only the killer would know this spot. If he made the killer think Kathy could still be alive, he or she would have to come back here—just to make sure Kathy was dead. That was why Adam rented that cabin nearby. That was why he had all that electronic equipment. To tape him. To have proof."

"Catching the killer returning to the scene of the crime," Jake said.

"Right."

"But I don't get something. Adam was killed before the magazine was mailed out. How did Christian find out about it?"

"He didn't. Remember, Adam was a pathologist. He wasn't an investigator. He overlooked a very important clue. At first anyway."

"What clue?"

"Kathy's clothes."

"What about them?"

"When Kathy's body was found, she was wearing a yellow sweater and a pair of gray sweat pants. Yet the sorority sisters said she was wearing blue when she left the house. The rapists said she was wearing blue. Dean Gordon said she was wearing blue. Ricky Lane said she was wearing blue. The sorority sisters were also positive that Kathy never returned to the house. So the question was: Where did the yellow sweater and gray sweat pants come from?"

Jake shrugged.

"It took Adam a while to realize the significance of the clothes. But when he did, he went to the most obvious source. Kathy's roommate."

"Nancy Serat."

"Right. But he didn't want to let on that Kathy's body had been found. So he asked Nancy where he could find her favorite yellow sweater, pretending to be a typical dad on some kind of nostalgic tour. But think about it. If Kathy didn't go back to her sorority house, where did she change clothes?"

Jake saw it now. "At Christian's," he said with a snap of the fingers. "Kathy slept there all the time. She must have kept clothes there."

"Right."

"And Nancy and Christian were friends," Jake said, picking up the thread. "She'd see nothing wrong with telling Christian all about Adam's visit. Probably thought the whole thing was kinda cute."

Myron turned toward Christian. "You got scared when you heard Adam had been asking about the yellow sweater. You knew he was getting close. So you followed him that night. You heard him fight with his wife. You saw him storm out of the house, and you figured this was the ideal opportunity to kill him. Another perfect misdirection."

Christian said nothing.

Jake said, "What do you mean, 'another perfect misdirection'?"

"When your investigation of Kathy's disappearance began," Myron said, "who did you focus in on?"

"Christian," Jake said. "Like I said, we always check out the boyfriend."

"So what did Christian do? With campus security combing the campus for clues, he planted the panties on the top of a garbage bin."

"The panties," Jake added, "with someone else's semen."

"Proof he didn't do it."

"Well, I'll be damned."

"He also misdirected us with Nancy Serat. He strangled Nancy. Then he planted one of Kathy's hairs at the scene."

"But where did he get the hair?"

"Kathy slept in his room all the time, right? She would have kept other stuff there besides her clothes. Stuff like a hairbrush."

"Son of a bitch."

"It was almost perfect. Blame someone who was dead. And if Kathy wasn't dead—if she had indeed survived—he'd make her look like a lunatic. Who'd believe the ravings of a girl who'd killed her old roommate? But Christian didn't count on Jessica showing up at Nancy's. He panicked. He hit her over the head and ran. Problem was, he'd left his fingerprints behind. But Christian was quick. He even used that to his advantage. When you dragged him in the next morning, he immediately admitted to being at Nancy's house. And then he came up with that wonderful story about sisters reuniting."

"Another perfect misdirection," Jake said.

"Except he forgot about the glass."

"What glass?"

"His fingerprints were found in several spots in the house, including a drinking glass. Yet Christian told us Nancy barely let him in the door, that she practically pushed him away mumbling about the reuniting sisters.

Under those circumstances, isn't it odd she'd offer him a drink?''

Myron looked at Christian. He lowered his eyes.

"I—I didn't mean to hurt any of them, Mr. Bolitar," he said.

"You were manipulative and calculating," Myron said. "You covered all the bases, even when you hired me. I was small-time. I could be controlled. You knew about my background, that I was an experienced investigator. You knew if any trouble arose, I'd keep things quiet. That I'd keep you informed. That I'd try to protect you. You played me for a sucker."

Everyone remained silent until Jake said, "All right. Get him out of here."

The uniformed officers led Christian away.

Myron looked back at Jessica. She still hadn't said a word. Tears slid down her cheeks. None of this morning's tears had been for her father. Maybe some of these were.

Win shook his head. " 'Squirrel lunch.' I can't believe I said 'squirrel lunch.' "

Jessica stopped crying. She even smiled a little. Myron put his arm around her and pulled her in close. Together they made their way back to the car.

Chapter 49

Three days later Myron drove Jessica to the airport.

"Just drop me off at the terminal," she said.

"I'll wait with you at the gate."

"You should head back."

"I have time."

"The traffic will be murder."

"I don't care."

"Myron?"

"What?"

"Just drop me off. Please. You know I hate scenes."

"I won't make a scene."

"You always make a scene."

Silence.

"What's going to happen to Gary Grady?" she asked.

"I've sent all the information to the school board and the local press. I don't know if he'll spend any time in jail, but he's finished.

"What about Dean Gordon?"

"He's resigned this morning. He's going to enter the private sector."

"And the rapists?"

"Cary Roland is the DA. This case means big headlines. He'll do his best. Ricky Lane is going to turn state's evidence."

"You dumped Ricky as a client?"

Myron nodded.

"And you lost Christian."

Another nod.

"All in all," she said, "this case hasn't had a real positive economic effect on you."

"I'm more worried about the personal effect."

"Meaning?"

"Meaning you're back in my life."

"Isn't that a good thing?"

"It is. Except you're leaving."

"Just for a month or two. It's a book tour."

He pulled up to the front of the terminal.

"I'll be back," she said.

He nodded.

Jessica kissed him. He held on. She finally pushed him back. He released her grudgingly.

"I love you," he said.

"I love you too." She stepped out of the car. "And I'll be back."

He watched her walk toward the entrance. He watched her pass through the sliding glass doors, watched her walk to the ticket gate, watched her disappear down an escalator. When she was out of sight, he still watched until a security guard knocked on his window.

"Unloading zone, bub. Move it!"

Myron looked back one more time. Then he drove back to the office.

There should have been a dark whisper in the wind. Or maybe a deep chill in the bone. Something. An ethereal song only Elizabeth or I could hear. A tightness in the air. Some textbook premonition. There are misfortunes we almost expect in life—what happened to my parents, for example—and then there are other dark moments, moments of sudden violence, that alter everything. There was my life before the tragedy. There is my life now. The two have painfully little in common.

Elizabeth was quiet for our anniversary drive, but that was hardly unusual. Even as a young girl, she'd possessed this unpredictable melancholy streak. She'd go quiet and drift into either deep contemplation or a deep funk, I never knew which. Part of the mystery, I guess, but for the first time, I could feel the chasm between us. Our relationship had survived so much. I wondered if it could survive the truth. Or for that matter, the unspoken lies.

The car's air-conditioning whirred at the blue MAX setting. The day was hot and sticky. Classically August. We crossed the Delaware Water Gap at the Milford Bridge and were welcomed to Pennsylvania by a friendly toll collector. Ten miles later, I spotted the stone sign that read Lake Charmaine—private. I turned onto the dirt road.

The tires bore down, kicking up dust like an Arabian stampede. Elizabeth flipped off the car stereo. Out of the corner of my eye, I could tell that she was studying my profile. I wondered what she saw, and my heart started fluttering. Two deer nibbled on some leaves on our right. They stopped, looked at us, saw we meant no harm, went back to nibbling. I kept driving and then the lake rose before us. The sun was now in its death throes, bruising the sky a coiling purple and orange. The tops of the trees seemed to be on fire.

"I can't believe we still do this," I said.

"You're the one who started it."

"Yeah, when I was twelve years old."

Elizabeth let the smile through. She didn't smile often, but when she did, *pow*, right to my heart.

"It's romantic," she insisted.

"It's goofy."

"I love romance."

"You love goofy."

"You get laid whenever we do this."

"Call me Mr. Romance," I said.

She laughed and took my hand. "Come on, Mr. Romance, it's getting dark."

Lake Charmaine. My grandfather had come up with that name, which pissed off my grandmother to no end. She wanted it named for her. Her name was Bertha. Lake Bertha. Grandpa wouldn't hear it. Two points for Grandpa.

Some fifty-odd years ago, Lake Charmaine had been the sight of a rich-kids summer camp. The owner had gone belly-up and Grandpa bought the entire lake and surrounding acreage on the cheap. He'd fixed up the camp director's house and tore down most of the lake-front buildings. But farther in the woods, where no one went anymore, he left the kids' bunks alone to rot. My sister, Linda, and I used to explore them, sifting through

2

their ruins for old treasures, playing hide-and-seek, daring ourselves to seek the Boogeyman we were sure watched and waited. Elizabeth rarely joined us. She liked to know where everything was. Hiding scared her.

When we stepped out of the car, I heard the ghosts. Lots of them here, too many, swirling and battling for my attention. My father's won out. The lake was hold-your-breath still, but I swore I could still hear Dad's howl of delight as he cannonballed off the dock, his knees pressed tightly against his chest, his smile just south of sane, the upcoming splash a virtual tidal wave in the eyes of his only son. Dad liked to land near my sunbathing mother's raft. She'd scold him, but she couldn't hide the laugh.

I blinked and the images were gone. But I remembered how the laugh and the howl and the splash would ripple and echo in the stillness of our lake, and I wondered if ripples and echoes like those ever fully die away, if somewhere in the woods my father's joyful yelps still bounced quietly off the trees. Silly thought, but there you go.

Memories, you see, hurt. The good ones most of all.

"You okay, Beck?" Elizabeth asked me.

I turned to her. "I'm going to get laid, right?"

"Perv."

She started walking up the path, her head high, her back straight. I watched her for a second, remembering the first time I'd seen that walk. I was seven years old, taking my bike—the one with the banana seat and Batman decal—for a plunge down Goodhart Road. Goodhart Road was steep and windy, the perfect thoroughfare for the discriminating Stingray driver. I rode downhill with no hands, feeling pretty much as cool and hip as a seven-year-old possibly could. The wind whipped back my hair and made my eyes water. I spotted the moving van in front of the Ruskins' old house, turned and—first pow—there she was, my Elizabeth, walking with that titanium spine, so poised, even then, even as a seven-year-old girl with Mary Janes and a friendship bracelet and too many freckles.

We met two weeks later in Miss Sobel's second-grade class, and from that moment on—please don't gag when I say this—we were soul mates. Adults found our relationship both cute and unhealthy—our inseparable tomboy-kickball friendship morphing into puppy love and adolescent preoccupation and hormonal high school dating. Everyone kept waiting for us to outgrow each other. Even us. We were both bright kids, especially Elizabeth, top students, rational even in the face of irrational love. We understood the odds.

But here we were, twenty-five-year-olds, married seven months now, back at the spot when at the age of twelve we'd shared our first real kiss.

Nauseating, I know.

We pushed past branches and through humidity thick enough to bind. The gummy smell of pine clawed the air. We trudged through high grass. Mosquitoes and the like buzzed upward in our wake. Trees cast long shadows that you could interpret any way you wanted, like trying to figure out what a cloud looked like or one of Rorschach's inkblots.

We ducked off the path and fought our way through thicker brush. Elizabeth led the way. I followed two paces back, an almost symbolic gesture when I think about it now. I always believed that nothing could drive us apart—certainly our history had proven that, hadn't it?—but now more than ever I could feel the guilt pushing her away.

4

My guilt.

Up ahead, Elizabeth made a right at the big semi-phallic rock and there, on the right, was our tree. Our initials were, yup, carved into the bark:

E.P.

+

D.B.

And yes, a heart surrounded it. Under the heart were twelve lines, one marking each anniversary of that first kiss. I was about to make a wisecrack about how nauseating we were, but when I saw Elizabeth's face, the freckles now either gone or darkened, the tilt of the chin, the long, graceful neck, the steady green eyes, the dark hair braided like thick rope down her back, I stopped. I almost told her right then and there, but something pulled me back.

"I love you," I said.

"You're already getting laid."

"Oh."

"I love you too."

"Okay, okay," I said, feigning being put out, "you'll get laid too."

She smiled, but I thought I saw hesitancy in it. I took her in my arms. When she was twelve and we finally worked up the courage to make out, she'd smelled wonderfully of clean hair and strawberry Pixie Stix. I'd been overwhelmed by the newness of it, of course, the excitement, the exploration. Today she smelled of lilacs and cinnamon. The kiss moved like a warm light from the center of my heart. When our tongues met, I still felt a jolt. Elizabeth pulled away, breathless.

"Do you want to do the honors?" she asked.

She handed me the knife, and I carved the thirteenth

line in the tree. Thirteen. In hindsight, maybe there had been a premonition.

It was dark when we got back to the lake. The pale moon broke through the black, a solo beacon. There were no sounds tonight, not even crickets. Elizabeth and I quickly stripped down. I looked at her in the moonlight and felt something catch in my throat. She dove in first, barely making a ripple. I clumsily followed. The lake was surprisingly warm. Elizabeth swam with clean, even strokes, slicing through the water as though it were making a path for her. I splashed after her. Our sounds skittered across the lake's surface like skipping stones. She turned into my arms. Her skin was warm and wet. I loved her skin. We held each other close. She pressed her breasts against my chest. I could feel her heart and I could hear her breathing. Life sounds. We kissed. My hand wandered down the delicious curve of her back.

When we finished—when everything felt so right again—I grabbed a raft and collapsed onto it. I panted, my legs splayed, my feet dangling in the water.

Elizabeth frowned. "What, you going to fall asleep now?"

"Snore."

"Such a man."

I put my hands behind my head and lay back. A cloud passed in front of the moon, turning the blue night into something pallid and gray. The air was still. I could hear Elizabeth getting out of the water and stepping onto the dock. My eyes tried to adjust. I could barely make out her naked silhouette. She was, quite simply, breathtaking. I watched her bend at the waist and wring the water out of her hair. Then she arched her spine and threw her head back.

My raft drifted farther away from shore. I tried to sift through what had happened to me, but even I didn't understand it all. The raft kept moving. I started losing sight of Elizabeth. As she faded into the dark, I made a decision: I would tell her. I would tell her everything.

I nodded to myself and closed my eyes. There was a lightness in my chest now. I listened to the water gently lap against my raft.

Then I heard a car door open.

I sat up.

"Elizabeth?"

Pure silence, except for my own breathing.

I looked for her silhouette again. It was hard to make out, but for a moment I saw it. Or I thought I saw it. I'm not sure anymore or even if it matters. Either way, Elizabeth was standing perfectly still, and maybe she was facing me.

I might have blinked—I'm really not sure about that either—and when I looked again, Elizabeth was gone.

My heart slammed into my throat. "Elizabeth!"

No answer.

The panic rose. I fell off the raft and started swimming toward the dock. But my strokes were loud, maddeningly loud, in my ears. I couldn't hear what, if anything, was happening. I stopped.

"Elizabeth!"

For a long while there was no sound. The cloud still blocked the moon. Maybe she had gone inside the cabin. Maybe she'd gotten something out of the car. I opened my mouth to call her name again.

That was when I heard her scream.

I lowered my head and swam, swam hard, my arms pumping, my legs kicking wildly. But I was still far from the dock. I tried to look as I swam, but it was too dark now, the moon offering just faint shafts of light, illuminating nothing.

I heard a scraping noise, like something being dragged.

Up ahead, I could see the dock. Twenty feet, no more. I swam harder. My lungs burned. I swallowed some water, my arms stretching forward, my hand fumbling blindly in the dark. Then I found it. The ladder. I grabbed hold, hoisted myself up, climbed out of the water. The dock was wet from Elizabeth. I looked toward the cabin. Too dark. I saw nothing.

"Elizabeth!"

Something like a baseball bat hit me square in the solar plexus. My eyes bulged. I folded at the waist, suffocating from within. No air. Another blow. This time it landed on the top of my skull. I heard a crack in my head, and it felt as though someone had hammered a nail through my temple. My legs buckled and I dropped to my knees. Totally disoriented now, I put my hands against the sides of my head and tried to cover up. The next blow—the final blow—hit me square in the face.

I toppled backward, back into the lake. My eyes closed. I heard Elizabeth scream again—she screamed my name this time—but the sound, all sound, gurgled away as I sank under the water.

1

Eight Years Later

Another girl was about to break my heart. She had brown eyes and kinky hair and a toothy smile. She also had braces and was fourteen years old and—

"Are you pregnant?" I asked.

"Yeah, Dr. Beck."

I managed not to close my eyes. This was not the first time I'd seen a pregnant teen. Not even the first time today. I've been a pediatrician at this Washington Heights clinic since I finished my residency at nearby Columbia-Presbyterian Medical Center five years ago. We serve a Medicaid (read: poor) population with general family health care, including obstetrics, internal medicine, and, of course, pediatrics. Many people believe this makes me a bleeding-heart do-gooder. It doesn't. I like being a pediatrician. I don't particularly like doing it out in the suburbs with soccer moms and manicured dads and, well, people like me.

"What do you plan on doing?" I asked.

"Me and Terrell. We're real happy, Dr. Beck."

"How old is Terrell?"

"Sixteen."

She looked up at me, happy and smiling. Again I managed not to close my eyes.

The thing that always surprises me—always—is that most of these pregnancies are not accidental. These babies want to have babies. No one gets that. They talk about birth control and abstinence and that's all fine

9

and good, but the truth is, their cool friends are having babies and their friends are getting all kinds of attention and so, hey, Terrell, why not us?

"He loves me," this fourteen-year-old told me.

"Have you told your mother?"

"Not yet." She squirmed and looked almost all her fourteen years. "I was hoping you could tell her with me."

I nodded. "Sure."

I've learned not to judge. I listen. I empathize. When I was a resident, I would lecture. I would look down from on high and bestow upon patients the knowledge of how self-destructive their behavior was. But on a cold Manhattan afternoon, a weary seventeen-year-old girl who was having her third kid with a third father looked me straight in the eye and spoke an indisputable truth: "You don't know my life."

It shut me up. So I listen now. I stopped playing Benevolent White Man and became a better doctor. I will give this fourteen-year-old and her baby the absolute best care possible. I won't tell her that Terrell will never stay, that she's just cut her future off at the pass, that if she is like most of the patients here, she'll be in a similar state with at least two more men before she turns twenty.

Think about it too much and you'll go nuts.

We spoke for a while—or, at least, she spoke and I listened. The examining room, which doubled as my office, was about the size of a prison cell (not that I know this from firsthand experience) and painted an institutional green, like the color of a bathroom in an elementary school. An eye chart, the one where you point in the directions the Es are facing, hung on the back of the door. Faded Disney decals spotted one wall while another was covered with a giant food pyramid poster. My fourteen-year-old patient sat on an examining table with a roll of sanitary paper we pulled down fresh for each kid. For some reason, the way the paper rolled out reminded me of wrapping a sandwich at the Carnegie Deli.

The radiator heat was beyond stifling, but you needed that in a place where kids were frequently getting undressed. I wore my customary pediatrician garb: blue jeans, Chuck Taylor Cons, a button-down oxford, and a bright Save the Children tie that screamed 1994. I didn't wear the white coat. I think it scares the kids.

My fourteen-year-old—yes, I couldn't get past her age—was a really good kid. Funny thing is, they all are. I referred her to an obstetrician I liked. Then I spoke to her mother. Nothing new or surprising. As I said, I do this almost every day. We hugged when she left. Over her shoulder, her mother and I exchanged a glance. Approximately twenty-five moms take their children to see me each day; at the end of the week, I can count on one hand how many are married.

Like I said, I don't judge. But I do observe.

After they left, I started jotting notes in the girl's chart. I flipped back a few pages. I'd been following her since I was a resident. That meant she started with me when she was eight years old. I looked at her growth chart. I remembered her as an eight-year-old, and then I thought about what she'd just looked like. She hadn't changed much. I finally closed my eyes and rubbed them.

Homer Simpson interrupted me by shouting, "The mail! The mail is here! Oooo!"

I opened my eyes and turned toward the monitor. This was Homer Simpson as in the TV show *The*

Simpsons. Someone had replaced the computer's droning "You've got mail" with this Homer audio wave. I liked it. I liked it a lot.

I was about to check my email when the intercom's squawking stopped my hand. Wanda, a receptionist, said, "You're, uh, hmm, you're, uh . . . Shauna is on the phone."

I understood the confusion. I thanked her and hit the blinking button. "Hello, sweetums."

"Never mind," she said. "I'm here."

Shauna hung up her cellular. I stood and walked down the corridor as Shauna made her entrance from the street. Shauna stalks into a room as though it offends her. She was a plus-size model, one of the few known by one name. Shauna. Like Cher or Fabio. She stood six one and weighed one hundred ninety pounds. She was, as you might expect, a head-turner, and all heads in the waiting room obliged.

Shauna did not bother stopping at Reception and Reception knew better than to try to stop her. She pulled open the door and greeted me with the words "Lunch. Now."

"I told you. I'm going to be busy."

"Put on a coat," she said. "It's cold out."

"Look, I'm fine. The anniversary isn't until tomorrow anyway."

"You're buying."

I hesitated and she knew she had me.

"Come on, Beck, it'll be fun. Like in college. Remember how we used to go out and scope hot babes together?"

"I never scoped hot babes."

"Oh, right, that was me. Go get your coat."

On the way back to my office, one of the mothers

gave me a big smile and pulled me aside. "She's even more beautiful in person," she whispered.

"Eh," I said.

"Are you and she . . ." The mother made a together motion with her hands.

"No, she's already involved with someone," I said.

"Really? Who?"

"My sister."

We ate at a crummy Chinese restaurant with a Chinese waiter who spoke only Spanish. Shauna, dressed impeccably in a blue suit with a neckline that plunged like Black Monday, frowned. "Moo shu pork in a tortilla shell?"

"Be adventurous," I said.

We met our first day of college. Someone in the registrar's office had screwed up and thought her name was Shaun, and we thus ended up roommates. We were all set to report the mistake when we started chatting. She bought me a beer. I started to like her. A few hours later, we decided to give it a go because our real roommates might be assholes.

I went to Amherst College, an exclusive small-Ivy institution in western Massachusetts, and if there is a preppier place on the planet, I don't know it. Elizabeth, our high school valedictorian, chose Yale. We could have gone to the same college, but we discussed it and decided that this would be yet another excellent test for our relationship. Again, we were doing the mature thing. The result? We missed each other like mad. The separation deepened our commitment and gave our love a new distance-makes-the-heart-grow-fonder dimension.

Nauseating, I know.

Between bites, Shauna asked, "Can you baby-sit Mark tonight?"

13

Mark was my five-year-old nephew. Sometime during our senior year, Shauna started dating my older sister, Linda. They had a commitment ceremony seven years ago. Mark was the by-product of, well, their love, with a little help from artificial insemination. Linda carried him to term and Shauna adopted him. Being somewhat old-fashioned, they wanted their son to have a male role model in his life. Enter me.

Next to what I see at work, we're talking *Ozzie and Harriet*.

"No prob," I said. "I want to see the new Disney film anyway."

"The new Disney chick is a babe and a half," Shauna said. "Their hottest since Pocahontas."

"Good to know," I said. "So where are you and Linda going?"

"Beats the hell out of me. Now that lesbians are chic, our social calendar is ridiculous. I almost long for the days when we hid in closets."

I ordered a beer. Probably shouldn't have, but one wouldn't hurt.

Shauna ordered one too. "So you broke up with what's-her-name," she said.

"Brandy."

"Right. Nice name, by the way. She have a sister named Whiskey?"

"We only went out twice."

"Good. She was a skinny witch. Besides, I got someone perfect for you."

"No, thanks," I said.

"She's got a killer bod."

"Don't set me up, Shauna. Please."

"Why not?"

"Remember the last time you set me up?"

"With Cassandra."

"Right."

"So what was wrong with her?"

"For one thing, she was a lesbian."

"Christ, Beck, you're such a bigot."

Her cell phone rang. She leaned back and answered it, but her eyes never left my face. She barked something and flipped the mouthpiece up. "I have to go," she said.

I signaled for the check.

"You're coming over tomorrow night," she pronounced.

I feigned a gasp. "The lesbians have no plans?"

"I don't. Your sister does. She's going stag to the big Brandon Scope formal."

"You're not going with her?"

"Nah."

"Why not?"

"We don't want to leave Mark without us two nights in a row. Linda has to go. She's running the trust now. Me, I'm taking the night off. So come over tomorrow night, okay? I'll order in, we'll watch videos with Mark."

Tomorrow was the anniversary. Had Elizabeth lived, we'd be scratching our twenty-first line in that tree. Strange as this might sound, tomorrow would not be a particularly hard day for me. For anniversaries or holidays or Elizabeth's birthday, I get so geared up that I usually handle them with no problems. It's the "regular" days that are hard. When I flip with the remote and stumble across a classic episode of *The Mary Tyler Moore Show* or *Cheers*. When I walk through a bookstore and see a new title by Alice Hoffman or Anne Tyler. When I listen to the O'Jays or the Four Tops or Nina Simone. Regular stuff.

"I told Elizabeth's mother I'd stop by," I said.

"Ah, Beck . . ." She was about to argue but caught herself. "How about after?"

"Sure," I said.

Shauna grabbed my arm. "You're disappearing again, Beck."

I didn't reply.

"I love you, you know. I mean, if you had any sort of sexual appeal whatsoever, I probably would have gone for you instead of your sister."

"I'm flattered," I said. "Really."

"Don't shut me out. If you shut me out, you shut everyone out. Talk to me, okay?"

"Okay," I said. But I can't.

I almost erased the email.

I get so much junk email, spam, bulk emails, you know the drill, I've become quite handy with the delete button. I read the sender's address first. If it's someone I know or from the hospital, fine. If not, I enthusiastically click the delete button.

I sat at my desk and checked the afternoon schedule. Chock-full, which was no surprise. I spun around in my chair and readied my delete finger. One email only. The one that made Homer shriek before. I did the quick scan, and my eyes got snagged on the first two letters of the subject.

What the—?

The way the window screen was formatted, all I could see were those two letters and the sender's email address. The address was unfamiliar to me. A bunch of numbers @comparama.com.

I narrowed my eyes and hit the right scroll button. The subject appeared a character at a time. With each click, my pulse raced a bit more. My breathing grew funny. I kept my finger on the scroll button and waited.

When I was done, when all the letters showed themselves, I read the subject again and when I did, I felt a deep, hard thud in my heart.

"Dr. Beck?"

My mouth wouldn't work.

"Dr. Beck?"

"Give me a minute, Wanda."

She hesitated. I could still hear her on the intercom. Then I heard it click off.

I kept staring at the screen:

To: dbeckmd@nyhosp.com
From: 13943928@comparama.com
Subject: E.P.+ D.B ///////////////////

Twenty-one lines. I've counted four times already.

It was a cruel, sick joke. I knew that. My hands tightened into fists. I wondered what chicken-shitted son of a bitch had sent it. It was easy to be anonymous in emails—the best refuge of the techno-coward. But the thing was, very few people knew about the tree or our anniversary. The media never learned about it. Shauna knew, of course. And Linda. Elizabeth might have told her parents or uncle. But outside of that . . .

So who sent it?

I wanted to read the message, of course, but something held me back. The truth is, I think about Elizabeth more than I let on—I don't think I'm fooling anyone there—but I never talk about her or what happened. People think I'm being macho or brave, that I'm trying to spare my friends or shunning people's pity or some such nonsense. That's not it. Talking about Elizabeth hurts. A lot. It brings back her last scream. It brings back all the unanswered questions. It brings back the might-have-beens (few things, I assure you, will devastate like the might-have-beens). It brings back the guilt, the feelings, no matter how irrational, that a stronger man—a better man—might have saved her.

They say it takes a long time to comprehend a tragedy. You're numb. You can't adequately accept the grim reality. Again, that's not true. Not for me anyway. I understood the full implications the moment they found Elizabeth's body. I understood that I would never see her again, that I would never hold her again, that we would never have children or grow old together. I understood that this was final, that there was no reprieve, that nothing could be bartered or negotiated.

I started crying immediately. Sobbing uncontrollably. I sobbed like that for almost a week without letup. I sobbed through the funeral. I let no one touch me, not even Shauna or Linda. I slept alone in our bed, burying my head in Elizabeth's pillow, trying to smell her. I went through her closets and pressed her clothes against my face. None of this was comforting. It was weird and it hurt. But it was her smell, a part of her, and I did it anyway.

Well-meaning friends—often the worst kind—handed me the usual clichés, and so I feel in a pretty good position to warn you: Just offer your deepest condolences. Don't tell me I'm young. Don't tell me it'll get better. Don't tell me she's in a better place. Don't tell me it's part of some divine plan. Don't tell me that I was lucky to have known such a love. Every one of those platitudes pissed me off. They made me—and this is going to sound uncharitable—stare at the idiot and wonder why he or she still breathed while my Elizabeth rotted.

I kept hearing that "better to have loved and lost" bullshit. Another falsehood. Trust me, it is not better. Don't show me paradise and then burn it down. That was part of it. The selfish part. What got to me more—what really hurt—was that Elizabeth was denied so much. I can't tell you how many times I see or do something and I think of how much Elizabeth would have loved it and the pang hits me anew.

People wonder if I have any regrets. The answer is, only one. I regret that there were moments I wasted doing something other than making Elizabeth happy.

"Dr. Beck?"

"One more second," I said.

I put my hand on the mouse and moved the cursor over the Read icon. I clicked it and the message came up:

To: dbeckmd@nyhosp.com
From: 13943928@comparama.com
Subject: E.P.+ D.B //////////////////
Message: Click on this hyperlink, kiss time, anniversary.

A lead block formed in my chest.

Kiss time?

It was a joke, had to be. I am not big on cryptic. I'm also not big on waiting.

I grabbed the mouse again and moved the arrow over the hyperlink. I clicked and heard the primordial modem screech the mating call of machinery. We have an old system at the clinic. It took a while for the Web browser to appear. I waited, thinking *kiss time, how do they know about kiss time?*

The browser came up. It read error.

I frowned. Who the hell sent this? I tried it a second time, and again the error message came up. It was a broken link.

Who the hell knew about kiss time?

I have never told anyone. Elizabeth and I didn't much discuss it, probably because it was no big deal. We were corny to the point of Pollyanna, so stuff like this we just kept to ourselves. It was embarrassing really, but when we kissed that first time twenty-one years ago, I noted the time. Just for fun. I pulled back and looked at my Casio watch and said, "Six-fifteen."

And Elizabeth said, *"Kiss time."*

I looked at the message yet again. I started getting pissed now. This was way beyond funny. It's one thing to send a cruel email, but . . .

Kiss time.

Well, kiss time was 6:15 p.m. tomorrow. I didn't have much choice. I'd have to wait until then.

So be it.

I saved the email onto a diskette just in case. I pulled down the print options and hit Print All. I don't know much about computers, but I know that you could sometimes trace the origin of a message from all that gobbledygook at the bottom. I heard the printer purr. I took another look at the subject. I counted the lines again. Still twenty-one.

I thought about that tree and that first kiss, and there in my tight, stifling office I started to smell the strawberry Pixie Stix.

2

At home, I found another shock from the past.

I live across the George Washington Bridge from Manhattan—in the typical American-dream suburb of Green River, New Jersey, a township with, despite the moniker, no river and shrinking amounts of green. Home is Grandpa's house. I moved in with him and a revolving door of foreign nurses when Nana died three years ago.

Grandpa has Alzheimer's. His mind is a bit like an old black-and-white TV with damaged rabbit-ear antennas. He goes in and out and some days are better than others and you have to hold the antennas a certain way and not move at all, and even then the picture does the intermittent vertical spin. At least, that was how it used to be. But lately—to keep within this metaphor—the TV barely flickers on.

I never really liked my grandfather. He was a domineering man, the kind of old-fashioned, lift-by-the-boot-straps type whose affection was meted out in direct proportion to your success. He was a gruff man of tough love and old-world machismo. A grandson who was both sensitive and unathletic, even with good grades, was easily dismissed.

The reason I agreed to move in with him was that I knew if I didn't, my sister would have taken him in. Linda was like that. When we sang at Brooklake summer camp that "He has the whole world in His hands," she took the meaning a little too much to heart. She would have felt obligated. But Linda had a son and a life partner and responsibilities. I did not. So I made a pre-emptive strike by moving in. I liked living here well enough, I guess. It was quiet.

Chloe, my dog, ran up to me, wagging her tail. I scratched her behind the floppy ears. She took it in for a moment or two and then started eyeing the leash.

"Give me a minute," I told her.

Chloe doesn't like this phrase. She gave me a look—no easy feat when your hair totally covers your eyes. Chloe is a bearded collie, a breed that appears far more like a sheepdog than any sort of collie I've ever seen. Elizabeth and I had bought Chloe right after we got married. Elizabeth had loved dogs. I hadn't. I do now.

Chloe leaned up against the front door. She looked at the door, then at me, then back at the door again. Hint, hint.

Grandpa was slumped in front of a TV game show. He didn't turn toward me, but then again, he didn't seem to be looking at the picture either. His face was stuck in what had become a steady, pallid death-freeze. The only time I saw the death-freeze melt was when he was having his diaper changed. When that happened, Grandpa's lips thinned and his face went slack. His eyes watered and sometimes a tear escaped. I think he is at his most lucid at the exact moment he craves senility.

God has some sense of humor.

The nurse had left the message on the kitchen table: CALL SHERIFF LOWELL.

There was a phone number scribbled under it.

My head began to pound. Since the attack, I suffer migraines. The blows cracked my skull. I was hospital-ized for five days, though one specialist, a classmate of mine at medical school, thinks the migraines are psychological rather than physiological in origin. Maybe he's right. Either way, both the pain and guilt remain. I should have ducked. I should have seen the blows coming. I shouldn't have fallen into the water. And finally, I somehow summoned up the strength to save myself—shouldn't I have been able to do the same to save Elizabeth?

Futile, I know.

I read the message again. Chloe started whining. I put up one finger. She stopped whining but started doing her glance-at-me-and-the-door again.

I hadn't heard from Sheriff Lowell in eight years, but I still remembered him looming over my hospital bed, his face etched with doubt and cynicism.

What could he want after all this time?

I picked up the phone and dialed. A voice answered on the first ring.

"Dr. Beck, thank you for calling me back."

I am not a big fan of caller ID—too Big Brother for my tastes. I cleared my throat and skipped the pleasantries. "What can I do for you, Sheriff?"

"I'm in the area," he said. "I'd very much like to stop by and see you, if that's okay."

"Is this a social call?" I asked.

"No, not really."

He waited for me to say something. I didn't.

"Would now be convenient?" Lowell asked.

"You mind telling me what it's about?"

"I'd rather wait until—"

"And I'd rather you didn't."

I could feel my grip on the receiver tighten.

"Okay, Dr. Beck, I understand." He cleared his throat in a way that indicated he was trying to buy some time. "Maybe you saw on the news that two bodies were found in Riley County."

I hadn't. "What about them?"

"They were found near your property."

"It's not my property. It's my grandfather's."

"But you're his legal custodian, right?"

"No," I said. "My sister is."

"Perhaps you could call her then. I'd like to speak with her too."

"The bodies were not found on Lake Charmaine, right?"

"That's correct. We found them on the western neighboring lot. County property actually."

"Then what do you want from us?"

There was a pause. "Look, I'll be there in an hour. Please see if you can get Linda to come by, will you?"

He hung up.

The eight years had not been kind to Sheriff Lowell, but then again, he hadn't been Mel Gibson to begin with. He was a mangy mutt of a man with features so extra-long hangdog that he made Nixon look as though he'd gotten a nip and tuck. The end of his nose was bulbous to the nth degree. He kept taking out a much-used hanky, carefully unfolding it, rubbing his nose, carefully refolding it, jamming it deep into his back pocket.

Linda had arrived. She leaned forward on the couch, ready to shield me. This was how she often sat. She was one of those people who gave you their full, undivided attention. She fixed you with those big brown eyes and you could look nowhere else. I'm definitely biased, but Linda is the best person I know. Corny, yes, but the fact that she exists gives me hope for this world. The fact that she loves me gives me whatever else I have left.

We sat in my grandparents' formal living room, which I usually do my utmost to avoid. The room was stale, creepy, and still had that old-people's-sofa smell. I found it hard to breathe. Sheriff Lowell took his time getting situated. He gave his nose a few more swipes, took out a pocket pad, licked his finger, found his page. He offered us his friendliest smile and started.

"Do you mind telling me when you were last at the lake?"

"I was there last month," Linda said.

But his eyes were on me. "And you, Dr. Beck?"

"Eight years ago."

He nodded as though he'd expected that response. "As I explained on the phone, we found two bodies near Lake Charmaine."

"Have you identified them yet?" Linda asked.

"No."

"Isn't that odd?"

Lowell thought about that one while leaning forward to pull out the hanky again. "We know that they're both male, both full-grown, both white. We're now searching through missing persons to see what we can come up with. The bodies are rather old."

"How old?" I asked.

Sheriff Lowell again found my eyes. "Hard to say. Forensics is still running tests, but we figure they've been dead at least five years. They were buried pretty good too. We'd never have found them except there was a landslide from that record rainfall, and a bear came up with an arm."

My sister and I looked at each other.

"Excuse me?" Linda said.

Sheriff Lowell nodded. "A hunter shot a bear and found a bone next to the body. It'd been in the bear's mouth. Turned out to be a human arm. We traced it back. Took some time, I can tell you. We're still excavating the area."

"You think there may be more bodies?"

"Can't say for sure."

I sat back. Linda stayed focused. "So are you here to get our permission to dig on Lake Charmaine property?"

"In part."

We waited for him to say more. He cleared his throat and looked at me again. "Dr. Beck, you're blood type B positive, isn't that right?"

I opened my mouth, but Linda put a protective hand on my knee. "What does that have to do with anything?" she asked.

"We found other things," he said. "At the grave site."

"What other things?"

"I'm sorry. That's confidential."

"Then get the hell out," I said.

Lowell did not seem particularly surprised by my outburst. "I'm just trying to conduct—"

"I said, get out."

Sheriff Lowell didn't move. "I know that your wife's murderer has already been brought to justice," he said. "And I know it must hurt like hell to bring this all up again."

"Don't patronize me," I said.

"That's not my intent."

"Eight years ago you thought I killed her."

"That's not true. You were her husband. In such cases, the odds of a family member's involvement—"

"Maybe if you didn't waste time with that crap, you would have found her before—" I jerked back, feeling myself choking up. I turned away. Damn. Damn him.

Linda reached for me, but I moved away.

"My job was to explore every possibility," he droned on. "We had the federal authorities helping us. Even your father-in-law and his brother were kept informed of all developments. We did everything we could."

I couldn't bear to hear another word. "What the hell do you want here, Lowell?"

He rose and hoisted his pants onto his gut. I think he wanted the height advantage. To intimidate or something. "A blood sample," he said. "From you."

"Why?"

"When your wife was abducted, you were assaulted."

"So?"

"You were hit with a blunt instrument."

"You know all this."

"Yes," Lowell said. He gave his nose another wipe, tucked the hanky away, and started pacing. "When we found the bodies, we also found a baseball bat."

The pain in my head started throbbing again. "A bat?"

Lowell nodded. "Buried in the ground with the bodies. There was a wooden bat."

Linda said, "I don't understand. What does this have to do with my brother?"

"We found dried blood on it. We've typed it as B positive." He tilted his head toward me. "Your blood type, Dr. Beck."

We went over it again. The tree-carving anniversary, the swim in the lake, the sound of the car door, my pitifully frantic swim to shore.

"You remember falling back in the lake?" Lowell asked me.

"Yes."

"And you heard your wife scream?"

"Yes."

"And then you passed out? In the water?"

I nodded.

"How deep would you say the water was? Where you fell in, I mean?"

"Didn't you check this eight years ago?" I asked.

"Bear with me, Dr. Beck."

"I don't know. Deep."

"Over-your-head deep?"

"Yes."

"Right, okay. Then what do you remember?"

"The hospital," I said.

"Nothing between the time you hit the water and the time you woke up at the hospital?"

"That's right."

"You don't remember getting out of the water? You don't remember making your way to the cabin or calling for an ambulance? You did all that, you know. We found you on the floor of the cabin. The phone was still off the hook."

"I know, but I don't remember."

Linda spoke up. "Do you think these two men are more victims of"—she hesitated—"KillRoy?"

She said it in a hush. KillRoy. Just uttering his name chilled the room.

Lowell coughed into his fist. "We're not sure, ma'am. KillRoy's only known victims are women. He never hid a body before—at least, none that we know about. And the two men's skin had rotted so we can't tell if they'd been branded."

Branded. I felt my head spin. I closed my eyes and tried not to hear any more.

This, like everything else, is for Anne.

The author wishes to thank Sunandan B. Singh, M.D., Chief Medical Examiner of Bergen County, New Jersey; Bob Richter; Rich Henshaw; Richard Curtis; Jacob Hoye; Shawn Coyne; and, of course, Dave Bolt.

Drop Shot

DEDICATION

For Anne and Charlotte,
from the luckiest man in the whole world

....

ACKNOWLEDGMENT

The author wishes to thank the following: my friends and college roommates James Bradbeer Jr. and Lawrence Vitale; David Pepe of Pro Agents Inc.; Peter Roisman of Advantage International; my editor and friend Jacob Hoye; Natalie Ayars, M.D.; E. W. Count; the AOL Writers Club; and, of course, Dave Bolt.

Chapter 1

"Cesar Romero," Myron said.

Win looked at him. "You're not serious."

"I'm starting off with an easy one."

On Stadium Court the players were changing sides. Myron's client, Duane Richwood, was shellacking the number-fifteen seed Ivan Something-okov, leading 5–0 in the third set after winning the first two sets 6–0, 6–2. An impressive U.S. Open debut for the unseeded twenty-one-year-old upstart from the streets (literally) of New York.

"Cesar Romero," Myron repeated. "Unless you don't know."

Win sighed. "The Joker."

"Frank Gorshin."

"The Riddler."

Ninety-second commercial break. Myron and Win were keeping themselves busy with a scintillating game of Name the *Batman* Criminal. The TV *Batman*. The *Batman* starring Adam West and Burt Ward and all those Pow, Bam, Slam balloons. The *real* Batman.

"Who played the second one?" Myron asked.

"The second Riddler?"

Myron nodded.

From across the court Duane Richwood flashed them a cocky smile. He sported garish aviator sunglasses with loud fluorescent green frames. The latest style from

Ray•Ban. Duane was never without them. He had become not only identified by the shades but defined by them. Ray•Ban was rather pleased.

Myron and Win sat in one of the two players' boxes reserved for celebrities and players' entourages. For most matches every seat in the box was filled. When Agassi played the night before, the box had overflowed with his family, friends, suck-ups, young lasses, environmentally correct movie stars, hair weaves—like an Aerosmith backstage party. But Duane had only three people in the box: agent Myron, financial consultant Win, and Duane's coach, Henry Hobman. Wanda, the love of Duane's life, got too nervous and preferred to stay home.

"John Astin," Win answered.

Myron nodded. "How about Shelley Winters."

"Ma Parker."

"Milton Berle."

"Louie the Lilac."

"Liberace."

"Chandell the Great."

"And?"

Win looked puzzled. "And what?"

"What other criminal did Liberace play?"

"What are you talking about? Liberace only appeared in that one episode."

Myron leaned back and smiled. "Are you sure?"

In his seat next to the umpire's chair Duane happily chugged down a bottle of Evian. He held the bottle so that the sponsor's name could be clearly seen by the television cameras. Smart kid. Knew how to please the sponsor. Myron had recently signed Duane to a simple deal with the natural water giant: during the U.S. Open Duane drank Evian in marked bottles. In return Evian paid him ten grand. That was water rights. Myron was negotiating Duane's soda rights with Pepsi and his electrolyte rights with Gatorade.

Ah, tennis.

"Liberace only appeared in that one episode," Win announced.

"Is that your final answer?"

"Yes. Liberace only appeared in that one episode."

Henry Hobman continued to study the court, scrutinizing with intense concentration, his line of vision swinging back and forth. Too bad no one was playing.

"Henry, you want to take a guess?"

Henry ignored them. Nothing new there.

"Liberace only appeared in that one episode," Win repeated, his nose in the air.

Myron made a soft buzzing sound. "Sorry, that answer is incorrect. What do we have for our player, Don? Well, Myron, Windsor gets the home version of our game plus a year's supply of Turtle Wax. And thank you for playing our game!"

Win was unmoved. "Liberace only appeared in that one episode."

"That your new mantra?"

"Until you prove otherwise."

Win—full name: Windsor Horne Lockwood III—steepled his manicured fingers. He did that a lot, steepling. Steepling fit him. Win looked liked his name. The poster boy for the quintessential WASP. Everything about his appearance reeked arrogance, elitism, *Town and Country* Parties Page, debutantes dressed in monogrammed sweaters and pearls with names like Babs, dry martinis at the clubhouse, stuffy old money—his fine blond hair, his pretty-boy patrician face, his lily-white complexion, his snotty Exeter accent. Except in Win's case some sort of chromosomal abnormality had slipped through the generations of careful breeding. In some ways Win was exactly what he appeared to be. But in many more ways—sometimes very frightening ways— Win was not.

"I'm waiting," Win said.

"You remember Liberace playing Chandell the Great?" Myron asked.

"Of course."

"But you forgot that Liberace also played Chandell's evil twin brother, Harry. In the same episode."

Win made a face. "You cannot be serious."

"What?"

"That doesn't count. Evil twin brothers."

"Where in the rule book does it say that?"

Win set his jutting jaw in that certain way.

The humidity was thick enough to wear as undergarments, especially in Flushing Meadows's windless stadium court. The stadium, named strangely enough for Louis Armstrong, was basically a giant billboard that also happened to have a tennis court in the middle. IBM had a sign above the speedometer that clocked the velocity of each player's serve. Citizen kept both the real time and how long the match had been going on. Visa had its name printed behind the service line. Reebok, Infiniti, Fuji Film, Clairol had their names plastered wherever there was a free spot. So did Heineken.

Heineken, the official beer of the U.S. Open.

The crowd was a complete mix. Down low—in the good seats—people had money. But anything went in the dress department. Some wore full suits and ties (like Win), some wore more casual Banana Republic–type clothes (like Myron), some wore jeans, some wore shorts. But Myron's personal favorite were the fans who came in full tennis gear—shirt, shorts, socks, tennis shoes, warm-up jacket, sweatbands, and tennis racket. Tennis racket. Like they might get called on to play. Like Sampras or Steffi or someone might suddenly point into the stands and say, "Hey, you with the racket. I need a doubles partner."

Win's turn. "Roddy McDowall," he began.

"The Bookworm."

"Vincent Price."

"Egghead."

"Joan Collins."

Myron hesitated. "Joan Collins? As in *Dynasty*?"

"I refuse to offer hints."

Myron ran episodes through his mind. On the court the umpire announced, "Time." The ninety-second commercial break was over. The players rose. Myron couldn't swear to it, but he thought he saw Henry blink.

"Give up?" Win asked.

"Shhh. They're about to play."

"And you call yourself a *Batman* fan."

The players took the court. They too were billboards, only smaller. Duane wore Nike sneakers and clothes. He used a Head tennis racket. Logos for McDonald's and Sony adorned his sleeves. His opponent wore Reebok. His logos featured Sharp electronics and Bic. Bic. The pen and razor company. Like someone was going to watch a tennis match, see the logo, and buy a pen.

Myron leaned toward Win. "Okay, I give," he whispered. "What criminal did Joan Collins play?"

Win shrugged. "I don't remember."

"What?"

"I know she was in an episode. But I don't remember her character's name."

"You can't do that."

Win smiled with perfect white teeth. "Where in the rule book does it say that?"

"You have to know the answer."

"Why?" Win countered. "Does Pat Sajak have to know every puzzle on *Wheel of Fortune*? Does Alex Trebeck have to know every question on *Jeopardy!*"

Pause. "Nice analogy, Win. Really."

"Thank you."

Then another voice said, "The Siren."

Myron and Win looked around. It seemed to have come from Henry.

"Did you say something?"

Henry's mouth did not appear to be moving. "The Siren," he repeated, his eyes still pasted to the court. "Joan Collins played the Siren. On *Batman*."

Myron and Win exchanged a glance.

"Nobody likes a know-it-all, Henry."

Henry's mouth might have moved. Might have been a smile.

On the court Duane opened the game with an ace that nearly bore a hole through a ball boy. The IBM speedometer clocked it at 128 mph. Myron shook his head in disbelief. So did Ivan What's-his-name. Duane was lining up for the second point when Myron's cellular phone rang.

Myron quickly picked it up. He was not the only person in the stands who was talking on a cellular phone. He was, however, the only one in a front row. Myron was about to disconnect the power when he realized it might be Jessica. Jessica. Just the thought quickened his pulse a little.

"Hello."

"It's not Jessica." It was Esperanza, his associate.

"I didn't think it was."

"Right," she said. "You always sound like a whimpering puppy when you answer the phone."

Myron gripped the receiver. The match continued without interruption, but sour faces spun to seek out the origin of the offending ring. "What do you want?" he whispered. "I'm in the stadium."

"I know. Bet you look like a pretentious asshole. Talking on a cellular phone at the match."

Now that she mentioned it . . .

The sour faces were glaring daggers now. In their eyes Myron had committed an unpardonable sin. Like molesting a child. Or using the salad fork on the entree. "What do you want?"

"They're showing you on TV right now. Jesus, it's true."

"What?"

"The TV does make you look heavier."

"What do you want?"

"Nothing much. I thought you might want to know I got you a meeting with Eddie Crane."

"You're kidding." Eddie Crane, one of the hottest tennis juniors in the country. He was seeing only the big-four agencies. ICM, TruPro, Advantage International, ProServ.

"No joke. Meet him and his parents by court sixteen after Duane's match."

"I love you, you know."

"Then pay me more," she said.

Duane hit a cross-court forehand winner. Thirty–love.

"Anything else?" Myron asked.

"Nothing important. Valerie Simpson. She's called three times."

"What did she want?"

"She wouldn't say. But the Ice Queen sounded ruffled."

"Don't call her that."

"Yeah, whatever."

Myron hung up. Win looked at him. "Problem?"

Valerie Simpson. A weird, albeit sad case. The former tennis wunderkind had visited Myron's office two days ago looking for someone—anyone—to represent her. "Don't think so."

Duane was up forty–love. Triple match point. Bud Collins, tennis columnist extraordinaire, was already waiting in the gangway for the postmatch interview. Bud's pants, always a Technicolor fashion risk, were particularly hideous today.

Duane took two balls from the ball boy and approached the line. Duane was a rare commodity in tennis. A black man. Not from India or Africa or even France. Duane was from New York City. Unlike just about every other player on the tour, Duane had not spent his life preparing for this moment. He hadn't been pushed by ambitious, carpooling parents. He hadn't worked with the world's top coaches in Florida or California since he was old enough to hold a racket. Duane was on the opposite end of the spectrum: a street kid who had run away at age fifteen and somehow survived on his own. He had learned tennis from the public courts, hanging around all day and challenging anyone who could hold a racket.

He was on the verge of winning his first Grand Slam match when the gunshot sounded.

The sound had been muffled, coming from outside the stadium. Most people did not panic, assuming the sound had come from a firecracker or car backfire. But Myron and Win had heard the sound too often. They

were up and moving before the screams. Inside the stadium the crowd began to mumble. More screams ensued.
Loud, hysterical screams. The court umpire in his infinite
wisdom impatiently shouted "Quiet, please!" into his
microphone.

Myron and Win sprinted up the metallic stairway.
They leaped over the white chain, put out by the ushers
so that no one could enter or leave the court until the
players switched sides, and ran outside. A small crowd
was beginning to gather in what was generously dubbed
the "Food Court." With a lot of work and patience the
Food Court hoped to one day reach the gastronomic levels of, say, its mall brethren.

They pushed through the crowd. Some people were
indeed hysterical but others hadn't moved at all. This
was, after all, New York. The lines for refreshments
were long. No one wanted to lose their place.

The girl was lying facedown in front of a stand serving Moët champagne at $7.50 a glass. Myron recognized
her immediately, even before he bent down and turned
her over. But when he saw her face, when he saw the
icy blue eyes stare back at him in a final, unbreakable
death gaze, his heart plummeted. He looked back at Win.
Win, as usual, had no expression on his face.

"So much," Win said, "for her comeback."

Chapter 2

"Maybe you should just let it go," Win said.

He whipped his Jaguar XJR onto the FDR Drive and headed south. The radio was tuned to WMXV, 105.1 FM. They played something called "Soft Rock." Michael Bolton was on. He was doing a remake of an old Four Tops classic. Painful. Like Bea Arthur doing a remake of a Marilyn Monroe film.

Maybe Soft Rock meant Really Bad Rock.

"Mind if I put on a cassette?" Myron said.

"Please."

Win swerved into a lane change. Win's driving could most kindly be described as creative. Myron tried not to look. He pushed in a cassette from the original production of *How to Succeed in Business Without Really Trying*. Like Myron, Win had a huge collection of old Broadway musicals. Robert Morse sang about a girl named Rosemary. But Myron's mind remained fixed on a girl named Valerie Simpson.

Valerie was dead. One bullet to the chest. Someone had shot her in the Food Court of the United States Tennis Association National Tennis Center during the opening round of America's sole Grand Slam event. Yet no one had seen a thing. Or at least no one was talking.

"You're making that face," Win said.

"What face?"

"The I-want-to-help-the-world face," Win said. "She wasn't a client."

"She was going to be."

"A large distinction. Her fate does not concern you."

"She called me three times today," Myron said. "When she couldn't reach me, she showed up at the tennis center. And then she was gunned down."

"A sad tale," Win said. "But one that does not concern you."

The speedometer hovered about eighty. "Uh, Win?"

"Yes."

"The left side of the road. It's for oncoming traffic."

Win spun the wheel, cut across two lanes, and swerved onto a ramp. Minutes later the Jag veered into the Kinney lot on Fifty-second Street. They gave the keys to Mario, the parking attendant. Manhattan was hot. City hot. The sidewalk scorched your feet right through your shoes. Exhaust fumes got stuck in the humidity, hanging in the air like fruit on a tree. Breathing was a chore. Sweating was not. The secret was to keep the sweat to a minimum while walking, hoping that the air-conditioning would dry off your clothes without giving you pneumonia.

Myron and Win walked south down Park Avenue toward the high-rise of Lock-Horne Investments & Securities. Win's family owned the building. The elevator stopped on the twelfth floor. Myron stepped out. Win stayed inside. His office at Lock-Horne was two floors up.

Before the elevator closed Win said, "I knew her."

"Who?"

"Valerie Simpson. I sent her to you."

"Why didn't you say anything?"

"No reason to."

"Were you close?"

"Depends on your definition. She's old money Philadelphia. Like my family. We were members of the same clubs, the same charities, that sort of thing. Our families occasionally summered together when we were kids. But I hadn't heard from her in years."

"She just called you out of the blue?" Myron asked.

"You could say that."

"What would you say?"

"Is this an interrogation?"

"No. Do you have any thoughts on who killed her?"

Win stood perfectly still. "We'll chat later," he said. "I have some business matters I must attend to first."

The elevator door slid closed. Myron waited for a moment, as though expecting the elevator to open again. Then he crossed the corridor and opened a door that read MB SportsReps Inc.

Esperanza looked up from her desk. "Jesus, you look like hell."

"You heard about Valerie?"

She nodded. If she felt guilty about calling her the Ice Queen moments before the murder, she didn't show it. "You have blood on your jacket."

"I know."

"Ned Tunwell from Nike is in the conference room."

"I guess I'll see him," Myron said. "No use moping around."

Esperanza looked at him. No expression.

"Don't get so upset," he continued. "I'm okay."

"I'm putting on a brave front," she said.

Ms. Compassion.

When Myron opened the conference room door, Ned Tunwell charged like a happy puppy. He smiled brightly, shook hands, slapped Myron on the back. Myron half-expected him to jump in his lap and lick his face.

Ned Tunwell looked to be in his early thirties, around Myron's age. His entire persona was always upbeat, like a Hare Krishna on speed—or worse, a *Family Feud* contestant. He wore a blue blazer, white shirt, khaki pants, loud tie, and of course, Nike tennis shoes. The new Duane Richwood line. His hair was yellow-blond and he had one of those milk-stain mustaches.

Ned finally calmed down enough to hold up a videotape. "Wait till you see this!" he raved. "Myron, you are going to love it. It's fantastic."

"Let's take a look."

"I'm telling you, Myron, it's fantastic. Just fantastic. Incredible. It came out better than I ever thought. Blows away the stuff we did with Courier and Agassi. You're gonna love it. It's fantastic. Fantastic, I tell you."

The key word here: *fantastic*.

Tunwell flipped the television on and put the tape in the VCR. Myron sat down and tried to push away the image of Valerie Simpson's corpse. He needed to concentrate. This—Duane's first national television commercial—was crucial. Truth was, an athlete's image was made more by these commercials than anything else—including how well he played or how he was portrayed by the media. Athletes became defined by the commercials. Everyone knew Michael Jordan as Air Jordan. Most fans couldn't tell you Larry Johnson played for the Charlotte Hornets, but they knew all about his Grandmama character. The right campaign made you. The wrong one could destroy you.

"When is it going to air?" Myron asked.

"During the quarter finals. We're gonna blitz the networks in a very big way."

The tape finished rewinding. Duane was on the verge
of becoming one of the most highly paid tennis players
in the world. Not from winning matches, though that
would help. But from endorsements. In most sports, the
big-name athletes made more money from sponsors than
from their teams. In the case of tennis, a lot more. A
hell of a lot more. The top ten players made maybe
fifteen percent of the money from winning matches. The
bulk was from endorsements, exhibition matches, and
guarantees—money paid big names to show up at a
given tournament no matter how they fared.

Tennis needed new blood, and Duane Richwood was
the most exhilarating transfusion to come along in years.
Courier and Sampras were about as exciting as dry dog
food. The Swedish players were always a snooze-a-thon.
Agassi's act was growing wearisome. McEnroe and
Connors were history.

So enter Duane Richwood. Colorful, funny, slightly
controversial, but not yet hated. He was black and he
was from the streets, but he was perceived as "safe"
street, "safe" black, the kind of guy even racists could
get behind to show they are not really racists.

"Just check this baby out, Myron. This spot, I'm telling you, it's . . . it's just . . ." Tunwell looked up, as
though searching for the word.

"Fantastic?" Myron tried.

Ned snapped his fingers and pointed. "Just wait till
you see. I get hard watching it. Shit, I get hard just
thinking about it. Swear to Christ, it's that good."

He pressed the PLAY button.

Two days ago Valerie Simpson.had sat in this very
room, coming in on the heels of his meeting with Duane
Richwood. The contrast was striking. Both were in their

twenties, but while one career was just blossoming, the other had already dried up and blown away. Twenty-four years old and Valerie had long been labeled a "has-been" or "never-was." Her behavior had been cold and arrogant (ergo Esperanza's Ice Queen comment), or perhaps she'd just been distant and distracted. Hard to know for sure. And yes, Valerie had been young, but she had not exactly been—to quote a cliché—full of life. Eerie to say it now, but her eyes seemed to have more life in death—more animated while frozen and staring—than when she'd sat across from him in this very room.

Why, Myron wondered, would someone want to kill Valerie Simpson? Why had she tried so desperately to reach him? Why had she gone to the tennis center? To check out the competition? Or to find Myron?

"Watch this, Myron," Tunwell repeated yet again. "It's so fantastic, I came. Really, swear to God. Right in my pants."

"Sorry I missed that," Myron said.

Ned whooped with pleasure.

The commercial finally began. Duane appeared, wearing his sunglasses, dashing back and forth on a tennis court. Lots of quick cuts, especially to his sneakers. Lots of bright colors. Pounding beat, mixed in with the sound of tennis balls being blasted across the net. Very MTV-like. Could have been a rock video. Then Duane's voice came on:

"Come to my court . . ."

A few more hard ground strokes, a few more quick cuts. Then everything suddenly stopped. Duane vanished. The color faded to black and white. Silence. Scene change. A stern-looking judge glared down from his bench. Duane's voice returned:

". . . and stay away from his court."

The rock music started up again. The color returned. The screen cut back to Duane hitting the ball, smiling through his sweat, his sunglasses reflecting the light. A Nike symbol appeared with the words COME TO DUANE'S COURT below them.

Fade to black.

Ned Tunwell groaned—actually groaned—in satisfaction.

"You want a cigarette?" Myron asked.

Tunwell's smile doubled in wattage. "What did I tell you, Myron? Huh? Fantastic or what?"

Myron nodded. It was good. Very good. Hip, well-made, responsible message but not too preachy. "I like it," he said.

"I told you. Didn't I tell you? I'm hard again. Swear to God, that's how much I like it. I might just come again. Right here, right now. As we speak."

"Good to know."

Tunwell broke into a seizurelike fit of laughter. He slapped Myron's shoulder.

"Ned?"

Tunwell's laughter faded away like the end of a song. He wiped his eyes. "You kill me, Myron. I can't stop laughing. You really kill me."

"Yeah, I'm a scream. Did you hear about Valerie Simpson's murder?"

"Sure. It was on the radio. I used to work with her, you know." He was still smiling, his eyes wide and bright.

"She was with Nike?" Myron asked.

"Yep. And let me tell you, she cost us a bundle. I mean, Valerie seemed like a sure thing. She was only sixteen years old when we signed her and she'd already reached the finals of the French Open. Plus she was good-looking, all-American, the works. And she was already developed, if you know what I mean. She wasn't a cute little kid who might turn into a beast when she got a little older. Like Capriatti. Valerie was a babe.''

"So what happened?"

Ned Tunwell shrugged. "She had a breakdown. Shit, it was in all the papers."

"What caused it?"

"Hell if I know. Lot of rumors."

"Like?"

He opened his mouth, then closed it. "I forget."

"You forget?"

"Look, Myron, most people thought it was just too much, you know? All that pressure. Valerie couldn't hack it. Most of these kids can't. They get it all, you know, reach such big heights and then poof, it's gone. You can't imagine what it's like to lose everything like . . . uh . . ." Ned stammered to a stop. Then he lowered his head. "Ah, shit."

Myron remained silent.

"I can't believe I said that, Myron. To you of all people."

"Forget it."

"No. I mean, look, I can pretend I didn't just put my foot in my mouth like that, but . . ."

Myron waved him off. "A knee injury isn't a mental breakdown, Ned."

"Yeah, I know but still . . ." He stopped again. "When the Celts drafted you, were you a Nike guy?"

"No. Converse."

"They dump you? I mean, right away?"

"I have no complaints."

Esperanza opened the door without knocking. Nothing new there. She never knocked. Ned Tunwell's smile quickly returned. Hard to keep the man down. He stared at Esperanza. Appreciatively. Most men did.

"Can I see you for second, Myron?"

Ned waved. "Hi, Esperanza."

She turned and looked right through him. One of her many talents.

Myron excused himself and followed her out. Esperanza's desk was bare except for two photographs. One was of her dog, an adorable shaggy pooch named Chloe, winning a dog show. Esperanza was into dog shows—a sport not exactly dominated by inner-city Latinos, though she seemed to do pretty well. The desk's other picture showed Esperanza wrestling another woman. Professionally wrestling, that is. The lovely and lithe Esperanza had once wrestled professionally under the name Little Pocahontas, the Indian Princess. For three years Little Pocahontas had been a crowd favorite of the Fabulous Ladies of Wrestling organization, popularly known as FLOW (someone had once suggested calling it the Beautiful Ladies of Wrestling, but the acronym was a problem for the networks). Esperanza's Little Pocahontas was a scantily clad (basically a suede bikini) sexpot whom fans cheered and leered at as she bravely took on enormous evil, cheating nemeses every week. A morality play, some called it. A classic reenactment of Good vs. Evil. But to Myron the weekly action was more like those women-in-prison films. Esperanza played the beautiful, naive prisoner stuck in cell block C. Her opponent was Olga, the sadistic prison matron.

"It's Duane," Esperanza said.

Myron took the call at her desk. "Hey, Duane. What's up?"

His voice came fast. "Get over here, man. Like now."

"What's the matter?"

"The cops are in my face. They're asking me all kinds of shit."

"About what?"

"That girl who got shot today. They think I got something to do with it."

Chapter 3

"Let me speak to the police officer," Myron told Duane.

Another voice came on the line. "This is homicide detective Roland Dimonte," the voice barked with pure cop impatience. "Who the hell is this?"

"I'm Myron Bolitar. Mr. Richwood's attorney."

"Attorney, huh? I thought you were his agent."

"I'm both," Myron said.

"That a fact?"

"Yes."

"You got a law degree?"

"It's hanging on my wall. But I can bring it if you'd like."

Dimonte made a noise. Might have been a snicker. "Ex-jock. Ex-fed. And now you tell me you're a goddamn lawyer?"

"I'm what you might call a Renaissance man," Myron said.

"Yeah? Tell me, Bolitar, what law school would let in someone like you?"

"Harvard," Myron said.

"Whoa, aren't we a big shot."

"You asked."

"Well, you got half an hour to get here. Then I drag your boy to the precinct. Got me?"

"I've really enjoyed this little chat, Rolly."

"You got twenty-nine minutes. And don't call me Rolly."

"I don't want my client questioned until I'm present. Understood?"

Roland Dimonte didn't answer.

"Understood?" Myron repeated.

Pause. Then: "Must be a bad connection, Bolitar." Dimonte hung up.

Pleasant guy.

Myron handed the phone back to Esperanza. "Mind getting rid of Ned for me?"

"Done."

Myron took the elevator to the ground floor and sprinted toward the Kinney lot. Someone shouted, "Go, O.J.!" at him. In New York everyone's a comedian. Mario tossed Myron the keys without glancing up from his newspaper.

Myron's car was parked on the ground floor. Unlike Win, Myron was not what one would label a "car guy." A car was a mode of transportation, nothing more. Myron drove a Ford Taurus. A gray Ford Taurus. When he cruised down the street, chicks did not exactly swarm.

He'd driven about twenty blocks when he spotted a powder-blue Cadillac with a canary-yellow roof. Something about it bothered Myron. The color maybe. Powder blue with a yellow roof? In Manhattan? A retirement community in Boca Raton, okay, driven by some guy named Sid who always had his left blinker on. Myron could see that. But not in Manhattan. And more to the point, Myron remembered sprinting past the exact same car on his way to the garage.

Was he being followed?

A possibility, though not a great one. This was midtown Manhattan and Myron was heading straight down

Seventh Avenue. About a million other cars were doing the same. Could be nothing. Probably was. Myron made a quick mental note and proceeded.

Duane had recently rented a place on the corner of Twelfth Street and Sixth Avenue. The John Adams Building, on the fringe of Greenwich Village. Myron illegally parked in front of a Chinese restaurant on Sixth, got passed through by the doorman, and took the elevator to Apartment 7G.

A man who had to be Detective Roland Dimonte answered the door. He was dressed in jeans, paisley green shirt, black leather vest. He also had on the ugliest pair of snakeskin boots—snow-white with flecks of purple— Myron had ever seen. His hair was greasy. Several strands were matted to his forehead like to flypaper. A toothpick—an actual toothpick—was jutting out of his mouth. His eyes were set deep in a pudgy face, like someone had stuck two brown pebbles in at the last minute.

Myron smiled. "Hi, Rolly."

"Let's get one thing straight, Bolitar. I know all about you. I know all about your glory days with the feds. I know all about how you like to play cop now. But I don't give a shit about none of that. Nor do I give a shit that your client is a public figure. I gotta job to do. You hear what I'm saying?"

Myron put his hand to his ear. "Must be a bad connection."

Roland Dimonte crossed his arms and gave Myron his most withering glare. The snakeskin boots had a high platform of some sort, pushing his height over six foot, but Myron still had a good three or four inches on him. A minute passed. Roland still glared. Then another minute. Roland gnawed on the toothpick. The glare persisted without a blink.

"On the inside," Myron said, "I'm quaking in fear."

"Go fuck yourself, Bolitar."

"Chewing the toothpick is a nice touch. A little cliché perhaps, but it works for you."

"Just keep it up, smart-ass."

"Mind if I come in," Myron said, "before I wet my pants?"

Dimonte moved out of the way. Slowly. The death glare was still locked on autopilot.

Myron found Duane sitting on the couch. He was wearing his Ray•Bans, but that was not surprising. He stroked his closely cropped beard with his left hand. Wanda, Duane's girlfriend, stood by the kitchen. She was tall, five-ten or so. Her figure was what was commonly referred to as tight or hard rather than muscular, and she was a stunner. Her eyes kept darting about like birds moving from branch to branch.

It was not a huge apartment. The decor was standard New York rental. Duane and Wanda had moved in only a few weeks ago. Month-to-month lease. No reason to fix the place up. With the money Duane was about to start making they could live anywhere they wanted to soon.

"Did you say anything to them?" Myron asked.

Duane shook his head. "Not yet."

"Want to tell me what's going on?"

Duane shook his head again. "I don't know."

There was another cop in the room. A younger guy. Much younger. He looked to be about twelve. Probably just made detective. He had his pad out, his pen at the ready.

Myron turned to Roland Dimonte. Dimonte had his

hands on his hips, emanating self-importance from every pore. "What's this all about?" Myron asked.

"We just want to ask your client a few questions."

"About what?"

"The murder of Valerie Simpson."

Myron looked over at Duane. "I don't know nothing," Duane said.

Dimonte sat down, making a big production out of it. King Lear. "Then you won't mind answering a few questions?"

Duane said, "No." But he didn't sound very confident about it.

"Where were you when the shooting occurred?"

Duane glanced at Myron. Myron nodded. "I was on Stadium Court."

"What were you doing?"

"Playing tennis."

"Who was your opponent?"

Myron nodded. "You're good, Rolly."

"Shut the fuck up, Bolitar."

Duane said, "Ivan Restovich."

"Did the match continue after the shooting?"

"Yeah. It was match point anyway."

"Did you hear the gunshot?"

"Yeah."

"What did you do?"

"Do?"

"When you heard the shot?"

Duane shrugged. "Nothing. I just stood there until the umpire told us to keep playing."

"You never left the court?"

"No."

The young cop kept scribbling, never looking up.

"Then what did you do?" Dimonte asked.

"When?"

"After the match."

"I did an interview."

"Who interviewed you?"

"Bud Collins and Tim Mayotte."

The young cop looked up for a moment, confused.

"Mayotte," Myron said. "M-A-Y-O-T-T-E."

He nodded and resumed his scribbling.

"What did you talk about?" Roland asked him.

"Huh?"

"During the interview. What did they ask you about?"

Dimonte shot a challenging glare at Myron. Myron responded with his warmest nod and a pilotlike thumbs up.

"I'm not going to tell you again, Bolitar. Cut the shit."

"Just admiring your technique."

"You'll admire it from a jail cell in a minute."

"Gasp!"

Another death glare from Roland Dimonte before he turned back to Duane. "Do you know Valerie Simpson?"

"Personally?"

"Yes."

Duane shook his head. "No."

"But you've met?"

"No."

"You don't know her at all?"

"That's right."

"You've never had any contact with her?"

"Never."

Roland Dimonte crossed his legs, resting his boot on his knee. His fingers caressed—actually caressed—the

white-and-purple snakeskin. Like it was a pet dog.
"How about you, miss?"

Wanda seemed startled. "Pardon me?"

"Have you ever met Valerie Simpson?"

"No." Her voice was barely audible.

Dimonte turned back to Duane. "Had you ever heard
of Valerie Simpson before today?"

Myron rolled his eyes. But for once he kept his mouth
shut. He didn't want to push it too far. Dimonte was not
as dumb as he appeared. No one was. He was trying to
lull Duane before the big whammy. Myron's job was to
disrupt his rhythm with a few choice interruptions. But
not too many.

Myron Bolitar, darling of the tightrope.

Duane said with a shrug, "Yeah, I heard of her."

"In what capacity?"

"She used to be on the circuit. Couple years back, I
think."

"The tennis circuit?"

"No, the nightclub circuit," Myron interjected. "She
used to open for Anthony Newley in Vegas."

So much for Mr. Restraint.

The glare was back. "Bolitar, you're really starting
to piss me off."

"Are you going to get to the point already?"

"I take my time with interrogations. I don't like to
rush."

"Should do the same," Myron said, "when purchasing footwear."

Dimonte's face reddened. Still glaring at Myron, he
said, "Mr. Richwood, how long have you been on the
circuit?"

"Six months."

"And in those six months you never saw Valerie Simpson?"

"That's right."

"Fine. Now let me see if I got this right: You were playing a match when the gun went off. You finished the match. You shook hands with your opponent. I assume you shook hands with your opponent?"

Duane nodded.

"Then you did an interview."

"Right."

"Did you shower before or after the interview?"

Myron held up his hands. "Okay, that's enough."

"You got a problem, Bolitar?"

"Yeah. Your questions are beyond idiotic. I'm now advising my client to stop answering them."

"Why? Your client got something to hide?"

"Yeah, Rolly, you're too clever for us. Duane killed her. Several million people were watching him on national television during the shooting. Several thousand more were watching him in person. But that wasn't him playing. It was really his identical twin, lost since birth. You're just too smart for us, Rolly. We confess."

"I haven't ruled that out," Dimonte countered.

"Haven't ruled what out?"

"That 'we' stuff. Maybe you had something to do with it. You and that psycho-yuppie friend of yours."

He meant Win. Lot of cops knew Win. None liked him. The feeling was mutual.

"We were in the stadium at the time of the shooting," Myron said. "A dozen witnesses will back that up. And if you really knew anything about Win, you'd know he'd never use a weapon that close up."

That made Dimonte hesitate. He nodded. Agreeing, for once.

"Are you through with Mr. Richwood?" Myron asked.

Dimonte suddenly smiled. It was a happy, expectant smile, like a school kid sitting by the radio on a snow day. Myron didn't like the smile.

"If you'll just humor me for another moment," he said with syrupy phoniness. He rose and moved toward his partner, the Pad. The Pad kept scribbling.

"Your client claims he didn't know Valerie Simpson."

"So?"

The Pad finally looked up. His eyes were as vacant as a court stenographer's. Dimonte nodded at him. The Pad handed him a small leather book encased in plastic.

"This is Valerie's calendar book," Dimonte said. "The last entry was made yesterday." His smile widened. His head was held high. His chest puffed out like a rooster about to get laid.

"Okay, poker face," Myron said. "What's it say?"

He handed Myron a photocopy. Yesterday's entry was fairly simple. Sprawled across the entire page it read:

D.R. 555-8705. Call!

555-8705. Duane's phone number. D.R. Duane Richwood.

Dimonte appeared gleeful.

"I'd like to talk to my client," Myron said. "Alone."

"No."

"Excuse me?"

"You're not going to duck away now that I have you on the ropes."

"I'm his attorney—"

"I don't give a rat's ass if you're the Chief Justice

of the Supreme Court. You take him away, I take him downtown in cuffs.''

''You don't have anything,'' Myron said. ''His phone number is in her book. Means nothing.''

Dimonte nodded. ''But how would it look? To the press, for example. Or the fans. Duane Richwood, tennis's newest hero, being dragged into the station with handcuffs on. Bet that would be hard to explain to the sponsors.''

''Are you threatening us?''

Dimonte put his hand to his chest. ''Heavens no. Would I do something like that, Krinsky?''

The Pad did not look up. ''Nope.''

''There. You see?''

''I'll sue your ass for wrongful arrest,'' Myron said.

''And you might even win, Bolitar. Years from now, when the courts actually hear the case. Lot of good that's going to do you.''

Dimonte looked a lot less stupid now.

Duane quickly stood and crossed the room. He snapped off the Ray•Bans, then, thinking better of it, put them back on. ''Look, man, I don't know why my number is in her book. I don't know her. I never spoke to her on the phone.''

''Your phone is unlisted. Is that correct, Mr. Richwood?''

''Yeah.''

''And you just moved in. Your phone's only been hooked up, what, two weeks?''

Wanda said, ''Three.'' She was hugging herself now, as though she were cold.

''Three,'' Roland Dimonte repeated. ''So how did Valerie get your number, Duane? How come some woman you don't know has your brand-new, unlisted number in her date book?''

"I don't know."

Roland skipped skeptical and moved directly to absolute disbelief. For the next hour he continued to hammer Duane, but Duane stuck to his story. He never met her, he said. He didn't know her. He never spoke to her. He had no idea how she could have gotten his phone number. Myron watched in silence. The sunglasses made it harder to read Duane, but his body language was all wrong. So was Wanda's.

With an angry sigh Roland Dimonte finally stood up. "Krinsky?"

The Pad looked up.

"Let's get the hell out of here."

The Pad closed the pad, joined his partner.

"I'll be back," Dimonte barked. Then pointing at no one in particular he added, "You hear me, Bolitar?"

"You'll be back," Myron said.

"Count on it, asshole."

"Aren't you going to warn us not to leave town? I love it when you cops do that."

Dimonte made a gun with his hand. He pointed it at Myron and lowered the thumb/hammer. Then he and the Pad disappeared out the door.

For several minutes no one said anything. Myron was about to break the silence when Duane started laughing. "You sure showed him, Myron. Tore him a whole new asshole—"

"Duane, we need—"

"I'm tired, Myron." He feigned a yawn. "I really need to get some sleep."

"We need to talk about this."

"About what?"

Myron looked at him.

Duane said, "Pretty weird coincidence, huh?"

Myron turned toward Wanda. She looked away, still hugging herself. "Duane, if you're in some kind of trouble—"

"Hey, tell me about the commercial," Duane interrupted. "How did it come out?"

"Good."

Duane smiled. "How did I look?"

"Too handsome. I'll be fighting off the movie offers."

Duane laughed too hard. Much too hard. Wanda did not laugh. Neither did Myron. Then Duane feigned another yawn, stretched and stood. "I really need to get some rest," he said. "Big match coming up. Hate to let all this bullshit distract me."

He showed Myron to the door. Wanda still had not moved from her spot by the kitchen door. She finally met Myron's eye.

"Good-bye, Myron," Wanda said.

The door closed. Myron took the elevator back down and walked to his car. A ticket was nestled between the windshield and the wiper. He grabbed it and started the car.

Three blocks away Myron spotted the same powder-blue Cadillac with the canary-yellow top.

Chapter 4

Yuppieville.

The fourteenth floor of Lock-Horne Investments & Securities reminded Myron of a medieval fortress. There was the vast space in the middle, and a thick, formidable wall—the big producers' offices—safeguarding the perimeter. The open area housed hundreds of mostly men, young men, combat soldiers easily sacrificed and replaced, a seemingly endless sea of them, bobbing and blending into the corporate-gray carpet, the identical desks, the identical rolling chairs, the computer terminals, the telephones, the fax machines. Like soldiers they wore uniforms—white button-down shirts, suspenders, bright ties strangling carotid arteries, suit jackets draped across the backs of the identical rolling chairs. There were loud noises, screams, rings, even something that sounded like death cries. Everyone was in motion. Everyone was scattering, panicked, under constant attack.

Yes, for here was one of the final strongholds of true yuppieism, a place where man was free to practice the religion of eighties greed, greed at all costs, without pretense of doing otherwise. No hypocrisy here. Investment houses were not about helping the world. They were not about providing a service to mankind or doing what was best for all. This haven had a simple, clear-cut, basic goal. Making money. Period.

Win had a spacious corner office overlooking Park and Fifty-second Street. A prime-time view for the company's number one producer. Myron knocked on the door.

"Enter," Win called out.

He was sitting in a full lotus on the floor, his expression serene, his thumbs and forefingers forming circles in each hand. Meditation. Win did it every day without fail. Usually more than once.

But as with most things with Win, his moments of inner solitude were a tad unconventional. For one, he liked to keep his eyes open when meditating, while most practitioners kept them closed. For another, he didn't imagine idyllic scenes of waterfalls or does in the forest; rather, Win opted for watching home videotapes—videos of himself and an interesting potpourri of lady friends in assorted throes of passion.

Myron made a face. "You mind turning that off?"

"Lisa Goldstein," Win said, motioning toward a mound of writhing flesh on the screen.

"Charmed, I'm sure."

"I don't think you ever met her."

"Hard to tell," Myron said. "I mean, I'm not even sure where her face is."

"Lovely lass. Jewish, you know."

"Lisa Goldstein? You're kidding."

Win smiled. He uncrossed his legs and stood in one fluid motion. He switched off the television, hit the EJECT button, put the tape back in a box marked *L.G.* He filed the box under the *G*'s in an oak cabinet. There were a lot of tapes already there.

"You realize," Myron said, "that you're quite deranged."

Win locked the cabinet with a key. Dr. Discretion. "Every man needs a hobby."

"You're a scratch golfer. You're a champion martial artist. Those are hobbies. This is deranged. Hobbies; deranged. See the difference?"

"Moralizing," Win said. "How nice."

Myron did not respond. They had been down this road many times since they were freshmen at Duke. It never led anywhere.

Win's office was pure, elitist WASP. Paintings of a fox hunt adorned paneled walls. Burgundy leather chairs ideally complemented the deep forest-green carpeting. An antique wooden globe stood next to an oak desk that could double as a squash court. The effect—not a subtle one, at that—could be summed up in two words: Serious. Cash.

Myron sat in one of the leather chairs. "You got a minute?"

"Of course." Win opened a cabinet in the bar behind his desk, revealing a small refrigerator. He took out a cold Yoo-Hoo and tossed it to Myron. Myron shook the can as per the instructions (*Shake! It's Great!*) while Win mixed himself a very dry martini.

Myron started off by telling Win about the police visit to Duane Richwood. Win remained impassive, allowing himself a small smile when he heard how Dimonte had called him a psycho-yuppie. Then Myron told him about the powder-blue Cadillac. Win sat back and steepled. He listened without interrupting. When Myron finished, Win rose from his seat and picked up a putter.

"So our friend Mr. Richwood is holding something back."

"We can't be sure."

Win raised a skeptical eyebrow. "Do you have any thoughts as to how Duane Richwood and Valerie Simpson are connected?"

"Nope. I was hoping you might."

"Moi?"

"You knew her," Myron said.

"She was an acquaintance."

"But you have a thought."

"About a connection between Duane and Valerie? No."

"Then what?"

Win strolled to a corner. A dozen golf balls were all in a line. He began to putt. "Are you really intent on pursuing this? Valerie's murder, I mean?"

"Yep."

"It might be none of your business."

"Might be," Myron agreed.

"Or you might unearth something unpleasant. Something you would rather not find."

"A distinct possibility."

Win nodded, checked the carpet's lie. "Wouldn't be the first time."

"No. Not the first time. Are you in?"

"There is nothing in this for us," Win said.

"Maybe not," Myron agreed.

"No financial gain."

"None at all."

"In fact there is never any profit in your holy crusades."

Myron waited.

Win lined up another put. "Stop making that face," he said. "I'm in."

"Good. Now tell me what you know about this."

"Nothing really. It's just a thought."

"I'm listening."

"You know, of course, about Valerie's breakdown," Win said.

"Yes."

"It was six years ago. She was only eighteen. The official word was that she collapsed under the pressure."

"The official word?"

"It may be the truth. The pressure on her was indeed awesome. Her rise had been nothing short of meteoric—but nowhere near as meteoric as the tennis world's expectations of her. Her subsequent fall—at least, up until the time of the breakdown—was slow and painful. Not at all like yours. Your fall, if you don't mind me using that word, was far swifter. Guillotinelike. One minute you were the Celtics' number one draft pick. The next minute you were finished. The end. But unlike Valerie, you had a freak injury and were thereby blameless. You were pitied. You cut a sympathetic figure. Valerie's demise, on the other hand, seemed to be of her own doing. She was a failure, ridiculed, but still no more than a child. To the world at large, the fickle finger of fate had ended the career of Myron Bolitar. But in the case of Valerie Simpson, she alone was culpable. In the eyes of the public she did not possess enough mental fortitude. Her fall, thus, was slow, torturous, brutal."

"So what does this have to do with the murder?"

"Perhaps nothing. But I always found the circumstances surrounding Valerie's mental collapse a bit disturbing."

"Why?"

"Her game had slipped, that much was true. Her coach—that famous gentleman who plays with all the celebrities . . ."

"Pavel Menansi."

"Whatever. He still believed Valerie could come back and win again. He said it all the time."

"Thereby putting more pressure on her."

Win hesitated. "Perhaps," he said slowly. "But there is another factor. Do you remember the murder of Alexander Cross?"

"The senator's son?"

"The senator from Pennsylvania," Win added.

"He was killed by robbers at his country club. Five, six years ago."

"Six. And it was a tennis club."

"You knew him?"

"Of course," Win said. "The Hornes have known every important Pennsylvania politician since William Penn. I grew up with Alexander Cross. We went to Exeter together."

"So what does he have to do with Valerie Simpson?"

"Alexander and Valerie were, shall we say, an item."

"A serious item?"

"Quite. They were about to announce their engagement when Alexander was killed. That night, as a matter of fact."

Myron did some quick mathematics in his head. Six years ago. Valerie would have been eighteen. "Let me guess. Valerie's breakdown took place right after his murder."

"Precisely."

"But I don't get something. The Cross murder was on the news every day for weeks. How come I never heard Valerie's name mentioned?"

"That," Win said, nailing another putt, "is why I find the circumstances disturbing."

Silence.

"We need to talk to Valerie's family," Myron said. "Maybe the senator's as well."

"Yes."

"You live in that world. You're one of them. They'd be more apt to talk to you."

Win shook his head. "They'll never talk to me. Being 'one of them,' as you put it, is a severe handicap. Their guard will be up with someone like me. But with you they won't be so concerned about facades. They'll perceive you as someone who doesn't matter, as someone inferior, as someone beneath them. A nobody."

"Gee, that's flattering."

Win smiled. "The way of the world, my friend. Many things change, but these people still consider themselves the true, original Americans. You and your kind are just hired help, shipped in from Russia or Eastern Europe or from whatever gulag or ghetto your people originated."

"I hope they don't hurt my feelings," Myron said.

"I'll arrange a meeting for you with Valerie's mother for tomorrow morning."

"You think she'll see me?"

"If I request it, yes."

"Groovy."

"Indeed." Win put down his putter. "In the meantime what do you suggest we do?"

Myron checked his watch. "One of Pavel Menansi's protégées is playing on Stadium Court in about an hour. I figured I'd pay him a visit."

"And *pour moi*?"

"Valerie spent the past week at the Plaza Hotel,"

Myron said. "I'd like you to look around, see if anybody remembers anything. Check her phone calls."

"See if she did indeed call Duane Richwood?"

"Yes."

"And if she did?"

"Then we have to look into that too," Myron said.

Chapter 5

The U.S.T.A. National Tennis Center is neatly snuggled into the bosom of Queens' top attractions: Shea Stadium (home of the New York Mets), Flushing Meadows Park (home of the 1964–65 World's Fair) and La Guardia Airport (home of, uh, delays).

Players used to complain about the La Guardia planes flying overhead, for the very simple reason that it made Stadium Court sound like a launch pad during an Apollo liftoff. Then-mayor David Dinkins, never one to let a terrible injustice go unheeded, immediately sprang into action. Using all his political might, the former mayor of New York City—who in a fascinating and almost eerie coincidence was also an enormous tennis fan—had La Guardia's offending runway halt operations for the duration of the Open. Tennis millionaires were grateful. In a show of mutual respect and admiration Mayor David Dinkins returned their gratitude by showing up at the matches every day for the two weeks of play, except— in yet another eerie coincidence—during election years.

Only two courts were used for the night sessions: Stadium Court and the adjacent Grandstand Court. The day sessions, Myron thought, were much more fun. Fifteen or sixteen matches might be going on at the same time. You could cruise around, catch a great five-set match on some obscure court, discover an up-and-coming player, see singles, doubles, and mixed doubles matches all in the glorious sunshine. But at night you basically sat in one seat and watched a match under lights. During the Open's first couple of days this match usually featured a top-seed mercilessly decapitating a qualifier.

Myron parked in the Shea Stadium lot and crossed the walking bridge over the No. 7 train. Someone had set up a booth with a radar gun where spectators could measure the speed of their own serve. Business was brisk. Ticket scalpers were also busy. So were the guys selling knockoff U.S. Open T-shirts. The knockoff T-shirts sold for five dollars, as opposed to the ones inside the gates that went for twenty-five dollars. Not a bad deal on the surface. Of course, after one wash the knockoff T-shirt could only be worn by a Barbie doll. But still.

Pavel Menansi was in one of the players' boxes, the same one Myron and Win had sat in earlier in the day. It was 6:45 P.M. The final day match was over. The first night match, featuring Pavel's latest protégée, fourteen-year old Janet Koffman, would not begin until 7:15 P.M. People were milling around during the day-to-night cusp. Myron spotted the usher from the day session.

"How ya doing, Mr. Bolitar?" the usher said.

"Fine, Bill. Just wanted to say a quick hello to a friend."

"Sure, no prob, go right ahead."

Myron headed down the steps. Without warning a man wearing a blue blazer and aviator sunglasses stepped in front of him. He was a big guy—six-four, two-twenty—just about Myron's size. His neatly combed hair sat above a pleasant though unyielding face. He expanded his chest into a paddleball wall, blocking Myron's path.

His voice said, "Can I help you, sir?" But his tone said, *Take a hike, bub.*

Myron looked at him. "Anyone ever tell you you look like Jack Lord?"

No reaction.

"You know," Myron said. "Jack Lord? *Hawaii Five-O*?"

"I'll have to ask you to leave, sir."

"It's not an insult. Many people find Jack Lord very attractive."

"Sir, this is the last time I'm going to ask nicely."

Myron studied his face. "You even have that Jack Lord surly grin. Remember it?" Myron imitated the grin for him, in case he'd never seen the show.

The face twitched. "Okay, buddy, you're out of here."

"I just want to speak to Mr. Menansi for a moment."

"I'm afraid that won't be possible at this time."

"Oh, okay." He spoke a little louder. "Just tell Mr. Menansi that Duane Richwood's agent wanted to discuss something very important with him. But if he's not interested I'll go elsewhere."

Pavel Menansi's head jerked around as though pulled by a string. His smile flicked on like a cigarette lighter. He rose, his eyes half open, his whole persona oozing that foreign charm that some women find irresistible and others find nauseating beyond words. Pavel was Romanian, one of tennis's original Bad Boys, the former doubles partner of Ilie "Nasty" Nastase. He was nearing fifty, his face tanned to the point of leathery. When he smiled, the leather cracked almost audibly.

"Pardon me," he said. His voice was smooth—part Romanian, part American, part Ricardo Montalban discussing Corinthian leather. "You are Myron Bolitar, are you not?"

"I am."

He dismissed Jack Lord with a nod. Big Jack was not happy about it, but he moved out of the way. His body swung to the side like a metal gate, allowing only Myron to enter. Pavel Menansi held out a hand. For a moment Myron thought he wanted him to kiss it, but it ended in a brief handshake.

"Please," Pavel said. "Sit here. Next to me."

Whoever was in the seat quickly made himself scarce. Myron sat. Pavel did likewise. "I apologize for my guard's zeal, but you must understand. People, they want autographs. Parents, they want to discuss their child's play. But here"—he spread his hands—"this is not the time or place."

"I understand," Myron said.

"I've heard quite a bit about you, Mr. Bolitar."

"Please call me Myron."

Pavel had the smile of a lifelong smoker, *sans* proper dental hygiene. "Only if you call me Pavel."

"Deal."

"Fine then. You discovered Duane Richwood, did you not?"

"Somebody pointed him out to me."

"But you saw the potential first," Pavel insisted. "He never played in the juniors, never went to college. That's why all the big agencies missed him, am I right?"

"I guess so."

"So now you have a top tennis contender. You are now competing with the big boys, yes?"

Myron knew that Pavel Menansi worked with TruPro, one of the country's largest sports agencies. Working with TruPro didn't automatically make you a sleazeball, but it brought you awfully close. Pavel was worth millions to them—not because of what he made as much as the young talent he brought in. Pavel got a Svengali-like hold on prodigies at the age of eight or ten, giving TruPro a hell of an advantage in getting them signed. TruPro had never been a reputable agency—almost a contradiction in terms anyway—but over the last year it had become mob-controlled, run by the appropriately named Ache brothers of New York City. The Ache brothers were into all the top mob favorites: drugs, numbers, prostitution, extortion, gambling. Sweethearts, those Aches.

"Your Duane Richwood," Pavel continued. "He played a fine match today. Fine match indeed. His potential is quite limitless. You agree?"

"He works very hard," Myron said.

"I'm sure he does. Tell me, Myron, who is Duane's present coach?" He said *present*, but it came out more like *former*.

"Henry Hobson."

"Ah." Pavel nodded with vigor, as though this response explained something very complex. He, of course, already knew who coached Duane. Pavel probably knew who coached every player on the circuit. "Henry Hobson is a fine man. A competent coach." He said *competent*, but it came out more like *crappy*.

"But I believe I can help him, Myron."

"I'm not here to talk about Duane," Myron said.

A shadow crossed his face. "Oh?"

"I want to discuss another client. Or should I say a once-potential client."

"And who would that be?"

"Valerie Simpson."

Myron looked for a reaction. He got one. Pavel lowered his head into his hands. "Oh, my God."

The box rumbled with overwrought concern. Comforting hands found their way to Pavel's shoulders, uttering his name in low voices. But Pavel pushed them
away. Very brave.

"Valerie came to me a few days ago," Myron continued. "She wanted to make a comeback."

Pavel took a deep breath. He made a show of putting
himself together a piece at a time. When he was able to
continue, he said, "The poor child. I can't believe it. I
just can't. . . . " He stopped. Overwhelmed again. Then:
"I was her coach, you know. During her glory years."

Myron nodded.

"To be shot down like that. Like a dog." He shook
his head dramatically.

"When was the last time you saw Valerie?"

"Several years ago," he said.

"Have you seen her since the breakdown?"

"No. Not since she went into the hospital."

"Spoken to her? On the phone maybe?"

Pavel shook his head again. Then he lowered it. "I
blame myself for what happened to her. I should have
looked out for her better."

"What do you mean?"

"When you coach one so young, you have responsibilities that go beyond her life on the court. She was
a child—a child growing up in the spotlight. The media,
they are savages, no? They don't understand what they
do to sell papers. I tried to cushion some of their blows.
I tried to protect her, to not let it eat her up inside. In
the end, I failed."

He sounded genuine, but Myron knew that meant
nothing. People were amazing liars. The more sincere

they sounded—the more they held your gaze and looked truthful—the more sociopathic they were. "Do you have any idea who would have wanted her dead?"

He looked puzzled by the question. "Why are you asking these questions, Myron?"

"I'm looking into something."

"Into what? If I may ask."

"It's kind of personal."

He studied Myron for a few seconds. The stench of tobacco was heavy on his breath. Myron was forced to inhale through his mouth. "I will tell you the same thing I told the police," Pavel said. "In my opinion Valerie's breakdown was not just from the usual tennis pressures."

Myron nodded, encouraging him to continue.

Pavel turned his palms toward the sky, as though seeking divine intervention. "Perhaps I am wrong. Perhaps I want to believe that to—how do you say?—soothe my own guilt. I don't know anymore. But I've had a lot of young people in my camp and never have I experienced anything like what happened to Valerie. No, Myron, her problems were caused by more than the pressures of big-time tennis."

"What then?"

"I'm not a medical doctor, you understand. I cannot say for sure. But you must remember that Valerie was being menaced."

Myron waited for him to elaborate. When he didn't, Myron said, "Menaced?" Probing interrogatories—one of Myron's strong suits.

"Stalked," he said with a finger snap. "That's the word they use nowadays. Valerie was being stalked."

"By whom?"

"A very sick man, Myron. A terrible man. After all

these years I still remember his name. Roger Quincy. Crazy animal. He wrote her love letters. He called all the time. He hung around her house, by her hotel, at every match she played.''

''When was this?''

''When she was on the tour, of course. It began—I don't know—six months before she was hospitalized.''

''Did you try to stop him?''

''Of course. We went to the police. They could do nothing. We tried to get a court order, but this Quincy never actually threatened her. He would say 'I love you, I want to be with you,' things like that. We did our best. We changed hotels, signed in under different aliases. But you have to remember, Valerie was just a child. She became paranoid. The pressure on her was already tremendous. But now she had to look over her shoulder all the time. This Roger Quincy, he was a crazy beast. That's what he was. He was the one who should have been gunned down.''

Myron nodded, waiting a beat. ''How did Alexander Cross react to Roger Quincy?''

The question stunned Pavel like a surprise left hook. Lennox Lewis vs. Frank Bruno. He hesitated, trying to regain his footing. The players came out of the tunnel. Applause began to build. The distraction worked like a standing eight count, giving Pavel time to recover.

''Why would you ask that?'' he asked.

''Weren't Alexander Cross and Valerie Simpson involved?''

''I guess you could say that.''

''Seriously?''

''She was away a lot. Traveling. But they seemed fond of each other.''

"And I assume their relationship was going on at the same time Quincy was stalking Valerie?"

"I believe the time periods overlapped, yes."

"So it's a natural question," Myron said. "How did Valerie's boyfriend react?"

"Natural, perhaps," he said. "But you must admit it is also a bizarre question. Alexander Cross has been dead for several years now. How is his reaction relevant to what happened to Valerie today?"

"For one, they were both murdered."

"You're not suggesting a connection?"

"I'm not suggesting anything," Myron said. "But I don't understand why you don't want to answer my question."

"It's not a matter of wanting or not wanting," Pavel replied. "It's a matter of doing what is right. You are delving into places where you do not belong. Personal places. Places that cannot possible have any relevance in today's world. I feel like I am betraying confidences. You see?"

"No."

Pavel looked back at Jack Lord. Jack's mouth twitched. He stood again. The chest self-inflated.

"The match is about to begin," Pavel said. "I hate to be rude, but I really must ask you to leave now."

"Hit a raw nerve, did I?"

"Yes. I cared for Valerie very deeply."

"That wasn't what I meant."

"Please leave. I must concentrate on this match."

Myron did not move. Jack Lord put a big mitt on Myron's shoulder. "You heard the man," he said. "Move out."

"Let go of my shoulder," Myron said.

Jack shook his head. "No more games, pal. It's time for you to get lost."

"If you don't move your hand," Myron explained calmly, "I'll hurt you. Maybe severely."

From behind his sunglasses Big Jack finally smiled. His grip on Myron's shoulder tightened. Myron quickly reached up with his right hand and grabbed the man's thumb. He locked the joint and pulled it back the wrong way. Jack dropped to one knee.

Myron lowered his mouth toward Jack's ear. "I don't want to make a scene, so I'm going to let you go," he whispered. "If you do anything but smile I will hurt you. Definitely severely. Nod if you understand."

He nodded, his face pale.

Myron let the thumb go. "Later, Pavel."

Pavel said nothing.

Myron walked past Jack. As ordered, Jack was smiling.

"Book 'em, Dann-o," Myron said.

Chapter 6

A stalker.

Could it be that simple? Could some deranged fan have put a bullet into Valerie Simpson because a voice told him to? Doesn't explain Duane Richwood's connection. But maybe there was no connection. Or maybe the connection had nothing to do with the murder and, more important, was none of Myron's business.

Myron turned onto Hobart Gap Road. He was only a mile from his home in Livingston, New Jersey. The powder-blue Caddy with the canary-yellow roof finally turned off, jumping on the JFK Parkway. Whoever it was must have figured Myron was going home for the night, and hence there was no reason to keep the tail. But if the Caddy was around tomorrow, Myron would have to take care of it—unmask the true identity of Mr. Miami Gin Tournament.

Right now he needed to concentrate on this whole stalker possibility.

If Valerie had been killed by Roger Quincy, then why had ol' Pavel gotten so antsy when Myron mentioned Alexander Cross? Or was it just like Pavel said—he didn't want to betray confidences? When you thought about it, wasn't it a hell of a lot more probable that Pavel just felt it was in his best interest to keep quiet? Senator Cross was an awfully powerful man. Spreading stories about his murdered son wasn't necessarily the wisest course of action. So there could be nothing there. Then again it could be something big. Or something small.

Thoughts like these are what made Myron a brilliant detective.

He parked in the driveway. His mom's car was in the garage. His dad's was nowhere in sight. He opened the door with his key.

"Myron?"

Myron. God, what a name. You'd think he'd be used to it by now, but occasionally the horror hit him anew. He had been dubbed Myron. A last-second decision, his parents claimed. Something Mom came up with at the hospital. But to name a kid Myron Bolitar? Was that fair? Was that ethical?

As a youngster Myron tried giving himself nick-names: Mike, Mickey, even Sweet J, for his famous jumpshot. Okay, maybe it was a good thing that Sweet J didn't stick. But still.

Warning to parents naming children: Let's be careful out there.

His mother called out, "Myron? Is that you?"

"Yeah, Mom."

"I'm in the den." She was wearing an exercise outfit, watching some kind of workout tape. She stood on one leg, crane stance à la *The Karate Kid*. On the television a familiar voice crooned, "Now flow-step to the left..."

David Carradine's T'ai Chi Workout. Wonderful.

"Hi, Mom."

"You're late," she said.

"I didn't realize I had a curfew."

"You said you'd be home by seven. It's past nine."

"Your point being?"

"I was worried. I saw on the news about that girl

getting shot at the Open. How did I know you weren't killed?''

Myron held back a sigh. "Did the news say I was killed? Did the news say anything about unidentified bodies? Or did they say only one girl named Valerie Simpson was shot?"

"They could have been lying."

"Excuse me?"

"Happens all the time. The police lie to the reporters until they notify the next of kin."

"Weren't you home all day?"

"What, the police have my phone number?"

"But they could . . ." He stopped. What was the point? "Next time a murder takes place within a three-mile radius of my being I'll be sure to call home."

"Good." She snapped off the tape. Then she placed a pillow in a corner and stood on her head.

"Mom?"

"What?"

"What are you doing?"

"What's it look like? I'm standing on my head. It's good exercise. Makes the blood flow. Makes me look my best. You know who used to stand on his head every day?"

Myron shook his head.

"David Ben-Gurion."

"And everyone knows what a looker he was," Myron said.

"Smart-mouth."

Mom was a major paradox. On the one hand she'd been a practicing attorney for the past twenty years. She was the first generation born in the United States, her parents coming over from Minsk or somewhere like that, living lives that as near as Myron could tell paralleled

Fiddler on the Roof. She became a sixties radical, an original bra burner, and experimented with various mind-altering drugs (hence naming a child Myron). She did not cook. Ever. She had no idea where the vacuum cleaner was stored. She did not know what an iron looked like, never mind whether or not she owned one. In the courtroom her crosses were legendary. She break-fasted on star witnesses. She was bright, frighteningly shrewd, and very modern.

On the other hand, all of this went out the window when it came to her son. She completely decompensated. She became her mother. And her mother before her. Only worse. Murphy Brown became Grandma Tzietl.

"Your father is picking up some Chinese food. I ordered enough for you."

"I'm not hungry, thanks."

"Spareribs, Myron. Sesame chicken." Meaningful pause. "Shrimp with lobster sauce."

"I'm really not hungry."

"Shrimp with lobster sauce," she repeated.

"Mom . . ."

"From Fong's Dragon House."

"No thanks."

"What? You love Fong's shrimp in lobster sauce. You're crazy about it."

"Maybe a little then." Easier.

She was still standing on her head. She began to whistle. Very casuallike. "So," she said in that strain-to-sound-aloof voice, "how's Jessica?"

"Butt out, Mom."

"Who's butting? I just asked a simple question."

"And I gave you a simple answer. Butt out."

"Fine. But don't go crying to me if something goes wrong."

Like that happens.

"Why has she been away so long anyway? What's she doing over there?"

"Thanks for butting out."

"I'm concerned," Mom said. "I just hope she's not up to something."

"Butt out."

"Is that all you can say? Butt out? What are you, a parrot? Where is she anyway?"

Myron opened his mouth, wrestled it closed, and stormed into the basement. His dwelling. He was almost thirty-two years old and still lived at home. He hadn't been here much the past few months. Most nights he'd spent at Jessica's place in the city. They had even talked about moving in together but decided to take it slow. Very slow. Easier said than done. The heart don't know from slow. At least Myron's didn't. As usual Mom had drilled into exposed nerve endings. Jessica was in Europe right now, but Myron had no idea where. He hadn't heard from her in two weeks. He missed her. And he was wondering too.

The doorbell rang.

"Your father," Mom called down. "Probably forgot his key again. I swear that man is getting senile."

A few seconds later he heard the basement door open. His mother's feet appeared. Then the rest of her. She beckoned him forward.

"What?"

"There's a young lady here to see you," she said. Then in a whisper, "She's black."

"Gasp!" Myron put his hand to his heart. "Hope the neighbors don't call the police."

"That's not what I meant, smart-mouth, and you know it. We have black families in the neighborhood now. The Wilsons. Lovely people. They live on Coventry Drive. In the old Dechtman home.''

"I know, Mom."

"I was just describing her for you. Like I might say she has blond hair. Or a nice smile. Or a harelip."

"Uh-huh."

"Or limp. Or she's tall. Or short. Or fat. Or—''

"I think I get the drift, Mom. Did you ask her name?"

She shook her head. "I didn't want to pry."

Right.

Myron headed up the stairs. It was Wanda, Duane's girlfriend. For some reason Myron was not surprised. She smiled nervously, waved quickly.

"I'm sorry to disturb you at home," she said.

"No problem. Please come in."

They headed down the basement. Myron had subdivided it into two rooms. One, a small sitting room he basically never used. Hence it was presentable and clean. The inside room, his living quarters, resembled a frat house after a major kegger.

Wanda's eyes darted around again, like they had when Dimonte had been at the apartment. "You live down here?"

"Only since I was sixteen."

"I think that's sweet. Living with your parents."

From upstairs: "If only you knew."

"Close the door, Mom."

Slam.

"Please," Myron said. "Sit down."

Wanda looked unsure but finally settled into a chair. She was wringing her hands nonstop. "I feel a little foolish," she said.

Myron gave her an understanding, encouraging smile—the Phil Donahue smile. *Caller, are you there?*

"Duane likes you," she said. "A lot."

"The feeling is mutual."

"The other agents, they call Duane all the time. All the big ones. They keep saying how you're too small-time to represent Duane. They keep saying they can help him make a lot more money."

"They might be right," Myron said.

She shook her head. "Duane doesn't think so. I don't think so either."

"That's nice of you to say."

"You know why Duane won't meet with those other agents?"

"Because he doesn't want to see me weep?"

She smiled at that one. The Master of Levity strikes again. Señor Self-Deprecation. "No," she said. "Duane trusts you."

"I'm glad."

"You're not just in it for the money."

"That nice of you to say, Wanda, but Duane is making me a lot of money. There's no denying that."

"I know," she said. "I don't want to sound naive here, but you put him first. Before the money. You look out for Duane Richwood the human being. You care about him."

Myron said nothing.

"Duane doesn't have many people," she continued. "He doesn't have any family. He lived on the streets since he was fifteen, scraping by. He wasn't an angel that whole time. He did some things he'd rather forget. But he never hurt anybody, never did anything serious. His whole life he never had anyone he could rely on. He had to take care of himself."

Silence.

"Does Duane know you're here?" Myron asked.

"No."

"Where is he?"

"I don't know. He just took off. He does that sometimes."

More silence.

"So anyway, like I said, Duane doesn't have anybody else. He trusts you. He trusts Win, too, but only because he's your best friend."

"Wanda, what you're saying is very nice, but I'm hardly driven by altruism. I'm well paid for what I do."

"But you care."

"Henry Hobson cares."

"Maybe. But his wagon is hitched to Duane's star. Duane is his ticket back to the bigs."

"Many would say the same for me," Myron countered. "Except that part about 'back,' since I've never been to the bigs. Duane's my only big tennis player. In fact Duane is the only player I've got in the U.S. Open."

She considered this for a moment, nodding. "Maybe that's all true," she said. "But when push came to shove—when trouble hit today—Duane came to you. And when push came to shove for me tonight, I came to you too. That's the bottom line."

The basement door opened.

"Would you kids like something to drink?"

"Got any Kool-Aid, Mom?"

Wanda laughed.

"Listen, smart-mouth, maybe your company is hungry."

"No, thank you, Mrs. Bolitar," Wanda shouted up.

"You sure, hon? Coffee maybe? A Coke?"

"Nothing, really, thank you."

"How about some Danish? I just bought some fresh at the Swiss House. Myron's favorite."

"Mom . . ."

"Okay, okay, I can take a hint."

Right. The Mistress of the Subtle Signal. The basement door closed.

"She's sweet," Wanda said.

"Yeah, adorable." Myron leaned forward. "Why don't you tell me why you're here?"

She started wringing her hands again. "I'm worried about Duane."

"If it's about Dimonte's visit, don't let him get to you. Being a horse's ass is part of his job."

"It's not that," she said. "Duane wouldn't hurt anybody. I know that. But something isn't right with him. He's tense all the time. He paces around the apartment. He flies off the handle at the littlest things."

"He's under a lot of pressure right now. It could just be nerves."

She shook her head. "Duane thrives on pressure. He loves competing, you know that. But the last day or two it's different. Something is really bothering him."

"Any idea what?"

"No."

Myron leaned forward. "Let me ask you the obvious question: Did Duane get a call from Valerie Simpson?"

She thought for a moment. "I don't know."

"Does he know her?"

"I don't know that either. But I know Duane. We've been together for three years, since we were both eighteen. He was still on the streets when we met. My father freaked out when he heard. He's a chiropractor. He makes a good living, worked hard to keep the bad element away from us. And here I was, dating a street kid, a runaway.''

She chuckled at the memory. Myron sat and waited.

"No one thought it would last,'' she continued. "I left college and got a job so he could pursue tennis. Now he's putting me through NYU. We love each other. We loved each other before all this tennis stuff started and we'll love each other long after he puts down the racket for good. But for the first time he's shutting me out.''

"And you think Valerie Simpson is somehow connected?''

She hesitated. "I guess I do.''

"How?''

"I have no idea.''

"What do you want me to do?''

She stood, paced in the small room. "I heard those policemen talking. They said you used to be a big deal with the government. You and Win. Something secretive with the FBI—after you recovered from the knee injury. Is that true?''

"Yes.''

"I thought maybe you could, I don't know, look into it?''

"You want me to investigate Duane?''

"He's hiding something, Myron. It has to come out.''

"You might not like what I find,'' he said, echoing Win's earlier words.

"I'm more afraid of going on like this.'' Wanda looked up at him. "Will you help him?''

He nodded. "I'll do what I can.''

Chapter 7

The phone rang.

Myron reached out blindly, swimming back to consciousness. He grabbed the receiver and croaked, "Hello?"

"Is this the Rent-a-Stud hotline?"

Her voice hit him like a jolt. "Jess?"

"Oh shit," Jessica said. "You were sleeping, right?"

"Sleeping?" Myron squinted at his digital. "At four-thirteen in the morning? Captain Midnight? Surely you jest."

"Sorry. I forgot about the time difference."

He sat up. "Where are you?"

"Greece," she said. "I miss you."

"You're just horny."

"Well, there's that."

"Captain Midnight is willing to help," he said.

"My fearless hero. I suppose you're not even a little horny."

"Captain Midnight lives chastely."

"Part of his image?"

"Exactly," he said.

"It's no fun," she said. "Being away from you."

His heart soared. "So come home."

"I am."

"When?"

"Soon." Jessica Culver, Miss Specific USA. "Tell me what's been going on," she said.

"You hear about the shooting at the Open?"

"Sure. The hotel has CNN."

Myron told her about Valerie Simpson. When he finished, her first comment was, "You didn't have to bend that clod's thumb back."

"But it was all very macho," Myron said.

"A real turn-on, I'm sure."

"Guess you had to be there," he said.

"Guess so. So are you going to find the killer?"

"I'm going to try."

"For Valerie's sake? Or for Wanda and Duane?"

"For all of them, I guess. But mostly Valerie. You should have seen her, Jess. She tried so hard to be sullen and unpleasant. A girl that young shouldn't have to try that hard."

"Do you have a plan?"

"Of course. First, I'm going to visit Valerie's mother tomorrow morning. In Philadelphia."

"And then?"

"Well, the plan isn't really that well developed. But I'm working on it."

"Please be careful."

"Captain Midnight is always careful."

"It's not just Captain Midnight I'm worried about it. It's his alter ego."

"And who might that be?"

"My Love Muffin."

Myron grinned into the receiver. "Hey, Jess, did you know Joan Collins was on *Batman*?"

"Of course," Jessica said. "She played the Siren."

"Oh yeah? Well, who did Liberace play?"

Chapter 8

Myron spent the rest of the night dreaming about Jessica, though as usual he could only remember meaningless scraps in the morning. Jessica was in his life again, but it was still new to him. Too new. He needed to hold back, to tread gently. He was afraid of being crushed under her heel again, of having his heart slammed in the door of love.

Door of love. Christ. He sounded like a bad country song.

He motored south on the famed New Jersey Turnpike. The powder-blue Cadillac with the canary-yellow top was four cars behind him. More than anything else, this stretch of roadway had made New Jersey the butt of so many jokes. He passed Newark Airport. Kind of ugly, but what airport isn't? Then he drove by the turnpike's pièce de résistance, its cause célèbre if you will— an enormous industrial power plant between exits 12 and 13 that closely resembled the futuristic nightmare world in the beginning of the *Terminator* movies. Thick smoke sprung from every orifice. Even in the bright sunshine the place looked dark, metallic, menacing, foreboding.

On the radio a rock group called the Motels were repeatedly singing the ingenious line *Take the L out of lover, and it's over.* Deep. Literal, but still deep. The Motels. Whatever happened to them?

Myron picked up the cellular phone and dialed. A familiar voice answered.

"Sheriff Courter speaking."

"Hey, Jake, it's Myron."

"I'm sorry. You must have the wrong number. Bye."

"Good one," Myron said. "Guess those night-school comedy courses are finally starting to pay off."

"What do you want, Myron?"

"Can't a friend just call and say hello?"

"So this is just a social call?" Jake said.

"Yes."

"I feel so blessed."

"Wait. It gets better. I'm going to be in your neck of the woods in a couple of hours."

"Be still my heart."

"I thought maybe we could meet for lunch. I'm buying."

"Uh-huh. You bringing Win?"

"No."

"Then okay. Guy gives me the creeps."

"You don't even know him."

"Cool by me. Now what do you want, Myron? This may be a surprise to you, but I work for a living."

"You still have friends on the Philadelphia force?"

"Sure."

"Can you get someone to fax you a homicide file?"

"Recent homicide?"

"Er, not exactly."

"How old?"

"Six years," Myron said.

"You're kidding, right?"

"It gets worse. The victim was Alexander Cross."

"The senator's kid?"

"Right."

"What the hell do you want that for?"

"I'll tell you about it when I get there."

"Someone is going to want to know why."

"Make something up."

Jake chewed on something that sounded like tree bark. "Yeah, all right. What time will you be here?"

"Probably around one. I'll call you."

"You're going to owe me, Myron. Owe me big."

"Didn't I mention I was buying lunch?"

Jake hung up.

Myron headed off at exit 6. The toll was almost four dollars. He was tempted to pay the Caddy's toll, but four dollars was a bit steep for the gesture. Myron handed the clerk the money. "I only wanted to drive on the road," Myron said. "Not buy it."

Not even a sympathetic smile. Complaining about toll prices. One of those signs you're becoming your father. Next thing you know Myron'd be screaming at someone for turning up the thermostat.

Altogether the trip to Philadelphia's wealthiest suburb took two hours. Gladwynne was old money. Plymouth Rock old money. Bloodlines were as important as credit lines. The house Valerie Simpson had grown up in was Gatsby-esque with signs of fray. The lawn was not quite manicured. The shrubbery was slightly overgrown. The paint was chipped in certain places. The ivy crawling along the walls seemed a tad too thick.

Still, the estate was huge. Myron parked so far away he almost waited for shuttle service. As he approached the front door Detectives Dimonte and Krinsky came out. In a major shock, Dimonte did not appear happy to see him. He put his hands on his hips. Important, impatient.

"What the fuck are you doing here?" he barked.

"Do you know what happened to the Motels?" Myron asked.

"The what?"

Myron shook his head. "How quickly they forget."

"Goddamn it, Bolitar, I asked you a question. What do you want here?"

"You left your underpants at my house last night," Myron said. "Jockey shorts. Size thirty-eight. Little bunny design."

Dimonte's face grew red. Most cops were homophobes. Best way to needle them was to play on it. "You better not be playing fucking Hardy Boys with my case, asshole. You and your pal Psycho-yuppie."

Krinsky laughed at that one. Psycho-yuppie. When ol' Rolly got hold of a good one he didn't let it go.

"Doesn't matter," Dimonte continued. "The case is just about wrapped up."

"And I'll be able to say I knew you when."

"You'll be happy to know your client is no longer my main suspect."

Myron nodded. "Roger Quincy the stalker is."

That didn't please Dimonte. "How the fuck do you know about that?"

"I am all-seeing, all-knowing."

"Doesn't mean your boy is fully in the clear. He's still lying about something. You know it. I know it. Krinsky here knows it."

Krinsky sort of nodded. Mr. Sidekick.

"But now we just figure your boy was porking her. You know, on the side."

"You have any evidence?"

"Don't need none. Don't give a shit. I want her killer, not her porker."

"Poetically put, Rolly."

"Ah screw it, I don't have time for your wit."

As they passed, Myron gave a little wave. "Nice talking to you, Krinsky."

Krinsky nodded.

Myron rang the doorbell. It rang dramatically. Sounded like an orchestra. Tchaikovsky maybe. Maybe not. A man of about thirty came to the door. He was dressed in a pink oxford shirt open at the neck. Ralph Lauren. Big dimple on chin. Hair so black it was almost blue, like Superman's.

He looked at Myron like he was a vagrant urinating on the steps. "Yes?"

"I'm here to see Mrs. Van Slyke." Valerie's mother had remarried.

"Now is not a good time," he said.

"I have an appointment."

"Perhaps you didn't hear me," he said in that haughty, Win-like accent. "Now is not a good time."

"Please tell Mrs. Van Slyke that Myron Bolitar is here," Myron persisted. "She is expecting me. Windsor Lockwood spoke with her last night."

"Mrs. Van Slyke isn't seeing anybody today. Her daughter was murdered yesterday."

"I'm aware of that."

"Then you'll understand—"

"Kenneth?"

A woman's voice.

"It's okay, Helen," the man said. "I'm handling the situation."

"Who is it, Kenneth?"

"No one."

Myron said, "Myron Bolitar."

Kenneth shot Myron a look. Myron held back the temptation to stick out his tongue. It wasn't easy.

She appeared in the foyer. All in black. Her eyes were red with equally red rims. She was an attractive woman, though Myron ventured to guess she was probably a lot more attractive twenty-four hours ago. Late forties. Blond hair, softly colored. Nicely coiffed. Not too bleachy.

"Please come in, Mr. Bolitar."

Kenneth said, "I don't think that's such a good idea, Helen."

"It's okay, Kenneth."

"You need your rest."

She took Myron's arm. "Please forgive my husband, Mr. Bolitar. He is just trying to protect me."

Husband? Did she say husband?

"Please follow me."

She led him into a room slightly larger than the Acropolis. Over the fireplace hung a gigantic portrait of a man with long sideburns and a walrus mustache. Kinda scary. The room was lit by a half dozen of those fixtures that look like candles. The furniture, while old-world tasteful, seemed a tad too worn. There wasn't a silver tea set, but there should have been. Myron sat in an antique chair about as comfortable as an iron lung. Kenneth kept his eye on Myron. Making sure he didn't pocket an ashtray or something.

Helen sat on the couch across from him. Kenneth stood behind her, hands on her shoulders. Would have made a nice photograph. Very regal. A little girl, no more than three or four, toddled into the room. "This is Cassie," Helen Van Slyke said. "Valerie's sister."

Myron smiled widely and leaned toward the little girl. "Hello, Cassie."

The little girl responded by bawling liked she'd just been stabbed.

Helen Van Slyke comforted her daughter, and after a few more wails Cassie stopped. She peeked out behind balled-up fists every once in a while to study Myron. Maybe she too feared for the safety of the ashtrays.

"Windsor tells me you're a sports agent," Helen Van Slyke said.

"Yes."

"Were you going to represent my daughter?"

"We were discussing the possibility."

Kenneth said, "I don't see why this conversation can't wait, Helen."

She ignored him. "So why did you want to see me, Mr. Bolitar?"

"I'd just like to ask you a few questions."

"What kind of questions?" Kenneth asked. Sneering suspicion.

Helen silenced him with her hand. "Please go ahead, Mr. Bolitar."

"I understand Valerie was hospitalized about six years ago."

"What does that have to do with anything?" Kenneth again.

"Kenneth, please leave us alone."

"But Helen—"

"Please. Take Cassie for a walk."

"Are you sure?"

"Yes."

He protested, but he was no match for her. She closed her eyes, signaling the argument's end. Grudgingly Kenneth took his daughter's hand. When they were out of earshot, she said, "He is a bit overprotective."

"It's understandable," Myron said. "Under the circumstances."

"Why do you want to know about Valerie's hospitalization?"

"I'm trying to put some loose ends together."

She studied his face for a moment. "You're trying to find my daughter's killer, aren't you?"

"Yes."

"May I ask why?"

"There are several reasons."

"I'll accept one."

"Valerie tried to reach me before the murder," Myron said. "She called my office three times."

"That hardly makes you responsible."

Myron said nothing.

Helen Van Slyke took a deep breath. "And you think her murder has something to do with her breakdown?"

"I don't know."

"The police feel quite certain the killer is a man who stalked Valerie."

"What do you think?"

She stayed perfectly still. "I don't know. Roger Quincy seemed harmless enough. But I guess they all seem harmless until something like this happens. He used to write her love letters all the time. They were sort of sweet, in a kooky kind of way."

"Do you still have them?"

"I just gave them to the police."

"Do you remember what they said?"

"They vacillated between almost normal courting words and outright obsession. Sometimes he would simply ask her on a date. Other times he would write about eternal love and how they were destined to be together forever."

"How did Valerie react?"

"Sometimes it scared her. Sometimes it amused her.

But mostly she ignored it. We all did. No one took it too seriously.''

"What about Pavel? Was he concerned?''

"Not overly.''

"Did he hire a bodyguard for Valerie?''

"No. He was dead set against the idea. He thought a bodyguard might spook her.''

Myron paused. Valerie hadn't needed a bodyguard against a stalker, yet Pavel needs one against pestering parents and autograph hounds. It made one wonder. "I'd like to talk about Valerie's breakdown, if that's all right.''

Helen Van Slyke stiffened slightly. "I think it's best to leave that alone, Mr. Bolitar.''

"Why?''

"It was painful. You have no idea how painful. My daughter had a mental collapse, Mr. Bolitar. She was only eighteen years old. Beautiful. Talented. A professional athlete. Successful by any rational measure. And she had a breakdown. It was stressful on all of us. We tried our best to help her get well, to keep it from getting in the papers and becoming public. We tried our best to keep it under wraps.''

She stopped then and closed her eyes.

"Mrs. Van Slyke.''

"I'm fine,'' she said.

Silence.

"You were saying how you tried to keep it under wraps,'' Myron prompted.

The eyes reopened. She smiled and sort of smoothed her skirt. "Yes, well, I didn't want this episode ruining her life. You know how people talk. For the rest of her life people would point and whisper. I didn't want that. And yes, I was embarrassed too. I was younger, Mr.

Bolitar. I was afraid of how her breakdown would reflect on the Brentman family name.''

"Brentman?"

"My maiden name. This estate is known as Brentman Hall. My first husband was named Simpson. A mistake. A social climber. Kenneth is my second husband. I know tongues wag about our age differences, but the Van Slykes are an old family. His great-great-grandfather and my great-grandfather were partners.''

Good reason to get married. "How long have you and Kenneth been married?"

"Six years last April."

"I see. So you got married around the same time Valerie was hospitalized."

Her eyes narrowed and her words came slower now. "What exactly are you implying, Mr. Bolitar?"

"Nothing," Myron said. "I wasn't implying anything. Really." Well, maybe a little. "Tell me about Alexander Cross."

She stiffened again, almost like a spasm. "What about him?" She sounded annoyed now.

"He and Valerie were serious?"

"Mr. Bolitar"—impatience creeping in—"Windsor Lockwood is an old family friend. He is the reason I agreed to see you. You earlier portrayed yourself as a man concerned with finding my daughter's killer."

"I am."

"Then please tell me what Alexander Cross or Valerie's breakdown or my own marriage has to do with your task?"

"I am making an assumption, Mrs. Van Slyke. I am assuming that this was not a random killing, that the person who shot your daughter was not a stranger. That means I have to know about her life. All of it. I don't ask these questions to amuse myself. I need to know who would have feared Valerie or hated her or had a lot to gain by her death. That means digging into all the unpleasantries of her life."

She held his gaze a beat too long and then looked away. "Just what do you know about my daughter, Mr. Bolitar?"

"The basics," Myron said. "Valerie became tennis's next wunderkind at the French Open when she was only sixteen. Expectations ran wild, but her play quickly leveled off. Then it grew worse. She was stalked by an obsessive fan named Roger Quincy. She had a relationship with the son of a prominent politician, who was later murdered. Then she had a mental collapse. Now I need to fill in—and illuminate—more pieces of this puzzle."

"It's very difficult to talk about all this."

"I understand that," Myron said gently. He opted now for the Alan Alda smile over the Phil Donahue. More teeth, moister eyes.

"There's nothing more I can tell you, Mr. Bolitar. I don't know why anyone would want to kill her."

"Perhaps you can tell me about the last few months," Myron said. "How was Valerie feeling? Did anything unusual happen?"

Helen fiddled with her strand of pearls, twisting them around her fingers until they made a red mark around her neck. "She finally started getting better," she said, her voice more of a choke now. "I think tennis helped. For years she wouldn't touch a racket. Then she started playing. A little at first. Just for fun."

The facade collapsed then. Helen Van Slyke lost it. The tears came hard. Myron took her hand. Her grip was both strong and shaky.

"I'm sorry," Myron said.

She shook her head, forcing the words out. "Valerie started playing every day. It made her stronger. Physically, emotionally. She finally seemed to be putting it all behind her. And then . . ." She stopped again, her eyes suddenly flat. "That bastard."

She might have been talking about the unknown killer. But somehow the anger seemed more specific.

"Who?" Myron tried.

"Helen?"

Kenneth was back. He quickly crossed the room and took his wife in his arms. Myron thought he saw her back away at his touch, but he couldn't be sure.

Kenneth looked over her shoulder at Myron. "See what you've done," he hissed. "Get out."

"Mrs. Van Slyke?"

She nodded. "Please leave, Mr. Bolitar. It's for the best."

"Are you sure?"

Kenneth bellowed again. "Get out! Now! Before I throw you out!"

Myron looked at him. Not the time or the place. "I'm sorry for the intrusion, Mrs. Van Slyke. My most sincere condolences."

Myron showed himself out.

Chapter 9

When Myron entered the small police station Jake's chin was coated with something red and sticky. Might have been from a jelly doughnut. Might have been from a small farm animal. Hard to tell with Jake.

Jake Courter had been elected sheriff of Reston, New Jersey two years before. In view of the fact that Jake was black in an almost entirely white community, most people considered the election result an upset. But not Jake. Reston was a college town. College towns were filled with liberal intellectuals who wanted to lift a black man up. Jake figured his skin color had been enough of a disadvantage over the years, might as well turn the tide. White guilt, he told Myron. The best vote-getter this side of Willie Horton ads.

Jake was in his early fifties. He'd been a cop in a half dozen major cities over the years—New York, Philadelphia, Boston, to name a few. Tired of chasing city scum, he'd moved out to the happy suburbs to chase suburban scum. Myron and Jake met a year ago, investigating the disappearance of Kathy Culver, Jessica's sister, a student at Reston University.

"Hey, Myron."

"Jake."

Jake looked, as always, rumpled. Everything about him. His hair. His clothes. Even his desk looked rumpled, like a cotton shirt kept in the bottom of a laundry hamper. The desk also had an assortment of goodies. A Pizza Hut box. A Wendy's bag. A Carvel ice-cream cup. A half-eaten sandwich from Blimpie. And, of course, a tin of Slim-Fast diet powder. Jake was closing in on two hundred and seventy-five pounds. His pants never fit right. They were too small for his stomach, too large for his waist. He was constantly adjusting them, searching for that one elusive point where they'd actually stay in place. The search required a team of top scientists and a really powerful microscope.

"Let's go grab a couple burgers," Jake said, wiping his face with a moist towelette. "I'm starving."

Myron picked up the Slim-Fast can and smiled sweetly. " 'A delicious shake for breakfast. Another for lunch. And then a sensible dinner.' "

"Bullshit. I gave it a try. The shit doesn't work."

"How long were you on it?"

"Almost a day. Zip, nothing. Not a pound gone."

"You should sue."

"Plus the stuff tastes like used gunpowder."

"You get the file on Alexander Cross?"

"Yeah, right here. Let's go."

Myron followed Jake down the street. They stopped at a place very generously dubbed the Royal Court Diner. A pit. If it were totally renovated, it might reach the sanitary status of an interstate public toilet.

Jake smiled. "Nice, huh?"

"My arteries are hardening from the smell," Myron said.

"For chrissake, man, don't inhale."

The table had one of those diner jukeboxes. The records hadn't been changed in a long time. The current number one single, according to the little advertisement, was Elton John's *Crocodile Rock*.

The waitress was standard diner issue. She was grumpy, mid-fifties, her hair a purplish tint not found anywhere in the state of nature.

"Hey, Millie," Jake said.

She tossed them menus, not speaking, barely breaking stride.

"That's Millie," Jake said.

"She seems great," Myron said. "Can I see the file?"

"Let's order first."

Myron picked up the menu. Vinyl. And sticky. Very sticky. Like someone had poured maple syrup on it. There were also bits of coagulated scrambled eggs in the crease. Myron was losing his appetite in a hurry.

Three seconds later Millie returned, sighed. "What'll it be?"

"Give me a cheeseburger deluxe," Jake said. "Double order of fries instead of the coleslaw. And a diet Coke."

Millie looked toward Myron. Impatiently.

Myron smiled at her. "Do you have a vegetarian menu?"

"A what?"

"Stop being an asshole," Jake said.

"A grilled cheese will be fine," Myron said.

"Fries with that?"

"No."

"To drink?"

"A Diet Coke. Like my low-cal buddy."

Millie eyed Myron, looked him up and down. "You're kinda cute."

Myron gave her the modest smile. The one that said, *Aw, shucks.*

"You also look familiar."

"I have that kind of face," Myron said. "Cute yet familiar."

"You date one of my daughters once? Gloria maybe. She works the night shift."

"I don't think so."

She looked him over again. "You married?"

"I'm involved with someone."

"Not what I asked you," she said. "You married?"

"No."

"All right then." She turned and left.

"What was that all about?"

Jake shrugged. "Hope she's not getting Gloria."

"Why?"

"She kinda looks like a white version of me," Jake said. "Only with a heavier beard."

"Sounds enticing."

"You still with Jessica Culver?"

"Guess so."

Jake shook his head. "Man, she's something else. I've never seen nothing that looked that good in real life."

Myron tried not to grin. "Hard to argue."

"She also got you wrapped around her finger."

"Hard to argue."

"Lots of worse places for a man to be wrapped around."

"Hard to argue."

Millie came back with the two Diet Cokes. This time she almost managed to smile at Myron. "Good-looking man like you shouldn't be single," she said.

"I'm wanted in several states," Myron said.

Millie did not seem discouraged. She shrugged, left. Myron turned back to Jake.

"All right," Myron said. "Where's the file?"

Jake flipped it open. He handed Myron a picture of a handsome, healthy man. Tan, fit, wearing tennis shorts. Myron had seen the picture in the paper after the murder.

"Meet Alexander Cross," Jake began. "Age twenty-four at the time of the murder. Wharton graduate. Son of United States senator Bradley Cross of Pennsylvania. On the night of July twenty-four, six years ago, he was attending a party at a tennis club called Old Oaks in Wayne, Pennsylvania. The esteemed senator was there. It's a pretty ritzy place—fancy food, indoor and outdoor courts, hard court, clay, lit, unlit, the works. Even grass courts."

"Okay."

"What happened next is a bit fuzzy, but here's what we have. Alexander Cross and three buddies were taking a walk around the grounds."

"At night? During a party?"

"Not unheard of."

"Not common either."

Jake shrugged. "Anyway, they heard a noise coming from the western end of the club. They went to check it out. They ran into two suspicious-looking youths."

"Suspicious-looking?"

"The youths were—what are they calling us today?— African American."

"Ah," Myron said. "Is it safe to assume that Old Oaks did not have a lot of African American members?"

"Like none. It's exclusive."

"So you and I could never be members."

"Real shame," Jake said. "I bet we'd have loved that party."

"So what happened next?"

"According to the witnesses, the white youths approached the black youths. One of the black youths—

later identified as one Errol Swade—reacted by whipping out a switchblade.''

Myron made a face. "A switchblade?"

"Yeah, I know. Such a cliché. No imagination. Anyway, an incident ensued. Alexander Cross was stabbed. The two youths ran. A few hours later the police caught up with them in north Philadelphia, not far from where the youths lived. During the apprehension, one of the punks pulled out a gun. A Curtis Yeller. Sixteen years old. A police officer shot him. Yeller's mother was at the scene, from what I understand. She was cradling the kid in her arms when he died."

"She saw him being shot?"

Jake shrugged. "Doesn't say."

"So what happened to Errol Swade?"

"He escaped. A nationwide manhunt began. His mug shot was in all the papers, sent to all the stations. Lot of cops on it, of course—the victim being the son of a U.S. senator and all. But here's where things get interesting."

Myron sipped the Diet Coke. Flat.

"They never found Errol Swade," Jake said.

Myron felt his heart sink. "Never?"

Jake shook his head.

"Are you telling me Swade escaped?"

"Appears so."

"How old was he?"

"Nineteen at the time of the incident."

Myron mulled that over a moment. "That would make him twenty-five now."

"Whoa. A math major."

Myron did not smile. Millie brought the food. She made another comment, but Myron did not hear it. Twenty-five years old. Myron couldn't help but wonder. It was a dumb thought. Unforgivable. And maybe even racist. But there it was. Twenty-five years old. Duane claimed to be twenty-one, but who knew for sure?

But no. It can't be.

Myron took another sip of the flat soda. "What do you know about Errol Swade?" he asked.

"A pedigree punk. He had already been in jail three times. First offense was stealing a car. He was twelve. Assorted felonies followed. Muggings, assaults, car thefts, armed robberies, drugs. Also a member of an ultraviolent street gang. Guess what the gang was called."

Myron shrugged. "Josie and the Pussycats?"

"Close. The Stains. Short for Bloodstains. They always wear a shirt dipped in a victim's blood. Kinda like a Boy Scout badge."

"Charming."

"Errol Swade and Curtis Yeller were also cousins. Swade had been living with the Yellers since his release a month earlier. Let's see what else. Swade was a dropout. Big surprise. A coke addict. Another shocker. And a major league moron."

"So how has he eluded the police for so long?"

Jake picked up his burger and took a bite. A big bite. Half the burger vanished. "He couldn't have," he said.

"Excuse me?"

"No way he could have stayed out of trouble this long. Impossible."

"Hold up. Did I miss something here?"

"Officially the police are still looking," Jake said. "But unofficially they're sure he's dead. The kid was a dumb punk. He couldn't find his ass with both hands, never mind hide from a nationwide dragnet."

"So what happened?"

"Rumor has it the senator got a favor from the mob. They knocked him off."

"Senator Cross put out a hit on him?"

"What, that surprises you? The guy's a politician. That's like a step below child molester."

"Weren't you *elected* sheriff?"

Jake nodded. "There you go."

Myron risked a bite of his sandwich. Tasted a bit like a sink sponge. "Do you have a physical description of Errol Swade?" he asked, almost hoping the answer was no.

"I got better. I got Swade's mugshot." Jake dusted his hands off, rubbed them on his shirt for good measure. Then he reached into the folder and withdrew a photograph. He handed it to Myron. Myron tried not to appear too eager.

It wasn't Duane.

Not even close. Not even with plastic surgery. For one, Errol Swade was much lighter skinned. Swade's head was shaped like a block, completely different from Duane's. His eyes were spaced too far apart. Everything was different. His height was listed as six-four, three inches taller than Duane. Can't fake being shorter.

Myron almost sighed with relief. "Does the name Valerie Simpson pop up in that file?" he asked.

Jake's eyes caught a little fire. "Who?"

"You heard me."

"Golly, Myron, that wouldn't be the same Valerie Simpson who was murdered yesterday?"

"By coincidence it is. Is her name in there?"

He handed Myron half the file. "Hell if I know. Help me look."

They went through it. Valerie's name was only on one sheet. A party guest list. Her name along with a hundred others. Myron jotted down the names and addresses of the witnesses to the murder—three friends of

Alexander Cross's. Nothing else of much interest in the file.

"So," Jake said, "what does the lovely and dead Valerie Simpson have to do with this?"

"I don't know."

"Jesus Christ." Jake shook his head. "You still yanking my chain?"

"I'm not yanking anything."

"What have you got so far?"

"Less than nothing."

"That's what you said about Kathy Culver."

"But this isn't your case, Jake."

"Maybe I can help."

"I really don't have anything. Valerie Simpson visited my office a few days ago. She wanted to make a comeback, but somebody killed her instead. I want to know who, that's all."

"You're full of shit."

Myron shrugged.

"The TV said something about a stalker doing the job," Jake said.

"Might be him. Probably is."

Silence.

"You're holding back again," Jake said. "Just like with Kathy Culver."

"It's confidential."

"You're not going to tell me?"

"Nope. It's confidential."

"Protecting someone again?"

"Confidential," Myron said. "As in not to be divulged. Communicated in the strictest of confidence. A secret."

"Fine, be that way," Jake said. "So how's your sandwich?"

Myron nodded. "Maybe the ambience isn't so good, but at least the food stinks."

Jake laughed. "Hey, you got tickets to the Open?"

"Yeah."

"How about getting me two?"

"For when?"

"The last Saturday."

The men's semis and women's finals. "Tough day," Myron said.

"But not for a big-time agent like yourself."

"Then we'll be even?"

"Yeah."

"I'll leave them at the on-call window."

"Make sure they're good seats."

"Who you taking?"

"My son Gerard."

Myron had played ball against Gerard in college. Gerard was a bull. No finesse about his game. "He still working homicide in New York?"

"Yep."

"Can he do me a little favor?"

"Shit. Like what?"

"The cop on Valerie's murder is a devout asshole."

"And you want to know what they have."

"Yeah."

"All right. I'll ask Gerard to give you a call."

Chapter 10

"Messages?"

Esperanza nodded. "About a million of them."

Myron fingered through the pile. "Any word on Eddie Crane?"

"You're having dinner with him and his folks."

He looked up. "When?"

"Tonight. Seven-thirty. At La Reserve. I already made a reservation. Make sure you use Win's name."

Win's name carried weight at many of New York's finest restaurants. "You realize, of course, that you're a genius."

She nodded. "Yeah."

"I want you to come too."

"Can't. School." Esperanza went to law school at night.

"Is Eddie still being coached by Pavel Menansi?" Myron asked.

"Yeah, why?"

"He and I had a discussion last night at the Open."

"What about?"

"He used to coach Valerie."

"And you two 'discussed' that?"

Myron nodded.

"May I assume you wowed him with your usual charm?"

"Something like that."

"So we don't have a chance with Eddie," she said.

"Not necessarily. If Eddie was really close to Pavel, then TruPro would have him signed by now. Maybe there's some friction there."

"Almost forgot." Esperanza picked up a small stack of papers. "This just came in by fax. They want it signed right away."

A contract for a baseball prospect named Sandy Repo. A pitcher. The Houston Astros had taken him in the first round. Myron scanned it over. The contract had been orally finalized yesterday morning, but Myron spotted the new paragraph right away. Sandwiched it in on the second-to-last page.

"Cute," he said.

"Who?"

"The Astros. Get me Bob Wasson on the line." The Astros' general manager.

Esperanza picked up the phone. "You're supposed to meet with Burger City tomorrow afternoon."

"Same time as Duane's match?"

She nodded.

"You mind handling it?" he asked.

"They're not going to like dealing with a receptionist," she said.

"You're an associate," Myron corrected. "A valued associate."

"Still not the main man. Still not Myron Bolitar."

"Ah, but who is?"

She rolled her eyes, picked up the phone, began dialing. She purposely did not look at him. "You really think I'm ready?"

The tone was hard to read. Myron couldn't tell if it signaled sarcasm or insecurity. Probably both.

"They're going to want Duane for their new promo,"

he said. "But Duane wants to wait for a national deal. Try to push someone else on them."

"Okay."

Myron went into his office. Home. Tara. He had a nice view of the Manhattan skyline. Not a corner office view like Win's, but not shabby either. On one wall he had movie stills. Everything from Bogie and Bacall to Woody and Diane. Another wall featured Broadway posters. Musicals mostly. Everything from Rodgers and Hammerstein to Andrew Lloyd Webber. The final wall was his client wall. Action photos of each player. He studied the picture of Duane, his body arched in a serving motion.

"What's going on, Duane?" Myron said out loud. "What are you hiding?"

The photo did not answer. Photos rarely did.

His phone buzzed. Esperanza came on the speaker. "I have Bob Wasson on the line."

"Okay."

"I can put him on hold. Until you're finished talking to your wall."

"No, I think I'll take it now." Wiseass. He hit the speakerphone. "Bob?"

"Goddamn it, Bolitar, take me off the speaker. You're not that goddamn important."

Myron picked up the receiver. "That better?"

"Yeah, great. What do you want?"

"I got the contract today."

"Well, yippee for you. Now, here's what you do next. Step one: Sign it where the X is. You know how to do that, don't you? I had your name typed under the X in case you're unsure of the spelling. And use a pen, Myron. Blue or black ink, please. No crayons. Step two:

Put the contract in the enclosed self-addressed envelope. Moisten the flap. With me so far?''

Good ol' Bob. Funny as a case of head lice. "There's a problem," Myron said.

"A what?''

"A problem.''

"Look, Bolitar, if you're trying to squeeze me for more dough, you can fuck yourself from behind.''

"Point thirty-seven. Paragraph C.''

"What about it?''

Myron read it out loud. '' 'The player agrees that he will not engage in sports endangering his health or safety including, but not limited to, professional boxing or wrestling, motorcycling, moped riding, auto racing, skydiving, hang gliding, hunting, et cetera, et cetera.' ''

"Yeah, so? It's a prohibited activities clause. We got it from the NBA.''

"The NBA's contract says nothing about hunting.''

"What?''

"Please, Bob, let's try to pretend I don't have a learning disability. You threw in the word *hunting*. Sneaked it in, if you will.''

"So what's the big deal? Your boy hunts. He hurt himself in a hunting incident two years ago and missed half his junior year. We want to make sure that doesn't happen again.''

"Then you have to compensate him for it," Myron said.

"What? Don't bust my balls, Bolitar. You want us to pay the kid if he gets hurt, right?''

"Right.''

"So we don't want him hunting. Suppose he shoots himself. Or suppose some other asshole mistakes him for a deer and shoots him. You know what that's going to cost us?"

"Your concern," Myron said, "is touching."

"Oh excuse me. A thousand pardons. I guess I should care more and pay less."

"Good point. Strike my last statement."

"So stricken. Can I go now?"

"My client enjoys hunting. It means a great deal to him."

"And his left arm means a lot to us."

"So I suggest a fair compromise."

"What?"

"A bonus. If Sandy doesn't hunt, you agree to pay him twenty thousand dollars at the end of the year."

Laughter. "You're out of your mind."

"Then take that clause out. It's not standard and we don't want it."

Pause. "Five grand. Not a penny more."

"Fifteen."

"Up yours, Myron. Eight."

"Fifteen," Myron said.

"I think you're forgetting how this is played," Bob said. "I say a number a little higher. You say a number a little lower. Then we meet somewhere in the middle."

"Fifteen, Bob. Take it or leave it."

Win opened the door and came in. He sat down silently, crossed his right ankle over his left thigh, and studied his manicured nails.

"Ten," Bob said.

"Fifteen."

The negotiation continued. Win stood, checked his reflection in the mirror behind the door. He was still fixing his hair five minutes later when Myron hung up.

Not a blond lock was out of place, but that never seemed to deter Win.

"What was the final number?" Win asked.

"Thirteen five."

Win nodded. He smiled at his reflection. "You know what I was just thinking?"

"What?"

"It must suck to be ugly."

"Uh-huh. Think you can tear yourself away for a second?"

Win sighed. "It won't be easy."

"Try to be brave."

"I guess I can always look again later."

"Right. It'll give you something to look forward to."

With one last hair pat, Win turned away and sat down. "So what's up?"

"The powder-blue Caddy is still following me."

Win looked pleased. "And you want me to find out who they are?"

"Something like that," Myron said.

"Excellent."

"But I don't want you to move in on them without me there."

"You don't trust my judgment?"

"Just don't, okay?"

Win shrugged. "So how was your visit to the Van Slykes' estate?"

"I met Kenneth. The two of us really hit it off."

"I can imagine."

"You know him?" Myron asked.

"Oh yes."

"Is he as big an asshole as I think?"

Win spread his hands wide. "Of biblical proportions."

"You know anything else about him?"

"Nothing significant."

"Can you check him out?"

"But of course. What else did you find out?"

Myron told him about his visits to both the Van Slykes and Jake.

"Curiouser and curiouser," Win said when he finished.

"Yes."

"So what's the next step?" Win asked.

"I want to attack this from several directions."

"Those being?"

"Valerie's psychiatrist, for one."

"Who will throw all kinds of terms like 'doctor-patient confidentiality' at you," Win said with a dismissive wave. "A waste of time. Who else?"

"Curtis Yeller's mother witnessed her son's shooting. She's also Errol Swade's aunt. Maybe she has some thoughts on all this."

"For example?"

"Maybe she knows what happened to Errol."

"And you—what?—expect her to tell you?"

"You never know."

Win made a face. "So basically your plan is to flail about helplessly."

"Pretty much. I will also need to talk to Senator Cross. Do you think you can arrange it?"

"I can try," Win said. "But you're not going to learn anything from him either."

"Boy, you're a bundle of optimism today."

"Just telling it like it is."

"Did you learn anything at the Plaza?"

"As a matter of fact, I did." Win leaned back and

steepled his fingers. "Valerie made only four calls in the past three days. All were to your office."

"One to make an appointment to see me," Myron said. "The other three on the day she died."

Win gave a quick whistle. "Very impressive. First you figure out Kenneth is an asshole and now this."

"Yeah, sometimes I even scare myself. Is there anything else?"

"A doorman at the Plaza remembered Valerie rather well," Win continued. "After I tipped him twenty dollars, he recalled that Valerie took a lot of quick walks. He found it curious, since guests normally leave for hours at a time, rather than scant minutes."

Myron felt a surge. "She was using a pay phone."

Win nodded. "I called Lisa at NYNEX. By the way, you now owe her two tickets to the Open."

Great. "What did she find out?"

"On the day before Valerie's murder, two calls were placed from a nearby pay phone at Fifth and Fifty-ninth to the residence of one Mr. Duane Richwood."

Myron felt a sinking feeling. "Shit."

"Indeed."

"So not only did Valerie call Duane," Myron said, "but she went out of her way to make sure no one would know."

"So it appears."

Silence.

Win said, "You'll have to talk to him."

"I know."

"Let it wait until after the tournament," Win added. "Between the Open and the big Nike campaign, there's no reason to distract him now. It will keep."

Myron shook his head. "I'll talk to Duane tomorrow. After his match."

Chapter 11

François, the maître d' at La Reserve, flitted about their table like a vulture awaiting death—or worse, a New York maître d' awaiting a very large tip. Since discovering that Myron was a close friend of Windsor Horne Lockwood III's, François had befriended Myron in the same way a dog befriends a man with raw meat in his pocket.

He recommended the thinly sliced salmon appetizer and the chef's special scrod as an entree. Myron took him up on both suggestions. So did the so-far silent Mrs. Crane. Mr. Crane ordered the onion soup and liver. Myron was not going to be kissing him anytime soon. Eddie ordered the escargot and lobster tails. The kid was learning fast.

François said, "May I recommend a wine, Mr. Bolitar?"

"You may."

Eighty-five bucks down the drain.

Mr. Crane took a sip. Nodded his approval. He had not smiled yet, had barely exchanged a pleasantry. Luckily for Myron, Eddie was a nice kid. Smart. Polite. A pleasure to talk to. But whenever Mr. Crane cleared his throat—as he did now—Eddie fell silent.

"I remember your basketball days at Duke, Mr. Bolitar," Crane began.

"Please call me Myron."

"Fine." Instead of reciprocating the informality, Crane knitted his eyebrows. The eyebrows were his most prominent feature—unusually thick and angry and constantly undulating above his eyes. They looked like small ferrets furrowing into his forehead. "You were captain of the team at Duke?" he began.

"For three years," Myron said.

"And you won two NCAA championships?"

"My team did, yes."

"I saw you play on several occasions. You were quite good."

"Thank you."

He leaned forward. The eyebrows grew somehow bushier. "If I recall," Crane continued, "the Celtics drafted you in the first round."

Myron nodded.

"How long did you play for them? Not long, as I recall."

"I hurt my knee during a preseason game my rookie year."

"You never played again?" It was Eddie. His eyes were young and wide.

"Never," Myron said steadily. Better lesson than any lecture he could give. Like the funeral of a high school classmate who died because he was D.U.I.

"Then what did you do with yourself?" Mr. Crane asked. "After the injury?"

The interview. Part of the process. It was harder when you were an ex-jock. People naturally assumed you were dumb.

"I went through rehab for a long while," Myron said. "I thought I could beat the odds, defy the doctors, come back. When I was able to face reality, I went to law school."

"Where?"

"At Harvard."

"Very impressive."

Myron tried to look humble. He almost batted his eyes.

"Did you make Law Review?"

"No."

"Do you have an MBA?"

"No."

"What did you do upon graduation?"

"I became an agent."

Mr. Crane frowned. "How long did it take you to graduate?"

"Five years."

"Why so long?"

"I was working at the same time."

"Doing what?"

"I worked for the government." Nice and vague. He hoped Crane didn't push it.

"I see." Crane frowned again. Every part of him frowned. His mouth, his forehead, even his ears frowned. "Why did you enter the field of sports representation?"

"Because I thought I'd like it. And I thought I'd be good at it."

"Your agency is small."

"True."

"You don't have the connections of some larger agencies."

"True."

"You certainly don't wield the power of ICM or TruPro or Advantage."

"True."

"You don't have too many successful tennis players."

"True."

Crane gave a disapproving scowl. "Then tell me, Mr. Bolitar, why should we choose you?"

"I'm a lot of fun at parties."

Mr. Crane did not break a smile. Eddie did. He caught himself, smothered the smile behind his hand.

"Is that supposed to be funny?" Crane said.

"Let me ask you a question, Mr. Crane. You live in Florida, right?"

"St. Petersburg."

"How did you get up to New York?"

"We flew."

"No. I mean, who paid for the tickets?"

The Cranes shared a wary glance.

"TruPro bought your tickets, right?"

Mr. Crane nodded tentatively.

"They had a limo meet you at the airport?" Myron continued.

Another nod.

"Your jacket, ma'am. It's new?"

"Yes." First time Mrs. Crane had spoken.

"Did one of the big agencies buy it for you?"

"Yes."

"The big agencies, they have wives or female associates who take you around town, show you the sights, do a little shopping, that sort of thing?"

"Yes."

"What's your point?" Crane interrupted.

"That kind of thing is not my bag," Myron said.

"What kind of thing?"

"Ass-kissing. I'm not very good at ass-kissing a client. And I'm terrible at ass-kissing the parents. Eddie?"

"Yes?"

"Did the big agencies promise to have someone at every match?"

He nodded.

"I won't do that," Myron said. "If you need me I'm available twenty-four hours a day, seven days a week. But I'm not physically there twenty-four hours a day, seven days a week. If you want your hand held at every match because Agassi's or Chang's is, go with one of the big agencies. They're better at it than I am. If you need someone to run errands or do your laundry, I'm not the guy either."

The Cranes shared another family glance. "Well," Mr. Crane said. "I heard you speak your mind, Mr. Bolitar. It appears you are living up to your reputation."

"You asked for a contrast between me and the others."

"So I did."

Myron focused his attention on Eddie. "My agency is small and simple. I will do all your negotiations—tournament guarantees, appearances, exhibitions, endorsements, whatever. But I won't sign anything you don't want to. Nothing is final until you look it over, understand it, and approve it yourself. Okay so far?"

Eddie nodded.

"As your father pointed out I am not an MBA. But I work with one. His name is Win Lockwood. He's considered one of the best financial consultants in the country. Win's theory is similar to mine: he wants you to understand and approve every investment he makes. I will insist that you meet with him at least five times a year, preferably more, so that you can set up solid, long-term financial and tax plans. I want you to know what your money is doing at all times. Too many athletes get taken advantage of—bad investments, trusting the wrong people, that sort of thing. That won't happen here because *you*—not just me, not just Win, not just your parents, but *you*—won't let it.''

François came by with the appetizers. He smiled brightly while the underlings served. Then he pointed and ordered them about in impatient French, like they couldn't possibly know how to put a plate down in front of a human being without his fretting.

''Is that everything?'' François asked.

''I think so.''

François sort of lowered his head. ''If there is any way I can make your dining experience more pleasurable, Mr. Bolitar, please do not hesitate to ask.''

Myron looked down at his salmon. ''How about some ketchup?''

François's face lost color. ''Pardon?''

''It's a joke, François.''

''And a funny one at that, Mr. Bolitar.''

François slithered away. Myron the Card strikes again.

''How about the young lady who set up this dinner?'' Mr. Crane asked. ''Miss Diaz. What's her function at your agency?''

''Esperanza is my associate. My right hand.''

''What's her work background?''

''She's currently goes to law school nights. That's why she couldn't join us tonight. She was also a professional wrestler.''

That piqued Eddie's interest. ''Really? Which one?''

''Little Pocahontas.''

''The Indian Princess? She and Big Chief Mama used to be the tag team champs.''

''Right.''

''Man, she is hot!''

"Yup."

Mrs. Crane nibbled at her salmon. Mr. Crane ignored his onion soup for the moment. "So tell me," Mr. Crane said, "what strategy would you employ for Eddie's career?"

"Depends," Myron said. "There's no set formula. You have two conflicting factors pulling at your son. On the one hand Eddie is only seventeen. He's a kid. Tennis shouldn't consume him to the point where he hates it. He should still have fun, try to do the things seventeen-year-olds do. On the other hand it's naive to think that tennis will still be just a game to him. Or that he'll be a 'normal' kid. This is about money. Big money. If Eddie does it right, if he makes some sacrifices now and works with Win, he can be financially set for life. It's a delicate balance—how many tournaments and exhibitions to play in, how many appearances, how many endorsements."

Crane's eyebrows nodded. They seemed to agree.

Myron turned his attention to Eddie. "You want to score a lot of money early, because you never know what can happen. I'm proof of that. But I don't want you sucked dry. Sometimes the hardest thing in the world is to say no to staggering amounts of money. But in the end it's your decision, not mine. It's your money. If you want to play in every tournament and every exhibition match, it's not my place to stop you. But you can't do it, Eddie. No one can. You're a good kid. You have your head on straight. You were raised right. But if you try to bend too far, you'll break. I've seen it happen too often.

"I want you to make a lot of money. But not every cent out there. I don't want to turn you into a money machine. I want you to have some fun. I want you to enjoy all of this. I want you to realize how lucky you are.''

The Cranes listened in rapt silence.

''That's my theory, Eddie, for what it's worth. You may make more money with the big agencies. I can't deny that. But in the long run, with a long and healthy career, with careful planning, I think you'll be wealthier and better off with MB SportsReps.''

Myron looked at Mr. Crane. ''Anything else you care to know?''

Crane sipped his wine, studied its color, put the glass down. He did the eyebrow mambo again. ''You came highly recommended to us, Mr. Bolitar. Or should I say to Eddie.''

''Oh?'' Myron said. ''By whom?''

Eddie looked away. Mrs. Crane put her hand on his arm. Mr. Crane provided the answer. ''Valerie Simpson.''

Myron was surprised. ''Valerie recommended me?''

''She thought you'd be good for Eddie.''

''She said that?''

''Yes.''

Myron turned to Eddie. He wasn't crying, but he looked on the verge. ''What else did she say, Eddie?''

Shrug. ''She thought you were honest. That you'd treat me right.''

''How did you know Valerie?''

''They met at Pavel's camp in Florida,'' Crane answered. ''She was sixteen when Eddie arrived. He was only nine. I think she looked after him a little.''

''They were quite close,'' Mrs. Crane added. ''Such a tragedy.''

''Did she say anything else, Eddie?''

Another shrug. Eddie finally looked up. Myron met his gaze, held it steady.

"It's important," Myron said.

"She told me not to work with TruPro," he said.

"Why?"

"She didn't say."

"My theory," Crane added, "is that she blamed them for her downfall."

"What do you think, Eddie?" Myron asked.

Yet another shrug. "Could be. I don't know."

"But you don't think so."

Nothing.

Mrs. Crane said, "I think that's enough for now. Valerie's murder has been very hard on Eddie."

The conversation slowly drifted back to business. But Eddie was silent now. Every once in a while he would open his mouth, then close it again. When they rose to leave, Eddie leaned toward Myron and whispered, "Why do you want to know so much about Valerie?"

Myron opted for the truth. "I'm trying to find out who killed her."

That widened his eyes. He looked behind him. His parents were busy saying good-bye to François. François kissed Mrs. Crane's hand.

"I think you might be able to help," Myron said.

"Me?" Eddie said. "I don't know anything."

"She was your friend. You were close to her."

"Eddie?"

Mr. Crane's voice.

"I have to go, Mr. Bolitar. Thank you for everything."

"Yes, thank you," Crane added. "We have a few more agencies to see, but we'll be in touch."

After they left, François came by with the bill. "Your tie is very becoming, Mr. Bolitar."

The man knew how to kiss ass. "You should have been an agent, François."

"Thank you, sir."

Myron gave him a Visa card and waited. He turned his cellular phone back on. A message from Win. Myron called him back.

"Where are you?" Myron asked.

"On Twenty-sixth Street, near Eighth," Win said. "There were two gentlemen—and I use that term in its absolute loosest sense—in the Cadillac. They followed you to La Reserve, sat outside for a while, and left about half an hour ago. They've just entered a drinking establishment of rather questionable repute."

"Questionable repute?"

"It's called the Beaver Hunt. Enough said?"

"Stay on them. I'm on my way down."

Chapter 12

Win was waiting across the street from the Beaver Hunt. The block was quiet, the only sound was the faint beat of music coming from inside the bar. A large neon sign said TOPLESS!

"Two of them," Win said. "The driver was a white man, approximately six-three. Overweight but powerfully built. I think you'll like his fashion sense."

"Meaning?"

"You'll see. He is with a black man. Six foot. Big scar on his right cheek. I guess you might describe him as thin and wiry."

Myron looked down the street. "Where did they park?"

"A lot on Eighth Avenue."

"Why not on the street? Plenty of spots."

"I believe our man is quite attached to his charming chariot." Win smiled. "If anything happened to it, I bet he'd be very upset."

"How difficult will it be to break in?"

Win looked insulted. "I'll pretend you didn't ask that."

"Fine, you check the car. I'll go inside."

Win snapped a salute. "Roger, Wilco."

They split up. Win headed for the lot, Myron for the bar. Myron would have preferred it the other way around, especially since the two men obviously knew what Myron looked like, but they needed to play their strengths. Win was far better at breaking into cars or handling anything mechanical. Myron was better at, well, this.

He entered the bar with his head lowered, just in case. No need. No one paid him any attention. There was no cover charge here. Myron looked around. Two words came to mind: major dive. The decor's theme was Early American Beer. The walls were ornamented with neon beer signs. The bar and table were crusted with beer rings. Behind the bar were pyramids of beer bottles from all over the land.

Of course, there were topless dancers. They lazily pranced atop small stages that looked like old stage props from *Wonderama*. Most of the dancers were not attractive. Far from it. The exercise craze had not yet hit the Beaver Hunt. Flesh jiggled. The place looked more like a cellulite test center than a male-fantasy cantina.

Myron moved to a corner table and sat by himself. There were a few suits, but for the most part the clientele was blue-collar. The well-to-do usually got their topless kicks at Goldfingers or Score, where the women were far more aesthetically pleasing, though their body parts were about as real as their inflatable brethren's.

Two men were laughing it up by center stage. One black, one white. They fit Win's description. When the dancers rotated stages, the one in front of them stepped off. Her downtime. The boys began to negotiate with her. In places like Goldfingers and Score, you paid about twenty or twenty-five dollars for a table dance. It was basically just what it sounded like. The girl took off her top and danced at your table for maybe five minutes. No touchy, no feely. At the Beaver Hunt, the order of the day was a recent craze known as the Lap Dance, which took place in discreet corners of the bar. The Lap Dance, known to young adolescents as the Dry Hump, consisted of a dancer gyrating on a man's crotch until he, well, orgasmed. Moral repugnancy aside, Myron had several questions about the technical aspects of such an act. Like after the act, how does a guy go around the rest of the night? Does he bring a change of underwear with him?

So many questions. So little time.

The two men and the dancer headed toward Myron's corner. Myron could now see clearly what Win had been talking about. The white guy did indeed have big arms, but he also had a protruding gut and flabby chest. Some of these flaws could be hidden with proper fashion sense, but the white guy was wearing a tight fishnet shirt. Fishnet. As in a lot of holes. As in practically no shirt at all. His chest hairs—and there were lots of them—were jutting through the holes. The hairs seemed unusually long, coiling around—and indeed getting enmeshed in—the many gold chains that were draped about his neck. As he walked by, Myron got a full view of his back, thank you very much, which was even hairier and somewhat oilier than the front.

Myron felt a little ill.

"Fifteen dollars for the first ten minutes," the girl said. "I can't do better than that."

"Don't jerk us around, whore," Fishnet said. "There's two of us here. Two for one."

"Yeah," the black guy chimed in. "Two for one."

"I can't do that," the girl said. If she seemed insulted by the name calling, it didn't show. Her voice was tired and matter-of-fact, like a diner waitress on the night shift.

Fishnet was not pleased by this. "Listen, bitch, don't get me angry."

"I'll get the manager," she said.

"The fuck you will. You ain't leaving here till I get my rocks off, slut."

"Yeah," the black guy added. "Me too. Slut."

"Look, I charge more for talking dirty," the girl said.

Fishnet looked at her in disbelief. "What did you say?"

"There's a surcharge for talking dirty."

"A surcharge?" Fishnet shouted. He was enraged now. "This might come as a surprise to a stupid whore, but we live in the U.S. of A. Land of the free, home of the brave. I can say whatever I want, slut—or haven't you ever heard of freedom of speech?"

A constitutional scholar, Myron thought. Nice to see a man defending the First Amendment.

"Look," the dancer said, "the price is twelve dollars for five minutes, twenty dollars for ten minutes. Plus tip. That's it."

"How about this," Fishnet said. "You dance on both of us at the same time."

"Huh?"

"Like you're dancing on me but stroking him. How's that sound, pig?"

"Yeah," the black guy said. "Pig."

"Look, fellas, there's no two-for-one deals," the dancer said. "Just let me get another girl. We'll take good care of you."

Myron stepped into view. "Will I do?"

No one moved.

"Gee," Myron said, "they're both so attractive. I just can't choose."

Fishnet looked at the black guy. The black guy looked at Fishnet.

Myron turned to the girl. "Do you have a preference?"

She shook her head no.

"Then I'll take him." Myron pointed to Fishnet. "He likes me. I can tell by the erect nipples."

The black guy said, "Hey, what's he doing here?"

Fishnet shot him a look.

"I mean, who is this guy?"

Myron nodded. "Nice recovery. Very smooth."

"What do you want, mister?" Fishnet asked.

"Actually, I was lying."

"What?"

"About how I knew you liked me. It wasn't just the erect nipples, though they were a noticeable—albeit nauseating—tip-off."

"What the fuck are you talking about?"

"Your following me around the past two days, that's what gave it away. Next time try the secret admirer route. Send flowers without signing for them. A nice Hallmark card. That kind of thing."

"Come on, Jim," Fishnet said to the black guy, "this guy's nuts. Let's get out of here."

The girl said, "No lap dance?"

"No. We gotta go."

"Someone's got to pay for this," the girl said. "Otherwise the manager's going to fry my ass."

"Get lost, whore. Or I'll whack you."

"Whoa, big man," Myron said.

"Look, mister, I don't got no beef with you. Just get out of my way."

"No lap dance for me either?"

"You're crazy."

"I can offer you a special discount," Myron said.

Fishnet's hands tightened into fists. He'd been ordered to follow Myron, not to be found out or get involved in a physical altercation. "Come on, Jim."

"Why have you been following me?" Myron asked.

"I don't know what you're talking about."

"Is it my hypnotic blue eyes? The strong features? The shapely derriere? By the way what do you think of these pants? They're not too tight, are they?"

"Fruitcake." They moved past him.

"Tell you what," Myron said. "You tell me who you're working for and I promise not to tell your boss."

They kept walking.

"Promise," Myron said.

They headed out the door. Another day, another friend. Myron had that knack.

Myron followed them out to the street. Fishnet and Jim hurried west.

Win appeared from the shadows across the street. "This way," he said.

They cut through an alley and arrived at the lot before Fishnet and Jim. It was an outdoor lot. The parking attendant was in a little booth watching a *Roseanne* rerun on a minuscule black-and-white TV. Win pointed out the Cadillac. They ducked behind an Oldsmobile parked two cars away and waited.

Fishnet and Jim approached the booth. They were still looking down the street. Jim was panicking. "How did he find us, Lee? Huh?"

"I don't know."

"What we gonna do?"

"Nothing. We'll change cars. Try again."

"You got another car, Lee?"

"No," Fishnet said. "We'll rent one."

They paid, got a receipt and their keys. Fishnet had insisted on parking the car himself.

"This," Win said, "should be fun."

When they arrived at the Cadillac, Fishnet put his key in the lock. He stopped, looked down, and began screaming.

"Shit! Goddamn fuck!"

Myron and Win stepped out of the shadows.

"Language, language," Myron said.

Fishnet stared down at his car in disbelief. Win had drilled a hole under the lock to break in. He didn't use that particular method when neatness counted, but this was an occasion when he thought it necessary. On top of that, Win's hand had "accidentally" slipped, scratching both driver's-side doors.

"You!" Fishnet shouted. He pointed at Myron, his face red and apoplectic. "You!"

Win turned to Myron. "Quite the vocabulary."

"Yeah, but it's the threads that really make me swoon."

"You!" Fishnet said. "You did this to my car?"

"Not him," Win said. "Me. And may I say you keep the inside lovely. I felt terrible about spilling that maple syrup all over the velour seats."

Fishnet's eyes popped. He looked inside, placed his hand on the inside, and screamed. The scream was deafening. It was so loud, the parking lot attendant almost stirred.

Myron looked at Win. "Maple syrup?"

"Log Cabin."

"I've always been an Aunt Jemima man myself," Myron said.

"To each his own."

"You find anything inside the car?"

"Not very much," Win said. "In the glove compartment were several parking stubs." He handed them to Myron. Myron took a quick glance.

"So," Myron called out, "who are you guys working for?"

Fishnet started walking over. "My car!" he shouted, his face red. "You . . . my car! My car!"

Win sighed. "Can we get past this, please? *Très* dull."

"You motherfucker! You . . ." Fishnet's hands were fists again. He stepped closer, smiling now at Win. It was an ugly smile in every way. "I'm going to break your fucking face, pretty boy."

Win looked at Myron. "Pretty boy?"

Myron shrugged.

Jim stood next to Fishnet. Neither one was armed with a gun, Myron could tell. They might have a blade hidden somewhere, but he wasn't worried.

Fishnet moved to within a yard of Win. Nothing unusual there. The bad guys always honed in on Win. He was smaller than Myron by nearly six inches and thirty-five pounds. Best of all, Win looked like a wimpy rich boy who raised his finger only to call for the butler—everything the discerning bully could want in a punching bag.

Fishnet took one more step and cocked his fist. Whoever had hired these guys had not briefed them well.

The punch whizzed toward Win's nose. He side-stepped it. Sometimes Myron thought Win moved like a cat. But that wasn't accurate. It was more ghostlike. One nanosecond he was there, the next he was two feet to the left. Fishnet tried again. Win blocked it this time. He grabbed Fishnet's fist with one hand and connected with a knife-hand strike to Fishnet's neck. Fishnet backed off, woozy. Jim stepped forward.

"Don't even think about it," Myron said.

Jim ran.

Myron Bolitar. The Intimidator.

Fishnet regained his footing. He charged Win, head lowered, attempting a tackle. Big mistake. Win hated it when an opponent tried to use superior size against him. Win had introduced Myron to tae kwon do during their freshman year at Duke, but he'd been studying it himself since he was five years old. He'd even spent three years in the Far East studying under some of the world's greatest masters.

"Aaaarrrrghhh!" Fishnet shouted.

Again Win stepped to the side, like the smoothest matador against the clumsiest bull. Win connected on a roundhouse kick to the solar plexus and followed up with a palm strike to the nose. There was a sharp crack and blood flowed. Fishnet screamed and went down. He did not get up again.

Win bent down. "Who are you working for?"

Fishnet looked at the blood in his hand. "You broke my nose!" His voice was nasally.

"Wrong answer," Win said. "Let me repeat the question. Who are you working for?"

"I ain't saying nothing!"

Win reached down, gripped the broken nose with two fingers. Fishnet's eyes bulged.

"Don't," Myron said.

Win looked up at him. "If you can't take it, leave." He turned his attention back to Fishnet. "Last chance. Then I start twisting. Who hired you?"

Fishnet said nothing. Win gave the nose a quick squeeze. The small bones grated against one another, making a sound like rain on a skylight. Fishnet bucked in agony. Win stifled his scream with his free hand.

"Enough," Myron said.

"He hasn't said anything yet."

"We're the good guys, remember?"

Win made a face. "You sound like an ACLU lawyer."

"He doesn't have to say anything."

"What?"

"He's a two-bit scum. He'd sell out his mother for a nickel."

"Meaning?"

"Meaning he's more terrified of opening his mouth than the pain."

Win smiled. "I can change him."

Myron held up one of the parking lot stubs. "This lot is at Fifty-fourth and Madison. It's under TruPro's building. Our pal here is working for the Ache brothers. They're the only ones who could put that kind of scare into a guy." Fishnet's face was pure white.

"Or Aaron," Win said.

Aaron.

"What about him?" Myron asked.

"The Aches could be using Aaron. He could put that kind of scare into a guy."

Aaron.

"He isn't working for Frank Ache anymore," Myron said. "At least, that's what I heard."

Win looked down at Fishnet. "The name Aaron mean anything to you?"

"No," he shouted. Quickly. Too quickly.

Myron lowered his head toward Fishnet. "Start talking or I'll tell Frank Ache you told us all about it."

"I didn't say nothing about no Frank Ache!"

"Triple negative," Win said. "Very impressive."

There were two Ache brothers. Herman and Frank.

Herman, the elder, was the boss, a sociopath responsible for countless murders and misery. But next to his whacked-out brother Frank, Herman Ache was Mary Poppins. Unfortunately, Frank ran TruPro.

"I didn't say nothing," Fishnet repeated. He was petting his nose like it was an abused dog. "Not a goddamn word."

"But how's Frank to know?" Myron asked. "You see, I'll tell Frank you sang like the tastiest of stool pigeons. And you know what? He'll believe me. How else would I know Frank hired you?"

Fishnet's face went from pale-white to a sort of seaweed-green.

"But if you cooperate," Myron said, "we'll all pretend this never happened. That I never spotted your tail. You'll be safe. Frank will never have to know about your little screwup."

Fishnet didn't have to think too long. "What do you want?"

"One of Ache's men hired you?"

"Yeah."

"Aaron?"

"No. Just some guy."

"What were you hired to do?"

"Follow you. Report wherever you went."

"For what reason?"

"I don't know."

"When did you get hired?"

"Yesterday afternoon."

"What time?"

"I don't remember. Two, three o'clock. I was told you were at the tennis match and to get over there right away."

That would have been almost immediately after Valerie's murder.

"That's all I know. I swear to God. That's it."

"Bull," Win said. But Myron waved him off. Fishnet knew nothing more of any real significance.

"Let him go," Myron said.

Chapter 13

Myron woke up early. He grabbed some cold cereal from the pantry. Something called Nutri-Grain. Yummy name. He read on the back of the box about the importance of fiber. Snore.

Myron longed for his childhood cereals: Cap'n Crunch, Froot Loops, Quisp. Quisp cereal. Who could forget Quisp, the cute alien who competed on TV commercials with some coal-miner loser named Quake? Quisp vs. Quake. Extraterrestrial vs. Mr. Blue-collar. Interesting concept. What happened to those two rivals? Has even lovable Quisp gone the way of the Motels?

Myron sighed. He was far too young for such bouts of nostalgia.

Esperanza had managed to track down an address for Curtis Yeller's mother. Deanna Yeller lived alone in a recently purchased house in Cherry Hill, New Jersey, a suburb outside Philadelphia. Myron made his way to his car. If he started out now, there would be time to drive to Cherry Hill, meet with Deanna Yeller, and get back to New York in time for Duane's match.

But would Deanna Yeller be home? Best to make sure.

Myron picked up the car phone and dialed. A woman's voice—probably Deanna Yeller—answered. "Hello?"

"Is Orson there?" Myron asked.

Warning: Clever deductive technique coming up. Those desiring professional pointers should pay strict attention.

"Who?" the woman asked.

"Orson."

"You have the wrong number."

"I'm sorry." Myron hung up.

Deduction: Deanna Yeller was home.

He pulled up to a modest but modern home on a classic New Jersey suburban street. Every house was more or less the same. Different colors maybe. The kitchen might be on the right instead of the left. But genetically they were clones. Nice. A sprinkling of kids on the street. A sprinkling of multicolored bicycles. Couple of squirrels. A far cry from west Philadelphia. It made him wonder.

Myron walked up the little brick walk and knocked on the door. A very attractive black woman answered, a pleasant smile at the ready. Her hair was tied back in a severe bun, emphasizing the high cheekbones. Age lines around the eyes and mouth, but nothing drastic. She was well dressed, kind of conservative. Anne Klein II. Her jewelry was noticeable but not too flashy. The overall impression: classy.

Her smile seemed to fade when she saw him. "Can I help you?"

"Mrs. Yeller?"

She nodded slowly, as though not sure.

"My name is Myron Bolitar. I'd like to ask you a few questions."

The smile fled completely. "What about?" Her diction was different now. Less suburban civil. More street suspicious.

"Your son."

"I ain't got a son."

"Curtis," Myron said.

Her eyes narrowed. "You a cop?"

"No."

"I ain't got the time. I'm on my way out."

"It won't take long."

She put her hands on her hips. "What's in it for me?"

"Pardon me?"

"Curtis is dead."

"I realize that."

"So what good is talking about it gonna do? He still gonna be dead, right?"

"Please, Mrs. Yeller, if I could just come in for a moment."

She thought about it a second or two, glanced around, then shrugged in tired surrender. She checked her watch. Piaget, Myron noticed. Could be a fake, but he doubted it.

The decor was basic. Lot of white. Lot of pinewood. Torchère lamps. Very Ikea. There were no photographs on the shelves or coffee table. Nothing personal at all. Deanna Yeller didn't sit. She didn't invite Myron to either.

Myron offered up his warmest, most trustworthy smile. One part Harry Smith, two parts John Tesh.

She crossed her arms. "What the hell you grinning at?"

Yep, another minute and she'd be curled up in his lap.

"I want to ask you about the night Curtis died," Myron said.

"Why? What's this got to do with you?"

"I'm investigating."

"Investigating what?"

"What really happened the night your son died."

"You a private eye?"

"No. Not really."

Silence.

"You got two minutes," she said. "That's it."

"According to the police your son drew a gun on a police officer."

"So they say."

"Did he?"

She shrugged. "Guess so."

"Did Curtis own a gun?"

Another shrug. "Guess he did."

"Did you see it that night?"

"I don't know."

"Did you ever see it before that night?"

"Maybe. I don't know."

Boy, was this helpful. "Why would your son and Errol break into the Old Oaks Club?"

She made a face. "You serious?"

"Yes."

"Why you think? To rob the place."

"Did Curtis do that a lot?"

"Do what?"

"Rob places."

Another shrug. "Places, people, whatever." Her tone was matter-of-fact. No shame, no embarrassment, no surprise, no revulsion.

"Curtis didn't have a record," Myron said.

Yet another shrug. Her shoulders would tire soon. "Guess I raised a smart boy," she said. "Until that night, anyhow." She made a show of looking at her watch again. "I gotta go now."

"Mrs. Yeller, have you heard from your nephew Errol Swade?"

"No."

"Do you know where he went after your son was shot?"

"No."

"What do you think happened to Errol?"

"He's dead." Again matter-of-fact. "I don't know what you want here, but this thing is finished. Finished a long time ago. No one cares anymore."

"How about you, Mrs. Yeller? Do you care?"

"It's done. Closed."

"You were there when the police shot your son?"

"No. I got there right after." Her voice sort of faded away.

"And you saw your son on the ground?"

She nodded.

Myron handed her his business card. "If you remember anything else . . ."

She didn't take it. "I won't."

"But if you do . . ."

"Curtis is dead. Nothing you can do can change that. Best to just forget it."

"It's that easy?"

"Been six years. Not like anybody misses Curtis."

"How about you, Mrs. Yeller? Do you miss him?"

She opened her mouth, closed it, opened it again. "Not like Curtis was a good kid or nothing. He was trouble."

"Doesn't mean he should have been killed," Myron said.

She looked up at him, held his gaze. "Don't matter. Dead is dead. Can't change that."

Myron said nothing.

"Can you change that, Mr. Bolitar?" she asked, challenging.

"No."

Deanna Yeller nodded, turned away, picked up her purse. "I have to go now," she said. "Best if you leave now too."

Chapter 14

Henry Hobman was the only one in the players' box.

"Hi, Henry," Myron said.

No one was playing yet, but Henry was still in his coach repose. Without turning away from the court, Henry muttered, "Heard you had a meeting with Pavel Menansi last night."

"So?"

"You unhappy with Duane's coaching?"

"No."

Henry almost nodded. End of conversation.

Duane and his opponent, a French Open finalist named Jacques Potiline, came onto the court. Duane looked himself. No signs of strain. He gave Myron and Henry a big smile, nodded. The weather was perfect for tennis. The sun was out, but a cool breeze gently purled through Stadium Court, staving off the humidity.

Myron glanced around courtside. There was a rather buxom blonde in the next box. She was packed into a white tank top. The word for today, boys and girls, is cleavage. Plenty of men ogled. Not Myron, of course. He was far too worldly. The blonde suddenly turned and caught Myron's eye. She smiled coyly, gave him a little wave. Myron waved back. He wasn't going to do anything about it, but yowzer!

Win materialized in the chair next to Myron. "She's smiling at me, you know."

"Dream on."

"Women find me irresistible," Win said. "They see me, they want me. It's a curse I live with every day of my life."

"Please," Myron said. "I just ate."

"Envy. It's so unattractive."

"So go for it, stud."

Win looked over at her. "Not my type."

"Gorgeous blondes aren't your type?"

"Her chest is too big. I have a new theory on that."

"What theory?"

"The bigger the breasts, the lousier the lay."

"Pardon me?"

"Think about it," Win said. "Well-endowed women—I am referring here to ones with mega-fronts— have a habit of laying back and relying on their, er, assets. The effort isn't always what it should be. What do you think?"

Myron shook his head. "I have several reactions," he replied, "but I think I'll stick with my initial one."

"Which is?"

"You're a pig."

Win smiled, sat back. "So how was your visit with Ms. Yeller?"

"She's hiding something too."

"Well, well. The plot doth thicken."

Myron nodded.

"In my experience," Win said, "there is only one thing that can silence the mother of a dead boy."

"And that is?"

"Cash. A great deal of it."

Mr. Warmth. But in truth the same thought had crossed Myron's mind. "Deanna Yeller lives in Cherry Hill now. In a house."

Win leapt on that one. "A single widow from the dumps of west Philadelphia moving to the 'burbs? Pray tell, how does she afford it?"

"Do you really think she's being bought?"

"Is there another explanation? According to what we know, the woman has no solid means of support. She spent her life in an impoverished area. Now all of a sudden she's Miss Better Homes and Gardens."

"Could be something else."

"For example?"

"A guy."

Win made a scoffing noise. "A forty-two-year-old ghetto woman does not find that kind of sugar daddy. It just doesn't happen."

Myron said nothing.

"Now," Win continued, "add into that equation Kenneth and Helen Van Slyke, the grieving parents of another dead child."

"What about them?"

"I've done a bit of checking. They too have no visible signs of support. Kenneth's family was already destitute when they married. As for Helen, whatever money she had Kenneth lost in his business ventures."

"You mean they're broke?"

"Completely," Win replied. "So pray tell, dear friend, how are they managing to carry on at Brentman Hall?"

Myron shook his head. "There has to be another explanation."

"Why?"

"One mother being bought off by her child's killer I *might* be able to buy. But two?"

Win said, "You have a rather rosy view of human nature."

"And you have a rather dim one."

"Which is why I'm usually correct in these matters," Win said.

Myron frowned. "What about TruPro's connection with this?"

"What about it?"

"Fishnet was hired to follow me immediately after the murder. Why?"

"The Ache brothers know you quite well by now. Perhaps they feared you'd investigate."

"So? What's their interest?"

Win thought a second. "Didn't TruPro used to represent Valerie?"

"But that was six years ago," Myron said. "Before the Ache brothers had even taken over the agency."

"Hmm. Perhaps you are barking up the wrong tree."

"What do you mean?" Myron asked.

"Perhaps there is no connection. TruPro is interested in signing Eddie Crane, correct?"

Myron nodded.

"And Eddie's mentor—this Pavel fellow—is closely associated with TruPro. Perhaps they feel you are moving in on their turf."

"Which the Ache brothers would not like," Myron added.

"Precisely."

A possibility. Myron tried it on and walked around a bit, but it just didn't feel right.

"Oh, one other thing," Win replied.

"What?"

"Aaron is in town."

Myron felt a quick chill. "What for?"

"I don't know."

"Probably just a coincidence," Myron said.

"Probably."

Silence.

Win sat back and steepled his fingers. The match began. Duane's play was nothing short of spectacular. He cruised through the first set 6–2. He stumbled a bit in the second, but came on to win it 7–5. Jacques Potiline had had enough. Duane whipped him in the final set 6–1.

Another impressive victory.

As the players left the court, Henry Hobman stood. His face remained locked on grim. He chewed at the inside of his mouth. "Better," he said tightly. "But not great."

"Stop gushing, Henry. It's embarrassing."

Ned Tunwell sprinted down the steps toward Myron. His arms were flapping like a kid making windmills in the snow. Several other Nike execs followed him. There were tears in Ned's eyes.

"I knew it!" Ned shouted in glee. He shook Myron's hand, hugged him, turned to Win, pumped his hand too. Win pulled his hand back and wiped it on his pants. "I just knew it!"

Myron simply nodded.

"Soon! So soon!" Ned cried. "The promo of the year begins! Everyone is going to know the name Duane Richwood! He was fantastic, utterly fantastic! I can't believe it. I swear, I don't think I've ever been this excited before!"

"You're not going to come again, are you, Ned?"

"Oh, Myron!" He nudged Win playfully with his elbow. "Is he a kidder or what?"

"A gifted comedian," Win agreed.

Ned slapped Win's shoulder. Win visibly winced but did not break the offending hand. Amazing restraint for Win.

"Look, guys," Ned said, "I'd love to stand here and chat all day. But I gotta run."

Win managed to hide his disappointment.

"Ciao for now. Myron, we'll talk, okay?"

Myron nodded.

"Bye, guys." Ned skipped—actually skipped—back up the stairs.

Win watched him depart with something approaching horror. "What," he asked, "was that?"

"A bad dream. I'll meet you back at the office."

"Where are you going?" Win asked.

"To talk to Duane. I have to ask him about Valerie's call."

"Let it go until after the tournament."

Myron shook his head. "Can't."

Chapter 15

Myron waited for the press conference to end. It took some time. Duane was holding court, firmly in his element. The media had a new darling. Duane Richwood. Cocky but not obnoxious. Confident yet gracious. Handsome. American.

When the hordes of press finally ran out of questions, Myron accompanied Duane back to the dressing room. He sat on a chair next to Duane's locker. Duane took off his sunglasses and put them on the top shelf.

"Some match, huh?" Duane said.

Myron nodded.

"Hey, this win oughta make Nike happy."

"Orgasmic," Myron agreed.

"They going to air the ad during my next match, right?"

"Yep."

Duane shook his head. "Quarterfinal, at the U.S. Open," he said in awe. "I can't believe it, Myron. We're on our way."

"Duane?"

"Yeah?"

"I know Valerie called you," Myron said.

Duane stopped. "What?"

"She called your apartment twice. From a pay phone near her hotel."

"I don't know what you're talking about."

Duane quickly reached for the sunglasses, fumbled them, put them on.

"I want to help you, Duane."

"Nothing to help with me."

"Duane . . ."

"Just leave me the fuck alone."

"I can't do that."

"Look, Myron, I don't need distractions right now. Just drop it."

"She's dead, Duane. That just won't go away."

Duane took off his shirt and began toweling off his chest. "Some stalker killed her," he said. "I saw it on the news. Got nothing to do with me."

"Why did she call you, Duane?"

His hands were clenching and unclenching. "You work for me, right?"

"Right."

"Then drop it or you're fired."

Myron looked at him. "No," he said.

Duane sunk into a chair, his head in his hands. "Shit, I'm sorry, Myron. I didn't mean that. It's just the pressure. What with this tournament and that Dimonte cop accusing me and all. Look, just forget I said anything, okay? Just forget this whole conversation happened."

"No."

"What?"

"Why did she call you, Duane?"

"Man, don't you listen?"

"Not well."

"Just stay out of it."

"No."

"It's got nothing to do with the murder."

"Then you admit she called you?"

Duane stood, turned his back toward Myron, leaned against his locker.

"Duane?"

His words were soft. "Yeah, she called me. So what?"

"Why?"

"Let's just say we were acquainted. Intimately, if you get my drift."

"You and Valerie . . . ?" Myron made futile hand gestures.

Duane nodded slowly. "It was no big thing. Just a few times."

"When did this start?"

"Couple of months ago."

"Where did you meet?"

He looked at Myron, confused. "At a tournament."

"Which one?"

"I don't remember. New Haven, I think. But it was over quick."

"So why did you lie to the police?"

"Why do you think?" he countered. "Wanda was standing right there. I love her, man. I made a mistake. I didn't want to hurt her. Is that so wrong?"

"So why wouldn't you tell me?"

"What?"

"When I asked you just now. Why didn't you tell me the truth?"

"Same reason."

"But Wanda isn't here."

"I was ashamed, okay?"

"Ashamed?"

"I'm not proud of what I did."

Myron watched him. With those sunglasses Duane's face looked sleek and robotic. But something wasn't right here. It was a nice sentiment, but twenty-one-year-old professional athletes, no matter how faithful to their partners, were not this ashamed of letting their agents know about an indiscretion. The excuse might be commendable, but it rang hollow. "If it was over, why was Valerie calling you?"

"I don't know. She wanted to see me again. One last fling, I guess."

"Did you agree to see her?"

"No. I told her we were finished."

"What else did you say?"

"Nothing."

"What else did she say?"

"Nothing."

"Are you sure? Do you remember anything at all?"

"No. Nothing."

"Did she seem distressed?"

"Not that I could tell."

The door opened. Players began to file in, many offering Duane icy congratulations. Rising stars were not big in the locker room. If someone new was joining the ultra-exclusive tennis club known as the "Top Ten," another member had to be thrown out. The way it was. No boardroom was this cutthroat. Everyone was a rival here. Everyone was competing for the same dollars and fame. Everyone was an enemy.

Duane suddenly looked very much alone.

"You hungry?" Myron asked.

"Starved," Duane said.

"You want anything in particular?"

"Pizza," Duane said. "Extra cheese and pepperoni."

"Get dressed. I'll meet you out front."

Chapter 16

"Myron Bolitar?"

The car phone. He'd just dropped Duane off at his apartment.

"Yes."

"This is Gerard Courter with the NYPD. Jake's son."

"Oh, right. How's it going, Gerard?"

"Can't complain. I doubt you remember but we played against each other once."

"Michigan State," Myron said. "I remember. And I have the bruises to prove it."

Gerard laughed. Sounded just like his old man. "Glad I was memorable."

"That's a polite word for what you were."

Another Jake-like guffaw. "My dad said you needed info on the Simpson homicide."

"I'd appreciate it."

"You probably heard there's a major suspect. Guy named Roger Quincy."

"The stalker."

"Yeah."

"Is there anything specific tying him to the murder?" Myron asked. "Besides the stalking?"

"He's on the run, for one thing. When they got to Quincy's apartment he was packed and gone. No one knows where he is."

"He might have just been scared," Myron said.

"Good reason to be."

"Why do you say that?"

"Roger Quincy was at the tennis center on the day of the murder."

"You have witnesses?"

"Several."

That slowed Myron down. "What else?"

* "She was shot with a thirty-eight. Very close range. We found the weapon in a garbage can ten yards away from the shooting. Smith & Wesson. It was in a Feron's bag. The bag had a bullet hole in it."

Feron's. Another tournament sponsor. They were licensed to sell "official tournament merchandise." Feron's had at least half a dozen stands selling to a zillion people. No way to trace it back. "So the killer walked up to her," Myron said, "shot her through the bag, kept walking, dumped the gun in the garbage, and headed out."

"That's how we see it," Gerard said.

"A cool customer."

"Very."

"Any prints on the gun?" Myron asked.

"Nope."

"Any witnesses to the shooting?"

"Several hundred. Unfortunately all anyone remembers is the sound of the gun, and Valerie toppling over."

Myron shook his head. "The killer took a hell of a chance. Shooting her in public like that."

"Yeah. A major case of brass balls."

"You got anything else?"

"Just a question," Gerard said.

"Shoot."

"Where are our seats for next Saturday?"

Chapter 17

Esperanza had neatly stacked two piles of six-year-old press clippings on Myron's desk. The pile on the right—the taller pile—was made up of articles on the murder of Alexander Cross. The smaller stack was on the hospitalization of Valerie Simpson.

Myron ignored the third stack—the one with his messages—and started sifting through the pile on Valerie. The story was already familiar to him. Valerie's family had claimed she was "taking time off," but a well-placed source leaked the truth to the press: the teen tennis star was actually a patient at the famed Dilworth Mental Health Facility. The family denied it for a few days—until a photograph of Valerie taking a walk on the Dilworth grounds appeared in the papers. A belated statement from the family claimed that Valerie was "resting from exhaustion caused by external pressures," whatever that meant.

The media coverage was only mildly intense. Valerie was already a has-been in the tennis world, ergo the press was interested but not ravenous. Still, rumors surfaced, especially in some of the fringe periodicals. One said that Valerie's breakdown had been the result of a sexual assault. Another said she'd been attacked by a stalker. Still another claimed Valerie had murdered someone in cold blood, though the article didn't bother the reader with mundane details—like the victim's name, how he or she was killed, why the police hadn't arrested Valerie, the little things.

But the most interesting rumor, the one that really snared Myron's attention, appeared in two separate papers. According to several "unnamed sources," Valerie Simpson had gone into hiding to cover up a pregnancy.

Might be something, might be nothing. Pregnancy rumors always surface when a young woman goes into hiding. Still . . .

He moved on to articles on Alexander Cross's murder. Esperanza had limited her search to Philadelphia area periodicals, but the material was still immense. The stories basically followed the police version. Alexander Cross had been at a party at his snooty tennis club. He stumbled across two burglars, Errol Swade and Curtis Yeller. He took chase, confronted them on the main grass court, and was stabbed by Errol Swade. The blade punctured Alexander's heart. Death was instantaneous.

Senator Cross and his family had not commented on the case. According to the senator's spokesman, the family was "in seclusion" and was "relying on law enforcement agencies and the justice system," whatever that meant.

The press focused on the manhunt for Errol Swade. The police were confident to the point of cocky that Swade would be captured within a matter of hours. But hours turned to days. Editorials harshly criticized the police for not being able to nab one nineteen-year-old drug addict, but the Cross family remained silent. The story provoked the standard public outrage—why, editorials demanded to know, had a lowlife like Errol Swade been let out on parole in the first place?

But the anger fizzled, as it always does in such cases.

Other stories began to take precedence. The coverage
trickled from front page to back page to oblivion.

Myron checked through the pile again. The police
shooting of Curtis Yeller had been neatly glossed over.
There was no mention of an internal affairs investigation
into the incident. None of the usual reactionaries protested the police "brutality," which was strange. Usually some whacko managed to get himself on television,
no matter what the facts, especially in the case of a black
teen being gunned down by a white cop. But not this
time. Or at least it wasn't covered by the press.

Wait. Hold the phone.

An article on Curtis Yeller. Myron had missed it the
first time because it'd been printed the day immediately
following the murder. Very early for this kind of piece.
Probably sneaked in before Senator Cross put his foot
down—but that might just be conspiracy paranoia on
Myron's part. Hard to tell.

It was a small article on the bottom corner of page
12 in the metro section. Myron read it twice. Then a
third time. The article was not on the shooting in west
Philly or even the police's role in said shooting. The
article was on Curtis Yeller himself.

It started out like any puff piece: Curtis Yeller was
described as an "honor roll student." Not a big deal
really. A psychotic child molester with the IQ of a citrus
beverage was suddenly dubbed an honor student when
killed prematurely. Very *Bonfire of the Vanities*. But this
story went a bit further. Mrs. Lucinda Elright, Curtis
Yeller's history teacher, described Curtis as her "best
pupil" and a boy who "had never even gotten a detention." Mr. Bernard Johnson, his English teacher, said
Curtis was "unusually bright and inquisitive," "one in
a million," and "like a son to me."

The usual death hyperbole?

Perhaps. But school records backed the teachers up. Curtis had never been on report. He also had the best attendance record in his grade. On top of that, his transcript reported a 3.9 average, his sole B coming in some sort of health class. Both teachers firmly believed that Curtis Yeller was incapable of violence. Mrs. Elright blamed Curtis's cousin Errol Swade, but no specifics were given.

Myron sat back. He stared at a movie still from *Casablanca* on the far wall. Sam was serenading Bogie and Bergman as the Nazis moved in. Here's looking at you, kid. We'll always have Paris. You're getting on that plane. Myron wondered if young Curtis Yeller had ever seen the movie, if he had had the opportunity to behold the celluloid image of Ingrid Bergman with tears in her eyes at a foggy airport.

He picked up the basketball from behind his desk and began spinning it on his finger. He slapped it at just the right angle to increase the speed rotation without dislodging the ball from its axis. He stared at his handiwork as though it were a Gypsy's crystal ball. He saw an alternate universe, one with a younger version of himself hitting a three-pointer at the buzzer on the Boston Garden's parquet floor. He tried not to let himself dwell on this image too long, but there it stayed, front and center, refusing to leave.

Esperanza came in. She sat down and waited in silence.

The ball stopped spinning. Myron put it down and handed her the article. "Take a look at this."

She read it. "A couple of teachers said something nice about a dead kid. So what? Probably misquoted anyway."

"But this is more than just a couple of casual comments. Curtis Yeller had no police record, no school record, a nearly perfect attendance record, and a 3.9 GPA. For most kids that's a hell of a statement. But this was a kid from one of the worst parts of Philadelphia."

Esperanza shrugged. "I don't see the relevance. What difference does it make if Yeller was Einstein or an idiot?"

"None. Except it's just one more thing that doesn't add up. Why did Curtis's mother say he was a no-good thief?"

"Maybe she knew more than his teachers."

Myron shook his head. He thought about Deanna Yeller. The proud, beautiful woman who answered the door. The suddenly hostile, defensive woman at the mention of her dead son. "She was lying."

"Why?"

"I don't know. Win thinks she's being bought off."

"Sounds like a good possibility," Esperanza said.

"What, a mother taking bribes to protect her son's murderer?"

Esperanza shrugged again. "Sure, why not?"

"You really think a mother . . . ?" Myron stopped. Esperanza's face was totally impassive—another one who always believed the worst. "Just look at this whole scenario for a second," he tried. "Curtis Yeller and Errol Swade break into this ritzy tennis club at night. Why? To rob the place? Of what? It was night. It wasn't like they were going to find wallets in the locker room. So what were they going to steal? Some tennis sneakers? A couple of rackets? That's a hell of a long way to go for some tennis equipment."

"Stereo equipment, maybe," Esperanza said. "The clubhouse could have a big-screen TV."

"Fine. Assume you're right. Problem is, the boys didn't take a car. They took public transportation and walked. How were they going to carry the loot? By hand?"

"Maybe they planned on stealing one."

"From the club's valet lot?"

She shrugged. "Could be," she said. Then: "Mind if I change subjects for a second?"

"Go ahead."

"How did it go with Eddie Crane last night?"

"He's a big fan of Little Pocahontas. He said she was 'hot.'"

"Hot?"

"Yup."

She shrugged. "Kid's got taste."

"Nice too. I liked him. He's smart, got his head on straight. Helluva good kid."

"You going to adopt him?"

"Uh, no."

"How about represent him?"

"They said they'll be in touch."

"What do you think?"

"Hard to say. The kid liked me. The parents are worried about me being small-time." Pause. "How did it go with Burger City?"

She handed him some papers. "Prelim contract for Phil Sorenson."

"TV commercial?"

"Yeah, but he has to dress up as a burger condiment."

"Which one?"

"Ketchup, I think. We're still talking."

"Fine. Just don't let it be mayonnaise or pickle." He studied the contract. "Nice work. Good figures."

Esperanza looked at him.

"Very good, in fact." He smiled at her. Widely.

"Is this the part where I get all excited by your praise?" she asked.

"Forget I said anything."

She pointed to the stack of articles. "I managed to track down Valerie's shrink from her days at Dilworth. Her name is Julie Abramson. She has a private office on Seventy-third Street. She won't see you, of course. Refuses to discuss her patient."

"A woman doctor," Myron mused. He put his hands behind his head. "Maybe I can entice her with my rapier wit and brawny body."

"Probably," Esperanza said, "but on the off chance she's not comatose, I went with an alternative plan."

"And that is?"

"I called her office back, changed my voice, and pretended you were a patient. I made an appointment for you to see her tomorrow morning. Nine o'clock."

"What's my psychosis?"

"Chronic priapism," she said. "But that's just my opinion."

"Funny."

"Actually, you've been much better since what's-her-name left town."

What's-her-name was Jessica, which Esperanza knew very well. Esperanza did not care much for the love of Myron's life. A casual observer might offer up jealousy as the culprit, but that'd be way off base. True, Esperanza was extraordinarily beautiful. Sure, there'd been moments of temptation between them, but one or the other had always been prudent enough to douse the flames before any real damage was done. There was also the fact that Esperanza liked a bit of diversity when it came to beaus—diversity that went well beyond tall or short, fat or thin, white or black. Right now, for example, Esperanza was dating a photographer. The photographer's name was Lucy. Lucy. As in a female, for those having trouble catching the drift.

No, the reason for her strong dislike was far simpler: Esperanza had been there when Jessica left the first time. She had seen it all firsthand. And Esperanza held grudges.

Myron returned to his original question. "So what did you tell them was wrong with me?"

"I was vague," she said. "You hear voices. You suffer from paranoid schizophrenia, delusions, hallucinations, something like that."

"How did you get an appointment so fast?"

"You're a very famous movie star."

"My name?"

"I didn't dare give one," Esperanza said. "You're that big."

Chapter 18

Dr. Julie Abramson's office was on the corner of Seventy-third Street and Central Park West. Ritzy address. One block north, overlooking the park, was the San Remo building. Dustin Hoffman and Diane Keaton lived there. Madonna had tried to move in, but the board decided she was not San Remo material. Win lived a block south, in the Dakota, where John Lennon had lived and literally died. Whenever you entered the Dakota's courtyard you crossed over the spot where Lennon had been gunned down. Myron had walked it a hundred times since the shooting, but he still felt the need to be silent when he did.

There was an ornate, wrought-iron gate on Dr. Abramson's door. Protective or decorative? Myron couldn't decide, but he saw some irony in a psychiatric office being guarded by a "wrought" iron gate.

Okay, not much irony but a little.

Myron pressed a doorbell. He heard the buzzer and let himself in. He was wearing his best pair of sunglasses for the occasion, even though it was cloudy outside. Mr. Movie Star.

The receptionist, a neatly attired man wearing fashionable spectacles, folded his hands and said, "Good morning," in a supposedly soothing voice that grated like a tortured cat's screech.

"I'm here to see Dr. Abramson. I have a nine o'clock appointment."

"I see." He perked up now, studying Myron's face, trying to guess who the big movie star was. Myron adjusted his sunglasses but kept them on. The receptionist wanted to ask for a name, but discretion got the better of him. Afraid of insulting the big-time celebrity.

"Could you fill out this form while you're waiting?" Myron tried to look annoyed by the inconvenience.

"It's just a formality," the receptionist said. "I'm sure you understand how these things are."

Myron sighed. "Very well then."

After it was filled out the receptionist asked for it back.

"I'd rather give it directly to Dr. Abramson," Myron said.

"Sir, I assure you—"

"Perhaps I didn't make myself clear." Mr. Difficult. Just like a real movie star. "I will give it to Dr. Abramson personally."

The receptionist sulked in silence. Several minutes later the intercom buzzed. The receptionist picked up the phone, listened for a second, hung up. "Right this way please."

Dr. Abramson was tiny—four-ten, tops, and seventy pounds soaking wet. Everything about her looked shrunken, scrunched up. Except for her eyes. They peered out of the diminutive face like two big, radiant, warm beacons that missed nothing.

She placed her child-size hand in his. Her handshake was surprisingly firm. "Please have a seat," she said.

Myron did. Dr. Abramson sat across from him. Her feet barely reached the ground. "May I have your sheet?" she asked.

"Of course." Myron handed it to her. She glanced down for a brief second.

"You're Bruce Willis?"

Myron gave her a cocky side smirk. Very *Die Hard*. "Didn't recognize me with the sunglasses, huh?"

"You look nothing like Bruce Willis."

"I would have put Harrison Ford, but he's too old."

"Still would have been a better choice." Then studying him a bit more she added, "Liam Neeson would have been better still." Dr. Abramson did not seem particularly upset by Myron's stunt. Then again, she was a trained psychiatrist and thus used to dealing with abnormal minds. "Why don't you tell me your real name."

"Myron Bolitar."

The little face broke open in a smile nearly as radiant as the eyes. "I thought I recognized you. You're the basketball star."

"I wouldn't say 'star' exactly." Blush, blush.

"Please, Mr. Bolitar, don't be so modest. First team all-American three years in a row. Two NCAA championships. One College Player of the Year. Eighth pick overall in the draft."

"You're a fan?"

"And so observant." She leaned back. Like a small child in a big rocking chair. "As I recall, you made the cover of *Sports Illustrated* twice. Unusual for a college player. You were also a good student, an academic all-American, popular with the press, and considered quite handsome. Am I correct?"

"Yes," Myron said. "Except maybe for that 'considered' part."

She laughed. It was a nice laugh. Her whole body seemed to join in. "Now why don't you tell me what this is all about, Mr. Bolitar."

"Please call me Myron."

"Fine. And you can call me Dr. Abramson. Now what seems to be the problem?"

"No, I'm fine."

"I see." She looked skeptical, but Myron sensed that the good doctor was having a little fun at his expense. "So you have a 'friend' with a problem. Tell me all about it."

"My friend," he said, "is Valerie Simpson."

That got her attention. "What?"

"I want to talk to you about Valerie Simpson."

The open face slammed shut. "You're not a reporter, are you?"

"No."

"I thought I read you were a sports agent."

"I am. Valerie Simpson was about to become a client."

"I see."

"When was the last time you saw Valerie?" Myron asked.

Dr. Abramson shook her head. "I can neither confirm nor deny that Valerie Simpson was ever a patient of mine."

"You don't have to confirm or deny it. I know she was."

"I repeat: I can neither confirm nor deny that Valerie Simpson was ever a patient of mine." She studied him for a moment. "Perhaps you can tell me what your interest is in this."

"Like I said before, I was going to represent her."

"That doesn't explain your visiting me incognito."

"I'm investigating her murder."

"Investigating?"

Myron nodded.

"Who hired you?"

"No one."

"Then why are you investigating?"

"I have my reasons."

She nodded. "What are those reasons, Myron? I'd like to hear about them."

Psychiatrists. "You want me to also tell you about the time I walked in on Mommy and Daddy?"

"If you want."

"I don't want. What I want is to know what caused Valerie's breakdown."

Her response was rote. "I can neither confirm nor deny that Valerie Simpson was ever a patient of mine."

"Doctor-patient privilege?"

"That's right."

"But Valerie is dead."

"That doesn't alter my obligation in the slightest."

"She's been murdered. Gunned down in cold blood."

"I understand that. Dramatics will not alter my obligation either."

"But you may know something helpful."

"Helpful in what way?"

"In finding the killer."

She folded the tiny hands in her lap. Like a little girl in church. "And that's what you're attempting to do? Find this woman's killer?"

"Yes."

"What about the police? I understood from news reports that they have a suspect."

"I don't trust authority types," Myron said.

"Oh?"

"It's one of the reasons I want to help."

Dr. Abramson fixed him with the big eyes. "I don't think so, Myron."

"No?"

"You look more like the rescue-complex sort to me. The kind of man who likes to play hero all the time, who sees himself as a knight in shining armor. What do you think?"

"I think we should save my analysis for later."

She shrugged her little shoulders. "Just giving my opinion. No extra charge."

"Fine." *Extra* charge? "I'm not so sure the police have the right man."

"Why not?"

"I was hoping you could help me with that. Valerie must have talked about Roger Quincy's stalking her. Did she think he was dangerous?"

"For the final time, I will neither confirm nor deny—"

"I'm not asking you to. I'm asking about Roger Quincy. You don't have a relationship with him, do you?"

"I also don't know him."

"Then how about one of those quick opinions. Like you did with me."

She shook her head. "I'm sorry."

"There's no way I can convince you to talk to me?"

"About a possible patient? No."

"Suppose I got parental consent."

"You won't."

Myron waited, watched. She was better at this than him. Her face gave away nothing, but the words couldn't be taken back. "How do you know that?" he asked.

She remained silent. Her eyes dropped to the floor. Myron wondered if the faux pas had been on purpose.

"They called you already, didn't they?" Myron said.

"I'm not at liberty to discuss any communications between myself and—"

"The family called. They hushed you up."

"I will neither confirm—"

"The body is barely cold and they're already covering their tracks," Myron went on. "You don't see anything wrong with that?"

Dr. Abramson cleared her throat. "I do not know what you're talking about it, but I will say this: it is not unreasonable in situations such as the one you've described to me for parents to want to protect their daughter's memory."

"Protect her memory"—Myron rose, put on his best lawyer-in-summation glower—"or her murderer?" Mr. High Drama.

"Now you're being silly," she said. "You surely don't suspect the young woman's family."

Myron sat back down. He gave his best anything's-possible head tilt. "Helen Van Slyke's daughter is killed. Within hours the grieving mother calls you to make sure you keep your mouth shut. You don't find that a tad odd?"

"I will neither confirm nor deny that I have ever heard the name Helen Van Slyke."

"I see," Myron said. "So you think this should all be shoved aside. Bottled up. Let the image rule over the reality. Somehow I don't think that sits well with you, Doc."

She said nothing.

"Your patient is dead," Myron continued. "Don't you think your obligation should be to her, not her mother?"

Dr. Abramson's hands tightened into small balls for

a moment, then relaxed. She took a deep breath, held it, let out it slowly. "Let us pretend—and just pretend—that I was the psychiatrist for this young woman. Wouldn't I have an obligation not to betray what she told me in the strictest of confidences? If the patient chose not to reveal any of this while alive, wouldn't I have an obligation to uphold that right for her in death?"

Myron stared at her. Dr. Abramson stared back. Unyielding. "Nice speech," he said. "But maybe Valerie wanted to reveal something. And maybe someone killed her to deny her that right."

The bright eyes blinked several times. "I think you should leave now," she said.

She pressed a button on her intercom. The receptionist appeared at the door. He crossed his arms and tried to look intimidating. The attempt was hardly a rousing success.

Myron rose. He knew he had planted a seed. He would have to give it time to germinate. "Will you at least think about it?" he added.

"Good-bye, Myron."

The receptionist stepped aside, allowing Myron room to pass.

Chapter 19

Of the three witnesses to the murder of Alexander Cross—all college chums of the deceased—only one lived in the New York area. Gregory Caufield, Jr., was now a young associate at daddy's law firm of Stillen, Caufield, and Weston, a high-powered, high-profile firm with offices in several states and foreign countries.

Myron dialed, asked for Gregory Caufield, Jr., and was put on hold. A woman came on the line several seconds later and said, "I'll put you straight through to Mr. Caufield."

A click. One ring. Then an enthusiastic voice said, "Well, hi!"

Well, hi?

"Is this Gregory Caufield?"

"Sure is. What can I do for you today?"

"My name is Myron Bolitar."

"Uh-huh."

"And I'd like to make an appointment to see you."

"Sure. When?"

"As soon as possible."

"How about half an hour from now? Will that be okay?"

"That'll be fine, thank you."

"Super, Myron. Looking forward to it."

Click. *Super?*

Fifteen minutes later Myron was on his way. He

walked up Park Avenue past the mosque steps where Myron and Win liked to lunch on summer days. Prime woman-watching perch. New York has the most beautiful women in the world, bar none. They wear business attire and sneakers and sunglasses. They walk with cool purpose, with no time to waste. Amazingly, none of the beautiful women checked Myron out. Probably just being discreet. Probably ogling him like crazy from behind those sunglasses.

Myron cut west to Madison Avenue. He passed a couple of electronics stores with the same GOING OUT OF BUSINESS signs they'd had up for at least a year. The sign was always the same—white sign, black letters. A blind man held out a cup. Didn't even give out pencils anymore. His seeing-eye dog looked dead. Two cops were laughing on the corner. They were eating croissants. Not doughnuts. Another cliché blown to hell.

There was a security guard by the elevator in the lobby.

"Yes?"

"Myron Bolitar to see Gregory Caufield."

"Oh yes, Mr. Bolitar. Twenty-second floor." Didn't call up. Didn't check his list. Hmm.

When the elevator opened, a pleasant-faced woman was standing there. "Good afternoon, Mr. Bolitar. If you'd please follow me."

Down a long corridor with an office-pink carpet, white walls, McKnight framed posters. No typewriters clicked, but Myron heard the whir of a laser printer. Someone was dialing a number on a speakerphone. A fax machine screeched its call to another fax machine. When they turned the corner, a second, equally pleasant-faced, woman approached. Plastic smiles all around.

"Hello, Mr. Bolitar," the second woman said. "Nice to see you today."

"Nice to see you too." Every line a lady-slayer.

The first woman handed him over to the second. Tag-team style. "Mr. Caufield is waiting for you in conference room C," the second woman said, her voice low, as if conference room C were a clandestine chamber in the bowels of the Pentagon.

She led him to a door very much like any other except it had a big bronze *C* on it. In a matter of seconds, Myron managed to deduce that the room was conference room C. The Adventures of Sherlock Bolitar. A man opened the door from the inside. He was young with a thick head of Stephanopoulos-like hair. He pumped Myron's hand enthusiastically. "Hi, Myron."

"Hi, Gregory." Like they actually knew each other.

"Please come in. There's someone here I'd like you to meet."

Myron stepped fully into the room. Big walnut table with dark leather chairs, the expensive kind, the kind with those little gold buttons on them. Oil portraits of stern-faced men on the walls. The room was empty, except for one man down the other end of the table. Though they had never met, Myron recognized the man immediately. He should have been surprised, but he wasn't.

Senator Bradley Cross.

Gregory did not bother with introductions. In fact he didn't bother staying. He slipped out the door, closing it behind him. The senator stood. His were a far cry from the classic patrician good looks one usually associates with political families. They say people look like their pets; in that case Senator Bradley Cross owned a basset hound. His features were long and malleable. His finely tailored suit did nothing to disguise his exaggerated pear build; on a woman, his hips would be called child-bearing. His hair was wispy gray strands that seemed to be suffering from static cling. He wore thick glasses and an off-center smile. Still, it was an endearing smile—indeed, an endearing, trustworthy face. The kind of face you'd vote for.

Senator Cross slowly put out his hand. "I'm sorry for the dramatics," he said, "but I thought we should meet."

They shook hands.

"Please have a seat. Make yourself comfortable. Can I get you something?"

"No, thank you," Myron said.

They sat facing each other. Myron waited. The senator seemed unsure how to begin. He coughed into his fists several times. Each cough made his jowls flap a bit.

"Do you know why I wanted to see you?" he asked.

"No," Myron said.

"I understand you've been asking a lot of questions about my son. More specifically, about his murder."

"Where did you hear that?"

"Around. Here and there. I am not without my sources." He tilted his head the way a basset hound does when he hears a strange sound. "I'd like to know why."

"Valerie Simpson was going to be a client of mine," Myron said.

"So I've been told."

"I'm looking into her murder."

"And you believe there might be a connection between Valerie's murder and Alexander's?"

Myron shrugged.

"My son was killed by a random street thug six years ago near Philadelphia. Valerie was killed almost gangland style at the U.S. Open in New York. What possible connection could there be?"

"Maybe none."

Cross leaned back, fiddled his thumbs. "I want to be up-front with you, Myron. I've looked into your background a bit. I know about your past work. Not the details, of course, but your reputation. I'm not trying to apply any influence here. It's not my style. I've never been comfortable at playing the tough guy." He smiled again. His eyes were wet now and there was a discernible quake in his voice. "I'm talking to you now not as a United States senator but as a grieving father. A grieving father who just wants to let his son rest in peace. I'm asking you to please stop what you're doing."

The pain in the man's voice was raw. Myron had not expected this. "I'm not sure I can, Senator."

The senator rubbed his entire face vigorously, using both hands. "You see two young people . . ." he began tiredly. "You see two young people with the whole world in front of them. Practically engaged to one another. And what happens to them? They're murdered in two separate incidents six years apart. The cruel coincidence is too much to fathom. You wonder about that, don't you, Myron?"

Myron nodded.

"So you begin to scrutinize their deaths. You look for something that might explain such a bizarre double tragedy. And in your search you find inconsistencies. You see pieces that just don't add up."

"Yes."

"And those inconsistencies lead you to believe that there is a connection between Alexander's murder and Valerie's."

"Maybe."

Cross glanced up at the ceiling and rested his index finger on his lip. "Will you take my word that those inconsistencies have nothing to do with Valerie Simpson?"

"No," Myron said. "I can't."

Senator Cross nodded, more to himself than Myron. "I didn't suspect you would," he said. "You don't have children, do you, Myron?"

"No."

"It doesn't matter. Even people who have children don't understand. They can't. What happened . . . it's not just the pain. The death is all-consuming. It never lets you go, never gives you a chance to catch your breath. My wife still has to be medicated almost daily. It's like someone scooped out everything inside of her and left behind only a pitiful shell. You can't imagine what it's like to see her like that."

"I don't mean to hurt anyone, Senator."

"But you won't stop either. And no matter how careful you are, someone is bound to get wind of your investigation, just as I did."

"I'll try to be discreet."

"You know that's impossible."

"I can't back away now. I'm sorry."

The senator gave himself the face massage again. He sighed deeply and said, "You leave me no choice. I'll have to tell you what happened. Maybe then you'll let it go."

Myron waited.

"You are an attorney, are you not?"

"Yes," Myron said.

"You're a member of the New York bar?"

"Yes."

Bradley Cross reached into his suit pocket. Sallow

skin hung off his face in uneven clumps. He took out a checkbook. "I'd like to hire you as my attorney," he said. "Will a five-thousand-dollar retainer be enough?"

"I don't understand."

"As my attorney, what I'm about to tell you falls under the jurisdiction of attorney-client privilege. You will not be allowed, even in a court of law, to repeat what I am about to tell you."

"You don't need to hire me for that."

"I'd prefer it."

"Fine. Make it a hundred dollars."

Bradley Cross wrote out the check and handed it to Myron.

"My son was on drugs," he said without preamble. "Cocaine mostly. Heroin too, but he'd only just started on it. I knew he was on something, but frankly I didn't think it was serious. I saw him high. I saw the red eyes. But I thought it was just marijuana. Hell, I've tried marijuana. Inhaled even."

Weak smile. Myron returned it, equally weak.

"Alexander and his friends weren't taking a casual stroll around the club grounds that night," he said. "They were going to get high. Alexander was found with a syringe in his pocket. There was cocaine found in the bushes not far from where the murder took place. And, of course, there were traces of both heroin and cocaine in Alexander's body. Not just in his fluids but in his tissue. I'm told that shows he'd been using for a while."

"I thought there was no autopsy," Myron said.

"It was kept secret. Nothing was reported or filed. It didn't matter anyway. A knife wound ended Alexander's life, not drugs. The fact that my son was taking illegal substances was irrelevant."

Maybe, Myron thought, keeping his expression blank.

Cross stared off for a while. After some time had passed he asked, "Where was I?"

"They left the party to get high."

"Right, thank you." He cleared his throat, sat up a little straighter. "The rest of the story is fairly straightforward. The boys stumbled upon Errol Swade and Curtis Yeller on one of the grass courts. The papers talked about how brave Alexander was, how he tried to thwart the evil-doers without concern for his own safety. My spin doctors at their best. But the truth is, he was flying so high he acted irrationally. He swooped in like some kind of superhero. The Yeller boy—the one the police shot—dropped everything and ran. But Errol Swade was a cooler customer. He took out a switchblade and punctured my boy's heart like a balloon. Casually, they say. Nonchalant."

Senator Cross stopped. Myron waited for him to continue. When it was clear he had reached the end of his saga, Myron asked, "Why were they at the club?"

"Who?"

"Swade and Yeller."

Senator Cross looked puzzled. "They were thieves."

"How do you know that?"

"What else would they have been doing here?"

Myron shrugged. "Selling drugs to your son. Dealing. It sounds a lot more plausible than a late-night robbery of a tennis club."

Cross shook his head. "They were carrying items. Tennis rackets. Tennis balls."

"According to whom?"

"According to Gregory and the others. The items were also found at the scene."

"Tennis rackets and balls?"

"There may have been other things, I don't remember."

"That's what they were after?" Myron said. "Some tennis gear?"

"The police believe that my son interrupted them before the robbery was complete."

"But your son stumbled across them *outside*. If they'd already stolen some gear, then they'd already been inside."

"So what are you suggesting?" the senator asked sharply. "That my son was murdered in a drug deal gone bad?"

"I'm just trying to see what sounds most plausible."

"Would a drug deal murder make a connection with Valerie more likely?"

"No."

"So what's your point?"

"No point. Just trying out different theories. What happened next? Directly after the murder?"

He looked off again, this time in the general direction of one of the portraits, but Myron didn't think he was actually seeing it. "Gregory and the other boys came running back into the party," he said in a hollow voice. "I followed them outside. Blood was bubbling out of Alexander's mouth. By the time I reached him he was dead."

Silence.

"You can pretty much figure out the rest. Everything switched over to autopilot. I really didn't do much. Aides did. Gregory's father—he's a senior partner here— helped too. I just stood and nodded numbly. I won't lie to you. I won't tell you I didn't know what was going on. I did. Old habits die hard, Myron. There is no creature more selfish than a politician. We so easily justify our selfishness as the 'common good.' So the cover-up was done.''

''And if the truth came out now?''

He smiled. ''I'd be destroyed. But I'm not really afraid of that anymore. Or maybe that's a lie too, who knows anymore?'' He threw up his hands, lowered them. ''But my wife never learned the truth. I don't know what it would do to her, I really don't. Alexander was a good kid, Mr. Bolitar. I don't want his memory ripped to shreds. In the end drugs do not make Errol Swade and Curtis Yeller any less culpable or my son any more guilty. He didn't ask to be stabbed.''

Myron waited a beat. Then the left-field question: ''What about Deanna Yeller?''

Puzzled. ''Who?''

''Curtis Yeller's mother.''

''What about her?''

''You have no relationship with her?''

More puzzled. ''Of course not. Why would you ask something like that?''

''You never paid to keep her silent?''

''About what?''

''About the circumstances of her son's death.''

''No. Why should I?''

''You know there was never an autopsy done on Curtis Yeller either. Strange, don't you think?''

''If you're insinuating that the police did not act strictly within regulations, I can't answer that because I don't know. I don't care either. Yes, I've wondered about the police shooting myself. Perhaps there was a second cover-up that night. If there was, I was not involved in it. And more important, I don't see what possible connection it could have with Valerie Simpson. In fact I don't see any connection in any of this with Valerie.''

"She was at the party that night?''

"Valerie? Of course.''

"Do you know where she was at the time Alexander was murdered?''

"No.''

"Do you remember how she reacted to his death?''

"She was devastated. Her fiancé had just been killed in cold blood. She was distraught and angry.''

"Did you approve of their relationship?''

"Yes, very much so. I thought Valerie was a bit troubled. A bit too sad. But I liked her. She and Alexander were good together.''

"Valerie's name was never mentioned in connection with your son's murder. Why?''

The jowls were quivering big-time. "You know why,'' he said. "Valerie Simpson was still something of a celebrity from her tennis days. We felt that there was already enough scrutiny without adding her name to the mix. It wasn't a question of liking or not liking Valerie. We just wanted to minimize the story as much as possible. Keep it off the front pages.''

"You got lucky then.''

"What do you mean?''

"Yeller was killed. Swade vanished.''

Cross blinked several times. "I'm not sure I understand.''

"If they were alive there would have been a trial. More media attention. Maybe too much media attention for even your spin doctors to handle.''

He smiled. "I see you've heard the rumors.''

"Rumors?''

"That I had Errol Swade killed. That the mob did me a favor or some such nonsense."

"You have to admit, Senator, their fates made for a convenient little public relations package. No one to dispute your spin on things."

"I don't cry over the fate of Curtis Yeller, and if Errol Swade was murdered I doubt I'd shed too many tears about that either. But I don't know any mobsters. That may sound silly, but I wouldn't know the first thing about enlisting the mob's help. I did hire a detective agency to look for Swade."

"Did they find anything?"

"No. They believe that Swade is dead. So do the police. He was a punk, Myron. He wasn't on a path that led to a long life even before this incident."

Myron followed up with a few more questions, but there was nothing more to learn. A few minutes later the two men stood.

"Would you mind if I spoke to Gregory Caufield before I leave?" Myron asked.

"I'd prefer it if you didn't."

"If there's nothing to hide—"

"I don't want him knowing I told you this. Attorney-client privilege, remember? He won't speak honestly to you anyway."

"He will if you tell him to."

Cross shook his head. "Gregory's father controls him. He won't talk."

Myron shrugged. The senator was probably right. The only leverage he could apply on Gregory would be what Cross just told him. Cross had neatly arranged it so Myron couldn't do that. He'd have to think of a way to end-run that. Caufield was an eyewitness. He'd be worth a few questions.

The two men shook hands, both making serious eye contact. Was Senator Cross a sweet old codger, a grieving father trying to protect his son's memory? Or had he calculated that this would be the most effective strategy for dealing with Myron? Was he cagey or sympathetic or both?

Cross gave him the endearing off-center smile again. "I hope I've satisfied your curiosity," he said.

He hadn't. Not even close. But Myron didn't bother telling him that.

Chapter 20

Myron left the building and strolled down Madison Avenue. Traffic was at a standstill. Big surprise in Manhattan. Five lanes were merging into one on Fifty-fourth Street. The other four lanes were blocked by one of those purely New York construction sites with steam pouring up out of the streets. Very Dante. What was with all that steam anyway?

He was about to cut across Fifty-third Street when he felt a sharp stab in his ribs.

"Give me an excuse, asshole."

Myron recognized the voice before seeing the taped nose and the black eyes. Fishnet. He was pressing a gun against Myron's rib cage, using his body to hide the gun from any curious onlookers.

"You're wearing the same shirt," Myron said. "Jesus Christ, you didn't even change."

Fishnet gave him a little gun jab. "You're going to wish you were never born, asshole. Get in the car."

The car—the powder-blue Caddy with thick scratches on the side—pulled alongside of them. Jim, Fishnet's partner, was driving, but Myron barely noticed him. His eyes immediately locked on the familiar figure in the backseat. The figure smiled and waved.

"Hey, Myron," he called out. "How's it going?"

Aaron.

"Bring him here, Lee," Aaron said.

Fishnet Lee gave Myron a nudge with the gun. "Let's go, asshole."

Myron got in the backseat with Aaron. Fishnet Lee joined Jim in the front. The front seats were both covered with plastic where Win had dumped the maple syrup.

Aaron was dressed in his customary garb. Pure-snow-white suit, white shoes. No socks. No shirt. Aaron never wore a shirt, preferring to display his tan pectorals. They gleamed from some sort of oil or grease. He always looked fresh out of the wax salon, his body smooth as a baby's bottom. Aaron was a big man, six-six, two-forty. The weight lifter's build was not merely for show. Aaron moved with a speed and grace that defied the bulk. His black hair was slicked back and tied into a long ponytail.

He gave Myron a game-show-host grin and held it.

Myron said, "Nice smile, Aaron. Lots of teeth."

"Proper dental hygiene. It's a passion of mine."

"You should share your passion with Lee," Myron said.

Fishnet's head spun. "What the fuck did you say, asshole?"

"Turn around, Lee," Aaron said to Fishnet. Fishnet glared a few more daggers. Myron yawned. Jim drove. Aaron sat back. He said nothing, smiling brightly. Every part of him glistened in the sunlight. After two blocks of this Myron pointed at Aaron's cleavage. "Your electrolysis missed a chest hair."

To Aaron's credit he didn't look. "We need to chat, Myron."

"What about?"

"Valerie Simpson. For once I think we're on the same side."

"Oh?"

"You want to capture Valerie Simpson's killer. So do we."

"You do?"

"Yes. Mr. Ache is determined to bring her killer to justice."

"That Frank. Always the good Samaritan."

Aaron chuckled. "Still the funny man, eh, Myron? Well, I admit it sounds a bit bizarre, but we'd like to help you."

"How?"

"We both know that Roger Quincy killed Valerie Simpson. Mr. Ache is willing to use his considerable influence to help locate him."

"And in return?"

Aaron feigned shock. He put a manicured hand the size of a manhole cover to his chest. "Myron, you wound me. Really. We try to extend the hand of friendship and you slap it away with an insult."

"Uh-huh."

"This is one of those rare win-win situations," Aaron said. "We're willing to help you get your killer."

"And you get?"

"Not a thing." He settled back into his seat. "If the killer is found, the police will move on to other matters. We will move on to other matters. And you, Myron, should also move on to other matters."

"Ah."

"Now, there's no reason to have a problem here," Aaron added. When the sun hit his chest at a certain angle, the reflection dazzled the eyes. "This isn't like some of our past encounters. We both want the same thing. We both want to put this tragic episode behind us. For you, that means finding the killer and bringing him to justice. For us, that means ending the investigation as soon as possible.''

''But suppose I'm not convinced Roger Quincy did it,'' Myron said.

Aaron raised an eyebrow. ''Come on now, Myron. You've seen the evidence.''

''It's circumstantial.''

''Since when has that bothered you? Oh by the way, a new witness has come forward. We just got wind of it.''

''What kind of witness?'' Myron asked.

''A witness who saw Roger Quincy talking to your beloved Valerie within ten minutes of the murder.''

Myron said nothing.

''You doubt my word?''

''Who's the witness, Aaron?''

''Some housewife. She was at the matches with her kids. And to answer your next question we have nothing to do with her.''

''So why the big fear?''

''What fear?''

''What's Ache so concerned about? Why hire Starsky and Hutch up there to follow me?''

Fishnet turned around. ''What the fuck did you call me, asshole?''

''Turn around, Lee,'' Aaron said.

''Ah, come off it, Aaron, let me fuck him up a little. You see what the motherfucker did to my car? And look at my fucking nose.'' Car first, then nose. Priorities. ''He and his faggot buddy jumped me. Two on one. When I wasn't looking. Let me teach him a little respect.''

''You couldn't, Lee. You and Jim together couldn't.''

''Fuck I couldn't. If I didn't have this busted nose—''

"Shut up, Lee," Aaron said.

Immediate silence.

Aaron rolled his eyes at Myron and spread his hands. "Rank amateurs," he said. "Frank is always trying to cut corners. Save a buck here. Save a buck there. In the end it always costs more."

"I thought you stopped working for the Ache brothers," Myron said.

"I work freelance now."

"So Frank just brought you in?"

"As of this morning."

"Must be something big," Myron said. "You don't come cheap."

Aaron gave him the teeth again, adjusted the jacket of his suit. "You want the best, you have to pay."

"So why's Frank so bent out of shape about this?"

"I have no idea. But make no mistake about it: Frank wants your investigation to end. Now. No excuses. Look, Myron, we both know you've been something of a pain in the ass to Frank. He doesn't like you. To be honest he'd like to ace you. That's no bullshit. I'm talking man to man here. Friend to friend. We're friends, right? Buddies?"

"Best of chums," Myron added. Shovel, shovel.

"But Frank is showing incredible restraint with you. Generosity even. He knows, for example, that you took Eddie Crane out to dinner. That alone would be reason for Frank to want you roughed up a bit. But he doesn't. In fact he's decided that if Eddie Crane chooses your agency, he won't get in the way."

"Big of him."

"But it *is* big of him," Aaron insisted. "He owns the kid's coach, for crying out loud. By all rights he belongs to TruPro. But Frank is willing to let him go, and he's willing to help you bring in Roger Quincy. Two very big favors. Gifts really. In exchange, you do nothing.''

Myron turned his palms up. "How can I pass up a deal like that?"

"Do I sense a whiff of sarcasm?"

Myron shrugged.

"Frank's trying to be fair, Myron."

"Yeah, the man's a prince."

"Don't push him on this. It's not worth it."

"Can I leave now?"

"I'd like your answer first."

"I'll have to think about it," Myron said. "But I'd be much more willing to let go if I knew what Frank was trying to hide."

Aaron shook his head. "Still the same old Myron, huh? You never change. I'm surprised no one has wasted you yet."

"I'm not easy to kill," Myron said.

"Maybe not."

"And I'm also a snazzy dancer. No one likes to kill a snazzy dancer. There're so few us left."

Aaron put his hand on Myron's knee and leaned toward him. "Can we stop the lunatic routine for a moment?"

Myron's eyes flicked down to the knee, then back to Aaron. "Uh, your hand?"

"You know about the carrot and the stick, Myron?"

"The what?"

"The carrot and the stick." The hand was still on Myron's knee.

"Oh. Sure. The carrot and the stick." *What?*

"So far I have shown you only the carrot. I would feel amiss if I did not also show a bit of stick."

In the front seat Fishnet and Jim shared a chuckle.

Aaron's fingers gave the knee a little squeeze. Like a hawk's talons. "Now you know me. I'm not a stick man. I'm the gentle sort. I'm kind. I'm nice. I'm..." He looked up as though searching for the word.

"A carrot," Myron finished.

"Right. A carrot."

Myron had seen Aaron kill a man. Snap his neck as though it were a twig. He'd also seen the results of Aaron's work in venues ranging from boxing rings to morgues. Some carrot.

"But nonetheless I need to add a bit of stick. Just for the record, you understand. It's expected. I know it's not necessary in your case. The stick, I mean."

"I'm listening," Myron said.

"Yeah," Fishnet added, "tell him, Aaron." Fishnet and Jim restarted the chuckle. Louder.

"Shut up," Aaron said softly.

Again immediate silence. Like they'd both been shot in the head.

Aaron swung his line of vision to Myron. His eyes were suddenly dark and hard. "There will be no further warnings. We will simply strike. I know you don't scare easily. I explained that to Frank. He doesn't care. He suggested striking places that another man might consider taboo."

"Like?"

"I understand Duane Richwood is playing well. I'd hate to see his career cut short." He gave the knee a harder squeeze. "Or take your beautiful Jessica, for example. Now I know she's out of the country right now. In Athens, in case you don't know. The Grand Bretagne Hotel. Room 207. Frank has friends in Greece."

Myron felt a cold chill. "Don't even think about it, Aaron."

"Not my decision." He finally let go of the knee. "It's Frank. He's adamant about this. He wants you to let go now. You know what they say about grabbing a tiger by the tail."

"If he touches her—"

Aaron waved him off. "Please, Myron, no threats. There's no reason for threats here. You can't win. You know that. The price of victory is too high. You and Win are only two men. Two good men. Two of the best. Worthy adversaries. But Frank has me, for one. And he has others. Many others. As many men as he needs. Men with no scruples. Men who would break into Jessica's room, take turns with her, and then blow her away. Men who would jump Esperanza on her way home from work. Men who would even do unspeakable things to your mother."

Myron stared at Aaron. Aaron did not blink. "You can't win, Myron. No matter how tough you are, you can't stand up to that kind of thing. We both know it."

Silence. The Caddy pulled up to the front of Myron's building.

"Can I have your answer now?" Aaron asked.

Myron tried not to shake as he got out of the car. Without glancing behind him he walked inside.

Chapter 21

Win worked the heavy bag. He was snapping side kicks that bent the eighty-pound bag almost in half. He threw kicks at every level. The opponent's knee. The abdomen. The neck. The face. He struck with his heel, his toes angled down. Myron went though several katas, or forms, concentrating on the precision of his strikes, imagining a person in front of him rather than the air. Sometimes the person was Aaron.

They were at Master Kwon's new downtown location. The *dojang* was divided into two sections. One looked like a dance studio. Hardwood floor and lots of mirrors. The other section had matted floors, dumbbells, a speed bag, a heavy bag, a jump rope. On the shelf were rubber knives and guns to practice take-away techniques. The American flag and Korean flag were hung near the doorway. Each student bowed to them as they entered and left. School rules were listed on a poster. Myron knew them by heart. His favorite was rule number ten. Always finish what you start.

Hmm. Good advice? Hard to say right now.

There were fourteen school rules in all. Every once in a while Master Kwon added a new one. Number fourteen had been put up two months ago: Do not overeat. "Students too fat," Master Kwon had explained. "Too much put in mouth." In the twenty years since Win had helped Kwon relocate to the United States, Kwon's English had continually degenerated. Myron suspected it was part of his image as a wise old man from the Far East. Playing Mr. Miyagi from the *Karate Kid* movies.

Win stopped. "Here," he said, gesturing to the bag. "You need this more than I do."

Myron began to hit the bag. Hard. He started with some punches. Tae kwon do's fighting stance is simple and practical, not all that different from a boxer's. Anyone who tried that crane-stance bullshit on the streets usually ended up on their ass. Myron followed up with some elbow and knee strikes. Elbows and knees were useful, particularly for fighting in close. Martial arts movies showed lots of spinning kicks to the head, jumping kicks to the chest, stuff like that. But street fighting was far simpler. You aimed for the groin, the knee, the neck, the nose, the eyes. Occasionally the solar plexus. The rest was wasteful. You get in a real life-or-death situation, you twist the guy's balls. You stick your fingers in his eyes. You throw an elbow to his throat.

Win walked over to a full-length mirror. "Let's review what we've learned so far," he said in the mock voice of a kindergarten teacher. He began to play air-golf, practicing his swing in the mirror. He did that a lot. "One, the esteemed senator from Pennsylvania wants you off this case. Two, a major mobster from New York wants you off this case. Three, your client, the womanizing Duane Richwood, wants you off this case. Have I left anybody out?"

"Deanna Yeller," Myron said. "And Helen Van Slyke. Kenneth too, don't forget Kenneth. Pavel Menansi." Myron thought a moment. "I think that's it."

"The police officer," Win added. "Detective Dimonte."

"Oh yeah, right. I forgot about Rolly."

Win checked the grip on his imaginary club. "Thus," he continued, "your cause is mustering its customary support—i.e., none."

Myron shrugged, threw a combination. " 'Can't please everyone, so you've got to please yourself.' "

Win made a face. "Quoting Ricky Nelson?"

"It's been a long day."

"I would say."

Myron back-kicked. A good countermove to almost any attack. "So why is everyone so afraid of Valerie Simpson? A United States senator sets up a clandestine meeting with me. Frank Ache brings in Aaron. Duane threatens to fire me. Why?"

Win took another air-golf swing in the mirror. He looked up after the shot, squinting, as though following the trajectory of the imaginary ball. He seemed displeased. Golfers.

The door to the *dojang* opened. Wanda peered inside, gave a shy wave.

"Hi," Myron said.

"Hi."

Myron smiled. He was happy to see her—someone who did indeed want him to continue his investigation. She wore a patterned, almost little-girlish summer dress. The dress was sleeveless, revealing her nicely toned arms. She wasn't wearing one of those big summer hats, but she should have been. Her makeup had been applied with a light hand. Gold hoop earrings hung from her lobes. She looked young and healthy and quite beautiful.

A sign beside the door read NO SHOES ALLOWED. Wanda obeyed, slipped her flats off before stepping inside the *dojang*. "Esperanza told me you'd be here," she said. "I'm really sorry about disturbing you outside the office again."

"Don't worry about it," he said. "You know Win."

"Yes," she said, turning to him. She managed a smile. "Nice to see you."

Win gave her an almost indiscernible head tilt. Stoic. Playing Tonto.

Wringing her hands together Wanda asked, "Can we talk for a moment?"

Win did not need prompting. He moved to the door, bowed deeply at the waist, left. They were alone.

She walked toward him deliberately, glancing around like she was on a house tour but not really interested in buying. "Do you come here a lot?" she asked.

"Here or one of Master Kwon's other *dojangs*."

"I thought they were called dojos," she said.

"Dojo is Japanese. *Dojang* is Korean."

She nodded as though this information had some significance in her life. She glanced around a bit more. "Have you studied this for a long time?"

"Yes."

"And Win?"

"Even longer."

"He doesn't look the fighting type," she said. "Except maybe in the eyes."

Myron had heard that before. He waited.

"I just wanted to know if you'd learned anything," she said. Her eyes flicked left, right, up, down.

"Not much," he said. Not exactly the truth, but Myron wasn't about to mention Duane's liaisons with Valerie.

She nodded again. Her hands were in constant motion, searching for something to occupy them. "Duane is acting even stranger," she said.

"How?"

"Just more of the same, I guess. He's on edge all the

time. He keeps getting these calls he takes in another room. When I answer the phone the caller hangs up. And he disappeared again last night. Said he needed some air, but he was gone for two hours.''

"Do you have any thoughts?" he asked.

She shook her head.

Myron aimed for his gentlest voice. "Could there be someone else?"

Her eyes stopped flicking and flared in his direction. "I'm not some hooker he picked up off the street."

"I know that."

"We love each other."

"I know that too. But I also know a lot of guys in love who still do dumb things." Women too. Jessica, for one. Four years ago with a guy named Doug. It still hurt. Guy named Doug. Go figure.

Wanda shook her head again firmly. Convincing herself or Myron? "It's not like that with us. I know I sound like a gullible idiot, but it's the way it is. I can't explain it."

"No need to. I was just seeing what you thought."

"Duane's not having an affair."

"Okay."

Her eyes were wet. She took a couple of deep breaths. "He's not sleeping at night. He paces. I ask him what's wrong, but he won't tell me. I tried eavesdropping on a call, but the only thing I picked up was your name."

"My name?"

She nodded. "He said it twice, but that's all I heard."

Myron thought a moment. "Suppose I put a tap on your phone."

"Do it."

"You don't have a problem with that?"

"No." The wet eyes broke into tears. She let out two

quick sobs, made herself stop. "It's getting worse, Myron. We have to find out what's going on."

"I'll do my best."

She gave him a brief hug. Myron wanted to stroke her hair and say something comforting. He didn't do either. She strode out slowly, head high. Myron watched. As soon as she was out of sight Win returned.

"Well?" Win asked.

"I like her," Myron said.

Win nodded. "Very shapely derriere."

"That's not what I meant. She's a good woman. And she's scared."

"Of course she's scared. Her meal ticket is about to go bye-bye."

The Return of Mr. Warmth. "It's not like that, Win. She loves him."

Win strummed a few notes on an air-violin. Couldn't talk to him about stuff like that. He just didn't get it. "What did she want?"

Myron filled him in on the conversation. Win spread his legs, dropping into a full split and then sliding back up. He repeated the move several times, faster and faster. Ladies and gentlemen, the Godfather of Soul, Mr. James Brown.

When Myron finished, Win said, "Sounds like Duane is trying to hide more than a quick fling."

"My thoughts exactly."

"You want me to watch him?"

"We can take shifts."

Win shook his head. "He knows you."

"He knows you too."

"Yes," Win said, "but I am invisible. I am the wind."

"Sure you don't mean passing wind?"

Win made a face. "That was a good one. I'm sure I'll laugh for days."

Truth was, Win could be nestled in your B.V.D.'s for a week and you'd never know. "Can you start tonight?" Myron asked.

Win nodded. "I'm already there."

Chapter 22

Myron shot baskets on the blacktop off the driveway. The long summer day was finally slipping into darkness, but the basket was illuminated with spotlights. He and his father had installed them when Myron was in the sixth grade. A variety of barbecue smells competed in the still air. Chicken from the Dempseys' house. Burgers from the Weinsteins'. Shish kebab at the Ruskins'.

Myron shot, rebounded, shot again. He got a little rhythm going, the ball back-spinning gently through the basket. Nothing but net. Sweat matted his gray T-shirt to his chest. Myron always did his best thinking out here, but right now his mind was a blank. There was nothing but the ball, the hoop, and the sweet arc after the release. It felt pure.

"Hey, Myron."

It was Timmy from next door. Timmy was ten.

"Bug off, kid. You're bothering me."

Timmy laughed and grabbed a rebound. It was an inside joke. Timmy's mother was convinced that her son was bothering Myron and that Myron should send Timmy home whenever he came over. Didn't stop Timmy. He and his friends always came over when Myron was shooting. Once in a while, when they needed an extra body, the kids would knock on the door and ask his mom if Myron could come out and play.

He and Timmy shot around for a while. They talked

about stuff that was important to little boys. A few other kids came by. The Daleys' boy. The Cohens' girl. Others. Bikes were parked at the end of the driveway. They started playing a game. Myron was designated steady passer. No one kept score accurately. Everyone laughed a lot. A few fathers came by and joined in. Arnie Stollman. Fred Dempsey. It'd been a while since they'd done this. A bit too Rockwellian for some, but it felt very right to Myron.

It was nearly ten when mothers started to call out for their children. From their front stoops the mothers smiled brightly and waved at Myron. Myron waved back. The kids "aw, Mom" 'd, but they listened.

Summer and school break. Still a touch of innocence. Kids were supposed to be different now. They had to deal with guns and drugs and crime and AIDS. But a summer night in middle-class suburbia was the great generational equalizer, a place far away from people like Aaron and the Ache brothers. A place far away from young women being murdered.

Valerie would have had fun tonight.

Mom opened the back door. "Telephone," she said shortly.

"Who is it?"

Her voice was like a closed fist. "Jessica." She made a face when she said it, like the name tasted bad on her lips.

Myron tried not to sprint. He walk/ran up the back steps and into the kitchen. The kitchen had been completely redone last year. Why, Myron couldn't say. No one in the house cooked, unless you count microwaving Celeste frozen pizzas.

"I'll take it in the basement," he said.

A grunt from Mom. No wisecrack. Like Esperanza,

Mom too held grudges. Especially when it came to her little boy.

He closed the door, grabbed the receiver, heard his mother hang up the extension. "Jess?"

"Is this Stallions 'R' Us?"

As usual her voice made him soar. "Why, yes it is. What can we do for you, ma'am?"

"I'm looking for a true stallion."

"You called the right place. Any preference?"

"Well hung," she replied. "But you'll do."

"Nice talk."

There was a lot of noise in the background. "What took you so long to pick up?" she asked.

"I was outside. Playing with Timmy and the kids."

"Did I interrupt?"

"Nope. Game just ended."

"Your mom sounded a tad frosty on the phone."

"She gets that way," Myron said.

"She used to like me."

"She still does."

"And Esperanza?"

"Esperanza never liked you."

"Oh yeah," she said.

"You still at the Grand Bretagne Hotel?" Myron asked. "Room 207?"

Pause. "Were you spying on me?"

"No."

"Then how do you know—"

"Long story. I'll tell you about it when you get home. Where are you?"

"Kennedy Airport. We just landed."

His heart did a quick twirl. "You're home?"

"I will be as soon as I find my luggage." She hesitated. "Will you come right over?"

"I'm on my way."

"Wear something I can easily rip off your bod," she said. "I'll be waiting in the tub with all kinds of exotic oils from overseas."

"Hussy."

There was another hesitation. Then Jessica said, "I love you, you know. I get funny sometimes, but I do love you."

"Never mind that. Tell me more about the oils."

She laughed. "Hurry now."

He put the receiver back in its cradle. He quickly stripped down and showered. A cold shower for the time being. He was whistling "Tonight" from *West Side Story*. He dried himself off and checked out his closet. Something in the easy-to-rip-off family. Found it. Snap buttons. He sprinkled on a little cologne. Myron rarely wore cologne, but Jess liked it. He heard the doorbell ring as he was bounding up the stairs.

"I'll get it," he called out.

Two uniformed police officers were at the door.

"Are you Myron Bolitar?" the taller one asked.

"Yes."

"Detective Roland Dimonte sent us. We would appreciate it if you would come with us."

"Where?"

"Queens Homicide."

"What for?"

"Roger Quincy has been captured. He's a suspect in the murder of Valerie Simpson."

"So?"

The shorter cop spoke for the first time. "Mr. Bolitar, do you know Roger Quincy?"

"No."

"You've never met him?"

"Not to my knowledge." Not to my knowledge. Lawyer talk for *no*.

The officers exchanged a glance.

"You better come with us," the taller cop said.

"Why?"

"Because Mr. Quincy refuses to make a statement until he talks with you."

Chapter 23

Myron called Jessica's place and left a message that he'd be late.

When they arrived at the precinct, Dimonte greeted Myron at the door. He was chewing a wad of gum or maybe it was spitting tobacco. And he was smiling a whole lot. He wore a different pair of boots this time. Still snakeskin, still hideous. But these were bright yellow with blue fringes.

"Glad you could make it," Dimonte said.

Myron pointed to the boots. "Mug a cheerleader, Rolly?"

Dimonte laughed. This wasn't good. "Come on, smart-guy," he said with something approaching good nature. He led Myron down a corridor, threading between lots of bored-looking cops. Almost every one of them had a cup of coffee in their hands, leaning against a wall or refreshment machine, pleading some pathetic case to a nodding head.

"No press," Myron noted.

"They haven't been told of Quincy's capture yet," Dimonte said. "But it'll leak soon enough."

"You going to leak it?"

He shrugged happily. "The public has a right to know."

"Sure."

"What about you, Bolitar? You want to come clean?"

"Come clean on what?"

He shrugged again. Mr. Carefree. "Suit yourself."

"I don't know him, Rolly."

"Guess he got your name out of the yellow pages, huh?"

Myron stayed silent. No point in arguing now.

Dimonte opened a door into a small interrogation room. Two cops were already in there. Their neckties were loosened low enough to double as a belt. They'd been working Roger Quincy over pretty good, but Quincy did not seem too agitated. In most movies or TV shows a prisoner in a holding cell wear stripes or grays. But in reality they wear loud, fluorescent orange. Better to see them should they opt to flee.

Roger Quincy's eyes lit up when he saw Myron. He was younger than Myron had expected—early thirties, though he probably could have passed for mid-twenties. He was thin, his face pretty in a feminine way. His fingers were graceful and elongated. He looked like a ballet dancer.

From his chair Roger Quincy waved and said, "Thanks for coming, Myron."

Myron looked at Dimonte. Dimonte smiled back. "Don't know him, huh?" He nodded to the other cops. "Come on, guys. Let's leave the two buddies alone."

A few quiet snickers later, the cops were gone. Myron sat in the chair across the table from Roger Quincy.

"Do I know you?" Myron asked.

"No, I don't think so." Quincy extended his hand. "I'm Roger Quincy."

Quincy's hand felt like a small bird. Myron gave it a quick shake. "How do you know my name?"

"Oh, I'm a big sports fan," he said. "I know I don't look the type, but I've been one for years. I don't follow basketball that closely anymore. Tennis is my favorite. Do you play at all?"

"Just a little."

"I'm not very good, but I try." His eyes lit up again. "Tennis is such a magnificent sport when you think about it. A competitive acrobatic dance really. A small ball hurls at you with unearthly velocity and you have to move, set your feet, hit the ball back using a racket. Everything has to be calculated in a matter of moments: the speed of the oncoming ball, the spot it will land, the spin on it, the angle of the bounce, the distance between your hand and the center of the racket head, the stroke you will use, the placement of your return. It's amazing when you think about it."

Two words: Looney Tunes.

"Uh, Roger, you didn't answer my question," Myron said. "How do you know me?"

"I'm sorry." He flashed a shy smile. "I get over-excited sometimes. Some people think it's a flaw. Me, I'd rather be like that than some couch potato. Did I mention that I'm also a basketball fan?"

"Yes."

"That's how I know your name. I saw you play at Duke." He smiled like that explained everything.

"Okay," Myron said, struggling to keep a patient tone. "So why did you tell the police you wanted to talk to me?"

"Because I did. Want to talk to you, that is."

"Why?"

"They think I killed Valerie, Myron."

"Did you?"

His mouth made a surprised little O. "Of course not. What kind of man do you think I am?"

Myron shrugged. "The kind who stalks young girls. The kind who harassed Valerie Simpson, who followed her around, called her repeatedly, wrote her long letters, frightened her."

He waved Myron off with those long fingers. "You're exaggerating," he said. "I courted Valerie Simpson. I loved her. I cared about her well-being. I was merely a persistent suitor."

"She wanted you to leave her alone."

He laughed. "So she turned me down. Big deal. Am I the first man ever rejected by a beautiful woman? I just don't give up as easily as most. I sent her flowers. I wrote her love letters. I asked her out again. I tried different tactics. Do you ever read romance novels?"

"Not really."

"The hero and heroine are always rejecting each other. Through wars or pirate attacks or high society parties, the couple fight and claw and seem to hate each other. But deep down they are in love. They're repressing their true feelings, see? That's how it was with Valerie and me. There was an undeniable tension there. A high-voltage surge between us."

"Uh-huh," Myron said. "Roger, why did you want to see me?"

"I thought you could talk to the police for me."

"And tell them what?"

"That I didn't kill Valerie. That she was in imminent danger from someone else."

"Who?"

"I thought you knew."

"What makes you think that?"

"Valerie told me. Right before she was murdered."

"She told you what exactly?"

"That she was in danger."

"In danger of what?"

"I thought you'd know."

Myron raised his hand. "Slow down a second, okay? Let's start at the beginning. You were at the U.S. Open."

"Yes."

"Why?"

"I go every year. I'm a big fan. I love to watch the matches. They're so mesmerizing—"

"I think we covered that already, Roger. So you went as a fan. Your going had nothing to do with Valerie Simpson? You didn't follow her there?"

"Of course not. I had no idea she'd even be there."

"Okay, so what happened?"

"I was sitting in the stadium watching Duane Richwood demolish Ivan Restovich. Incredible performance. I mean, Duane slaughtered him." He smiled. "But why am I telling you this? You're his agent, right?"

"Yes."

"Can you get me his autograph?"

"Sure."

"Not tonight, of course. Tomorrow maybe?"

"Maybe." Earth to Roger. "But let's stick with Valerie right now. You were watching Duane's match."

"Exactly." His voice grew serious. "I wish I'd known you were Duane Richwood's agent then, Myron. Maybe everything would have been okay then. Maybe Valerie would still be alive and I'd be the hero who saved her and she'd have to stop denying her true feelings and let me into her life and let me protect her forevermore."

Myron remembered a quote from *Man of La Mancha:*

"I can see the coo-coo singing in the coo-coo berry tree."

"What happened, Roger?"

"The match was basically over so I checked my program. Arantxa Sanchez-Vicario was about to start her match on court sixteen, so I figured I'd go over there and get a good seat. Arantxa's a wonderful player. Such a hustler. Her brothers Emilio and Javier are pros also. Nice players, but they don't have her heart."

"So you left the stadium," Myron tried

"I left the stadium. I had a few minutes, so I went over to the booth near the front entrance. The one with all the TV monitors giving the scores of the other matches. I saw that Steffi had already won and that Michael Chang had been dragged into a fifth set. I was checking out some doubles matches on the board. Men's doubles, I think. Ken Flach was one of the people. No, it was . . . I can't remember."

"Stay with me, Roger."

"Anyway, that's when I saw Valerie."

"Where?"

"By the front gate. She was trying to get in, but the guard wouldn't let her. She didn't have a ticket. She was very upset, that was clear. You know, the Open is always sold out. Every year. But I still couldn't believe what I was seeing. The guard wouldn't let her in. Valerie Simpson. He didn't even recognize her. So naturally I went to her aid."

Naturally. "What did you do?"

"I got my hand stamped by another guard and walked outside the gate. Then I came up behind her and tapped her on the shoulder. When she turned around I couldn't believe what I saw."

"What?"

"I know Valerie Simpson," he said, his words slower now. "Even you will have to concede that. I've seen every match she ever played in. I saw her at work. I saw her at play. I've seen her on the streets, on the court, at her house, practicing with that slimy coach of hers. I've seen her happy and sad, up and down, in triumph and defeat. I saw her progress from an enthusiastic teenager to a fierce competitor to a despondent, lifeless beauty. My heart has ached for her so many times, I've lost count. But I'd never seen her like this."

"Like what?"

"So scared. She was absolutely terrified."

Little wonder, Myron thought. Daffy Duck here sneaks up behind her and taps her on her shoulder. "Did she recognize you?"

"Of course."

"What did she do then?"

"She asked for my help."

Myron arched a skeptical eyebrow. He'd learned the technique from Win.

"It's true," Roger insisted. "She said she was in danger. She said she needed to get in and see you."

"She mentioned me by name?"

"Yes. I'm telling you, she was desperate. She pleaded with the guard, but he wouldn't listen. So I came up with an idea."

"What was that?"

"Scalp a ticket," he answered. He was clearly pleased with himself. "There were dozens of scalpers hanging around the subway entrance. I found one. A black man. Nice enough fellow. He wanted a hundred and fifty dollars. I told him that was way too much. They always start high. The scalpers, I mean. You have to negotiate with them. They expect it. But Valerie would have none of that. She just accepted his price. That's Valerie. No head for money. If we'd gotten married, I would have had to handle the finances. She's too impulsive.''

''Focus with me, Roger. What happened after you bought the ticket?''

His face went soft and dreamy. ''She thanked me,'' he said, like he'd seen a burning bush. ''It was the first time she ever opened up to me. I knew then that my patience had won out. After all this time I'd finally cracked the face. Funny, isn't it? For years I tried so hard to make her love me. And then when I least expect it, boom!—love crashed into my life.''

I, me, I, me, I, me. Even Valerie's murder he could only see in terms of himself. ''What did she do then?'' Myron asked.

''I escorted her through the gates. She asked me if I knew what you looked liked. I said, you mean Myron Bolitar the basketball player? She said yes. I said yes, I knew. She said she needed to find you.'' He leaned forward. Earnest. ''You see what I mean? If I had known you were Duane's agent I would have known exactly where you were. I would have led her right to you. Then everything would have been all right. I'd have gotten a bigger thank-you and that priceless Valerie Simpson smile all for me. I'd have saved her life. I would have been her hero.'' He shook his head for what might have been. ''It would have been perfect.''

''But instead?'' Myron tried.

''We split up. She asked me to cover the outside courts while she searched the Food Court and the stadium area. We were going to meet back by the Perrier booth every fifteen minutes. I took off and began my search. I was anxious. Finding you would have proved my undying love—''

''Yeah, I got that part.'' This guy must have been gobs of fun for ol' Rolly to interrogate. ''What happened next?''

''I heard a gunshot,'' Quincy continued. ''Then I heard screams. I ran back toward the Food Court. By the time I got there a crowd had formed. You were running toward the body. She was on the ground. So still. You bent down and cradled her body. My dreams. My life. My happiness. Dead. I knew what the police would think. They tormented me for courting her. Called me names. Heck, they threatened to put me in jail for asking her out—what were they going to think now? They never understood the bond between us. The attraction.''

''So you ran,'' Myron said.

''Yes. I went to my place and packed a bag. Then I took out the maximum amount on my MAC card. I saw on TV once how the police tracked a guy down by where he used his credit cards, so I wanted to make sure I had enough cash. Smart, huh?''

''Ingenious,'' Myron agreed. But he felt his heart sink. Valerie Simpson had had no one. She'd been alone. When danger struck she turned to Myron, a man she barely knew. And someone had murdered her. A painful pang consumed him.

''I stayed in crummy motels and used fake names,'' Quincy rambled. ''But someone must have recognized me. Well, you know the rest. When they caught me, I asked for you. I thought you'd be able to explain to them what really happened.'' Quincy leaned forward, whispered conspiratorially. ''That Detective Dimonte can be rather hostile.''

''Uh-huh.''

"The only time he smiled was when I mentioned your name."

"Oh?"

"I told him you and I were friends. I hope you don't mind."

"Not at all," Myron said.

Chapter 24

Myron faced Dimonte and sidekick Krinsky in the adjoining interrogation room. It was identical to the other one in every way. Dimonte was still gleeful.

"Would you care for an attorney?" he asked sweetly.

Myron looked at him. "Your face is positively beaming, Rolly. New moisturizer?"

The smile stayed. "I'll take that as a no."

"Am I under arrest?"

"Of course not. Have a seat. Care for a drink?"

"Sure."

"What would you like?" Quite the host, that Rolly. "Coke? Coffee? Orange juice?"

"Got any Yoo-Hoo?"

Dimonte looked at Krinsky. Krinsky shrugged and went to check. Dimonte folded his hands and put them on the table. "Myron, why did Roger Quincy ask for you?"

"He wanted to speak to me."

Dimonte smiled. Mr. Patience. "Yes, but why you?"

"I'm afraid I can't answer that."

"Can't," Dimonte said. "Or won't?"

"Can't."

"Why can't you?"

"I think it falls under attorney-client privilege. I have to check."

"Check with who?"

"With whom," Myron said.

"What?"

"Check with whom. Not who, whom. Prepositional phrase."

Dimonte nodded. "So it's going to be like that, is it?"

"Like what?"

His voice was a little rougher now. "You're a suspect, Bolitar. No, check that. You're *the* suspect."

"What about Roger?"

"He's the trigger man. I'm sure of that. But he's too much of a nut job to have done it on his own. Way we figure it, you set the whole thing up. Had him do the dirty work."

"Uh-huh. And my motive?"

"Valerie Simpson was having an affair with Duane Richwood. That's why his phone number was in her book. A white girl with a black guy. How would the sponsors have reacted to that?"

"It's the nineties, Rolly. There's even a mixed marriage on the Supreme Court."

Dimonte put a boot up on a chair and leaned on the raised knee. "Times may change, Bolitar, but sponsors still don't like black boys boffing white chicks." He tickled his chin with two fingers. "Let me run this by you, see how it sounds: Duane is a bit of a coonhound. He sniffs out white meat. He nails Valerie Simpson, but she doesn't fancy the idea of being a one-nighter. We know she's a bit of a fruitcake, spent time in an asylum. Probably a bunny burner to boot."

"Bunny burner?"

"You seen *Fatal Attraction*?"

Myron nodded. "Oh. Bunny burner. Right."

"So like I said, Valerie Simpson is crazy. Her elevator don't stop at every floor. But now she's also pissed off. So she calls up Duane just like it says in her little diary and threatens to go to the press. Duane is scared. Like he was yesterday when I came by. So who does he call? You. That's when you hatch your little scheme."

Myron nodded. "That'll hold up in court."

"What? Greed isn't a good motive?"

"I might as well confess right here."

"Fine, smart-guy. You play it that way."

Krinsky returned. He shook his head. No Yoo-Hoo.

"You want to tell me why Quincy called you first?" Dimonte continued.

"Nope."

"Why the hell not?"

"Because you've hurt my feelings."

"Don't fuck with me, Bolitar. I'll throw your ass into a holding cell with twenty psychos and tell them you're a child molester." He smiled. "He'll like that, won't he, Krinsky?"

"Yeah," Krinsky said, mirroring Dimonte's smile.

Myron nodded. "Right. Okay, now I say, what do you mean? Then you say, a tasty morsel like you will be popular in the slammer. Then I say, please don't. Then you say, don't bend over to pick up the soap. Then you both give me a cop snicker."

"What the fuck you talking about?"

"Don't waste my time, Rolly."

"You think I won't throw your ass in jail?"

Myron stood. "I know you won't. If you thought you could I'd be handcuffed by now."

"Where the fuck do you think you're going?"

"Arrest me or get out of my way. I got places to go, people to see."

"I know you're dirty, Bolitar. That whacko didn't ask

for you by accident. He thought you could save him.
That's why you've been playing cop with us. Pretending
to investigate on your own. You just wanted to stay
close, find out what we knew.''

"You got it all figured out, Rolly."

"We'll grill him and grill him and grill him until he
gives you up."

"No, you won't. As his attorney I am forbidding any
interrogation of my client."

"You can't represent him. Ever heard of conflict of
interest?"

"Until I find him someone else I'm still his attorney
of record."

Myron opened the door and stepped into the corridor.
He was surprised to see Esperanza. So were the cops.
Every one of them up and down the corridor stared at
her hungrily. Probably just being careful, Myron mused,
afraid maybe Esperanza had a concealed weapon in her
tight jeans. Yeah, that was probably it.

"Win called," she said. "He's looking for you."

"What's up?"

"He followed Duane. There's something he thinks
you should see."

Chapter 25

Esperanza and Myron shared a yellow cab to the Chelsea Hotel on Twenty-third Street between Seventh and Eighth. The cab smelled like a Turkish whorehouse, which was an improvement over most.

"Win will be seated in a red chair near the house phones," she told him when they stopped. "It's to the right of the concierge's desk. He'll be reading a newspaper. If he's not reading a newspaper, the coast isn't clear. Ignore him and walk out. He'll meet you at the Billiards Club."

"Win said that?"

"Yes."

"Even that part about the coast not being clear?"

"Yes."

Myron shook his head. "You want to come?"

"Can't. I still have studying to do."

"Thanks for finding me."

She nodded.

Win was seated where advertised. He was reading the *Wall Street Journal* so the coast was clear. Oooo. Win looked exactly like himself, except a black wig covered the blond locks. Dr. Disguise. Myron sat next to him and whispered, "The white rabbit turns yellow when the black dog urinates on him."

Win continued to read. "You said to contact you if Duane did anything unusual."

"Yep."

"He arrived here about two hours ago. He took the elevator to the third floor and knocked on the door to room 322. A woman answered. They embraced. He entered. The door closed."

"That's not good," Myron said.

Win turned the page. Bored.

"Do you know who the woman is?" Myron asked.

He shook his head. "Black. Five-seven, five-eight. Slim. I took the liberty of booking room 323. The peephole has a view of Duane's door."

Myron thought of Jessica waiting for him. In a warm tub. With those exotic oils.

Damn.

"I'll stay if you want," Win said.

"No. I'll handle this."

"Fine." Win stood. "I'll see you at the match tomorrow, if our boy isn't too tired to play."

Myron took the stairs to the third floor. He peered out into the corridor. No one. With key in hand he hurried down to room 323 and went inside. Win, as usual, was right. From the keyhole he had a good, albeit convex, view of the door to room 322. Now he had to wait.

But wait for what?

What the hell was he doing here? Jessica was waiting for him in a bathtub filled with exotic oils—the thought made his body both sing and ache—and here he was, playing Peeping Tom over . . .

Over what?

What was he after anyway? Duane had explained his connection to Valerie Simpson. They'd briefly been lovers. What was so weird about that? They were both attractive, both in their early twenties, both tennis players. So what was the big deal? The racial thing? Nothing

unusual about that anymore. Hadn't he just pointed that
out to Dimonte?

So what was Myron doing with his eye pressed
against a peephole? Duane was a client, for chrissake,
an important client. What right did Myron have to in-
vade his privacy like this? And for what reason—because his girlfriend didn't like the fact that Duane was
having affairs? So what? That wasn't Myron's concern.
Myron wasn't Duane's social worker, parole officer,
priest, shrink—he was his agent. His job was to get the
maximum return for his client, not make morality judgments.

On the other hand, what the hell was Duane doing
here? Maybe he liked to play the field, fine and dandy,
no problem. But tonight of all nights? It's crazy. Tomorrow was the biggest day of Duane's career. Nationally televised match. His first U.S. Open quarterfinal. His
first match against a seeded player. The launching of the
Nike spots. Kind of a strange night for a romantic tryst
in a hotel room.

Duane Richwood, the Wilt Chamberlain of professional tennis.

Myron didn't like it.

Duane had always been a bit of a mystery. In reality
Myron knew nothing about his past. He'd been a runaway, or so Duane said, but who knew for sure? Why
had he run in the first place? Where was his family now?
Myron had created a spin on the facts—portraying
Duane as the poor street kid struggling to escape the
shackles of poverty. But was that the truth? Duane
seemed like a good kid—intelligent, well-spoken, well-
mannered—but could that all be an act? The young man
Myron had known would not be spending such an im-

portant night screwing in a strange hotel room—which, of course, circled Myron back to the question:

So what?

Myron was his agent. Period. The kid had talent to burn and a terrific court sense. He was good-looking and could make a lot of money in endorsements. In the end, that was all that mattered to an agent. Not a player's love life. The kid was a dream on the court. Who cared what he was like off it? Myron was getting too close to this. He had no perspective anymore. He had a business to run, and spying on one of his biggest clients, invading that client's privacy, was not good business sense.

He should leave. He should go to Jessica and talk to her about it, see what she thought.

Ten more minutes.

He needed only two. He switched eyes just as the door to room 322 opened. Duane appeared, or at least the back of him. Myron saw a woman's arms go around his neck, pulling him down. They embraced. He couldn't see the woman's face, just the arms. Myron thought about Wanda's intuition. She had been so sure of herself, so blind to this possibility. Myron understood. He'd been there. Love has a way of putting on the blinders.

"Putting on the blinders," Myron muttered to himself. "Unbelievable."

After the hug broke, Duane straightened up. The woman's arms dropped out of sight. Duane looked ready to leave. Myron pushed his eye closer to the peephole. Duane spun and looked directly at Myron's door. Myron almost jumped back. For a second it was like Duane was looking right at Myron, like he knew Myron was there.

Once again Myron wondered how he had ended up here. If his job included checking on the promiscuity of every athlete he represented, he would spend his life peering through peepholes. Duane was a kid. Twenty-one years old. He wasn't even married or officially engaged. Nothing Myron was seeing was connected in any way with Valerie Simpson's murder.

Until Duane finally stepped away.

Duane had given the woman one more brief hug. There had been muffled voices, but Myron couldn't make out any specific words. Duane looked left, then right, then moved away. The woman was already starting to close the door, but she glanced out one last time. And that was when Myron saw her.

The woman was Deanna Yeller.

Chapter 26

The morning.

Myron had not confronted Duane. He'd stumbled to Jessica's in something of a daze. He'd opened the door with his key and said, "I'm sorry. I had to—"

Jessica shushed him with a kiss. Then a bigger kiss. Hungrier kiss. Myron tried to fight off her advances, though some might call his struggle less than valiant.

He rolled over in the bed. Jessica was gently padding across the room. Naked. She slipped into a silk robe. He watched, as he always did, with utter fascination. "You're so hot," he said, "you make my teeth sweat."

She smiled. There is something that happens to men when Jessica looks at them. Shallow breathing. Fluttering stomach. A cruel longing. But her smile raised all those symptoms to the tenth power.

"Good morning," she said. She bent down and kissed him gently. "How are you feeling?"

"My ears are still popping from last night."

"Nice to know I still have the touch," she said.

The understatement of the millennium. "Tell me about your trip."

"Tell me about your murder first."

He did. Jess was a great listener. She never interrupted, except to ask the right question. She looked at him steadily without a lot of that phony head nodding or out-of-context smiling. Her eyes focused in on him as if he were the only person in the world. He felt light-headed and happy and scared.

"This Valerie got to you," Jessica said when he finished.

"She had no one. Her life was in danger and she had no one."

"She had you."

"I only met her once. She wasn't even signed yet."

"Doesn't matter. She knew what you were. If I were in trouble, you'd be the person I'd run to." She tilted her head. "How did you know my room number and hotel?"

"Aaron. He was trying to be intimidating. He succeeded."

"Aaron threatened to hurt me?"

"You, me, my mom, Esperanza."

She hesitated, thinking. "Esperanza would be my choice. I mean, if it has to be one of us."

"I'll tell him." He took her hand. "I'm glad you're home."

"No third degree?"

Myron shook his head.

"But I owe you an explanation."

"I don't want one," he said. "I just want to be with you. I love you. I've always loved you. We are soul mates."

"Soul mates?"

He nodded.

"When did you decide this?" she asked.

"A long time ago."

"So why not tell me before now?"

He shrugged. "I didn't want to scare you off."

"And now?"

"Now it's more important to tell you how I feel."

The room was still. "What am I supposed to say to that?" she asked.

"Nothing."

"I do love you, Myron. You know that."

"I know."

Silence. A long silence.

Jessica crossed the room. Naked. She was not self-conscious about her body. Then again, she had no reason to be. "It seems to me," she began, "there are a lot of weird connections with this murder. But there is one overriding constant."

Change of subjects. That was okay. Enough had been said for one day. "What?" Myron asked.

"Tennis," she said. "Alexander Cross is killed at a tennis club. Valerie Simpson is murdered at the national tennis center. Valerie and Duane have an affair—both are professional tennis players. Those two kids who supposedly killed Alexander Cross—what's their names?"

"Errol Swade and Curtis Yeller."

"Swade and Yeller," she repeated. "They were both up to no good at a tennis club. The Ache brothers and Aaron are connected to an agency who deals with tennis players. That leaves us with Deanna Yeller."

"What about her?"

"Her sleeping with Duane. It can't just be a coincidence."

"So?"

"So how would she have met Duane?"

"I don't know," Myron said.

"Does she play tennis?"

"What if she does?"

"Keeps things constant." She stopped. "I don't know. I'm ranting. It's just that everything circles back to tennis—except for Deanna Yeller."

Myron thought about it a moment. Nothing clicked, but something did rumble somewhere in the back of his brain.

"Just a thought," she said.

He sat up. "Before you said 'supposedly' killed Alexander Cross. What did you mean?"

"What real evidence do you have that Swade and Yeller murdered the Cross kid?" she asked. "They might have just been convenient scapegoats. Think about it a second. Yeller was conveniently killed by the police. Swade has conveniently fallen off the face of the earth. Who better to take the fall?"

"Then who do you think killed Alexander Cross?" he asked.

She shrugged. "Probably Swade and Yeller. But who knows for sure?"

More rumbling in the brain. But still nothing surfaced. Myron checked his watch. Seven-thirty.

"You in a rush?" she asked.

"A little."

"I thought Duane Richwood doesn't play until one," she said.

"I'm trying to land a kid named Eddie Crane. He's playing in the juniors at ten."

"Can I come along?" she asked.

"Sure."

"What are your chances of landing him?" she asked.

"I think they're pretty good. His father might be a problem."

"The father doesn't like you?"

"I think he'd prefer a bigger agency," Myron said.

"Should I smile sweetly at him?" she asked.

Myron thought a moment. "Flash a little cleavage. I'm not sure this guy's into subtle."

"Anything to get a client," she said.

"Maybe you should practice a little first," he said.

"Practice what?"

"Flashing cleavage. I'm told it's something of an art."

"I see. And on whom should I practice?"

Myron spread his hands. "I'm willing to volunteer my services."

"The sacrifices you make for clients," she said. "It's heroic, really."

"So what do you say?"

Jessica gave him a look. *The* look, actually. Myron felt it in his toes, to name one place. She leaned toward him. "No."

"No?"

She put her lips to his ear. "Let's try out my new oils first."

One word: Yowzer.

Chapter 27

Jessica hadn't need to flash cleavage.

Both Cranes were immediately entranced. Mrs. Crane chatted with Jess about her books. Mr. Crane couldn't stop smiling and sucking in his gut. At the start of the second set Mr. Crane tried to chew down the commission a half point. A very good sign. Myron made a mental note to bring Jess to more business gatherings.

There were other agents there. Lots of them. Most wore business suits and had their hair slicked back. They ranged in age, but most looked pretty young. Several tried to approach, but Mr. Crane shooed them away.

"Vultures," Jessica whispered to Myron as one forced his card on Mr. Crane.

"Just trying to hustle business," Myron said.

"You're defending them?"

"I do the same thing, Jess. If they're not aggressive they don't have a chance. You think the Cranes are going to come to them?"

"But still. You don't hang around like these guys."

"What exactly am I doing now?"

Jessica thought a second. "Yeah, but you're cute."

Hard to argue. Eddie crushed his opponent 6–0, 6–0, but the match was not as close as the score indicated. Eddie lacked finesse. He relied on power. But what power. His racket ripped through the still air like the reaper's scythe. The ball shot off the strings as though from a bazooka. The finesse would come. But for now the awesome power was more than enough.

After the players shook hands Eddie's parents went onto the court.

"Do me a favor," Myron said to Jess.

"What?"

"Get rid of the parents for a couple of minutes. I want to talk to Eddie alone."

She did it with a lunch invitation. Jessica escorted Mr. and Mrs. Crane to the Racquets restaurant overlooking the Grandstand. Myron accompanied Eddie to the locker room. The kid had barely broken a sweat. Myron had exerted himself more just watching. Eddie walked with big, unhurried steps, a towel draped around his neck, completely relaxed.

"I told TruPro I wasn't interested," Eddie said.

Myron nodded. That explained Aaron's generous offer to let Myron represent Eddie. "How did they respond?"

"They were pretty pissed," Eddie said.

"I bet."

"I think I want to go with your agency," he said.

"How do your parents feel?"

"Doesn't matter really. They both know it's my decision."

They walked a few more steps.

"Eddie, I need to ask you about Valerie."

He half-smiled. "Are you really trying to find her killer?"

"Yes."

"Why?"

"I don't know. It's just something I have to do."

Eddie nodded. The answer was good enough for him. "Shoot."

"You first met Valerie at Pavel's camp in Florida?"

"Right."

"How did you two become friends?"

"You ever been to Pavel's academy?" Eddie asked.

"No."

"You might not get it." Eddie Crane stopped, brushed the hair from his eyes, continued. "It probably sounds weird—a sixteen-year-old girl and a nine-year-old boy being close friends. That's pretty normal in tennis. You don't make friends with kids your own age. They're the enemy. Val and I were both lonely, I guess. And because of our differences we weren't threats to each other. I guess that's how it started."

"Did she ever mention Alexander Cross?"

"Yeah, a couple of times. They dated or something."

"Did you get the impression they were serious?"

He shrugged. The guard checked their passes and let them enter. "Not really. Tennis was her life. Boyfriends were peripheral."

"Tell me more about Pavel's academy. What was it like for Valerie?"

"What was it like?" Eddie grinned sadly, shook his head. "It was like one big game of King of the Mountain. Every kid is trying to knock off every other kid."

"And Valerie was king of the woman's side?"

Eddie nodded. "The undisputed king."

"Did Pavel and Valerie get along?"

"Yeah. At first anyway. He motivated Val like no one else could. She would practice for hours with his assistants, and just when you thought she couldn't take one more step Pavel would come out and boom! it was like an energy boost. Val was a great player, but Pavel knew how to get her competitive juices really flowing. When he was there, she blew away everyone else. Diving, stretching, running down every lob. She was incredible."

"So when did things start going wrong?"

Eddie shrugged. "When she started losing." He said it like it was the most natural thing in the world.

"What happened?"

"I don't know." He stopped again, thinking. "She stopped caring, I guess. It happens to a lot of the players. They burn out. Too much pressure too fast."

"What did Pavel do?"

"He tried all his old tricks. You see, Pavel fostered the whole dog-eat-dog atmosphere. It weeded out the weak, he told me. But Valerie wasn't responding anymore. She still beat most of the girls. But when she played against the game's greats—Steffi, Monica, Gabriela, Martina—she didn't have the heart to beat them anymore."

Eddie sat in a chair in front of his locker. Very few people were around. The floor, carpeted in an office-brown, was littered with little pieces of wrap and band-aging. Myron sat down next to him. "You told me you saw Valerie a few days before she died."

"Yeah," Eddie said. "In the lobby of the Plaza." He took off his shirt. The kid was bony. The kind of bony where it appears the chest concaves into the heart. "I hadn't seen her in a long time."

"What did she say to you?"

"She was going to make a comeback. She seemed pretty excited about the idea, kinda like the old Val. Then she gave me your number and told me to stay away from Pavel and TruPro."

"Did she say why you should stay away?"

"No."

"Did she say anything else?"

He paused, his mind flashing back. "Not really. She was kinda in a hurry. She said she had to go out and settle something."

"Settle what?"

"I don't know. She didn't say."

"What day was this?" Myron asked.

"Thursday, I think."

"Do you remember the time?"

"Must have been around six."

Valerie had called Duane's apartment Thursday at six-fifteen. Settle something. Settle what? Settle her relationship with Duane? Or expose it? And what if she did threaten that? Would Duane kill her to stop her? Myron didn't think so, especially in light of the fact that Duane was serving a tennis ball in front of several thousand people when she was shot.

Eddie slipped out of his sneakers and socks.

"I got two tickets to the Yankees for Wednesday night," Myron said. "You want to go?"

Eddie smiled. "I thought you didn't do that."

"Do what?"

"That ass-kissing stuff."

"I do. Every agent does. I'm not above it. But in this case I actually thought it might be fun."

Eddie stood. "Should I be skeptical of your motives?" he asked.

"Only if you're smart."

Duane liked to be alone before a match. Win had taught him meditation techniques, *sans* the dirty videotapes, and you could usually find him curled up in a corner, sitting in the lotus position with his eyes closed. He didn't like to be disturbed, which was good. Myron wasn't sure he wanted to see him right now anyway. His main responsibility, he knew, was still to help his client perform his best—especially on this, the most important day of Duane's career. Raising the issue of Duane's late-night rendezvous with Deanna Yeller would be a distraction. A major distraction.

It would have to wait.

The crowd was huge. Everyone had been waiting for this match between the upstart American Duane Rich-wood and the cool Czech Michel Brishny, a former number one player now ranked fifth. Myron and Jessica took their seats in the front row. Jess looked incredible in a simple yellow sundress. Spectators gaped. Nothing new there. Without a doubt, the TV cameras would be getting plenty of shots of the box today. Between Jess's beauty and her fame in the literary world they wouldn't be able to resist.

Myron debated having her hold up one of his business cards. Nah. Too tacky.

A bevy of favorites was already in their seats. Ned Tunwell and other Nike VIPs crowded a corner box. Ned waved like a windmill on LSD. Myron gave a small wave back. Two boxes behind them sat chubby Roy O'Connor, the rotund president of TruPro. Sitting with him was Aaron. Aaron had his face tilted to the sun, soaking up the rays. He was garbed in his usual attire—white suit, no shirt. Across the way Myron also spotted Senator Cross in a box jammed with gray-haired lawyer types—the exception being Gregory Caufield. Myron still wanted to talk to Gregory. Perhaps an opportunity would present itself after the match. The buxom blonde from the other day was back in the same seat. The shapely lass gave Myron another small wave. He didn't wave back.

Myron turned to Jessica. She smiled at him.

"You're beautiful," he said.

"More beautiful than the blonde with the big boobs?" she asked.

"Who?" Myron said.

"The Silicone She-Beast giving you the eye."

"I don't know what you mean." Then: "How do you know they're silicone?"

The players took the court for warm-ups. Two minutes later Pavel Menansi made his grand entrance. There was a smattering of applause. Pavel displayed his gratitude with a circular hand gesture. Very popelike. He wore tennis whites, with a green sweater tied around his neck. The smile was on full blast. Pavel made his way toward the TruPro box. Aaron rose, let him in, then sat back down. Pavel and Roy O'Connor shook hands.

It hit Myron like a shot to the solar plexus. "Oh no," he said.

"What?" Jessica asked.

Myron stood. "I've got to go."

"Now?"

"I'll be back. Make my excuses."

Chapter 28

The match was on the car radio. WFAN, 66 AM. From the sound of it Duane was not playing well. He had just dropped the first set 6–3 when Myron pulled into a lot off Central Park West in Manhattan.

Dr. Julie Abramson lived in a town house half a block down from her office. Myron rang the bell. There was a buzzing noise and then her voice came over the intercom.

"Who is it?"

"Myron Bolitar. It's urgent."

There were a few seconds of silence. Then: "Second floor." The buzzer sounded again. Myron pushed the door open. Julie Abramson was waiting for him on the stairwell.

"Did you call and hang up on me?" she asked.

"Yes."

"Why?"

"To see if you were home."

He arrived at her door. They stood and faced each other. With their height difference—she well under five feet, he six-four—the sight was almost comical.

She looked up. Way up. "I still can't deny or confirm that Valerie Simpson was ever a patient of mine," she said.

"That's okay. I want to ask you about a hypothetical situation."

"A hypothetical situation?"

He nodded.

"And that couldn't wait until Monday?"

"No."

Dr. Abramson sighed. "Come on in."

She had the television turned on to the match. "I should have known," she said. "The TV keeps flashing to Jessica Culver in the players' box, but never you."

"With her there they wouldn't show me anyway."

"The sportscaster says you two are an item. Is that true?"

Myron shrugged. Noncommittal. "What's the score now?" he asked.

"Your client lost the first set 6–3," she said. "He's down 2–0 in this set." She switched off the television with the remote and signaled to a chair. They both sat. "So tell me about your hypothetical situation, Myron."

"I want to start off with a young girl. Fifteen years old. Pretty. From a well-to-do family, parents divorced, the father absent. She dates a boy from a prominent family. She's also a tennis protégée."

"This isn't sounding too hypothetical," Dr. Abramson said.

"Just bear with me a second. The young girl is such a great tennis player that her mother ships her off to an academy run by a world-famous tennis coach. When this young girl arrives at the academy she finds the competition cutthroat. Tennis is the most individual of sports. There is no team spirit here. There is no camaraderie. Everybody is vying for the approval of the world-famous coach. Tennis is not conducive to making friends." Echoing Eddie's words. "It isolates. Would you say that's true, Doctor?"

"On the level you're talking about, yes."

"So when this young girl is uprooted from the life she has known and tossed into this rather hostile environment, she is not made to feel welcome. Far from it. The other girls see this new tennis protégée as a threat and when they realize what a magnificent player she is, the threat becomes reality. The other girls shun her all the more. She grows even more isolated."

"Okay."

"Now, this world-famous coach, he's a bit Darwinian. Survival of the fittest and all that. He sort of plays a dual role here. On the one hand this isolation will force the girl to search for an escape, a place where she can thrive."

"The tennis court?" Abramson said.

"Exactly. The young girl begins to practice even harder than before. But at the same time the world-famous coach is nice to her. While everyone else is cruel, the world-famous coach praises her. He spends time with her. He gets the most out of her."

"Which in turn," Dr. Abramson interjected, "isolates her from the other girls all the more."

"Right. The young girl becomes dependent on the coach. She thinks he cares and like any eager student she wants—needs—his approval. She begins to play even harder. She also knows that pleasing the world-famous coach will also please her mother. She tries even harder. The cycle continues."

Dr. Abramson had to see where Myron was going with this, but her face remained blank. "Go on," she said.

"The tennis academy is not the real world. It's a secluded domain ruled by the world-famous coach. But he acts like he cares for the young girl. He treats her like she's something special. The young girl plays even

harder, pushing herself more than she could ever imagine—not for herself, but to please him. Maybe he offers
her a pat on the back after practice. Maybe he rubs her
sore shoulders. Maybe they have dinner one night to
discuss her tennis. Who knows how it started?''

"How what started?'' Abramson asked.

Myron chose to ignore the question. For now. "The
young girl and world-famous coach start touring together,'' he continued. "She starts playing competitive
tennis against women who again treat her as a feared
rival. But now the young girl and the world-famous
coach are alone. On the road. Staying in hotels.''

"More isolation,'' Abramson offered.

"She plays well. She's beautiful, she's young, she's
American. The press begins to swarm. The sudden attention frightens her. But the world-famous coach is
there to protect her.''

"She becomes more dependent on him.''

Myron nodded. "Now let's remember that the world-
famous coach is a former world-famous player himself.
He is accustomed to the narcissistic lifestyle that goes
along with being a professional athlete. He is used to
doing as he pleases. And that's exactly what he does
with this girl.''

Silence.

"Could this happen, Doc? In theory?''

Dr. Abramson cleared her throat. "In theory, yes.
Whenever a man yields power and authority over a
woman the potential for abuse is high. But in your scenario the potential for abuse is maximized. The man is
older, the woman no more than a child. A teacher or a
boss might control their victim for a few hours a day,
but in your scenario the coach is both omnipotent and
omnipresent.''

They looked at each other.

"The girl in my scenario," Myron said softly. "Her play would deteriorate if he abused her?"

"Without question."

"What else would happen to her?"

"Every case is different," Abramson replied as though giving a dissertation. "But the results would invariably be catastrophic. A scenario like yours would probably start out for the young girl as nothing more than a crush. This sophisticated, older man is nice to her when nobody else is. He understands and cares about her. She probably doesn't have to invite his advances—they just sort of happen. The young girl may encourage them at first, but probably not. She may even resist, but at the same time she feels responsible. She blames herself."

Myron felt something in the pit of his stomach open wide. "Which causes more problems."

"Yes. You talked about how the world-famous coach isolates her," Abramson continued. "But in your scenario he does more than that. He dehumanizes her. Her adolescence is turned upside down by her tennis greatness. Her life is not about school and friends and family. It's about money and winning. She's become a commodity. She knows that if she displeases him, the commodity becomes worthless. And her being a commodity makes it easier on him too."

"How?" Myron asked.

"A commodity is far easier to abuse than a human being."

Silence.

"So what happens when it's all over?" Myron asked. "When the world-famous coach uses up the commodity, what happens to her?"

"The young girl would reach out for something—anything—that she thinks might save her."

"The old boyfriend maybe?"

"Perhaps."

"She might even want to get engaged right away."

"That's possible, yes. She may see the old boyfriend as a return to her innocence. In her mind the boyfriend may be raised to savior status."

"And suppose this boyfriend was murdered?"

"You've pulled out the final block," Abramson replied softly. "The young girl was already in need of serious therapy. Now a complete mental breakdown is a very real possibility. Maybe even a likelihood."

Myron felt his heart crumble.

Dr. Abramson looked away for a moment. "But there are other aspects to your scenario that need to be explored," she said, trying to sound offhanded.

"Like?"

"Like what actually occurred during the abuse. If, as you say, the world-famous coach was a narcissistic man, he would only concern himself with his pleasure. He wouldn't worry about her. He probably wouldn't, for example, wear protection. And since this girl is rather young and probably not sexually active, she wouldn't be using oral contraceptives."

Dread flooded Myron's chest. He remembered the rumors. "He got her pregnant."

"In the realm of your scenario," Abramson said, "that is certainly a possibility."

"What would happen . . . ?" Myron stopped. The answer was obvious. "The world-famous coach would make her get an abortion."

"I imagine so, yes."

Silence.

Myron felt something well up in his eyes. "What she went though..." He shook his head. "Everyone thought Valerie was so weak. But in reality—"

"Not Valerie," Abramson corrected. "A young girl. A theoretical young girl in a theoretical situation."

Myron looked up. "Still trying to protect your ass, Doc?"

"You can't say anything, Myron. It's all hypothetical. I will neither confirm nor deny that Valerie Simpson was ever a patient of mine."

He shook his head, stood, and headed for the door. When he reached it, he turned back toward her. "One more hypothetical question," he said. "The world-famous coach. If he's willing to abuse one child, how likely is it he'll do it again?"

Dr. Abramson did not face him. "Very likely," she said.

Chapter 29

By the time Myron got back to Stadium Court, Duane had dropped the first two sets 6–3, 6–1, and it was 2–2 in the third set. Myron sat between Jessica and Win. Pavel Menansi, he immediately noticed, was no longer in his seat. Aaron was still there. Senator Cross and Gregory Caufield were in their box too. Ned Tunwell still sat with his Nike colleagues. Ned was no longer waving. He was, in fact, crying. The entire Nike box looked like a deflated balloon. Henry Hobman was still as a Rodin.

Myron turned to Jessica. She looked concerned but said nothing. She took his hand and gave it a little squeeze. He squeezed back and gave her a small smile. He noticed that she was now wearing a bright pink Ray•Ban cap.

"What's with the cap?" he asked.

"A guy offered me a thousand dollars to wear it."

Myron was familiar with the old advertising trick. Companies—in this case, Ray•Ban—paid anyone seated in the players' boxes to wear the caps during matches, figuring, of course, that there was an excellent chance the person and hence the hat would show up on television. Relatively cheap and effective exposure.

Myron looked at Win. "What about you?"

"I don't do caps," Win replied. "They muss my hair."

"That," Jessica added, "and the guy only offered him five hundred dollars."

Win shrugged. "Sexual discrimination. It's an ugly thing."

More like smart business. Five hundred dollars was the normal rate. But somebody at Ray•Ban realized Jess was both attractive and a celebrity—ergo, extra exposure.

Duane dropped another game. Down 3–2 after losing the first two sets. Not good. The players collapsed in their chairs on either side of the umpire for the change-over. Duane toweled down his racket. He changed shirts. Some female fans whistled. Duane did not smile. He glanced over at their box. Unlike just about any other sport in the world, tennis players are not allowed to talk to their coaches during the match. But Henry did move. He took his hand off his chin and made a fist. Duane nodded.

"Time," the chair ump said.

That was when Pavel made his return.

He entered through the portal on the right near the grandstand carrying an Evian in his hand. Myron's eyes locked on to him. He felt his pulse quicken. Pavel Menansi was still wearing the sweater tied around his neck. He took his seat behind Aaron. Pavel Menansi. He smiled. He laughed. He sipped a cold Evian. He breathed in and out. He lived. People patted his back. Someone asked for an autograph. A young girl. Pavel said something to her. The young girl giggled behind her hand.

"Burgess Meredith," Win said. He was looking at the court, not Myron.

"What?"

"Burgess Meredith."

More Name the *Batman* Criminal. "Not now," Myron said.

"Now. Burgess Meredith."

"Why?"

"Because you're staring. Aaron will pick it up." Win adjusted his sunglasses. "Burgess Meredith."

He was right. "The Penguin."

"Victor Buono."

"King Tut."

"Bruce Lee."

Jessica leaned over. "Trick question," she said.

"No hints," Win said.

"He played Kato," Myron said. "Green Hornet's sidekick. He guest-starred on one episode. I don't know if you could call him a criminal."

"Correct." Silence. Then Win said: "That bad?"

"Worse."

"The police released Valerie's body," Win said. "The funeral is tomorrow."

Myron nodded. On the court Duane served up an ace. Only his second of the match. Myron said, "It may get ugly now."

"How so?"

"I know why the Ache brothers want us out."

"Ah," Win said. "May I assume the Aches will not want you to disseminate this information to the general public?"

"Correct assumption."

"And may I further assume this information is worth the cost of Aaron and an all-star cast?"

"Another correct assumption."

Win sat back. He was very still. He was also smiling. Myron turned to Jessica. Her hand still held his.

"If you get killed," she whispered, "I'll kill you. Soul mate."

Silence.

On the court Duane hit two more aces and then an overhead to tie the third set at three games apiece. Duane looked over at the box. The reflection of the sun off his sunglasses was blinding, giving him a sleek, robotic look. But something in his face had changed. Duane made the fist again.

Henry spoke for the first time. "He's baaack."

Chapter 30

Henry Hobman was good as his word. Duane rallied. He took the third set 6–4. Ned Tunwell stopped crying. The fourth set went to a tiebreaker, which Duane won 9–7, saving three match points. Ned started the windmill wave again. Duane won the fifth set 6–2. Ned had to change his underwear.

Final score of the marathon match: 3–6, 1–6, 6–4, 7–6, (9–7), 6–2. Before the combatants had even left the court the word *classic* was being bantered about.

By the time all the congratulations and news conferences ended it was getting late. Jess borrowed Myron's car to visit her mother. Win dropped him off at the office. Esperanza was still there.

"Big win," she said.

"Yup."

"Duane played like shit in the first two sets."

"He had a long night," Myron said. "What have we got?"

Esperanza handed him a stack of papers. "Prenuptial agreement for Jerry Prince. Final copy."

Ah, the beloved prenup. A necessary evil. Myron hated to recommend them. Marriage should be about love and romance. A prenup, frankly speaking, was about as romantic as licking a litter box. Still, Myron had an obligation to guard the financial well-being of his clients. Too many of these marriages ended in quickie divorces. Gold-digging, it used to be called. Some mistook his concern for sexism. It wasn't. Well-to-do female athletes should do the same.

"What else?" he asked.

"Emmett Roberts wants you to call. He needs your opinion on a car he's buying."

Myron drove a Ford Taurus, hardly qualifying him as *MotorTrend*'s Man of the Year.

Emmett was a fringe basketball player who bounced between bench-sitting in the NBA and starring in the Continental Basketball Association—a sort of basketball minor league where players do nothing but try to impress NBA scouts. Very few do. There were exceptions. John Starks and Anthony Mason of the Knicks, to name two. But for the most part the CBA gymnasiums were yet another haven of shattered dreams, a bottom rung on the ladder before slipping off altogether.

Myron fingered through his Rolodex. Esperanza was good about keeping it up-to-date and in alphabetical order for him. Raston. Ratner. Rextell. Rippard. Roberts. There. Emmett Roberts.

Myron stopped.

"Where's Duane's card?" he asked.

"What?"

Myron quickly skimmed through the rest of the *R*'s. "Duane Richwood isn't in my Rolodex. Could you have misfiled it?"

She dismissed that possibility with a glare. "Look around. It's probably on your desk someplace."

Not on the desk. Myron tried the *D*'s. No Duane.

"I'll make you up a new one," she said, heading for the door. "Try not to lose it this time."

"Thanks a bunch," he said. Still, the missing card

gnawed at him. Another coincidence involving Duane? He dialed Emmett Roberts's phone. Emmett answered.

"Hey, Myron. How's it going?"

"Good, Emmett. What's this about buying a car?"

"I saw this Porsche today. Red. Fully loaded. Seventy Gs. I was thinking about using the play-off bonus money to buy it."

"If that's what you want," Myron said.

"Man, you sound like my mother. I wanted your opinion."

"Buy something cheaper," Myron said. "A lot cheaper."

"But the car is so hot, Myron. If you could just see it . . ."

"Then buy it, Emmett. You're an adult. You don't need my blessing." Myron hesitated. "Did I ever tell you about Norm Booker?"

"Who?"

How soon they forget.

"I was maybe fifteen or sixteen years old," Myron said, "and I was working at this summer camp in Massachusetts. It was a Celtics camp. They used to have their rookie tryouts there. I was basically a towel boy. I met a lot of the draft picks back then. Cedric Maxwell. Larry Bird. But my first year the Celtics had a first-round pick named Norm Booker. I think he was out of Iowa State."

"Yeah, so?"

"Norm was a great player. Six-seven, smooth moves, nice touch. Strong as an ox. And nice guy too. He talked to me. Lot of the guys ignored the towel boys, but Norm wasn't like that. I remember he used to shoot foul shots with his back to the basket. He'd toss the ball over his shoulder. He had such a great touch that he could make better than fifty percent that way.''

"So what happened to him?''

"He sat the bench as a rookie. The Celtics cut him the next year. He scrounged around a bit and then he landed with the Portland Trailblazers. He mostly rode the bench, played garbage time, that sort of thing. When the Trailblazers made the play-offs Norm got the usual bonus. He was so excited about it he went out and bought a Rolls-Royce. Dropped every dime he had on that car. But he wasn't worried. There was always next year. And the year after that. Only thing was, Portland cut him. He tried out with a couple of other clubs, but nobody wanted him. Last I heard Norm had to sell the car to feed his family.''

Silence.

After some time passed Emmett said, "I also saw this Honda Accord. They had a pretty good lease deal.''

"Go for it, Emmett.''

They hung up a few minutes later. Myron hadn't thought about Norm Booker in a long time. He wondered what became of him.

Esperanza came back in. She put a new card for Duane Richwood in his Rolodex. "Happy?''

"Yes.'' He handed her two sheets of paper. "This is a party list for the night Alexander Cross was killed.''

"What am I looking for?''

"Heck if I know. A familiar name. Something that leaps out at you.''

She nodded. "You know about the funeral tomorrow?''

Myron nodded.

"You going?'' she asked.

"Yes.''

"I tracked down one of the schoolteachers from the article on Curtis Yeller."

"Which one?"

"Mrs. Lucinda Elright. She's retired now, lives in Philadelphia. She'll see you tomorrow afternoon. You can go right after the funeral."

Myron leaned back. "I'm not sure that's necessary anymore."

"You want me to cancel?"

Myron thought a moment. In light of what he'd learned about Pavel Menansi, the connection between Valerie's murder and what happened to Curtis Yeller seemed more tenuous than ever. The murder of Alexander Cross had not caused Valerie's downfall. It wasn't even the final push. Pavel Menansi had pushed Valerie off the cliff years before. He had watched her slowly plummet, tumbling over jagged rocks on her painful way down. Alexander Cross's death had marked the end of the descent. The ground, if you will. The final crash. Nothing more. Clearly there was no connection between Valerie's death and the events of six years ago. There was also no connection between Duane and Valerie other than what Duane had said—they slept together. No big deal.

Except . . .

Except for last night's rendezvous between Duane and Curtis Yeller's mother.

If not for that—if Myron hadn't seen them together at the hotel—he would be able to dismiss them both entirely. But Duane and Deanna Yeller having an affair—it was too much of a coincidence. There had to be a connection.

"Don't cancel," Myron said.

Chapter 31

Valerie's funeral was strictly cookie-cutter.

The reverend, a porky man with a red nose, hadn't known her with any depth. He listed achievements as though reading from a résumé. He mixed in a few oldies but goodies: loving daughter; so full of life; taken so young; God has a plan. An organ sounded self-righteous indignation. Tacky flowers, like something you'd find draped around a winning horse, adorned the chapel. Stern stain-glass figures peered from above.

The crowd did not linger long. They stopped by Helen and Kenneth Van Slyke, not so much to offer comfort but to be sure they'd been seen and recognized, which was the real reason they'd come in the first place. Helen Van Slyke shook hands with her head high. She did not blink. She did not smile. She did not cry. Her jaw was set. Myron waited in the receiving line with Win. As they got closer they could hear Helen repeat the same phrases—"Good of you to come, thank you for coming, good of you to come, thank you for coming"—in a singsong voice reminiscent of a flight attendant upon disembarkation.

When it was Myron's turn Helen gripped his hand hard. "Do you know who hurt Valerie?"

"Yes." She had said hurt, Myron noted. Not kill.

Helen Van Slyke looked at Win for confirmation. Win nodded.

"Come back to the house," she said. "There's going to be a reception." She turned to the next mourner and hit PLAY on her internal tape recorder. "Good of you to come, thank you for coming, good of you to come . . ."

Myron and Win did as she asked. The mood at Brentman Hall was neither Irish wake–like nor devastating grief. There were no tears. No laughter. Either would have been more welcome than this room completely void of any emotion. "Mourners" milled around like they were at an office cocktail party.

"No one cares," Myron said. "She's gone and no one cares."

Win shrugged. "No one ever does." The eternal optimist.

The first person to approach them was Kenneth. He was dressed in proper black with well-shined shoes. He greeted Win with a back slap and a firm handshake. He ignored Myron.

"How are you holding up?" Win asked. Like he cared.

"Oh I'm doing okay," he said with a heavy sigh. Mr. Brave. "But I'm worried about Helen. We've had to medicate her."

"I'm sorry to hear that," Myron said.

Kenneth turned to him, as though seeing him for the first time. He made a face like he was sucking on a lemon. "Do you mean that?" he asked.

Myron and Win shared a glance. "Yes, I do, Kenneth," Myron said.

"Then do me the courtesy of staying away from my wife. She was very upset after your visit the other day."

"I meant no harm."

"Well, you caused plenty of it, I can tell you. I think it's high time, Mr. Bolitar, you showed some respect.

Leave my wife alone. We are grieving here. She's lost her daughter and I've lost my stepdaughter.''

Win rolled his eyes.

Myron said, "You have my word, Kenneth."

Kenneth nodded a manly nod and moved away.

"His stepdaughter," Win said in disgust. "Bah."

From across the room Myron caught Helen Van Slyke's eye. She made a gesture toward a door on her right and slipped through it. Like they were meeting for a secret liaison.

"Keep Kenneth away," Myron said.

Win feigned surprise. "But you gave Kenneth your word."

"Bah," Myron said. Whatever that meant.

He ducked through the doorway and followed Helen. She too wore all black, a suit of some sort with the skirt cut just low enough to be sexy yet proper. Good legs, he noticed, and felt like a pig for thinking such a thing at such a time. She led him to a small room down the end of an ornate corridor and closed the door behind them. The room looked like a miniature version of the living room. The chandelier was smaller. The couch was smaller. The fireplace was smaller. The portrait over the mantel was smaller.

"This is the drawing room," Helen Van Slyke explained.

"Oh," Myron said. He'd always wanted to know what a drawing room was. Now that he was in one he still had no idea.

"Would you care for some tea?"

"No thanks."

"Do you mind if I have some?"

"Not at all," he said.

She sat demurely and poured herself a cup from the

silver set on the table. Myron noticed that there were two tea sets on the table. He wondered if that was a clue as to the definition of drawing room.

"Kenneth tells me you're on medication," he said.

"Kenneth is full of shit."

Big surprise.

"Are you still investigating Valerie's murder?" she asked. There was almost a mocking quality in her voice. Her words also seemed just a tad slurred, and Myron wondered if perhaps she was indeed being medicated or if she'd added a little home brew to her tea.

"Yes," he said.

"Do you still feel some chivalrous responsibility toward her?"

"I never did."

"Then why do you do it?"

Myron shrugged. "Someone should care."

She looked up, searching his face for a shred of sarcasm. "I see," she said. "So tell me: what have you learned from your investigation?"

"Pavel Menansi abused your daughter."

Myron watched for a reaction. Helen Van Slyke smiled semi-teasingly and put a sugar cube in her tea. Not exactly the reaction he had in mind. "You can't be serious," she said.

"I am."

"What do you mean, abused?"

"Sexual abuse."

"As in rape?"

"You may call it that, yes."

She made a scoffing noise. "Come now, Mr. Bolitar. Isn't that a tad extreme?"

"No."

"It is not as though Pavel forced himself on her, is it? They had an affair. It's hardly unheard of."

"You knew about it?"

"Of course. And frankly, I was quite displeased. Pavel showed poor judgment. But my daughter was sixteen years old at the time—maybe seventeen, I'm not really sure. Anyway, she was certainly of legal age. Calling it rape or sexual abuse, well, I think that's being a tad overdramatic, don't you?"

Maybe both medication and booze. Maybe even mixing them. "Valerie was a young girl," he said. "Pavel Menansi was her coach, a man of nearly fifty."

"Would it have made it any better if he was forty? Or thirty?"

"No," Myron said.

"So why bring up their age difference?" She put down the tea. The smile was again toying with her lips. "Let me ask you a question, Mr. Bolitar. If Valerie was a sixteen-year-old boy and he had an affair with a beautiful female coach who was, let's say, thirty—would you call that sexual abuse? Would you call that rape?"

Myron hesitated for a second. It was a second too long.

"I thought so," she said triumphantly. "You're a sexist, Mr. Bolitar. Valerie had an affair with an older man. It happens all the time." Again the playful smile. "To me even."

"Did you have a breakdown after it was over?"

She raised an eyebrow. "So that's your definition of abuse?" she asked. "A breakdown?"

"You entrusted your daughter to this man," Myron said. "He was supposed to help her. But he used her instead. He tore her down. He destroyed and discarded her."

"Tore? Destroyed? Discarded? My, my, Mr. Bolitar, we are out for shock effect, aren't we?"

"You don't see anything wrong with what he did?"

She put down her tea and took a cigarette. She lit it, inhaled deeply with her eyes closed, and let it all out. "If it makes you happy to blame me for what happened, fine, blame me. I was a lousy mother. The worst. Is that better?"

Myron watched her calmly smoking her cigarette and sipping her tea. Too calmly. Did she really buy this crap she was peddling? Or was it an act? Was she just deluding herself or . . .

"Pavel bought you off," Myron said.

"No."

"TruPro and Pavel are paying—"

"That's not it at all," she interrupted.

"We know about the money, Mrs. Van Slyke."

"You don't understand. Pavel blames himself for what happened. He took it upon himself to remedy the situation in the only way he could."

"By paying you off."

"By providing us with some of the funds Valerie may have earned had her career continued. He didn't have to do that. The affair wasn't necessarily the cause—"

"It's called hush money."

"Never," she said in a near-hiss. "Valerie was my daughter."

"And you sold her for cash."

She shook her head. "I did what I thought was best for my daughter."

"He abused her. You took his money. You let him get away with it."

"There was nothing I could do," she said. "We

didn't want to make it public. Valerie wanted to put it behind her. She wanted to keep it confidential. We all did."

"Why?" Myron said. "It was just an affair with an older man. Happens all the time. To you even."

She bit down on her lip for a moment. When she spoke again her voice was softer. "There was nothing I could do," she repeated. "It was in everyone's best interest to keep it quiet."

"Bullshit," Myron said. He realized he was pushing too hard, but something inside of him wouldn't let him back off. "You sold your daughter."

She was silent for a few moments, concentrating only on her cigarette, watching the ash grow longer and longer. In the distance they could hear the low rumble from the funeral crowd. Glasses clinking. A polite titter.

"They threatened Valerie," she said.

"Who?"

"I don't know. Men who work with Pavel. They made it very clear that if she opened her mouth she was dead." She looked up, pleading. "Don't you see? What option did we have? No good could come from talking. They'd kill her. I was afraid for Valerie. Kenneth—well, I think Kenneth was more interested in the money. Hindsight may be twenty-twenty, but at the time I believed it was the best thing."

"You were protecting your daughter," Myron said.

"Yes."

"But she's dead now."

Helen was puzzled. "I don't understand."

"You don't have to worry about her being hurt anymore. She's dead. You're free to do as you please."

She opened her mouth, closed it, tried again. "I have another daughter," she managed. "I have a husband."

"So then what was all that talk before about protecting Valerie?"

"It . . . I was trying . . ." Her voice churned to a silence.

"You took the hush money," Myron said. He tried to remind himself that the woman who sat before him had buried her daughter today, but not even that fact could slow him down. If anything, it seemed to fuel him. "Don't blame your husband. He's a spineless worm. You were Valerie's mother. You took money to protect a man who abused your daughter. And now you'll keep taking money to protect a man who might have killed her."

"You have no proof Pavel had anything to do with her murder."

"The murder, no. His other crimes against Valerie—that's a different story."

She closed her eyes. "It's too late."

"It's not too late. He's still doing it, you know. Guys like Pavel don't stop. They just find new victims."

"There's nothing I can do."

"I have a friend," Myron said. "Her name is Jessica Culver. She's a writer."

"I know who she is."

He handed her Jess's card. "Tell her the story. She'll write it up. Put it in a major publication. *Sports Illustrated* maybe. It'll be out before Pavel's people even know about it. They're bad men, but they're not wasteful or stupid. Once it's published there'll be no reason to go after your family anymore. It'll end him."

"I'm sorry." She lowered her head. "I can't do it."

She was crumbling. Her whole body was slumped and shaking. Myron watched her, tried to muster up some pity, couldn't do it. "You left her alone with him," he continued. "You didn't look after her. And when you had the chance to help her, you told her to bury it. You took money."

Her body racked. Probably from a sob. Attacking a mother at her own daughter's funeral, Myron thought. What could he do for an encore? Drown newborn kittens in the neighbor's pool?

"Perhaps," he went on, "Valerie wanted to tell the truth. Maybe she needed that to put it all behind her. And maybe that's why she was murdered."

Silence. Then without warning Helen Van Slyke raised her head. She stood and left without saying another word. Myron followed. When he reentered the living room he could hear her voice.

"Good of you to come. Thank you for coming."

Chapter 32

Lucinda Elright was big and warm with thick, jiggly arms and an easy laugh. The kind of woman that as a child you feared would hug you too hard and as an adult you wish like hell she would.

"Come on in," she said, shooing several small children away from the door.

"Thank you," Myron said.

"You want something to eat?"

"No thanks."

"How about some cookies?" There were at least ten kids in the apartment. All black, none over the age of seven or eight. Some were using a paint set. Some were building a castle out of sugar cubes. One, a boy about six years old, was sticking his tongue out at Myron. "Not homemade, you understand. I can't cook worth spit."

"Actually, cookies sound good."

She smiled. "I do day care now that I'm retired. Hope you don't mind."

"Not at all."

Mrs. Elright went into the kitchen. The little boy waited until she was out of the room. Then he stuck his tongue out again. Myron stuck his tongue out back. Mr. Mature. The kid giggled.

"Now sit, Myron. Right over there." She knocked

various paraphernalia off the sofa. The plate was full of the classics. Oreos. Chips Ahoys. Fig Newtons.

"Eat," she said.

Myron reached for a cookie. The little boy stood behind Mrs. Elright so he couldn't be seen. He stuck his tongue out again. Without so much as a backward glance Mrs. Elright said, "Gerald, you stick your tongue out one more time, I'll cut it off with my pruning shears."

Gerald rolled his tongue back. "What's pruning shears?"

"Never you mind. Just go over there and play now, you hear? And don't you be causing no trouble."

"Yes, ma'am."

When he was out of earshot Mrs. Elright said, "I like them better at this age. They break my heart when they get a little older."

Myron nodded, pulled apart an Oreo. He didn't lick out the cream. Very adult.

"Your friend Esperanza," Mrs. Elright began, grabbing a Fig Newton. "She said you wanted to talk about Curtis Yeller."

"Yes, ma'am." He handed her the article. "Were you correctly quoted in this article?"

She lifted her half-moon reading glasses from her hefty bosom and scanned the page. "Yes, I said that."

"Did you mean it?"

"This wasn't just talk, if that's what you're getting at. I taught high school for twenty-seven years. I've seen lots of kids go to jail. I've seen lots of kids die in the streets. Never said a word to the newspapers about any of them. See this scar?" She pointed to an immense, fleshy bicep.

Myron nodded.

"Knife wound. From a student. I got shot at once

too. I've confiscated more weapons than any damn metal detector.'' She put her arm down. ''That's what I mean when I say I like them younger. Before they get like that.''

''But Curtis was different?''

''Curtis was more than just a good boy,'' she said. ''He was one of the best students I ever had. He was always polite and friendly and never caused a lick of trouble. But he wasn't a sissy either, you understand. He was still popular with the other boys. Good at all kinds of sports. I'm telling you, the boy was one in a million.''

''What about his mother?'' Myron asked. ''What was she like?''

''Deanna?'' Lucinda sat a little straighter. ''Fine woman. Like so many of them young mothers today. Single. Proud. Did whatever she had to to get by. But Deanna was smart. She set rules. Curtis had a curfew. Kids today don't even know what curfew means anymore. Couple nights ago, a ten-year-old boy got shot at three in the morning. Now you tell me, Myron—what's a ten-year-old boy doing out on the streets at three in the morning?''

''I wish I knew.''

She waved a hand at the air. ''Anyway you don't want to hear no old woman rambling on.''

''I got time.''

''You're a sweet man, but you're here for a reason. A good reason, I think.''

She looked at Myron. He nodded but said nothing.

''Now,'' she continued, slapping her thighs with her palms, ''what were we talking about?''

''Deanna Yeller.''

''That's right. Deanna. You know, I think about her a lot too. She was such a caring mother. She came to every open house. She loved parent-teacher conferences. She basked in all that praise we heaped on her boy.''

"Did you talk to her after his death?"

"Nope." She shook her head hard and let out a sigh. "Never heard from Deanna again, poor woman. No funeral. No nothing. I called her a couple of times, but nobody ever answered. Like she fell off the face of the earth. But I understood. She'd always had it rough. From the start. She used to be a street girl, you know."

"I didn't know. When?"

"Oh, a long time ago. She doesn't even know who Curtis's father really was. But she quit. Got herself cleaned up. Worked like a dog, any job she could get. All for her boy. And then, just like that . . ." She shook her head. "Gone."

"Did you know Errol Swade?" Myron asked.

"Just enough to know he was trouble. In and out of prison his whole life. He was Deanna's sister's boy. The sister was a junkie. Ended up dying of an overdose. Deanna had to take Errol in. He was family. She was a responsible woman."

"How did Errol get along with Curtis?"

"Actually, they got along pretty good—considering how different they were."

"Well, maybe they weren't so different," Myron said.

"What do you mean?"

"Errol got him to break into that tennis club."

Lucinda Elright watched him a moment before she picked up a cookie and began to nibble. A small smile toyed with her lips. "Come on, Myron, you know better than that," she said. "You're a smart boy. So was Curtis. What would he want to steal way out there? It don't make sense, robbing a place like that at night. Think about it."

Myron had already. He was glad to see someone else had the same trouble with the official scenario. "So what do you think happened?"

"I've thought a lot about it, but I don't really know. Nothing makes much sense to me about that whole night. But I do think Curtis and Errol were set up. Even if Curtis decided to steal—and even if he was dumb enough to break in to this club—I can't believe he'd shoot at a police officer. A boy can change, but that's like the tiger changing his stripes. It's just too incredible." She sat up, adjusting herself on the couch. "I think some fool thing happened at the rich white club and they needed a couple of black boys to take the fall. Now, I'm not that way. I'm not one of those who think the white man is always plotting against the black man. It's just not in my nature. But in this case I don't know what else could have happened."

"Thank you, Mrs. Elright."

"Lucinda. And Myron, do me a favor."

"What?"

"When you find out what really happened to Curtis, let me know."

Chapter 33

Myron and Jessica drove out to New Jersey for dinner at Baumgart's. They ate there at least twice a week. Baumgart's was a strange combination. For half a century it had been a popular soda fountain and deli, the kind of place neighbors went for lunch and Archie took Veronica for an after-school smooch. Eight years ago a Chinese immigrant named Peter Li bought the place and turned it into the best Chinese around—but without getting rid of the old soda fountain. You could still twirl on a stool at the counter, surrounded by chrome and blenders and ice-cream scoops in hot water. You could order a milkshake with your dim sum and have french fries with your General Tso's chicken. When they first lived together, Myron and Jess had come at least once a week. Now that they were back together, the tradition had resumed.

"It's the Alexander Cross murder," Myron said. "I can't stop thinking about it."

Before Jess could answer, Peter Li arrived. Myron and Jess never ordered. Peter chose for them. "Coral shrimp for the beautiful lady," he said, putting down her plate, "and Baumgart's Szechuan chicken and eggplant for the man not fit to grovel at her feet."

"Good one," Myron said. "Very funny."

Peter bowed. "In my country they consider me a man of great humor."

"Must be a lot of laughs in your country." Myron looked down at his plate. "I hate eggplant, Peter."

"You'll eat it and beg for more," he said. He smiled at Jess. "Enjoy." He left.

"Okay," Jess said, "so what about Alexander Cross?"

"It's not Alexander, per se. It's actually Curtis Yeller. Everyone says he was a great kid. His mom was very involved, loved him like mad, the whole nine yards. Now she acts like nothing happened."

" 'There's a grief that can't be spoken,' " Jessica replied. " 'There's a pain goes on and on.' "

Myron thought a second. "*Les Mis*?" The ongoing game of Guess the Quote.

"Correct, but what character said it?"

"Valjean?"

"No, sorry. Marius."

Myron nodded. "Either way," he said, "it's a lousy quote."

"I know. I was listening to the tape in the car," she said. "But it might not be that far off the mark."

"A grief that can't be spoken?"

"Yes."

He took a sip of water. "So it make sense to you, the mother acting like nothing happened."

Jessica shrugged. "It's been six years. What do you want her to do—break down and cry every time you come around?"

"No," Myron said, "but I'd think she'd want to know who killed her son."

Before touching her shrimp, Jessica reached across the table and forked a piece of Myron's chicken. Not the eggplant. The chicken. "Maybe she already knows," Jess said.

"What, you think she's being bought off too?"

Jess shrugged. "Maybe. But that's not what's really bugging you."

"Oh?"

Jess chewed daintily. Even the way she chewed food was a thing to behold. "Seeing Duane in that hotel room with Curtis Yeller's mother," she replied. "That's what's got to you."

"You must admit it's a hell of a coincidence," he said.

"Do you have a theory?" she asked.

Myron thought a moment. "No."

Jessica forked another piece of chicken. "You could ask Duane," she said.

"Sure. I could just say, 'Gee, Duane, I was following you around and noticed you're shacking up with an older woman. Care to tell me about it?' "

"Yeah, that could be a problem," she agreed. "Of course, you could approach it from the other direction."

"Deanna Yeller?"

Jessica nodded.

Myron took a taste of his chicken. Before Jess finished the whole thing. "Worth a try," he said. "You want to come along?"

"I'll scare her off," Jess said. "Just drop me off at my place."

They finished eating. Myron even ate the eggplant. It was pretty good. Peter brought them a rich chocolate dessert—the kind of dessert you could gain weight just looking at. Jess dove in. Myron held back. They drove back over the George Washington Bridge to the Henry Hudson and down the west side. He dropped her off at her loft on Spring Street in Soho. She leaned back into the car.

"You'll come by after?" she said.

"Sure. Put on that little French maid's uniform and wait."

"I don't have a French maid's uniform."

"Oh."

"Maybe we can pick one up in the morning," she said. "In the meantime I'll find something suitable."

"Groovy," Myron said.

Jess got out of the car then. She made her way up the stairs to the third floor. Her loft took up half the floor. She turned the key and entered. When she flicked on the lights she was startled to see Aaron lounging on her couch.

Before she could move, another man—a man with a fishnet shirt—came up behind her and put a gun to her temple. A third man—a black man—locked the door and turned the dead bolt. He too had a gun.

Aaron smiled at her. "Hello, Jessica."

Chapter 34

Myron's car phone rang.

"Hello."

"*Bubbe*, it's your aunt Clara. Thanks for the referral."

Clara wasn't really his aunt. Aunt Clara and Uncle Sidney were just longtime friends of his parents. Clara had gone to law school with Myron's mom. Myron had set her up to represent Roger Quincy.

"How's it going?" Myron asked.

"My client wanted me to give you an important message," Clara said "He stressed that I, his attorney, should treat this as my number one priority."

"What?"

"Mr. Quincy said you promised him an autograph of Duane Richwood. Well, he'd like it to be an autographed *picture* of Duane Richwood, not just an autograph. *Color* picture, if that's not too much trouble. And he'd like it inscribed to him, thank you very much. By the way, did he tell you he was a tennis fan?"

"I think he might have mentioned it. Fun guy, huh?"

"A constant party. Laughs galore. My sides are aching from all the laughing. It's like representing Jackie Mason."

"So what do you think?" Myron asked.

"In legal terms? The man is a major fruitcake. But

is he guilty of murder—and more important, can the
D.A. prove it?—that's a different kettle of gefilte.''

"What do they have?"

"Circumstantial nothings. He was at the Open. Big
deal, so were a zillion other people. He has a weird past.
So what, he never made any overt threats that I'm aware
of. No one saw him shoot her. No tests link him to the
gun or that Feron's bag with the bullet hole. Like I said,
circumstantial nothings."

"For what's it worth," Myron said, "I believe him."

"Uh-huh." Clara wouldn't say if she believed him
or not. It didn't matter. "I'll speak to you later, doll-
face. Take care of yourself."

"You too."

He hung up and dialed Jake.

A gruff voice said, "Sheriff Courter's office."

"It's me, Jake."

"What the fuck do you want now?"

"My, what a charming salutation," Myron said. "I
must use it sometime."

"Jesus, you're a pain in the ass."

"You know," Myron said, "I can't for the life of
me understand why you're not invited to more parties."

Jake blew his nose. Loudly. Geese in the tristate area
scattered. "Before I'm left mortally wounded by your
caustic wit," he said, "tell me what you want."

"You still have your copy of the Cross file?" Myron
asked.

"Yeah."

"I'd like to meet the coroner on the case and the cop
who shot Yeller," Myron said. "Think you can set it
up?"

"I thought there was no autopsy."

"Nothing formal, but the senator said someone did some work on him."

"Yeah, all right," Jake said. "But I know the cop who did the shooting. Jimmy Blaine. A good man, but he ain't gonna talk to you."

"I'm not interested in bringing him down."

"That's a big comfort," Jake said.

"I just want some information."

"Jimmy won't see you, I'm sure of it. Why do you need all this anyway?"

"I see a connection between Valerie's murder and Alexander Cross's."

"What connection?"

Myron explained. When he finished, Jake said, "I still don't see it, but I'll call you if I get something."

He hung up.

Myron lucked out and found a spot within two blocks of the hotel. He walked in like he belonged and took the elevator to the third floor. He stopped in front of room 322 and knocked.

"Who is it?" Deanna Yeller's voice was cheerful, singsong.

"Bellhop," Myron said. "Flowers for you."

She flung open the door with a wide smile. Just like the first time they'd met. When she saw no flowers—and more to the point, when she saw Myron—the smile fled. Again, just like the first time.

"Enjoying your stay?" Myron said.

She didn't bother hiding her exasperation. "What do you want?"

"I can't believe you came to town and didn't call me. A less mature man would be insulted."

"I got nothing to say to you." She began to close the door.

"Guess who I just spoke to?"

"I don't care."

"Lucinda Elright."

The door stopped. With Deanna looking slightly dazed, Myron slid through the opening.

Deanna recovered. "Who?"

"Lucinda Elright. One of your son's teachers."

"I don't remember none of his teachers."

"Oh but she remembers you. She said you were a wonderful mother to Curtis."

"So?"

"She also said that Curtis was a wonderful student, one of the best she ever had. She said he had a bright future. She said he never got into trouble."

Deanna Yeller put her hand on her hips. "There a point to all this?"

"Your son had no police record. He had a perfect school record, not so much as a detention. He was one of the top students in his class, if not *the* top student. You were clearly involved in his activities. You were an excellent mother, raising an excellent young man."

She looked away. She might have been looking out the window, except the blinds were drawn. The TV was humming softly. A commercial for men's pickup trucks featuring a soap opera star. Soap opera star, pickup trucks—what advertising genius came up with that combo?

"This is none of your business," she whispered.

"Did you love your son, Ms. Yeller?"

"What?"

"Did you love your son?"

"Get out. Now."

"If you cared about him at all, help me find out what happened to him."

She glared at him. "Don't give me that," she countered. "You don't care about my boy. You're trying to find out who killed that white girl."

"Maybe. But Valerie Simpson's death and your son's are connected. That's why I need your help."

She shook her head. "You don't listen too good, do you? I told you before: Curtis is dead. Can't change that."

"Your son wasn't the type to rob. He wasn't the type to carry a gun or threaten the police with one. That's just not the boy you raised."

"Don't matter," she said. "He's dead. Can't bring him back."

"What was he doing at the tennis club that night?"

"I don't know."

"Where did you suddenly get all your money?"

Pow. Deanna Yeller looked up, startled. The old change-topic attention-getter. Works every time. "What?"

"Your house in Cherry Hills," Myron said. "It was a cash deal four months ago. And your bank account at First Jersey. All cash deposits within the past half year. Where did the money come from, Deanna?"

Her face grew angry. Then suddenly she relaxed and smiled eerily. "Maybe I stole it," she said, "just like my son. You gonna report me?"

"Or maybe it's a payoff."

"A payoff? For what?"

"You tell me."

"No," she said. "I don't have to tell you nothing. Get out."

"Why are you here in New York?"

"To see the sights. Now leave."

"One of those sights Duane Richwood?"

Double pow. She stopped. "What?"

"Duane Richwood. The man who was in your room the other night."

She stared at him. "You were following us?"

"No. Just him."

Deanna Yeller looked horror-stricken. "What kind of man are you?" she said slowly. "You get off on that kind of thing, watching other people and all? Checking their bank accounts? Following them around like a Peeping Tom?" She opened the door. "Don't you have no shame at all?"

The argument was a little too close for comfort. "I'm trying to find a killer," Myron argued, but his tone rang lamely in his own ears. "Maybe the person who killed your son."

"And it don't matter who you hurt to do it, right?"

"That's not true."

"If you really want to do some good, then just drop this whole thing."

"What so you mean by that?"

She shook her head. "Curtis is dead. So is Valerie Simpson. Errol . . ." She stopped. "It's enough."

"What's enough? What about Errol?"

But she kept shaking her head. "Just let it go, Myron. For everyone's sake. Just let it go."

Chapter 35

Jessica felt the cold barrel of the gun against her temple.

"What do you want?" she asked.

Aaron signaled. The man behind her covered her mouth with his free hand. He pressed her hard against him. Jessica could feel hot spittle on her neck. It was hard to breathe. She twisted her head back and forth. Her chest hitched as she scrambled for more air. Panic seized her.

Aaron rose off the couch. The black man moved a step closer, his gun still pointed at her.

"No reason for preliminaries," Aaron said calmly. He took off his white jacket. He wore no shirt underneath, revealing instead the hairless, bodybuilder physique. He flexed a little. His pectoral muscles made ripples, like a stadium crowd doing the wave. "If you can still speak when we're through, make sure you tell Myron it was me." He cracked his knuckles. "I'd hate for my work to go unaccredited."

"Should I break her jaw?" the man with the fishnet asked. "So she can't yell or nothing."

Aaron thought a moment. "No," he said. "I kind of enjoy a good yell now and again."

All three men laughed.

"I go second," the black man said.

"Like hell," the man with the fishnet countered.

"You always go before me," the black man whined.

"All right, we'll flip for it."

"You got a coin? I never carry change.".

"Shut up," Aaron said.

Silence.

Jessica struggled feverishly, but the man in the fishnet was too strong. She bit down and managed to skim one of his fingers. He yelped and called her a bitch. Then he bent her head back in a way it was never supposed to go. Pain shot down her spine. Her eyes widened.

Aaron was about to unbutton his pants when it happened.

A gunshot. Or more than one gunshot. It sounded to Jessica like only one, but it had to be more. The hand pressed hard against her mouth slackened and slid off. The gun against her temple dropped to the floor. She turned just enough to see the man behind her no longer had a face or even much of a head. He was dead well before his legs realized it and let him cave onto the floor.

At seemingly the same time, the back half of the black man's head flew across the room. He too fell to the floor in a bloody heap.

Aaron's speed was uncanny. Seemingly before the first bullet even hit its target he had rolled into a crouch and whipped out a gun. Everything—the shots, the men going down, Aaron rolling to safety—had taken less than two seconds. Aaron came up aiming his gun at Win, who aimed his right back. Jessica stood frozen. Win must have come in through the terrace window, though how he could have gotten there and how long he'd been there Jessica could not say.

Win smiled casually and gave a half-nod. "My, my, Aaron, you're looking rather buff."

"I try to stay in shape," Aaron said. "Nice of you to notice."

The two men continued to aim their guns at each other. Neither blinked. Neither stopped smiling. Jessica had not moved. Her body quaked as though from fever. She felt something sticky on her face and realized it was probably brain matter from the man at her feet.

"I have an idea," Aaron said.

"An idea?"

"For how to end this deadlock. One I think you'll like, Win."

"Do tell," Win said.

"We both put our guns down at the same time."

"So far it doesn't sound very appealing," Win said.

"I'm not finished."

"How rude of me. Please continue."

"We've both killed men with our bare hands," Aaron said. "We both know we like it. A lot. We both know there are very few worthy adversaries in this world. We both know we are rarely if ever seriously challenged."

"So?"

"So I'm suggesting the ultimate test." Aaron's grin grew brighter. "You and me. Man to man, hand-to-hand combat. What do you say?"

Win chewed on his upper lip. "Intriguing," he said.

Jessica tried to say something, but her tongue would not obey. She just stood there, stone-faced; the thing that used to wear fishnet shirts bled without a twitch.

"One condition," Win said.

"What's that?"

"No matter who wins, Jessica goes free."

Aaron shrugged. "Doesn't matter. Frank will get her some other time."

"Maybe. But not tonight."

"Fine then," Aaron said. "But she can't leave until it's over."

Win nodded at her. "Wait by the door, Jessica. When the fight ends, run."

"But you have to wait until it's over," Aaron added.

Jessica found her voice. "How will I know when it's over?"

"One of us will be dead," Win said.

She nodded numbly. She couldn't stop shaking. Both men were still pointing the guns at one another.

"You know the drill?" Aaron asked.

"Of course."

Still holding the guns, both men placed their hand on the floor. At the same time, they twisted their weapons so that the barrel was no longer pointing at the other man. They both released their weapons at the same time. They both stood at the same time. They both kicked the weapons into a corner at the same time.

Aaron grinned. "It's done," he said.

Win nodded.

They approached each other slowly. Aaron's grin spread into something fully maniacal. He got into some weird fighting position—dragon or grasshopper or something—and beckoned with his left hand. His body was sleek, all muscle. He towered over Win. "You forgot the basic premise of the martial arts," Aaron said.

"What's that?" Win asked.

"A good big man will always beat a good little man."

"And you forgot the basic premise of Windsor Horne Lockwood III."

"Oh?"

"He always carries two guns."

Almost nonchalantly, Win reached into his leg holster, took out his gun, and fired. Aaron ducked, but the bullet still hit him in the head. The second bullet also hit Aaron's head. So too, Jessica guessed, did the third.

The big man fell to the ground. Win walked over and studied the still figure, tilting his head from side to side like a dog hearing a strange sound.

Jessica watched him in silence.

"Are you okay?" he asked.

"Yes."

Win continued to look down. He shook his head and made a *tsk, tsk* noise.

"What is it?" she asked.

Win turned to her, an almost shy smile toying with his lips. He gave a half-shrug. "I guess I'm not much for fair fights."

He looked back down at the body and started to laugh.

Chapter 36

Jessica didn't want to talk about it. She wanted to make love. Myron understood. Death and violence do that to a person. The fine line. There was definitely something to that "reaffirming life" stuff after facing down the Grim Reaper.

When they were spent, Jessica lay her head on his chest, her hair a wonderful fan. For a long time she didn't say anything. Myron stroked her back. Finally she spoke. "He enjoys it, doesn't he?"

Myron knew she meant Win. "Yes."

"Do you?" she asked.

"Not like Win."

She lifted her head and looked at him. "That sounded a tad evasive."

"Part of me hates it more than you can imagine."

"And another part of you?" she prompted.

"It's the ultimate test. There's an undeniable rush to that. But it's not like what happens with Win. He craves it. He needs it."

"And you don't?"

"I like to think I loathe it."

"But do you?"

"I don't know," Myron said.

"It was scary," she said. "Win was scary."

"He also saved your life."

"Yes."

"It's what Win does. He's good at it—the best I've ever seen. Everything with him is black and white. He has no moral ambiguities. If you cross the line, there is no reprieve, no mercy, no chance to talk your way out of it. You're dead. Period. Those men came to harm you. Win wasn't interested in rehabilitating them. They made their choice. The moment they entered your apartment they were doomed."

"It sounds like the theory of massive retaliation," she said. "You kill one of ours, we kill ten of yours."

"Colder," Myron said. "Win's not interested in teaching a lesson. He sees it as extermination. They're no more than pestering fleas to him."

"And you agree with that?"

"Not always. But I understand it. Win's moral code is not mine. We've both known that for a long time. But he's my best friend and I'd trust him with my life."

"Or mine," she said.

"Right."

"So what is your moral code?" she asked.

"It's flexible. Let's leave it at that."

Jessica nodded. She lay her head back down on his chest. The warmth of her felt good against his heartbeat. "Their heads," she said. "They just exploded like melons."

"Win doctors the bullets to maximize impact."

"Where did he take the bodies?" she asked.

"I don't know."

"Will they be found?"

"Only if he wants them to be."

A few minutes later Jessica's eyes closed and her breathing grew deep. Myron watched her drift into a sound sleep. She cuddled closer to him, looking small and frail. He knew what would happen tomorrow. She'd still be in some form of shock—not a dazed shock as much as a denial. She'd go about her day as though nothing had happened, straining extra-hard for normalcy but falling just short of achieving it. Everything would be just a little different than yesterday. Nothing drastic, just the little things. Her food would taste a little different. The air would smell a little different. Colors would have an almost indiscernibly different hue.

At six in the morning, Myron got out of bed and showered. When he came back she was sitting up. "Where are you going?" she asked.

"To see Pavel Menansi."

"This early?"

"They'll think Aaron took care of the problem last night. I might catch them off guard."

She pulled the covers over her. "I've been thinking about what you said last night at dinner. About the connection to the Alexander Cross murder."

"And?"

"Suppose you're right. Suppose something else happened that night six years ago."

"Like?"

She sat upright, leaning against the headboard. "Suppose Errol Swade didn't kill Alexander Cross," she said.

"Uh-huh."

"Well, suppose Valerie saw what really happened to Alexander Cross. And suppose that whatever she saw pushed her already battered psyche over the edge. She had already been weakened by what Pavel Menansi did to her. But now suppose whatever she saw was the ultimate cause of her breakdown."

Myron nodded. "Go on."

"And now suppose years pass. Valerie gets stronger. She makes a remarkable recovery. She even wants to

play tennis again. But most of all, she wants to face up
to her darkest fear: the truth of what really happened
that night.''

He saw where she was going with this. ''She'd have
to be silenced,'' he said.

''Yes.''

Myron slipped a pair of pants on. Over the past few
months his clothes had begun a slow migration to Jess's
loft. About a third of his wardrobe now resided here. ''If
you're right,'' he said, ''we now have two people who
want to silence Valerie: Pavel Menansi and whoever
killed Alexander Cross.''

''Or someone who wants to protect those two.''

He finished dressing. Jess hated his tie and told him
to change it. He complied. When he was ready to leave,
Myron said, ''You'll be safe this morning, but I want to
move you someplace out of town for a little while.''

''For how long?'' she asked.

''I don't know. Few days. Maybe longer. Just until I
can get this situation under control.''

''I see,'' she said.

''Are you going to fight me on this?''

She got out of bed and pattered across the room. She
wore no clothes. Myron's mouth went a little dry. He
stared. He could stare all day. She walked with the ease
of a panther. Every movement was supple and marvelous
and rawly sensual. She slipped into a silk robe. ''I know
this is the part where I'm supposed to get all indignant
and say that I'm not going to change my life,'' she said.
''But I'm scared. I'm also a writer who could use a few
days of solitude. So I'll go. No arguments.''

He hugged her. ''You're always a surprise,'' he said.

''What?''

''Being reasonable. Who would have thought?''

"I'm trying to keep the mystery alive," she said.

They kissed. Passionately. Her skin felt wonderfully warm.

"Why don't you stay a little longer?" she whispered.

He shook his head. "I want to get to Pavel before Ache realizes what happened."

"One more kiss then."

He stepped away. "Not unless you want to pack me in ice." He blew her a kiss and left the bedroom area. Clumps of blood were stuck to the exposed brick wall by the door. Courtesy of Fishnet Lee's head.

Outside, Win was nowhere in sight, but Myron knew he was there. Jess would be safe until they moved her.

Pavel Menansi was staying at the Omni Park Central on Seventh Avenue, across the street from Carnegie Hall. Myron would have preferred to go in with backup, but it was better Win wasn't there. There had been a bond between Win and Valerie—more than just the family-friend variety. Myron didn't know what that bond was. Win cared about very few people, but for those select few he would go to any lengths. The rest of the world meant nothing to him. Somehow Valerie had entered that protective circle. Myron would have enough trouble keeping his own rage in check. If Win were here—if Win were to question Pavel about his "affair" with Valerie—it wouldn't be a very pretty sight.

Pavel was staying in room 719. Myron checked his watch. Six-thirty. Not much activity in the lobby. The floor was being mopped. An exhausted family was checking out. Three kids, all whining. The parents looked like they could use a vacation. Myron walked purposefully onto an elevator, like he belonged. He pressed the button for the seventh floor.

The corridor was empty. When Myron reached the

door to Pavel's room, he knocked. No answer. He knocked again. Still no answer. He tried once again. Nothing. He was about to go downstairs and try the house phone when a sound made him stop. He listened again. The sound was barely perceptible. He pressed his ear against the door.

"Hello?" he called out.

Crying. Faint. Growing stronger. The cries of a little girl.

Myron pounded the door this time. The crying picked up a little steam now, becoming more a sob. "Are you okay?" Myron asked. More crying, but still no words. A minute or so more of this and Myron began to look for the familiar sight of the maid cart and her passkey. But it was six-thirty in the morning. The maid wasn't on her run yet.

Picking locks was not Myron's forte. Win was a lot better at it. Plus he didn't have the tools. Another cry from the room. "Open the door," he shouted. The only answer was more cries.

To hell with it, he thought.

Leading with his shoulder, Myron pile-drove his body into the door. It stung him pretty good, but the lock gave way. The cries were still muffled, but for a moment Myron forgot about them. Sprawled across the bed was Pavel Menansi. His eyes were wide open but unseeing. His mouth was frozen in a surprised oval. Dried, dark blood was caked on his chest where the bullet had entered.

He was naked.

Myron stared for a few moments before the renewed cries snapped him out of it. He turned to his right. The sound emanated from behind the bathroom door. Myron moved toward it. There was a plastic Feron's bag on the floor. The same kind they used at the U.S. Open. The same kind they found at Val's murder.

The bag had a bullet hole in it.

In front of the bathroom door, jammed under the knob, was a chair. Myron kicked it out of the way and opened the door. A young girl was sitting on the tile, her knees pulled up to her chest. She was huddled in a corner against the toilet. Myron recognized her right away. It was Janet Koffman, Pavel's newest protégée. Fourteen years old.

She too was naked.

Janet looked up at him. Her eyes were large and red and puffy. Her lower lip quivered. "We were just talking tennis," she said in a dead voice. "He's my coach. We were just talking about a match. That's all."

Myron nodded. Janet started to cry again. He bent down and wrapped a towel around her. He reached out, but she shrank away.

"It's okay now," he said, not knowing what else to say. "You're going to be okay."

Chapter 37

Janet Koffman had stopped crying. She was sitting on the loveseat by the window. Her back was to the bed and hence Pavel's corpse. From what Myron could get out of her she had been in the bathroom when someone locked her in with the chair and killed Pavel. She hadn't seen a thing. She was still sticking to her other story too: she and her coach had been talking tennis. Myron chose not to probe into the small details—like why, for example, they would have this particular discussion in the nude.

He had called the police. They'd be here any minute now. The question was, what should he do with Janet? On the one hand, he wanted to protect her from all of this; on the other, he knew she had to deal with what she had been through, that she couldn't just pretend nothing had happened to her. So what should Myron do—tamper with a police investigation or expose her to the brutish ways of the cops and worse, the press? What message of shame would hiding the truth send her? Then again, what would happen to this young girl if the story hit the airwaves?

Myron didn't have a clue.

"He was a good coach," Janet said softly.

"You did nothing wrong," Myron said, again realizing how lame he sounded. "Whatever else happens, remember that. You did absolutely nothing wrong."

She nodded slowly, but Myron wasn't sure if she'd even heard him.

Ten minutes later the police arrived, led by Dimonte. Rolly looked like something the proverbial cat had dragged in. He was unshaven. His shirt was untucked and buttoned wrong. His hair was all over the place. He had sleep-buggers in both eyes. Still, the boots were nicely polished. He charged up to Myron. "Returning to the scene of the crime, asshole?"

"Yeah," Myron said, "that's it."

The press rounded the corner. Flashbulbs started strobing. "Keep those assholes downstairs!" Dimonte hollered. Some uniformed cops pushed them back. "Downstairs, I said! No one on this floor."

Dimonte turned back to Myron. Krinsky came in and stood next to him. His pad was out.

"Hey, Krinsky," Myron said.

Krinsky nodded.

"So what the hell happened?" Dimonte demanded.

"I came up to see him. I found him like this."

"Stop fucking with me, asshole."

Myron didn't bother with a retort. Cops were all over the place. The coroner was slitting a hole in Pavel's torso with a surgical scalpel. The liver area, Myron knew. Trying to get a liver temperature reading to find out time of death.

Dimonte spotted the Feron's bag on the floor. "You touch this?"

Myron shook his head.

Dimonte bent down and looked at the bullet hole. "Cute," he said.

"You going to let Roger Quincy go now?"

"Why should I?"

"You didn't have squat on him before. Now you have less than squat."

Dimonte shrugged. "Could just be a copycat. Or"—he snapped his fingers—"or it could be someone who wants to get Quincy off." A smile. "Someone like you, Bolitar."

"Yeah," Myron said, "that's it."

Dimonte stepped closer. He gave Myron the tough-guy glare again. Then, as though suddenly remembering it, he quickly whipped out his toothpick and put it in his mouth. He glared again and gnawed the toothpick.

"I was wrong before," Myron said.

"What?"

"About the toothpick being cliché. It's actually very intimidating."

"Keep it up, funny man."

"It's too early for this, Rolly."

"Listen, asshole, I want to know what you're doing here."

"I told you. I came to see Pavel."

"Why?"

"To talk about him coaching a player of mine."

"At six-thirty in the morning?"

"I'm an early riser. It's why they call me Mr. Sunbeam."

"They should call you Mister Lying Sack of Shit."

"Oooo," Myron said. "That hurt."

Dimonte started gnawing on the toothpick with renewed vigor. You could almost hear something churn inside his head. "So tell me, Bolitar," he said with the beginnings of a smile, "you came to the hotel to talk business. You took the elevator up to see our victim here. You knocked on the door. No one answered. Right so far?"

"Yep."

"So then you kicked the door in, right?"

Myron said nothing.

Dimonte turned to Krinsky. "That make sense to you, Krinsky? Kicking in the door like that?"

Krinsky looked up from his pad, shook his head, looked back down.

"You always do that when no one answers a door, asshole? Kick it down?"

"I didn't kick it. I used my shoulder."

"Don't bullshit me, Bolitar. You didn't come here to talk business. And you didn't kick down the door just because no one answered."

The coroner tapped Dimonte on the shoulder. "Bullet to the heart. Clean shot. Death was instantaneous."

"Time of death?" Rolly asked.

"He's been dead six, maybe seven hours."

Dimonte looked at his watch. "It's seven now. That would mean he was killed between midnight and one."

Myron turned to Krinsky. "And he didn't even see you use his fingers."

Krinsky almost smiled.

Dimonte tossed out another glare. "You got an alibi, Bolitar?"

"I was with a lady friend."

"That Jessica Culver?"

"Correct." Myron waited for Krinsky to look up. When he did, Myron said, "Her number is 555-8420."

Krinsky wrote it down.

"All right, Bolitar, now stop busting my balls. Why did you kick down the door?"

Myron hesitated. He looked at Dimonte. Dimonte looked back and said, "Well?"

"Come with me," Myron said in a quiet voice. He began to leave the room.

"Hey, where the fuck do you think you're going?"

"For once, Rolly, don't be an ass. Just shut up and follow me."

To Myron's surprise Dimonte kept quiet. They went down the corridor in silence. Krinsky stayed at the crime scene. Myron stopped in front of a door, took out a key, and opened it. Janet Koffman was sitting on the bed. She was wearing a hotel bathrobe. If she realized they were there, she didn't show it. Janet rocked back and forth, humming to herself.

Dimonte looked a question at Myron.

"Her name is Janet Koffman."

"The tennis player?"

Myron nodded. "The killer locked her in the bathroom before he shot Menansi. I heard her crying when I knocked on the door. That's why I kicked it in."

Dimonte looked at Myron. "You mean she and Menansi were . . . ?"

Myron nodded.

"Christ, how old is she?"

"Fourteen, I think."

Dimonte closed his eyes. "We have someone down at the precinct," he said softly. "A doctor. She's good with this stuff. I'll talk to the Manhattan cop in charge about sneaking her out, see if he can keep the press away. I'll try to keep the victim's name out of the papers for a while."

"Thank you."

"I've seen this kinda thing before, Bolitar. The girl is going to need help."

"I know."

"Any chance she offed him herself? Frankly I wouldn't give a shit but . . ."

Myron shook his head. "She was locked in from the outside with a chair. It couldn't have been her."

Dimonte gave the toothpick a little chew. "Thoughtful killer," he said.

"What do you mean?"

"He didn't want the girl to see what happened. He made sure she had an alibi by locking her in with the chair. And most of all he saved her from going through any more of Menansi's hell." He looked at Myron. "I'd probably pin a medal on the guy if he hadn't also killed Valerie Simpson."

Myron said, "Me too." It made him wonder.

Chapter 38

The office was only about ten blocks away. Myron decided to walk it. Cars sat completely still on Sixth Avenue, though the lights were green and there was no visible construction. Everyone honked their horns. Like this ever does any good. A well-groomed man got out of a taxi. He wore a pin-striped suit, a gold Tag Heuer watch, and Gucci shoes. He also wore a green pinwheel hat and plastic Spock ears. New York—my kind of town.

Myron ignored the fumes and tried to think the whole thing through. The popular theory—the main theory, if you will—had gone something like this: Valerie Simpson had been abused by Pavel Menansi. Regaining her mental strength, she had decided to expose him. This exposure would have been detrimental to the financial well-being of TruPro and the Ache brothers. So they eliminated her before she could do any damage. It all added up. It all made sense.

Until this morning.

A major monkey wrench had been tossed into the main theory: Pavel Menansi had been murdered too, in a fashion similar to Valerie Simpson. Under the main theory, the murders of Valerie Simpson and Pavel Menansi were at cross-purposes. Why kill Valerie Simpson to protect Pavel Menansi, only to go ahead and kill Pavel

Menansi? It didn't mesh. It wasn't profitable for TruPro
or the Aches.

Of course, there was the possibility that Frank Ache
had decided Menansi was too big a risk, that exposure
was imminent and losses might as well be cut right now.
But if Frank had wanted Pavel dead, he would have had
Aaron do it. Pavel had been murdered between midnight
and one. Aaron was dead by midnight. Myron mulled
this over a bit and decided that Aaron's being dead made
it extremely unlikely he was the killer. And moreover,
if Frank had intended to kill Pavel, there would have
been no reason to scare Myron off with the attack on
Jessica.

On the street in front of him a pale woman with a
bullhorn screamed that she had recently met Jesus face-
to-face. She stuffed a pamphlet into Myron's hand.

"Jesus sent me back with this message," she said.

Myron nodded, glanced down at the ink smears on
the pamphlet. "Too bad he didn't give you a decent
printer."

She gave him a funny look and went back to her
bullhorn. Myron stuffed the pamphlet into his pocket and
continued walking. His mind returned to the problem at
hand.

Frank Ache wasn't behind Pavel's murder, he
thought. To the contrary, Frank Ache wanted Pavel
saved because Pavel meant mucho dinero to TruPro.
Frank Ache had even brought Aaron in to protect Pavel.
He had ordered Aaron to harm Jessica and to protect
Pavel. Killing TruPro's main tennis drawing card would
make no sense.

So what did that leave us?

Two possibilities. One, we were dealing with two
separate killers with two separate agendas. Seeing an

opportunity, Pavel's killer had left behind a Feron's bag
to put the blame on Valerie's killer. Or two, there was
some other linkage between Valerie and Pavel, one that
was not readily apparent. Myron favored this possibility,
and of course it led back to Myron's earlier obsession:

The murder of Alexander Cross.

Both Valerie Simpson and Pavel Menansi had been
at the Old Oaks tennis club that night six years ago. Both
had been attending the party for Alexander Cross. But
so what? Let's suppose Jessica had been right this morning. Suppose Valerie Simpson had seen something that
night, maybe even the identity of the real murderer. Suppose she'd been about to reveal the truth. Suppose that
was why she'd been killed. How would that tie in to
Pavel Menansi? Even if he had seen the same thing, he
hadn't opened his mouth in years. Why would Pavel
start now? It's not as though he'd come forward to help
poor Valerie. So what is the connection? And what about
Duane Richwood? How did he fit into this equation, if
at all? And Deanna Yeller? And where was Errol
Swade? Was he still alive?

He headed east three blocks and then turned down
Park Avenue. The majestic (if not ostentatious) Helms-
ley Palace or Helmsley Castle or Helmsley whatever sat
straight ahead, seemingly in the middle of the street; the
MetLife building huddled over it like a protective parent.
For eons the MetLife building had been something of a
New York landmark known as the Pan Am building.
Myron couldn't get used to the change. Every time he
turned the corner he still expected to see the Pan Am
logo.

Activity was brisk in the front of Myron's building.
He headed past the modern sculpture that adorned the
entrance. The sculpture was hideous. It looked very

much like a giant intestinal tract. Myron had looked for a name on the sculpture once, but in a typical New York move, someone had pried off the name plaque. What someone did with an ugly sculpture's name plaque was beyond comprehension. Maybe they sold it. Maybe there was an underground market for name plaques from works of art—for those who couldn't afford actual stolen artworks and thus settled for the plaques.

Interesting theory.

He entered the lobby. Three Lock-Horne hostesses sat on stools behind a tall counter, smiling plastically. They wore enough makeup to double as cosmetic counter girls at Bloomies. Of course, they didn't wear the official white lab coat of genuine Bloomie counter girls, so you could tell they weren't professional makeup people. Still, all three were attractive—model wanna-bes who found this more enjoyable (and put them in touch with more potential bigwigs) than waiting tables. Myron walked past them, smiled, nodded. None gave him the eye. Hmm. They must know how committed he was to Jessica. Yeah, that must be it.

When the elevator opened on his floor, he walked toward Esperanza. Her white blouse was a nice contrast against her dark, flawless skin. She'd have been great on one of those Bain de Soleil commercials. The Santa Fe tan without any sun.

"Hi," he said.

Esperanza cupped the phone against her shoulder. "It's Jake. You want to take it?"

He nodded. She handed him the phone.

"Hey, Jake."

"Some girl did a partial autopsy on Curtis Yeller," Jake said. "She'll see you."

Myron said, "Some girl?"

"Mea culpa for not being politically sensitive," Jake said. "Sometimes I still refer to myself as black."

"That's because you're too lazy to say African American," Myron said.

"Is it African or Afro?"

"African now," Myron said.

"When in doubt," Jake said, "ask a honky."

"Honky," Myron repeated. "Now there's a word you don't hear much anymore."

"Damn shame too. Anyway, the assistant M.E. is Amanda West. She seemed anxious to talk." Jake gave him the address.

"What about the cop?" Myron asked. "Jimmy Blaine?"

"No dice."

"He still with force?"

"Nope. He retired."

"You have his address?"

"Yes," Jake said.

Silence. Esperanza kept her eyes on her computer screen.

"Could you give it to me?" Myron asked.

"Nope."

"I won't hassle him, Jake."

"I said no."

"You know I can find the address on my own."

"Fine, but I'm not giving it to you. Jimmy is one of the good guys, Myron."

"So am I," Myron said.

"Maybe. But sometimes the innocent get hurt in your little crusades."

"What's that supposed to mean?"

"Nothing. Just leave him alone."

"And why so defensive?" Myron continued. "I just want to ask him a couple of questions."

Silence. Esperanza didn't look up.

Myron continued, "Unless he did something he shouldn't have."

"Don't matter," Jake said.

"Even if he—"

"Even if. Good-bye, Myron."

The phone went dead. Myron stared at it a second. "That was bizarre."

"Uh-huh." Esperanza still stared at her computer screen. "Messages on your desk. Lots of them."

"Have you seen Win?"

Esperanza shook her head.

"Pavel Menansi is dead," Myron said. "Someone murdered him last night."

"The guy who molested Valerie Simpson?"

"Yep."

"Gee, I'm so brokenhearted. I hope I don't lose too much sleep." Esperanza finally flicked a glance away from the screen. "Did you know he was on that party list you gave me?"

"Yeah. You find any other interesting names?"

She almost smiled. "One."

"Who?"

"Think puppy dog," Esperanza said.

Myron shook his head.

"Think Nike," she continued. "Think Duane's contact with Nike."

Myron froze. "Ned Tunwell?"

"Correct answer." Everyone in Myron's life was a game show host. "Listed as E. Tunwell on the list. His real name is Edward. So I did a little digging. Guess who first signed Valerie Simpson to a Nike deal."

"Ned Tunwell."

"And guess who had plenty of egg on his face when her career took a nosedive."

"Ned Tunwell."

"Wow," she said dryly, "it's like you're clairvoyant." She lowered her eyes back to her computer screen and started typing.

Myron waited. Then: "Anything else?"

"Just a very unsubstantiated rumor."

"What?"

"The usual in a situation like this," Esperanza said, her eyes still on the screen. "That Ned Tunwell and Valerie Simpson were more than friends."

"Get Ned on the phone," Myron said. "Tell him I need—"

"I already made the appointment," she said. "He'll be here at seven tonight."

Chapter 39

Dr. Amanda West now worked as chief pathologist at St. Joseph Medical Center in Doylestown, not too far from Philadelphia. Myron pulled into the hospital parking lot. On the radio was the classic Doobie Brothers song "China Grove." Myron sang along with the chorus, which basically consisted of saying "Oh, Oh, China Grove" repeatedly. Myron sang it louder now, wondering—not for the first time—what a "China Grove" actually was.

As he took a parking ticket from the attendant the car phone rang.

"Jessica is hidden," Win said.

"Thanks."

"See you at the match tomorrow."

Click. Abrupt, even for Win.

Inside Myron asked the receptionist where the morgue was. The receptionist looked at him like he was nuts and said, "The basement, of course."

"Oh, right. Like on *Quincy*."

He took the elevator down a level. No one was around. He found a door marked MORGUE, and again using his powers of deductive reasoning, quickly realized that this was probably the morgue. Myron the Medium. He braced himself and knocked.

A friendly female voice chimed, "Come in."

The room was tiny and smelled like Janitor-in-a-

Drum. The decor theme was metal. Two desks facing each other, both metal, took up half the room. Metal bookshelves. Metal chairs. Lots of stainless steel trays and bins all over the place. No blood in them. No organs. All shiny and clean. Myron had indeed seen plenty of violence, but the sight of blood still made him queasy once the danger passed. He didn't like violence, no matter what he'd told Jessica before. He was good at it, no denying that, but he did not like it. Yes, violence was the closest modern man came to his true primitive self, the closest he came to the intended state of nature, to the Lockean ideal, if you will. And yes, violence was the ultimate test of man, a test of both physical strength and animalistic cunning. But it was still sickening. Man had—in theory anyway—evolved for a reason. In the final analysis, violence was indeed a rush. But so was skydiving without a parachute.

"Can I help you?" the friendly voiced woman asked.

"I'm looking for Dr. West," he said.

"You found her." She stood and extended her hand. "You must be Myron Bolitar."

Amanda West smiled a bright, clear smile, which illuminated even this room. She was blond and perky with a cute little upturned nose—the complete opposite of what he'd expected. Not to be stereotyping, but she seemed a tad too sunny, too upbeat, for someone handling rotting corpses all day. He tried to picture her cheerful face splitting open a dead body with a Y-incision. The picture wouldn't hold.

"You wanted to know about Curtis Yeller?" she asked.

"Yes."

"Been waiting six years for someone to ask," she said. "Come on in. There's more room in the back."

She opened a door behind her. "You squeamish?"

"Uh, no." Mr. Tough-guy.

Amanda West smiled again. "There's nothing to see really. Just that some people get freaked out by all the drawers."

He entered the room. The drawers. There was a wall of huge drawers. Floor to ceiling. Five drawers up. Eight across. That equals forty drawers. Mr. Multiplication Tables. Forty dead bodies could fit in here. Forty dead rotting corpses that used to have lives and families, that used to love and be loved, that once cared and struggled and dreamed. Freaked out? By a bunch of drawers? Surely you jest.

"Jake said you remembered Curtis Yeller," he said.

"Sure. It was my biggest case."

"Pardon me if I sound out of line," Myron said, "but you look awfully young to have been an M.E. six years ago."

"You're not out of line," she said, still smiling sweetly. Myron smiled back with equal sweetness. "I had just finished my residency and worked there two nights a week. The chief M.E. was with the corpse of Alexander Cross. Both bodies came in nearly the same time. So I did the prelim on Curtis Yeller. I didn't get the chance to do anything resembling a full autopsy—not that I needed one to know how he was killed."

"How was he killed?"

"Bullet wound. He was shot twice. Once in the lower left rib cage"—she leaned to the side and pointed at her own—"and once in the face."

"Did you know which was one fatal?"

"The shot to the ribs didn't do much damage," she said. Amanda West was, Myron decided, cute. She tilted her head a lot when she talked. Jess did that too. "But

the bullet in Yeller's head ripped off his face like it was
Silly Putty. There was no nose. Both cheekbones were
barely splinters. It was a mess. The shot was at very
close range. I didn't get a chance to run all the tests, but
I'd say the gun was either pressed against his face or no
more than a foot away.''

Myron almost took a step back. "Are you saying a
cop shot him in the face at point-blank range?"

Water dripped into a stainless steel sink, echoing in the room. "I'm just giving you the facts,"
Amanda West said steadily. "You draw your own con-
clusions."

"Who else knows about this?" he asked.

"I'm not sure. It was a zoo in there that night. I
usually worked alone, but there must have been half a
dozen other guys with me on this one. None of them
worked for the coroner's office."

"Who were they?"

"Cops and government guys," she replied.

"Government guys?"

She nodded. "That's what I was told. They worked
for Senator Cross. Secret service or something like that.
They confiscated everything—tissue samples, the slugs
I extracted, everything. They told me it was a matter of
national security. The whole night was crazy. Yeller's
mother even managed to get in the room once. She
started screaming at me."

"What was she screaming about?"

"She was very insistent that there should be no autopsy. She wanted her son back immediately. She got
her wish too. For once the police acquiesced. They
weren't interested in having anyone look too closely at
this, so it worked out for all concerned." She smiled
again. "Funny thing, don't you think?"

"The mother not wanting an autopsy?"

"Yes."

Myron shrugged. "I've heard of parents not wanting autopsies before."

"Right, because they want the body preserved for a decent burial. But this kid wasn't buried. He was cremated." She offered up another smile, this one more saccharine.

"I see," Myron said. "So any evidence of police wrongdoing would have been burned up with Curtis Yeller."

"Right," she said.

"So you think—what—someone got to her?"

Amanda West put her hands up in surrender. "Hey, I said it was a funny thing. Not ha-ha funny, just strange funny. The rest is up to you. I'm just an M.E."

Myron nodded again. "You find anything else?"

"Yes," she said. "And this too I found funny. Very funny."

"Ha-ha funny or strange funny?"

"You decide," she said. She smoothed her lab coat. "I'm no ballistics expert, but I know a little something about bullet slugs. I pulled two slugs from Yeller. One from the rib cage, one from the head."

"Yeah so?"

"The two slugs were of different calibers." Amanda West put up her index finger. All traces of a smile were gone now. Her face was clear and determined. "Understand what I'm telling you, Mr. Bolitar. I'm not just saying two different guns here. I'm talking about different caliber. And here's the funny part: all the officers on the Philadelphia force use the same caliber weapon."

Myron felt a chill. "So one of the two bullets came from someone other than a cop."

"And," she continued, "all those secret service men were carrying guns."

Silence.

"So," she said, "ha-ha funny or strange funny?"

Myron looked at her. "You don't hear me laughing."

Chapter 40

Myron decided to ignore Jake's advice. Especially after listening to Amanda West.

Finding Officer Jimmy Blaine's current address had not been easy. The man had retired two years ago. Still Esperanza found out he lived alone on some small lake in the Poconos. Myron drove through the wilderness for two hours until he pulled into what he hoped was the right driveway. He checked his watch. He still had plenty of time to see Jimmy Blaine and get back to the office in time for his meeting with Ned Tunwell.

The house was rustic and quaint, about what you'd expect to find nestled away in the Poconos. Gravel driveway. Dozens of small wooden animals guarded a front porch. The air was heavy and still. Everything—the weather vane, the American flag, the rocking chair, all the leaves and blades of grass—stood frighteningly motionless, as if inanimate objects had the ability to hold their breaths. As Myron climbed up the porch stairs, he noticed a modern-looking wheelchair ramp that also led to the front door. The ramp looked out of place here, like a doughnut in a health food store. There was no doorbell, so he knocked.

No one answered. Curious. Myron had called ten minutes ago, had heard a man answer, and hung up. Could be out back. Myron circled around the house. As he hit the backyard, the lake stared him in the face. It

was a spectacular picture. The sun shone off the still—
again, frighteningly motionless—water and made Myron
squint. Placid. Tranquil. Myron felt the muscles in his
shoulders start to unbunch.

Sitting in a wheelchair facing the lake was a man. A
Saint Bernard lay by his feet. The dog too was frighteningly motionless. As Myron approached he saw that
the man was whittling wood.

"Hi," Myron called out.

The man barely raised his eyes. He wore a red T-
shirt and a John Deere cap pulled down over a weathered
face. His legs were covered with a blanket, even in this
heat. There was a portable phone within reach. "Hi."
He went back to whittling. If he was surprised or upset
to have company he was certainly taking it all in stride.

"Beautiful day," Myron said. Mr. Engaging Neighbor.

"Yep."

"Are you Jimmy Blaine?"

"Yep."

Even without the wheelchair it was hard to picture
this guy working the city bowels of Philadelphia for
eighteen years. Then again, it was hard to picture the
bowels of Philadelphia, period, when you were out here.

Silence. No birds or crickets or anything but the whittling.

After some time had passed, Myron asked, "Had
much rain this year?" Myron Bolitar, Salt of the Earth.
Mr. Farmer's Almanac.

"Some."

"This your dog?"

"Yep. Name is Fred."

"Hi, Fred." Myron scratched the dog behind the

ears. The dog wagged its tail without moving any other part of its body. Then it farted loudly.

"Great place you have here," Myron tried. Yep, just two good ol' boys shooting the breeze. Eb and Mr. Haney on *Green Acres*. Myron half expected denim overalls to materialize on his body.

"Uh-huh." Whittle, whittle.

"Listen, Mr. Blaine, my name is—"

"Myron Bolitar," Blaine finished for him. "I know who you are. Been expecting you."

He shouldn't have been surprised. "Jake called you?"

Blaine nodded without looking up from his whittling. "He said you were stubborn. Said you wouldn't listen to him."

"I just want to ask you a few questions."

"Nothing I care to say to you though."

"I'm not here to hound you, Mr. Blaine."

He nodded again. "Jake told me that too. Said you were okay. Said you liked to right wrongs, is all."

"What else did he say?"

"That you don't know how to mind your own business. That you're a wiseass. And that you're a major pain in the butt."

"He left out snazzy dancer," Myron said.

For the first time since he arrived Jimmy Blaine stopped whittling. "You trying to right the wrong done to Curtis Yeller?"

"I'm trying to find out who killed him."

"Simple," Blaine said. "Me."

"No, I don't think so."

That stopped him for a brief moment. He gave Myron the once-over and then began whittling again.

"Could you tell me what happened that night?" Myron asked.

"The boy pulled a gun. I shot him. That's it."

"How far away were you when you shot him?"

He shrugged, whittled. "Thirty feet. Maybe forty."

"How many shots did you fire?"

"Two."

"And he just dropped?"

"Nope. He swung around the corner with the other
one—that Swade kid, I guess. They disappeared."

"You shot a man in the face and ribs and he kept
running?"

"I didn't say they kept running. The two of them
were by a corner. They disappeared around it. Didn't
know it at the time, but the Yellers lived right there.
They must have climbed in a window."

"With a bullet in his skull?"

Jimmy Blaine shrugged again. "The Swade kid probably helped him," he said.

"That's not how it happened," Myron said. "You
didn't kill him."

Blaine eyed him and then went back to his whittling.
"Second time you've said that," he noted. "You want
to explain what you mean?"

"Two bullets hit Yeller."

"I just told you I shot twice."

"But two different caliber slugs were pulled out of
him. One of the shots—the one in the head—was from
close range. Less than a foot away."

Jimmy Blaine said nothing. He concentrated hard on
his whittling. It looked like he was sculpting an animal
of some sort, like the ones on the front porch. "Two
different calibers, you say?" He aimed for nonchalance,
but he wasn't making it.

"Yes."

"That kid I shot didn't have a record," Blaine continued. "You know what the odds are of that? In that part of the city?"

Myron nodded.

"I checked up on him," Blaine continued. "On my own. His name was Curtis Yeller. He was sixteen years old. He did well in school. He was a good kid. He had a chance at a good life until that night."

"You didn't kill him," Myron said.

Blaine whittled with a bit more intensity now. He blinked a lot. "How did you find out about those slugs?"

"The assistant M.E. told me," Myron said. "You never knew?"

He shook his head. "I guess it makes sense though," he said. "Blame me for it. Why not? It's easier. It's a legit shooting. No one questioned it. IAD barely broke a sweat. It didn't hurt my record. Didn't hurt anyone. No harm done, they figured."

Myron waited for him to say more, but he just kept whittling. Two long ears were now evident in the wood. Maybe he was making a rabbit. "Do you know who really killed Curtis Yeller?" Myron asked.

There was a long moment of the same whittle-filled silence. Fred farted again and wagged his tail. Myron's eyes kept going back to the lake. He stared out at the silver water. The effect was hypnotizing.

"No harm done," Jimmy Blaine said again. "That's what they all probably thought. Good ol' Jimmy. We won't let him take the rap. It'll be washed clean from his record. No one will know. Hell, some of the guys will even treat him special—making a shooting like that. They'll say he saved his partner's life. Good ol' Jimmy will come out of this looking like a hero. Except for one thing.''

Myron was tempted to ask what, but he sensed the answer was coming.

"I saw that boy dead," Blaine continued. "I saw Curtis Yeller lying in his own blood. I saw his mother hold him in her arms and cry. Sixteen years old. If he was a street punk or a drug addict or . . ." He stopped. "But he wasn't any of those things. Not this kid. He was one of the good ones. I found out later he never even touched the senator's kid. The other one—the Swade punk—he did the stabbing.''

Two ducks splashed madly for a second, then stopped. Blaine put down the whittling, then thinking better of it, picked it back up again. "I replayed that night a lot of times in my head. It was dark, you know. There was barely any light. Maybe the Yeller kid wasn't going to fire the gun. Maybe what I saw wasn't even a gun. Or maybe none of that mattered. Maybe it was a legit shooting, but the pieces still never quite added up. I kept hearing the mother's screams. I kept seeing her press her dead boy's bloody face into her bosom. And I think about it, you know, and thinking ain't always a good thing for a cop to do. And four years.later, the next time a kid is pointing a gun at me, I think about seeing another crying mother. I think long and hard. Too long.''

He pointed to his legs. "And this is the result." He changed tools and kept whittling. "Nope, no harm done.''

Silence.

Myron now understood Jake's attitude on the phone. Jimmy Blaine had gone through enough. If he'd done wrong in the case of Curtis Yeller, he had already paid an enormous price. Problem was, Jimmy Blaine hadn't done wrong. He hadn't killed Curtis Yeller—legit shooting or not. In the end Jimmy Blaine was yet another victim of that night.

After some time had passed, Myron tried again. "Do you know who killed Curtis Yeller?"

"No, not really."

"But you have a thought."

"A thought maybe."

"You mind telling me?"

Blaine looked down at Fred, as if looking for an answer. The dog maintained his bear-rug pose. "Henry and I—he was my partner—got the call at a little past midnight," he began. "The two suspects had stolen a car from a driveway three blocks from the Old Oaks tennis club. A dark blue Cadillac Seville. We spotted a vehicle matching the description coming off the Roosevelt Expressway twenty minutes later. When we pulled up behind the stolen vehicle, the suspects sped off. We then engaged in a high-speed pursuit."

His voice had changed. He was a cop again, reading from a notepad he had read too many times in the past. "Henry and I followed the vehicle down an alley not far from Hunting Park Avenue, off Broad. The chase then proceeded on foot. At the time we had no identification on the two youths and thus no address. We only had the car. The chase proceeded for several blocks. As we turned a corner, the driver drew a firearm. My partner told him to freeze and drop his weapon. Yeller responded by aiming the firearm at Henry. I then fired two shots. The youth fell or stumbled out of sight beyond the next corner. By the time Henry and I turned the same corner, there was no sign of either youth. We figured that they were hiding in the nearby vicinity and awaited backup before proceeding. We secured the area as best we could. But the cops didn't get there first. The so-called secret service guys did."

"Senator Cross's men?"

Blaine nodded. "They called themselves 'national security,' but they were probably mob guys."

"Senator Cross told me he had no mob connections," Myron said.

Jimmy Blaine raised an eyebrow. "You serious?"

"Yes."

"The mob owns Bradley Cross," Blaine said. "More specifically, the Perretti family. Cross is a major gambler. I know he's also been arrested twice with prostitutes. One of his early opponents—this is back when he was just a congressman—ended up in the river during the primaries."

"And you traced it back to Cross?"

"Nothing anyone could prove. But we knew."

Myron considered this for a moment. Clearly, the beloved senator had lied to him. Big surprise. He had played Myron for a sucker. Another big surprise. Win was right. Myron always went astray when he believed the best about people. "So what happened next?"

"The senator's hoods were at the scene almost immediately. Been monitoring our radio. We'd been told over the air to cooperate with them one hundred percent. A real community effort finding these two kids. I'm surprised we spotted them first. Mob goons are usually better at this stuff than we are, you know?"

Myron knew. The mob had all the advantages over the police. They were closer to the city's underbelly. They could pay top dollar. They didn't have to worry about rules or laws or constitutional rights. They could inspire genuine fear.

"So what happened?" Myron asked.

"We started combing the area with flashlights, checking garbage Dumpsters, the whole bit. Cops and goons hand in hand. We found nothing for a while. Then we heard some gunshots. Henry and I ran to some dumpy apartment adjacent to where I'd shot Yeller. But Senator Cross's men were already there."

Blaine stopped. He leaned and gave Fred a good ear scratch. Fred still didn't move except for the thumping tail. Still scratching his dog, Blaine said, "Well, you know what we found." His voice was low and dead. "Yeller was dead. His mother was cradling him in her arms. She went through all these stages. First she just kept calling out his name over and over. Sweetly sometimes. Like she was trying to wake him up for school. Then she stroked the back of his head and rocked him and told him to go back to sleep. We all stood around and watched. Even the goons didn't bother her."

"What about the other gunshots?" Myron asked.

"What about them?"

"Didn't you wonder where they had come from?"

"I guess I did," he replied. "But I figured the security guys had shot after Swade. I didn't think they'd be dumb enough to admit it, but that's what I thought."

"It never crossed your mind they might have shot Yeller?"

"No."

"Why not?"

"I told you the mother went through stages."

"Right."

"Once she realized her boy wasn't waking up again, she started pointing fingers and screaming. She wanted to know who had shot her boy. She wanted to look the killer in the eyes, the murderer who had shot her son on the street in cold blood. She said that Swade had dragged her boy in like that. Already shot up and dead.''

"She said all that? That Swade dragged him in and that he was already shot?"

"Yes."

Silence. No water rippling. No birds chirping. Not even whittling. Several minutes passed before Blaine looked up and squinted. Then he said, "Cold."

"What?" Myron asked.

"That mother. If she was lying about who killed her boy. I always wondered why there were no repercussions. The mother never made a fuss. She didn't go to the newspapers. She didn't press charges. She didn't demand an explanation.'' He shook his head. "But what could have made her do that to her own flesh and blood? How could they have gotten to her so fast? With money? With threats? What?"

"I don't know," Myron said.

Jimmy Blaine finished whittling. It was a rabbit. Pretty good one too. A bird finally chirped, but it wasn't a pretty sound. More like a caw than a melody. Blaine spun his wheelchair around. "You want something to eat?" he asked. "I'm about to make lunch."

Myron looked at his watch. It was getting late. He had to get back to the office for his meeting with Ned Tunwell. "Thanks, but I really have to get going."

"Some other time then. When you're all done with this.''

"Yes," Myron said.

Blaine blew the wood dust off the rabbit. "Still don't get it," he said.

"What?"

He stared at his finished handiwork, turning the rabbit over in his hand, studying it from every angle. "Could the mother have really been that frosty?'' he asked. "How much money did they offer her? How much fright did they put into her? Hell, is there enough money or frights in the world for a mother to do that to her son?'' He shook his head, dropped the wooden rabbit into his lap. "I just don't get it."

Myron didn't get it either.

Chapter 41

Myron got back into his Ford Taurus and headed east. He drove several miles without seeing a car. Mostly he saw trees. Lots of trees. Yes, the great outdoors. Myron was not an outdoors kind of guy. He didn't hunt or fish or do any of that. The appeal seemed clear, but it just wasn't for him. Something about being alone in the woods always reminded him of Ned Beatty in *Deliverance*. He needed people. He needed movement. He needed noise. City noise—as opposed to squeal-like-a-pig noise.

He now knew a lot more about the deaths of both Alexander Cross and Curtis Yeller than he'd known twenty-four hours ago, but he still didn't know if any of it was relevant to what happened to Valerie Simpson. And that was what he was after. Digging into a sensational six-year-old murder might be fun, but it was beside the point. He wanted Valerie Simpson's murderer. He wanted to find the person who had decided to snuff out that young, tortured life. Call it righting a wrong. Call it having a rescue or hero complex. Call it chivalry. Didn't matter. It was far simpler to Myron: Valerie deserved better.

The roads were still abandoned. The foliage on both sides of the road blurred into green walls. He started putting together what he knew. Errol Swade and Curtis Yeller had been spotted by Jimmy Blaine and his partner. A chase had ensued. Leaving aside the question of whether it was a legitimate shooting or not, Jimmy Blaine fired at Curtis Yeller. One of Blaine's bullets probably hit Curtis Yeller in the ribs, but the key fact is that somebody else shot Yeller in the head at close range. Somebody who was using a different caliber gun. Somebody who was not a cop.

So who shot Curtis Yeller?

The answer now seemed fairly obvious. Senator Cross's men—thugs or security forces or whatever they were—had been carrying firearms. Both Amanda West and Jimmy Blaine had confirmed that. They certainly had the opportunity. They certainly had the motive. It didn't matter if Cross had lied to Myron or not. Either way it would be in the senator's best interest for Curtis Yeller and Errol Swade to end up dead. Live suspects could talk. Live suspects could tell tales of drug use. Live suspects could counter the claim that Alexander Cross had died a hero. Dead men tell no tales. More important, dead men do not dispute spin doctors.

As for Errol Swade—the mysterious "escapee"— he'd almost assuredly been killed, probably in that gunfire Jimmy Blaine heard. The senator's men could have hid the body and dumped it later. Not definite, but again most likely. Errol Swade had a lot working against him. He was no genius. He was six-four. Myron knew from personal experience it was difficult to hide when you were that big. The odds of Swade eluding the police dragnet for so long—not to mention the mob's underworld army—were, as they say, statistically insignificant.

The sun was beginning to lower. The beams were now positioned in that one spot high enough to be in Myron's eyes but still low enough to avoid the sun visor.

Myron squinted and slowed. His mind shifted gears again, this time to the aftermath of the Yeller shooting. Somehow Curtis Yeller ended up in his mother's arms, and somehow somebody got to her. Through either money or fear of reprisal—probably a combination of both—Deanna Yeller had been convinced to let the death of her son slide.

There were problems with this scenario, of course. For example, the money. Deanna Yeller's son had been murdered six years ago—yet the first big deposit in her account had occurred five months ago. Why the time lapse? She could have been biding her time, hiding the money under a mattress or something. But that didn't feel right. On the other hand, if the money was indeed new, the questions became more focused: why, all of a sudden, was Deanna getting this money? Why, all of a sudden, had Valerie been murdered? And how did Pavel fit in?

Good questions. No answers yet, but good questions. Maybe Ned Tunwell would know something useful.

Something caught Myron's eye. He glanced up. A car grew suddenly large in the rearview mirror. A big car. Black with a tinted windshield so you couldn't see inside. The license plate was New York.

The black car moved to its right, disappearing from the rearview mirror and appearing in the passenger-side mirror. Myron watched its progress. The imprint in the mirror reminded him that objects may be closer than they appear. Thanks for the clue. The black car picked up a little speed. As it came alongside of him, Myron could see it was a stretch limousine. A Lincoln Continental stretch. Extra-long stretch. The side windows too were tinted so you couldn't look in. It was like staring into a pair of giant aviator sunglasses. Myron could see himself in the reflection. He smiled and waved. His reflection smiled and waved back. Handsome devil.

The limo was dead-even with Myron's car now. The back window on the driver's side began to slide open. Myron half expected an elderly man to stick his head out and ask for Grey Poupon. Imagine his surprise when, instead, a gun appeared.

Without warning the gun fired twice, hitting the front and back tires on the passenger side of Myron's car. Myron swerved. He fought to regain control. The car veered off the road. Myron twisted the wheel and skidded away from a tree. The Ford Taurus came to a stop with a thud.

Two men jumped out of the limousine and headed toward him. Both wore blue suits. One also wore a Yankees cap. Business suit, baseball cap—an interesting fashion combo. They also carried guns. Their faces were stern and ready. Myron felt his heart in his throat. He was unarmed. He didn't like carrying guns, not for some moral reason but because they were bulky and uncomfortable and he so rarely ever used one. Win had warned him, but who listens to Win on a subject like this? But Myron had been careless. He was pissing off some powerful people and he should have been better prepared. He should have at least kept one in the glove compartment.

A little late for self-admonishments. Then again he might never have the chance again.

The two men approached. Not knowing what else to do, Myron ducked out of sight. He started dialing the car phone.

"Get your ass out of the car," one of the men barked.

Myron said, "Take another step and I'll drop you where you stand." Mr. Bluff.

Silence.

Myron dialed furiously and hit the send button. At that exact moment, he heard a sound like a twig breaking and then static. The goon with the Yankees cap had snapped off his antenna. This wasn't good. Myron kept himself low. He opened the glove compartment and reached inside. Nothing but maps and registration. His eyes searched the floor anxiously for some sort of weapon. The only thing he saw was the car cigarette lighter. Somehow he doubted that it would be effective against two armed goons. Maps, registration card, cigarette lighter. Unless Myron suddenly became MacGyver, he was in serious trouble.

He could hear footsteps shuffling about now. Myron's mind raced for an answer. Nothing came to him. Then he heard the car door of the limo open again. A quiet curse followed. Sounded like "Shit." Then a deep sigh.

"Bolitar, I ain't here to play no fucking games."

The voice sent a chill through Myron. Something hardened in his chest. New York accent. More specifically, a Bensonhurst accent. Frank Ache.

This was not good.

"Get the fuck out of the car now, ass-wipe. I ain't here to kill you."

"Your men just shot out my tires," Myron called back.

"Right, and if I wanted you dead, they would have shot out your fucking head."

Myron mulled that one over. "Good point," he said.

"Yeah, how about this one? I got two AK's sitting in the back here. If I wanted you dead, I could have Billy and Tony spray-paint this piece of shit you call a car with them."

"Another good point," Myron said.

"Now get the fuck out here," Frank barked. "I don't got all goddamn day. Ass-wipe."

Myron didn't really have a choice. He opened the car and stood. Frank Ache ducked back into the backseat. Billy and Tony scowled at him.

"Get in here," Frank called out.

Myron walked to the car. Billy and Tony blocked his path. "Give me your gun," the one with the Yankees cap said.

"Are you Billy or Tony?"

"The gun. Now."

Myron squinted at the baseball cap. "Wait a second, I get it. Plugs, right?"

"What?"

"Wearing a baseball cap with a suit. You're covering up new hair plugs."

The two men exchanged a glance. *Bingo*, Myron thought.

"Now, ass-wipe," the cap man said. "The gun."

Ass-wipe. The goon word of the week. "You didn't say please."

Frank's voice came from inside the car. "Jesus Christ, Billy, he don't have no piece. He was just yanking your hardware."

Billy's scowl grew angrier. Myron smiled, turned his palms to the sky, shrugged.

Tony opened the door. Myron slid into the backseat. Tony and Billy moved into the front. Frank pressed a button and a partition slid up, separating the back compartment from the front seats. The limo had a wet bar and television with VCR. The inside was sort of a royal red, blood-red actually, which, knowing Frank's history, probably helped cut down on the cost of cleanings.

"Nice wheels, Frank," Myron said.

Frank wore his customary garb—a velour sweat suit a couple of sizes too small. This one was green with yellow trim. The front zipper was down midway, like those guys in the seventies wore at discos. His gut was enormous enough to be mistaken for a multiple gestation. He was bald. He stared at Myron for several seconds before he spoke.

"You enjoy crawling up my ass crack, Bolitar?"

Myron blinked. "Gee, Frank, there's an appetizing thought."

"You're a crazy fuck, you know that? Why you always trying to piss me off? Huh?"

"Hey, I'm not the one who sent goons to rape his girlfriend," Myron said.

Frank pointed his finger at Myron's chest. "And what—you didn't have that coming? You didn't ask for that?"

Myron remained still. Stupid to raise Jessica with this man. Impossible as it seemed, you couldn't let it get personal. You had to separate, to stop thinking of Frank as the man who tried to do grievous harm to the love of your life. To think such thoughts would be at best counterproductive. At worst, suicide.

"I warned you," Frank continued. "I even sent Aaron so you'd know I was serious. You know what Aaron costs per day?"

"Not much anymore," Myron said.

"Ho, ho, I'm dying of laughter," Frank countered, but he wasn't laughing. "I tried to be reasonable with you. I let you have that Crane kid. And how do you thank me? By fucking around with my business."

"I'm trying to find a killer," Myron said.

"And I'm supposed to give a rat's ass? You want to

go play fucking Batman, fine, do it without costing me any money. Once you cost me money, you cross the line. Pavel meant money to me.''

"Pavel also slept with underage girls," Myron said.

Frank held up his hands. "Hey, what a guy does in the privacy of his own bedroom, that don't concern me.''

"You're so progressive, Frank. You voting Democratic now?''

"Look, ass-wipe, you want to hear I knew about Pavel? Fine, I knew. I knew Pavel fucked kiddies. So what? I work with guys who make Pavel Menansi looked like Mother Teresa. I can't go picking and choosing in my line of work. So I ask myself one simple question: Is the guy making me money? If the answer is yes, then that's it. That's my rule. Pavel was making me money. End of story.''

Myron said nothing. He was waiting for Ache to get to the point, which he sincerely hoped was not a bullet in the skull.

Frank took out a packet of chewing gum. Dentyne. He popped one in his mouth. "But I ain't here to get in no philosophy talk with you. Fact is, Pavel is dead. He's not making me money anymore, so my rule don't apply no more. You see?''

"Yes."

"I'm a simple businessman," Frank went on. "Pavel can't make me money no more. That means you and me don't have a beef no more. So you get to live. Wasting you would no longer be profitable to me. You understand?''

Myron nodded. "Are we having a tender moment, Frank?''

Frank leaned forward. His eyes were small and black. "No, ass-wipe, we're not. Next time I ain't gonna fuck around. Hiding your girlfriend won't help you. I'll find her. Or I'll waste someone else instead. Your mommy, your daddy, your friends—hell, even your fucking barber."

"His name is Pierre. And he prefers the term 'beauty technician.' "

Frank looked him square in the eye. "You fucking joking with me?"

"You just threatened my parents," Myron said. "What's the proper way to respond?"

Frank nodded slowly and sat back. "It's over. For now." He pressed a button and the partition slid down.

Billy said, "Yes, Mr. Ache?"

"Call a towing service for Bolitar's car."

"Yes, Mr. Ache."

Frank turned back to Myron. "Get the fuck out of my car."

"No hug first?"

"Out."

"Can I ask you one quick question?"

"What?"

"Did you have Valerie killed to protect Pavel?"

Frank grinned with bad, ferretlike teeth. "Get out," he said. "Or I'll use your nuts for snack foods."

"Right, thanks. Nice chatting with you, Frank, stay in touch." He opened the door and got out.

Frank slid across the seat and leaned his head through the open door. "You tell Win we talked, okay?"

"Why?"

"None of your business why. You just tell Win. Got it?"

"Got it," Myron said.

Frank closed the door. The limo drove away.

Chapter 42

Triple A got there pretty quickly. Myron reached his office at six-thirty. Ned wasn't there yet. Esperanza handed him his messages. He went into his office and returned calls.

Esperanza buzzed. "The bitch. Line three."

"Stop calling her that." He picked up the phone. "You're back at the loft?"

"Yes," Jessica said. "That didn't take long."

"I work fast," he said.

"And yet I never complain," she said.

"Ouch."

"So what happened?" she asked.

"Someone murdered Pavel Menansi. There's nothing for Ache to protect anymore."

"It's that simple?"

"It's business. Business with these guys is very simple."

"No profit, no kill."

"The cardinal rule," Myron said.

"Will you come over tonight?" she asked.

"Yes."

"But one rule of our own," she said.

"Oh?"

"No talking about Valerie Simpson or murder or any of this. We forget it all."

"What will we do instead?" Myron asked.

"Screw each other's brains out."

Myron said, "I guess I can live with that."

Esperanza leaned her head in and said, "He's heeeee-ere."

He nodded at Esperanza and said to Jessica, "I'll call you later."

Myron put the phone back in the cradle. He stood and waited. An evening alone with Jessica. Sounded perfect. It also sounded scary. Things were moving too fast. He had no control. Jess was back and things appeared to be better than ever. Myron wondered about that. Mostly he wondered if he could survive another crash like last time, if he could go through the pain again. He also wondered what he could do to protect himself, realized the answer was nothing, and wished he was better at putting up defenses.

Ned Tunwell practically leaped into his office, hand extended—like an enthusiastic late-show guest coming through a curtain. Myron half expected him to wave to the crowd. He pumped Myron's hand. "Hey, Myron!"

"Hi, Ned. Have a seat."

Ned's smile dropped at Myron's tone. "Hey, there's nothing wrong with Duane, is there?"

"No."

Still standing but his voice was panicky. "He's not hurt?"

"No, Duane is fine."

"Great." The smile was back. Tough to keep a good man down. "That match yesterday—he was fantastic. Fantastic, Myron. I tell you, the way he came back—it's all anyone's talking about. The exposure was awesome. Simply awesome. We couldn't have scripted it better. I practically wet myself."

"Uh-huh. Sit down, Ned."

"Sure." Ned sat. Myron hoped he wouldn't leave a stain on the seat. "Just a few hours away, Myron. The big day. The Saturday Semis. Big live crowd, huge TV audience. You think Duane's got a shot against Craig? Papers don't seem to think so."

Thomas Craig, the second seed and the game's premier serve-and-volley player, was currently playing his career-best tennis. "Yes," Myron said. "I think Duane's got a shot."

Ned's eyes were bright. "Wow. If he could somehow pull it off . . ." He stopped and just shook his head and grinned.

"Ned?"

He looked up. Wide-eyed. "Yes?"

"How well did you know Valerie Simpson?"

Ned hesitated. The eyes dulled a bit. "Me?"

Myron nodded.

"A little, I guess."

"Just a little?"

"Yeah." He flashed a nervous smile, struggled to hold it. "Why, what's up?"

"I heard differently."

"Oh?"

"I heard you were the one who got Nike to sign her. That you handled her account."

He squirmed a bit. "Yeah, well, I guess so."

"So you must have known her pretty well then."

"Maybe, I guess. Why are you asking me this, Myron? What's the big deal?"

"Do you trust me, Ned?"

"With my life, Myron. You know that. But this subject is painful for me. You understand?"

"You mean her dying and all?"

Ned made a lemon-sucking face. "No," he said. "I

mean her career plummet. She was the first person I signed for Nike. I thought she'd launch me to the top. Instead she set me back five years. It was painful."

Another Mr. Sensitive.

"When she flopped," Ned continued, "guess who took the fall? Go ahead, guess."

Myron thought the question was rhetorical, but Ned waited with that expectant face of his. Myron finally said, "Would that be you, Ned?"

"Damn straight, me. I was thrown to the bottom. Just dumped there. I had to start climbing up all over again. Because of Valerie and her collapse. Don't get me wrong, Myron. I'm doing okay now—knock wood." He rapped his knuckles on the desk.

Myron knocked wood too. The sarcasm was lost on Ned. "Did you know Alexander Cross?" Myron asked.

Both Ned's eyebrows jumped. "Hey, what's the deal here?"

"Trust me, Ned."

"I do, Myron, really, but come on . . ."

"It's a simple question: Did you know Alexander Cross?"

"I may have met him once, I don't remember. Through Valerie, of course. They were something of an item."

"How about you and Valerie?"

"What about me and Valerie?"

"Were you two an item?"

He put his hand out in a gesture of *stop*. "Hey, hold up. Look, Myron, I like you, I really do. You're an honest Joe. A straight shooter just like me—"

"No, Ned, you're not a straight shooter. You're jerking me around. You knew Alexander Cross. In fact you were at the Old Oaks tennis club the night he was murdered.''

Ned opened his mouth but no sounds came out. He managed to shake his head no.

"Here." Myron stood and handed him the party guest list. "In yellow highlighter. E. Tunwell. Edward né Ned."

Ned looked down at the paper, looked up, looked down again. "This was a long time ago," he said. "What does this have to do with anything?"

"Why are you lying about it?"

"I'm not lying."

"You're hiding something, Ned."

"No, I'm not."

Myron stared down at him. Ned's eyes scattered, searching for safe haven and finding none. "Look, Myron, it's not what you think."

"I don't think anything." Then: "Did you sleep with her?"

"No!" Ned finally looked up and held a steady gaze. "That damn rumor almost ended my career. It's a lie that slimeball Menansi made up about me. It's a lie, Myron, I swear."

"Pavel Menansi told people that?"

Ned nodded. "He is a sick son of a bitch."

"Was."

"What?"

"Pavel Menansi is dead. Someone killed him last night. Shot in the chest. Very similar to what happened to Valerie." Myron waited two beats. Then he pointed his finger at Ned. "Where were you last night?"

Ned's eyes were two golf balls. "You can't think . . ."

Myron shrugged. "If you've got nothing to hide . . ."

"I don't!"

"Then tell me what happened."

"Nothing happened."

"What aren't you telling me, Ned?"

"It was nothing, Myron. I swear—"

Myron sighed. "You admit Valerie Simpson severely damaged your career. You admit you're still 'pained' by what she did. You've also told me that Pavel Menansi spread rumors about you. In fact you referred to a recent murder victim as—and I quote—'a sick son of a bitch.' "

"Hey, come on, Myron, that was just talk." Ned tried to smile his way out of it, but Myron kept his face stern. "It didn't mean anything."

"Maybe, maybe not. But I wonder how your superiors at Nike are going to react to the publicity."

The smile stayed in place, but there was nothing behind it. "Hey, you can't be serious. You can't go around spreading rumors like that."

"Why?" Myron asked. "You going to kill me too?"

"I didn't kill anyone!" Ned shouted.

Myron feigned fear. "I don't know . . ."

"Look, Valerie took me outside that night, okay, that's all. We kissed, but it went no further, I swear."

"Whoa, back up a second," Myron said. "Start at the beginning. You were at the party."

Ned slid to the tip of his chair, his words came fast now. "Right, I was at the party, okay? So was Valerie. We arrived together. She was very excited because Alexander was going to announce their engagement. But when he backed out, she got really pissed off."

"Why did he back out?"

"His father. He made Alexander call it off."

"Senator Cross?"

"Uh-huh."

"Why?" Myron asked.

"How the hell am I supposed to know? Valerie told me the man was a major prick. She hated him. But when Alexander bowed to his whim like that, she blew her stack. She wanted revenge. A little payback."

"And you were handy?"

Ned snapped his fingers. "Right, exactly, I was handy. That's all. It wasn't my fault, Myron. I was at the wrong place at the wrong time. You understand, right?"

"So you two went outside," Myron prompted.

"We went outside and found a spot behind a shed. We only kissed, I swear. Nothing more. Just kissed. Then we heard some noise, so we stopped."

Myron sat back down. "What noise?"

"First it was just someone hitting tennis balls. But then we heard raised voices. One of them was Alexander's. Then we heard this awful scream."

"What did you do?" Myron asked.

"Me? Nothing at first. Valerie screamed too. Then she broke into a run. I followed her. I lost her for a second. Then I came around a bend and saw her up ahead just standing there. When I got to her I saw what she was staring at. Alexander was bleeding all over the grass. His friends were starting to run away. The big black guy was standing over the body. He had a tennis racket in one hand, a big knife in the other."

Myron leaned forward. "You saw the murderer?"

Ned nodded. "Up close and personal."

"And he was a big black guy?"

"Yep."

"How many of them were there?"

"Two. Both black."

So much for the setup theory. Unless Ned was lying, which Myron doubted. "So what happened next?"

Ned paused for a second. "You ever see Valerie in her prime? On the court, I mean."

"Yes."

"You ever see that look in her eyes?"

"What look?"

"Certain athletes get it. Larry Bird used to. Joe Montana. Michael Jordan. Maybe you used to too. Well, Val had it, and she had it now. The smaller black guy started screaming at the big one, saying stuff like, 'Look what you did,' 'Are you crazy,' stuff like that. Then they started to run. They ran right toward us. Me, I ran. I'm no fool. But not Val. She just stood there and waited. When they got close she let out this big scream and dove at the little guy. I couldn't believe it. She tackled him like a linebacker. They both ended up on the ground. The little guy whacked her with his tennis racket and managed to pull away."

"Did you get a good look at them?"

"Pretty good, I guess."

"Did you ever see pictures of Errol Swade?"

"Yeah, sure, his picture was on the news every day for a while."

"Was it the same guy you saw?"

"Definitely," he said without hesitation. "No question about it."

Myron mulled this over. They'd been there that night. At the Old Oaks Club. Myron had been wrong. Lucinda Elright had been wrong. Swade and Yeller were not just casual fall guys. "So what did you two do then?" Myron asked.

"Hey, her career was in enough trouble. We didn't need this kind of press. So I brought her back to the party. Didn't say anything to anyone about it. Val was out of it anyway—in a real funk, but that wasn't any surprise. I mean, think about it. She takes me outside to cheat on her boyfriend at the exact moment he's getting murdered. Weird, huh?''

Myron nodded. "Very."

And, Myron thought, the kind of thing that would push a troubled soul over the final ledge.

Chapter 43

Myron and Jessica kept their promise. They did not talk about the murders. They snuggled and watched *Strangers on a Train* on AMC while eating Thai takeout. They made love. They snuggled and watched *Rear Window* while downing some Häagen-Dazs. They made love again.

Myron felt light-headed. For one night he actually forgot all about the world of Valerie Simpson and Alexander Cross and Curtis Yeller and Errol Swade and Frank Ache. It felt good. Too good. He started thinking about the suburbs and the hoop in the driveway and then he made himself stop thinking such thoughts.

Several hours later the morning sunlight drop-kicked him back into the real world. The escape had been paradise and for a fleeting moment, as he lay in bed with Jessica, he considered wrapping his arms around her and not going anywhere. Why move? What was out there that could come close to this?

He had no answer. Jessica hugged him a little tighter, as though reading his thoughts, but it didn't last long. They both dressed in silence and drove to Flushing Meadows. Today was the big match. The last Tuesday of the U.S. Open. The women's finals sandwiched by the men's semifinals. First match of the day featured the number-two seed, Thomas Craig, vs. the tournament's biggest surprise, Duane Richwood.

After they passed through the gate Myron gave Jessica a ticket stub. "I'll meet you inside. I want to talk to Duane."

"Now?" she said. "Before the biggest match of his career?"

"Just for a second."

She shrugged, gave him a skeptical eye, took the ticket.

He hurried over to the players' lounge, showed his ID to the guard at the gate, and entered. The room was fairly unspectacular, considering that it was the players' lounge for a Grand Slam event. It reeked of baby powder. Duane sat alone in a corner. He had his Walkman on and his head tilted back. Myron couldn't tell if his eyes were opened or closed because, as always, Duane had on his sunglasses.

When he approached, Duane's finger switched off the music. He tilted his face up toward Myron. Myron could see himself in the reflection of the sunglasses. It reminded him of the windows in Frank's limo.

Duane's face was a rigid mask. He slowly slid the headphones off his ears and let them hang around his neck like a horseshoe. "She's gone," Duane said slowly. "Wanda left me."

"When?" Myron asked. The question was stupid and irrelevant, but he wasn't sure what else to say.

"This morning. What did you tell her?"

"Nothing."

"I heard she came to you," Duane said.

Myron said nothing.

"Did you tell her about seeing me at the hotel?"

"No."

Duane changed tapes in the Walkman. "Get out of here," he said.

"She cares about you, Duane."

"Funny way of showing it."

"She just wants to know what's wrong."

"Nothing's wrong."

The sunglasses were disconcerting. He looked straight up at Myron; it appeared as though they were making eye contact, but who knew? "This match is important," Myron said, "but not like Wanda."

"You think I don't know that?" he snapped.

"Then tell her the truth."

Duane's chiseled face smiled slowly. "You don't understand," he said.

"Make me understand."

He fiddled with the Walkman, popping the tape out, pushing it back in. "You think telling the truth will make it better, but you don't know what the truth is. You talking like 'The truth will set you free' when you don't even know the truth. The truth don't always set you free, Myron. Sometimes the truth can kill."

"Hiding the truth isn't working," Myron said.

"It would if you'd let it lie."

"Someone was murdered. That's not something you can just let lie."

Duane put the Walkman's headphones back on his ears. "Maybe it should be," he said.

Silence.

The two men stared dares. Myron could hear the faint din coming from the Walkman. Then he said to Duane, "You were there the night Alexander Cross was murdered. You were at the club with Yeller and Swade."

The stares continued. Behind them, Thomas Craig lined up by the door. He carried several tennis rackets and what looked like an overnight bag. Security was there too with walkie-talkies and earplugs. They nodded toward Duane. "Show time, Mr. Richwood."

Duane stood. "Excuse me," he said to Myron. "I have a match to play."

He walked behind Thomas Craig. Thomas Craig smiled politely. Duane did likewise. Very civil, tennis. Myron watched them leave. He sat there for a few minutes in the abandoned locker room. In the distance he heard the cheers as both men entered the court.

Show time.

Myron found his way to his seat. It was during the match—in the fourth set actually—when he finally figured out who murdered Valerie Simpson.

Chapter 44

Stadium Court was packed by the time Myron sat down. Duane and Thomas Craig were still warming up, each taking turns lofting easy lobs for the other to slam way. The fans floated and mingled and socialized and made sure they were seen. The usual celebs were there: Johnny Carson, Alan King, David Dinkins, Renee Richards, Barbra Streisand, Ivana Trump.

Jake and his son Gerard came down to the box.

"I see you got the tickets okay," Myron said.

Jake nodded. "Great seats."

"Nothing's too good for my friends."

"No," Jake said, "I meant yours."

Ever the wiseass.

Jake and Gerard chatted a moment with Jessica before moving up to their seats, which were by any stretch of the imagination excellently situated. Myron scanned the crowd. A lot of familiar faces. Senator Bradley Cross was there with his entourage, including his son's old chum Gregory Caufield. Frank Ache had shown up wearing the same sweat suit Myron had seen him in yesterday. Frank nodded toward Myron. Myron did not nod back. Kenneth and Helen Van Slyke were there too—surprise, surprise. They were sitting a few boxes over. Myron tried to catch Helen's eye, but she was trying very hard to pretend she didn't see him. Ned Tunwell and Friends (not to be confused with Barney and

Friends, though the confusion would be understandable) were in their usual box. Ned too was doing his utmost not to see Myron. He seemed less animated today.

"I'll be right back," Jessica said.

Myron sat. Henry Hobman was already in game mode. Myron said, "Hi, Henry."

"Stop messing with his head," Henry said. "Your job is to keep him happy."

Myron didn't bother responding.

Win finally showed up. He wore a pink shirt from some golf club, bright green pants, white bucks, and a yellow sweater tied around his neck. "Hello," Win said.

Myron shook his head. "Who dresses you?"

"It's the latest in sophisticated wear."

"You clash with the world."

"Pardon *moi*, Monsieur Saint Laurent." Win sat down. "Did you talk to Duane?"

"Just a little pep talk."

Jessica returned. She greeted Win with a kiss on the cheek. "Thank you," she whispered to him.

Win said nothing.

They stood for the national anthem. When it was over, the English-accented voice on the loudspeaker asked everyone to lower their heads for a moment of silence to remember the great Pavel Menansi. Heads lowered. The crowd hushed. Someone sniffled. Win rolled his eyes. Two minutes later the match began.

The play was incredible. Both men were power hitters, but no one expected anything like this. The pace was like something from another planet. A far faster planet. The IBM serve speedometer drew constant "Ooo"'s from the crowd. Rallies didn't last very long. Mistakes were made, but so were incredible shots. This was serve and volley in the old tradition taken to the

tenth power. Duane was unconscious. He whacked at the
ball with uncommon fury, as though the ball had personally offended him. Myron had never seen either man
play better.

Win leaned over and whispered, "Must have been
some pep talk."

"Wanda left him."

"Ah," Win said with a nod. "That explains it. The
shackles are off."

"I don't think that's it, Win."

"If you say so."

Myron didn't bother. It was like talking colors with
a blind man.

Duane won the first set 6–2. The second set went into
a tie-breaker, which Thomas Craig won. As the third set
opened, Win said, "What have you learned?"

Myron filled him in, trying to keep his voice down.
At one point, Ivana Trump shushed him. Win waved a
hand in her direction. "She digs me. Big-time."

"Get real," Myron said.

During a change of sides in the third set, Win said,
"So first we believed that Valerie was eliminated because she knew something harmful about Pavel Menansi. Now we believe that she was eliminated because
she saw something the night Alexander Cross was
killed."

"A possibility," Myron said.

During the next change of sides, Myron felt a tap on
his shoulder. He looked down—way down—and was
surprised. "Dr. Abramson," he said.

"Hello, Myron."

"Nice to see you, Doc."

"Nice to see you too," she said. "Your client is playing very well. You must be pleased."

"I'm sorry," Myron said. "I can neither confirm nor deny that Duane Richwood is a client of mine."

She didn't smile. "Was that supposed to be funny?"

"Guess not," Myron said "I didn't know you were a tennis fan."

"I come every year." She spotted Win. "Hello, Mr. Lockwood."

Win nodded. "Dr. Abramson."

"This is my friend Jessica Culver," Myron said.

The two women shook hands and exchanged polite smiles. "A pleasure," Dr. Abramson said. "Well, I don't want to keep you. I just wanted to say a quick hello."

"Can we talk a little later?" Myron asked.

"No, I don't think so. Good-bye."

"Did you know that Kenneth and Helen Van Slyke are here?"

"Yes. And I also know they just stepped out for a moment."

Myron looked toward their seats. Empty. He smiled. "You crafty shrink. Coming over to say hello when they weren't looking."

"And to say good-bye," she said, returning the smile. She turned away and left. The match started up again. During the next change of sides, the Van Slykes returned. Myron leaned over to Win. "How do you know Dr. Abramson?"

"I visited Valerie," he said.

"Often?"

Win didn't answer. He might have shrugged, might not. Either way it told Myron to mind his own business. Myron looked at Jessica. She shrugged too.

On the court Duane was growing more erratic, but he was still hitting enough winners to maintain the edge.

He won the third set 7–5. He was up two sets to one—
one set away from the U.S. Open finals. The Nike box
was animated. Hands were slapping Ned's back. Even
Ned seemed to be perking up now. Hard to keep a good
man down.

Senator Cross watched in silence. No one talked to
him, and he talked to no one. Not even during breaks.
He had met Myron's eyes only once. He stared for a
long time, but did not move. Helen and Kenneth Van
Slyke spoke to the people around them, but they both
looked uncomfortable. Frank Ache adjusted his crotch
and jabbered with Roy O'Connor, the president of
TruPro. Frank looked comfortable. Roy looked like he
wanted to puke. Ivana Trump glanced about her surroundings. Every time she looked near Win, he blew her
kisses.

It was during a serve in the third set when Myron
finally began to see it. It started small, a statement made
by Jimmy Blaine that did not compute. Something about
the foot chase in Philadelphia. The rest sort of tumbled
into place. When the final piece clicked, he sat up.

Win and Jessica traded glances. Myron stared off.

"What is it?" Jessica asked.

Myron turned to Win. "I need to talk to Gregory
Caufield."

"When?"

"Right away, next break. Can you get him alone?"
Win nodded. "Done."

Chapter 45

In the tournament's first few rounds it was not uncommon for fifteen or more matches to be going on at the same time. The biggest names usually stayed on Stadium Court or the Grandstand, while other matches took place in smaller venues, some with no seating. Today those courts were so barren, Myron half expected a tumbleweed to blow through. He waited by court sixteen, a semimajor court. It had the most seating next to the Stadium and Grandstand, though less than most high school gyms.

He sat on an aluminum bench in the front row. The sun had gained strength and was now at its most potent. Every once in a while he heard cheers erupt from the Stadium's crowd a hundred yards or so away. Sometimes tennis fans sounded like they were having an orgasm during particularly brilliant points. It sort of built up slowly with a low oh-oh-oh, and then increased Oh-Oh, and finally the big OH-OH-OH, followed by a loud sigh and clapping.

Weird thought.

Distracting thought too.

He heard Gregory Caufield well before he saw him. That same creepy, money accent that Win possessed said, "Windsor, where on earth are we going?"

"Just over here, Gregory."

"Are you sure this couldn't wait, old boy?"

Old boy. Neither one of them was thirty-five yet and he was using term *old boy*.

"No, Gregory, it can't."

They rounded the corner. Gregory's eyes widened a bit when he saw Myron, but he recovered fast. He smiled and stuck out his hand. "Hello, Myron."

"Hi, Greg."

His face flinched for a second. He was Gregory, not Greg.

"What's this all about, Windsor? I thought you had something private to tell me."

Win shrugged. "I lied," he said. "Myron needs to speak with you. He needs your cooperation."

Gregory turned to Myron and waited.

"I want to talk to you about the night Alexander Cross was murdered."

"I know nothing about it," Gregory said.

"You know plenty about it, but I just have one question for you."

"I'm sorry," Gregory said. "I must be getting back now." He turned to leave. Win blocked his path. Gregory looked puzzled.

"Just one question," Myron said.

Gregory ignored him. "Please move out of my way, Windsor."

Win said, "No."

Gregory could not believe what he was hearing. He half-smiled and put a hand through his unruly hair. "Are you prepared to use force to keep me here?"

"Yes."

"Please, Windsor, this is no longer amusing."

"Myron needs your cooperation."

"And I am not prepared to give it to him. Now I insist you move."

Win did not move. "Are you telling me you will not cooperate, Gregory?"

"That is precisely what I am telling you."

Win's palm shot out and hit the solar plexus. The wind gushed from Gregory. He collapsed to one knee, his face pale and shocked. Myron shook his head at Win, but he understood what he was doing. To people like Gregory—actually, to most people—violence is abstract. They read about it. They see it in movies and in the newspapers. But it never really touches them. It simply doesn't exist in their world. Win had shown Gregory how quickly that can change. Gregory had now experienced physical pain from the hands of a fellow human being. He would be different now. Not just here, not just today.

Gregory held his chest. He was on the verge of tears.

"Do not make me strike you again," Win said.

Myron stepped toward him but did not help him up. "Gregory, we know all about that night," he said. "I have just one question. I don't care what you were doing out there. I don't care if you were snorting or shooting illegal substances. That doesn't interest me in the least. What you say will in no way incriminate you—unless you lie to me."

Gregory looked up at him. His face was completely void of any color.

"They weren't robbing the club, were they?" Myron asked.

Gregory did not answer.

"Errol Swade and Curtis Yeller hadn't broken into the club to rob it," Myron said. "And they weren't there selling drugs either. Am I right? If I am, just nod."

Gregory looked at Win, then back to Myron. He nodded.

"Tell me what they were doing," Myron said.

Gregory didn't say anything.

"Just say it," Myron continued. "I already know the answer. I just need you to say it. What were they doing there that night?"

Gregory's breathing was returning to normal now. He reached out his hand. Myron took it. He stood up and looked Myron straight in the eye.

"What were they doing?" Myron asked. "Tell me."

And then Gregory Caufield said exactly what Myron had expected. "They were playing tennis."

Chapter 46

Myron ran to his car.

Duane was ahead two sets to one, 4–2 in the fourth set. He was two games away from reaching the U.S. Open finals, but that no longer seemed like such a big deal. Myron now knew what happened. He knew what happened to Alexander Cross and Curtis Yeller and Errol Swade and Valerie Simpson and maybe even Pavel Menansi.

He picked up the car phone and began placing calls. His second call was to Esperanza's house. She picked up.

"I'm with Lucy," she said. Esperanza had been dating a woman named Lucy for a couple months now. They seemed serious. Of course, Myron thought Esperanza was serious with a guy named Max just a few months earlier. Dating a Max, then a Lucy. Never a dull moment.

"Do you have the appointment book?" Myron asked.

"I got a copy on my computer here."

"The last day Valerie Simpson was in our office, who had the appointment right before her?"

"Give me a second." He heard her clack some keys. "Duane."

As he thought. "Thanks."

"You're not at the match?"

"No."

"Where are you?"

"In my car."

"Is Win with you?" she asked.

"No."

"How about the witch?"

"I'm alone."

"Swing by and pick me up then. Lucy's leaving anyway."

"No."

He hung up and switched on the radio. Duane was up 5–2. One game away. He dialed the home number of Amanda West, M.E. Then he called Jimmy Blaine. It all checked out. Myron felt something very cold caress his spine.

His hand actually trembled when he called Lucinda Elright. The old teacher answered on the first ring.

"Can you see me today?" Myron asked.

"Yes, of course."

"I should be there in a couple of hours."

"I'll be here," Lucinda said. She asked no questions, wanted no explanations. She simply said, "Good-bye."

Duane won the final set 6–2. He was in the finals of the U.S. Open, but the postgame wrap-up was short for several reasons. First, the women's finals came up right on the heels of Duane's impressive win. Second, the colorful Duane Richwood had run out without doing any interviews. The radio broadcasters seemed surprised.

Myron was not.

He reached Lucinda Elright's apartment in less than two hours. He stayed less than five minutes, but the visit was the final confirmation Myron needed. There was no longer any doubt. He took the book and got back in his car. Half an hour later he parked in the driveway. Myron

rang the doorbell. No smile this time when the door
opened. No surprise this time either.

"I know what happened to Errol Swade," Myron
said. "He's dead."

Deanna Yeller blinked. "I told you that the first time
you came by."

"But," Myron said, "you didn't tell me you killed
him."

Chapter 47

Myron didn't wait for an invitation. He pushed past her. Again he was struck by the impersonal feel of this house. Not one picture. Not one remembrance. But now he understood why. The TV was tuned on the tennis match. No surprise there. The women were midway through the first set.

Deanna Yeller followed him.

"It must torture you," he said.

"What?"

"Watching Duane on TV. Instead of in person."

"It was just a fling," she said in a monotone. "It didn't mean anything."

"Duane was just a one-nighter?"

"Something like that."

"I don't think so," Myron said. "Duane Richwood is your son."

"What are you talking about? I only had one son."

"That's true."

"And he's dead. They killed him, remember?"

"That's not true. Errol Swade was killed. Not Curtis."

"I don't know what you're talking about," she said. But there wasn't much conviction in her voice. She sounded tired, like she was going through the motions— or maybe she just realized that Myron was beyond buying the lies.

"I know now." Myron showed her the book in his hand. "Do you know what this is?"

She looked at the book, her face blank.

"It's the yearbook from Curtis's high school. I just got it from Lucinda Elright."

Deanna Yeller looked so frail, a stiff breeze would send her crashing into the wall. Myron opened the yearbook. "Duane has had a nose job since then. Maybe some other surgery too, I can't be sure. His hair is different. He's gotten a lot more muscular, but then again, he's not a skinny sixteen-year-old anymore. Plus he always wears sunglasses in public. Always. Who would recognize him? Who would even imagine Duane Richwood was a murder suspect killed six years ago?"

Deanna stumbled over to a table. She sat down. She pointed weakly to the chair across from her. Myron took it.

"Curtis was a great athlete," Myron continued, fingering through the pages. "He was only a sophomore, but he was already starting varsity football and basketball. The high school he went to didn't have a tennis team, but Lucinda told me that didn't stop him. He played as often as he could. He loved the game."

Deanna Yeller remained still.

"You see, from the beginning I never bought the robbery angle," Myron said. "You were quick to call your son a thief, Deanna, but the facts didn't back it up. He was a good kid. He had no record. And he was smart. There was nothing to steal out there. Then I thought maybe it was a drug deal gone bad. That made the most sense. Alexander Cross was a user. Errol Swade was a seller. But that didn't explain why your son was there. I even thought for a while that Curtis and Errol had never gone to the club, that they were just scapegoats.

But a fairly reliable witness swears he saw them both. He also said he heard tennis balls being hit at night. He also saw Curtis and Errol each carrying one tennis racket. Why? If you're robbing the place, you carry as many rackets as you can. If you're doing a drug deal, you don't carry any rackets. The answer was obvious in the end: they were there to play tennis. They jumped the fence not to rob the place, but because Curtis wanted to play tennis."

Deanna lifted her head up. She was hollow-eyed. Her movements were sparse and slow. "It was a grass court," she said. "He'd watched Wimbledon on TV that week. He just wanted to play on a grass court, that's all."

"Unfortunately Alexander Cross and his buddies were outside getting high," Myron went on. "They heard Curtis and Errol. What happened next is not exactly clear, but I think we can probably take Senator Cross's word on this one. Alexander, high as a kite, created a conflict. Maybe he didn't like the idea of a couple of black kids playing on his court. Or maybe he really thought they were there to rob the club. It doesn't matter. What does matter is that Errol Swade took out a knife and killed him. It might have been self-defense, but I doubt it."

"He just reacted," Deanna said. "Stupid kid saw a bunch of white boys, so he stabbed. Errol didn't know any different."

Myron nodded. "They ran away then, but Curtis got tackled in the bushes by Valerie Simpson. They struggled. Valerie got a good look at Curtis. A very good look. When you are fighting with someone you believed killed your fiancé, you don't forget the face. Curtis managed to break away. He and Errol jumped the fence and ran down the block. They found a car in a driveway. Errol had been arrested several times already for stealing cars. Breaking in and hot-wiring one was no problem for him. That's what first gave it to me. I talked to the officer who supposedly shot your son. His name is Jimmy Blaine. Jimmy said he shot the *driver* of the car, not the passenger. But Curtis wouldn't have been driving. That wouldn't make any sense. The driver was the experienced thief, not the good kid. So then it dawned on me: Jimmy Blaine didn't shoot Curtis Yeller. He shot Errol Swade.''

Deanna Yeller sat still as a stone.

"The bullet hit Errol in the ribs. With Curtis's help they managed to round the corner and crawl in through the fire escape. They made their way to your apartment. By now sirens were sounding all over the place. They were closing in on all of you. Errol and Curtis were probably in a state of panic. It was pandemonium. They told you what happened. You knew what this meant—a rich white boy shot at a fancy rich white club. Your son was doomed. Even if Curtis had only been standing there—even if Errol told the police that it was all his fault—Curtis was finished."

"I knew more than that," Deanna interjected. "It'd been almost an hour since the murder. The radio already said who the victim was. Not just a rich white boy, but the son of a United States senator."

"And," Myron continued, "you knew Errol had a long record. You knew it was his fault. You knew he was going away for good this time. Errol's life was over, and he had no one to blame but himself. But Curtis was innocent. Curtis was a good boy. He'd done everything right, and now because of the stupidity of his cousin, his life was about to be flushed away."

Deanna looked up. "But that was all true," she insisted, sparking up just a bit. "Can't deny any of that,
can you? Can you?"

"No," Myron said. "I guess I can't. What you did
next probably didn't take much thought. You'd heard
the police fire two bullets. You saw only one in Errol.
Most important, Curtis didn't have a record. His mug
shot wasn't on file. His description wasn't on file." He
stopped. Her eyes were clear and on him. "Whose gun
was it, Deanna?"

"Errol's."

"He had it with him?"

She nodded.

"So you took the gun. You pressed it against Errol's
cheek. And you fired."

She nodded again.

"You blew his face right off," Myron continued. "I
wondered about that too. Why would someone shoot him
up close in the face? Why not in the back of the head
or the heart? The answer is, you didn't want anyone to
see his face. You wanted him to be an unrecognizable
lump. Then you put on your big act. You cradled him
in your arms and cried while the police and the senator's
hoods came crashing in. It was so simple really. I asked
the medical examiner how they identified Curtis's body.
She scoffed at such a ridiculous question. The usual way,
she told me. The next of kin. You, Deanna. The mother.
What else did they need? Why question that? The cops
were thrilled you didn't want to make a big deal over it,
so they didn't look too closely. And just to cement your
plan, you were smart enough to have the body cremated
immediately. Even if someone wanted to go back and
check, the evidence was ashes.

"As for Curtis, his escape was easy. A nationwide

manhunt began for Errol Swade, a six-foot four-inch man who looked nothing like your son. No one was looking for Curtis Yeller. He was dead.''

''It wasn't quite that easy,'' Deanna said. ''Curtis and I were careful. Powerful men were in this. The police scared me, sure, but not as much as those men who worked for the senator. And then the papers all made that Cross boy out to be a hero. Curtis knew the truth. If the senator ever got a hold of my boy . . .'' She shrugged away the obvious.

Myron nodded. He'd thought the same thing too. Dead men tell no tales. ''So Curtis spent the next five years underground?'' he asked.

''I guess you could call it that,'' Deanna said. ''He roamed around, scraped by on whatever he could. I sent him money when I had some, but I told him to never come back to Philadelphia. We'd arrange times to talk on public phones and stuff. He grew up on his own. He lived on the streets, but he was well-spoken enough to get some decent jobs. He worked for three years at a tennis club near Boston. He played all the time, even hustled a few games. I saved up enough for him to get a little plastic surgery done. Just some little touches, you know, in case he ran into someone he knew. Like you said, he got a lot bigger. He grew an inch and put on thirty pounds. He also wore those sunglasses, though I always thought that was going a little too far. No one's gonna recognize him, I thought. Not anymore. It'd been too long. Worst thing happen, someone might think he resembles a dead boy they used to know. I mean, five years passed. We thought he was safe.''

''That's why you started getting money recently,'' Myron said. ''It wasn't a pay-off. The money came from Duane's turning pro. He bought you this house.''

She nodded.

"And when I saw you two at the hotel that night, I immediately jumped to the conclusion that you were lovers. But it was actually a son visiting his mother. The embrace I saw when he left your room—it wasn't the embrace of lovers, but a mother hugging her son goodbye. In fact Duane hadn't slept around at all. That was an act on his part. Wanda was right all along. He loved her. He never cheated on her. Not with you. And not with Valerie Simpson."

She nodded again. "He loves that girl. He and Wanda are good together."

"Everything was going just fine until Valerie spotted Duane in my office," Myron continued. "His sunglasses were off. She saw him up close, and like I said before, you don't forget the face of the man you think killed your fiancé. She recognized him. She stole his card from my Rolodex and called. What happened next, Deanna? Did she threaten to expose him?"

"There's some stuff we left out," Deanna said. "I just want to be clear, okay?"

Myron nodded.

"Curtis didn't know I was going to kill Errol that night," she said. "I just told him to hide in the basement. There was a closed-off tunnel down there. I knew he'd be safe for a while. I told Errol to stay with me, I'd fix his ribs. When Curtis was out of the room, I shot Errol."

"Did Curtis ever learn the truth?"

"He figured it out later. But he didn't know then. He had nothing to do with it."

"So what about Valerie? Was she going to talk?"

"Yes."

Their eyes met.

"So you killed her," Myron said.

For a few moments Deanna said nothing. She stared down at her hands, as though looking for something. "She wouldn't listen to reason," she said softly. "Duane told me that Valerie called him. He tried to convince her she had the wrong man, but she wouldn't hear it. So I met up with her at the hotel. I tried to persuade her too. I told her he'd done nothing wrong, but she just kept talking this nonsense about not hiding things anymore—how she'd buried too many things and it had to all come out." Deanna Yeller closed her eyes and shook her head. "The girl left me no choice. I watched her hotel. I saw her rush out. I saw her rush to the matches, and I knew she was scared and I knew she was going to say something and I knew I couldn't wait anymore, that I had to stop her now or . . ." She sat still. Then she moved her hands off the table and folded them on her lap. "I had no choice."

Myron remained quiet.

"I did the only thing I could," she said. "It was her life or my son's life."

"So for the second time you chose your son."

"Yes. And if you turn me in, it'll all be for nothing. The truth will come out, and they'll kill my boy. You know they will."

"I'll protect him," Myron said.

"No, that's my job."

Tires squealed in the driveway. Myron rose and looked out the window. It was Duane. He threw the car in park and leaped out.

"Keep him out," Deanna said, suddenly out of her chair. "Please."

"What?"

She ran to the door and threw the dead bolt. "I don't want him to see."

"See what?"

But now Myron did see. She turned toward him. She had a gun in her hand. "I've already killed twice to save him. What's a third?"

Myron looked for a safe place to dive, but for the second time in this case he'd been careless. He was out in the open. It would be impossible to miss. "Killing me won't make it go away," he said.

"I know," she replied.

There was a pounding at the door. Duane shouted, "Open up! Don't say anything to him!" More pounding.

Deanna's eyes welled with tears. "Don't tell anyone, Myron. No need to say anything anymore. The guilty will have all been punished."

She placed the barrel of the gun against her head.

"Don't," Myron whispered.

From outside the door, Duane shouted, "Mama! Open up, Mama!"

She turned toward the voice. Myron tried to reach her in time, but he had no chance. She pulled the trigger and made one final sacrifice for her son.

Chapter 48

Time passed. Myron had to persuade Duane to leave his mother alone. It was what she would have wanted, Myron reminded him. When they were both far enough away, Myron placed an anonymous call to the Cherry Hill police. "I think I heard a gunshot," he said. He gave the address and hung up.

They met up at a stop along the New Jersey Turnpike. Duane was no longer crying.

"Are you going to tell?" Duane asked.

"No," Myron said.

"Not even Valerie's mother?"

"I don't owe her anything."

Silence. Then Duane started tearing again.

"Did the truth set you free, Myron?"

He ignored the question. "Tell Wanda," Myron said. "If you really love her, tell her everything. It's the only chance you have."

"You can't be my agent anymore," Duane said.

"I know," Myron said.

"There was no other way for her. She had to protect me."

"There was another way."

"What? If it was your kid, what would you have done?"

Myron didn't have the answer. He only knew that

killing Valerie Simpson was not it. "Are you going to play tomorrow?"

"Yes," he said. He climbed back in his car. "And I'm going to win."

Myron did not doubt it.

It was late when he got back to New York. He parked the car at the Kinney lot and headed past the ugly intestinal sculpture and into the building. The security guard greeted him. It was Saturday night. Practically no one was there. But even on street level Myron had seen the light on.

He took the elevator to the fourteenth floor. The customary hubbub of activity at Lock-Horne Securities was absent. The floor was dark. Most of the computers had been turned off and covered with plastic, though a few were left on, the bizarre screen savers dancing streaks of lights across the desk. Myron walked toward the light in the corner office. Win was sitting at his desk, reading a book in Korean. He looked up when Myron entered.

"So tell me," Win said.

Myron did. The whole story.

"Ironic," Win said when he'd finished.

"What?"

"We kept wondering how a mother could care so little for her son when in reality the problem was just the opposite. She cared too much."

Myron nodded.

Silence.

Then Win said, "You know?"

"Yes."

"How?"

"Dr. Abramson," Myron said. "Your visiting Valerie enough for her to know your name. It got me think-ing.''

Win nodded. ''I was going to tell you.''

''You didn't have to kill him,'' Myron said.

''You're a child sometimes,'' Win said. ''I did what had to be done.''

''You didn't have to kill him.''

''Frank Ache would have killed us,'' Win said. ''The only reason he chose to back off was because Pavel Menansi was dead—ergo the profit was gone. By elim-inating Pavel, I took away his motive. Our options were clear: we could have taken on the mob and eventually gotten killed, or we could exterminate a vermin. In the end, sacrificing scum saved our lives.''

''What else did you do to Ache?'' Myron asked.

''What do you mean?''

''Frank didn't show up in the woods just to call off a hit. Something had scared him. He told me to mention our meeting to you.''

''Oh,'' Win said, ''that.'' He stood and grabbed his putter. He dropped a few golf balls on the floor. ''I sent him a little package.''

''What package?''

''One containing Aaron's right testicle. That, added together with Pavel's death, was enough to convince him that it would be in all of our interests to drop the mat-ter.''

Myron shook his head. ''What separates you from Deanna Yeller?''

''Just one thing,'' Win said. He lined up a putt and sank it. ''I don't fault her for what she did the night Alexander Cross was murdered. It was practical. It made sense. She didn't trust the justice system. She didn't trust a United States senator. In both cases, she was undoubtedly right. And what did she sacrifice? Her lowlife nephew who would have spent his life behind bars anyway. No, in that case we were the same.''

He lined up over the next putt and checked the lie. ''Where we differ, however, is that she killed an innocent person the second time around. I did not.''

''You're drawing a pretty thin line,'' Myron said.

''The world is made up of thin lines, my friend. I was there. I visited Valerie every week in the institution. Did you know that?''

Myron shook his head. He was probably closer to Win than anyone, and he hadn't known that. He hadn't even known he knew Valerie Simpson.

Win took another putt. ''From the first moment I saw her in that godforsaken place I wanted to know what changed her. I wanted to know what monstrosity had deadened the spirit that had soared so. You were the one who figured it out. Pavel Menansi did that to her, just as he would have done it to Janet Koffman if I hadn't stopped him.'' Win looked over at Myron. ''You already know this, but I'll say it just the same: the fact that killing Pavel helped us with Frank Ache was just a bonus. I would have killed him anyway. I really didn't need any justification.''

''There were other ways to make him pay,'' Myron said.

''How?'' Win scoffed. ''By arresting him? No one would press charges. And even if all was revealed as per your plan, what would happen to him? He'd probably write a book and go on *Oprah*. He'd tell the world how he'd been abused as a child or some such nonsense. He'd be an even bigger celebrity.'' Win took another putt. Another make. ''We're not the same, you and I. We both know that. But it's okay.''

"It's not okay."

"Yes, it is. If we were the same it wouldn't work. We'd both be dead by now. Or insane. We balance each other. It's why you're my best friend. It's why I love you."

Silence.

"Don't do it again," Myron said.

Win did not reply. He lined up another putt.

"Did you hear me?"

"It's time to move on," Win said. "This incident is in the past. You know better than to try to control the future."

More silence. Win sank another putt.

"Jessica is waiting," Win said. "She told me to remind you about her new oils."

Myron turned and left then. He felt unclean and unsure. But he knew Win was right: it was over. It would just take a bit of time for things to feel normal again. He would recover.

And, Myron thought as he headed into the elevator, what better way to start the healing process than with Jessica's oils?

1

Three days before her death, my mother told me—these weren't her last words, but they were pretty close—that my brother was still alive.

That was all she said. She didn't elaborate. She said it only once. And she wasn't doing very well. Morphine had already applied its endgame heart squeeze. Her skin was in that cusp between jaundice and fading summer tan. Her eyes had sunken deep into her skull. She slept most of the time. She would, in fact, have only one more lucid moment—if indeed this had been a lucid moment, which I very much doubted—and that would be a chance for me to tell her that she had been a wonderful mother, that I loved her very much, and good-bye. We never said anything about my brother. That didn't mean we weren't thinking about him as though he were sitting bedside too.

"He's alive."

Those were her exact words. And if they were true, I didn't know if it would be a good thing or bad.

We buried my mother four days later.

When we returned to the house to sit shivah, my father stormed through the semi-shag in the living room. His face was red with rage. I was there, of course. My sister, Melissa, had flown in from Seattle with her husband, Ralph. Aunt Selma and Uncle Murray paced. Sheila, my soul mate, sat next to me and held my hand.

That was pretty much the sum total.

There was only one flower arrangement, a wonderful monster of a thing. Sheila smiled and squeezed my hand when she saw the card. No words, no message, just the drawing

⊞

Dad kept glancing out the bay windows—the same windows that had been shot out with a BB gun twice in the past eleven years—and muttered under his breath, "Sons of bitches." He'd turn around and think of someone else who hadn't shown. "For God's sake, you'd think the Bergmans would have at least made a goddamn appearance." Then he'd close his eyes and look away. The anger would consume him anew, blending with the grief into something I didn't have the strength to face.

One more betrayal in a decade filled with them.

I needed air.

I got to my feet. Sheila looked up at me with concern. "I'm going to take a walk," I said softly.

"You want company?"

"I don't think so."

Sheila nodded. We had been together nearly a year. I've never had a partner so in sync with my rather odd vibes. She gave my hand another I-love-you squeeze, and the warmth spread through me.

Our front-door welcome mat was harsh faux grass, like something stolen from a driving range, with a plastic daisy in the upper left-hand corner. I stepped over it and strolled up Downing Place. The street was lined with numbingly ordinary aluminum-sided split-levels, circa 1962. I still wore my dark gray suit. It itched in the heat. The savage sun beat down like a drum, and a perverse part of me thought that it was a wonderful day to decay. An image of my mother's light-the-world smile—the one before it all happened—flashed in front of my eyes. I shoved it away.

I knew where I was headed, though I doubt if I would have admitted it to myself. I was drawn there, pulled by some unseen force. Some would call it masochistic.

Others would note that maybe it had something to do with closure. I thought it was probably neither.

I just wanted to look at the spot where it all ended.

The sights and sounds of summer suburbia assaulted me. Kids squealed by on their bicycles. Mr. Cirino, who owned the Ford/Mercury dealership on Route 10, mowed his lawn. The Steins—they'd built up a chain of appliance stores that were swallowed up by a bigger chain—were taking a stroll hand in hand, There was a touch football game going on at the Levines' house, though I didn't know any of the participants. Barbecue smoke took flight from the Kaufmans' backyard.

I passed by the Glassmans' old place. Mark "the Doof" Glassman had jumped through the sliding glass doors when he was six. He was playing Superman. I remembered the scream and the blood. He needed over forty stitches. The Doof grew up and became some kind of IPO-start-up zillionaire. I don't think they call him the Doof anymore, but you never know.

The Marianos' house, still that horrid shade of phlegm yellow with a plastic deer guarding the front walk, was on the bend. Angela Mariano, our local bad girl, was two years older than us and like some superior, awe-inducing species. Watching Angela sunning in her backyard in a gravity-defying ribbed halter top, I had felt the first painful thrusts of deep hormonal longing. My mouth would actually water. Angela used to fight with her parents and sneak smokes in the toolshed behind her house. Her boyfriend drove a motorcycle. I ran into her last year on Madison Avenue in midtown. I expected her to look awful—that was what you always hear happens to that first lust-crush—but Angela looked great and seemed happy.

A lawn sprinkler did the slow wave in front of Eric Frankel's house at 23 Downing Place. Eric had a space-travel-themed bar mitzvah at the Chanticleer in Short Hills when we were both in seventh grade. The ceiling was done up planetarium style—a black sky with star constellations. My seating card told me that I was sitting at "Table Apollo 14." The centerpiece was an ornate model rocket on a green fauna launching pad. The waiters, adorned in realistic space suits, were each supposed to be one of the Mercury 7. "John Glenn" served us. Cindi Shapiro and I had sneaked into the chapel room and made out for over an hour. It was my first time. I didn't know what I was doing. Cindi did. I remember it was glorious, the way her tongue caressed and jolted me in unexpected ways. But I also remember my initial wonderment evolving after twenty minutes or so into, well, boredom—a confused "what next?" along with a naïve "is that all there is?"

When Cindi and I stealthily returned to Cape Kennedy's Table Apollo 14, ruffled and in fine post-smooch form (the Herbie Zane Band serenading the crowd with "Fly Me to the Moon"), my brother, Ken, pulled me to the side and demanded details. I, of course, too gladly gave them. He awarded me with that smile and slapped me five. That night, as we lay on the bunk beds, Ken on the top, me on the bottom, the stereo playing Blue Oyster Cult's "Don't Fear the Reaper" (Ken's favorite), my older brother explained to me the facts of life as seen by a ninth-grader. I'd later learn he was mostly wrong (a little too much emphasis on the breast), but when I think back to that night, I always smile.

"He's alive. . . ."

I shook my head and turned right at Coddington Terrace by the Holders' old house. This was the same route Ken and I had taken to get to Burnet Hill Elementary School. There used to be a paved path between two houses to make the trip shorter. I wondered if it was still there. My mother—everyone, even kids, had called her Sunny—used to follow us to school quasi-surreptitiously. Ken and I would roll our eyes as she ducked behind trees. I smiled, thinking about her overprotectiveness now. It

4

used to embarrass me, but Ken would simply shrug. My brother was securely cool enough to let it slide. I wasn't.

I felt a pang and moved on.

Maybe it was just my imagination, but people began to stare. The bicycles, the dribbling basketballs, the sprinklers and lawn mowers, the cries of touch footballers—they all seemed to hush as I passed. Some stared out of curiosity because a strange man strolling in a dark gray suit on a summer evening was something of an oddity. But most, or again so it seemed, looked on in horror because they recognized me and couldn't believe that I would dare tread upon this sacred soil.

I approached the house at 147 Coddington Terrace without hesitation. My tie was loosened. I jammed my hands in my pockets. I toed the spot where curb met pavement. Why was I here? I saw a curtain move in the den. Mrs. Miller's face appeared at the window, gaunt and ghostlike. She glared at me. I didn't move or look away. She glared some more—and then to my surprise, her face softened. It was as though our mutual agony had made some sort of connection. Mrs. Miller nodded at me. I nodded back and felt the tears begin to well up.

You may have seen the story on 20/20 or *PrimeTime Live* or some other television equivalent of fish wrap. For those who haven't, here's the official account: On October 17 eleven years ago, in the township of Livingston, New Jersey, my brother, Ken Klein, then twenty-four, brutally raped and strangled our neighbor Julie Miller.

In her basement. At 147 Coddington Terrace.

That was where her body was found. The evidence wasn't conclusive as to if she'd actually been murdered in that poorly finished subdwelling or if she'd been dumped postmortem behind the water-stained zebra-striped couch. Most assume the former. My brother escaped capture and ran off to parts unknown—at least, again, according to the official account.

Over the past eleven years, Ken has eluded an international dragnet. There have however been "sightings."

The first came about a year after the murder from a small fishing village in northern Sweden. Interpol swooped in, but somehow my brother evaded their grasp. Supposedly he was tipped off. I can't imagine how or by whom.

The next sighting occurred four years later in Barcelona. Ken had rented—to quote the newspaper accounts—"an oceanview hacienda" (Barcelona is not on an ocean) with—again I will quote—"a lithe, dark-haired woman, perhaps a flamenco dancer." A vacationing Livingston resident, no less, reported seeing Ken and his Castilian paramour dining beachside. My brother was described as tan and fit and wore a white shirt opened at the collar and loafers without socks. The Livingstonite, one Rick Horowitz, had been a classmate of mine in Mr. Hunt's fourth-grade class. During a three-month period, Rick entertained us by eating caterpillars during recess.

Barcelona Ken yet again slipped through the law's fingers.

The last time my brother was purportedly spotted he was skiing down the expert hills in the French Alps (interestingly enough, Ken never skied before the murder). Nothing came of it, except a story on *48 Hours*. Over the years, my brother's fugitive status had become the criminal version of a VH1 *Where Are They Now?*, popping up whenever any sort of rumor skimmed the surface or, more likely, when one of the network's fish wraps was low on material.

I naturally hated television's "team coverage" of "suburbia gone wrong" or whatever similar cute moniker they came up with. Their "special reports" (just once, I'd like to see them call it a "normal report, everyone has done this story") always featured the same photographs of Ken in his tennis whites—he was a nationally ranked player at one time—looking his most pompous. I can't imagine where they got them. In them Ken looked handsome in that way people hate right away. Haughty, Kennedy hair, suntan bold against the whites, toothy grin, Photograph Ken looked like one of those people of privilege (he was not) who coasted through life on his charm (a little) and trust account (he had none).

I had appeared on one of those magazine shows. A producer reached me—this was pretty early on in the coverage—and claimed that he wanted to present "both sides fairly." They had plenty of people ready to lynch my brother, he noted. What they truly needed for the sake of "balance" was someone who could describe the "real Ken" to the folks back home.

I fell for it.

A frosted-blond anchorwoman with a sympathetic manner interviewed me for over an hour. I enjoyed the process actually. It was therapeutic. She thanked me and ushered me out and when the episode aired, they used only one snippet, removing her question ("But surely, you're not going to tell us that your brother was perfect, are you? You're not trying to tell us he was a saint, right?") and editing my line so that I appeared in nose-pore-enhancing extreme close-up with dramatic music as my cue, saying, "Ken was no saint, Diane."

Anyway, that was the official account of what happened.

I've never believed it. I'm not saying it's not possible. But I believe a much more likely scenario is that my brother is dead—that he has been dead for the past eleven years.

More to the point, my mother always believed that Ken was dead. She believed it firmly. Without reservation. Her son was not a murderer. Her son was a victim.

"He's alive. . . .He didn't do it."

The front door of the Miller house opened. Mr. Miller stepped through it. He pushed his glasses up his nose. His fists rested on his hips in a pitiful Superman stance.

"Get the hell out of here, Will," Mr. Miller said to me. And I did.

The next big shock occurred an hour later.

Sheila and I were up in my parents' bedroom. The same furniture, a sturdy, faded swirling gray with blue trim, had adorned this room for as long as I could remember. We sat on the king-size bed with the weak-springed mattress. My mother's most personal items—the stuff she kept in her bloated nightstand drawers—were scattered over the duvet. My father was still downstairs by the bay windows, staring out defiantly.

I don't know why I wanted to sift through the things my mother found valuable enough to preserve and keep near her. It would hurt. I knew that. There is an interesting correlation between intentional pain infliction and comfort, a sort of playing-with-fire approach to grieving. I needed to do that, I guess.

I looked at Sheila's lovely face—tilted to the left, eyes down and focused—and I felt my heart soar. This is going to sound a little weird, but I could stare at Sheila for hours. It was not just her beauty—hers was not what one would call classical anyway, her features a bit off center from either genetics or, more likely, her murky past—but there was an animation there, an inquisitiveness, a delicacy too, as if one more blow would shatter her irreparably. Sheila made me want to—bear with me here—be brave for her.

Without looking up, Sheila gave a half-smile and said, "Cut it out."

"I'm not doing anything."

She finally looked up and saw the expression on my face. "What?" she asked.

I shrugged. "You're my world," I said simply.

"You're pretty hot stuff yourself."

"Yeah," I said. "Yeah, that's true."

She feigned a slap in my direction. "I love you, you know."

"What's not to love?"

She rolled her eyes. Then her gaze fell back onto the side of my mother's bed. Her face quieted.

"What are you thinking about?" I asked.

"Your mother." Sheila smiled. "I really liked her."

"I wish you had known her before."

"Me too."

We started going through the laminated yellow clippings. Birth announcements—Melissa's, Ken's, mine. There were articles on Ken's tennis exploits. His trophies, all those bronze men in miniature in mid-serve, still swarmed his old bedroom. There were photographs, mostly old ones from before the murder. Sunny. It had been my mother's nickname since childhood. It suited her. I found a photo of her as PTA president. I don't know what she was doing, but she was onstage and wearing a goofy hat and all the other mothers were cracking up. There was another one of her running the school fair. She was dressed in a clown suit. Sunny was the favorite grown-up among my friends. They liked when she drove the carpool. They wanted the class picnic at our house. Sunny was parental cool without being cloying, just "off" enough, a little crazy perhaps, so that you never knew exactly what she would do next. There had always been an excitement—a crackle if you will—around my mother.

We kept it up for more than two hours. Sheila took her time, looking thoughtfully at every picture. When she stopped at one in particular, her eyes narrowed. "Who's that?"

She handed me the photograph. On the left was my mother in a semi-obscene yellow bikini, I'd say, 1972ish, looking very curvy. She had her arm around a short man with a dark mustache and happy smile.

"King Hussein," I said.

"Pardon me?"

I nodded.

"As in the kingdom of Jordan?"

"Yep. Mom and Dad saw him at the Fontainebleau in Miami."

"And?"

"Mom asked him if he'd pose for a picture."

"You're kidding."

"There's the proof."

"Didn't he have guards or something?"

"I guess she didn't look armed."

Sheila laughed. I remember Mom telling me about the incident. Her posing with King Hussein, Dad's camera not working, his muttering under his breath, his trying to fix it, her glaring at him to hurry, the king standing patiently, his chief of security checking the camera, finding the problem, fixing it, handing it back to Dad.

My mom, Sunny.

"She was so lovely," Sheila said.

It's an awful cliché to say that a part of her died when they found Julie Miller's body, but the thing about clichés is that they're often dead-on. My mother's crackle quieted, smothered. After hearing about the murder, she never threw a tantrum or cried hysterically. I often wish she had. My volatile mother became frighteningly even. Her whole manner became flat, monotone—*passionless* would be the best way to describe it—which in someone like her was more agonizing to witness than the most bizarre histrionics.

The front doorbell rang. I looked out the bedroom window and saw the Eppes-Essen deli delivery van. Sloppy joes for the, uh, mourners. Dad had optimistically ordered too many platters. Delusional to the end. He stayed in this house like the captain of the *Titanic*. I remember the first time the windows had been shot out with the BB gun not long after the murder—the way he shook his fist with defiance. Mom, I think, wanted to move. Dad would not. Moving would be a surrender in his eyes. Moving would be admitting their son's guilt. Moving would be a betrayal.

Dumb.

Sheila had her eyes on me. Her warmth was almost palpable, more sunbeam on my face, and for a moment I just let myself bathe in it. We'd met at work about a year before. I'm the senior director of Covenant House on 41st Street in New York City. We're a charitable foundation that helps young runaways survive the streets. Sheila had come in as a volunteer. She was from a small town in Idaho, though she seemed to have very little small-town girl left in her. She told me that many years ago, she too had been a runaway. That was all she would tell me about her past.

"I love you," I said.

"What's not to love?" she countered.

I did not roll my eyes. Sheila had been good to my mother toward the end. She'd take the Community Bus Line from Port Authority to Northfield Avenue and walk over to the St. Barnabas Medical Center. Before her illness, the last time my mom had stayed at St. Barnabas was when she delivered me. There was probably something poignantly life-cycling about that, but I couldn't see it just then.

I had however seen Sheila with my mother. And it made me wonder. I took a risk.

"You should call your parents," I said softly.

Sheila looked at me as though I'd just slapped her across the face. She slid off the bed.

"Sheila?"

"This isn't the time, Will."

I picked up a picture frame that held a photo of my tanned parents on vacation. "Seems as good as any."

"You don't know anything about my parents."

"I'd like to," I said.

She turned her back to me. "You've worked with runaways," she said.

"So?"

"You know how bad it can be."

I did. I thought again about her slightly off-center features—the nose, for example, with the telltale bump—and wondered. "I also know it's worse if you don't talk about it."

"I've talked about it, Will."

"Not with me."

"You're not my therapist."

"I'm the man you love."

"Yes." She turned to me. "But not now, okay? Please."

I had no response to that one, but perhaps she was right. My fingers were absently toying with the picture frame. And that was when it happened.

The photograph in the frame slid a little.

I looked down. Another photograph started peeking out from underneath. I moved the top one a little farther. A hand appeared in the bottom photograph. I tried pushing it some more, but it wouldn't go. My finger found the clips on back. I slid them to the side and let the back of the frame drop to the bed. Two photographs floated down behind it.

One—the top one—was of my parents on a cruise, looking happy and healthy and relaxed in a way I barely remember them ever being. But it was the second photograph, the hidden one, that caught my eye.

The red-stamped date on the bottom was from less than two years ago. The picture was taken atop a field or hill or something. I saw no houses in the background, just snowcapped mountains like something from the opening scene of *The Sound of Music*. The man in the picture wore shorts and a backpack and sunglasses and scuffed hiking boots. His smile was familiar. So was his face, though it was more lined now. His hair was longer. His beard had gray in it. But there was no mistake.

The man in the picture was my brother, Ken.

2

My father was alone on the back patio. Night had fallen. He sat very still and stared out at the black. As I came up behind him, a jarring memory rocked me.

About four months after Julie's murder, I found my father in the basement with his back to me just like this. He thought that the house was empty. Resting in his right palm was his Ruger, a .22 caliber gun. He cradled the weapon tenderly, as though it were a small animal, and I never felt so frightened in my entire life. I stood there, frozen. He kept his eyes on the gun. After a few long minutes, I quickly tiptoed to the top of the stairs and faked like I'd just come in. By the time I trudged down the steps, the weapon was gone.

I didn't leave his side for a week.

I slipped now through the sliding glass door. "Hey," I said to him.

He spun around, his face already breaking into a wide smile. He always had one for me. "Hey, Will," he said, the gravel voice turning tender. Dad was always happy to see his children. Before all this happened, my father was a fairly popular man. People liked him. He was friendly and dependable, if not a little gruff, which just made him seem all the more dependable. But while my father might smile at you, he didn't care a lick. His world was his family. No one else mattered to him. The suffering of strangers and even friends never really reached him—a sort of family-centeredness.

I sat in the lounge chair next to him, not sure how to raise the subject. I took a few deep breaths and listened to him do the same. I felt wonderfully safe with him. He might be older and more withered, and by now I was the taller, stronger man—but I knew that if trouble surfaced, he'd still step up and take the hit for me.

And that I'd still slip back and let him.

"Have to cut that branch back," he said, pointing into the dark.

I couldn't see it. "Yeah," I said.

The light from the sliding glass doors hit his profile. The anger had dissolved now, and the shattered look had returned. Sometimes I think that he had indeed tried to step up and take the hit when Julie died, but it had knocked him on his ass. His eyes still had that burst-from-within look, that look of someone who had unexpectedly been punched in the gut and didn't know why.

"You okay?" he asked me. His standard opening refrain.

"I'm fine. I mean, not fine but . . ."

Dad waved his hand. "Yeah, dumb question," he said.

We fell back into silence. He lit a cigarette. Dad never smoked at home. His children's health and all that. He took a drag and then, as if suddenly remembering, he looked at me and stamped it out.

"It's all right," I said.

"Your mother and I agreed that I would never smoke at home."

I didn't argue with him. I folded my hands and put them on my lap. Then I dived in. "Mom told me something before she died."

His eyes slid toward me.

"She said that Ken was still alive."

Dad stiffened, but only for a second. A sad smile came to his face. "It was the drugs, Will."

"That's what I thought," I said. "At first."

"And now?"

I looked at his face, searching for some sign of deception. There had been rumors, of course. Ken wasn't wealthy. Many wondered how my brother could have afforded to live in hiding for so long. My answer, of course, was that he hadn't—that he died that night too. Others, maybe most people, believed that my parents somehow sneaked him money.

I shrugged. "I wonder why after all these years she would say that."

"The drugs," he repeated. "And she was dying, Will."

The second part of that answer seemed to encompass so much. I let it hang a moment. Then I asked, "Do you think Ken's alive?"

"No," he said. And then he looked away.

"Did Mom say anything to you?"

"About your brother?"

"Yes."

"Pretty much what she told you," he said.

"That Ken was alive?"

"Yes."

"Anything else?"

Dad shrugged. "She said he didn't kill Julie. She said he'd be back by now except he had to do something first."

"Do what?"

"She wasn't making sense, Will."

"Did you ask her?"

"Of course. But she was just ranting. She couldn't hear me anymore. I shushed her. I told her it'd be okay."

He looked away again. I thought about showing him the photograph of Ken but decided against it. I wanted to think it through before I started us down that path.

"I told her it'd be okay," he repeated.

Through the sliding glass door, I could see one of those photo cubes, the old color images sun-faded into a blur of yellow-green. There were no recent pictures in the room. Our house was trapped in a time warp, frozen solid eleven years ago, like in that old song where the grandfather clock stops when the old man dies.

"I'll be right back," Dad said.

I watched him stand and walk until he thought he was out of sight. But I could see his outline in the dark. I saw him lower his head. His shoulders started to shake. I don't think that I had ever seen my father cry. I didn't want to start now.

I turned away and remembered the other photograph, the one still upstairs of my parents on the cruise looking tan and happy, and I wondered if maybe he was thinking about that too.

When I woke late that night, Sheila wasn't in bed.

I sat up and listened. Nothing. At least, not in the apartment. I could hear the normal late-night street hum drifting up from three floors below. I looked over toward the bathroom. The light was out. All lights, in fact, were out.

I thought about calling out to her, but there was something fragile about the quiet, something bubblelike. I slipped out of bed. My feet touched down on the wall-to-wall carpet, the kind apartment buildings make you use so as to stifle noise from below or above.

The apartment wasn't big, just one bedroom. I padded toward the living room and peeked in. Sheila was there. She sat on the windowsill and looked down toward the street. I stared at her back, the swan neck, the wonderful shoulders, the way her hair flowed down the white skin, and again I felt the stir. Our relationship was still on the border of the early throes, the gee-it's-great-to-be-alive love where you can't get enough of each other, that wonderful run-across-the-park-to-see-her stomach-flutter that you know, *know*, would soon darken into something richer and deeper.

I'd been in love only once before. And that was a very long time ago.

"Hey," I said.

She turned just a little, but it was enough. There were tears on her cheeks. I could see them sliding down in the moonlight. She didn't make a sound—no cries or sobs or hitching chest. Just the tears. I stayed in the doorway and wondered what I should do.

"Sheila?"

On our second date, Sheila performed a card trick. It involved my picking two cards, putting them in the middle of the deck while she turned her head, and her throwing the entire deck save my two cards onto the floor. She smiled widely after performing this feat, holding up the two cards for my inspection. I smiled back. It was—how to put this?—goofy. Sheila was indeed goofy. She liked card tricks and cherry Kool-Aid and boy bands. She sang opera and read voraciously and cried at Hallmark commercials. She could do a mean imitation of Homer Simpson and Mr. Burns, though her Smithers and Apu were on the weak side. And most of all, Sheila loved to dance. She loved to close her eyes and put her head on my shoulder and fade away.

"I'm sorry, Will," Sheila said without turning around.

"For what?" I said.

She kept her eyes on the view. "Go back to bed. I'll be there in a few minutes."

I wanted to stay or offer up words of comfort. I didn't. She wasn't reachable right now. Something had pulled her away. Words or action would be either superfluous or harmful. At least, that was what I told myself. So I made a huge mistake. I went back to bed and waited.

But Sheila never came back.

3

Las Vegas, Nevada

Morty Meyer was in bed, dead asleep on his back, when he felt the gun muzzle against his forehead.

"Wake up," a voice said.

Morty's eyes went wide. The bedroom was dark. He tried to raise his head, but the gun held him down. His gaze slid toward the illuminated clock-radio on the night table. But there was no clock there. He hadn't owned one in years, now that he thought about it. Not since Leah died. Not since he'd sold the four-bedroom colonial.

"Hey, I'm good for it," Morty said. "You guys know that."

"Get up."

The man moved the gun away. Morty lifted his head. With his eyes adjusting, he could make out a scarf over the man's face. Morty remembered the radio program *The Shadow* from his childhood. "What do you want?"

"I need your help, Morty."

"We know each other?"

"Get up."

Morty obeyed. He swung his legs out of bed. When he stood, his head reeled in protest. He staggered, caught in that place where the drunk-buzz is winding down and the hangover is gathering strength like an oncoming storm.

"Where's your medical bag?" the man asked.

Relief flooded Morty's veins. So that was what this was about. Morty looked for a wound, but it was too dark. "You?" he asked.

"No. She's in the basement."

She?

Morty reached under the bed and pulled out his leather medical bag. It was old and worn. His initials, once shiny in gold leaf, were gone now. The zipper didn't close all the way. Leah had bought it when he'd graduated from Columbia University's medical school more than forty years before. He'd been an internist in Great Neck for the three decades following that. He and Leah had raised three boys. Now here he was, approaching seventy, living in a one-bedroom dump and owing money and favors to pretty much everyone.

Gambling. That'd been Morty's addiction of choice. For years, he'd been something of a functioning gamble-holic, fraternizing with those particular inner demons yet keeping them on the fringe. Eventually, however, the demons caught up to him. They always do. Some had claimed that Leah had been a facilitator. Maybe that was true. But once she died, there was no reason to fight anymore. He let the demons claw in and do their worst.

Morty had lost everything, including his medical license. He moved out west to this shithole. He gambled pretty much every night. His boys—all grown and with families—didn't call him anymore. They blamed him for their mother's death. They said that he'd aged Leah before her time. They were probably right.

"Hurry," the man said.

"Right."

They started down the basement stairs. Morty could see the light was on. This building, his crappy new abode, used to be a funeral home. Morty rented a bedroom on the ground floor. That gave him use of the basement—where the bodies used to be stored and embalmed.

In the basement's back corner, a rusted playground slide ran down from the back parking lot. That was how they used to bring the bodies down—park-'n-slide. The walls were blanketed with tiles, though many were crumbling from years of neglect. You had to use a pair of pliers to get the water running. Most of the cabinet doors were gone. The death stench still hovered, an old ghost refusing to leave.

The injured woman was lying on a steel table. Morty could see right away that this didn't look good. He turned back to the Shadow.

"Help her," he said.

Morty didn't like the timbre of the man's voice. There was anger there, yes, but the overriding emotion was naked desperation, his voice more a plea than anything else. "She doesn't look good," Morty said.

The man pressed the gun against Morty's chest. "If she dies, you die."

Morty swallowed. Clear enough. He moved toward her. Over the years, he'd treated plenty of men down here—but this would be the first woman. That was how Morty made his quasi-living. Stitch and run. If you go to an emergency room with a bullet or stab wound, the doctor on duty had a legal obligation to report it. So they came instead to Morty's makeshift hospital.

He flashed back to the triage lessons of medical school. The ABCs, if you will. Airway, Breathing, Circulation. Her breaths were raspy and filled with spittle.

"You did this to her?"

The man did not reply.

Morty worked on her the best he could. Patchwork really. Get her stabilized, he thought. Stabilized and out of here.

When he was done, the man lifted her gently. "If you say anything—"

"I've been threatened by worse."

The man hurried out with the woman. Morty stayed in the basement. His nerves felt frayed from the surprise wake-up. He sighed and decided to head back to bed. But before he went up the stairs, Morty Meyer made a crucial error.

He looked out the back window.

The man carried the woman to the car. He carefully, almost tenderly, laid her down in the back. Morty watched the scene. And then he saw movement.

He squinted. And that was when he felt the shudder rip through him.

Another passenger.

There was a passenger in the back of the car. A passenger who very much did not belong. Morty automatically reached for the phone, but before he even picked up the receiver, he stopped. Who would he call? What would he say?

Morty closed his eyes, fought it off. He trudged back up the steps. He crawled back into bed and pulled the covers up over him. He stared at the ceiling and tried to forget.

All Orion/Phoenix titles are available at your local bookshop or from the following address:

Mail Order Department
Littlehampton Book Services
FREEPOST BR535
Worthing, West Sussex, BNI3 3BR
telephone 01903 828503, *facsimile* 01903 828802
e-mail MailOrders@lbsltd.co.uk
(Please ensure that you include full postal address details)

Payment can be made either by credit/debit card (Visa, Mastercard, Access and Switch accepted) or by sending a £ Sterling cheque or postal order made payable to *Littlehampton Book Services*.
DO NOT SEND CASH OR CURRENCY.

Please add the following to cover postage and packing

UK and BFPO:
£1.50 for the first book, and 50p for each additional book to a maximum of £3.50

Overseas and Eire:
£2.50 for the first book plus £1.00 for the second book and 50p for each additional book ordered

---

BLOCK CAPITALS PLEASE

name of cardholder

*delivery address
(if different from cardholder)*

address of cardholder

postcode

postcode

☐ I enclose my remittance for £

☐ please debit my Mastercard/Visa/Access/Switch (delete as appropriate)

card number ⬚⬚⬚⬚⬚⬚⬚⬚⬚⬚⬚⬚⬚⬚⬚⬚

expiry date ⬚⬚⬚⬚   Switch issue no. ⬚⬚

signature

prices and availability are subject to change without notice